Big Band of
BACHELORS BOOK

SEAL Brotherhood

SHARON HAMILTON

SHARON HAMILTON'S BOOK LIST

SEAL BROTHERHOOD BOOKS

SEAL BROTHERHOOD SERIES
Accidental SEAL Book 1
Fallen SEAL Legacy Book 2
SEAL Under Covers Book 3
SEAL The Deal Book 4
Cruisin' For A SEAL Book 5
SEAL My Destiny Book 6
SEAL of My Heart Book 7
Fredo's Dream Book 8
SEAL My Love Book 9
SEAL Encounter Prequel to Book 1
SEAL Endeavor Prequel to Book 2
Ultimate SEAL Collection Vol. 1 Books 1-4 /2 Prequels
Ultimate SEAL Collection Vol. 2 Books 5-7

BAD BOYS OF SEAL TEAM 3 SERIES
SEAL's Promise Book 1
SEAL My Home Book 2
SEAL's Code Book 3
Big Bad Boys Bundle Books 1-3

BAND OF BACHELORS SERIES
Lucas Book 1
Alex Book 2
Jake Book 3
Jake 2 Book 4
Big Band of Bachelors Bundle

BONE FROG BROTHERHOOD SERIES
New Year's SEAL Dream Book 1
SEALed At The Altar Book 2
SEALed Forever Book 3
SEAL's Rescue Book 4
SEALed Protection Book 5

SILVER SEALS SERIES
SEAL Love's Legacy

SLEEPER SEALS SERIES
Bachelor SEAL

SUNSET SEALS SERIES
SEALed at Sunset
Second Chance SEAL
Treasure Island SEAL
Escape to Sunset

STAND ALONE BOOKS & SERIES
SEAL's Goal: The Beautiful Game
Nashville SEAL: Jameson
True Blue SEALS Zak
Paradise: In Search of Love
Love Me Tender, Love You Hard

NOVELLAS
SEAL You In My Dreams Magnolias and Moonshine

PARANORMALS

GOLDEN VAMPIRES OF TUSCANY SERIES
Honeymoon Bite Book 1
Mortal Bite Book 2
Christmas Bite Book 3
Midnight Bite Book 4

THE GUARDIANS
Heavenly Lover Book 1
Underworld Lover Book 2
Underworld Queen Book 3

FALL FROM GRACE SERIES
Gideon: Heavenly Fall

NOVELLAS
SEAL Of Time Trident Legacy

All of Sharon's books are available on Audible, narrated by the talented
J.D. Hart.

ABOUT THE BOOK

Band of Bachelors: Lucas

Special Operator Lucas Shipley thought his living arrangement was temporary, since getting booted from the house by his wife. He sleeps on a couch in the apartment with four other divorced Navy SEALs, thinking he'll get the call to come home any day. He ignores the not-so-helpful advice his buddies are giving him about marriage, women and romance. Until he gets served with divorce papers.

Realtor Marcy Gelland is hired by Lucas' soon-to-be ex-wife to liquidate all their real estate holdings and help her orchestrate a speedy departure from Lucas' life. Based on what the hot-headed SEAL wife has told her, Marcy understands Lucas deserves every ounce of pain coming his way.

But when Marcy and Lucas are left alone together in a remote Northern California woods, they ignite a personal bonfire that threatens to burn down the whole forest. Marcy is forced to see she is wrong about Lucas.

Amidst the backdrop of hardened bachelor SEALs with their unsolicited, anti-long-term relationship advice, and a terrorist training camp operating nearby, Lucas must do what he's always done: be the hero and save the day. But will it be in time to save Marcy?

Band of Bachelors: Alex

Adrenaline junkie and Navy SEAL Alex Kowicki is one of four bachelor SEALs trying to navigate his successful military career while achieving his goals as a first class connoisseur of beautiful women. He isn't ready to jump back into anything but his free falls, HALO drops or his missions overseas. He trusts his buddies to fix him up with another blind date that won't be as dangerous as his last ones.

But Sydney Robinson has other plans. A beach volleyball player who can spike better than most men, and block with explosive speed to defend her side of the net, she executes a series of events to include stalking the handsome SEAL all the way to Sonoma County wine country, and delivering his carcass to her bed. Having achieved her first goal, she sets about to become a pro AVP player.

When duty calls and Alex is pulled back to Iraq to complete a failed mission, neither expects to find that the real danger is lurking very much close to home. But this fight might cost one of them their lives.

Band of Bachelors: Jake

Navy SEAL Jake Green wakes up in the Honeymoon Suite at the Desert Oasis Motel in Las Vegas and can't remember how he got there. But that's not the only thing he doesn't remember. A bachelor, his left hand now sports a gold wedding ring.

Band of Bachelors: Jake2

Navy SEAL Jake Green comes home from deployment to a family in turmoil. With the recent death of his father, his ex-wives, mother and brother are thrown into a snakepit left by his father's poor choices. Jake and Ginger attempt to strengthen their marriage and young family amidst a dangerous deployment to Baja California. Jake's got alimony and child support, a blown up will he's the executor of, illegitimate siblings and a Mexican General gunning for him. It's one thing to come home in one piece from a SEAL mission. But which mission is more dangerous?

AUTHOR'S NOTE

I always dedicate my SEAL Brotherhood books to the brave men and women who defend our shores and keep us safe. Without their sacrifice, and that of their families—because a warrior's fight always includes his or her family—I wouldn't have the freedom and opportunity to make a living writing these stories. They sometimes pay the ultimate price so we can debate, argue, go have coffee with friends, raise our children and see them have children of their own.

One of my favorite tributes to warriors resides on many memorials, including one I saw honoring the fallen of WWII on an island in the Pacific:

> "When you go home
> Tell them of us, and say
> For your tomorrow,
> We gave our today."

These are my stories created out of my own imagination. Anything that is inaccurately portrayed is either my mistake, or done intentionally to disguise something I might have overheard over a beer or in the corner of one of the hangouts along the Coronado Strand.

I support two main charities. Navy SEAL/UDT Museum operates in Ft. Pierce, Florida. Please learn about this wonderful museum, all run by active and former SEALs and their friends and families, and who rely on public support, not that of the U.S. Government. www.navysealmuseum.org

IF YOU GOT ANY CLOSER, YOU WOULD HAVE TO ENLIST

I also support Wounded Warriors, who tirelessly bring together the warrior as well as the family members who are just learning to deal with their soldier's condition and have nowhere to turn. It is a long path to becoming well, but I've seen first-hand what this organization does for its warriors and the families who love them. Please give what your heart tells you is right. If you cannot give, volunteer at one of the many service centers all over the United States. Get involved. Do something meaningful for someone who gave so much of themselves, to families who have paid the price for your freedom. You'll find a family there unlike any other on the planet. www.woundedwarriorproject.org

LUCAS

Band of Bachelors
Book 1

SHARON HAMILTON

CHAPTER 1

L UCAS WOKE UP with the sun slicing daggers of light into his eyes.
Fuck me.

He rolled over to shield his face from the bright morning and fell off the couch, right onto his tailbone.

Goddamit. The sharp pain added to the bruise he'd already created from previous sleepless nights. His ass had made divots between the second and third cushions of the sectional, which was as equally uncomfortable to sit on. The couch's grey scratchy fabric was Scotchguarded, making his back and balls itch. His buddies on SEAL Team 3 had picked up this wonderful piece of *loungery* for two hundred bucks four months back. The San Diego Goodwill had been so happy to get rid of it, they gave the team the matching loveseat without charging a penny extra.

From the floor, Lucas stared eye-level at the hunk of junk he'd battled with all night long and knew it would still go up like a torch regardless of the Scotchguard. As he pulled his body up, the matching loveseat veering off to the right gaped at him, its bent footrests looking like huge gumless jaws. The thing was laughing at him.

It was nothing like his king-size bed with the Egyptian cotton sheets at home—the home he'd been kicked out of a month prior. He hadn't expected to have to sleep on his buddies' couch this long. When he'd first been shown the door, he hadn't been too worried, convinced Connie would soon change her mind and invite him back.

He'd envisioned that 'welcome home' party every day and night, in spite of the fact that his last vision of her was of her screaming at the top of her lungs, those delicious blue veins at the sides of her neck protruding like they were fat, blue birthday candles. His sobbing three-year-old daughter stood next to her mother, burying her face in Connie's thigh as the toddler screamed in her arms. It broke Lucas' heart to see his wife clutch the baby, his horror-filled expression showing fear and confusion.

That was one shitty day, but he knew in his heart of hearts that at any time, she'd soften and he'd be back home, in their bed, sliding against her smooth thighs and kissing the place between her legs, making her scream his name. Oh, he was the candy man, all right. His dick got hard just thinking about it. She'd never had a man go down on her before they got together. She'd been a good Catholic girl, and the nuns had filled her head with stories of how the germs from his hot tongue would poison her womb.

As if they knew.

His arousal meant only one thing: he'd have to finish it in the shower or he wouldn't be able to get his jeans on without pain.

Someone swung open one of the four bedroom doors with enough force they nearly ripped it off its hinges. "What the fuck just happened?" asked Jake, his mop of black hair sticking straight up like an unclipped Mohawk. "We just have an earthquake, Lucas?"

Lucas grimaced. "No, that would be my ass hitting the ground."

"Would you quit that? You'll wake up the whole fuckin' household."

Lucas stood in his shorts, bare-chested and barefoot. He inclined his head to the side, arms outstretched, palms up as if listening for the complaints—which didn't materialize—from the other three rooms. "And your point is?" Lucas asked, after a few seconds of silence.

"Geez, Lucas, would you put your fire hose away? I've seen it, remember?" Jake pointed to Lucas' groin.

Standing at full attention, Lucas' *unit* had found freedom from the hole in his American flag shorts and was ready to par-tay. He quickly tucked it back in, but it popped out again. That time, he turned his back to Jake, properly stowed his cannon, then whipped around to find that Jake had disappeared back into his room.

Only two of the bedrooms had their own private bath with a shower, since the guest bath only contained a toilet with a cracked seat and a sink. Lucas didn't want to wake anyone else up, so he headed for the half bath, looking forward to perhaps working on his aim while studying the raunchy posters pinned up all around the little room. They didn't have to worry about entertaining females in the men's club of an apartment, since most of the SEALs who lived there had sworn off any women, except professionals who would definitely not be looking at the posters.

He washed his hands twice, feeling more relaxed, then padded into the kitchen to make some coffee. He covered the coffee grinder with a towel to muffle the sound and inhaled the only luxury the boys allowed themselves: fresh ground coffee.

He paused his musing to glare at the coffee pot, performing its death gurgle. He surveyed his temporary 'home sweet home'. The garbage can was overflowing—even the recycle side—with beer bottles, pizza boxes, and half-gallon plastic orange juice containers. A wet bath sheet and t-shirt hung over an old, paint-splattered folding chair, one of four, surrounding a square card table with coffee rings stained into it. Their big-screen TV sat on top of two pallets they'd hauled from the dumpster. The light beige rug was mostly *dark* beige from oil, food, and coffee stains, and one plate-sized red stain from someone's Hawaiian Punch spilled a week back. They'd been trying to clean up each little accident, until the punch mishap. After that, they understood that when they deployed, they'd not get their deposit back on the apartment. Ryan said they might even owe the landlord something.

Look at me...already considering myself part of this sorry band of bachelors.

Lucas chastised himself for even considering this to be the case. He'd be out of there so fast it would take them a couple of days to miss him.

Sorry-assed sailors. Unlike his Connie, the bachelor frogs had only themselves to blame for their poor choices. Jake had children littered all over the world, just like their old pal, Gunny, who used to own the gym they all trained at. He wasn't exactly sure how many he'd fathered, but knew it would take two hands to count.

The coffee pot began to shut down, as he took stock of his friends.

Cory Brown was a preacher's son, way too trusting, and had started dating girls from his father's church after high school, until several parents complained he was deflowering the future generation of Sunday school teachers. And then he knocked one up, and that was it. Reverend Brown made sure the right thing happened. That marriage didn't last more than a month after the baby was born, and then Cory was being sued for child support that would take over half his pay, including his SEAL bonus.

Ryan and Alex got married in a double ceremony in Las Vegas, and had similar stories of woe.

No, none of them had spent much time finding a fine, quality girl like Connie. Yes, she was a bit hotheaded, but Lucas kind of liked it when she got steamed up, as long as it was something he could wiggle his way out of. The unfortunate bachelor party in Vegas was the last straw, though. And the stripper he'd had his photograph taken with turned out to be a transvestite, not that it made any difference to Connie. Lucas had been hoping it would.

But all that would be over soon.

He turned off the coffee maker, poured himself a cup, added a shot glass full of real Half and Half and walked out onto the deck overlooking the valley below and Coronado Island in the distance. He considered getting the boys up because a Specialist from Virginia was coming to do some training with them, even though it was Saturday. The military didn't observe weekends if the upcoming mission was urgent. This one apparently was.

Below him in the parking lot, a sweet brunette in an impossibly tight, short skirt stepped out of a cherry-red VW convertible. She looked up at him, shielding her eyes with one hand and slinging her large bag over her shoulder with the other. Lucas straightened himself up and sucked in his gut, smiling as her gaze found him and gave him an appreciative perusal.

He told himself it wasn't really a bad thing. One thing to look, another to, well, partake. He didn't want to blow his chances of sliding back into Connie's expensive silk sheets, or being buried deep inside her sweet little jellyroll. But looking was okay. He'd just not chat her up. So he waved.

Her grin was fine. She looked like the kind of girl who had all manner of dirty little thoughts. She licked her lips, straightened her upper torso and smoothed over her tummy and hips with those palms of hers. One wrist had a charm bracelet that tinkled in the distance. Without an invitation, she headed straight for the entrance to the upper floors, right below him.

Holy hotness. Did she think I invited her up?

Inside, he found Ryan, Alex and Cory up and showered, making a barefoot line in the kitchen like old men at a rescue mission.

"I say strawberry waffles before we head over to the base," said Cory as he poured his coffee.

"Ask them to leave the whipped cream can this time," said Ryan.

Jake exited from his bedroom, followed by a cloud of steam, matching the shirtless wonders in the kitchen.

Cory nearly spit out his mug of Joe. "Dayum, Shipley. Good thing we're not shooting this morning. I'm going to be shaking for a week," barked Cory.

"Use more cream," was Lucas' answer. "Hey, guys, you know anything about this Thom guy? He's some kind of security expert?"

"Something to do with a little pod of terrorists they encountered over in Mosul." Alex sat down on the floor, back straight against the wall, his feet out in front of him. Ryan soon joined him.

"Kyle said they've got information the group plans to do something here in California. A retaliation," added Jake.

"Helluva thing to do on a Saturday, haul us in there," said Cory.

"What the fuck difference does it make?" Jake wrinkled his nose and forehead. "Not like I've got a date."

Lucas snorted. "Oh, so you call those hookups 'dates' now? You really go on dates, Jake? Man, I must be rubbing off on you."

"You should talk." Alex and Ryan were punching each other in the arm, which escalated into a coffee fight. Alex continued, caramel-colored liquid dripping off his chin. "Don't see you dating anytime soon, shitface."

Lucas hated the fact that his last name had taken the ugly moniker ever since the unfortunate bachelor party he didn't remember.

"Geez. I hang around you guys too much and I might stop believing in true love."

Lucas was pelted with coffee, one of the SEALs throwing the ceramic mug itself, which hit him at bicep level.

"Okay, okay. I get it. It's just that I'm not ready to give up on my marriage like you guys. I may not have as many kids as you do, Jake, and I may only have known her a little bit longer than you two knew your wives, Groves and Kowicki, but I *definitely* know how to fuckin' use a condom, Cory—*especially* if I'm gonna screw a girl in the back of my father's sanctuary."

"Hallelujah, praise the Lord," someone shouted.

"A fuckin' religious experience, I call it," Jake said as he high-fived Cory.

"See, that's where you guys go wrong. You don't treat women with respect."

No one said a word. Then the unofficial spokesman for the group, Jake, inserted his opinion. "So, if you feel like you don't fit in, why don't you fuckin' leave?"

The silence that followed made Lucas nervous. He could sense more than a couple of his buddies felt he'd crossed the line. There were some hurt feelings they often didn't verbalize, but he sure could feel it. He knew he had to be careful.

"You don't know a damned thing until you've really walked around in another man's shoes. Or, in Cory's case, his high heels." Lucas delivered it straight and for just one second he thought he'd made thing worse.

But then the catcalls began, which was a signal things were returning to normal. Lucas relaxed enough to apologize and make it sound like he meant it. And he did. The doorbell buzzed.

"You know," said Jake, who walked over to Lucas and fist-bumped him, "you're probably right. You're the one who's gonna make it in this relationship game. For us assholes, well, I think we're pretty much fucked."

All of them laughed.

The doorbell buzzed again twice this time, and Cory jogged over and opened it. Lucas couldn't hear anything but a sweet voice asking if she could talk to Lucas. He didn't know how, but he just knew it belonged to the lady in the red VW. *She knows my name?* He was flattered, until he remembered his situation, and Connie.

"Sure, come right in, ma'am," Cory offered, showing her the way with his arm.

Her bright red lips were the same color as the VW. She had the whole ladybug thing going on—with her black skirt, the black and white polka-dot blouse that was a bit sheer, showing him she wore bright white, lacy underthings—his personal favorite. She kept her knees together as she carefully stepped over their dirty carpet, her spiked heels making her balance a little difficult. She extended her hand with the charm bracelet softly clinking, and he extended his.

"Holy crap, Shipley, you've been holding out on us," someone said. The team separated and gave Lucas and the girl space like a drop of oil in water.

"So, you're Lucas Shipley," she said sweetly, and then gave him a devilish smile that made his shorts erupt.

He nodded nervously as she shifted her bag, which had fallen off her shoulder.

"Excuse me," she said as she extracted her hand and unzipped her purse. Bringing out a large white envelope, she didn't give him time to stop admiring her shapely form.

"You've been served."

CHAPTER 2

M ARCY GELLAND LOOKED over at the woman who was ending her marriage of five years. Connie Shipley was initialing and signing where the little orange arrows indicated. It wasn't easy, Marcy knew, to just wash your hands of a marriage, especially a marriage with property and children. She saw how resolute Connie was, how firmly she pressed, signing her name with a big script flourish like she was auto-graphing a bestseller in front of a crowd of people. The baby was trying to grab her pen, then her hair, the top of her dress, her earrings, but still Connie persisted, gently peeling back his chubby hands. Her young daughter was coloring with felt-tipped pens on the dark blue carpet at her feet.

She knew there would come a time during the process when Connie would wonder if she was doing the right thing. That was always the risk in taking on real estate listings where the couple was divorcing. One moment they hated each other, then the next they were doing the hot and dirty on the kitchen floor. She'd worked with couples who started out being adversaries, requiring her to take a neutral stance. But if one of them wanted to keep the marriage together, it was a fifty-fifty chance that party would prevail, and then suddenly representing them became impossible. Harder still were the cases when the house had already sold, and the buyers were looking forward to moving in.

But as she watched Connie with the paperwork and discussed the numbers with her, Marcy had the impression the woman was complete-ly sure of her decision.

"So, when can I get Lucas' signature?" Marcy asked the attractive blonde Navy wife as she bounced her baby on her knee.

"Sorry. That's your job, Marcy. I'm hoping he'll cooperate, but I'm not sure."

"So you are the one forcing this, then?"

The baby was fussing. Connie drew a bottle from the large satchel under the table and unceremoniously stuffed the nipple in the baby's mouth. "Excuse me. What did you ask?" She frowned, bouncing the youngster.

"It was *your* decision to sell everything off, then? Did you try to work it out, go to counseling?"

Connie gave her a look she knew quite well. Her half-lidded eyes told her she was tired of trying to explain it, even to herself. "Not sure whose great idea it was to post the pictures of the SEAL bachelor party online, but it was irrefutable evidence."

"Ah." Marcy studied her. She decided to let it go without asking for further clarification. "But he won't be surprised, I guess."

Mrs. Shipley laughed, tossing back her head. The baby's arm had traveled down Connie's shirt, between her breasts, while his other hand fisted his blond curls at the temples. That's when Marcy saw an anchor tat on Connie's right breast, and underneath the anchor was the name *Lucas*, written in fancy script. She wondered what Connie would do to cover up or alter that message.

"I'm pretty sure he expected to be invited back. But I don't think it was me he wanted. Just my bed." Connie followed the comment by raising her right eyebrow and giving Marcy a sultry look.

Marcy sensed it was not a good idea to pry any further, but she did need some help getting the listing contract signed.

Connie put the empty bottle back in the diaper bag and put the baby over her shoulder. Marcy thought she handled the little one with callused indifference, as she lifted him up and down against her shoulder and chest until they heard a gargantuan burp followed by sounds of spillage.

"Dammit," Connie said as she stood up, handed the baby to Marcy, and then retrieved a cotton cloth from the bag, wiping her neck and shoulder, her front, and her back. Then she wiped down the chair and dabbed the carpet.

Marcy had never held a baby before, so she continued to grip him under his armpits as the blue-eyed cherub stared back, then promptly spit-up clotted milk, which dripped down his chin and soaked into his cotton t-shirt.

Connie came to her side, taking away the baby before the smelly liquid fell on Marcy. "Did he get you wet? Oh, Marcy, I'm so sorry," she said, holding out her cloth.

"He's got a bunch of stuff—," but before Marcy could complete her sentence, Connie had eliminated the evidence.

"Look, next is going to be a huge explosion," Connie said as she patted the baby's underside, "and you don't want to be around for that one. So I've got about two minutes." She fished out a card and handed it to Marcy. "Here's his cell phone, but the email no longer works. He's getting something else set up, since he no longer lives at the house."

"Gotcha. So I should call him?"

"Yes. Now, let me just tell you a couple of quick things and then—" Connie sniffed in the baby's diaper area—"so far so good. I feel like I should warn you: do not believe a word the man says. He's a sweet talker, and he might even come onto you, you know, try to seduce you so you'll go easy on him?"

"Oh, not to worry, Connie. Besides, I have a boyfriend," Marcy lied.

"Well, that doesn't matter one whit to him. I could tell you stories. I got tired of being all alone and scared to death while he was overseas. And then when he came home, he either wanted to screw day and night or he wouldn't want to do anything. He'd just watch TV. The kids would be screaming, and he'd be near comatose. I needed a big fuckin' break. I'd been stuck with them for months sometimes and here he couldn't help out, lift a finger."

Marcy was filled with compassion for the woman who felt abandoned, tied down with kids she was responsible for raising nearly on her own. Whatever glue had held this marriage together was gone.

"Then there was the staying out late, drinking with the guys—Marcy, he was hanging out more with them than with me. If he didn't have some bar thing to go to, some fuckin' *Macho Brotherhood* thing to do, he was in bed." She wiped a tear from her cheek. "Those guys are always getting married, divorced, their ladies leaving them. It's all just one excuse to Par-Tay. And he's got these loser friends who have messed up their marriages, too. They're a bad influence on him."

Marcy had gotten the picture minutes ago, but Connie seemed hell-bent on smashing her points in with a dull knife. "What about counseling?" she asked.

"Counseling? Those guys don't do that. Deathly afraid someone will label them as unstable and they'll lose their precious Trident. He didn't like to talk about feelings, especially *my* feelings. He was like, 'So, join a gym, or why not take up a hobby, like quilting or gardening.'" Connie rolled her eyes. "I mean, really? I'm trying to raise two kids all by myself, and he was streaking out there clear across the world from me, and doing who knows what that he couldn't talk about. Marcy, it was all just too much."

Like it was an exclamation mark to Connie's speech, they both heard the explosion in the baby's diaper. Those big blue eyes looked to Marcy as if she had an answer for him.

Marcy wrinkled her nose at the smell. "What do you need?"

"I need to get my life back. I need a nanny."

AFTER CONNIE LEFT, Marcy gave the SEAL a call. She heard loud music in the background, some whistles and "Oh yeah, yeah, baby." Marcy knew Lucas Shipley was at some sort of strip club.

"Hallo?" The husky, inebriated voice boomed in her ear.

"Is this Lucas Shipley?" she asked timidly.

"Who the fuck wants to know? You drive a red Volkswagen?"

"Pardon?"

"It's a simple question," he slurred. "Do you fuckin' drive a red Volkswagen? Inquiring minds want to know, darlin'. You might as well jump on in with the good news. Everyone else has."

"No."

A loud cheer went up as she heard a female voice in the background. The bump and grind music was so loud, the phone was beginning to cut out.

"Hello, baby. You have a fine ass." His sexy whisper was barely audible.

"Excuse me?" Marcy's back straightened as she felt the jolt travel down her spine.

"Ah, fuck, honey. I'm hanging up the phone right now." He whispered to Marcy, "'Excuse me, it's been nice, but I gotta go." She heard him shout out to the stripper, "No! Baby, don't go!"

The line went dead.

Marcy nearly threw her phone against the wall. It was all the evidence she needed to be totally convinced Connie Shipley was indeed doing the right thing for herself and her young family. She could completely understand why she wanted to separate from this scumbag of a husband.

Marcy was going to help her make him pay.

CHAPTER 3

THE MORNING BEGAN just like it always did. Lucas fell off the couch. Behind Jake's closed door, Lucas heard, "Fuck!" Climbing back onto the scratchy couch, he tried to bury his head under his pillow as Jake let loose a string of invectives. That started another SEAL yelling at him, and then Cory swung open his door and came running out so fast, Lucas thought he was going to get thrown over the balcony.

"Would you fuckin' quit this shit, Lucas? We gotta tie you to the sofa?"

"Maybe I should get a rollaway?"

Alex appeared right behind Cory with his eyes narrowing. "I think you need to get yourself another crash pad, Lucas. It's clear this is a more permanent arrangement—and you're becoming a pain in the ass. Around here, sleeping in on Sunday mornings is sacred. *Sacred!* You need to find yourself another king-sized bed somewhere, and fast."

Lucas thought about the night before. They'd dropped Thom off at his hotel, but the SEAL from Virginia Beach couldn't walk, so they'd had to carry him into the room. It had fallen to Lucas to fish the room key out of the man's pants, and that wasn't pleasant at all.

He vaguely remembered Thom's wife calling. *Wait a minute.*

"Did Connie call?" he asked, sure someone's wife called. Or girlfriend. His mind was totally fuzzy.

He was about to ask the little crowd gathered again when the sound of the coffee grinder jolted him harder than if he'd been hit in the eye socket with a dull spear. Holding his ears with his palms did nothing to stop the pain.

Lucas collapsed again and waited for silence.

"Check your phone, asshole," Jake barked. "Now, in addition to having you over here at no rent, out of the goodness of our hearts, you want us to be your answering service, as well?"

"Okay, fair enough," Lucas said as he checked his cell. "I don't recognize this number." He hesitated and decided to hit redial later. "So, on that other point, I'm willing to share in the rent. I can pay in advance, up front. Question is where do I sleep?"

The unanimous answer was, "Not in my room."

Jake stepped up to deliver the final ultimatum. "I think you're shit out of luck, sailor. You need to find some place permanent."

"I really think she's gonna change her mind. Something tells me she's just bluffing." Lucas thought about all those deployments he came home and all he wanted to do was stay in bed and screw. Connie wanted relief from the kids. Why didn't he see that? But Lucas was so damned happy to be alive, to be home, to be in his bed again with the woman who made him feel terrific, when she was into it, he thought she'd be just as into him. Wasn't that what she missed all the time he was away? He couldn't figure her out. He was, after doing it for Connie, for all the people in this wonderful country. Why couldn't she get that?

"Seriously? You really think she'd go to all the trouble and expense of filing for divorce—that had to cost her at least a grand—*and* have it served, and you're still thinking she's gonna take you back?" Alex was shaking his head, his mouth puckered like he'd just taken a spoonful of motor oil.

"What fuckin' planet are you on, man?" Ryan asked.

Connie had accused him of being insensitive. But he *was* being sensitive. He was going out with his buds, not leaving them alone. Some of them had gotten home to find their wives with other men, even pregnant by other men. Other fuckin *regular Navy* guys and that was just tight. Nothing good about that. They were all responsible for each other. He wouldn't expect they'd abandon him, so why shouldn't he support them? It wasn't about the drinking or the strippers, it was about the community, and the healing that occurred when they all hung out together. Everyone returning home whole meant fixing stuff on the way back, as well as the adjustment to being home.

He could see now this would never be good enough for Connie. She had to be the center of attention, even ahead of the kids, and that bothered him. She just didn't get it. And she never would. She was like a clock that had been over sprung and would never again purr like that kitten he liked in bed, the lady who drove him wild with fantasies all during his time overseas.

"Redial, my man. Then I'm going back to bed," Jake added.

Lucas punched the red arrow on his phone, and the call was connected.

'This is Marcy Gelland from the Coronado Bay Realty. I'm either on the other line or assisting clients. If you would leave your name and number and the reason for your call, I'll get back to you as soon as I'm free. Thanks, and make it a great day!"

Lucas hung up. "Realtor," he said sheepishly. The day was suddenly turning dark.

Jake started to laugh. "You son of a gun, Lucas. Don't you have a clue what's happening to you? Your wife is trying to sell the house right out from under you."

"I'll just give my tenants notice and move into it. Mom left it to me when she passed. I can't afford both houses anyway," Lucas answered. "She's stupid to sell it. Don't know how she'll afford to get another place since she's not working."

Ryan leaned in, handing Lucas a fresh mug of coffee with the usual dosage of cream. "She doesn't have to work, my man. *You* do."

MARCY SOUNDED A bit frosty on the phone, Lucas thought. She insisted on a meeting, requesting he come down to her real estate office.

"Couldn't we meet at the house? Haven't seen the kids for a week, and you'll need Connie's signature anyway."

"Already got it, and I don't think she wants to see you."

It pissed him off that she would have such an opinion about the details of his marriage, since she'd only been hired to sell the property.

"Lucas, I can't find the information I need on the home at Linda Lane, and the property in Sonoma County. Do you have mortgages on those?"

Lucas fisted his right hand and nearly cracked the cell with his left. "Wait a minute. My mother left that house on Linda Lane to me. That's *my* house."

"Did you ever get the transfer done after your mother's death?"

"You're not hearing me. I'm not selling that house. I'm keeping it. I need some place to live."

"I'll require the rent rolls and how much the taxes are. Is there a mortgage? Connie thought it was given to you free and clear."

"You know, I'm talking and you're not hearing me. That was *my* house left to me by *my* mother."

"Except you were married at the time."

"So?"

"So, half of it belongs to Connie. You know California's a community property state. I'm no attorney, Lucas, but I think maybe you should get one and right away. Connie intends to sell this property, and the house up in Sonoma County, too."

"That fuckin hunting cabin has been in my family for a hundred years." His voice cracked like a teenager. "No way is that going to Connie."

"Look, go get an attorney. In fact, I insist you do so."

The cold bitch didn't sound like she had an ounce of compassion.

"I could give you three names as recommendations. But in the meantime, you can't stop Connie from putting the house, the house you two lived in together, on the market. She can't *sell* it without your permission, but she can encumber her half. And if she goes to court, the judge will order it."

He felt her voice soften just a touch, but she was still all business and still too pushy.

"Maybe if she gets the house sold, and she gets some money, she'll ease up on the other properties. Maybe not. But you need to get an attorney right away, and you need to meet with me to get this paper-work signed."

"I need time to digest all this. I just got served with papers yester-day."

"Oh." He heard the hesitation in Marcy's voice. "So, this was a sur-prise, then?"

"Yeah, it was pretty much a surprise."

"Can we compromise?"

He could hear some sweetness, but he didn't trust his ears yet.

"I won't have you give me any signatures on the Linda property and the cabin in Cloverdale, but can we at least do the paperwork on the house so I can get it on the market Monday morning?"

He'd agreed because he didn't know what else to do. He'd trained for everything under the sun, every eventuality, but he'd not been prepared for the attack coming from the one person in the world he always thought would be there for him.

Connie was taking the house they'd picked out together as newly-weds, with money for the down payment that came from his SEAL signing bonus. She could try to take what his mother had left him, as well as the cabin up in the woods, but she could *not* take his dignity. That, no woman would ever have, *especially* not Connie.

CHAPTER 4

MARCY DIDN'T EXPECT the tall SEAL to arrive so soon. She'd been involved in checking the new listings and had begun to upload some of the Shipley house information to the multiple listing service. She was waiting for his signature before she hit send.

The pink stucco home was on one of San Diego's nicer streets. The picture she'd taken that morning didn't do it justice. It had a rounded doorway like many of the bungalows in the area, with a red-tiled roof and iron grates over the tiny windows on the whole front side of the building, including the front door. Built just after the Depression, every house in town of that vintage was nearly identical, except for some interior remodeling and reversal of floor plan. The living room was always on the right or left and the kitchen was opposite, on the other side of the dining area. The homes had been built for younger families, but younger families could barely afford them anymore without help from outside.

She was admiring the pleasant picture on the screen when she heard his deep voice behind her.

"You're Marcy Gelland?"

When she turned, his dark hair and deep blue eyes threw her off-balance for a bit. He was stuffed into jeans that were baggy at the calves and knees, but well filled out in the butt and groin area. And he'd caught her checking him out.

His eyes smiled while his lips didn't move except for a tiny muscle on his left, which was a good thing. The resulting dimple at the left side of his mouth was giving her palpitations.

Well, of course he's handsome, Marcy. What did you expect?

He smelled of fresh soap, wore a white button-down shirt with rolled-up long sleeves, showing his corded muscles and multiple forearm tats, including a string of frog prints going from his wrist to the crook in his arm. She was glad she'd decided to wear her dark blue suit, her power suit. She needed the strength and resolve it gave her.

Standing, she extended her hand and felt him give her a full-contact handshake ending with a little squeeze. He returned her palm in an altered state. Her heart was pounding so hard she was sure her little dangle earrings were shaking.

Picking up her file, she asked him to follow her to the conference room. She could easily imagine him gazing at the movement of her hips under her skirt, so she attempted to walk completely without swagger, so as not to encourage him further. His mannerism wasn't at all what she expected when he pulled out a chair for her. She was forced to say thank you, and then felt his fingertips glide across the top of her shoulders as he returned to his side of the table, sat with his fingers folded on the tabletop in front of him.

Marcy recalled what Connie had told her. He could be a charmer, and no doubt he was on his best behavior right that moment. If he expected any special favors, he was sorely mistaken. She inhaled, elongated her neck, settled her jaw and applied her professional mask as she met his stare.

He was stoic, seemingly unaffected by her in the slightest, leaning back against the padding in the office chair, breathing shallowly, but drilling her with his gaze. She could tell he was checking her out elsewhere, with his peripheral vision, but was skilled enough to hide it.

In spite of herself, she was dying to know if she'd measured up.

Get hold of yourself. He's a predator, after all. Good at sizing up people, assessing his odds and calculating weaknesses. "So, Mr. Shipley—"

"Lucas. You can call me Lucas if you're going to rob me. No need to be all formal about it."

"I'm not robbing you—"

He put one paw on her hand, the one clutching the legal-sized manila folder with the listing information in it. The action made her jump and immediately pull away.

"Marcy, may I call you Marcy?" He didn't wait for an answer. "Let's cut the crap. I've given it some thought for, oh," he pulled out his cell phone and checked the time, "about thirty minutes. She can have the house. She can keep it, sell it, give it away to a homeless shelter for all I care about it. That's no longer a place I want to have anything to do with," he said, pointing to the folder.

"Mr. Shipley—"

"I said call me Lucas," he interrupted.

"Mr. Shipley, this hasn't been negotiated and until you get yourself an attorney, you shouldn't be offering anything like that to me. I'm supposed to be an impartial neutral party to this transaction, representing both of you—"

"Sure you are." His arms were crossed and his left eye squinted, pulling up the left side of his lip.

"Well, you're certainly not making it very easy for me."

"What freakin' rule says I'm supposed to make it easy for *you?* You think this is freakin' easy for *me?*"

"No. But I'm here to get your signature on the listing contract for the house. *Only* the house. I'm going to tell your wife—"

"Soon-to-be ex-wife."

Marcy nodded and stared back at his oversized fingers. She saw cut marks on the inside of his bent and misshapen forefinger and a scar running up from the knuckle of his middle digit to above his wrist. The scar was nearly covered by a patch of dark body hair. He was missing the last joint on his fourth and little fingers. The vision distracted her until she saw him dip his head down, looking up and across to her side of the table, expecting an answer.

"You were saying something about my ex-wife?"

She took a deep inhale. "Mr. Shipley, I was offering a peace pipe, of sorts. We can do this contract, and I can get the house on MLS tonight or first thing in the morning. I'll tell her you wouldn't agree to the other two houses. Perhaps, with your cooperation here, this afternoon, I can convince her not to pursue the other two homes."

He leaned back in the chair, hiding his hands underneath the table. His chest fully rose as he gulped in air, and then his shoulders dropped as he exhaled. The scent of his body laced with what smelled like menthol shaving soap hit her in the face like a blast furnace and, in spite of herself, made her panties wet.

"And just why would you do that?"

She didn't really have an answer, because it had just come to her as a strategy and she had no idea from where. "Just…I don't know." She shrugged, seeking words to describe what she couldn't. Her insides were a jumbled mess. "I guess I feel like we should take this in little bites. The whole enchilada is probably hard to swallow at this point in time, Mr. Shipley."

Oh, no. There it is again, looking at me that way. The edge of his upper lip curled in amusement. If they were familiar, if they were a – *What in the devil are you doing, Marcy?* By the arch of his dark brow, she could tell he was tempted to say something dirty about the size of her mouth and the whole enchilada, and she worked very hard to put it out of her mind.

She closed her eyes so as not to watch him, putting her forehead into her palm, trying to seize back control of the conversation. It was no use, when she opened her eyes, and regarded the hunky SEAL sitting in front of her, with that sexy way he objected to everything she was trying to do, even the favor she was trying to bestow on him, the butterflies in her stomach instantly multiplied. Connie was right. He was a charmer of the professional class. A sheer force of nature. Her heart was beating like she'd just run a marathon.

Normally, the calmest person during a negotiation, but today, right then, she was losing it, big time. She'd never before met someone who affected her so. Was she excited for the challenge, or was it something else?

God help me.

CHAPTER 5

THOM GRANDE WAS waiting in the warehouse where the rest of Kyle's squad assembled. The SEAL from DEVGRU in Virginia studied each man carefully, as Lucas knew he'd been trained to do. Lucas had deployed with the Varsity Group, as Team 6 was known, two summers before, although not during the deployment that took out BinLaden. It was a special operation of four weeks, which gave him a nice signing bonus—enough for the down payment on the house Connie now wanted to sell.

When Thom's blue eyes met Lucas', he winked, acknowledging the antics of the night before at the strip club. Lucas wished he could remember more of it. He hoped he hadn't blown his chances to do a rotation with them, or perhaps join Team 6 in the future. Since he didn't have anyone around to hold him back, doing the most dangerous tours overseas was suddenly looking like the cure he needed. Way better than waiting for legal papers and the inside of courtrooms. He'd be crying, the kids would be crying, and sure as shit, Connie would drill him with a look that would send him straight to Hell.

Thom walked over to him, and they shook hands.

"How's your head, Shitface?"

Lucas turned to Jake, who snickered.

"I'm fine," Lucas mumbled. To Ryan and Jake, he whispered, "You fuckin' told him?"

"It slipped," Ryan whispered back. "But it was kind of obvious."

Jeffrey and Danny entered the room, and Kyle called the meeting.

"Okay, gents, yesterday was the briefing on that terrorist Jihadi John and what Thom and his boys have been dancing with. We have some late-breaking intel we were waiting for before we gave you the whole story."

They waited. Thom stepped forward and stood next to Kyle.

"So, I've got some bad news, gents," Kyle said.

Lucas could taste the juicy deployment he knew was coming up. Wouldn't that make his soon-to-be ex shit her pants? Turf the little hottie realtor, although he wouldn't mind hanging out with her again. He'd enjoyed the sparring the previous afternoon. He hadn't been able to sleep much that night, thinking about all the things he could do with her, all the positions...

"You think something's funny, son?" Kyle said.

Lucas saw bodies turn in his direction. His shit-eating grin and pleasant fantasy went right out the window as he realized they were waiting for him to respond.

"Yeah, asshole, I'm talking to you." Kyle had his hands on his hips and a mean scowl on his face.

"Sorry, sir. Was thinking about something else for a second."

Kyle's jaw clenched. "You see what I'm talking about? You guys do that over there and you'll get your brains splashed over all your buddies. Focus, goddammit. We're not in high school." Kyle sighed and continued with the monologue, but gave Lucas a nasty glare. Thom was standing half a body width behind Kyle, with his palm to his lips, having a hard time keeping a straight face, so the SEAL looked down.

Alex rubbed his dick against Lucas' left butt cheek, messing with Lucas' concentration, so he whipped around and tried to pop him.

"You wanna just sit this one out, Shipley?" Kyle barked.

Lucas knew if he told on Alex, he'd lose the respect of the team. He had to take it on by himself. "Chief Lansdowne, I got the runs. Got them last night. I was going to make a dash for the head, but I suddenly got control."

He knew they were all busting a gut inside. Thom broke out in a full smile that Kyle couldn't see.

"You want to go to the little girl's room, then, Shipley? Or are we good now? Can we go on with our meeting?"

"Yes, Chief Petty Officer Lansdowne. I'm good."

Kyle took one step back, folding his hands at his waist behind his back. "This here is SO Thom Grande, and he's going to tell us what we just learned today."

"Thanks, Chief Petty Officer Lansdowne," Thom Grande said in a soft voice.

His smirk was subtle. Lucas could see his affable nature made him a natural-born leader. He couldn't remember everything that was said the night before, but he remembered SO Grande had confided he'd had his share of difficulty with an ex-wife himself.

"We spent about four months last year on deployment, jumping in and out of Mosul, trying to rescue sensitive information and looking for one mean motherfucker, Jihadi John. I'm glad to say drone strikes have nearly wiped out the network he created and grew. But we don't really know anything further since that region is off limits to us now, as you know, or at least officially."

Thom paced in front of the thirty-man squad, walking a nearly straight line right down the middle of one crack between two poured slabs of concrete flooring, like the precision footwork was enjoyable to him.

"The nature of the enemy—of any enemy, for that matter—is to adapt to their environment and to stop doing what's not working and expand what is. This cell is no different. The drone strikes and night raids we used to do a couple of years ago were eating into the propaganda value of their campaign. They went quiet after we captured the cluster of leaders at the top, and those bastards are now housed in Kurdish prisons, guarded by men who would rather kill them than guard them."

Lucas waited for the first shoe to drop. He was salivating, the mantra *deployment* ringing in his ears.

"And when they went quiet, we thought perhaps they'd had a change of heart, or that the younger generation didn't have the stomach for war. We considered it a good sign."

Thom stood within two feet of the front line of SEALs from Alpha squad. "I was sent here because we received some intel we think is credible, and it involves Teams 3 and 5. Today, it was confirmed, and that confirmation was what I was waiting for before I could level with you all, completely." He locked gazes with everyone in the front row. Then he paced back the way he came, gaining eye contact with every man in the second.

Kyle watched them all, as well. Thom completed his analysis of what was to be their future. Lucas couldn't wait to hear the words, *We'll be deploying within the week.*

"We have reason to believe there was a death squad sent specifically to go after members of Teams 3 and 5, as retaliation."

He let it sink in a bit. No one said a word.

"Somehow, they got it that Team 3 and Team 5 were the ones who rounded up their leaders. They intend to bring some of you boys back home with them as hostages. To return the favor, so to speak. To show that it can be done—"

Lucas was hearing things he never thought possible, things so far from his imagination he had a hard time understanding the actual words. It was as if Grande was speaking Pashtu.

"—that terrorists could come here on U.S. soil, could kidnap a bunch of Navy SEALs and bring them back to Iraq. Their own twisted version of a snatch and grab."

The squad erupted in a string of expletives, each mumbling their favorite words of disgust.

Jake was the first to speak coherently. "You have to be shittin' me. That's the dumbest idea I've ever heard."

Thom smiled, even though his gaze remained hard. "I agree. It sounds farfetched." He looked right at Lucas as he continued, "But *if* they could, and that's a pretty big *if,* the propaganda factor would be huge. Even if they halfway carried some part of it off, their mission would make headlines all over the world."

Kyle took one long step, coming to sharp attention as he joined

Grande. "Unlike our side, those bastards don't care about the loss of life. They're looking for sensational things they can do to swell the ranks with new recruits. Trust me, gents, something like this would be huge for them, even if they fail. And make no doubt about it—they *will* fail."

Lucas still had one last hope for deployment. "So, what is it we do, exactly? Like when do we leave and get these assholes before they try to come over here and attempt their suicide mission?"

"You boys aren't going anywhere overseas; not yet, anyways. You're not due to deploy for another five months, at least. You get to stay here while the other teams are out. Team 5 will deploy in thirty days, as planned. But you guys—you? You get to hang around Coronado and become bait."

Lucas was getting sick to his stomach.

Alex rolled his shoulder and growled, "SO Grande? Could you answer a question that's bugging me?"

"Sure. Go ahead. I'm here for your questions. All of them," answered the Varsity SEAL.

"Why don't we just meet them in combat over there, like Lucas here just said?"

It was Kyle's turn. Sucking in air, his back erect, he answered, "Because, Kowicki, they're already here."

CHAPTER 6

MARCY WAS UPLOADING the rest of her listing, sending out the reverse match emails to agents who were looking for property in this price range and location, when her cell phone rang. It was Connie.

"Hi, there. Just uploading your listing right now, Connie."

"Thank God. Do you have to inspect the other two houses, Marcy? I found keys for both of them."

"Well, Connie, I was going to talk to you about that." Marcy was trying to dart between the divorcing couple, noticing how anxious Connie was to untie their bond of marriage. "Why don't we just take it one step at a time? I think Lucas has shown some cooperation. Maybe we can get a great offer on your house right off the bat, and that would take some of the financial pressure off you both for a bit until you get settled. We can always handle those other two listings later. We could perhaps offer to be reasonable if he cooperates, which would be much better for you."

"And why would I do that?" Connie's cold tone sent Marcy a chill.

"Well, I think it's in your best interest to have his full cooperation on the sale of the house, Connie, don't you?"

"I don't care about getting cooperation. I want to make him pay."

"But Connie, don't you want to walk away with the most amount of money?"

"You mean, would I rather walk away with a ton of money or the satisfaction of screwing him six ways to Sunday? If you have to ask that question, Marcy, you don't know me very well."

The baby started crying in the background, and Connie went to retrieve him. Marcy really didn't know Connie as well as she was going to, but she did know this wasn't headed anywhere good.

Connie picked up the phone again and continued, "If you're coming out here today to put the lockbox on, I can give you both keys. I have no idea if either of them are occupied—"

"He told me the house on Linda Lane had a tenant in it."

"See? I told you he'd cooperate. That's more than he's told me. He hides that rent money, spends it on God knows what. Gambling. Girls. Drugs—"

"Drugs?" Marcy's hackles raised a bit. The suggestion seemed to be completely out of character, even for Lucas. He was, after all, an elite Navy man.

"Sure, why not? I mean, he does everything else. The man's a fuckin' human tornado. He and those boys of his are wreaking havoc wherever they drop their pants—"

"Look, Connie, I don't want to—"

"Maaaaar Seee. Did that asshole try to charm his way into your pants? He can, you know. I told you he can."

The dance Marcy had started became very tedious and she began to wonder if she had the skill to stay out of the frying pan, or avoid getting hit by it as it went flying past her head. "Look, Connie, can we just keep it simple? I don't think he wants any trouble, he just—"

"That sweet-talkin' dickwad."

Marcy was walking on quicksand. These two were going to be a real piece of work. Suddenly, she wasn't so confident she'd be able to keep them in their own corners and avoid killing each other. "You have to give the tenant notice for those kinds of things. I don't even have any way to contact them."

"Then I'll go. I'll just fuckin' walk right up to the house, knock on the door, put little Jack on my boob, and ask to fuckin' walk around the house that I half-own. I can take pictures, right?"

"Connie, you're not hearing me."

"I'll tell them if they want to stay, they'd better cooperate with open houses, tours coming through, people walking through at all times of the day and night."

"All things you'll put up with on your house, is that correct?"

"*Hell, no.*"

Jack started to fuss. Again.

"Look, you've talked with him about it. He didn't react."

"He most certainly *did* react. He strongly objected. Only way I could get him to sign the contract for your house was by telling him we'd do it one step at a time. Same as I'm telling you now, Connie. Seriously, this is in your best interest."

"Why don't you just fill out the paperwork, and I'll sign those two new contracts today. He can sign when he realizes I'm serious. Oh. And how much equity is in both?"

Marcy was beginning to see why they were divorcing. Connie was every bit the piece of work he was. "He didn't tell me about the mortgages or taxes, but I did ask him."

"That jerkoff."

"I don't think he would have signed the listing agreement on your house if I held him up for all three listings, Connie." How many times did she have to repeat that fact before it sunk in?

She could hear Connie telling something to their daughter. "I have to go, Marcy. What time will you be here?"

"I can get there within an hour. After I finish a couple of things, I'll be right over."

Connie hung up without saying another word.

ON THE WAY over to Connie's, Marcy couldn't understand how two people could make babies together and still act like children themselves. And how he could go through the grueling training to become a Navy SEAL, have all the stamina—mental stamina—to do that job and not be able to reel in his emotions. That was her first thought.

Her second thought was about how completely *unboring* the guy was. She imagined he would be a piece of work in the bedroom if he loved like he argued. He had skin in the game. Life mattered to him.

Things mattered to him. Was it because he had to control his breathing, his fear, and his thoughts of impending death so many times in the battlefield he just let it all hang out in real life?

Yeah, that's probably it. Being a trained warrior, he was out of his element stateside, having to do things like be soft and gentle and worry about someone else's feelings. He'd married someone else who also had a hair-trigger and needed the intense relationship a guy like him could bring. That not only wasn't in his training, but he'd probably been trained to funnel everything emotional away from the job as a stress-coping mechanism.

And so the wife and family received the brunt of his inability to connect. The family got what was left over after his deployments, not his best side, either.

Still, she wondered what they'd been like when they first married. She imagined they'd exploded like rockets lighting up the sky. Those two were probably incapable of doing anything halfway.

She allowed herself a smile. Maybe she was going about it wrong. Maybe she should just sit back and enjoy the show. At least they weren't turning on her.

Not yet.

She rang the doorbell, and Connie's disembodied voice told her to come in. She laid her paperwork down on the dining room table, including the folder with his signature on the contracts and disclosure statements, and then sat and waited. She needed Connie's John Hancock on the disclosures.

Connie wafted into the room wearing the tightest pair of jeans Marcy had seen, along with a push-up, low-cut cotton top that revealed her ample cleavage.

"He filled out the Transfer Disclosure, Connie. I gotta have you review what he put down, initial and sign these."

The SEAL wife sneered at the stack of papers. "Wow. He musta been there for hours and hours. The guy can't read, you know. He covers it up well, but the Neanderthal doesn't read anything. He likes graphic novels and—"

"Connie, he reads just fine. It didn't take long. I helped him with some of it, but he filled it all out."

Connie crossed her arms over her chest, sending her boobs north. "Sure you did." Connie's look was a challenge.

"What does that mean?"

She huffed and leaned over Marcy's shoulder, grabbing a pen. "Just sayin'. Okay, where do I sign?"

Marcy indicated where she was to initial and then sign beneath his signature. "Fuckin' jerk signed in my spot."

"Makes no difference—"

"So, you don't think it makes a difference who's on top?" She wiggled her eyebrows.

Marcy looked away and felt heat creep across her cheeks.

Connie laughed. "I'll bet this is the last divorcing SEAL you'll ever represent, huh?"

"No. It isn't the first, and it most certainly won't be my last, either."

"Well, if you can keep the cows in the barn and keep his pants on, you might get paid. One of my best friends is a realtor, and she wouldn't touch this with a ten-foot pole."

"I'll bet," Marcy said under her breath, slipping the contracts into the folder. So much for feeling lucky about winning the listing from the agents she'd had to battle it out with. Unless that was a lie, too. Sensing Connie's unfriendly stare on the top of her head, she pulled out the blue lockbox and held it up. "This goes on a water pipe or, if there is none, the front door, but it scratches the wood. It has to be on something that won't go anywhere."

"Put it on his fuckin' flagpole. And I'm not talking about his dick."

The woman's cursing was beginning to wear on every last one of her nerves. She'd never have guessed wives cursed like sailors, too. Marcy fought for composure. "So, that's where, exactly?"

"Oh, that's right. His huge honker of an American flag isn't on it. Some days, when the breeze picks up, I'd have to battle that damned thing so I could get out the front door. He likes 'em big, like everything, except his women. He likes them with huge tits in fancy white lace, likes skinny waists and loves to talk dirty in bed."

Marcy felt heat begin to crawl up her neck, but managed to will away the blush. She wondered how the Lucas she'd met could have hooked up with this woman, and though it wasn't really her business, for her own sake, she needed to know. A slight worry for the health of the children began to grow as well.

Connie gave her a little wink and a half-smile.

"Gonna miss that part of things a bit. But I'm working hard to find me a replacement—quick."

CHAPTER 7

AFTER THE MEETING, Thom Grande came up to Lucas, the rest of the team barely within earshot. "Understand you're having trouble with the missus."

"That's fuckin' putting it mildly."

"So that explains your behavior last night. Not that I minded tagging along."

"You forget yourself, Grande. I think you forgot the part about us helping you walk and plopping your sorry ass on the bed at your motel. Or don't you remember that?"

Thom nodded and grinned at his cowboy boots. They looked expensive to Lucas, but then Lucas, being a California kid, didn't know anything about boots.

The SEAL peered up at Lucas and gave him that knowing look. "Been there, done that."

"What, the going to strip clubs or the domestic wars?"

"Guilty on both counts. But that kind of action at clubs and bars and shit, Lucas, there's nothing there except a fake good time. It's all fake, man. Save your marriage if you can."

Lucas started to chuckle. "Well, it isn't up to me, Grande. The woman has her own ideas of where the boundary lines are, and I fuckin' crossed into enemy territory when I wasn't looking."

"And she won't forgive you?"

"Nothing to forgive. She thinks I did the thing with a transvestite who takes a really good picture. Not that the big guy wasn't attractive, just not my thing. I've never been unfaithful to Connie, but I can't convince her otherwise."

"So, you keep pushing the envelope, hoping some woman will just grab your balls and make you forget your wife? That's your plan? That what you're saying? You know how dangerous that is?"

"Look, man, this is all good here, but you're not my fuckin' psychiatrist. No offense intended. I got Kyle and the guys here watching out for me. I'm good. I'm just going through a rough patch. I got kids I won't be able to see, a wife who wants to have nothing to do with me for nothing I've done, and now she's taking me to the cleaners. I fucking re-upped for four years to get the down payment for this fuckin' house she's taking away from me. And now the bitch wants my granddad's hunting cabin and the house my mother left me."

Grande stepped back. "No worries. I feel you. Didn't mean to butt in, Shipley." He held his palms out to the sides as if demonstrating he didn't hold a weapon. "Just if there's any advice I can give you, the best advice I didn't get until it was too late, is to get a good divorce attorney."

"Fuck it. She can have it all."

"And she'll keep taking it until you fight her, my man," Alex said as he slapped Lucas on the back.

"Listen to him, Shitface. This guy has the scars to prove it," added Jake.

"Come on, assholes," Kyle called out. "Get the hell out of the building. I gotta lock up."

THEY MET FOR beers at the Scupper. The usual parade of high school students and college party girls was in and around the bar, sliding up and down seats like they were working a pole at a club, the skirts shorter and tighter than Lucas remembered. They were looking younger and prettier the more beers he drank.

One of Kyle's old-timers, Calvin Cooper, sat down across the table. "You're gonna have to face your demons, Lucas, or you'll be no good to us. Being sober is no joke, my man."

Cooper's gentle rolling voice was soothing, but a warning nonetheless. His plain talk and even sharper stare made Lucas sit up. Coop's huge six-foot-four frame loomed over the table like he was the king at court.

"I can handle it."

"Oh, sure you can. Until you can't, and then you'll be balling one of those sixteen-year-olds with a fake I.D., and bam, you're off the teams. You gotta ask yourself what's really more important, being married or being a SEAL. 'Cause right now, you can't do both. It's eating you alive, man. You're hooked up with a woman who can't handle the heat. She's gone over the edge. She's bent. And you're in some la-la land, thinking you can turn her back into the little kitten she was when you married her."

"How many times you been married, Coop?" Lucas liked the big SEAL medic.

"Mentally? Lots of times. But nah, I tried out a lot for all those teams, but in the end, there was only one lady for me. Just once, man."

"So, how can you talk?"

"You forget I've been doing this over eleven years. I've seen it all. If Kyle doesn't toss you, I will. I'll give you a mental so fast you won't be able to find your dick. Just imagine how the Navy will put you to use with that in your folder."

As one of the team medics, Coop could easily end his career. He wouldn't want to, of course, but if it meant saving the life of the others on the team, weeding out someone who wasn't paying attention, it would be something he'd have to do for everyone's safety. And though Lucas would be off the teams, his obligation to the Navy would continue. He'd get stuck cleaning toilets on a ship or perhaps being a BUD/S instructor and dishing out his brand of hate on all the young, new recruits.

"One more piece of advice, and then I'm going to get these gentlemen to escort you home. Get yourself a fuckin' lawyer. Stop feeling sorry for yourself. Quit reacting and start making a plan. Either walk away or fight. Those are your only two choices."

The giant stood, threw down a twenty, even though he'd been drinking mineral water, and in a couple of long strides was out the doorway.

Minutes later, Lucas left as well. The night air was crisp and the stars were out. The warm, salty breeze was something Lucas loved more than just about anything.

Just about.

They had five days until they started training for hostage rescue and house-to-house searches. They'd all have to requalify on the range, and anything less than expert was not acceptable. Lucas decided he'd go visit the cabin, get in touch with his childhood and see what the ghosts of Northern California had to say to him.

Besides, it beat waiting for Connie to serve him with more papers. And the ghosts were a helluva lot kinder than Connie's mouth.

But his dick still got hard when he thought about what wonders she could do with that mouth.

CHAPTER 8

MARCY HAD A friend from college who lived in Sonoma County and sold real estate. And she happened to be married to an ex-SEAL. They had a small winery operation a lot of the San Diego crowd had invested in. She decided to call her.

"Hey, Devon. I've got a property I need to check out in Cloverdale. Was thinking maybe I'd drive up and see you and Nick for a day or two. What do you say?"

"That would be great. You want my help with the listing in any way?"

"I don't have the listing yet. Divorcing couple. He's a SEAL, and they don't exactly see eye to eye on everything yet."

Devon giggled. "They never do, unless *you* screw up, then they get reunited."

"In this case, I'd actually walk away. They have two beautiful kids. A shame, really."

"Not everyone can make it. Lots of divorces in the community. What day are you coming?"

"How about tomorrow?"

"Sure. My place is open. We just finished the guest cottage, and I don't have anyone renting it until the weekend. The place is yours."

"Thanks."

"Does Nick know him?"

"The SEAL? Name's Shipley, Lucas Shipley."

"I'll ask him. Safe journeys. Why don't you fly up? We got direct flights now, just like in the big city. I'll pick you up at the airport. Would save you a whole day each way, unless you want the drive to ease your mind."

"You know, I think I'll do that. But let me pick up a car at the airport. I'm going to need my own wheels."

"Yup, unless you want to drive one of our tractors."

MARCY DROVE FROM the Charles Schulz airport down the freeway into Santa Rosa, and then took the two-lane country road to Bennett Valley. A small shingle sign at the end of a crushed granite driveway marked the property as Sophie's Vineyard. The rows of lush green vines under a bright blue cloudless sky welcomed her. The rich black soil of Sonoma County provided stark contrast to the colors of the fresh crushed straw covering it. Something emotional was building inside, and she wasn't quite sure what was happening. She felt like there was a new adventure looming—something unexpected was about to happen. It would alter her path forever.

Devon and Nick's modern home was built on the site of Nick's sister's nursery grounds, a nursery that had failed as an enterprise, but succeeded in bringing together Nick and Devon, a couple who were living out their dreams in the wine country. Though Nick had retired from the teams without a pension, he was more than content running the day-to-day operations of the small winery. Devon made enough money for them to live on while the grapes were developing. It was a storybook romance from beginning to end.

Devon wrapped her arms around Marcy and gave her a squeeze. "So great to see you, Marcy. Wow. Things in San Diego must agree with you."

"Thanks." Marcy blushed. "I've been lucky, I guess."

Nick appeared at the doorway. He was as handsome as Marcy remembered—tall with wide shoulders, blond hair and green eyes. Wearing jeans with suspenders and a khaki long-sleeved shirt rolled up at the sleeves, he was wiping his hands on a rag.

"Hey there, Marcy," he said as he gave her a quick hug and kiss on the cheek.

"You're looking all farm boy-like, Nick. No body armor, guns, or tats covering half your body?"

"Oh, I got the tats," Nick said, showing her the line of frog prints extending from his wrist to inside his elbow joint, just like Lucas had.

"All the guys on Kyle's squad have them. Sort of a rite of passage. You're working for one of us?" Nick squinted and asked, tossing the rag onto the seat of a riding mower.

"Lucas Shipley. You know him?"

"Yeah, Devon asked me. Can't say that I do, but there were a bunch of guys at the end, coming on board. How long's he been with the teams?"

"All I know is he re-upped a couple of years ago. His bonus was what gave them the down payment on the house I'm selling." She allowed her voice to trail off. This was part of her job she wasn't proud of.

"Ohhh, ouch. Well then, I probably knew him. Some of the guys do extra training, though. Languages, medic long course, details at Quantico, burn center in Texas. He could have been doing one of those."

"And you took a lot of time off, Nick, when Sophie—"

Marcy had been told the story of how Nick's sister had been poisoned with arsenic in her well water by a neighbor who was now serving time for her murder.

Devon frowned and then drew herself out of her private thought. "Well, I'm not being very hospitable leaving you out here. Nick, you want to get Marcy's bags?"

Marcy opened the truck as Nick picked up two overnight suitcases and slung her briefcase over his shoulder.

"I still get to do all the heavy lifting around here," he said as he widened his eyes and pretended to be overloaded.

Devon slipped an arm around Marcy's waist. "So, tell me about yourself. What's new? And I need to hear about all the hunks in San Diego you're dating."

As Marcy stepped into the doorway, she was stunned. Far from looking like a house, the place more aptly resembled a church. The living room was two stories tall, with a large glass garage door facing out to the hillside garden beyond. The carefully crafted rock walls and meandering garden paths she could see from the large window were stunning. Inside, the living and dining room contained eclectic things from all over the world, including a couple of flower boats from India and a carved sandalwood cabinet that looked like it came from a palace. She smelled fresh coffee and heard light jazz playing in the beautiful room.

"This is amazing. I guess I had a hard time visualizing it when I was up here for the wedding." She turned around a couple of revolutions. "It doesn't look like the same place."

"That was before we got all the furniture in the house. Was a great place for a wedding, though," Devon said.

Nick came back from the hallway and took his wife's hand. "I've set your things on the bed in there. You have a fireplace, but I'd keep it off. We're getting some heat these days. The pilot light keeps the room toasty, sometimes too warm."

"Thank you so much," Marcy said.

"You want something to drink? We were going to have an early supper."

"Wine. You have any wine?"

Nick walked over to a huge floor-to-ceiling wine refrigerator cabinet with double doors, housing more than a hundred bottles of wine. He turned to Marcy and said, "We got white. We got red. You get to pick."

"You have any that came from here? I'd love a red wine."

"Excellent choice." Nick presented the cool bottle to Marcy, where she read the label, *Sophie's Choice.*

CHAPTER 9

THE TRIP UP the coast was always enjoyable. Except for a couple of areas of commuter congestion, the ride was uneventful and stress-free. Lucas used the time to listen to several audio books he'd not made time for in San Diego. The beautiful ride went by quickly, even with the three stops for gas. Like most men on SEAL Team 3, he owned a Hummer, something Connie had been bugging him to get rid of because of the expense. Today, he was glad he'd prevailed in this one thing.

Watching the landscape change from ocean to rocky shoreline in the Monterey area, back to farmland north to Silicon Valley, and then back out to the coast at Marin, all the way nearly to Bodega Bay, it was hard to envision the beautiful scenery as a war zone. But if Thom was right, that's exactly what it was. Stopping for oysters at Marshall's Cove, he drank a beer and watched the sun as it began dropping to the water's horizon. A local motorcycle club was loud and apparently staying nearby. Listening to their language, he pegged them for cops, not bandits.

It touched him as he watched the band of brothers play together, how the cops from the East Bay were trying so hard to have a normal life, just like he and his SEAL buddies did in Coronado. These men had seen the carnage left by society and chose to serve honorably, just like the SEALs. And just like the SEALs, in their off time, they didn't want to look anything like cops. They wore their red bandanas and black leathers. Beefy arms sported tats. And every one of them had all manner of ear piercings. Some of the bikers were alone, some with wives or girlfriends. The ladies were in all sizes, shapes, and ages.

Good for them.

The public had no idea what evils lay out there, even in the brown and green hills of the wine country of California. Evil was everywhere. Lucas knew it was his job to keep evil at bay. And now he'd be doing that at home, as well.

He knew from the talk and the reaction from the other guys that this was a hard thing to wrap their minds around. Danger at home. Sure, the cops were used to it, but SEALs? Having to watch their six at home, in the land of freedom? Where everything was apple pie, and it was easier to tell the good guys from the bad guys?

Forget politics. Leave it to a bunch of politicians to make treaties and agreements they knew no one would keep, and leave it all to the fighting men and women to enforce the unenforceable. Wasn't their fault they were losing the war, and now was it really coming over here? No one could win that kind of war. Even the zealots wouldn't win.

It was just like the cops, trying to deal with the complexities and political decisions of local laws. Up to them to enforce the unenforceable, too.

He finished his oysters as he mentally said goodbye to the guys acting like badasses down at the designated fire pits on the beach. He drove east, and then in an hour arrived in Cloverdale.

He'd forgotten how the sound of the crickets made him feel safe. As long as they were doing their two-toned chirp thing, it meant no strange animal or person was on their way. Just like frogs at the local frog pond he'd played at as a child. When the din stopped suddenly, that was when you paid attention to your surroundings. His grandfather had taught him that.

Lucas fished for the old brass key, slipped it into the lock and instantly he was taken back twenty years, even though it had only been less than ten since he'd been here. That was the summer Granddad had passed away, and his dad soon after that, as if the two were brothers, instead of a very close father and son.

He'd always envied his dad's relationship with his grandfather, probably forged because he'd been raised without a mother and there wasn't anyone to dilute their relationship.

Their whispers in every corner still haunted him as he examined the crude, knotty pine cupboards the three of them had made one summer. He opened the cabinet next to the sink and, sure as shit, there were the holes in the cabinet door where he'd had to re-drill for the screws attaching the hinges three times. His dad wanted him to do it, until he learned how to do it right. The puttied holes were testament to a lesson learned, and no one ever talked about it after it was accomplished. As he grew into a teen and came up to hunt with the two most important men in his life, he liked to look at that door just to remind himself of where he'd come from. It was like proof of his existence.

The cabin had only one bedroom. The old brass bed sported the quilt his mother had made, and when he checked out the spongy mattress that always squeaked when his father happened to take his mother up sometimes, a small cloud of dust rose. Lucas quickly removed the quilt and took it outside, shaking it furiously. He left the colorful patchwork quilt over the porch handrail to air out.

Lucas reset the refrigerator switch and plugged it in, hearing the familiar purring of the old turquoise Philco appliance, stowing the milk, eggs and beer he'd brought, along with some meat for a barbeque he was looking forward to the following night. He found rags and cleaning supplies and did a thorough scrub down of the whole cabin, working until well after midnight. It was a labor of love, homage to a time long past and perhaps never coming again. Just like the refrigerator, he felt his reset switch had been tripped. He was ready for the change.

The cold shower he took before bed was exhilarating after the twelve-hour drive. He found a flannel nightshirt of his father's in the bureau drawer, stowed his Sig Sauer under his pillow, brought the quilt from the porch inside and, draping it over the bed, crashed.

At first light, the birds began chirping, and Lucas found it impossible to sleep any further. He checked his gun, made his bed and unpacked the few things he'd brought with him. The tall highboy dresser with its cracked mirror stood faithfully to serve him, like a butler, showing a reflection of himself in the darkened glass. He took another cold shower, this time not feeling so cold, considered shaving and decided against it. He put on his jeans, a new t-shirt, and then a sweater of his father's he'd found hanging in the closet.

He was going to make some coffee when he heard a car drive up. Quickly stowing his gun in the back waistband of his pants, covered by the sweater, he looked through the window to the driveway outside. Next to his burgundy Hummer, a white sedan was parking. Out stepped Marcy Gelland.

He opened the front door and leaned into the frame, arms crossed, until she looked up and saw him.

"Oh. It's you!"

"Yes, Miss Gelland. I do own this cabin—at least for a little while longer, anyway."

Her oversized satchel was slung over her shoulder. She had on a pair of forest green recycled ankle gardening boots, and a big white, silk shirt with a pocket stitched over one breast, covering long, tan slacks that were going to be way too warm in a couple of hours. She'd done her hair up in a clip, and she wore no makeup. He liked her better that way.

"You following me now?" he asked, not moving from the spot, daring her to try to gain entry into his private domain. "I told you I wasn't going to sell this place."

She turned around, glancing at the tree line before her eyes at last landed on the thatched roof of the cabin. Then she tilted her head and spoke to him. "Beautiful here. I don't blame you a bit."

"So, you've seen it. Now, you can go, Miss Gelland—or is it Mrs. Gelland?"

Her lips parted slightly, one side turned up, amused. "Marcy. You can call me Marcy. Unlike you, I've never been married."

"Touché." The sting in her comment hurt like a pinprick, but it sucked him back into his impending court battle with Connie. He dropped his arms at the sides, suddenly not knowing what to do with them. "Well, that's it. Show's over. I have nothing else left to offer, unless you like strong coffee and scrambled eggs."

"I love strong coffee and scrambled eggs. I'm afraid I can't make either one successfully."

He didn't know why he said it, but before he could take it back, found himself whispering, "Well, perhaps you're better at other things."

"I should hope so," she said timidly. "I guess, according to you, I rob people for a living."

"Ah, an honest woman who admits her vices. How refreshing. Do you ask for forgiveness before or after you fleece them?"

At first, she didn't smile, just stared back at him. She wasn't afraid, which was such a turn-on. "I solve problems. Most of my day is spent solving other people's mistakes and problems. And I'm damn good at it." She narrowed her eyes, as if taunting him to say something nasty.

Lucas was struck with the inability to fight with her. Whatever was going on, he couldn't dislike her, and he wanted to, perhaps needed to.

Marcy still didn't move an inch. There she was in the middle of the fuckin' forest, way far away from anyone who could hear her scream. He was trying to stand up to her, trying to hate her and everything she stood for. He wanted to blame her for what his life was going to become. She was a willing accomplice to his wife's selfish attitude.

She remained standing, as if waiting for instructions. Defiant, almost petulant, daring him to cave in and show his ungentlemanly side. She hugged her file folder and oversized purse, looking way more desirable than she probably knew. But when she broke a smile and stepped closer to his perch, she finally dropped the hand with the folder, catching it at the side of her hip, and giving him the view of her chest he'd wanted to see. Although he wasn't going to let her catch him at it, his peripheral vision took in the whole lovely sight of her.

She glanced up, recognizing something, and gave him a playful, narrowed look. "I think we got off to a bad start. I'm not here to cause you any pain, or to rob you. Mr.—"

"Lucas. If I'm calling you Marcy, you're calling me Lucas."

"Yessir," she said as she straightened her spine, her pert little lips doing that pouty thing.

What a blessing she was. What a fresh piece of something he'd never had and wanted desperately.

"Like I was saying, *Lucas…*"

Her large brown eyes smiled up at him, and his heart melted. He hadn't realized he was so starved for mature female attention, the kind that wasn't tipped or bought and paid for.

"I think you misunderstand my intentions. I'm not here to sell your cabin. As a matter of fact, I'm not sure I can, or that Connie has the right to order either of them sold. That will have to be worked out in a settlement agreement between the two of you."

He could see that the longer he watched her speak and focused on her lips, the more talkative she became. Words were nervously stringing together, and all he could think of was her light pink tongue darting out behind her white teeth, and the way she licked her lips and nervously bit her bottom one.

"You haven't taken my suggestion and gotten an attorney yet, have you?" she finished and took in a deep breath.

"That was only a little over a day ago, Marcy." He was thinking to himself that his perspective was changing by the minute. "But I'm all ears. Perhaps you can recommend someone for me."

The double meaning seemed to make her blink very slowly, considering what he'd said. She quickly looked downward toward her ridiculous boots.

"Where'd you get those?" he asked with a chuckle.

"Costco."

"No socks. Can't go into the woods without socks. You'll get ticks on your ankles, or worse, traveling up your pant legs."

Marcy cocked her head and frowned then gave him that full gaze that did him in. She forged her response. "You going to continue to defend the perimeter, or am I invited in for those scrambled eggs and strong coffee? Or have I said something to cause you to change your mind?"

There was an exchange between them without words. It fell to him to speak up first, perhaps acknowledge what was going on inside him, hopefully inside her, too. He knew when a woman liked what she saw, and she was definitely transmitting it. "On the contrary. But enter at your own risk."

He let his words linger there until she dropped her gaze again. Stepping aside, he turned and opened the door for her to walk into his life.

Once inside, she slowly took stock of the place, carefully examining the pictures on the walls, the cabinets, the hooked rug in front of the fireplace, the kitchen area, and the sparse furniture of the living room with one table lamp he'd made as a Boy Scout.

"It's lovely. I can see why it has special meaning to you. Lots of memories here. I can feel them, I think."

He'd been holding his breath. "Thank you." He stepped closer to her, and slowly brought his palm to her cheek and cupped it. Letting his fingers brush against her flawless skin, and then dropped his hand. He wanted to be careful, not push his boundaries, but the granite in his pants was making him very uncomfortable.

She turned once again, and he wanted to lace his fingers through her hair, take that damned clip out and muss it all up real good, before he gave her the kiss she so deserved. Hell, *he* deserved that kiss. It had been a long, insane dry spell.

She set her folder down on the table, placing her bag on top of it. "Can I help you with something?"

Oh, yeah, darlin'. You can help me heal that big wound in my soul. Get me feeling right about myself again, about the world. "Let's see. Can you crack eggs?" he asked as he brought out a carton from the refrigerator and set them next to a green bowl from the cupboard. "I even have the right implements." He drew out a wire whisk from one of the drawers.

Her fingers wrapped around the base of the whisk, and for a moment, their fingers touched. It would have been so easy to curl her into his chest, kiss the top of her head, and feel her blood pumping in her neck as he nibbled there. She smelled divine, and he was fairly sure her temperature had risen, since there were tiny beads of sweat on her upper lip.

He moved away from her to light the propane stove and pull out an iron skillet. As she cracked several eggs, he brushed behind her to get the butter. He felt her jump at his proximity, and it gladdened him. He would take the whole day cracking eggs and eating breakfast if she'd let him. Suddenly, he wasn't in a hurry to go anywhere or do anything.

He poured water from a gallon jug into a saucepan on the stove, and after boiling it and cooking the eggs, filled the coned coffee filter to the top and watched as it drained into a ceramic pitcher.

He added cheese and some spices to the eggs, made toast in the frying pan, poured their coffee, and put the cream on the table.

"Breakfast is served, Madame," he said with a bow, placing the two plates on the table across from each other.

"So how often did you come here growing up?" she asked.

"Some of the best times of my life. My grandfather and father used to bring me up every summer. Sometimes my mom, but only occasionally. Learned to hunt and fish. They told stories about being a man that scared this little boy to death."

Lucas worried he'd revealed something perhaps he shouldn't.

The silence was awkward and in need of filling. Marcy beat him to it. "Wow. These eggs are terrific—I think the best I've had."

"Not my best skill," he said, smiling into his coffee mug.

She answered him with a smile. "You want an update on the house?"

"I don't care about that right now, really."

"Okay."

"No offense."

"None taken," she said breathlessly. "Lucas, this property was yours before your marriage, from what I can see. Unless you encumbered it in some way." Her eyes were soft.

"The bank asked me to use it as additional collateral on the loan, because Connie had a couple late payments on her student loan."

"But you didn't borrow against it, right? Pull any money out of it?"

"No. Just used it as a kind of guarantee for the house loan."

"So, if *that's* paid off through escrow, then *this* house would be, what, free and clear?"

"Yes, ma'am."

"I'm no attorney, but I understand that if it was yours before you got married, it remains your sole and separate property. I don't think you can be forced to sell it."

"That's good news," he said, letting out a breath. "So, I have a question for you, Marcy, since we're talking about business sorts of things." He was about to risk a little more, feeling suddenly comfortable and intrigued.

"Shoot," she said as she finished her eggs and took a gulp of coffee.

"Why are you here?" Her eyes widened at first, and then she returned his honest gaze.

"Well, you'll probably have to submit a valuation for this place during your divorce proceedings, when they start. And, I don't know." She shrugged, brushing some crumbs from her lap. "I guess I was looking for something. Not sure what."

Those eyes again searched his face.

"Did you find what you were looking for?" he asked as he covered her hand with one of his.

She hesitated a bit, giving a jolt as their fingers wove together, and then he drew her hand to his face and kissed her palm.

She swallowed hard. "Yes. I think I did."

"Is this wise, Marcy? You're going to have to stop me, you know, because I can't."

She closed her eyes again, as if searching the back reaches of her mind. "I don't want you to stop," she said, her eyes still closed.

CHAPTER 10

MARCY QUIVERED WITH anticipation as he took her by the hand and, without looking back, brought her to the little bedroom. In front of the patchwork quilt, he reached around her waist and drew her to him, holding her as her hands traveled up his arms. She arched back and they parted. He bent and kissed her. When his kiss went deep, she was lost.

This wasn't the smart thing to do. Somewhere, she knew this, but she'd been starved for this meal. She knew deep inside, she'd always regret it if she didn't just take a chance and let herself glide into something unwise and dangerous—with him.

I'm going to have to cancel the listing and give it to someone else in the office, she thought while he kissed her neck. He removed her hair clip, tossing it to the corner, his fingers lacing through her hair.

Other equally ridiculous thoughts flew past her when his fingers probed down her front as he slowly unbuttoned her shirt. She'd worn a lace bra. White. Exactly what Connie had said. The look on Lucas' face told her it wasn't a lie. *Lucas likes his women big-chested,* which Marcy was, *and in white lace,* which she also was.

"Lucas, wait a minute."

"No." He continued exploring her top, trying to get his tongue into the cup of white lace to taste her nipple, kissing her in other impossible places.

"If we do this—"

"Honey, we're doing this."

"Then I can't represent you."

"Ask me if I care," he whispered in her ear. "I need this. I think you do, too."

He was right, of course. But her job, her morals, every alarm and bell were sounding off the wall.

"I—I don't think this is a good idea."

"Same answer. Ask me if I care."

"I feel like I'm taking advantage of my position."

He continued kissing her neck and between her breasts. In spite of herself, she felt his hard ridge, and instead of backing away, she pressed into him.

"I intend to take full advantage of you taking advantage of me," he answered in a whisper.

"It isn't wise."

"No, it isn't."

"It isn't smart." She sighed as her lips told him something else.

"Not smart at all," he murmured before he completely covered her mouth.

When their lips parted, she was leaning in to him, holding on to him like he was her lifeline.

"But is it right, Marcy? Ask your soul. Is this something you should have, something you *deserve*?" He ducked his head a bit to gaze into her eyes. She could see he was giving her the choice.

"Is it, Marcy? Is it right for you, because it's sure right for me." His thumb brushed against her lips.

"Would you stop if I asked you?"

"Yes, after I kissed every inch of your body. After I made you come so many times, you didn't remember your name, baby. Yes, I'd stop. If you begged me."

Dayum. Dayum.

"I don't do this. I'm not that kind of girl."

"I know what kind of girl you are. The kind of girl you're showing me is just fine. I like your kind of girl very much," he said as he continued kissing her, his long fingers reaching into the top of her panties after his other hand unzipped her skirt, and it dropped to the floor. The heavy bulge in his jeans against her nearly nude sex was such a turn-on she sparked a fever.

She crossed her arms behind his neck, pulling his head down to hers. "I'm lost, Lucas. Help me."

His long groan had her bud pulsing. She could feel the moisture preparing her channel for him. He lowered his crooked forefinger, and she sucked in air as he inserted it in her opening. "Does that help, baby?"

"Oh, yes, Lucas. But I need more."

"Of course you do. Show me. Show me what you want."

Suddenly, she was timid, but she smoothed over his button fly.

He groaned. "You want that, baby? I want to fuck you so bad right now. Take it out for me, sweetheart. Let me feel your fingers around me."

She undid the top three buttons on his fly. He was commando, no underwear. "You like it quick," she heard herself say.

"No, sweetheart. I like to be ready, is all. Not quick. I like it slow. I like you to ache when I ram my cock inside you."

She had never been more ready in her life. His jeans fell to the floor. She took the enormous girth of him, squeezing him, pressing him between their abdomens. She whimpered when she saw a little of his pre-cum leaking. Her ears were buzzing. He was peeling away all the layers of her ladyhood, all the good girl parts of her, leaving the wild child unfettered and free and aching to perform on a stage for him.

She opened his shirt, popping the buttons.

The rest of the clothes went quickly. As she stood before him completely naked, he dropped to his knees and kissed her leg from her knee all the way up. When he reached her sex, she jumped and her lower lip quivered. She gripped the tops of his shoulders at the intimate act.

"Tell me what you're thinking," he whispered against her mound.

"I'm scared, Lucas."

He leaned back on his haunches, grinned with lips wet with her own moisture, and then dropped his gaze to between her legs again.

"You've never done this before?" He reached out and touched her. "Has a man ever played with this?"

She couldn't speak; all she could do was nod. She'd had a man touch her there, once. And she'd asked him to move his hand away.

His gaze narrowed. "But you're not a virgin, right?"

"No, just not—"

"Ah! Now I understand. Just not this. You haven't done this," he whispered as he moved forward, looking up at her while he lapped at the slit between her legs. "Baby, you taste sweet. You like that?"

"Yes."

"You want more?"

"Oh, my God, yes."

"That's my girl. Ride my hand while I taste your juices. Just a little." He held her hip and tilted her pelvis back and forth, dipping his head to bury his tongue inside her as he rocked her back and forth.

God, it was getting hot in the room. The backs of his fingers rubbed against her thighs, gently smoothing and parting them. "That little bud is working hard, Marcy. You feel the pressure there?"

"Yes," she whispered.

"I'm gonna take some of the pressure off, so it doesn't ache so much. You okay with that, honey?"

"Um, oh, yes." She couldn't think.

He sucked the lips of her sex and slid his fingers up and down. "You tell me if you want me to stop, and I'll stop." He slipped both thumbs inside her opening, breaching her core, giving him full access.

"Don't—"

His head jerked up.

"God, *don't stop*, Lucas. Please. Don't. Stop."

"I have no intention of stopping. We got all day and no where else to go."

His tongue found her opening again.

She felt an orgasm coming on quickly. She pinched her own breasts, and then looked down on his head buried between her legs, where he feasted.

"Come for me, baby. Let me taste it, sweetheart," he whispered below her.

The friction of his tongue against her clit made her shudder as she felt herself lose control. His deep guttural moan told her he tasted the gold he was seeking. "God, Marcy, more, give me more," he said just before he dove in again.

As the spasms overtook her, she was filled with crazy need to have him inside her channel while she pulsed against him. "I need this so much, Lucas. God, I can't tell you how much I need this."

He withdrew his hands. "I know, baby." He fished for something in his pants, she heard the tearing of a foil packet and then he stood. Her hands went down to his shaft. She rubbed the ridged surface of the condom, and her eyes grew wide.

"Something else new, am I right? Oh, baby, what I'm going to do to you," he said as he picked her up quickly and dropped her back on the bed. "I'd normally like to get you screaming before I come inside, but I think you're there already and I can't wait any longer."

He mounted her, spreading her thighs. He yanked two pillows from the head of the bed, stuffed them under her pelvis and let a finger rub up and down her wet slit so achingly slow; she arched back and spread her legs further apart.

With his gaze locking with hers, he put his forefinger in his mouth. "Ah, baby, choices, choices." The tip of the condom had filled slightly and the plastic looked like it was going to burst.

"Lucas, please. Don't tease me any longer. Please."

"Please what, sweetheart?"

"I need you. Inside me."

He let the tip rub up and down, and then he pushed enough to have just the head inside her and held.

"Please, Lucas," she said, raking her nails over his chest.

"Ask me. Beg me, baby."

"Please, I need you to…"

"To what? What do you need me to do? Tell me, sweetheart."

"I need you inside me."

"Yes, baby, but ask me nice and sweet. Tell me what you want."

His gaze became devilishly dark as he stroked himself, ready for entry. "I need the command, baby."

She inhaled as his large hand squeezed her breast so hard it nearly hurt.

"That, that thing you were thinking. That thought. I want to hear that thought," he said as he smiled, squeezed, and slid his knees under her thighs, readying himself.

"Fuck me, Lucas."

"Yes, my dear. That's exactly what I'm going to do. With pleasure." He grinned again. "Pull me inside, baby."

She leaned forward, gripping his buttocks, and pulled him with her muscles deep inside her, holding him there, milking his length and feeling the hardness of his tip against her cervix. The dull ache had her squeezing her eyes shut. She rolled back and arched her abdomen. His hands held her hips, then pulled her knees up over his shoulders, and he ground down into her, rotating and drilling, holding firm and then deepening his pressure. "Is this what you need, baby?" he asked.

She couldn't speak. He thrust and held her tight, holding his breath as she did the same, then released her and soon thrust deep inside again. Her spine began to tingle as the little precursor to her orgasm began. She desperately needed him to fill every part of her insides. The calm between his powerful hip thrusts left her vacant and needy.

"Deeper," she whispered.

He hitched her knees up again, burying his shaft without holding back. "God, Marcy. I can't get enough."

The soft hairs at the back of her neck began to stiffen. She felt her internal muscles clamp down on him hard. Her breasts felt hot, her nipples engorged. Her body was at the edge of an explosion of passion unlike she'd felt before. Her eyes flew open and through her hair, she saw the smile cross his lips as he felt her pulse against him, as he watched her pleasure, kissing her eyes, her neck, the warm space between her breasts.

Then a sudden frown wrinkled his forehead and his lips formed a perfect O. "God, I can't help it," he said with difficulty as he exhaled, pumped and held, until he collapsed on top of her. As her breathing slowed and perspiration traveled from his chest to hers, she allowed her fingers to sift through his hair, pushing it off his forehead. He kissed her nipples gently, then tucked his head into the space beneath her chin and pressed his cheek to her.

IN THE LAST few moments before she fell into a deep sleep, Lucas still buried deep inside her, she played with the damp curls at the back of his neck. Her fingers stroked up and down his spine and she squeezed his butt cheeks. His enormous torso pressed her breasts until their bodies breathed in tandem. Holding him, she'd never felt happier, and she knew, if she ever had to let this man go, she'd miss him the rest of her life.

CHAPTER 11

THEY NEEDED A cold shower after the third time they made love. Lucas insisted on washing her all over, slipping fingers into every crevice, because it was like seeing her all over again. Her body was like silk. The bubbles over her breasts made them slippery. She was built perfectly for him, and he loved the feeling of her slick body brushing up against his torso.

He tried to envision the faces of other lovers and exciting conquests from his past, but he couldn't see a single one. He couldn't even picture Connie's face anymore. The connection was so strong between him and Marcy he didn't care if they never left the cabin.

Where was it all going? And did it matter, really? He knew Connie would blow a gasket, and he hoped she wouldn't retaliate against this lovely creature he'd found, this woman he barely knew. He wasn't going to fuck it up. Not this time. The bonfire they could build together would be enough to last their lifetimes.

What the fuck am I saying? he asked himself as he watched the water sluice down her perfect back, ending at that perfect ass. She was using his palms as her washcloth, letting him touch every inch of her.

He knew they needed to talk, but he wasn't in any hurry. This was what he knew: The sight of her nude body shuddering in front of him, and her little shouts and wiggles as the cold made her jump, had him smiling and fucking melted his heart.

Oh, he was snagged all right. He was so fuckin' hooked and hog-tied. There was no way out. No way he'd let anyone get between them.

But then he remembered he was a team guy. He was a warrior, and there was a job to do in just a couple of days. They'd have to talk between their fucking. She liked to talk during sex, just like he did. He could pump her little pussy until her lips were so swollen she'd walk funny. And even then, it wouldn't be enough.

"Are you hungry, Marcy?" he dared to whisper. He hated to end their little romp in the shower, but he honestly wasn't sure if they hadn't already drained the well. "We're gonna burn up the pump if we keep this up," he said as he kissed her under her ear.

She turned, and her smile tempted him further. Half-lidded eyes did him in. "I'm starved. What did you have in mind, sailor?"

THEY ATE THAI food on Cloverdale Boulevard. He began to get his bearings, watching people through the dirty glass window. He liked the little town. Things hadn't become all yuppified. There were cowboys, jazz musicians, pot smokers, and little hotties trying to get modeling jobs in San Francisco, so they could escape from their little town. He couldn't blame them. People lived here because they didn't aspire to do many big things. And that meant things were safe—if there ever was a really safe town in the U.S. anymore.

He pushed his leftover food aside and took her hand. "I gotta explain a couple of things to you."

She set down her fork, took a sip of water, and gave him a sober look.

"You know what I do, right?"

"I do."

"So, I don't think I'm breaching protocol when I tell you the world is a much more dangerous place than everyone thinks."

She shrugged. "I know that."

"No, sweetheart," he said as he leaned in, putting his elbows on the table. "You don't know the half of it. Involving you in my life, and I'm assuming we'll be involved—"

"Involved?" She raised her eyebrows.

"Well, pardon me, but I just assumed that—"

She giggled, and it was such a wonderful sound. "You and I are in a boatload of trouble, Lucas. We just jumped out of an airplane without a parachute."

A smile tugged at his lips. "That's a pretty good way to put it, honey." He could see she was hesitant to say something.

"I'd say we're more like blended. Like all those bodily fluids we exchanged all morning."

"I like all those bodily fluids. I want to make more," he whispered.

Marcy blushed.

"What is it? You re-thinking all this?"

"Not sure I can. It's just that I can't believe I'm here, with you. Connie was all wrong about you. I'll bet you never cheated on her either."

"Never. Not after we got married."

"For the life of me, I don't understand why she thought you did, how she could just could walk away."

He stiffened. He didn't want to talk about Connie. "Long sad, story, Marcy. We sure had fun, but we had no staying power. She had one station, Marcy. It was to be all Connie's way. Always Connie's way. She could never understand why I wanted to do this. Looking back on it, I don't think she really supported my decision to become a SEAL. Not really."

"So much for easing into things to find out what's going on, Lucas."

"You and me? I told you it wasn't smart."

"You did. And I didn't listen. I've been a bad girl." Her eyes sparkled as she dipped her chin in an obvious flirtation.

Oh, that was such a dangerous thing to do to him. If she only knew.

"I haven't even gotten started, Marcy, with all the things I want to do with you."

She blushed and looked down at her lap. "Are we going to think about all this before we spend another few hours getting lost in each other's arms?"

"That's exactly what we're doing right now, honey."

She watched their entwined fingers, his thumb caressing the back of her hand. "No, *you* were starting to warn me about something," she said.

He adjusted his hips, rolled his shoulders and tried to get comfortable. "We're deploying in a few months, but in the meantime, we're doing some training out of state."

"What kind of training?"

"See, that's the problem—I can't tell you."

"Are there girls there?"

"Honey, there are girls everywhere. Anywhere there are SEALs, there are girls. But if you don't stop letting those nasty thoughts run naked around that cute little pink brain of yours, I'm gonna spank your sweet ass until it's welted and red."

Her eyes widened. "Another thing I haven't tried before."

It was no use. Only thing left to do was work up a good appetite for that nice steak barbeque he'd planned. The big difference was that this time, he was going to do it all naked.

CHAPTER 12

MARCY CALLED DEVON and Nick and told them she was going to stay in Cloverdale and wasn't coming home until tomorrow.

The following day, she and Lucas shopped for provisions in town, and then about noon, went to Nick and Devon's home, where Lucas seemed impressed with the small winery.

Devon was giving them scrutiny after Marcy introduced Lucas to both of them. Marcy could tell she'd figured out who Lucas was, and what they'd been doing.

"I'd heard about this place from some of the old guys," Lucas said. Nick's head jerked up.

"Old?"

"Well, the guys who have been in longer than ten years. You got out at ten, right? About the time I joined Team 3."

"That's right."

"You okay with leaving the teams, Nick? I mean, did it give you trouble?"

"You heard I got injured? It was an easy choice after that. And Devon does really well. I think it would be harder if we lived down in San Diego, seeing all the guys every day. Here, we just blend in, man. It's a good life."

Lucas' phone chirped. "Hallo," he said as he watched Devon and Marcy whispering in the kitchen. He recognized the number as Kyle's.

"We've stepped up the training, Lucas. I gotta ask you to come back."

"When?"

"Yesterday." Kyle's tone told him not to argue. It was a command.

"What's up?" This wasn't anything good. Something big had happened.

"Not over the phone."

"Okay, well, I'll get going tonight. Be home in about twelve hours."

"No can do. Bought you a ticket; it's waiting for you at Sonoma County Airport."

"Today, as in this afternoon?"

"Yessir. That direct flight leaves at three. You better be on it."

"I got my truck, Kyle."

"So get someone else to drive it home, Lucas. This is something we can't wait about."

It wasn't optimum, but Marcy agreed to drive Lucas' truck back to San Diego. "You can stay a couple of days up here with Nick and Devon, if you want. Makes no difference to me when I get the truck back. I won't be anywhere I'll need it."

He knew Marcy wanted to ask him where he was going. He liked that she didn't even try. He worked to calm his breathing. He didn't want her to get as nervous as he was. "I can't even go back up to Cloverdale to clear out the place, and there's one thing I don't like leaving there."

"No worries, Lucas. I can bring your things back."

"Cabin's pretty out in the middle of nowhere, Marcy. I don't want you going up without someone to help." Nick was watching nearby.

"Promise."

"You unplug the refrigerator and take home all the food. Make sure the water's shut off. I got a couple of things in the closet, in particular, a heavy black zipper bag full of crap. Don't forget that one, Marcy." Lucas saw the black bag registered with Nick, who added his nod.

"We'll go up there tomorrow. Soonest I can do it."

"Thanks, Nick."

"So, other than making sure everything is locked up tight, nothing else needs to be done." He handed her the truck keys and watched her frown with downcast eyes. "Marcy, honey, no worries. You guys get up to Cloverdale tomorrow. You show them the way, okay?"

Marcy agreed.

"Some of that stuff's heavy. Especially that bag." He glanced over at Nick, and they shared a look. "You don't know the area and there's some crazy shit going on."

Nick gave him another brief nod.

Marcy reached for his arm. "I'll be fine, Lucas. You just come home safe," she whispered.

He put his arms around her and felt her shaking as he held her close. "I will, baby. You just keep the truck until I get back into town." He paused. "And I can't tell you when, either, but I'll call when I can."

Marcy took him to the airport in Lucas' truck so she could practice working the stick shift. He showed her all the little gadgets, like the keyless entry and the locked storage compartment she was never to open, which sat underneath the front seat. "You put the heavy black bag here in the back seat and you cover it up with the blanket there. Don't forget it, promise?"

"What's—?"

"Don't ask, Marcy. Just have Nick help you with it."

When they arrived at Schulz International, Sonoma County's only airport, Lucas checked his duty bag separately, having the talk with the security agent. He had to take some of his things with him, since he really didn't want to leave all of his firearms back with Marcy for the road trip home.

As they waited for his plane to San Diego, she brought it up first. "I'm going to have to tell Connie, Lucas. I just wanted you to know."

"Your funeral." The line was getting shorter, and then he was at the x-ray machine. "Tell her we don't get along."

"And what if she sees me driving your truck when I return it. What's she going to say then?"

"The likelihood of that is nil, Marcy. You know that. I doubt she'd ever come over to the place. She never has. You want to avoid Connie at all costs."

"I have to cancel the listing, Lucas, have to give her a reason."

"Don't mess with her, Marcy. If she does find out, don't be surprised if she doesn't try to go after your license or something like that."

"Just such a risk. I'll park the truck at your place, maybe get someone to help me with your stuff. And mysteriously slip away. Geez, Lucas I'm so nervous about all of this. I hate all this sneaking around."

"You go by Gunny's Gym and ask for Sinouk, the owner's son. He can help you with the stuff." Lucas saw she'd been pouting. "Hey, not to worry." He elicited a smile from her as he coaxed another kiss from her lips. God, he hated to leave her now.

"Sir, I'm afraid visiting hours are over," the guard barked. "You're gonna miss your plane."

He gripped the back of Marcy's hair. "We'll talk, Marcy. Not to worry. We'll figure something out."

"But I'm going to give up the listing anyway, Lucas. I just can't in good conscience—"

"*Sir!*"

"Just one fuckin' minute, okay?" Lucas shouted over the small crowd. A mother shushed him and covered her daughter's ears. "She's gonna have a pretty hard time getting my signature now, Marcy." He was rewarded with a smile, and a kiss.

His parting thought as he turned and headed for the plane: *I like the way you do business, Marcy Gelland!* He hoped he had one more time to say goodbye before they deployed in earnest. Finally, he tore himself away and tried to focus on the mission at hand.

SHE WATCHED HIM walk out onto the windy tarmac, following a trail of travelers, including one older man in a wheelchair. He quickly turned around and ran past the security guard, who chased him back inside the terminal.

On the other side of the glass security doors, he pounded with his fists and shouted, "Marry me, Marcy Gelland!"

"Yes. Yes, I'll marry you, Lucas Shipley," she shouted back, her heart bursting, crazy, totally crazy for the guy and completely not caring about any of the reality of what she'd just plunged herself into. One thimbleful of rational thought made its way out at last.

"But first, you gotta get divorced."

CHAPTER 13

MARCY DECIDED TO go straight up to the house in Cloverdale after dropping Lucas off at the airport. She didn't want to bother Devon and Nick, who would be waiting for her to stay over tonight. Driving all the way back down to Santa Rosa, picking them up, and then going north to the cabin and then back home was just too many trips on the 101 Freeway, and inconsiderate of her friend's time. And she wanted to do the lockup in the daylight hours.

She'd promised Lucas she wouldn't go up there alone, and now she was going to violate that promise. *Always easier to ask for forgiveness than permission.* It had served her well for most of her life. Now was certainly no exception.

Traffic was coming the opposite direction as she headed north. When she pulled into the little town of Cloverdale, she stopped at a coffee shop and picked up a cappuccino and a sandwich, then took the winding road off into the woods north of town.

She took one wrong turn, then doubled back and found the correct trail to the cabin. Using the large brass key, she let herself in. As she stood, feeling the warmth and the wash of memories of what they'd been doing for the past twenty-four hours there, she blushed. It was so peaceful and quiet. On the front stoop all she could hear were the sounds of the tall trees rustling in the wind and an occasional bird. Somewhere off in the blue, cloudless sky a small plane sputtered on its way. A faint smell of campfire and woods was soothing to her nerves. It made her sleepy being so peacefully alone.

Back inside, she washed the dishes and put them away, unplugged the refrigerator and shut off the water main to the house. She made the bed, folded and straightened the towels in the bath, put Lucas' clothes in another nylon shoulder bag she found in the closet, and added her own clothes. She picked up the heavy black bag Lucas had mentioned and gingerly carried it to the truck, depositing it on the rear floor like she had been instructed, covering it with the old blanket. Returning to the house, she took one more look around, loaded the other bags up, and then went back, pulling out all the supplies from the refrigerator and put them in brown paper bags, and locked the door behind her.

Before taking off, she walked around the outside of the cabin to make sure all the windows were secured.

The roadway going out looked different than she'd remembered and again, she took a wrong turn. The drive ended in another cabin nearby, with several metal outbuildings and a stable behind it. A slim man in jeans and a light blue shirt was working with a hoe in the front yard where he was growing a small vegetable garden. A battered red pickup truck and a rusted white passenger van were parked at the side of the structure. The man looked up. He wore wire-rimmed glasses and sported a full beard.

Marcy knew there were communes and pot growers out in the woods between here and Mendocino County. The young man looked like he could have been a settler from a Jewish kibbutz with his full beard and well-tanned skin. He leaned on his hoe and squinted in the late afternoon light at her, frowning, his wire-rimmed glasses glinting in the sunlight.

She rolled down her window, leaning out. "Sorry. I'm a bit lost. Looking for the way out to the highway."

She noticed the front door of the cabin opened and she could see a face, perhaps two in the crack created. The man looked up to the door and shouted something and the door immediately shut.

He walked toward her, pointed with a thin finger, and in accent he said, "Left. Then right. All the way right."

"Okay, so I go out this driveway, turn left, and then take the first right?"

"First right, all the way right," he repeated in his thick accent. "Freeway." He nodded.

"Thank you very much."

The man bowed slightly, smiling as if blushing, averting his eyes down and away from her. Marcy put the truck in reverse, grinding the gears, which had the stranger abruptly raise his head in alarm. She hit the gas and too quickly let out the clutch and the truck stalled. She put the truck in neutral, restarted it, and took off down the road in a cloud of dust. In the rearview mirror she saw two other young men leave the front door, both standing side by side, intent on watching her truck barrel along the dusty drive. Just before she turned left, she noticed a small wooden sign she'd missed on the way in. It was the sign of the cross, with sunlight grooved in and painted in faded yellow. Underneath the insignia were the words, "Sonshine Haven."

Marcy made a mental note to ask Lucas and perhaps Nick and Devon about this obviously Christian camp so close to Lucas' cabin. In a way, it was reassuring to have a neighbor so close nearby, in case anything were to happen with the cabin.

By the time she hit Highway 101, the sun had fallen low. She got a text message that Lucas had arrived safely in San Diego and would call when he could, later tonight or tomorrow morning. She texted back hearts and kisses to him, which he returned.

Next, Marcy telephoned Devon, gave her the news and told her she was on her way back to their house.

Nick was particularly quiet over dinner, causing Devon to ask him what was wrong.

The handsome green-eyed former SEAL gave Marcy a serious look, cocking his head to the side. "Marcy, I don't know you very well but I'm bothered about one thing. And you're gonna have to forgive me on this. I'm a very careful man."

"Okay, shoot," Marcy said.

"Nick?" Devon slipped her arm under Nick's and squeezed herself next to him. "What's up?"

Nick smiled at his wife, but it quickly evaporated.

"Lucas told you not to go up there alone, and the very first thing you did when he was on that plane was go right up there."

Marcy felt her cheeks flush. Nick's direct approach to her disobedience made her feel ashamed, naked in front of them. It was time to beg for forgiveness.

"I didn't want to bother you guys—"

"But Lucas asked you *not* to do that. He made quite a point about it, and probably had good reason for that, Marcy. It has to do with your safety."

"Nick, come on," Devon pestered him.

Nick stiffened, removed Devon's arms from his, separating himself from her, and sat up straight. "It's not funny, you two. If Lucas mentioned it, then it was important. You have to trust him when he tells you things like that, Marcy. You don't know what's at stake."

"I know, but nothing happened. I just got all the things out, did what he asked, and I buttoned up the house so you guys don't have to be bothered with it."

"Except he's going to want me to go up there and make sure it's okay. So you didn't save me a trip after all."

"Nick? What the heck is going on?" Devon asked. Her frown cut deep into the bridge of her nose.

"These are strange times. Lucas even said it. I've been told about all sorts of stuff you guys don't want to know about. It's for your protection you not know. But you have to follow directions. Nothing optional about it."

Marcy knew he was right, but she didn't care for Nick's method of delivery. She felt prickly. Devon had obviously picked it up.

"Nick, get over it, will you? No harm no foul. That's one of your favorite expressions. So just chill. The main thing is that she got it done. Lucas' stuff is safely back down here."

"Not the point, Devon."

"I'm done with this, Nick. You need to go to bed. Now." Devon was getting angry. "Marcy and I will clean up here."

Devon pointed to the stairs.

Nick gave her a hug and quick kiss. Then he addressed Marcy. "Sorry, kid. I'm going to be a stickler about this. Tomorrow we go back up there and double check everything, not that you didn't do everything correctly, but he wanted me to go so I could confirm that it was all done. We're like that. Thorough. Checking, double-checking. Sometimes our life depends on it. No reflection on you."

"I understand." Marcy thought she did a pretty good job of hiding her hurt feelings.

Nick turned and ran upstairs. Marcy followed Devon to the kitchen, and then remembered the food she'd left in the truck. "Holy crap. I've probably got a back seat full of sour milk and melted cheese."

"I'll help you."

The two of them carried the two boxes inside the kitchen. Marcy was going to get the other bags later. They stowed the perishables, cleaned up the dinner and placed dishes in the dishwasher, turning it on. Devon made a couple of glasses of ice water and handed one to Marcy. "Come on, let's sit in the living room for a bit."

"I'm for that," said Marcy settling into the comfortable couch.

"Let's catch up on some juicy gossip," Devon started. "I want to know all about Lucas' wife, or soon-to-be ex-wife. What's she like?"

"She's a piece of work, Dev. Gorgeous, but a basket case. She's bitter, and I don't think he did anything to deserve that. She's jealous of his connection with the Brotherhood."

"From what I've heard, some of the guys play around a lot. Father children all over the place. Many of them lack good judgement. Don't get yourself caught, Marcy. Be careful."

"I might be stupid, but I believe Lucas. I really do," admitted Marcy.

"Some women aren't made for this lifestyle. I might not have been very good at it, actually."

"I don't know much about the community. Maybe you can help me there. All I know is Lucas is on her list. She seems to genuinely hate him. I feel sorry for those kids. Just too bad what she's doing."

"They're pretty intense. But I remember I asked one of the wives about them before Nick and I got married one time when I visited—have you been to any of their get-togethers?"

"No. This happened so fast. I mean, we're only at day three here."

"Right. I forget, Marcy. They rarely let in outsiders, so having you here, involved with him like this, well, it brings you into the inner circle. They have a funny way about them, a code. You're either in, or you're out. You're in, Marcy, and Connie is out. But none of the guys will date her. If she's out, she's out."

"It just seems over the top."

Devon laughed. "In the beginning, I thought so, too. I mean, Nick seemed just like a total asshole at first. So full of himself. But boy, when we got involved, man did sparks fly."

Marcy felt her cheeks pink up again.

"You have to love the way they live, their intensity. Sometimes they're right on, and sometimes they have shit for brains." Devon continued. "They get all this training, all this fantastic equipment. They pretty much feel invincible. Hard for them when they come home. The wives are taking care of everything, running the house, paying the bills, and then he comes home and suddenly he's the king. All she wants to do is get some help. Especially with the kids."

"Makes sense. Connie more or less told me the same thing." Marcy was hesitant to ask Devon so she started softly. "You guys going to try anytime soon, Devon?"

"Have been. It will happen when it happens. At least I don't have to try to space the births around deployments, like some of the other wives do."

"Impossible." Marcy shook her head. How *did* women handle all that, not knowing if their men would come home? But she realized it was what women and families of soldiers have to deal with all the time. Always been that way for those who chose to love warriors, not a stock broker, insurance man, or another realtor.

"So what's her main beef with Lucas?"

"I think the tipping point was a bachelor party, and some of the pictures taken were a little revealing." Marcy giggled. "They had some dancers and such."

"Strippers," interrupted Devon. "Seems to be a custom for these guys. I don't even ask what Nick's party was like."

"Well this one was worse, from what I understand."

Devon frowned.

"Someone posted them on Facebook, and when Connie saw them, she flipped out."

"You can be sure I didn't check Nick's FB page for a month afterward."

"Smart. But, honestly, I think Connie didn't want anything coming between her and Lucas. I think she began to resent the Navy, resent his closeness to the other team guys, perhaps asking him to choose between her and the brotherhood."

"Ouch! Not smart."

"Just my guess, Dev. So when Lucas didn't agree or side with her, I think she decided she was done. I hate to think it's about the money she'll make with the sale of the house, but you know, Devon, I couldn't even rule *that* out. She's one of the meanest people I've ever met."

"And you have to deal with her?"

"I think I'm handing the listing over to someone else."

"Probably wise. I mean, I can only imagine what would happen if she found out—"

"Gives me chills, Dev. Not looking forward to that."

"And you have to drive his truck all the way back to San Diego, too?"

Marcy shrugged.

"How is the market down there?"

"Going gangbusters. That's why I have to get back. Been one of the busiest times I've had. How about you?"

"You know what they say. How do you make a small fortune in the wine business? Start with a large fortune and you'll soon have a small fortune."

They shared a laugh.

"Everything I saved and did has gone into the winery. We start crush soon, fingers crossed for nice temperate weather for harvest. Hoping we get a good yield and the grapes are better than last year. We're at year five now. Another two to go and we'll know."

"Are you still selling real estate as much as before?"

"As much as I can. But Nick needs my help here, too. I represent some big investors who are buying right now, so that part's been good for me. We have investors too, some of the SEAL families are part owners, so that takes the burden off, but adds the pressure to turn a profit."

Marcy looked around the house, hearing the crickets through the screens overlooking the patio. The large harvest moon was just rising over the vineyards in the distance. It was a special evening. Felt like the calm before the storm, for some reason, and she was grateful her college friend could give her the time to just sit and chat.

"You own a little piece of Heaven, Devon."

"That we do. Sophie, Nick's sister, always said so, and she was right. I wouldn't trade my lifestyle for anywhere else in the world. I'd like to raise my family here one day. I'd love this to be a Northern California Wine Retreat for SEALs and their families."

"Wouldn't that be something?"

CHAPTER 14

L
UCAS WAS MET at the airport by Jake and Alex. The warm night air smelled of the salty inlet, something he'd forgotten he missed.

"So what's up with your truck, man?" Jake asked as Lucas climbed into the second seat of the Hummer.

"It's getting driven back in the next day or two. Kyle wanted me back here ASAP. You tell me, what the fuck's going on?"

"All shit is hitting the fan. We got a lot of chatter about some groups all over the U.S. They're making us do some specialized training with the guys from Little Creek. Team 6 uncovered some stuff in Turkey. And someone tried to take out a military surgeon on vacation in Oregon with his family. They were just camping."

Lucas felt guilty he'd been so head over heels loving Marcy, he hadn't been watching the news. Other than X-rated movies, international news was as popular as sports at the bachelor pad.

"Everyone okay?"

"Cut up, especially his wife, but the kids were okay. Lucky thing he was carrying a gun, though he'll get written up for it." Jake drove them in the opposite direction of the apartment.

"You're shitting me," Lucas said.

"Federal lands. Not allowed to carry," Alex said over the back of the seat. "They might not have survived without it, though."

"That's messed up," said Lucas. No one said a word. Lucas noticed they seemed to be headed toward Coronado. "Hey, we going over to the Team Building?"

"Yup," said Jake.

The injustice of the attack and the fact that the man might get in trouble for defending his family had him fuming. "Just can't believe they'd actually put a letter in his file." Lucas continued to shake his head as he watched the lights of the Coronado base come into view.

"Kyle thinks they'll go light on him, but they have to make note of it." Jake's shoulders rounded as he continued, "A very strange world out there, Lucas."

"That it is. You guys do any training yesterday or day before?" Lucas asked.

"Nope. We start the briefing tonight. Couple of guys coming in tomorrow," answered Jake.

They passed the guard shack, parked the Hummer, and walked toward the entrance to their building. Kyle was locked in serious conversation with a small group of team guys, including T.J., Cooper, Tyler, Rory, and Luke. All of them looked up and behind Lucas as the team erupted in a warm welcome for a dark-skinned man wearing western wear, including cowboy boots.

Kyle put his arm around Jake, as he pulled a group of newbies over to introduce them. "This here is the baddest motherfucker on the whole planet."

The dark-skinned man nodded and looked down at his boots. Though he wasn't one of the newbies, Lucas had never met the man before, even on his DEVGRU deployment.

In a heavily accented voice, the newcomer answered, "Only when I have you guys at my back, or dropping in like flies all around me. Then I can be very, very brave. By myself, not so much."

T.J. and Luke came over and gave the man a bear hug. "Come here you lying sonofabitch," T.J. said to his ear. He made a grand gesture of kissing him on the side of the face. "How the fuck are you?"

"I'm good. My wife's pregnant again. Hoping to create one of those, how you say, 'anchor babies'?"

"Why am I not surprised?" Rory Kennedy said.

When T.J. let go of him, Kyle stepped up and repeated the hug. He turned and presented the man to Lucas, Jake, Alex, and several newbies at the end. "This here is Jackie Daniels, our interpreter. We don't know his real name—"

A couple of the older SEALs started laughing. Lucas hadn't seen so many white teeth since the last time they'd had a bachelor party and half of them were completely shitfaced. Fredo and Armani entered the warehouse building, along with several others Lucas thought looked like transplants from other teams.

Cooper added his hug to the lineup. "Yeah, if he told us, he'd have to kill us, so we call him Jackie. And T.J.'s right, he's the baddest motherfucker in the whole Navy."

"No. Your government will not make me a Navy man. I am working on my citizenship, but soon, they will give it to me, and then I can be a taxi driver like all of my other countrymen."

Jake stepped forward and shook Jackie's hand. "Honor to meet you. Heard a lot about you, Mr. Daniels."

"Jackie," the interpreter corrected. "Mr. Daniels sounds like some guy who is the principal at my daughter's school."

Jackie gripped Lucas's hand, tilting his head and giving him a wide smile, but his eyes didn't blink or waver, and Lucas felt like he'd just had his mind read. Jackie took a respectful step back and seemed to sense the new introductions had some uneasy around him. Lucas also knew it didn't bother the terp, Jackie, one bit.

They'd been told the stories about how he'd risked his life on several missions with their team, as well as several others he'd worked with in the past. Their highest level capture was on a mission that nearly cost six SEALs and a CIA agent their lives. Unlike several of the other interpreters, Jackie was not opposed to be carrying a weapon and protected them on this mission when they freed several SEAL hostages taken captive. This was before Lucas joined the team.

Like a skilled warrior, Jackie didn't force himself on any of them, nor make them show loyalty without it being earned. Lucas knew he was a big-time asset to whatever mission they would be tasked with.

Kyle came to attention, regarding several men in and out of uniform who walked through the Team 3 Building doors. Lucas and everyone else faced them, and several addressed the new audience in hushed tones.

Collins, their SEAL liaison, walked over to a small group of tables and chairs, followed by one Lt. Commander and a non-uniformed, who Lucas judged to be CIA. Kyle took his place next to them, making a fourth. Lucas knew something big was going on as another couple of unidentified, but well-built, gentlemen took to some rear seats in the pit. This was a nighttime briefing, conducted without the whole Charlie Team being present, which meant they were in a hurry. He was glad he'd texted Marcy when he landed, since he doubted he'd be able to be in much communication very soon.

"Gentlemen, take your seats," Kyle said to the group, who had already started doing so before the order was given. Lucas sat next to Jake and Ryan. Looking around, he nodded to Alex, Cory, and several others.

No one standing was smiling. T.J. and Luke sandwiched Jackie, the terp. Danny and Jeffrey sat together in the back row, both wearing sunglasses, though the building was low lit. Rory sat just in front of them.

"This here is Lt. Commander Ian Forsythe, Office of Naval Intelligence. He's going to brief you on a situation we have going on now. Lt. Commander?" Kyle backed up and the highly decorated veteran cleared his throat and took the center stage. Though the SEALs were not required to salute, each man in his own way sat up straighter, uncrossed their arms, and showed they were paying attention, unlike their normal demeanor.

"You've been briefed before about terrorist group formations in this country. I know you had a representative of DEVGRU, SO Thom Grand, speaking with you recently about death teams who we now know have landed here. We have it on good authority some have been spotted in several areas in the southwest, south, and now with this recent incident in Oregon, we believe some are in the Pacific Northwest. We're still scrambling a bit to gather all that intelligence without tipping our hand."

Lucas' stomach lurched as he realized he hadn't eaten anything since boarding the plane, except for some peanuts and a coke. Or, maybe it was the news. He would have anticipated getting geared up and ready to roll if he was with Team 6 again, or even Team 3 in Iraq. But he wasn't sure what the plan of action was for the situation at hand. This was a threat on U.S. soil, after all.

Forsythe continued. "We know members of the military, especially SEALs, are being targeted. Our families are in danger. Our friends too, perhaps. Time to take measures, hopefully preventative measures to ensure our community stays safe."

Forsythe turned to Collins, who stepped up next to him. "Gentlemen, we're going to institute some rules that will not be broken, do I make myself clear?"

Affirmations trickled from the group, a combination of nods and whispers and grunts.

"While we are doing some specialized training, and this will all be explained to you in detail, we're going to organize a com schedule, so no one on this team is out of the loop. And this is going to extend to your wives. And I gotta also mention there will not be the usual recreational use of females, or something that involves you getting shitfaced and making a scene, or getting caught in some place by yourself with people you don't know. We aren't sure how they'll come after us, but we're staying vigilant and, of course, prepared. Being prepared keeps us alive, right, gents?"

Again a wave of affirmations filled the room.

Kyle added his comments. "Newbies especially, listen up. We're doing something that's never been done before. We're going to create an old-fashioned phone list. You are to be in phone contact with five other men on our team every day, morning and evening. And you are to pass along anything you see that is out of the ordinary. Each five-man group will have a senior man who will be responsible for relaying information. But, make no mistake, you can't get hold of someone? You call me, you call Coop here, Fredo, Armani, or Collins."

Forsythe added, "Your training is going to coincidentally take place next to two well-known and documented terrorist training camps. Active camps. Camps we believe have recently imported some talent, and that talent has been kept hidden, which means they know we're surveilling them, and they're still doing it."

A hushed silence fell over the group. Someone let out a loud and long, "Fuuuuck."

"Gentlemen, those of you who've been over in the arena know that not many of these guys fear death. They don't fear getting caught, because that makes the news. Making the news is what they're after. They won't win in the end, but they want to make the US of A feel like a self-imposed prison camp." Forsythe exhaled and paced back and forth.

So that was the gig, Lucas thought. They were supposed to look like they were just living their lives as usual, but they were going to go dangerously close to the bee and not get stung, or be ready for the swarm. They were going to tempt the group to try and snag one of them. But he wasn't sure, so he thought he'd asked.

"Sir, SO Shipley here. May I ask a question?" Lucas stood.

"Go ahead, son," Forsythe answered.

"I'm just not clear, and you probably have much more to tell us, but from what our brothers at DEVGRU, SEAL Team 6, told us, weren't they interested in perhaps doing a reverse snatch and grab?" Lucas could see a couple of newbies had no clue what he was saying.

"That's right. We think they're looking to take a target back with them, possibly a SEAL, and more specifically, one from Team 3 or 5."

More muttering and private discussions continued until Lucas continued. "Okay, then. Why are we going to train near them, if our goal is to avoid being captured or killed?"

Kyle inserted himself before Forsythe could answer. "You mean did we just confirm the CIA and Naval Intelligence is using us as bait? That your question, SO Shipley?"

Lucas nodded his head. "Yes, Chief." He heard a couple of the older SEALs swear, crossing their arms and legs. It was something apparently, several of them were thinking about, but none were excited by the idea.

"Who else would you suggest, SO Shipley?" began Forsythe. "Your wives and children, innocent civilians?" Forsythe drilled his stare into Lucas, his breathing very slow and deep, like he was bracing for a punch and was completely calm and ready for whatever anyone would dish out. All sound was sucked out of the room and nobody moved. "I'm asking you a serious question. I'm as serious as a heart attack, Shipley."

T.J. Talbot snarled out, "Oh yeah. 'Come on over here said the spider to the fly.'" The big SEAL examined the fingernails on his right hand as Jackie and Luke started chuckling. Lucas sat.

Coop was more sober. "I'm going to ask you what I always need to know, sir."

"All ears here," answered Forsythe.

"The women and children. What the fuck are we supposed to do with them?"

After a brief moment of silence, while everyone looked at Kyle, Jones added his comments. "You dumb-fuck." Jones waved his long arms around his head. "You white boys are real slow in the bedroom. You're supposed to keep them barefoot and happy. Nekked I think, too. Yo mamas never teach you nothin?"

Everyone started adding their two cents. But Coop and Kyle were staring at each other like they shared something no one else knew about. Kyle hushed the raucous spouting off. Lucas knew it was nervous repartee, helping to mask how uneasy everyone felt about this whole situation. "Wait a minute guys," Kyle continued. "Coop has a point. So listen up." He turned to Collins and then glanced over at Forsythe.

"I'll take that," said Forsythe. "We're instituting something for them, too. Similar. We're going to embed some extra protection. We're also coordinating with the local sheriff and police, on a very limited basis, not with the rank and file, so while you're gone on training, or, if we don't have a more favorable outcome, we may delay deployment. Just not sure yet what that's going to look like."

"In the meantime, we're traveling out of state," said Kyle.

Fredo shouted out, "Snow gear or swim trunks?"

Some of their jungle training was in Baja, some in Florida, or desert training in Las Vegas. Alaska was always good for cold-weather exercises.

"Neither," barked Forsythe. He took two steps to the side, assuming the wide stance some of the officers were known for, arms crossed behind his back. He inhaled sharply, gave them a half smile and shouted, "Gentlemen, we're headed to Tennessee."

CHAPTER 15

MARCY AND NICK drove up to Cloverdale in Lucas' truck mid-morning.

"Sorry about the inconvenience, Nick. I thought I was saving you some time."

"No need to apologize, but you gotta pay attention, Marcy. It comes with the territory."

She knew he was right. "You know we hardly know each other, Nick. There is so much about Lucas I'm just learning."

"Afraid I can't help you there. But even if I could, we don't do that."

Marcy knew it was an uphill battle. It was a long-shot that the two of them would wind up together, and now she began to feel guilty she'd said yes to marrying him. In fact, as she thought about all the decisions she'd made, especially the one about "screwing the husband of the divorcing clients," which was a huge no-no on every scale possible, she was ashamed. She might have even jeopardized her job at Coronado Bay.

Nick tuned in on a country satellite station, taking some of the tension out of the air. She crossed and uncrossed her arms and legs and began chewing down a nail. The countryside was green with rows of vineyards, but the brown earth and commercial buildings detracted from the beauty of the several wineries they passed on their way. Traffic bothered her. The bugs on the truck's windshield bothered her. She didn't like one of the songs, and she wished she was back in San Diego, near the ocean, near the blue water and the breeze that was ever present.

Her cell rang. Nick turned down the radio station so she could answer it. "This is Marcy."

"Where the devil are you, Marcy?" Her broker's voice sounded shrill.

"Sorry, Joe. I'm up here in Sonoma County, looking at my client's real estate. She asked me to do it."

"Are you sure about that?"

"Yes." Marcy's stomach flip-flopped, and she squeezed the phone against her ear.

"I've had some complaints from other agents; they can't get hold of you."

"I've gotten no calls, Joe. I'll be back in a day or two."

"Good idea, Marcy. Say, you give that SEAL's wife your cell?"

"I did. Why?"

"Not sure, but she's been talking to Gail here in the office, you know, the new agent married to the football player?"

"Oh yes."

"I guess they're friends. I'd watch my back on that one."

"Joe, there's a little situation there I need to go over with you." Marcy looked sideways at Nick who was pretending he couldn't hear. "I'm going to give up their listing. Coming up here, well, it's changed my perspective a bit." Then she felt Nick's eyes on her as she tried to speak to the passenger window softly, seeking some privacy. "I just can't represent them. I don't feel like I can get along with Connie."

"Then talk with Gail, or someone else about referring it, Marcy. But do it quick."

"Will do. As soon as I get back."

"I'd do it by phone. I'd talk to your client today." Joe hung up.

Was she ready to confront Connie, and do it by phone, not in person like she'd planned? She'd thought she would have the long drive home to San Diego to rehearse and think about how to tell Connie, so it wouldn't blow up in her face. Not being present in person was more dangerous.

"So the wifey doesn't know you and Lucas are an item? That what I'm hearing?" Nick asked.

"Afraid so."

Nick was mercifully quiet. Marcy knew what he was thinking. This also wasn't a very good way to gain points with her college friend and her husband either. Marcy sighed. She was messing up on all fronts.

"I really screwed things up, Nick," she said at last.

"Roger that, Marcy. You got yourself one hell of a problem. And it's going to be a problem for Lucas, too, even if he didn't think about all this beforehand."

No, they certainly hadn't thought about anything. All that mattered at the time, and for the two days afterward, was the chemistry between them, how she felt being around Lucas.

The sounds of the truck filled the deadly silence between them.

Nick continued. "We do so many things well overseas, because we're trained to do it over and over again. All this stuff? Divorce, selling houses, dating? I can't say our community does it very well. We're used to jumping in without thinking. Can't do that at home. And that's a hard lesson to learn. Took me awhile to settle down to being a civilian."

She appreciated his candor and realized she was getting more of a glimpse of the community, way more than she probably deserved.

"But you eventually did, Nick? You eventually made the switch over?"

He nodded, staring right as they pulled off into the woods north of town. "I got injured and that helped the choice. But I couldn't do it back down there in San Diego. It would've driven me nuts. But yes, eventually." He smiled back at her, his honest green eyes giving her a steady hand-up. "Not saying I don't miss it sometimes, though." He splayed his right hand as it rested on top of the steering wheel. "Just being perfectly honest."

Marcy gave him instructions, and in a few minutes they pulled down the now-familiar dirt driveway.

"I can see why he wanted you to come here in the daytime. And you *do* know there are pot growers all over here, right?"

"He told me."

"Used to be a big problem when people would stumble onto some-one's field and get shot. Now I think these people grow inside temperature-controlled buildings, the big operations, that is. And they don't do the pot forests like the old days."

"Speaking from first-hand knowledge?" Marcy said as she opened her door and hopped out.

"Not me. My folks, believe it or not."

"You know I got lost coming here yesterday. There are little roads and trails all over the place up here. When I came the first time, I used my GPS. But not everything up here is on that map."

Nick walked to the front stoop. "Nice up here. Very remote, though. You don't ever want to be at this place alone."

Marcy nodded and inserted the key into the front door. Fear coursed through her when she discovered it was unlocked. She was sure she had locked it when she left.

She instantly knew someone had been inside the home even before she saw the mess left behind. The cupboards had been ransacked. Cushions in the living room had been torn open, white pieces of cotton stuffing fell like snow over the floor. A long wooden cabinet door was broken off the hinges, splinters covering the braided rug in front of it. A metal lock was discarded. Nick ran to the bare cabinet first.

"Was this empty?"

"I have no idea."

He peered through checkerboard kitchen window curtains, while Marcy noticed someone had thrown darts, hitting the wall instead of the game board. Nick searched the rest of the cabin, including the closets and the bathroom.

"I'm going to go look around outside. You check for anything that might be missing, if you can tell."

Contents had been removed from the bathroom cabinet and strewn over the floor. Several vitamin and aspirin bottles had been opened and their tablets were absorbing water, turning to paste. Someone had used the toilet, not been very careful about their aim and not flushed it.

Marcy checked the bedroom closet. Every box or bag was opened, and open-ended. Books were removed from the desk in the corner. The cushions on the overstuffed reading chair were sliced open and stuffing was removed just like in the living room.

She wondered what the motive of the break-in had been. The urine left in the toilet made her think druggie kids might be the culprits.

Nick entered the bedroom just as she'd discovered the bedroom window latch had been pried off the wooden sash, which still remained open. "I think this is how they got in," she told him.

Nick fingered the cut marks in the window frame. "I'm not liking this. I've got to get hold of Lucas. You sure you never saw this gun cabinet loaded with weapons?"

"No. I think the weapons are still in the second seat of the truck."

"What the fuck?" Nick's eyes squinted. He cocked his head. "What are you saying, Marcy?"

"The large black bag he was most concerned about is in the back seat of his truck. He wanted me to make sure you helped me. I forgot all about it when I got home last night. It's still there."

Nick ran outside, ripping open the second seat door, removing the blanket and placed the bag over the other items on the bench. As he unzipped it, Marcy could see over his shoulder a huge weapon nearly four feet long. There were several smaller bags, which Nick quickly checked through, and she noticed several contained large sharply-tipped brass rounds in neat rows. Another weapon, much shorter and stubby, looking like a small machine gun, was wrapped in a dirty blue towel. He undid pockets on the front of the bag, pulling out a couple thick knives with serrated edges. Marcy was looking at the bag belonging to a killing machine. Something deep in her stomach churned and her mouth became parched.

The sun was making her dizzy and she stepped back.

Nick made sure the black nylon was well hidden under the old blanket, and turned to address her.

"You're not used to all this, so I have to forgive you for some of your stupid mistakes, but Marcy, no more. You've made a whole boatload of bad decisions, starting with leaving unattended a very dangerous weapon and enough rounds of ammo to kill a hundred people. In the wrong hands, these things are deadly. Could cost you and everyone you love their lives. So, I'm going to give it to you straight. Don't make this fuckin' mistake again. I'm not letting you drive to San Diego alone to return them to Lucas. And I know sure as shit he's going to need them very soon."

"Sorry."

"No. Just doing what he'd do if he was here. Marcy," He stepped forward so quickly she jumped, flinching when he grabbed her shoulders. "You don't do shit like this again. You watch everything. You never leave a weapon lying around where it can be stolen, or found by police, understood?"

"Yes." She couldn't help it, but her lower lip was quivering. If she wasn't so afraid, she'd be breaking down into a sob, seeking the comfort of Nick's arms.

"Okay, gotta call Lucas. You feel okay about starting to clean up in there?"

"Yes. Again, Nick, I'm—"

Nick had dialed Lucas and interrupted her. "Hey, asshole. You wanna tell me what you were doing with an M27 and a fuckin' MP5 in the back seat while your girlfriend and my wife go shopping for bagels and coffee and shit?"

Marcy was glad she couldn't hear Lucas' response.

CHAPTER 16

MOUSTAFA WAS GLAD he'd seen the woman who was fated to come into his web yesterday. He'd dreamt about her all night long as he pleasured himself lying on the mattress out under the stars. When he'd heard an owl hooting in the distance, he grew cautious, washed his hands in the hose bib by the garden and retired inside for the rest of the evening.

His two recruits read their books by candlelight. Moustafa was trying to use as little energy as he could, and liked the idea that the boys were learning their sacred studies just as the Prophet had centuries ago, by candlelight.

God is great.

He knew where she had come from, and he'd scouted the little cabin earlier in the month. So he had reason to go back now. As the dawn was breaking he and the others hiked a path through the heavy woods. He chuckled that the recruits would be scratching their skin off the next day, as the forest was full of poison oak. Moustafa knew the best thing was to take a cold shower afterwards, use his Tech-Nu and then blot his skin dry. He wouldn't get the pox of western man that way. But the boys needed to experience the uncomfortable results while they meditated and did their prayers.

God is great.

He'd seen the gun cabinet on the previous scouting and was most anxious to open it and steal what he thought would surely be some weaponry inside. But that was not to be. The flimsy pine cabinet only held cobwebs and spiders. Even the refrigerator was empty.

He relished shredding the couch pillows, tossing all the dishes and glassware like they were made of paper. His recruits took his lead and destroyed the bathroom. Nothing was found that was of use. The books were unreadable, the magazines worse, although his recruits stole the ones with the naked women in them, thinking Moustafa wouldn't catch them hiding the folded lust books in their clothes. They were like schoolboys upset with being harshly punished, angry that there wasn't anything to eat in the refrigerator, which was still partially cold, justified to help themselves to the infidel's debauched way of life.

He was going to turn on the water and let it run, perhaps burn up the pump and drain the well, but he wanted to watch her shower again, like he'd watched the night before when the big man was there fucking her on his knees with his lips, fucking her from behind and letting her fuck him between her breasts. He would enjoy taking her apart bit by bit, if the opportunity presented itself. It could be a teaching moment for his recruits, who would soon have to do the same. He'd show them an infidel was not like a real woman, one of their believers. They were too used to their mothers and sisters, but they'd learn, in time. Showing them how to properly kill an infidel would toughen them up.

He heard the high-pitched whine of the infidel's truck from a mile away only an hour after they'd started searching the cabin. They'd had just enough time to run back toward the mother house. Moustafa jumped in the shower and put on clean pajama pants and a loose fitting Humboldt State t-shirt, watching as one by one, both of his new recruits began to scratch their skin. He didn't feel a thing.

God is great.

By now, she would have found the cabin altered. Moustafa would wait until nightfall and then creep back and perhaps spy on her sleeping there. Perhaps look for items in the vehicle she wouldn't think to lock up.

He got out his yellow-lined tablet, working on his plan for new recruits arriving this fall, all arranged through a refugee humanitarian program administered by the church group they bought the camp from.

God is great.

America was indeed the land of opportunity. They had no idea what they were willingly giving away. It was a sign from the Prophet they could walk right in and claim what was theirs. The Kingdom of Heaven would reign supreme for all the true believers. And those who did not submit, would be eliminated. There was only one path to Heaven and all roads led there, whether or not the hapless Americans knew it or not.

He smiled as he looked out the window at the bright sunshine. In the dialect of his adopted home, Northern California, he said to himself, 'God is Awesome!'

CHAPTER 17

LUCAS HADN'T BEEN able to reach Marcy, but the call with Nick got him worried. They'd all been asked to stay off their cells, unless it was an emergency, so he'd had to end the call quickly without asking how she was doing.

"Can't talk, Nick. I'll be dark for a few. Bring that shit home." He hated to hang up like that, do that to a former teammate, even though they hadn't served together. But he knew Nick would figure it out.

Their transport was waiting on the tarmac near lunchtime, the big beast gobbling all sixteen of them, with another group coming the following week from two other teams that were redeployed from the Pacific and East Africa. They landed in Park Field as part of the Naval Mid-South command base. The temporary training hangar and cyclone workout area looked like old prison grounds. A small track bordering a roughly patched lawn with goalposts at the end seemed out of place in the dusty heat of the afternoon.

Tyler Gray was the first to say something after they walked their gear toward the yard. "Holy mother fuck. We got ourselves a soccer field."

Fredo nodded his head. T.J. and Cooper looked toward the sky at the heat of the sun and shook their heads. Lucas stood next to them all, feeling suddenly joyful. "We can have ourselves a scrimmage, gents."

"Gets mighty hot this time of year," said Rory.

Lucas turned back to survey the rest of the base. Old planes and bunk buildings, long since unused, littered the area. It did not look like a high-level SEAL facility, but Lucas reminded himself it didn't take lots of shiny new equipment and paint to make a good target. Even a fresh patch of green lawn wouldn't do it. They weren't there to impress anyone. They were flesh and blood bait on a stick.

The team was greeted by a petite woman in blue camo. She wore a whistle around her neck and a stopwatch. She singled out Kyle somehow and shook his hand. "Donna Grant. I'm one of your trainers here."

Several of the team regarded the diminutive woman, but respectfully not a word was spoken. "Chief Petty Officer Kyle Lansdowne. Where you want us, ma'am?"

She dropped her hand and did an about face, motioning him to follow toward one of the run-down barracks. Several vans were parked nearby and a Skilsaw was being operated inside one of the rooms.

"We don't have much, but what we have is yours, Chief. Had to install internet and some extra plugs, replace part of the bathroom fixtures, some broken windows, and got rid of the crusty urinals. These buildings haven't been used for over twenty years." She turned to the group, smiling tightly. "Downsizing and all that shit," she said, wiggling her eyebrows.

Kyle angled his head and frowned, but his eyes grew to twice their size. "Good to know." He winked at Coop and Fredo.

Lucas regarded the grins and white teeth surrounding him and knew the little lady had just made one hell of an impression on the whole group. Someone mumbled, "I think I might like this training after all."

Donna walked like a basketball player, but without the tall lanky build. The hallway floor was covered with speckled puce gray vinyl tiles the Navy used boatloads of all over the world. The building was cool and dark. When she flipped on the buzzing overhead lights, some of them blinking and barely glowing behind yellowed plastic covers, it wasn't much of an improvement.

"Okay, you campers can choose your rooms. Trust me, take the ones on the ground floor. Upstairs can be for the poor frogs who have to come next week."

The rooms were not large, but bedrooms opened to a central quad area, so four men could share the common area. Single mattresses in each room were brand new, still in plastic, one set of white sheets and a pillowcase folded neatly and perfectly centered. The rec room at the end of the building was completely sparse. No TVs, tables, or couches were anywhere in sight. A stainless steel all-in-one sink, stove, and dishwasher was bordered by light green Formica countertops with stainless steel, real authentic retro trim. Plywood cabinets overhead had no doors on them.

"Looks like a Costco run is in order, gents," whispered Kyle.

"Do they even have a fuckin' Costco in Tennessee?" asked Fredo.

"Oh yes. We have three," added Donna. "We got more bars, more churches, and the biggest Costco in the whole state not more than a few miles away."

Donna announced the evening dinner would be served at twenty-hundred and pointed to the hall where it would be served. "And tonight, we have something special for you. Providing you behave yourselves, you'll get to train with the Navy Soccer team. They're joining us for dinner tonight, gentlemen."

Lucas and Tyler grinned at each other. Both of them had played with the boys before and were looking to a rematch.

"When do they arrive?" asked Tyler.

Donna checked her watch. "They're on their way now. Just finished up a game against Tennessee State, and they won, so the ladies are going to want to celebrate."

"Ladies?" Lucas asked.

"Yes. Didn't I tell you? They're the Navy *Women's* Soccer Team."

The announcement had room choices happening quickly and the showers were suddenly full, which limited the water pressure to a trickle.

KYLE CONDUCTED A briefing before dinner. "We're about ten miles from the camp run by the MOA group here. Occasionally we'll see members on the freeway, or in town at various places, primarily grocery outlets and secondhand stores. You are not to engage them. I'm good with you looking casual, sharp and military, but no insignias of any branch, please. I'm okay if they think you're a paramilitary defense contractor group here for some specialized training, or, better yet, Army Corps of Engineers working on one of the dams or waterways nearby. But don't volunteer one fuckin' thing. Don't talk to them, or to the locals who have befriended them. You can't trust a one, not one."

Kyle continued with some of the ground rules. "Any of you want to grow beards, be my guest. You know how that registers and identifies us overseas. But again, and I can't stress this enough, you stay off social media as far as posting pictures and letting people at home know you're okay or where you are exactly. Only cell phones, and only if it's extremely important. We have internet just to get and send information about our finds, and not for your pleasure, okay?"

The team grumbled.

Kyle handed out a list of names. "This is your phone tree, like your mom had when you were playing soccer. You check in with your men on this list every morning and every night. You know where they are, when they'll be back, when they get up, and when they go to bed."

"Do we have to find out when they take a shit?" T.J. asked. The group started adding other bits of helpful advice.

"I'm thinking no," said Kyle, who grinned neatly and then turned to all business.

Lucas had chosen a room with Jake, Alex, and Ryan. They'd already made a list of furniture for their crib, as well as the electronic equipment, including a big screen TV and a couple of blenders.

"We gonna be allowed to watch streaming video?" Jake asked.

"Working on it, Jake. Security is our main concern, so stuff like that has to be checked out, and the ONI office hasn't finished their work. We'll work something out."

Kyle distributed pictures of the camp bordered with tall metal fencing covered with razor wire in the remote forested region up the road, which also encompassed a rocky crag nearly two hundred feet tall. Kyle told them the group had twenty-four-seven guards posted in pairs atop this vantage point.

He also told them all aerial surveillance was current. The group had purchased a small dozer-tractor and they appeared to be enlarging a large swale or earthen dam, harnessing one of the tributaries into a man-made lake that had begun to fill. "We don't know what's going on here, but if you'll notice they have some small watercraft so we're guessing some kind of amphibious training exercise area." He showed them a picture of a target range and one long metal hangar with no doors or windows in it. The structure looked brand new.

"We are trying to find out what that building is. I'm sending a couple of you over to the contractor's office to find out. Whatever it is, you can bet it's no good. We don't have authority to trespass, so keep your distance, but understand these guys are for real, and they've spent a lot of money getting set up."

The jovial nature of the possible meetup with the soccer players was dashed as the team studied the glossy pictures being passed around. Kyle held up a picture of a graying rotund gentleman in a long Afghani robe and gray pakol cap. His wide face and near mid-chest level beard streaked with light brown made him look grandfatherly and harmless. Lucas had seen many of these tribal members before on previous deployments and it was difficult to tell the good guys from the bad guys.

"You see this guy, you let me or Lt. Commander Forsythe know right away. This is Sheik Hammid Rushti. He hasn't been picked up by birds in a month or more, so he's either escaped without detection or he's still inside. And if he is, we'd guess he'd be here." Kyle pointed to the long, ominous building.

Kyle went over the training schedule as Donna Grant entered the building and announced dinner.

Most the SEALs wore white V-necked t-shirts, and jeans or cargo pants, and canvas slip-ons. There was more aftershave and clean-shaven cheeks than Lucas had remembered at a high school dance. He knew, after tonight, everyone who would be growing beards.

He'd gotten two text messages marked urgent from both Nick and

Marcy to call, so he tried to reach Marcy first.

"Lucas, someone's broken into the cabin."

"What? You get my black bag?" He tried to hide the edge to his voice.

"Yes, not to worry. That bag and all your things came back with me. Everything you asked me to get, I did."

"So, what do you mean? Broken in and busted the place up?"

"Yes."

"Nick was there with you?"

"Yes, he went with me to, well, to double-check everything I'd done. I came right up after I dropped you at the airport." Marcy was hesitant to finish. "And I cleaned out your place, like you asked, but I did it alone. So he took me up there this morning—"

He swore and hoped she didn't hear it. "Marcy, I told you not to do that."

"I know, Lucas. I've already gotten the lecture."

"So what did they take?"

"Nothing. Just threw things around the house, broke the dishes, and messed up the couches and bathroom. Nothing that couldn't be fixed."

"How'd they get in? You *did* lock it, right?"

"Of course. Looks like they pried open the bedroom window and came through that way. Didn't break a window, just trashed the contents, the furniture, and…and your gun case. *Was* that a gun case?"

Lucas concentrated and didn't remember checking the case, which had been locked. He'd lost the key years ago.

"It was, but I don't think there was anything in there. Haven't opened it since high school, but my dad and grandpa never left weapons up there. We always brought everything."

"Well, that's good. That's the one thing Nick asked me about."

"I'll bet. So they busted it open?"

"Shattered it."

"Is Nick there?"

"He's outside checking the perimeter. We're preparing to leave here in a few. He's gonna be responsible for that heavy black bag getting to your apartment. That *is* where you want it, right?"

"I'm thinking my locker at the team building. No one's at the apartment."

"Where are you?"

"Can't say."

"You can reach Nick on his cell. We'll be driving all night, so call us anytime you can."

"Thanks, Marcy. Glad you weren't hurt." His mind was racing to think who could have damaged the cabin. It had been there so long without an incident, it was so unusual, but then, lots of unusual things were happening.

"I'm fine. Don't worry about me. And Nick will drive with me all the way to San Diego."

Lucas saw the others gathering for dinner. "I have to go. Tell Nick I'll call later, if I can."

"Will do. Miss you, Lucas."

"Me too, Marcy. You have that talk with Connie yet?"

"Was going to wait until I got there, but don't think I can now. She's already making a little stir at the office."

"Do *not* tell her about us, Marcy. Big mistake. Trust me on that."

"No argument here, Lucas. You take care of yourself. Is it customary to say keep your head down? Like 'break a leg' for an actor?"

Lucas found himself smiling and it felt good. "Would be better if you told me you were in the shower rubbing that gel all over your body."

"Well then, sailor. I'd say it's still appropriate to say, 'keep your head down.'"

"Roger that, baby. Soon. Be safe. Be smart."

"Love you, Lucas."

He hadn't heard those words for at least two years. Marcy's confession of love to him was just in time, too. Not that he needed something to live for. "Love you too, kid. Talk soon."

He hung up, the hard-on in his pants very inconvenient, but easily covered up by a food tray. He hoped.

While they waited for their food, the soccer team bus drew up and one by one the ladies exited, each carrying a large blue and gold leather bag. The players unceremoniously slipped the leather straps off their shoulders and dropped them just inside the doorway. Several disappeared into the restroom while others washed their faces and hands in the cool drinking water dispenser and sauntered over to the food line in their matching blue and yellow flip-flops with the large block letter *N* on the outer edge.

Tyler was the first to speak to them. "Congrats on the win."

One player towered over all the others, being nearly Coop's height, which would make her nearly six and a half feet tall. She cut in front of the line without looking at any of the SEALs, without asking permission. Their captain was still wearing her red armband.

"Thanks," the captain said. "And we beat the *guys* in a twenty minute friendly game too." She flashed a perfect white smile back at Tyler, then winked up at Jake.

Their shorts and tanned legs were scoring big-time points with the team, both married and single guys. All of Lucas' bachelor buddies were pulling out chairs, tucking napkins into their shirts, and asking politely for salt and pepper instead of standing to reach in front of each other. They brought glasses and pitchers of iced tea for the ladies, not paying attention to a couple of SEALs who had their hand out for a cup. The swearing was clipped as well.

Kyle, Cooper, Fredo, and Armani sat together at one end of the table with several other of the married guys. Though married, Tyler sat next to their captain and the two started talking soccer immediately.

Lucas overheard Tyler whisper, "Who's the Amazon?" to his neighbor.

"By the way, it's Lacey," she said shaking Tyler's hand.

Tyler began, "This is Jack, Lucas, Alex, Connor, Danny, Jeffrey, and the rest of the guys are married."

"And what are you, Tyler?" said Danny Begay. "Lacey, don't trust him. We're both married."

Lacey began her team introductions, and then added, "Husbands and boyfriends are not suitable topics of conversation on the road."

Jake and Alex shared a smile.

"But I'd recommend staying away from our keeper, Chloe. She's the short one in her family and her dad plays for the Suns."

Chloe lifted a fork and nodded acknowledgement, but otherwise sat expressionless and focused on her food.

One of the pretty blonde-haired brown-eyed players asked the table a general question. "So why are you guys way out here? And how come we've been sent to babysit you? Aren't you guys SEALs?"

The question left the table completely quiet.

CHAPTER 18

MARCY AND NICK started to drive Lucas' truck back to San Diego in the afternoon. He called in at dusk, and Nick reassured him he was going to keep Marcy in plain sight.

"Honestly, Lucas, the gun cabinet would have been of interest to anyone. Because it had a lock on it, it was attractive to kids. That's who I think they were. Normal thieves don't do destruction. They just look for valuables. This was a concerted effort to damage and destroy."

She watched the dusk send an orange glow to the western horizon. They'd gotten so busy cleaning everything up and disposing of the broken things, she'd completely forgotten to call Connie. They had another six hours to drive, so she decided to put it off until she could do the *in person* conversation.

Nick chuckled. "Nothing like that. But they did pee all over the toilet." Nick gave Marcy a wink. "Your lady made that place shine when we were done. I screwed the window frame shut because I didn't have a new latch. You'll have to fix that when you return."

He finally asked Lucas the question Marcy was wondering. "You in country or out?"

She heard the, "Yes," in response from Lucas.

"Meaning you are or are not out of country?"

She heard the tinny, "Yes" from the other end of the phone.

"You asshole."

Lucas said something else while Marcy waited to get her chance to talk to him.

"Hey, punk, you have any beefs with your neighbors?" Nick rolled his eyes and gave her another wide smile.

She heard the scratchy swearing and objection on the other end.

"I know, I know. You guys were angels growing up. I can only imagine you terrorizing the little church goin' sweethearts when your dad and grandpa weren't paying attention. No, asshole, I'm talking about the fuckin' neighbors who live in that commune next door." Nick held the squawking phone out to Marcy. "You tell him."

"Nice to hear your voice twice in one day, Lucas," said Marcy. "Everything okay?"

Lucas laughed. "The beach is awesome, babe. Those umbrella drinks are strong. Good music. Missing you real bad."

"That's the only part of this conversation I believe, Lucas."

"Nick said we have new neighbors? What's this about a commune?"

"Well, looks to me like they've been there for awhile. Doing a bunch of things. Buildings out back. Nick said it was an old Christian camp. Sonshine Haven. You hear of it?"

"Nobody has used that place for years, Marcy. I didn't think they even had a road cleared anymore."

"Trust me, it's been worked on. Bunkhouse-like cabin in front and a covered riding arena in the back. Some new metal stables, and hay barns. The guy tending the vegetable garden looked like he could be a pot grower."

Lucas didn't say a word. "You stay away from there, Marcy. I'll check it out when I get home, but for now, no one goes up there."

"Don't you think someone should check on your place for you? How long will you be gone?"

"Not your concern, and to be honest, none of us knows that. But you stay away. Understood?"

"Yessir."

"Seriously, Marcy. Especially with the break-in, you don't go up there anymore."

Marcy agreed with him completely.

They said their goodbyes and Marcy handed the phone back to

Nick with a "Thanks."

Checking her cell phone, she noticed she'd missed a call from Connie Shipley. "Oh shoot. I had the ringer turned off. I have to call my client."

"I'm going to pull over for a quick bite. You want a burger or something? There's a great Mexican restaurant a couple of miles west."

"I'm game. Let's go Mexican. I'll finish my call with Connie and then meet you inside."

Connie's phone went to voicemail right away. "Hey, Connie. This is Marcy Gelland with Coronado Bay Realty. I'm—"

Just as she watched Nick walk inside the restaurant, she saw Connie had returned her call. She hung up the message and answered her.

"Sorry to call you so late, Connie. I'm on my way back to San Diego. Thought maybe we—"

"Well, holy shit, Marcy. How good of you to wake the baby up."

"Sorry. I can call in the morning—"

"No. You don't get off that easy."

"Pardon?"

"I've got a screaming baby, but I got a boob that will do just fine."

"Okay." Marcy tried a nervous laugh on for size. Connie was more than prickly.

"All good now. Little shit won't sleep the night, but then that's nothing new." Connie took a deep breath and let it out before she continued. "So, I've been doing a little research. Very interesting what you can find out if you ask the right questions."

"Not sure what you mean, Connie. What questions?"

"When were you going to tell me you were fucking my husband?"

CHAPTER 19

P T STARTED AT o-six-hundred with a timed five-mile run around the track. The girls joined them. On the other side of the cafeteria was a small gym with rusty equipment Lucas could smell just as soon as he walked through the old double doors. One window had been duct taped down the middle, cheaply repairing a crack that threatened to destroy the whole frame. Fredo was making a list of things to get at Costco. He'd put down a water dispenser, some white towels to wipe the equipment down with, cleaning supplies and some free weights.

The smell of fresh coffee reminded Lucas of home, causing a twinge of homesickness. He missed her.

The training went by fast as they focused on pull-ups and sit-ups before they began doing stretching exercises. Several of the team guys remarked they missed the ocean. Coop and Fredo had created a ritual of diving in after an especially long and arduous workout.

Kyle asked T.J., Armando, Lucas, and Jake to join him for a hike up toward the ridge overlooking the camp's compound. It was classified a training exercise.

The five of them made less noise than one of the local deer as they jogged through sparse woods and a meadow with a small stream coursing through the middle. Close to the compound, the terrain was dotted with large granite boulders and became steep. Midway up the bluff, Kyle motioned with hand signals pointing to a sentry. The team fanned out around the back side of the outcropping so his line of sight would miss them. The thin, dark-skinned man was wearing shabby ill-fitting clothes and shoes that laced up, but appeared several sizes too large for him.

T.J. nearly ran into another sentry sitting on a large boulder, an AK-47 resting across his thighs. T.J. signaled and everyone froze in place.

The team waited nearly an hour, settling against rocky crags and high meadow brush, easily camouflaged, to make sure no one else appeared in the area. Since these men were not breaking the law, the SEALs were only tasked with observing, making note of what they found and not to engage. Unless fired upon, they would not be allowed to use their weaponry, either.

They heard a vehicle approach from several hundred yards behind them. Country music was rising into the blue overcast sky. The heat was stifling hot, and Lucas studied the gray clouds with more than a passing interest. A quick shower, even a downpour would be welcome in the nearly one-hundred-degree noonday heat.

The vehicle came into view. Both sentries watched the red Jeep advance into the woods, following the off-road trail. They were speaking to each other from about ten yards apart, their dialect sounding Pashtu, but Lucas couldn't be sure. Kyle held up a small recording device with a plastic cone boost, trying to capture what was being said.

Two young girls in tank tops and cutoffs were in the front seat of the open-air Jeep, wearing baseball caps and sunglasses. One was singing to the words of the song on the radio.

Lucas was concerned at first they were wandering into a den of bad guys, but when one of the sentries waved to the driver of the Jeep, and the other one didn't ready his weapon, he knew it was a planned or announced visit. The girls did not look Middle Eastern, but extremely westernized and young.

Lucas quietly cleaned the lenses on his binoculars, wiped down the scope he'd mounted to his H&K, inserted his fifteen round magazine, and then clicked off the safety, which was all they could do, since they weren't on a snatch and grab or kill on sight mission. Armani was laying flat and had already sighted the camp below, while Kyle was focused on the sentries. That left Jake to be their eyes behind them his Glock at the ready.

Below them, the Jeep stopped, motor running, as the two girls inside began a conversation with the perimeter guards. The ladies turned down their radio and spoke with one of two guards, who leaned over the door of the Jeep as the other scanned the roadway and the hill above. Without knowing it, the guard looked directly at the Team's position, and Lucas heard Armani hold his breath as his finger rested against the trigger mechanism after selecting his firing safety setting. As the guard looked away and the girls were waved through, Lucas noted Armando quietly release his breath, closed his eyes, and then retreated back.

Kyle took pictures of the compound, the approach, and close-ups of the guard gate and the sentries and where they were placed. There were several large trucks with closed beds parked at the side of the long building. A satellite dish and radio tower was installed atop one of the pine trees nearby. Kyle took pictures of that too.

Their LPO motioned for them to make their way back down the hill, and once at the bottom and out of sight, sprinted the way back to the creek, where they splashed water on their faces and down their shirts. Then they continued with the jog until they got back to their camp mid-afternoon. Lucas headed for the shower, for a cold one, soon followed by Kyle and the others.

Alex and Ryan hung around the doorway, waiting for him to finish in privacy.

"So what'd you find out?" Alex asked.

Kyle put his head under the water, rinsing off before he answered. "They're used to having female visitors."

"How'd you get that?" Alex asked, scrunching his eyebrows and forehead.

"They didn't make the local girls cover up. Especially their heads."

"Then there were the cut-offs," Lucas added.

Alex was still not convinced. So Kyle hammered it in. "That would *never* happen to an un-westernized Iraqi." He dried off and threw the skimpy towel around his waist. "Still can't decide what's in that building, but they're moving something in and out of there with those trucks. They're smart not to have people out in the daytime for the birds to spy overhead. We need to get our IR gear and visit them after dark. Begay has natural night vision so he's coming. You in, Alex?"

"Sure, anything, Chief. After all, I don't got a date."

"He's working to fix that as soon as is humanly possible. But the job comes first," added Ryan.

"Tyler's got his eye on Captain Blondie, that married sonofabitch," said Armando.

"I think she's sweet on Jake, from what I can see," said Alex.

Lucas knew Tyler would not go outside his marriage, that the chance to converse with someone about soccer was the real draw. "I agree. Never thought the bachelors would hook up on this training. God is looking out for you guys."

"*You* guys?" asked Kyle. The skimpy white towel barely tucked around Kyle's trim waist and narrow hips. "Aren't you in that league, Lucas? Connie's got you by the balls, I hear."

Lucas nodded in agreement. "Actually, I'm a little attached to my realtor. Got serious quick."

"Holy fuck. You're dumber than I thought, Lucas," said Kyle. "That the realtor Connie hired?"

Lucas didn't see any point to keeping it a secret. "Well, yes."

"You ain't even fuckin' divorced yet."

"That's been pointed out to me, Chief," Lucas answered.

"Unbelievable," Kyle said as he pushed his way past the crowd.

Back at their room, Jake sat down on Lucas' bed. "I need to talk to you a minute."

Lucas was putting on his jeans and a black Team 3 t-shirt.

"He said no logos."

"Shit, you're right. Just second nature." Lucas removed the shirt, tossing it in the built-in cabinet, and unwrapped a new white t-shirt. He slipped it over his head. "Thanks, man." He could see Jake was conflicted about something. "You okay?"

Jake looked at his hands, forearms resting on his thighs. "I've been dating that friend of Connie's, remember?"

Lucas had forgotten all about it, mostly because, since his divorce, Jake never stayed serious with one woman for more than about a month. He figured that ship had sunk long ago.

"So this is serious then, that what you're about to tell me?"

Jake grinned. "You know me. Fucked it up good this time. How did I know she had a sister that didn't look anything like her? Still a babe and all, but man, I had no idea sisters could look so opposite and yet act so competitive. Real catfight. And then they turned it all on me."

"Some people like that action, Jake."

"Shut the fuck up motherfucker. I'm not talking about *that*."

"Come on, Jake, you know sisters are bad news."

"Like I said, I didn't know!"

"Sounds like you dodged a bullet, my man." Lucas slipped on his shoes. He combed his hair and put on aftershave. "Weren't you the one all spouting off to me about staying single? Distrusting women? Didn't we have that conversation? So she, or they, whichever it is, broke up with you. Big deal."

"Well, yeah, that part's okay. I mean, I'm used to it. But boy, these ladies these days talk. They even talked to my ex. Connie gave me an earful."

"Well, you didn't exactly behave, Jake. I mean, mine was just a picture. You went and did the dirty."

"Not with a transvestite hooker."

"*Dancer*. I don't go with hookers."

"That you know of."

"Jake, just where the hell is this conversation going? You know full well I don't date or sleep around at all. And I never did that while married."

"You're married now, asshole."

"Yup, but she served papers on me."

"You're still legally married, you dumb-fuck."

"That's a minor detail. Thing is, Connie got some bad information, and believed I was—"

"That's what I have to talk to you about."

"Okay, I'm listening." Lucas could see Jake didn't want to tell him something and it was eating a hole in his gut.

"So the four of them are having lunch together, and—"

"Jake, you are one unlucky motherfucker. The four of them? Your ex, the sisters you've been banging and who else? Someone *else* you were banging?"

"No. Not exactly."

"Jake what part of *'banging'* don't you understand? That's like being just a little pregnant. We've had that talk, too."

Jake's expression became more painful.

"Holy fuck, you got the sisters pregnant, both of them?"

"Nah, man. Like I said, the four of them were having lunch, and apparently they told Connie—"

"Wait a minute, *my* Connie?"

"She isn't *your* Connie anymore, Lucas."

Alex and Ryan appeared at the doorway, as if on cue. Lucas glanced over at them and then put his hands on his hips. "Fuckit," he said as he grabbed Jake by the shirt. "You fucked Connie, too?"

Alex and Ryan sprang to action and separated them.

"No way, Lucas. I wouldn't do that. Honest." Jake's eyebrows tented upward, eyes squinting like he'd just smelled something terrible. He rubbed his forearm where Alex had grabbed him roughly. "I must have mentioned it to the one gal on our way out here. They wanted to arrange a double-double when we got back. Remember those, Lucas? Like we did before you married Connie?

Lucas could never forget those nights. "Before you were married, too, asshole."

"That's right. So, I told them you were seeing this realtor Connie had hired. They told Connie you were banging the realtor."

Even though he'd confirmed one of his best friends hadn't slept with his wife, Lucas still wanted to punch Jake as the deliverer of the bad news. Very bad news.

"Why did you have to tell me this?"

"Because it's the truth, man. Thought you ought to know, since you said you were sweet on her. Knowing Connie and her temper, I'd put protection on your lady, Lucas."

"Except I'm stuck in fuckin' Tennessee. How the hell am I supposed to do that?"

"Well, call her, when you get the chance. At least give her a warning."

Kyle stood behind Ryan and Alex. "We good here?" he asked.

Lucas nodded his head while the others just watched.

"We're meeting in five. Rec Room." Kyle said as he left.

Lucas knew it was the end of their private conversation. He was good at burying all his feelings over any deployment. One by one, the team collected in the rec area, as instructed.

Kyle was poring over his computer. "Okay, I've uploaded the photos and sent the audio clip back to Coronado. Hoping we can get some confirmation on what to do next."

Rory asked the next question. "You make them out to be Afghani? You think they were speaking Pashtu?"

"Yes," T.J. said. His language training was the best in the team. "See if you can amplify it, Kyle and I'll take a listen."

"Roger that, T.J."

The door burst open at the end of the bunkhouse and in walked Fredo, carrying boxes. "Hola, amigos! We got our Costco shit here,"

Accompanying him were Coop, Jeffrey, and Danny. Coop and Fredo unloaded boxes to the kitchen counters while Danny and Jeffrey sat down to assemble two tables and chairs and a TV stand which had all come in boxes. Soon several other members of the team took up positions in a circle.

"Okay, we got nice, fluffy towels," said Fredo. We got two cases of beer, some waters, and sodas and shit. Kyle, got your fuckin' turkey jerky."

"Thanks man," said Kyle.

"I bought condoms, toothpaste, deodorant, and aftershave for those dating, Red Bull, Gatorade, Monkey Butt powder, moist towelettes and some medicated ones for the old guys, hand sanitizer, detergent and dish soap," Fredo continued. "Coop got his dryer sheets and mineral waters too, so he's happy."

"Razors?" Lucas asked. "Forgot to mention it."

Fredo came over and put an arm on his shoulder. "Got you covered, my man, since you're beard is ugly as shit."

Lucas punched him in the arm.

"And for the record, no tofu or fresh vegetables. I figure frozen shit will work, lots of tortilla chips and salsa. Those of you into the healthier lifestyle can go to the fuckin' market tomorrow."

"Awesome!" Jake said as he opened up a box of chocolate bars.

Within ten minutes, all the furniture was assembled without anyone being in charge. The directions were passed around as needed. It was obvious the TV stand needed something on top, which would be one of the missions for tomorrow.

Two blenders and a coffee maker were set on the countertop. Coop filled new ice cube trays and placed them in the freezer. Fredo doled out a towel for each man.

"Okay, I'm going to say this one time, because about six of you have asked me," started Kyle. "Yes, we're having the ladies over tonight for a meet and greet. And here are some of the ground rules."

Lucas and Jake looked at each other and rolled their eyes. The disagreement of earlier seemed to have dissipated.

"First, the bedroom doors are to remain open while they're here. If you're going to be unsociable and go to bed early, you go to bed with your door open and the light on in your quad room. Got it?"

The grumbling continued until Donna Grant showed up to announce dinner.

"Hold on, Boy Scouts," Kyle shouted. "Got two more things to say. I need a volunteer to organize a scrimmage tomorrow afternoon."

Lucas and Tyler's hands shot up.

"Okay, we got two. Perfect." Kyle looked over at Fredo. "You need a donation of how much, Fredo?"

"Hundred bucks, gents," Fredo said.

"That has to happen before the weekend. We have a signup list over on the refrigerator for anything you want that you can share. No promises, of course. Fredo here keeps all the money and there are no refunds."

Lucas noticed a lined piece of yellow paper had been pasted to the refrigerator door with duct tape.

"I'm going to choose several to go up later tonight for a look-see at the camp with some IRs. We aren't telling the girls anything about this, get my drift?" Kyle surveyed his men in front of him. "We might get a visit from DC and Forsythe in a few days, depending on what we find up there at the camp. He's to bring some equipment I've requested. Again, no word of this to the ladies."

Alex asked if the phone tree was in effect tonight.

"What do you think?"

That seemed to settle it.

"I'm sending Coop and Lucas to town tomorrow to talk to the barn contractor. On the way back, they're to pick up a big screen and Blu-ray. We'll wait for them before we start the scrimmage, okay?"

Lucas nodded to Coop, who returned his acknowledgement. They both understood neither would have the night shift tonight. It also meant Lucas might be able to call Nick and Marcy, and perhaps use the internet at a coffee shop.

"Anything else you need to know about?" Kyle searched the room. "Everyone good on the home front?"

Jake and Ryan punched Lucas in the arm.

"Not you, Lucas, you're fucked," said Armando.

Several of the men started to chuckle. He had to defend himself. "At least I'm not the only one. How many times has she taken you to court, Jake?"

"Every time I knocked her up."

Amid the laughter, Kyle signed them off. "Okay, then. We'll have a briefing after PT in the morning. Be safe tonight and get to bed at a decent hour. The midnight hike will be with Armani, Fredo, Danny and

Alex."

Kyle let them head for dinner. On their way to the door, he announced behind them, "Last one up cleans up the kitchen."

Lucas knew that meant there'd be a race for early bedtimes, which was probably what his LPO intended.

CHAPTER 20

NICK AND MARCY arrived in the early dawn, stopped for breakfast, and then drove to Lucas' apartment, the place he told them was temporary and shared with the other bachelors.

"This is going to be new for me too, Marcy. Never met Lucas before you came into the picture."

"Do you know Connie?"

"Only by reputation. You've got your hands full."

"Tricky part is getting someone *else* to keep the listing. I can't in good conscience represent them. I mean, I *could*, but the appearance would be otherwise."

"I totally get it. Devon has had similar issues."

Marcy checked out Nick's expression. "Not really," she said with a teasing smile, followed by a wink.

"Oh, yes. She gets divorcing couples all the time. About half her business."

Marcy had to laugh at how naïve Nick was, something she also saw in Lucas. Here he was this big tough guy and was completely blind to some personal things. "I think I went a little beyond where Devon has gone. I know her and she'd never do what I did."

Nick blushed and would not look back at her. "Gotcha. Sorry. It didn't even cross my mind."

He set the black clothes bag on the floor near the front door. "Don't know which is his room," he added as he began searching the bedrooms for something that would indicate it belonged to Lucas. "You recognize anything?" he asked as he walked out of one bedroom into the next.

"Afraid not," she sighed. "And I don't know the other guys either."

Marcy unzipped the duffel and pulled out clothes she'd added back at the cabin. Some of her underwear accidentally dangled from one hand in front of Nick.

"You need a bag," he said, and pretended he'd not seen the unmentionables. Returning with a recycled plastic shopping bag from the kitchen, he continued not making eye contact.

Marcy loaded up and dropped the bag by the door. Then she walked slowly through the apartment. The living room couch and matching loveseat looked more than well-used and wasn't anything she'd sit down on. There were nude posters in every room. Several hard-oiled women in handcuffs, blindfolds, and various states of mostly undress lined the walls of the guest bath.

A set of folding chairs sat around a small stained table in the kitchen. The rugs were brightly stained. The slider to the balcony overlooking the valley below was covered with handprints and a torn screen hanging on a bent frame.

Two of the bedrooms had cultures growing from half-eaten food or glasses. The kitchen sink was filled with four bowls with old cold cereal stuck to the sides.

"If I had a couple of hours, I could fix this place up," she said.

Nick smirked.

Marcy continued. "And I'm thinking they'd hate it. Am I right?"

"With those guys? From what I understand, anything approaching domestic bliss would be totally off limits."

"Okay, so what's next?"

"I was thinking I'd get the equipment bag over to the Team building, but I'm detached, so I'll have to get someone else to do it. Can you drop me off? I'll stay there tonight and try to take a plane up to Santa Rosa in the morning."

"Sure thing. Thought the whole team was with Lucas."

"They have someone who injured his leg in a jump and didn't go."

MARCY SLIPPED BEHIND the wheel of Lucas' truck and watched as the sandy-haired ex-SEAL hoisted the heavy weapons bag over his shoulder and resumed a path to his friend's front door. He met another well-built young man with an ankle to hip cast on his leg. Marcy shook her head.

Am I ready for all this? She'd barely knew Lucas, and already she was running guns, cleaning up ransacked cabins, and riding in his truck with another SEAL she barely knew. And somehow, she was *okay* with it?

How my life has changed. With a heavy dose of apprehension, Marcy noted how fast her world had tilted on its axis. She waved goodbye to Nick and his friend like they were people she'd known her whole life. The day was already getting long and she needed a shower and an early to bed.

But first, she had to face the wife of the man she was screwing.

THE CORONADO BAY Realty office was on a corner in the neighborhood of expensive designer boutiques, high-end burger bars, vegetarian restaurants, art galleries and espresso coffeehouses. Marcy had always enjoyed working at the attractive, highly-visible, upscale office, unlike some of her other realtor friends. Many of the agents there didn't need the income and worked there just to hobnob with local celebrities and wealthy businessmen. It was also known far and wide as a great place to pick up a wealthy second or third husband for singles or soon-to-be singles, either male or female. She was one of the few who did not have all the cosmetic surgery to make themselves into sufficient eye candy.

Their lobby was decorated by a designer regularly featured in Architectural Digest. Imitating an abandoned villa in Tuscany, broken pots spilled water fountains and colorful beds of flowers decorated outside the entrance doors. The lobby featured a large, textured steel waterfall, giving a serene and peaceful effect, like a high-end spa. Bird calls and a Tuscan orange room scent piped into the air ducts drifted around the reception and waiting area.

Today, none of those things did anything to cheer her mood.

Gail Burnett, married to the famous wide receiver, Barry Burnett, was the first to greet her. She had been chatting with the young receptionist, her long, tanned form outfitted in a white designer suit. Her blonde hair cascaded over her shoulders and back like spun gold. As she turned to face Marcy, her eyelids closed slightly. She licked her lips and tilted her chin up. Her green eyes sparkled with mischief. On another day and under different circumstances, she would have been someone Marcy could enjoy spending time with. But as a competitor, she was a feral cat used to successfully taking down lions.

Gail was all the wrong kinds of dangerous.

"There you are, sweetie."

It always annoyed Marcy when someone only a few years older could take on the aura of a critical parent.

"Hi, Gail." It was always wise to give the realtor what she wanted. "You look terrific today."

"And you look like you've just come from a demolition derby." Gail winked at her, making it overly obvious she didn't really mean the comment.

Except she did.

"Just got back from up north."

"Yes, heard about your interesting road trip." Gail checked her nails and then fluffed her hair.

Marcy wondered why her broker would have disclosed this little factoid. She put it out of her mind. "How's everything around here? Keeping busy?"

Gail smiled. Marcy held her breath.

"Can't complain. Barry's in Detroit, so I'm actually getting some work done."

Marcy figured Detroit wasn't the shopping destination Chicago or New York or even Atlanta would be. "Well, good. I've got some catching up to do myself," Marcy answered. "Let me get settled, and then could you and I have a little chat in the conference room?"

The receptionist, seated behind the curved bamboo counter, tore her eyes off her computer screen and shot a worried glance at Gail's profile.

"Sure thing, Marcy. Kind of wanted to talk to you as well." The fetching smile she used on her best clients looked dangerous.

"Give me about five. I'll meet you there."

"You bet." Gail turned and continued her conversation with the receptionist. Her skirt could not have been any tighter, revealing she wasn't embarrassed to show she wore thong underwear.

Several minutes later, Marcy and Gail stepped into the warm bisque-themed meeting space. A mural of vineyards and tiled roof spires perched atop rolling hills was painted along the long wall. Marcy sat at the head of the table, laying down her listing information and several other forms she'd dug out.

Gail had a thin file folder she held in long tapered fingers accented with pearlescent polish. Her open-toed sandals made small scratching sounds as she took up her place on Marcy's right, and sat.

Marcy looked at the painting before her and took in a deep breath as if she was vacationing in the little Tuscan village, not staring at a plastered wall. Her nervousness was uncharacteristic, but then, there were so many things she hadn't fully thought out. Normally, she liked to calculate every move in this chess game of real estate sales. Now she was trying to execute a retreat with her job and her pride still intact.

It was not what she was used to doing.

"Gail, I've taken this listing for a house on Apricot Way, and—"

"Connie and Lucas' house. I know it well," Gail interrupted.

"Good. Well, I've decided I'm going to refer their listing, and wanted to know if you'd be interested in taking over for me." She didn't spell out that normally there would be a referral fee shared between the agents, and just decided to let the implication stand, without bringing attention to it.

Gail hesitated a couple of seconds, tapping her fingernails on top of her file folder, as if she was considering a move she wasn't sure of. Her surgically plumped lips pulled back, without a wrinkle, into a thin line. Her eyes were able to give more expression. "Your timing is pretty good, Marcy." She opened the folder. "Because I got this letter from

Connie earlier this morning."

She handed the sheet of paper across the table. Marcy read:

'To: Marcy Gelland

I hereby request that you withdraw my listing at 442 Apricot Way, San Diego, California, immediately. I no longer wish to be represented by you.

The letter was signed by Connie Shipley and dated this morning.

Marcy sat back and waited for the other shoe to drop.

"You know we're always trained to give the client whatever they want, Marcy. I didn't solicit this, not in any way." Gail watched her words sink in. "Marcy, she wants *me* to represent them. Connie feels there's a conflict of interest." Gail's eyes got hard and cold. No smile lines appeared on her flawless face.

Marcy was going to sidestep the elephant in the room, hoping she wouldn't have to bring it out into the open. Instead, she decided, again, to give Gail what she wanted.

"Well, Gail, I agree and have no objection to this. Like I said, I wanted to—"

"And I'm *not* paying a referral fee, Marcy. Don't you think it's a little beyond that anyway?"

"Fine."

"Really?" Gail made a point to raise her eyebrows and bat her big green eyes with the eyelash extensions.

Marcy didn't want to press a fight. If all this could just go away, she'd be fine with the lack of income. She didn't have Barry Burnett's income as backup, but she was the top office producer and could absorb the cut in pay. What was more valuable than the commission earned was her standing in the office, especially with her broker, Joe.

She pulled out a Change Order form and began to fill it out for Gail, when they heard noise coming from the lobby. Marcy had just signed her name to the form when Connie Shipley appeared at the conference room door, her left hand splayed as she slapped the glass, her wedding ring making the metallic tapping sound. She was holding the baby in her right.

Marcy didn't realize Gail had locked the door, so when Connie began yanking on the burnished copper handles, the rattling sound shook most the nearby walls. Connie's face was shriveled in anger. "You let me in there, right now. Where the fuck is Lucas?"

Gail stood to unlock the door, but before she could get there, Connie continued with her tirade.

"Release me from your fuckin' listing contract or I'll tell the whole world you're fuckin' my husband!"

Even through the thick glass, Connie's voice was loud and menacing, but not nearly as loud as Marcy knew it was to the whole office. It would be impossible for anyone present to miss Connie's accusations.

So much for a clean exit.

CHAPTER 21

A FTER DINNER, THE music began. Jake was the center of attention, often dancing with three or four soccer players. He kept encouraging Lucas to join in, but Lucas was preoccupied with the reveal Jake had given him about Connie, and he worried about Marcy and how she was doing.

He slipped into the bathroom and tried to text her, but couldn't get a signal. In the old days, he'd have been mixing the margaritas and making sure everyone had a generous helping of alcohol, but this time they'd only bought a limited amount and that was mostly beer. He started a list he'd be going over tomorrow when he and Coop paid the visit to the contractor and the shopping trip planned for afterward.

A coed poker game was in full swing. Lucas was normally right in the middle of the action, but his somber attitude prevailed.

Donna Grant wasn't participating in the alcohol, the dancing or the cards. She took a seat next to him and toasted his beer with her mineral water.

"You got a girl at home, Lucas?" she asked. The lady was probably five years his senior, but he'd seen lots of relationships with older military women and the young SEALs. It gave them a problem sometimes with the other branches of service they had to work with closely.

"Complicated, but yes," he answered her. If she wore a little makeup, she'd be pretty. He noticed she had a barbed wire tat around her left wrist. Her hair was cut short, but was shiny brown. With her large brown eyes, she had a classic look and would be stunning if she wanted to be. That had him curious.

"What exactly does that mean?" she asked, without looking at him.

"Means my wife's divorcing me, and I recently found a girlfriend."

"Can't live with them and can't live without them, that right?" she answered.

Lucas rolled his shoulder and cracked his neck. The loud noise had her wincing and even caught the attention of a couple of the card players. "That sounded painful. You better get that checked out."

"I'm fine. You?"

"I like the travel, and I prefer working with men on the job."

Lucas pegged her for being perhaps sweet on women. He nodded, not bothered one way or the other.

She smiled to her shoes. "I like men all right, Lucas. I'm just more of the best friend kind of person. Don't much care for chasing after the steamy romance, if you know what I mean."

No, he didn't know what she meant.

"Sometimes, Donna, it just comes to you. Sometimes you don't have to chase after it at all."

"That happen to you?"

"Sometimes," he answered.

"So that's what happened to your marriage, then?"

"No. That's not what I meant. I'm not like that, although my wife—" He stopped himself until the alarms in his head stopped screaming. "All that was before I got married. My wife is the one who found and chose me."

Donna peeled her gaze from the poker table and looked at him honestly. "And here I would have thought you knew."

"Knew what?"

"The woman always chooses, my friend. That's why you guys have to wait. When you're single, that means no woman has chosen you yet."

He wasn't sure he liked the tone of her implication. She was complicated. Secretive. That was a dangerous combination.

"I still say you be patient. It will happen for you. You just wait and you'll see."

"Great advice, but I'm afraid it doesn't really apply to me."

"But you *are* looking?"

She rocked her head from side to side. "Everybody looks, Lucas. I apologize, but it's a long story. It's not that I'm into ladies, I just have issues with men."

"Except you like to work with them?"

"I know, sounds nuts, doesn't it?" She smiled and he did think she was pretty. "You trying to pick a fight?"

"No, ma'am. I don't fight with women."

She giggled and said something under her breath that sounded like a swear word. "Long story, my frog prince, and I don't know you well enough."

He decided to add a little levity into the conversation, since he was getting a bit uneasy with her secrets, not that he had any right to them of course, but he was used to being direct and forthright, answering and asking questions. He thought he'd just push a little to see if he could crack that tough exterior. "I don't have to worry about you taking a knife to my throat late some night, right? You're not one of those?"

She showed him her white teeth again in a grin. "Only if we're forced to sleep in the same bed and you snore, which I can already tell you do, so give it up, sailor, and leave me alone." She stood and walked away, still looking like an athlete slowly departing a basketball court or a track somewhere. He realized she was probably way stronger than he'd given her credit for.

And lethal.

EVERYONE TURNED IN before nine o'clock, with the exception of the group going with Kyle to the top of the hill.

"I'm good if you need me, Chief," said Lucas.

"Sure you're just trying to get out of cleaning up? But if you want to tag along, be my guest. You got your FLIRs?" he asked, meaning the SEAL-issued forward-looking infrared goggles.

"Roger that."

"Okay, you still up to the shopping trip tomorrow with Coop?"

"Fuckin' A, Chief."

Kyle and Danny led the team back through the woods. With their thermal gear, they saw eyes of forest animals such as fox, raccoon and deer light up and move quietly out of their path. The sky was cloudy, which was good for visibility. The moon was over half full and very bright.

Lucas was amazed how much easier it was to see the outline of the lone sentry with the equipment they brought. They would be back up as time permitted on other nights, just to verify the single guard was not an anomaly.

Kyle directed Danny and Armando to position themselves higher than the sentry to give the rest of the team cover in case they were discovered. The rest of the team took the best clear vantage point nearly twenty yards below the sentry so they could get a closer wide-angled look.

Scanning the campground, Lucas watched the end on the long metal building slowly move to the side, its large, metal, gear-type wheels squealing as the metal door rolled out of the way. Inside, he saw what looked like a warehouse with tables and storage shelves. But down the center of the building was a lush garden of plants, reminding Lucas of pictures he'd seen of the Panhandle in Golden Gate Park. He counted approximately twenty men, all carrying small automatic weapons similar to their short barrel H&Ks slung over their shoulders.

Lucas heard the whir and click of the scope camera as Kyle documented everything, including the sentry. Lucas adjusted his magnification, got out his vest pocket spiral and jotted down the license plates of every van or truck he could identify. Kyle gave him a thumbs-up, adjusted his scope, and took more photos.

Boxes were being loaded onto dollies and placed inside rear doors of two trucks they'd seen earlier that day. Just before the door shut, Lucas caught a glimpse of a sandaled pair of feet peering out of a long kaftan, or robe.

He tapped Alex on the shoulder, pointing straight ahead and saw the faint nod of acknowledgement in return. Alex laid a hand gently on

Kyle's shoulder, passing the information along. Lucas could see he'd already started taking pictures of the figure in the doorway.

He wasn't surprised when the gentleman didn't go fully outside, but remained in the doorway. Lucas could see he had a long beard, which the goggles showed in near-perfect detail. With the man's wire-rimmed glasses, the girth of his upper torso, his height, and the tribal cap he wore, Lucas knew he was looking at pure evil.

Fucking Sheik Hammid Rushti!

There was no doubt in his mind this was the gentleman whose picture they'd been shown yesterday. He was amazed at the quality of equipment they'd been issued and the detail it provided.

God bless the U.S. taxpayer and the United States Navy Spec Ops Command.

Surveying the rest of the area, he found someone sitting in a small sedan, under cover of a large willow tree. Once again he gave the signal to Alex, while Fredo watched from Lucas' left side. Kyle took photos of the car.

The howl of a dog of some kind startled Lucas and nearly had him lose his footing. Pitching forward, he braced himself, which knocked a small round rock loose. It slid down the hillside, picking up steam along the way, making too much noise on its journey. The sentry turned in their direction, angling his gun to waist height. Lucas, Alex, Fredo, and Kyle stayed perfectly still, holding their breath.

Lucas wondered where the animal noise had come from since the sound reverberated all over the small canyon. Without turning his head, he glanced to the left and saw two scrawny dogs playing in the dusty campground yard below. The man in the sedan got out, whistled to the dogs who jumped to him and whined as he chained them to a metal clothesline dog run. The movement distracted the sentry, who sat with his rifle across his thighs, studying the compound below.

Kyle and the rest of them stayed calm and within seconds their in-frared picked up the shape of Danny backing away from the guard not more than a few feet behind the man. Their only Native American SEAL, Danny made a habit of sneaking up on everyone on the team and playing pranks. Lucas was pretty darned glad he was part of the mission today. If need be, that guard wouldn't have heard a thing before Danny's blade did its job. It was reassuring to know someone so skilled was there to protect them all.

They waited until they could no longer see Danny's outline before Kyle ordered them to get ready to return to camp. His Chief whispered something to Danny, who got out his slingshot, picked up a pea-shaped pebble, aimed without use of the IR goggles at one of the dogs. The animal yelped and started to howl, backing up in circles and trying to get loose of the chain. In the safety of the noise the commotion caused, the team retreated and was halfway down the back side of the hill before it got quiet again.

Lucas realized he'd been holding his breath nearly the whole way down.

CHAPTER 22

T HE DAY ENDED mercifully and at last Marcy got her long bubble
bath She retired early, which was also something she needed. She
propped up pillows and took out her favorite romance book. She loved
the lavender hand and body crème she'd used; it would calmly put her
to sleep. Just before cracking open the book, she checked her phone.
Still no text or call from Lucas.

She fell into the love story, feeling sad she was missing Lucas. That
new scratchy feeling in the pit of her stomach, indicating a new love
and desire to grow and explore that love brought delicious anticipation.
It was something she'd only felt a few times in her life. This was not just
the lusty parts of their steamy and rather sudden crash into each other.
It felt like something long sleeping had been awakened. The passion
and intensity of this SEAL took her breath away. She knew a relationship with him would be a wild ride, and not all of it would be fun.

But, boy, would it be exciting.

She snuggled in bed, relaxed but unable to sleep. She could still feel
his callused hands move up and down her thighs, the way his stiff
fingers moved the hair around the back of her ears, or unclipped her
hair to let it fall. He didn't make love to her, he *consumed* her like a
man who'd been starving. His neediness was something that filled a
void. She also realized very few people would ever see that neediness, or
how strong his desire was to love and be loved fully. Every other man
she'd ever been with was a pale copy of the color and life and energy
Lucas brought her. It was something the SEAL training would never

drum into him. It was who he was and what he brought to the SEAL team. It wasn't anything a man could learn.

As her eyes closed, the screaming and yelling of this afternoon faded into a sensual dream. Connie's ugly face, the screaming baby and scared to death toddler weren't so scary as she felt Lucas's body behind her, warming her back, his hands around her waist, holding and protecting her, while his lips and tongue tasted the sensitive skin at the back of her neck.

It was what life was all about: the ugly and the beautiful. One woman's horror was another woman's lifeblood. She was sure she was the woman for him, just as she'd felt the first time she'd kissed him and her eyes opened for the very first time to what could be her new future.

THE MORNING LIGHT brought fresh appreciation for the warm glow she felt inside. She lay back in the soft pillows, hearing the diffused spray of a sprinkler outside her bedroom window. The day would be a tough one. But for right now, she was savoring one of the first mornings of her new life. Someday, she'd look back on it and remember how she felt, and perhaps she'd tell someone, perhaps a son or daughter, what it felt like to fall in love.

She held that thought, letting her heart beat faster, feeling the blood pumping all the way to her fingertips. She never wanted this feeling to end.

And then her phone rang. It was her broker, Joe Reed.

"Marcy, we need to talk. Can I buy you lunch or a cup of coffee when you can spare some time?"

"Sure, Joe. I was planning on coming in to the office in an hour or so. Have some paperwork to handle."

"Well, you know what? I'd like to talk to you some place private. There's a lot of stuff going on right now, and I just needed a private place to clear the air a bit. That okay with you?"

"Absolutely. The Coffee Bean near the office?"

"Maybe some place else. We'll run into agents on their way in. I just need to talk, Marcy."

Her stomach fell to the floor. His normal friendly tone was distinctly missing, though she could tell he was working hard to mask it. "Okay. Where and when?"

"That new place off the strand? They have ice cream, candy, and coffee? How about that one? Haven't been in there yet and my kids are dying to go there."

"Sounds good. In an hour?"

"Perfect."

Marcy decided to finish shattering the rest of her bucolic morning by asking a question she didn't want to ask. But it would prepare her for the meeting, and that was the best she could do right now. "Is there a problem?"

"Marcy, I like you, but yes, there's a big problem, I'm afraid."

MARCY FOUND A parking place for the truck in a lot behind one of the storefronts that was under remodel. She'd planned on dropping it off at Lucas' place and then taking a taxi back to pick up her own car. Rounding the corner, she walked down the half block to the little specialty shop. She didn't see Joe anywhere until she heard the tinkle of the front door bell and saw him standing right beside her.

Joe had been a good mentor, although they hadn't been close. He'd helped her get started in the business and ran a very tight office for a local celebrity chef, who owned Coronado Bay Realty. One of the things Joe did exceedingly well, and the reason he was such a good manager to work for, is that he had a no-drama policy at work, and so his stable of agents weren't going and coming like so many of the offices in San Diego. Everyone was happy, and Joe didn't hire people without something to bring to the company. Several retired Navy veterans with heavy combat experience, pilots, and sports figures worked at the office.

"Always be the calming voice in the negotiation," he'd taught her. Marcy knew some of the drama now occurring between her and Connie was not anything he'd be happy with. She hoped Gail had backed her up, somehow shifting some of the blame off her shoulders.

"You go get us a table. What can I get you?" he asked with a smile that looked difficult to produce.

"Latte. Medium."

Marcy found a corner and sat against the wall, leaving the comfortable plastic padded bench to Joe. He'd put on a little weight in his middle, but he was still an attractive man with a dusting of gray hair. The office had been very busy with the uptick in sales all summer long, and she thought perhaps he'd not made the time to go to the gym.

He came back bearing two identical coffee drinks, set one down in front of her and slid into the padded seat. After his first sip, he opened his eyes and peered right into hers, slight worry lines developing between his eyebrows that all of a sudden disappeared as he began to talk.

"Thanks for coming, Marcy. I've been talking with Gail Burnett."

"Yes, I met with her yesterday afternoon, and my client on Apricot came by the office. I transferred the paperwork to Gail."

"Okay. She told me as much." He let his fingers scratch at the brown cardboard heat sleeve on the side of the cup. "Your former client, Connie Shipley, has been very vocal, even after yesterday. She barged into the office this morning and broke up a meeting with the staff. I couldn't get her out fast enough."

"Where was Gail?"

"Not in yet. But Connie came in to see me. Insisted on it."

Marcy waited for him to gather his thoughts. She knew this was difficult for Joe. Whatever he was going to say next, she wasn't going to like.

"She's made some rather severe accusations." His sad eyes were apologetic. He slowly inhaled, his chest getting full and his shoulders rising. He leaned over the table and bent down, coaching his words, lowering the timbre to a whisper. "She said that you had sex with her husband, *while* you had the listing." His eyes did not smile. He tilted his head in the other direction, but didn't take his gaze from her. "We don't do that here at Coronado Bay, Marcy. And I know you know that."

She had wanted to return his gaze, but inside she felt ashamed. "I'm sorry, Joe. It was a mistake," she said to the tabletop.

He sighed with the confirmation she'd given him, shook his head, and looked up to the ceiling as if he'd find an answer there. "God, I was hoping you'd say she got it wrong." He looked out the window onto the traffic passing by on the Strand.

"I'm not going to lie, Joe. It was just plain and simple a mistake. I'm sorry."

"Damned *right* it was a mistake," he said, his temper beginning to flare. She'd never seen that in him before. "She's talking about suing the company."

Her steely resolve, the fantasyland that everything would turn out somehow crashed all around her like a porcelain doll. Her eyes got hot, and soon tears welled up and started running down her cheeks. Joe handed her a napkin which she used to dab her eyes with.

"What in the devil were you thinking?"

"I wasn't. That's the problem."

Joe sat back and watched her work to repair her composure. With his back erect, he examined the coffee shop, making note of the clerks behind the bar and the new customers who'd entered. His eyes also lighted on the empty seat on his left. "Well, here's the thing, your problem has now become my problem. My problem will be Guy's problem and I don't want to lose my job."

He didn't have to tell her anything more. She was going to try one more time to save the situation. "Is there something I can do to fix this?"

"Not really. I'm in damage control here. I have to tell Guy, and your little lady has a big mouth on her."

"She's mean and vindictive."

"She has some choice words for you too, Marcy. Words she's screamed all over the office. We had clients in the conference room, sitting at agent's desks who heard all this. It was the last thing I wanted to hear at the top of her lungs. We handle a lot of divorcing couples, as you know. That's all we need is to have some divorcing wife hear our agents sleep with their husbands. Get my drift?"

"Yes. I fully understand. I take full responsibility, Joe."

"And you of all people. From a nice family. I mean I have gold-diggers in this office. I try to weed them out before they get hired, but you know this can be a problem. I never expected this from you. You are usually so levelheaded. What the devil got into you?"

If she was crass, she would tell him exactly what had gotten into her, or whom. Now she understood why Lucas wanted her to lie, but that wasn't going to be the way. She knew that was wrong. Why didn't she stop herself from making the other mistake that would, in all likelihood, cost her her job?

"Joe, tell me what I can do, and I'll do it. Anything. You want me to talk to Guy?"

"God no!"

"What can I do to fix this situation for you? Forget about me. What can I do to make it up to you, to the company and its reputation?"

He bit his lower lip, then he smiled. "I'm going to have to ask you to leave."

Marcy expected it, but it still didn't take away the shock of hearing the words delivered to her. Her parents would be so disappointed in her. Every meeting she would go to from now on would be painful. She could feel the whispers behind her back, the gossip. All the embellishments to her character as salacious details were spread throughout the professional community. And it would be more vicious because of the company's long-standing reputation for being more professional and a cut above the rest of the offices in town.

"I understand. I wish there was some way I could get a second chance. Believe me when I say it will never happen again."

"Well, you're right about one thing. It *will* never happen again at my company." He stood, extending his hand to her. "I'm sorry, Marcy. Very, very sorry. You get your things taken care of, I want you releasing all your listings and we'll close the escrows you have, send you a check. But after today, I'm going to ask for your key and ask you to vacate your desk."

She shook his hand and tried to be firm about it. "Okay, I'll get right on it today. Do—does anyone know yet?"

"The secretaries, that's all."

That meant Gail and the rest of the gossip crew knew every detail, and what they didn't know, they were making up. She wanted to go home and just throw herself in her bed, but it wouldn't get any easier than this morning, before the office got busy, to remove all her things. Someone walking out with a Banker's Box full of stuff always indicated one thing: they were permanently leaving. And in her case, everyone would know she was fired.

Marcy watched Joe walk out into the sunlight, the glass door shutting behind him, ringing the tinkle bell. Her stomach was in knots. She picked up her half-sipped Latte and tossed it in the garbage.

Walking toward the burgundy Hummer, her cell phone rang.

It was Lucas.

CHAPTER 23

"**W**HAT'S WRONG?" LUCAS asked.

"I was asked to leave."

"Leave? From where?"

"Basically, the company fired me, Lucas."

Lucas knew this had something to do with Connie. Hell, it had something to do with him, too. Guilt was not an easy emotion to feel, and he found it stuck like black tar in the pit of his stomach. "What are you going to do?" He held off saying he was sorry, as that cow had already gotten out of the barn.

"You mean right now?"

He felt Marcy's defenses rising. Perhaps his making the phone call was a bad idea. But being in town, he had to try.

"What are you going to do about your job?"

"I don't have a job, Lucas. I'm not sure what I can do. First, I'm going to deliver your truck back to your apartment. Then go by and pick up my stuff at the office. Then look for a job, I guess.

"So this have to do with us?"

"Of course it does. Connie found out, you know."

"Yes, that was partly why I was calling. I just discovered that out too. Jake had dated one of her friends. I think that's how it got to Connie."

"God, Lucas, you guys sound like a bunch of gossipy women."

It frustrated him, too. So many uncertainties about relationships, and women were so darned complicated. He didn't have that with any of the guys he served with. But then, it was life and death and a little screwing around in between. They got serious about really serious things. Everything else was like quicksand, something to avoid at all costs, and usually meant someone other than himself would be crying. He'd be left with that uneasy feeling in the pit of his stomach that he'd been a disappointment, but was powerless to sort it out and make things right. He didn't like not being in control.

So now he'd gotten her fired. That was on him, not her. And that just wasn't fair. She'd been a casualty of his desires. Oh yes, the desires were real, but she paid a heavy price for it. And could he be trusted, really?

Now, so far away from her, maybe that was the safest for her. Not for him. God, he wanted to see her, but it was better for *her*.

Her frustration speared him through the long, tired sigh he heard over the phone. He'd wanted just to touch base, yet he couldn't tell her anything about what he was doing. Nothing like, "Oh, we're just having a normal day, checking out terrorists, searching for bad guys at midnight, fraternizing with the Navy Women's Soccer team. We're buying big screen TVs and checking out contractors and little hottie Nashville chicks who want to hang out with these assholes we're watching. We're locked and loaded and nearly cut a guy's head off last night, but other than that, we're fine."

He really didn't know what to say. And he knew he should say something, and quick, too.

"That's too bad, Marcy." He winced, doubling over, socking his thighs with his fists. Coop looked up from his computer and grimaced at him. The tall SEAL held his palms out to the sides as if telling him, *'What the fuck are you doing?'*

"Too bad? Did I hear you right, Lucas?" He deserved every bit of her frostiness.

"I mean, what do you want me to do?" He tried to be soft. He was listening for every little detail over the phone, any sigh, anything at all telling him she was okay with it. But he had a really bad feeling about their chemistry right now.

The silence sliced down on the back of his neck. *Shit. Here it comes.*

"You know, I might be some minor inconvenience to you, Lucas, and I do appreciate the call, but right now, I've got to sort out the rest of my life, since I don't have a job and I won't be able to afford to live in my place for more than a couple of months and no one in San Diego will hire me anyway."

"You're being a little dramatic, aren't you?" He bit his tongue at what an asshole he was being, but if there was nothing he could do, why pretend? She needed to calm down and solutions would come to her. In any high-stress situation, making a decision while upset could get you killed in the battlefield. And this was beginning to feel like a war. The love wars, like the boys had been telling him. But he also knew he was sounding like a royal jerk to suggest it. He didn't know what to say to her. He cared about her so much and wanted to spend the rest of his life with her, but he freakin' didn't know what to say right now.

He could feel what her face probably looked like. He knew she'd be bright red now. Her chest would be blotchy and she'd be shaking like a leaf.

The last line she delivered, he knew he fully deserved.

"You know, Lucas? I didn't understand how Connie felt until today. Now I do. You are every bit the asshole she said you were—"

"Marcy, wait—"

"Wait? Wait for you to come back here to California so you can charm the pants off me again? You know, Connie warned me about you. I didn't believe her. Now I'm thinking—no, I'm *knowing* she's right."

"Marcy, calm down. You don't have to get upset—"

Coop was looking at him like he had black warts all over his face.

"No, of course not. Who needs a fuckin' job, Lucas?" She sucked in air. "I could go stand on a street corner here and pick up SEALs who want to screw, maybe make a few bucks to tide me over—"

"No, Marcy. That's just nuts."

"You know what's nuts? Believing your horseshit. You remind me of the guy my sister dated. He'd put a big fuckin' engagement ring on someone's finger so he could get all the sex he wanted. When he broke it off, she gave the ring back. It was the best deal in the world for him."

"I didn't get you a ring. I have no ring."

"Which means it was an even worse idea to agree to marry you."

"Marcy—"

"Please, Lucas. I don't want to hear another word. Let me cling to that tiny ounce of self-respect I have left. I thought you really cared."

"I did."

He realized he put closure to their entire relationship with that one. Coop covered his face with his hand and was shaking his head.

"Oh yeah? Well listen here, sailor. I never did."

The line went dead.

"Fuck," he said and almost tossed the phone.

"You are a seriously stupid asshole, Lucas. I don't think I've ever heard anyone at your level. Ever. So all the stories are true. You and that stripper?"

"Dancer."

"The trani dancer?"

He was going to argue the point, but looking at Coop, he knew he should just shut up and get drunk.

LUCAS WAS STILL festering, consumed in his head as they drove over to the building contractor's office.

"Would you stop with the fuckin' sighing, Lucas? You're acting like a teenager." Cooper downshifted the van and pulled around the corner, sending Lucas into the passenger door. "Get your fuckin' seatbelt on, man."

Lucas complied.

"And get your mind off that phone call. We have to concentrate here."

"I know," he said softly. He told himself he wouldn't have taken it so personally if he'd been overseas. Over there, you knew you had to concentrate. Here, on home soil, it was something he was having a hard time getting used to. Terrorists here. Possibility of danger. Here. In

Tennessee, of all fuckin' places. It just didn't fit.

Coop drove them to the office of the contractor who built the barn at the complex.

Inside the front door, a large fuzzy-haired dog slept by the metal reception desk. He rose up, blinking his dark eyes underneath soft bangs, regarded them casually and then laid his head back down over his outstretched paws.

They were greeted by a young, ponytailed blonde girl who appeared to be high school age.

"Can I help you?" She wore tight blue jeans, ones she looked poured into, and a pink flannel shirt in a plaid design, and pink cowboy boots. Her drawl was soft and sexy and Lucas again cursed his lack of judgment.

Coop cleared his throat and took out a piece of yellow-lined paper with a building design drawn on it. "We're looking to get some quotes on a building for my friend's ranch. He drew this from a magazine."

She took the paper, regarding Lucas briefly, and then studied the drawing.

"Let me get my dad. Just a minute." With the drawing in hand, she exited through the glass door to the shop area in the rear. Lucas couldn't help but follow her perfectly formed ass through the doorway. He told himself it reminded him of Marcy, but he cursed himself for the lie.

A country station was playing in the background. Pictures of stalls, hay barns, and paddocks adorned the walls. The owner apparently supported several kids' baseball and soccer teams. Framed letters from satisfied customers also cluttered the walls in small black frames. Although clean, the office was sparse. Two imitation leather chairs in an olive green color sat in the corner, bordering a corner table with a large amber lamp that looked like it had come from someone's living room thirty years ago. A space heater in the opposite corner next to the dog kicked in, but the dog didn't move.

"Where did you get the picture?" Lucas asked.

"Traced it from one of those farming magazines."

"Looks like the one—"

"Shhh. Sort of. That was the idea."

Lucas took three steps to the side and bent down to pet the dog, who promptly rolled over and exposed his full underside, including an empty ball sac.

"Sorry there, boy," Lucas said to him. "You're a friendly thing aren't you?"

A red-faced gentleman with a belly bump walked through from the back with the paper in his hand. He extended his hand. "Hunter Boles. I'm the owner."

His thick accent was difficult for Lucas to understand. Coop returned the shake. "Calvin Cooper here, and this here is Lucas."

Boles pursed his lips, a frown developing on his forehead. "Hey, Jake, get over here," he ordered the dog. The animal scrambled to obey. His legs were long and thin, with a slim waist and large chest. Lucas thought he might be part Greyhound. "Some guard dog, right?"

Cooper gave him a half smile. "I got a dog, Bay. About the same size, and he's real friendly when I'm around. Not so much when I'm not. I'm sure your dog is the same way."

Lucas saw Jake hang his head as the door was opened and he walked slowly to the back. "Yeah, well, he's supposed to earn his keep. My wife doesn't like him at home because he sheds on everything, so this here's his home and he's workin."

Boles put the paper on the desk, smoothing it over.

"This is just a rough drawing of what he saw."

"This your friend here?" Boles said, pointing to Lucas.

"No. My friend lives west of here."

"Um hum." Boles studied the drawing again, tilting his head to the side and scratching the back of his neck, then stood to address Coop. "So what's he doing with the building, then?" Boles squinted up to Coop's considerable six-foot-four frame.

"Hell if I know. Gentleman farmer. Grows pot? He hasn't told me. And I don't ask."

"Gotcha. Yeah, we got a few of those around here."

"He's got money."

"I would expect he'd pay cash." Boles said as he narrowed his eyes.

"Sure. He's just looking for a good deal."

"So how did you get my name?"

Coop shrugged. "No clue."

The owner pulled his pants up onto his waist, which was wider than his hips. "So don't 'spose you know what size he wants, either."

"Big."

Boles grinned and Lucas could see a wad of tobacco stuck to his upper teeth, staining them a dark brown and making him look like he was missing them.

"No windows, I guess."

"That's what he drew. I thought he just forgot to put them in here. I mean, why would anyone want a building like that without windows?"

"Well, it kinda depends on what you're doin' inside, Mr. Cooper. If you don't want anyone to know, whole lot safer not to have windows."

"You build anything like this he can take a look at?"

"Sure. Baptist Free Will Church over near Paris, but that one has windows. This here is really a warehouse. No animals?"

"Again, Mr. Boles, I have no idea."

"Well, I need to know that. Ventilation? Air conditioning? He want it on a slab?

"I'm guessing so, yes."

"Well, keeps the varmints out, too. Until it rusts." He held the paper up. "Can I make a copy of this?"

"Help yourself," Coop said.

Boles handed him back the drawing. "I'm a little uncomfortable talking price without the owner, you know, the guy who's paying for it, being present. Don't like to talk to representatives, no offense."

"No offense taken, sir."

"You shopping this around?" he asked Coop.

"You're the first person we came to."

"Why don't you let me have a first crack at it? I'll see if I can find you an overrun or slightly damaged building, if that's not important to him?"

"Sounds good to me. If I don't have to drive halfway across the state, I'm happy with that."

"You fellas aren't from around here, are you? You sound like a Midwestern boy."

"That's right. Nebraska."

"I knew it."

"And I'm from California," added Lucas. Boles completely ignored him.

"Well, Mr. Cooper, I'm going to need the size, though, so you'll have to get him to give me a call with that. I'll have to see the site, study the road access for the trucks carrying the steel."

"Of course."

"How soon does he want this?"

"He said as soon as possible."

Boles studied both of them slowly, focusing on their shoulders, forearms, taking special note of their tats. Cooper had turned his forearm toward his side, as did Lucas, to hide the identical frog print tats that nearly everyone on Kyle's team had from inside their elbow to their wrists. Lucas made a note to himself to wear something long sleeved the next time.

"You boys military?" Boles had taken on a somber tone, trying to sound more casual than he was thinking.

"Ex," said Coop.

That seemed to satisfy Boles. He handed Coop a couple of business cards. "That's got my cell phone on it. Use that number. I pick it up all the time, day or night, but never when I'm on top of a building doing an erection, okay?"

"Thanks, sir. I'll have my friend call you."

They both turned to go, Lucas opening the outside door first. From behind them, he heard Boles shout out, "What's your friend's name?"

Coop slowly turned. "Kyle. Kyle Lansdowne."

Boles shook his head. "Never heard of him."

CHAPTER 24

MARCY DROVE LUCAS' Hummer to the complex the bachelors lived in. Of course, she felt completely different now than when she and Nick had returned Lucas' items. She had been in some fog then, clinging to some oversexed belief this was true love and Lucas was The One.

Thank God for reality, she thought. Though painful, she made a mental note that a fresh start was what she needed. And maybe San Diego would remind her too much of the failed experiment that was her SEAL, Lucas. It would be a good thing if she never had to talk to another SEAL for the rest of her life. Except Nick, of course. But then, he wouldn't really count, since he was out and Devon was her friend.

Thinking about Devon's career in Sonoma County gave Marcy an idea as she turned off the truck. She fiddled with the keys and saw what looked like a front door key on the fob. Perhaps that was to the apartment. She decided to try it, and perhaps call the Taxi from inside Lucas' place.

She examined the area, including the parking lot that was near drained of cars. *That's right. Everyone's at work.*

She told herself it would get easier. Shrinking from the reality of her firing wouldn't help. She'd face it head-on. Get used to the idea that, unlike the rest of the world, she was on a precarious footing, but she would definitely find a way out. And whatever was out there, was going to be a good thing. *Not* a bad thing. When had she not landed on her feet?

Marcy knocked on the front door, and when no one answered, used her key. "Hello? Anyone home?" she said out of practice. The place smelled just like before. It was still a man cave. If she still harbored any warm loving feelings for Lucas, she'd stay and clean the place up, but she figured they wouldn't notice any tidying up, and it would send the wrong message. The men had nothing living in the place that needed tending, like plants or fish tanks. Everything could be left to rot or dry up as she was sure they were used to doing.

She examined the sagging ugly brown couch, and got the impression perhaps this was Lucas' bed. *Serves him right.* The SEAL was freeloading on his buds too.

She walked toward the dirty sliding glass door entrance to the balcony overlooking the parking lot. The barbeque was still covered in plastic, but the wheels and undercarriage were getting rusty from the salty air. The view was nice, seeing the bay and a large cruise ship pulling out, getting ready for a grand voyage.

Maybe I should sail away. Take a vacation.

She thought of Nick and Devon's place, the winery, the beautiful scenery she'd seen on her way up to the house in Cloverdale. She did have a California Real Estate license, so relocating up there might work. Might. Maybe Devon could grease the way a bit. Hanging around Nick would be safe too, since he wasn't really close to Lucas and probably wouldn't have much to do with him. And somehow, she trusted him.

Marcy discovered there was no apartment phone, but she did find a phone book and called a taxi with her cell, instructing him to meet her next to the Hummer. She peeked one more time at the four bedrooms, and again at the disgusting hallway bathroom with the raunchy posters and, as if she was saying goodbye one final time to Lucas, did a complete 360, not finding anything she wanted to memorialize. She was done. Time to go. Next fish to fry was moving all her stuff out of the office. She dropped the keys under the sand-filled ashtray pot standing guard by the front door.

Halfway down the hallway, she ran straight into Connie Shipley, who was carrying a Banker's Box. She had the baby in a front backpack and the little girl was tugging at her impossibly tight jeans.

"You just keep turning up like a bad penny, Marcy," the SEAL's wife said.

"Just dropping something off." It was a partial truth, though she really had no reason to be inside the apartment.

"Well then, you can open the door so I can give Lucas this shit."

"He's not here."

"Do I care? Did I ask that?" Connie balanced the box on the metal railing. The toddler was yanking on her leg, begging for something.

"Well, I'm just leaving." Marcy tried to walk past Connie, but her former client stepped into her path.

"Hey. You got a key? Then I don't have to leave these outside the door."

Marcy cursed inside at the thought Connie would leave a man's stuff outside for anyone to steal. She knew Lucas wouldn't be back right away, and she guessed Connie did as well. "Yes. I have a key. You don't?"

"Of course not. So you can let me in, and then leave it with me."

Marcy wasn't sure what to do with that one. She whirled around, walked past Connie, stooped down and found the key and unlocked the door. She stood next to the frame while Connie and her box and two children entered. The way the woman wandered around, Marcy ascertained she'd never been inside the place before.

"Where's his bedroom, Marcy?" Connie asked, pursing her lips and raising her eyebrows. She was still holding the box, while the little girl began running from room to room. "Lindsay, stop it," Connie yelled.

"I have no idea. I was never here when Lucas was."

"So how come you have a key?"

"Because I drove Lucas' truck home from Sonoma County with Nick, his friend."

"Oh, so now we're working on another SEAL? Is that right? He *is* another SEAL?"

Marcy wanted to get herself as far away from this woman as she could. She was having unclean thoughts about saying or doing something unladylike. "Connie, Lucas was called away so fast, he had to fly back. That left the truck behind, and I was conveniently available to drive it back."

"With your new boyfriend."

"I don't *have* a boyfriend. And what difference does it make to you, anyway? Let's just get this over with, and then we don't have to speak to each other again, okay?"

"Fine." She dropped the box beside the entrance to one of the bedrooms. Marcy could hear something clatter inside, perhaps break. "Lindsay, we're going."

The little one grabbed onto her mother's hand and continued looking back at Marcy with wide eyes, her little feet running to keep up with her mother.

Marcy locked the door, tucking the keys back into her pocket this time, and followed behind them. At the parking lot, she stood by Lucas' Hummer to wait for the taxi she'd called. She would ask Nick for the name of someone in the area she could safely leave Lucas' keys with.

Connie hadn't forgotten her earlier request. Holding out her hand, she gave a triumphant smile. "The keys."

"I'm sorry, those weren't Lucas' instructions."

"You have no right to my husband's truck keys or the keys to his apartment!"

Marcy's fury didn't interfere with her judgment and she bit her tongue, swallowed, and reeled in everything she had to stay calm. "I'm afraid you'll have to take it up with him. I'm merely following orders. But in case it matters, I'm not coming over here or taking his truck anywhere."

The unkind scowl Connie gave her did nothing to her already churning insides. Marcy was confused, hurt, angry, and tired of everything, ready to put it all behind her as quickly as possible.

"You know, Marcy, my divorce attorney has suggested I sue your broker."

"Really? That surprises me," Marcy lied. She thought perhaps the woman wanted to gloat about something. "I'd love to stand here and chitchat," she said as the yellow taxi pulled up and she waved to the driver, "but I have to go over to the office to pick up my things. As you may or may not know, they fired me because of the stink you caused. So I get to move on with my life. I guess I should thank you. But I do have work to do."

She didn't look back at Connie as the taxi did a U-turn and came back the way it had entered the parking lot.

IN FIFTEEN MINUTES, Marcy was at her own apartment, located within walking distance to the Coronado Bay Realty office. Once inside the door, her defenses dropped and she ran to her favorite overstuffed reading chair. Her tears had begun before she hit the cushions. The familiar hollow angst in her chest, the hole through her heart, was something that began to spread all over her body, causing her to shake. The tears desperately tried to wash away the hurt and memory of something lost, perhaps something that never was. Her neck ached.

She leaned her head on the padded back of the chair, staring up at the watery ceiling. Big gulps of air helped, and she began to calm with each deep breath she drew in. At last, the warm familiar aura of the place she'd enjoyed living in finished the soothing job of bringing her back to herself—the self that she'd relied on, the person who had been successful, enjoyed life, and made good decisions. Not the reckless self so easily influenced by that wrecking ball of a man. He was like an Alaskan ice breaker ship, crashing through all her defenses, making a waterway for himself where there wasn't one before.

She'd been so dumb. She'd been no match for his intensity. And yet, being perfectly honest, that intensity was what she had been attracted to in the first place. She was like a moth to the flame, and, unlike her usual self, powerless to stop it.

Marcy decided to call Devon in the privacy of her own space. She made herself a glass of ice water, brought it back to the chair, and dialed.

"Hola, Marcy. How are things?"

"Nick get back okay?"

"Fine. He had a good time driving down with you."

Marcy's stomach lurched. She'd not had breakfast, just the coffee. "He's a really nice guy. You're a lucky woman."

"Hey, hands off."

It was a light-hearted comment, but it cut to the bone. She covered the phone in case Devon would be able to hear the heavy breathing that came along with more tears. She tried to speak, but the words were more like a whisper.

"Marcy? Are you okay? What's wrong?"

"They fired me." There. She'd said it.

"Oh my God. When did this happen?"

"Just today, just now really. It's a mess, Devon."

"Yeah. I can imagine. Your broker is taking a hard line. You gave up the listing, of course?"

"Absolutely. But Connie—that's the wife—she's a real pistol. Lots of drama with that lady, and, well, she caused a scene in our office, with all the high-end clientele, celebrities, and such. My manager worries about—"

Oh hell, who am I kidding? I made a mistake!

"It's all my fault. Never should have happened." She tried to laugh, but it didn't come out right. "Devon, I was such an idiot."

"Love is blind."

"And stupid. There isn't anything there. I gave up my career—a good career too—for a couple of days of self-indulgence. That's the long and short of it. I'm ashamed."

"Oh stop it. I think you guys are great together."

"Except that's not happening either."

"What?"

"Lucas called right after I met with my manager. I know I was upset, but he sounded like such an asshole. I ended it, Devon."

"Oh no! I'm sorry to hear that."

"Well, Dev, this has been a couple of just terrible days. I'm working to get my head on straight. And I was wondering—"

"*Of course.* You get your butt up here. You can stay as long as you like."

"Under the circumstances, I've had to turn over all my listings to the office, so there isn't any reason for me to stay down here. I really appreciate it if I could bunk up there until I sort out what I'm going to do. But I'm not one to impose."

"Nonsense. You can help me with the crush and all the holiday party planning, Marcy. Get your mind off everything. Just get the soonest flight out you can."

"I think I'm going to drive, bring a few of my things, if that's okay. *Not* moving in, of course, but I will need a car. I plan to look for work up there. Maybe, you know, a winery hiring?"

"You can use ours—the old beater or the Kubota, of course!"

They both laughed.

"I'll get your room ready and you just let me know when you leave. We'd love to have you."

"Thanks, Devon. Really appreciate this."

"You'd do the same for me."

"I would."

Marcy was about to sign off, when Devon added, "Hey, and sorry about the comment about hands off on Nick. I didn't realize—"

"I'm so over that, Devon. How would you have known? Eventually, I'd like to find someone just like Nick. When I'm ready. Right now, I just gotta land on my feet, figure out what I want to do."

"I got it. And where, right? You need to figure out where you're going to live? You're not giving up real estate, are you?"

"Well, perhaps we could talk about that too, but let's just wait and see where this takes me. I do appreciate all your help."

"I'm going to talk to my broker, or do you not want me to do that?"

"Hold off for now. I'll see you in a couple of days."

"No problem. But get up here so I can keep an eye on you, okay? I'm going to worry myself sick until I see your smiling face."

Marcy was so filled with gratitude, she nearly started crying again. It wouldn't totally fill the hole in her heart, but it lessened the size and gave her the doorway to another future, so she could turn her back on the poor decisions of her recent past. In time, she knew she'd scratch her head and wonder what had come over her. It would look like just a little blip on her timeline. She'd be able to notice it without feeling like she'd lost something.

After all, she *was* gaining a future, somehow. It just wouldn't be with Lucas.

CHAPTER 25

L UCAS DIDN'T LIKE the contractor. "You trust this guy?"

"Well, we're not going to fuckin' build a building on the Navy site. Not sure how much trust we need."

Coop's steps were longer than Lucas' He began to speed up to stay slightly ahead of the tall medic.

"But with the proper encouragement, I think we can get his cooperation."

Lucas stopped in his tracks. Looking up to Coop, he asked the question: "How we going to do that?"

"Up to Kyle. He has ways, believe me, and he knows more about this whole thing than he lets on."

Lucas nodded. He knew Coop was out of sorts about something. He could ask the giant about it, but decided he'd wait for Coop to seek him out. He didn't have to wait long.

"Look, Lucas. I'm going to say this once to you, and then I'm going to shut up about it because I really shouldn't be having this talk with you."

Oh fuck, here it comes.

"Ladies. This is about ladies."

"I don't need it, man." Lucas wondered why everyone felt they had the right to tell him where he'd fucked up. "I'm not a perfect man, Coop. I make mistakes just like the other guy. I don't need to hear all about it, is all." His shoulder ached and he rotated it while cracking his neck.

"Holy shit, Lucas. You gotta get that looked at."

"Shut up and go ahead, tell me what I can't stop you from saying. Just for the record, and for the second time, I. Don't. Need. It."

"Oh, you're gonna need it, or you won't make it on the team. I've seen guys…" He was quiet as a couple of young girls passed by them, giving them a long hungry stare. Coop turned around to make sure they were out of earshot, and Lucas heard their giggles. "Girls are funny," the tall SEAL whispered.

"I don't get that same reaction, Coop."

"You know what it is? They know I'm nice to them. I've never mistreated a lady. Worst thing I ever did was turn them down, and that's hard. But sometimes, it's the most compassionate thing to do."

Lucas tried to let Coop think he was considering his words, but he didn't believe a word of it.

"A man wants to do things, you know, sweet talk himself into a little nice situation. A little pleasure party, you know. It makes us feel good. Makes us feel like a man when the ladies fall for us. Flirting is one thing, being a gentleman is another thing. *Not* being a gentleman or not realizing the consequences of your actions is very dangerous."

Lucas was hoping Coop would shut up soon or he was going to lose it.

"THEN YOU'LL BE like your friends at the bachelor pad. Hating women. Leaving them crying all over the place. Kids in every port, you know what I'm sayin'?"

"Coop, that's not me. I used a condom."

"Fuck's sake, Lucas. I think you're the dumbest frog I've ever met. You seriously think that ends your responsibility? How the hell'd they let you on the teams with that attitude?"

"No one asked me about condoms, man."

"I can't believe what I'm hearing," Coop said. "Unbelievable."

Lucas was starting to get pissed off. "Coop, could we just stop talking about all this shit and go buy the fuckin' TV and maybe some groceries, including some beer—a lot of beer—and then you can leave me to have my own pity party?"

"Sure. I expect you'll be rooming with those guys for the next ten years. Better start looking for a five bedroom place, or you'll start sleeping with each other."

"Asshole."

"I've been called that before. I expect you'll be called that a whole lot now. Good luck with that, by the way." Coop stopped in his tracks. "One more thing—"

"You said that already. This makes the second thing."

Coop ignored his words and punched him in the chest with his forefinger. "You stay the hell away from my wife, Libby, or any of her friends. And if she's real nice to you and tries to fix you up with one of her lady friends, you just say no. You stay away from all of them, you hear?"

"Sure, Coop." He had to look up to the tall Nebraska former farm boy, but he wasn't intimidated. "I can do that. Your lady and her friends are probably way out of my league, anyway."

"You just have to learn the facts of life, Lucas. Don't listen to Jake and Ryan and those losers."

"They're not losers. And Connie and I had a great time in the beginning."

Coop started laughing. "I'll bet you did. Not doubting that."

Lucas still didn't like the advice giving, but Coop was senior to him on the team and he knew it was smart to show him the respect he was owed, even if he didn't agree or like the advice.

"You'll figure it out, kid."

He didn't take offense at Coop's comments, even though they weren't even ten years apart. But Coop had paid his dues, and Lucas had one third the deployments the tall medic had.

That counted for a lot. He figured he could put up with some of Coop's shit and then go his own way. No need to start another confrontation, or a fire.

THEY BROUGHT THE large screen TV into the temporary team building to much celebration. With quiet concentration, the Blu-ray and cable was connected, and soon the 55" screen was streaming action-adventure films. Another poker game was started, but Lucas grabbed a couple of beers and retreated to his bedroom. He thought about his conversation with Marcy, especially her words that Connie had been right. Were they both right? Perhaps he had no business being with a woman.

When he'd moved in with Jake and Alex and the rest of the boys, he thought it would be a temporary gig, that Connie would tire of her single life, she'd start to miss him, and voila, they'd be back together again.

He'd been wrong on that one.

Then he found himself attracted to Marcy. That was not only wrong from her standpoint, it made things worse with Connie. And it ruined Marcy's employment situation. He never intended for this to happen. He didn't wish any ill to come to either of them. Was he really that dangerous?

He finished his first beer, set the bottle down on the concrete floor, where it tipped over. Jake was at his doorway in an instant.

"You're being rather unsociable, my friend."

"Bad news. That stuff with Connie is a real mess. Wish Connie hadn't been told."

"Hey, I wish a lot of things. I wish my ex hadn't gotten the hots for the pharmacist. I wish I hadn't been on such a long deployment. I wish I hadn't dated the sisters—"

"That one," Lucas said as he pointed to Jake while still holding the bottle, "that's the one that fucked us both up, and got Marcy fired."

"Fired?"

"Yes. Fired."

"Wow, that sucks."

"Jake, the company she worked for is real high-brow and everything. Not everyone understands these things. I mean, we do, but it didn't go over very well with her boss."

"Geez. I'd never make it there," said Jake.

"No kidding."

"Half the population screws around, and here it was just one night of sin and all."

"It was a couple. But that's not the point, Jake. She was working for both Connie and I, and how do you suppose Connie took it?"

"Yeah. I knew that." Jake sat down with his beer. "So what's your plan?"

"What do you mean?"

"Well, what did you tell her?"

"Oh that." Lucas sat up, rubbed the back of his neck and took another long sip of the second beer, finishing it as well. "We're done."

"Done?"

"Yup. I screwed this one up royally. Really great lady. I wasn't thinkin'. She's better off without me." Lucas looked at the bottle and set this one down carefully beside the first one.

"If it makes you feel any better, I've been told that a time or two."

Lucas nodded his head and he imagined Jake had been told that many times over. "We aren't the type who are good for women, Jake. I didn't believe it at first, but you know, in the brief time since I've been bunking with you guys, you've got me convinced."

"Well, glad we could help on that score at least," Jake said as he stood up. "Come on, it's going to be time for dinner soon, and then maybe we can wreck some hearts on the Navy soccer team. You game for that?"

"Not sure about the girls, but the food? Yeah. I could take some right about now. And then I'm going to have a few more beers and see where it leads me."

"That's a good plan, Lucas."

Lucas watched him leave the room while he stayed behind, sitting on the bed, with the light of the day waning, waiting for dinner, considering having one more beer before.

It was a shame Marcy had to pay the price for his stupid mistake. But hell, at the time, it sure didn't feel like a mistake at all. It felt like one of the best couple of days of his life. Everything was possible. He was finally into a woman who was just as into him. How in the world could that be a bad thing?

CHAPTER 26

MARCY WAS GOING to attend to her office things, but after the call with Devon, she started making a plan, writing a list of things she would pack and take up to Sonoma County. To heck with the prying eyes of the office. Besides, if she went in there right now, she would be the talk of the place. Marcy decided to wait until late in the day when she knew the office would be completely deserted.

She picked through her clothes, thinking there could be a few boxes she would give away. She straightened up her apartment, changed her sheets and towels. Something about this little ritual made her feel more like a whole woman. She lit two new candles and played a streaming Spa Radio channel. She made herself a light lunch, brewed some fresh, strong coffee, sat at her tiny dining table overlooking the flowering crepe myrtle tree that went up three stories, its showy deep rose pink flowers blooming happily just for her. It had been a nice place to stay, but she realized she would move on without regret. Some place equally as nice in Sonoma County awaited her. And in the meantime, Devon and Nick's home was a safe place to land for a few days.

She called her hairdresser and found out she'd had a cancellation, so Marcy took the time to have some highlights and a trim. Next were her nails and a pedicure at her favorite Asian spa with the waterfall. She even managed to return Lucas' keys to the friend who had taken the heavy duffel. She no longer trusted leaving them at Lucas' apartment, where Connie had watched her retrieve them.

Strengthened by doing all the things she liked, she decided to go face the office, just as the sun was hanging low and threatening to melt into the ocean. Tomorrow morning she'd get up early and go to the gym in the complex, finish her packing, and then perhaps leave for up North early the next day.

All the good self care she'd done buoyed her mood, so that when she pulled into the parking lot at the Coronado Bay Realty company's lot, squeezing her Nissan between large Mercedes, Teslas and Bentleys, the three cars of choice for the Realtors in her office, she felt strong and ready to take on anyone or anything.

Until she rounded the corner to her semi-private office. Someone had already started moving her things and had brought in several boxes of their own. Marcy's plaques and awards, even the oil painting a client had done for her as a thank you, some of the celebrity photos she'd had signed, were all stuffed roughly into a couple of cardboard boxes without being careful about the quality of the packing job. It was an obvious slight. The painting had a small hole in the bottom right corner of the canvas where a sharp cornered black-framed award had poked its way into it.

Son of a bitch. She worked on keeping her emotions in check, the painful memory of Lucas' advice to do so washing a prickling wave over her skin surface, making her hot, frustrated and needing to take it out on something. She kicked the brown box belonging to a stranger, heard something inside tinkle like it had broken and frowned.

"Hey, Marcy. That's my stuff," Gail said to her back.

Of course it would be Gail.

Whipping around, Marcy stared back at the woman who was dressed in skinny jeans and an expensive designer t-shirt, showing her ample surgically enhanced cleavage, dressed for a designer work day. "Who gave you authorization to take my stuff down? You put a hole in my painting."

Gail sneered, reared her head backwards like Marcy's comment had an odor. "Geez, Marcy. That thing? I'm sorry. I thought a little kid did it. I was careful with your awards." She crossed her chest, arms revealing long white fingernails. "As for who gave me authorization? Joe did.

He said he'd *fired* you." Her eyelids lowered and Gail didn't seem to have any trouble using that "F" word. She examined Marcy's face through the bottom half of her eyes, head thrown back again. "Sorry about how all this has happened."

"I'll bet," Marcy mumbled. Her composure had flown right out of the room. "I need a little privacy to go through my things, if you don't mind." She took two steps toward Gail, pulled the door away from the wall and swung it in front of the agent's body. Gail had to step back to avoid getting it slammed in her face. Marcy made sure she gave it an extra push for the satisfying sound effect as it rattled the other doors and windows in the building.

She pushed Gail's boxes to the corner and out of the way first. Then she loaded up the items on her desktop so she could use it as a staging area for other things she needed to quickly go through. Gail stood outside the glass window overlooking the bullpen of other agent's desks, talking on her cell phone, while giving a disapproving look back to Marcy. The agent's lack of consideration for anyone else's feelings actually helped with the process. Marcy was looking forward not to have to deal with Gail and the other whispering hens who could say whatever they wanted, once Marcy was safely away, living a great life in Sonoma County.

Surprised it only took barely a half hour to complete the sorting, Marcy brought a large box of papers and folders to the shred bin in the reception area, unlocked the box, and dumped her things inside. The rest of her things fit into three remaining boxes. She'd been short one, so removed the contents of Gail's things from one box and placed them on the near-empty desktop.

A picture of Gail and Connie caught her eye. It was taken in Hawaii, in happier times. The two ladies were tanned, drinking umbrella drinks at sunset. Behind them were two tanned men: Lucas Shipley and Barry Burnett. The visceral reaction she had seeing Lucas' face was a surprise to her. His wide smile and white teeth contrasted the twinkle in his eye. She could see all the way through to his bad boy soul. It made her heart beat faster.

Damn.

Carefully, Marcy grabbed the framed picture and turned it over on the desk top. She loaded up her items and took each box out to her car. Before she removed the last box, she righted the foursome picture, turning it to face the side wall, surrounding it with other things from Gail's collection, turned around and left without searching back.

"All yours," she said with a quick smile. Gail stood in the lobby area alone, without expression.

"Good luck to you, Marcy. Where are you going to work?"

"Not sure yet."

"Well, I can call your cell, then?"

"Excuse me?" Marcy set the heavy box down on a reception chair.

"If I have questions about your other listings."

So Joe had given them all to Gail, which felt like a stab in the back. Suddenly her trusted feeling towards her broker was gone.

Better. You are so outta here, Marcy. Who cares what any of them do now. Not. Your. Concern.

"I'm probably not going to be available, Gail. It's up to you."

"Oh."

Marcy was planning on calling all her former clients, to say a proper good bye. Perhaps lay the seed they could still use someone else from the office if they were unhappy with her replacement. Something like that. Do it classy and quick. Let them know it wasn't her choice.

"Where are you going, then?"

"Gail, I have no idea." One of the receptionists was leaning to the side to watch her communication with Gail. Marcy walked up to her and presented her office key. "Give this to Joe, okay?"

"Sure will."

Marcy walked out the lobby doors, past the scored faux columns and broken pottery vases bursting forth with color, down the crushed granite walkway to the parking lot beyond and set the box down in the trunk. Marcy and her Murano drove off. She had no impulse to want to see what the office looked like. There was nothing there any longer she wanted to remember.

THE TRIP UP to Sonoma County the next day began after Marcy did one last hard workout in her complex gym. The morning commute was thinning. She texted Devon before leaving and then promised she'd let her know when she was near San Francisco. She double-checked messages and confirmed Lucas had not called, which was as she expected.

Near dusk, she was close to San Francisco, stopping by an Italian place she knew about, had some soup and good San Francisco French Bread, a cappuccino, and then texted Devon she was an hour and a half away. Devon texted her back a smilie face and a heart, *'Can't wait.'*

Near eight o'clock she turned down the winding Bennett Valley Road, into the crushed granite driveway of Sophie's Choice Vineyard. The stress of driving the distance and the awkward meeting at her office lifted as she pulled up to the beautiful modern home, golden lights from the many windows illuminating the silent green vineyards tucked in neat rows.

Devon ran outside, grabbed her Murano's door handle and swung it wide. "Welcome home!" She nearly pulled Marcy from the little SUV and then gave her a big hug. "So glad you made it safe and sound."

Devon was quickly trying to struggle with Marcy's bags when Nick appeared. "Hold it there. You get your butt inside the house, little one. I got this."

Marcy started to take one of the bags and Nick swatted her hand away.

"I *said* I got this." Then he broke a smile. "Welcome." His familiar blue-green eyes were warm and friendly. With his straight jaw, slightly unshaven stubble, his blond hair wildly growing like cropped golden hills of California, he exuded confidence, health and a good dose of sex appeal. She had trusted him since the first time she'd met him, but now, she realized she'd missed their easy conversation and banter on the trip down to San Diego.

As the tingling began forming in her belly it dawned on her that the person she was really missing was Lucas. The loss of that sexy friendship she had with him hurt like a wound that would never heal.

She and Devon laced their elbows together as Marcy slung her red computer case over her shoulder and walked arm in arm with her best friend. Her eyes filled with water with the welcoming she'd received in just under a minute. It was something that helped take away the bitter sting of her firing and painful scrutiny in San Diego.

They were playing soft music that echoed up throughout the house. A melodic soft African singer's voice filled the large rooms with warm sound.

"You have dinner? Want anything?" Devon asked.

"I'm fine. I stopped in San Francisco and had some soup and French bread."

"Vesuvio's?"

"What do you think?"

"How about some hot chocolate?"

"Sounds perfect."

Devon pointed through the sliding glass door off the kitchen, "You go on outside to the guest house and get yourself situated. I'll brew you some hot chocolate with a little chili, okay? Come on in after you get settled."

Marcy set her computer case down and crossed the kitchen in three long strides to hug Devon. "Thanks so much, Dev. You guys are a lifesaver."

Devon's body was warm, returning her hug with a squeeze. "I'm just so excited to have you here. We've got some wonderful news I'll tell you all about it after you come back. Now scoot." She said as she spanked Marcy on the rear.

The cottage brought back the memory of when she first came up to Sonoma County, the day she met Lucas. It was the cottage she'd hoped to spend a few nights with him in, before he was called away. A single lemon-scented candle glowed on the glass coffee table in front of the burgundy loveseat at the foot of the bed. Bright oil paintings adorned the walls as well as collages of work done to the winery. She examined one picture with a bunch of boys working shirtless, spraying each other and dancing. She saw Lucas among them.

"Where do you want these?" Nick asked, standing in the doorway behind her.

"Just put them on the bed. I'll unpack later tonight and tuck them away." She smiled up at him as he lay the suitcases down on the bed, waved and started to leave.

At the doorway, he turned to ask her a question, "So Marcy, you hear from Lucas?"

"No. Not sure I will ever again."

"Ever is a long time." He was right, of course, but Nick's wicked red eyes bored into her like she was target practice.

"I know, Nick. I appreciate all you guys are trying to do for me. This was very generous of you."

He departed.

The property had been Sophie's struggling nursery and Marcy could still feel her presence, her spirit somewhere. Sophie had been Devon's mentor and friend, but she was also the older sister of Nick. Marcy knew the story of how she'd died at the old home, had been poisoned with arsenic in the water tank. Shortly before her death she had to endure the fire that nearly burned everything to the ground. She looked at a picture of Nick and a very frail and thin Sophie, which must have been taken just before her death.

Marcy washed her face, put on a stretchy top and bottoms she could sleep in, hung up a few things and placed underwear and other items in the dresser drawers she'd been provided. She removed her shoes and slid into some felt slippers, making her way back outside along the pathway nearly overgrown with honeysuckle, to the rear kitchen door. Devon had just poured them each a steaming mug of hot chocolate.

"Here you go. Let's sit here for a bit," Devon pointed to one of the overstuffed chairs in the living room. A fountain outside bubbled and spattered loudly, working its magic on Marcy's soul and she relaxed further. Nick sat on the wide arm of Devon's chair, making her look like a child easily lost in the big cushions. Devon's feet couldn't touch the ground when she was seated all the way to the back.

"So, can I ask you what happened with you and Lucas?"

"Nick, stop it. None of our business," Devon interrupted him. It elicited a shrug from Nick.

"Sorry."

"If it makes you feel any better, when Lucas gets home, I'm sure we'll talk. But only if he initiates it. Not holding my breath," said Marcy. "In all fairness, it was just one conversation, a long-distance conversation." She examined her fingernails. "Nothing I can do about any of it until he's back. I could tell his focus had changed. He was a bit stressed."

"I'll bet," Nick whispered looking far away.

"What's happening, Nick?" asked Marcy.

"Crazy sh—stuff." He shook his head. "We are living in strange times."

"Well these are certainly strange times. I meet Lucas, and less than a week later, I'm without a job, relocating to Northern California. I'll be lucky if I still have my real estate license left when all the dust settles."

"Lucas is a one-man wrecking crew."

"We all are," Nick corrected her. "Remember, Devon? We get this tunnel vision, especially when we're on deployments. I've seen guys lose it when they get into arguments with their girlfriends or wives. Here they are, hiding in some boxcar of a home, hot, tired and maybe a little scared. Waiting for all the action to start and wham, a call to or from home, puts them on their ladies' shit list. Not a damned thing we can do about it, either."

"So, maybe it's best that everything is over before too much is made of it." Marcy's words trailed off and she slowly felt herself getting sleepy. "I gotta turn in."

"Me too. We'll talk in the morning. I have a noon appointment in the office, so why don't you plan on going in with me and I'll introduce you to my manager. That sound good?"

"Thanks, Devon."

On the way back to the cottage, Marcy saw a shooting star, and made a wish, just as she'd always done as a child.

"If there's a way, and a reason for it, bring him back. If you can. And only if he wants."

CHAPTER 27

T HE SOCCER GAME after lunch between the Navy players and the SEALs was a complete wipeout—for the SEALs. The girl's goalkeeper wasn't afraid of a muscled hero coming at her. What she couldn't stop with her body, she would push back with her spikes. She drew blood on three forwards, tackled another and did a from behind slide tackle as her only defense of the box when she'd been caught off guard by a quick pass. With no refs to call a maybe questionable foul, she got away with it. What was apparent was that, for all their strength and stamina, because the SEALs had not worked together as a team on the field, the girls would be able to kick their butt each time they played. And the games wouldn't be close either. They called it quits after an hour, and although there was a dispute about the actual score, what wasn't in question was that the girls scored at least ten times, and the SEALs had only made one.

It was something that would eventually even out, but it would take several more games than they had.

A party was arranged to go up to spy on the training camp in the daylight. This time, Lucas stayed back at base. Jeffrey had brought a prototype of his new Battlefield Zombies video game Lucas and Jake lost themselves in.

"Holy shit, Jeffrey, do you suppose you could have any more blood in it? Alex asked the handsome former Bachelorette contestant.

The game had blood spurting in every direction when one of the good guys died, and greenish black ooze that worked like acid on the good guy's skin for the zombies. Lucas laughed when a new zombie appeared dressed as a cheerleader, complete with a couple of heads she used as pompons she held by long stringy hair. He wasn't so sure he'd have much of an appetite for dinner. It didn't affect his ability to drink red bull and beer in alternate doses.

"Red sells really well in China," Jeffrey answered.

"That's death to Chinese."

"Prosperity and long life, good luck too," he answered. "That's what they asked for. Lots of red."

"Who the fuck is supposed to win?" Jake asked. "Looks to me the zombies have an edge."

"Can't make it too easy. I think they expect for a novice there'll be lots of red. They asked for that. Then we get the kids to watch the online tutorial I'm working on now. You tell me what parts you like, would like to see more of."

Lucas switched with Rory and T.J. while Lucas, Jake and Ryan went outside, sitting on foldup lawn chairs he and Cooper brought back.

"So you guys think we can find a five bedroom in the complex?" Lucas asked.

Ryan sniffed the air, "You smell that, Jake? I can smell it a mile away. This here is a kiss-up."

"Nice and sweet," He smiled back at Lucas. "You stay the hell away from me in the shower. Recent breakups can do a lot to a guy, and you got two inside of one week, my friend."

"Shut up. You should talk."

"Seriously, Lucas," Began Ryan, "You're lucky man. I'd say you dodged a big ol' bullet. These married guys, they can talk all they want, but we all know what some of those ladies can turn into. And as you've noticed, you don't get any warning or chance to plan."

"Ryan's right. You're much better off playing the field."

They all turned their heads when Rory screamed, "Fuckin' A" so loud it nearly rattled the windows. The video game was getting lots of attention. The noise made it difficult to talk, so the three bachelors retired to Lucas and Jake's bedroom.

"In time, it goes away, and then you wonder what the big deal was," said Jake, pulling from a bag of chips.

"What goes away?" Lucas wondered.

"You know, dreaming about your ex, and trying to get back together. That goes away in time."

"What about your kids, Jake?" Lucas had identified what the real pain was.

"I get to see them. They're actually happier to see me when they don't see me every day. Our times are special now. And they can't say no."

Lucas had to laugh again. "You should see mine. Connie's scared the shit out of them. They cry whenever –well I've only seen them once since the—the—"

"You just got served man. You haven't had enough time for them to adjust. Now for another piece of advice?" Jake started. "Get back in good with that Realtor, and make Connie jealous. She'll start trying to get you back, Lucas. Women like a little competition."

"You don't know Connie."

"No. Sadly, no," Ryan said.

Lucas threw his beer at him and the arc of amber liquid sprayed across Jake's chest. It started a pileon—Jake was on Lucas immediately and then Ryan jumped the pile, causing them all to hit the floor.

Rory and Jeffrey appeared and quickly separated the brawl by pulling Jake and Ryan up to standing position, then shoving them out into the common area between the two bedrooms.

Lucas tore himself off the bed, straightened the mattress that had been dislodged from its base. He wanted to watch some news, feeling a little isolated from the rest of the world, but the game players were monopolizing the big screen. Depending on how long they were there, another TV might be in order to satisfy all camps.

Kyle and the rest of the men who had gone with him up to the hills made their entrance. Kyle headed for the bedroom he shared with Coop, who was burdened with some equipment in a pack that looked heavy. In his other hand, he held a camera with long lens attached.

Lucas walked over to his LPO, leaning into the doorway. Kyle sat at a makeshift desk, and was writing some notes, copying some measurements from a crumpled piece of paper they'd prepared in the field.

"What's up, Chief?" Lucas asked, but he looked at Cooper.

"No sign of Rushti. Kind of a quiet day," Coop said. Kyle's back was to the two of them, until he turned around to face them.

"I gotta call CentCom, gentlemen. I'm gonna need a little privacy."

"Sure thing." Coop set the equipment on a table against the wall, which also housed three black duty bags Lucas knew to be filled with ammo and IEDs. Lucas entered the hallway with Cooper right behind him, closing the door.

"We saw him though, right? I mean they know that back in San Diego?"

"And D.C."

"You know what the plan is?"

Cooper grinned.

"There is a plan, right?"

"Oh yeah, there's a plan."

"Spill."

They heard the hallway door open. Lacey and several members of the soccer team sauntered in, freshly washed, looking lovely, and smelling even lovelier. Lucas momentarily forgot his question to Cooper, until the giant stepped on his big toe.

"The plan is that we focus on what the plan is, young froglet. Keep your eyes and ears open."

Several of the girls shuffled slowly past them, their running shoes barely making a sound. Cooper nodded. Lucas mumbled, "Ladies."

"We weren't sure we'd be welcome after today's game," started Lacey. She gave Lucas a wink.

Jake and Ryan had joined the group. "Apology accepted. But you owe us," Jake said. The two accompanied the girls to the living room/kitchen. Rory demonstrated the new video toy.

Coop cleared his throat. "So the plan is that we don't do anything to provoke them. Can't do a damned thing until we get the okay. Now, if they pick a fight, well then, all bets are off."

"You don't think they'd be stupid enough to—"

"Stupid's got nothing to do with it, Lucas. They're worked up with the heavenly fever, I call it. That knife cuts both ways."

"That it does," Kyle said behind Coop. "We stop talking about this right now. We have company."

"Roger that," Coop said. "Lucas, you hang with Kyle and I and stay away from those friends of yours or you'll go crazy. There's a reason they're single and we're married."

Lucas thought about the comment from Jake about being better off, and he agreed with his buddy one hundred percent. That's when he decided Cooper wasn't nearly as smart as he thought he was when it came to women. Eventually, he'd find out.

CHAPTER 28

DEVON AND MARCY rode together to Devon's office for a scheduled appointment with her Broker/Manager.

"I know about Coronado Bay. Good company. We've shared referrals over the years, although we don't get many coming up here from San Diego," Ted told the two women.

"Just want to be totally honest and above-board," Marcy began. "I made a terrible mistake, and this lapse in judgment isn't something I'm very known for. I've never been close to this. Ever. I think this couple just rattled me. I've worked with very high-end and powerful people, Admirals, CEOs and heads of hospitals who are used to hiring and firing doctors, and never had a problem."

Ted smiled. "Well, Devon's husband is the exception, of course, but most these guys are pretty wound up tight. I can see where that would bring some extra tension into an already stressful situation."

"Thank you, sir."

"So is there any fall-out about all this? Are you being sued? The company being sued? Anything like that and I need to know? Anything that comes up, I have t be kept in the loop."

"Of course. No. Nothing like that. I've turned over all my listings to another agent in the office, as instructed. I have nothing that should pull me back there. I need—" Marcy's left eye twitched as she stared down at the carpeting. "I want," she corrected, "to make a fresh start of it. I know Devon. I hope to make friends and get involved in the community and perhaps forget I was ever in San Diego. Besides, it's lovely up here."

"It is. Don't let the people fool you. Lots of money here. We are what they call the blue jeans tofu crowd."

All three of them chuckled.

"Down south, they try to show their opulence. Opposite up here. We don't like that sort of thing. We hate scandal, drama, too much rushing around, being cutthroat or unfair. Most agents here don't care how much they do, as long as they do it right. And I couldn't agree more. Lucky, really, to live here."

"I can see that. Well, if you'll give me a chance, I'd like to join your team."

"I think you'd fit in well, Marcy. Welcome aboard." He leaned over the desk and gave her a firm handshake. "I'll have the Independent Contractor agreement drafted for you in the morning, and of course we'll have to request your license."

Marcy held out her business card for him to get the broker address and her license number. "That's my cell."

"You want a desk here? Or, are you working out of Devon's house, like she does?"

Marcy smiled at her friend. "I'm going to impose as little as possible on Devon and Nick, although I'll be staying there until I can find my own place. So yes, assign me a desk and I'll try to start as soon as it's arranged. That way I'll be around your staff and people who can show me what to do until I learn.

They got up to leave, shaking the Broker's hand, and he tilted his head to the side. "You still seeing the SEAL?"

"Well, he's on deployment, but no, I don't think so. Part of the reason I need a fresh start."

"I understand completely. It's a shame, Marcy. Sorry for all this mess. But I figure you'll want to get busy to bring in some income. That works for me."

The two women had lunch downtown at an open-air pizza restaurant, watching people, sitting in the late autumn sun.

"I'm going to go looking for a place to stay, Devon. I intend not to be a burden to you guys."

"Don't be ridiculous. You've been through a lot—"

"Everything of my own making."

"Yes, that's true, but what kind of a friend would I be to dump you out on your own? You take as long as you want. Why don't you start making some calls for me? We could share the listings, if you get the appointments for me. We can work as a team."

"I don't want to impose."

"Now you're just being silly. I've got phone lists at home. You could even get started today, if you wanted."

Devon stopped for a newspaper, handing the classified section over to Marcy to search for properties.

At home, Marcy called on several rental cabins. Not being familiar with the area, she ran the addresses by Devon, who immediately eliminated those that she wouldn't find to her liking. Marcy was left alone when Nick returned and took Devon shopping.

Her rental car had GPS, so when she found a cabin up in the woods near Lucas' cabin, she decided to head up to Cloverdale area and check it out. Along the freeway she passed rows of vineyards, splaying out in order, leaves beginning to turn yellow and red at their tips. Assorted white tents were set up in the rows as a sun shield for field workers picking the grapes for harvest. Underneath the green and golden leaves, the ground was a rich charcoal color. Bins of grapes stacked up between rows. Several large estate wineries were perched like crystals atop rolling golden hillsides.

Cloverdale came up soon after. The two lane road through the center of town was nearly devoid of traffic. A dog made his way across the highway, barely glancing in Marcy's direction, sensing she'd slow down and let him cross without him having to make a run for it.

Before she made it off the highway, she stopped for a coffee. Espresso machines squealed their protest. The heavily tatted barista was playing light jazz in the background. Marcy examined artwork hung along the bright orange walls of the little coffee house. A lending library stood in the corner with a full two rows of books, several of the romance. It was a place she could sit and think about things, on another day when she wasn't on a mission. Some day, when she could ponder the complexities of life. She got in her car and headed left when she passed the outskirts of the town, as her GPS had instructed.

The drive through the redwoods was lush and green. Unlike the scrubby oak and madrone wilderness where Lucas' family home was located, this area was cooler, closer to the ocean by a few miles, the damp green carpet of foliage making a perfect place for a nap in the forest. The tall trees were thicker and let in little light. The road soon turned to a red-brown color. Her GPS instructed to go further, when all of a sudden, something hit her rear bumper from behind. She dared not look into the rear view mirror since she was having so much difficulty maneuvering her car, but one quick glance and she saw a dirty white van with tinted windshield. In the limited light from the forest, she couldn't tell who was driving. The van continued to push her car as she fishtailed in front of it. Unable to keep up with the switching back and forth. Eventually she was forced off the road, down a small embankment and into the path of a redwood tree.

In a flash of color, she saw the impact. Her windshield cracked and burst forth into a rain of crystals while her head was forced into the steering wheel, and then ripped backward from the impact of the crash. The airbags deployed before her head could hit the steering wheel a second time.

The last thing she heard was a door opening with a squeak. It wasn't from her vehicle. She smelled gasoline and wondered if she'd be able to move if the auto should catch fire. Black spots appeared in front of her eyes. She felt something warm trickle from the side of her mouth as her forehead pressed into the sticky wet plastic of the white airbag. Blackness shrouded her in a deafening silence.

CHAPTER 29

LUCAS TRIED HIS hand at Jeffrey's game after dinner. He noted Donna was sitting just a little too close to him, and her thigh stretched the length of his. While he didn't think she meant anything by it, he also felt it was more than a sexual advance. Her close proximity, her scent, the way she laughed and so expertly worked the controls of the game when it was her turn, and competitively tried to beat him at every round, intrigued him. But he also felt something dark was looming just under her surface. She wasn't a woman to talk much, and she'd been blabbing all evening, and drinking more beer than he'd seen her do the previous two days.

Something had shifted. She trusted him. He wondered if that was very wise.

Kyle went outside to greet someone who drove up in what sounded like a large diesel truck. Lucas tried to angle a way to see through the building windows, but couldn't make out who it was.

"The barn builder," Coop said.

Lucas excused himself and followed Cooper outside. When Boles laid eyes on them, he didn't smile or extend his hand like he had in the shop.

"You guys got a lot of fuckin' nerve getting me to come out here after dinner. Urgent, you said. What the fuck's so urgent about this place? This is government land. I don't want any of that goddamned paperwork filled out in quadruplicate cluttering up my system. I deal with small time rural farmers." His face was bright red. One eye had a popped blood vessel, which was new. Lucas saw he could have a temper. "I don't have to wait months and months for my cash. I get it before or the day of installation."

"We had to do it this way, sir," Coop started in. He peered over at Kyle, asking for help. They'd not discussed him coming over today. Kyle must have gotten the urgent call from Forsythe and made the invite himself.

His LPO sat down on a picnic table, leaned into his thighs and spoke slowly to the man, who was scanning the scene in front of him. Boles scratched the back of his neck and breathed hard like he had a medical issue.

"We're looking for information about our neighbor over the hill there." Kyle pointed to the ridge of dark green trees casually. By the way he studied the builder, Lucas could see he didn't trust him either.

"Not sure what you mean by that, son."

"You know, the people who have the little group thing over the hill. You've been there I'm sure. You helped them build it, am I right?"

"Of course. But if you think I'm going to go gossip about them— you guys have no right coming in here under false pretenses. I keep to myself. I don't ask questions and I certainly fuckin' don't answer any asshole's questions unless I got a good reason to do so."

Kyle stood up and was toe-to-toe with the man. The contractor's belly pushed into Kyle's abdomen but neither man backed up. "I got a good reason. Trust me I got a good reason," Kyle said between his teeth.

Boles managed to take a step back. "You guys military? You look military. What, we gonna have a fuckin' war on our hands here in the great state of Tennessee?

"Not if we can help it sir, and that's where you come in." Kyle's voice was practiced and gentle. Calming. It did little good.

"Like I said, I don't want any trouble."

"And we're not looking for trouble either," answered Kyle.

Boles scanned the three of their faces. He nearly jumped out of his pants when the back door to the building opened and out poured several SEALs. Lacey came behind them, kicking a soccer ball. Two of her teammates had removed their jerseys, exposing their sports bras underneath, and stuck the t-shirts inside the backs of their pants. The SEALs were bare chested, having tucked their shirts in similar fashion. Within seconds a lively pickup game of grab ass ensued, both sides trying to capture jerseys while others members attempting to bury the soccer ball into the post nets on either side. One goal was well defended, the other had no keeper.

Fredo had been on the sidelines and at last jumped in. With his speed and superior ball handling skills, he was dodging other players and easily scored a goal. He was on his way to scoring a second, when Chloe tackled him and left him limping for a bench.

"Who the hell are all these?" Boles finally asked.

"U.S. Navy Women's Soccer Team," Kyle answered.

"Navy, huh? So you guys are Navy?" Boles squinted into the remaining sunlight. The lights on the field came on as the dusk sensors kicked in.

"Um hum," Kyle answered him and didn't break his line of sight.

"Fuckin special forces. That's what you are." The builder spit on the ground.

Lucas cracked his neck again and all three turned quickly, alarm written all over their faces.

Kyle refocused on Boles. "So all we want is information." He brought a picture from his vest. "This man. Did you see this man?"

"Never saw him before."

Lucas didn't believe him. The telltale widening of the eyes before his uber-quick response told him the contractor had seen him, maybe even talked with him.

"Try again," Coop said as he picked up the contractor by his western style denim shirt. Lucas heard a loud rip in the fabric. His feet nearly dragged in the dirt although he probably outweighed Coop by forty pounds. Coop let loose of him, brushing the fabric flat against the man's chest. "I apologize for ruining your pretty shirt. I'll see to it Uncle Sam brings you another one."

"Get your fuckin' hands off me. You think I'm stupid?" Boles adjusted his clothes, stepping back for a safe distance.

Kyle looked at Cooper and then to Lucas and shrugged. All of them shook their heads. "No sir," Lucas said. "None of us thinks you're stupid. That's why you're gonna cooperate with us."

"This isn't fuckin' Afghanistan or Iraq. You can't just come in here and manhandle me!" His voice was attracting attention from the field. Fredo limped over to add assistance. Two of the girls stopped and put their hands on their hips. Even Chloe stopped, holding the ball at her hip with one palm.

"So, I'm gonna ask you one more time. Have you seen this man?" Kyle held the picture of the Shiek up to the builder's nose.

"He was there. Didn't talk to him, though."

"How many are they?"

"How the fuck do I know? They have some young ones that stay in the other buildings. Saw them through the windows. Never saw them outside. I only went inside their bunkhouse one time when I got paid. We made a point not to stare, if you know what I mean."

"Sure." Kyle sighed. "So guess. Humor me."

"Thirty? No telling how many inside those other buildings."

"So what's the scene like? You were there, what, three days?"

"Four."

"Okay, so what did you see that you remember? Anything unusual?"

"What, besides the fact that they pray several times a day? They wear long white robes in the fuckin' ninety degree afternoon? They got sandals instead of cowboy boots? You wear sandals here when you're a full grown man and you're, well, we don't do that here."

"I got you. So they're different. What else. What about this guy?" Kyle tapped on the picture.

"His look. The way he looked at me."

"How was that?"

"He looked like he fuckin' hated me." He pulled his jeans up, bringing his belt buckle up into the middle of his "pregnant" belly. "After the first day, I had the creeps. I asked for all my money. I gave it to my wife in case I didn't make it out of that place alive. The Mexicans in my crew didn't seem to have a problem with them. They're used to not understanding the conversations I have with clients."

"So what gave *you* the creeps?"

He looked up at the trees as if the camp's spies were looking down on all of them, and bit his lip, following along the horizon. He watched the soccer players for a few silent seconds without showing any expression, his lips pursing in fleshy puckers, and then smoothing back into a grimace. At last he took a deep breath and made a line in the dusty dirt with the side of his cowboy boot. When he looked up at Kyle, the man's eyes didn't stray a quarter of an inch from side to side. Lucas could see there was a little courage, a little fight left in the man. But not much. And though he was trying to mask it, Lucas could tell he was more than a little intimidated.

"One night we were working late. I saw this guy walk between the buildings. The sun had gone down. They'd finished their prayers. We were picking up our tools but the moon was bright so we could see. I wanted to get out of there so fast it made me sick to my stomach. We knew we'd be done in one more day, and that was one day too long."

"Okay. So what happened?"

"He walked into one of the houses. Before that, I never once saw or heard a woman. But that night, I heard a woman crying, like things were being done to her, you know? Those animals were doing things to her."

Lucas could see Kyle wanted to punch the guy, but his mission was more important than his own satisfaction. Instead of chastising him, Kyle showed mercy. Not many men, especially men who weren't trained to see the kinds of things they saw over in the arena, would know how to deal with this. It wasn't something people in the U.S. were used to seeing. Unfortunately, it was something all three of the SEALs standing before this man knew without a doubt occurred in the world of evil men. Lucas knew it hit all three of them the same. Someone innocent was being violated. Someone needed rescuing.

Kyle spoke softly, making the man lean towards him to hear. "Now you know why we must be here."

CHAPTER 30

MARCY'S HEAD HURT with a dull ache, which is what woke her up. She was confused, but gradually the fog lifted and she remembered what had happened before she'd passed out. She also remembered hearing voices in a strange dialect, and hands holding her body, carrying her somewhere. But the splitting pain forced her to keep her eyes closed, keeping the room from spinning, knowing even limited light would hurt worse. And then things would go black again. This happened several times before she woke in earnest.

Now, nausea plagued her. She needed to roll over and vomit, but when she tried, discovered she couldn't move. As she struggled with her own mind, trying to will her legs to slide off the bed, and found she wasn't on a bed at all, but a hospital gurney. She smelled the sweat from her body and knew she'd been there more than a day. She had to go to the bathroom.

The tiny room was cold, like a closet off a main living area, without heat. Someone had covered her with a blanket that smelled like it hadn't been washed in months. And then she discovered she was nude underneath the blanket. So where were her clothes? Did she require surgery? Was she in a hospital or clinic of some kind?

Light crept under the doorway, where she heard muffled talking, again in a foreign tongue.

She checked herself over, closing her eyes and concentrating on what hurt and what didn't, discovering her head was still the most painful. She willed her bladder to hold and to her surprise, it worked.

Wiggling her eyebrows up and down, she felt the welt on the right side of her forehead. The rusty taste in her mouth and clots of blood on her lip made her heart beat faster. It was one thing to be involved in an accident. But to be drugged and kept in a storage closet, without any medical care, meant only one thing: the accident had been anything but an accident, and the same people who caused it now held her.

They hadn't gagged her, so Marcy deduced they weren't concerned about her screaming for help. She guessed they were somewhere out in the boonies, since she could hear neither traffic, airplanes or other sounds of civilization, except for the faint middle eastern music and the sing song of the unfamiliar dialogue in the background.

The room smelled of bleach, or some sort of pungent cleaning fluid she didn't recognize.

Because one ankle strap immobilized her left foot, toes pointing down, Marcy developed a calf cramp in her left leg that began to drive her wild. She focused on the cramp, pushing into it, while her other leg developed another cramp. She willed herself into accepting it and stopped fighting, which gradually sent the dual cramps into remission.

She steadied her breathing, promising herself that, as more and more memory began to dawn on her, that she would not panic. What had Lucas said?

'Aren't you being overly dramatic?'

"Fuck," she muttered softly. She hated to admit it, but being overly excited *would* interfere with her problem solving, and she most definitely had a problem. A life or death problem. She harbored no illusions as to their intentions.

Marcy struggled against her foot binding and a small metal tray fell from the gurney, crashing onto a concrete floor. The door to the lighted room opened, flooding her with bright white light. She squeezed her eyes shut.

Someone closed the door partially, giving her eyes time to adjust. Standing before her was a young man in white robes. His full beard framed the smooth, young face of the man she recognized near Lucas' cabin from three days ago. He saw in her eyes the recognition she bore.

His teeth were white and perfectly straight. His smile tilted upward to the left as he scratched his chin. But the eyes of this man carried a coldness she'd not seen before.

He removed a large ugly knife, brandishing it from palm to palm, showing off the highly polished glint of the blade. His eyes studied her as he peeled back the top of the blanket and lowered the tip of the knife to her abdomen. He jerked it upward, tickling her skin without penetrating. Still dangerously clutching the handle in one hand, the man pulled back the blanket to below her belly button. His sharp inhale told her he was turned on by the violence he anticipated. She braced for a stabbing, a deep cut, or perhaps a beheading.

One more time the blade was lowered and this time she felt the cold metal on the flesh of her upper abdomen, causing her to shiver. With a flick of the wrist her captor scraped her left nipple. He stared down at her chest, licking his lips.

He was muttering a prayer. Marcy accepted the fact that there was nothing she could do, except perhaps throw her weight to the side and topple them both. But being strapped to the gurney would put her at a disadvantage.

And then it hit her. They wouldn't kill her until they abused her. The way this man looked at her flesh, she became convinced his pleasure would be extracted from her pain. If she showed fear, or struggled, it would enhance the experience for him.

She vowed to hold out for as long as she could.

The robed man shouted several Arabic names and instantly the room was filled with several young boys barely old enough to shave.

He waved the tip of the blade at her while he spoke to them. None of them would look her in the eyes, but remained focused on her breasts. The robed one squeezed her left breast first, muttering something in a sneer, citing a verse the rest of the room repeated. He fondled her right breast, but this time, tweaked her nipple, twisting it until it caused pain.

She arched up as much as she could, but did not scream. That action drew a reaction from the young boys. One by one, they each took a nipple, twisted it until Marcy finally cried out. She watched in horror as the boys were encouraged by her terror.

Her stomach finally could hold out no longer as the nausea swept up from her abdomen, quickly sending bile and contents of her lunch up and out her mouth, spraying the group with her vomit. Pandemonium spread over the little gathering, as the room emptied, no doubt sending the boys to the showers to wash up.

She got what she'd been hoping for and didn't have time to brace herself against. The robed man's hand came crashing down against her left cheekbone and again the room went black.

CHAPTER 31

E ARLY NEXT MORNING, Donna Grant went for her usual five mile run. The faint scent of burning leaves was in the air. Heat from yesterday's sun had soaked into the soil and the asphalt she ran on at the side of the country lane, but the air was crisp and cool, perfect for her run.

As the road veered off to the left, she heard a vehicle approach from behind so she moved further onto the shoulder to make sure to give the driver clearance. But the motor slowed and began following close behind her. She tapped her watch, sending her personal signal through the Apple device. The watch would clock her location and send that information as well.

The motor continued to run but when she turned to look behind, three dark-skinned men in green camo caught up to her, despite the fact she'd put on the speedburner sprint most men had difficulty keeping up with. They grabbed her arms, one of them put his hand over her mouth where she was able to bite down and take a sizeable chunk from the man's palm. She could feel freedom within reach when suddenly a moist rag was placed over her nose and mouth and she succumbed to spotted dizziness fading to black.

"FORSYTHE IS COMING today. We're gonna show him the camp. He's bringing sat photos, and another special honored guest," Kyle reported to the group before breakfast. "We do our PT here. No one leaves the compound until Forsythe okays it, understood?"

"Who's Forsythe bringin'?" asked T.J.

"T.J. because I'm not totally positive he's coming, I'm going to wait. But you'll find out when all the rest of us do."

Tyler raised his arm and was called on. "How about a rematch with the ladies? We're looking at O for three."

"Not a fuckin' chance. Besides, I think they're leaving soon, maybe even today. I don't want Forsythe to get the impression this is a Club Tennessee all inclusive fucking resort, catch my drift?"

Lucas noted how disappointed Tyler was. "I'll kick the ball around with you after breakfast, if you want. We can do that without the girls, right? You still remember how to play with men, don't you?"

The team laughed at Tyler's expense. Tyler took off his sweaty shirt and threw it at Lucas.

Breakfast was somber. The girls obviously noted none of the SEALs sat with them, as was the custom. Everyone on Team 3 had one eye on the entrance to the mess hall's doors, looking for Forsythe.

Lacey cornered Tyler when he went back for seconds. "You guys sore losers?" she asked loud enough for the entire room to hear.

"Nah. We got—" he looked at Kyle for reassurance he could mention Forsythe and got the nod, "We got brass coming in today. We're supposed to show our bad-ass side, not the fraternizing side. Nothing against you ladies."

"What a load," Chloe said under her breath as she walked past the men on her way to hand in her tray. Lucas thought it was funny as hell.

"See, that's what's wrong with women," Jake started. "They win a little bit, and then they take over. Mess with your head. Talk about sore losers. They hate to waste an opportunity to pound us into the ground."

"Fuck sake," said Alex. "It's their job to win. That's what they train for. We train for something else. They get in your head, Jake, because you let them get inside your head. Your fault, man."

Cooper leaned forward to be able to deliver his message to both Jake and Alex. "Boys, I'm having a hard time imagining you ever being married. I mean ever. This isn't about winning. You don't treat a woman like that. You continue with that shit and you'll be jerking off to the TV when you're seventy. Broke and lonely."

"Fuck, already broke," Jake said after standing. Tyler nodded to Lucas and the two of them cleared their spots, then headed over to the bunkhouse to retrieve the soccer ball.

A black SUV with darkened windows pulled up and three men stepped out. The security team consisted of the driver and two details. Ian Forsythe extricated himself from the rear passenger side, while Jackie Daniels got out on the other side behind the driver. Kyle was quick to appear and give the man a shake, and give Jackie a bear hug.

Jackie was roundly welcomed. Lucas knew then, that if the mission was successful, they'd be interrogating the Sheik or his underlings, and that would require someone with native language skills. Jackie was the only man any of them trusted for this job. And he had saved their lives on several other missions. Not only was he deadly with his interpreting, he was deadly with any weapon they gave him, and never hesitated to use it. He was as close to an Afghani SEAL there was.

Several minutes later, the team was briefed. Forsythe showed photos of satellite surveillance on the camp.

"You'll see these trucks are in constant use. We've tracked them as far as we can. Gonna have to paint them somehow, or install tracking devices. We're bringing in some drones, but understand only Coop operates them. I don't want any incidents, or alerting the camp to our presence."

Coop nodded. "Can I take pictures?"

"Being fitted now as we speak, Coop. Daytime only, I'm afraid, though."

"We'll do the best we can."

"Chatter is up, indicating we got something coming very soon. The Oregon incident was apparently orchestrated by a group in Northern California, but you know as well as I do, there are over thirty training camps operating in the U.S. today. Our leadership hasn't been comfortable spying on them, although God knows they should be. I mean what the fuck do they want with training camps, learning how to shoot while crawling on their bellies, breech boats and blow shit up."

"Wonder if that guy who got away—remember that guy, Rory?"

"Sure do. The sidekick of the dude Megan went all Bobbitt on," said Fredo.

Jackie piped up. "I do not understand why your government does nothing. They know. It's like they want to allow these people to do evil things to the good citizens of the United States. This should never have been allowed."

"And it's getting worse," Forsythe said.

"Not like it's a church or Boy Scout camp," added Jackie. He continued to shake his head.

There was a general mumble of approval from the group.

"You know what they say. Evil exists when good men do nothing." He paused. "When Kyle reported your builder guy heard a woman crying out, that escalated this mission into a primary target. We can't engage unless they engage first. Be very clear about that. We in no way want to bring in local news crews or garner criticism about SEALs doing work inside the U.S. borders, so we're still considered a training mission. Doesn't hurt to take pictures, and if need be, stage a rescue if we can get the approval."

Armando stood. "Sir, wouldn't it be a good idea to inform the locals? Isn't this something the Sheriff's Department or Marshall's Service should know about?"

"We're studying the situation. Not sure it will work that smoothly. We got three jurisdictions and they don't always cooperate. But yes, we will if we can. If we have time. That would be ideal. But gentlemen, we're here to learn about this verified threat of militias kidnapping and taking hostages—SEALs, *not* civilians. So we're taking the broad interpretation it's our mission. But again, I have to underscore we keep it tight. We say nothing to anyone. No one. Understood?"

The Team was in agreement.

"We will have to verify there's a hostage situation. We can't just send guys in there, even locals, unless we can verify this. So far, we have nothing on what we've taken by air. Hope the drones work better, Coop."

"If she's able to be seen, we'll find her."

"I'm working on VIR equipment for your two drones, too," said Forsythe.

"Two? Hot damn!"

Lucas knew Cooper was their gadget guy and could rig up anything to look harmful or not harmful, depending on the requirement. In his single days he lived in a motorhome by the beach, outfitted with more devices than some small police departments had. His home on wheels, before his marriage to Libby, was affectionately called the Babemobile and had been used on some surveillance and rescues in the past, before Lucas' time on the Team.

Jackie Daniels spoke up. "You get something to record their conversations, and that will be more incriminating. They have to speak to someone by cell. They probably have computers, which would be good to try to capture."

"I got some little devices with a pretty good range. Problem is, we need to be line of sight to work them. That means someone has to stay buried up on top of the mountain."

"Then we'll plan that. You look today for what you'd need and plan where we put them. We'll do the rest," answered Kyle.

"Okay, then. Kyle, give me the grand tour," said Forsythe.

Lucas accompanied Forsythe and Kyle, Cooper, Armando, Jackie and Fredo to the top of the ridge. They were surprised to find two guards posted on the hill today, and, unlike before, one was upper ridge, one was lower ridge. With his high-powered scope, Armando was able to determine there were two other sentries across the small valley overlooking the camp. This meant they had beefed up security, for some reason. Nothing could be discussed until they were away from earshot.

Lucas heard the buzz of a high-flying drone before anyone else did, and he pointed it out to Coop.

"Shit," he said softly. He pointed to his chest, shook his head, "Not ours," he whispered.

Armando finished taking pictures. Lucas noted the vans were lined up as they always were, with the exception of one backed up to the end of a building. The doors were not visible.

Forsythe was comparing their photos with what he was seeing live and made a couple notations to Kyle. Lucas kept scanning the skies for evidence of the drone's return. Movement down in the valley piqued his attention and he found a drone operator using a small laptop computer was guiding it home. He handed his scope, taken from his H&K, to Coop. After several seconds of study, and watching the drone land near the lake's shore, Coop nodded and handed him back the scope.

"All good," he whispered.

Lucas gave him the thumb's up.

They began to leave the site when they heard a car approach the guard gate to the camp. The occupants were two ponytailed blonde ladies, both wearing short shorts and tank tops. Lucas examined the ladies as they were ushered through the gate. What he saw made the hair stand up all over his body.

"Holy fuck!" he whispered.

Kyle faced him and angled his head.

He whispered, "Builder's daughter" to Kyle's ear. Armando had them in his site as well.

"Wonder if papa knows," said Armani.

"I'm guessing not." Kyle added, "If he felt the creeps when he was there, I'd have a hard time thinking he'd let his daughter go there."

"He must have told her, right?" Lucas asked.

Armando shook his head. "I say no. She's doing her little wild child thing, but that's a dangerous game. Very dangerous."

The ladies parked outside one of the buildings and were shown the way to the building doorway. The girls looked at each other, shrugged and walked inside.

The SEALs waited a half hour without further incident. It appeared no foul play was at hand, or whatever the girls were doing was consensual, so Kyle and Forsythe checked with Jackie for any clues, and then called their surveillance off and the group headed back to camp.

After they arrived at the meadow at the base of the ridge, Lucas asked Coop what he was dying to know. "What the hell are they doing with that drone?"

"Same thing we are. We gotta hope to God they don't know we're here," Coop answered him. "Hard to tell, but I didn't see any equipment saddled on her, so I think she's not taking pictures, but you never know. They get hold of one of those micro cameras and we may be on their evening news."

Forsythe turned to them. "We're going to have to consider not going up anymore in the daytime. At least at night, we aren't as discernable."

"But our signature will stand out more," said Kyle.

"Only reason you'll be there is if we can't get the air support, if we go in. We need eyes on the ground," said Forsythe. "I'm going to get on the horn and find out if there are any updates. But I think our next mission will be to verify there is a hostage there."

Lucas didn't like the fact that, due to it being on U.S. soil, they'd have to be extra careful before they were granted permission to go forward. Going in and still having to get permission to go forward didn't seem tactically sound. But he wasn't the one calling the shots.

CHAPTER 32

M OUSTAFA INTENDED MARCY would be the training whore for his young men, something to use as reward for jobs well done. He cleaned her body and even put first aid salve on some of her scrapes and the bump on her forehead. He enjoyed washing her, preparing her. The training would be long and delicious.

He found that forbidden fruit was the best kind of motivator. They studied it was wrong to have sex with an infidel, but an infidel being used to train boys into becoming men, was allowed. The fact that she would never give her consent made the whole scenario complete. Consensual sex with an infidel was punishable by death. Rape with a subhuman infidel was not only allowed, it was doing the Prophet's work and moving them all toward the Kingdom of Heaven. Moustafa knew he'd be rewarded.

In the meantime, he'd be quiet about his designs on the woman. He would let them touch her, pinch and lick her, perhaps draw a little blood, but the first entry into her body would be performed by him. He'd like to do it in private, but it was important to show the men how it was done. In the old days, they would have themselves to practice on, but now they had a live woman, a woman they could defile and not be punished.

God is good.

He'd given her another dose of heroin, when she started to come to as he was washing her. She quickly succumbed to a deep sleep and he could do anything he wanted to her. Such a thought was thrilling.

The heroin was part of the supply they were leaching out into the local high schools in Northern California, which accomplished two things: they raised funds for their cause, and they got the local population hooked on the substance. As far as he knew, they were off the radar.

The government was not only letting them operate these training camps, which emboldened his leaders back in Iran, but had expressly put out public communications to law enforcement they were to be protected. How the Prophet managed to arrange this, Moustafa could never figure. But it was a fact, they had nearly full immunity from prosecution, or persecution. Being isolated in the woods made them virtually invisible. Only thing missing was a fence. Every other compound had installed one. His would be coming soon.

God is good.

Marcy was in such a state that the restraints were not necessary. Besides, he liked having her drape over his body, her limp form still lusciously curvy in all the right places. He loved the smell of her perspiration, and the scent of old cologne behind her ears, on her wrists and between her breasts.

Today, while the boys were delivering their drugs to Cloverdale High School, he locked himself in the room with her, removing all their clothes and let her sleep on top of him. He fingered her clit, stuck a thumb into her anus and she moaned like it was pleasurable. But he knew better.

It had been a stroke of luck when they'd found her at the coffee shop. He'd hungrily watched her athletic body order her coffee, watched her out of the corner of his eye as she added cream and stirred the liquid mixture. Her backward tilt of the head exposed the silky white flesh of her neck. The more he watched her, the more he felt he owned her. His fantasies came in wild colors as he imagined things he could do to her, things like that warrior had done. He knew what her skin looked like at midnight, in the shower, even when she was relieving herself. He'd watched her shave her legs, shave other parts of her more intimately. Just for him.

They'd followed her at a distance, but when she drove off the main road leading to the coast, and onto the dusty dirt roads of the redwood forest, he decided on his bold plan. He would take her and the taking would happen nearly five miles from where they were living. It would surely take a week or more to find her car, locate her body, if at all. That was more than enough time for the events he knew were coming.

Capturing her was thrilling. He allowed someone else to drive while he made sure her body was sufficiently intact. Her arms were strong, thighs unharmed. Her forehead was bruised, but her abdomen was flat and unmarked. Her butt cheeks smooth and squeezable. He took just a few liberties, when the students were not looking over at him.

Soon it would be time to use her the way the Prophet intended.

His erection was deliciously hard. She was unconscious. He grasped her hand and squeezed her fingers around his shaft, jerking off into her belly button. He longed for the day he could take her several times and spend an entire day doing it.

When he heard the boys' van drive up, he quickly clothed himself, gave her another dose of heroin, placed her still naked body under the fleece blanket he'd taken off his own bed, and left her alone in the dark.

"Have you found anything?" he asked his young apprentices.

"Nothing."

"Then have you developed our next target?"

They nodded. "She's under age, Moustafa. Does it still count?"

"It counts double."

His young students beamed with delight and anticipation, handing him all the money they'd raised.

"Tomorrow, then. We will continue our training with the infidel whore. Later in the week, you all will become men together. Then you will have the chance to choose your own vessel. After that, we will kill them all. Together."

God is indeed good.

CHAPTER 33

R EVEREND TRAVIS BANKS ministered to his flock at Riverbend Maximum Security Prison, ten miles away from their base camp. Banks had met T.J. Talbot at the request of T.J.'s dying father, who was an inmate at Riverbend before he passed.

Because the SEAL team was asked not to leave camp, T.J. asked for and was granted permission to have him come visit at the camp the next morning. A year ago, Banks had informed T.J. about some of the activity that had been going on in the greater Nashville area, and the trending toward radicalization in the local prison population. T.J. thought perhaps Banks could be of some use.

The giant of a man with the gold front tooth made even T.J. look small, something that never happened.

"You never did stop by and I been waitin', T.J. We gots some catching up to do," Banks said, showing off his tooth in the wide smile pasted to his face.

"No excuses. But with little Courtney, it's been tough. We're expecting again."

"Halleluiah. God blesses those who do the good work."

"If that was the case, you'd have a dozen kids."

Travis stopped a bit, tilted his head and dropped his smile, as if offended.

"Oh shit, Travis, I'm so sor—"

"Jes messin' with ya."

Lucas could see T.J. was relieved. "Honored to meet you, Reverend

Banks. T.J. has talked about you non-stop since we found out you were coming out here," Lucas said as he shook the pastor's massive hand.

Forsythe was going over some photos and stopped to greet T.J.'s friend. "We're most grateful for any help you can give us."

"That's partly why I'm here."

Kyle showed Banks the photo of the Sheik. "This is the guy we're looking for, reverend."

Banks studied the photo. "Hmm. Reminds me of a real bad dude came through here last year, just before Christmas, but it wasn't this guy. Big, grown bad-ass men at the prison were bowing on their knees to him. He swept through here, had a couple huge services at the Mosque and there were crowds clear across the street, blocking traffic. Police had to shut down the whole area and it was on the news. I don't remember his name, but he was someone big, very big in their circle."

"Like an advanced guard," Forsythe commented.

"Kyle," Jackie slipped between them. "You guys find some news footage. Let me listen to what he's saying and I'll tell you exactly what he was all about. This guy I don't know, but he must be a powerful Imam from Iraq, maybe Syria," offered Jackie Daniels.

Forsythe indicated he'd get someone working on it.

"So you wanna catch us up as far as what's been happening in the community?" T.J. asked.

"Word has it there's going to be a coordinated effort at a strike, or something of that nature. But the thing that bothers me is that this prison isn't the only place. I got a friend out west works in the central valley of California, and he's run across the same thing. This Imam I was telling you about went to all those places, too." Banks looked around him at all the SEALs. "So what're you doing here in Tennessee? Not exactly a place I'd expect to see this kind of crowd."

"Training mission," Kyle said. His voice was flat, but Lucas knew it belied apprehension. Kyle wore the mantle of leadership well, but anyone who spent any time around him knew he carried more than they saw publically.

Reverend Banks was hesitant to offer more help but finally agreed to check the visitor logs, which was a violation of his volunteer agreement.

"Now can me and T.J. here just sit and shoot the bull a bit? Or is this all serious, being that it's a *training mission*." He winked at T.J.

After getting permission, the two men headed to the corner. "Your sister looks good, T.J." Lucas heard the pastor say as they left earshot.

"How did we not know this, Forsythe. You guys uncover this?"

"I'm sure the Bureau has knowledge of it. Politics, Kyle. Stay as far away as possible from politics. No winners there, except the most ambitious, the ones who will do anything."

"That kinda fits us. We'd do anything to save this country," said Coop.

"Ambitious here, to make sure everyone stays safe. A lot of our guys are dying out there and it's still coming this way," said Lucas.

"Well, that's geography catching up to us. We can be thankful for that big old Atlantic. Pacific too, for that matter," answered Forsythe. "With limited resources and the public retreating from their taste for war, as opposed to 9-11, we have to decide what to put to good use. Can't do it all. People need to understand that."

"Until something big hits us," whispered Kyle staring off into space.

"And maybe that's coming," said Forsythe. "Either that or we'll be ready. That's why you boys are here, mainly to watch and learn. We weren't putting you into the middle of a fight, but right next to the bad guys."

Lucas couldn't help but think about the timing of all this. Someone knew a confrontation was brewing. With over thirty camps in the U.S. it wasn't going to be possible to stop them all. Maybe, just maybe, they could stop one here in Tennessee.

He thought about Marcy and was glad she was some distance from harm's way, living in San Diego, where there were more military and retired military per square mile than just about anywhere. Even if he couldn't, some soldier down there would make sure she was safe. Of that he was sure.

CHAPTER 34

DONNA GRANT HEARD the voice of another woman, which was odd because she lived alone. But within mere seconds, she heard not one voice, but several. And they were all women's voices. One was sobbing uncontrollably.

She wondered if one of the soccer players had managed to call a meeting with several of the others while she was sleeping. It felt like she'd slept a whole week, and then remembered she'd been drugged. Then Donna recalled the strange truck, the rag across her mouth and nose, and the odd noises while she fell backward into someone's arms.

She'd been running. That was the part she was sure about. And they'd come up behind her and—and they'd kidnapped her! She remembered sending off the text SOS just before they came up behind her with the rag.

The sobbing continued. Several women's voices tried to soothe the pain, but if anything, the crying continued at an even higher decibel. Donna was now wrestling with two conflicting feelings. She felt perhaps they were all in danger, but before she could do anything, she needed to know whether or not she was intact or gravely injured. It was her training: to assess the damage to her own person first before attending to someone else's.

Her left shoulder was sore. Her head felt groggy, but other than that, she was good to go, provided they stopped giving her the heroin. She assumed that was what it was from her previous experience in Iran.

That had been nearly four years ago when their convoy had been picked off by a warlord and his small band of militia. While most of her unit was killed, they'd taken her captive. The days and nights blurred into one long nightmare that lasted nearly a whole month before she'd been rescued by SEAL Team 5.

But now it was happening all over again. She was a captive this time in the U.S., not some foreign hellhole. And there were other women here as well.

She arched her back and found she had no pain. She brushed the hair from her forehead, opened her eyes and began to feel her life had been spared so she could exact revenge. That required clear-headedness, planning. Taking in a deep breath, she pushed the scream-ing voices of insanity rattling around in her brain all the way to the back of her skull, where it could sit in a corner until she was ready to call it out. It was time to focus on what lay in front.

The zip ties they'd fastened to her wrists were easily removed by wiggling the ends back and forth until they crumbled in her fingers. She did the same with her ankle restraints.

"Who's here?" she called out.

The sobbing stopped immediately.

"I'm Jenna, and I'm here with Shelley. There's another young girl here, very young, but she doesn't speak English."

"Anyone know how long I've been here?" Donna asked.

"They brought you in this morning."

"Okay, I'm Donna. Coming over. Don't be afraid," she said.

She felt her way on the concrete floor stained with water and what smelled like blood, until her eyes adjusted and she could see the outline of three women in seated position.

"Anyone hurt?" she asked.

"She is," one of the girls said. We just got thrown in here. But from the feel of her face, she's been cut and beaten."

Donna reached out to the girl and immediately the poor thing jolt-ed and pulled away, working against her restraints.

"They even have a collar around her neck," one of the girls said.

Donna used soothing words like she would do to a frightened

young child, holding out her hand until she felt the familiar leather collar she knew all too well. The pictures of her abuse flooded her brain until she closed her eyes and willed them to be gone.

"There should be a buckle at the back, or perhaps a lace up device. Do you have use of your hands?" she asked them.

"Yes." She heard the clanging of metal as the collar was removed. The young woman spoke in a Pashtu dialect. Donna remembered the word *whore*, and *animal*, shouted to her multiple times, and she heard those words again uttered by a frail young girl.

She spoke a few words to the girl, and got some single word answers she could barely understand. Donna put her palm on the girl's shoulder and told her that there were people near who could help them all. It was the truth, however, getting word to those people, her SEAL friends, would be a whole other problem.

Her wrist hurt and that's when she discovered they'd not taken her watch, probably not realizing it had internet and wifi capacity. Donna pushed the light button on the right of the small screen and noted she had a decent signal. She tapped in an SOS to her procurement officer's cell phone in Norfolk. She didn't have time to look for a return signal, but started to focus on the other women.

Donna removed the zip ties from the others while one of the American girls held the light for her. Her fingers were stiff and swollen from the drugs, but eventually the plastic ties fell away.

The young girl looked to be no more than a preteen, which sickened her. Her clothes were in rags. Her pretty face was marred with large purple and blue bruises that had been dished out over multiple incidents. The girl's right wrist also appeared to be broken, the swelling forming a lopsided red lump that was hot to the touch. If she had time, Donna would make a sling to immobilize it, but for now she had to address the issue of where they were and what their options were.

"Why are you here?" she asked the American girls.

"Well, we know these guys. We've been coming here for weeks."

"Where is here?"

"Their retreat, you know, this is where they bring in the people from the cities and give them some country experience."

Donna couldn't believe what she was hearing.

"So this is the camp on Pine Flat Road?"

"Yes."

They heard voices outside the door. Donna scooted over to the other wall, lay on her side and pretended to be sleeping.

The door opened and a slice of yellow light fell on the room. Donna heard the young Middle Eastern girl whimpering as two men yelled at her and threatened to hit her about the face. Donna could tell they wanted to know how she'd managed to get out of her restraints. The girl didn't have to act to be scared, and didn't give them an answer. They grabbed her by the elbows, lifted her up, and despite her protests, carried her out of the room.

Donna heard the distinctive beep of her watch, thankfully just after the door was closed behind the enemy. She disabled the sound and then looked at the words on her tiny screen.

Message received. ST3 en route.

She doubted no text message would ever make her so happy again as those few little words.

"Okay, we got help coming I think."

"That the special forces guys?"

Donna's hackles stood up. "Who said anything about special forces guys?"

"My dad. He built this complex, well most of it."

"Okay. So he knows you've been coming over here?"

"No. He'd be pissed. We just like to hang out, you know. They have some awesome weed. They've been really nice to us."

"You call this *nice?*"

"Up until today," the other American girl said.

"Yeah," the other one whispered, her voice fading.

"So that should tell you, what?" Donna answered. "How long have you been here?"

"Since yesterday afternoon," one of the girls said.

They were silent. Finally one of the girls spoke up. "We came over to warn them. We thought they were friends."

"Friends?"

"People don't understand them. Once they get to know them—"

"No. I don't want to hear any more of this folly," said Donna. She looked for a window and found none. The only way out of the room was the door they'd come in through.

The air was punctuated by the sounds of their young co-captive screaming. "Still think they are friends?" Donna willed her nerves to calm, but terror was looming at the edges of her mind. She knew what a full on panic attack felt like, and she was close. She needed to be able to think.

The room was some sort of storage closet. With her wristband light, she was able to see cleaning supplies and an old mop, a broken wooden chair. All of a sudden she remembered what the girl had said. "Warn them about what?"

"We wanted them to know about the Special Forces guys who came in to town asking questions. I think they put us here just to ask us some questions. They're not going to harm us, you don't think?"

"They've been holding you against your will."

"Maybe they were provoked. They almost seemed happy about what we told them."

"I'll bet. Part of that devious plan they have. You've put yourself right in the middle of extreme danger. These are bad men. This is a terrorist training camp, not a Boy Scout camp for R&R. I can't believe how stupid you were." Donna took the broom, laying it against the wall on the floor. Her fingers squeezed the wooden handle, as if there was some support there. She sat back and tried to breathe. There wasn't anything in this closet she could defend herself with, except for this broom. After a few seconds she sent another text.

4 of us here. One young girl badly beaten.

Donna's eyes began to water. Her face began to flush, her fingers swollen and stiff. Her mouth was parched. Her heartbeat nearly threw her against the wall. She wondered how long before she'd completely lose it. She had to get out. Being confined for any length of time would kill her, not to mention what the group's intentions were, and she had a pretty good guess at those, too.

Memories began to sift into her head. Those long thirty days came flooding back again and she knew it was useless to try to push them aside now. Donna began to shake. She closed her eyes and banged her head against the concrete walls of their prison, like she had done before. After awhile, she knew it would no longer hurt. The back of her head would hurt later, if she survived.

But today she couldn't knock those visions out of her head. The trauma she'd suffered, the acts of debasement she'd had to undergo were so horrible, she'd become grateful for the heavy doses of heroin they'd given her that day and the days after.

Donna watched the outline of the two girls who had been unwilling accomplices. More memories poured in, her shakes became more pronounced. All of a sudden, she was transported back there as if it was happening all over again, right here, right now. She inhaled and braced herself for what she knew was going to happen next.

She remembered on that worst day, when she'd been forced to have sex with multiple men in an endless stream of hell, she wished they'd just given her an overdose. She'd tried to fight the effects of the drug, to make them give her more. She'd sought death with everything inside her. The more she fought, the more they beat her. She fought the cattle prods, the foreign objects forced into her mouth, her vagina and her ass, defying them, seeking to draw their anger to perhaps finish her off.

That day, she crossed the threshold between life and death. It wouldn't matter what they did to her. She felt like she was dead already. There wasn't anything further they could take. She was sure they'd already taken away her womb, cut and disfigured her such that her life as a normal woman would forever be lost to her. But while they'd altered her physical appearance and capabilities of her body, they didn't change the woman she was on the inside.

At the end of that day, she'd come up with a slogan that sustained her, "Dead people feel no pain."

She'd lived through that. She could wait the time it might take for the SEALs to stage a rescue. She hoped the tipoff didn't mean the SEALs would be running right into an ambush.

Donna left one more message for her boss.

They know you're coming.

CHAPTER 35

JACKIE THREW HIS headset down on the table. "This is definitely the Sheik."

Lucas ran to find Kyle, who was on the phone. He gave his LPO a thumb's up.

"Okay, Jackie says it's him," Kyle said into the phone.

Jackie came up behind speaking over Lucas' shoulder. "The girl they are holding is from Michigan," he said in his heavily accented dialect. "I cannot make out the name, but she's been given in exchange for favors. She herself was a ransom."

Kyle relayed the information into the phone.

Lucas couldn't believe what he was hearing.

"Chief Kyle, she's only thirteen years old," Jackie added.

"Fuck me," Lucas said. "Sorry."

"No I completely agree," said the terp.

Could this mean they were getting permission to actually perform a rescue mission in the states? As far as he understood, this was the first of its kind performed by a SEAL Team on U.S. soil.

"How's Donna holding up, do you know?" Kyle was looking right at him while talking on the phone with someone from SOC.

Lucas felt like the air had been knocked out of him. Could Donna be in danger?

He ran to the poker game. "Anyone seen Donna?"

"Last I saw, she was going for a run," said Rory. "But geez, that was hours ago."

"Kyle's talking to command, and asked how she was doing."

Cooper shot up to his feet and ran to where Kyle was just finishing his call. They shared a private conversation, then Cooper departed to his room. Lucas guessed it was to retrieve his medical kit. That meant something big was happening.

Lucas began letting the other members know something was up. The faces of their team went from relaxed to stoic attention. The games were left right where they'd been played. Cards left overturned at each man's seat. The activity level began to intensify.

"Jake, we're gonna go do something. Get your shit together," he said to his roommate who was outside reading a book.

"Gotcha."

Lucas changed his clothes and put on his full camo gear even though it would be hotter than hell. He heard Kyle shout orders and they all came running to the common area.

"Okay, I've just been given the go-ahead for a mission to rescue confirmed hostages, one of whom may need serious medical attention over at the training camp."

The audience of SEALs were silent, except for some muttered cursing.

Lucas interrupted Kyle. "Excuse me, sir, but is Donna among the hostages, or do we know?"

"That's a confirmed yes. And we don't believe she's injured at this point, but we really don't know. There appear to be four."

The room erupted in every man's personal choice of profanity, so Kyle had to draw them to order.

"Listen up! We have permission to engage only if fired upon first. This is a rescue, not a search and destroy mission, and I want every man to fully understand that." Then he added, "Get your shit together and let's be on the road in thirty."

"We're driving?"

"We're borrowing Donna's two vans. I'm hoping she won't be too pissed."

Everyone grinned.

As the orders sunk in, the group got vocal, as had been their routine on deployments. Conducting a mission was what Lucas lived for. All the cares and concerns for his personal life, including Marcy and his kids, were secondary to the mission. It pained him that there was no one to call, no one to leave a message for. Before he allowed it to rot a hole in his heart, he sucked it up, took on a deep breath and started packing gear.

Kyle pulled the barn builder's card out of his pocket. "Lucas, go call him and find out where his daughter is. See if she's missing, okay?"

"Roger that."

"Hold it there, son. Get your gear together first. Then you call him. We think we already have the answer."

"Got it. So the girls we saw yesterday are still there, then?"

"That's what I want you to find out. There are at least four hostages right now. We just don't know who anyone is, except Donna. You get on the horn when you're done getting you shit."

"I'm on it."

Lucas moved down the hall, walking just outside the barracks doors and dialed the number. He got a recording.

This is Hunter Boles. I'm not available to—the phone message was interrupted by Boles' gruff voice.

"Mr. Boles, this is Special Operator Lucas Shipley. We have a situation here and wondered if you could give us some information."

"I'll do what I can." Boles sounded pissed he'd been interrupted from something and was helping out begrudgingly. "I'm a little short staffed here today, so you'll have to forgive me. Let's keep this short."

Lucas could hear another phone ringing in the background.

"That's partly what I'm calling about, sir. Do you know the whereabouts of your daughter, sir?"

The silence on the other end of the line screamed volumes.

"I have no fuckin' idea where she is. She's not at work, that's for sure. You know anything I should know?"

"When was the last time you saw her?"

"Yesterday afternoon. Just after lunch. But she's not here today. She and her girlfriend took off to run some errands yesterday, and I just figured she stayed with her friend Jenna last night. She does that all the time."

"Have you tried to call her?"

"Well, of course I have. Her phone doesn't pick up. Is she in some kind of trouble, Lucas—was it Lucas?"

"Yes, sir. We think we may have located her."

"Where?"

"Not at liberty to tell yet, but as far as we know, she's not injured and she went of her own will."

"What the hell's that supposed to mean? You mean like she wasn't kidnapped or something? That what you're sayin'?"

"In essence, yes. We'll let you know as soon as we have anything further."

"So if I was going to go look for my daughter, give me a guess where I should start."

"Does she often stay out of communication this long, sir?"

"No."

Lucas knew he couldn't reveal anything to the girl's father. "Her phone's probably dead. When we can, we'll have her contact you. Keep the phone by your side, okay?"

"Will do."

Lucas was going to hang up when he heard Boles ask him another question he didn't want to answer.

"Should I be wearing a gun?"

Lucas decided to give the man something to do. "I'd say stay armed until we find her. Now, if you'll excuse me—"

"Wait, wait, where is my daughter? You gotta tell me!"

"I promise to let you know just as soon as we confirm a few things."

When Lucas returned to Kyle, he shook his head.

"She didn't come home. He hasn't seen her since yesterday after lunch."

"That's what I was afraid of. Hey, thanks, Lucas. You packed?"

"Yup."

"Okay, see you out front in a couple."

"Chief? Can I ask a question?"

"Shoot."

"So are other places, like San Diego—are they experiencing this type of behavior too? I mean, how safe is it near one of these camps?"

"Right now I think your girl, the girl you broke up with, is safe, Shipley. We don't have any intel this is going on in any coordinated effort. We just know they're up to something. But as far as I know, no one else has experienced a hostage situation."

"Except there is that girl Jackie says was from Michigan."

"And that's a different story. Unfortunately, that was cultural blackmail. Any way you slice it, we gotta rescue those ladies quickly. We can't wait for a terrorism task force to get assembled."

"Thanks."

But Lucas decided he would have to swallow his pride, and as soon as they were back from whatever mission this was, he was going to find Marcy, apologize for being a complete dickwad.

CHAPTER 36

I T WASN'T THE nakedness that bothered Marcy, it was the fact that she'd been injected with so much heroin she could hardly think.

The "boys" in the compound were getting bolder, showing their disgust of her, which of course she did in return. She felt like a piece of meat in their eyes. She was a plaything for amusement, similar to what a person would do if they were going to torture an animal. But she knew the longer she held out, the better chance she had of survival. She had no illusions the wait would be in any way pleasant.

Thinking about these men, she understood a little more where Lucas went on deployments, mentally. There was evil in the world. She'd seen her share of wicked people, but pure evil—until now—she'd never been exposed to it. If the world knew what she knew, what Lucas and his brothers knew, they'd spend less time being politically correct trying to run a gentlemen's war and more time seeking results. She knew that she was the least of those being tortured, held captive just for believing what they believed, for being an American, for having a lifestyle worthy of the envy of the whole rest of the world.

Lucas was part of that line of defense of the Homeland. And he was paying the price for it. He did and always would come to the aid of his brothers in arms, even though it would look like he was abandoning his wife and children. He had to have that singleness of focus. She understood that now more than anything.

How ironic, she thought, that now, after they'd broken up at her call, not his, that she should figure that out. She was grateful for what he had to do. She understood now what he needed in life: a woman to help him heal, bring him back, not make him jump through a bunch of hoops of her own selfish choosing. She also understood how Connie felt, but she was sure the woman had her own set of issues that warped her worldview and made it impossible for her to be the support he needed. Being totally honest with herself, Marcy wasn't sure she had it in her either. But she knew she'd feel like a complete heel if she didn't at least try. She owed the man an apology.

She closed her eyes and pretended to be asleep when she heard footsteps at the door.

The familiar voice of her oldest captor spoke in broken English. "You are awake I think. Time to prepare you for your new life as the vessel of our pleasure."

"I'm not the vessel of your pleasure, or anyone's pleasure. I'm a woman whose freedom has been taken from her, but who still has her dignity left. Nothing will ever make me a vessel."

He smiled and patted her arm. "We'll see about that." He pulled back the blanket and peered down at her naked body. "I can help you with a shower, if you like. Would you prefer to wash up before we get started?"

Marcy calculated what she'd have to give up for the chance to have her wounds cleaned and decided the most important part of her current survival plan was her health. She attempted to sit up and found she had been bound about the waist, to the rolling hospital cart. Her arms felt heavy and though unrestrained, were useless to her. She suspected her legs would be the same as she couldn't feel her toes.

"Yes, the effects are wearing off, so I had to restrain you. That means I will have to help you to the shower."

She wished she had more choices, but needed to see what was outside the room, and she needed to get as clean as possible.

"Yes."

"Yes, what?" he asked.

"Yes, I'd like a shower."

"Very well. The boys will be pleased when they get back, that you have prepared yourself for them." He pulled back the brown blanket that stunk of him, unbuckled the large leather strap around her waist, and slipped an arm beneath her, lifting her to sitting position. She tried to lean away from him, but there was nothing to hold her up. He adjusted her balance so she didn't do a backward roll off the gurney, bringing her forward and against his chest and abdomen.

His hand softly thread through her hair while she drooled a bloody mixture down his shirt, unable to stop him. His wild scent as pungent, without cologne, smelling more of rancid oils mixed with days of sweat. Her stomach churned and she heaved, but without anything in her aching stomach, she produced nothing.

"Yes, a little nourishment, too. Would you like that?"

She didn't trust his feigned sweetness. She tried to imagine what he'd look like eviscerated, or hanging from a tree, or torn limb from limb. The violent thoughts came easily, her fear fueling her imagination. Or perhaps it was the effects of the drug he'd given her.

"Water. I need some water," she managed to mumble.

"You can drink in the shower."

He was a small man, and had difficulty getting her out to the living quarters off the storeroom, down the hallway to the bathroom. Her toes dragged on the concrete surface and she knew they were bloody with patches of skin scraped off. Again she tried to raise her elbows, and was more successful than before, but at last her strength gave way and she allowed them to flop down over his arms wrapped around her waist. As he moved her into the shower, her head bobbed back, and although she tried, she was unable to hold it upright.

He sat her on the tiled handicap bench seat, leaning her back against the cool tile wall of the shower. She looked at her bloody feet as he disrobed, slipped off his sandals and then stepped close to her.

"I have watched you shave yourself."

She tried not to react. The water began to flow ice cold, and she shuddered. "Sorry we have no hot water here, but I think you'll enjoy this anyway."

He hoisted her up, into the spray and she stiffened, found the cold sent blood pumping to her legs and for a minute, she had enough traction to fight him off. But it was short-lived. Her knees collapsed and he was once again propping her up, facing into the spray. She opened her mouth and drank the cool water. It smelled of sulfur and rust. The drain and shower floor was light orange.

Marcy felt tingling in her extremities and allowed her heart a moment's triumph. It did feel good to get the sweat and remaining vomit from last night off her. It felt invigorating to have a drink of water. When he positioned her back onto the wooden bench seat in the corner she looked at his face for the first time that morning.

Though the young man smiled, his eyes were hard and did not smile. The covetous stares seemed to inflame something inside him that did not appear human. She could see how mad he truly was. He was living in a bonfire of hell, and it was of his own choosing.

She slumped forward involuntarily, and he pushed her back again as her head lolled forward.

Her eyes were focused on the tiled floor, fixated on something that was blurry at first. As her eyes came into focus, she saw a bottle with a large plastic pump spout in the corner. He bent and squeezed some of the clear gel into his palm, rubbed his hands together making a lather and began to rub his palms over her now-slippery flesh at the shoulders and then on to her breasts. She couldn't react as he squeezed her flesh, as he pinched her nipples. Her eyes continued to focus on the shower gel in the corner.

Slowly he lathered her arms, her belly, her thighs and legs, kneeling like a servant in front of her. Though she didn't show it, her spine became rigid. She could push her feet against the floor of the shower, felt the cool water and for the first time, she was able to squeeze her fingers into a fist.

Staring at the bottle still, she pushed herself forward over his shoulder, draping her body over him, and then allowed herself to topple, sliding down to the floor. He was frantically trying to right her, but with her slippery skin not giving traction, was unable to lift her up to set her back down on the bench. Her right hand reached for the shower gel and she watched as she tried to hold it one-handed, which would have been impossible even without the drugs, and the bottle tipped, scooting out of reach. She released the support from her legs and she collapsed to the floor under the stream, her back curved against the wall, her feet pushing against the wall perpendicular to it.

Her captor began to say things she didn't understand. But he was unhappy and getting more agitated by the minute.

Bending over her, he managed to get his arms around her lower back and tried to pull her up, but Marcy resisted, feigning lack of control. She rotated to her upper torso, to her back, looking up to him. His feet were slipping on the slick shower surface. He was focused on his arms, and when he squeezed his eyes shut to pull her limp body up, Marcy put both palms around the shower gel bottle and with all her might, forced the spout into his neck just below his chin. Even after the spout entered his skin, she pushed, feeling the delicious crunch of cartilage that was his windpipe.

Her captor screamed. The spray from his blood covered the walls and poured over her, coating her with the deep red of his precious fluids, momentarily blinding her. She pushed with her legs and managed to head butt the man out of the shower, where he fell onto the bathroom floor, still struggling to get the spout from his neck. His legs frantically bicycle-kicked as he tried to find something else to push against. He was trying to get air. His gurgling screams got less intense. His almond-shaped eyes stared back at her in panic, and she realized the same time he did that she had just successfully inflicted a mortal wound.

His struggle was over. A light bloody spittle leaked from the right side of his mouth. With brown eyes fixated on her, she saw the moment when life left his body. She continued to lay on her belly, gasping for air, the water sluicing over her backside and upper thighs, sending her ribbons of calm and bursts of hope. She didn't know how she was going to function against the men who would be coming back, but she knew she couldn't wait around to find out. Somehow, she had to get out of the cabin and to some place safe. Some place that had tools and sharp objects she could use to defend herself.

Carefully she sat up. Her legs were coming back to near full strength, the activity in the shower and adrenalin pumping through her veins apparently aiding this process. Marcy grasped the wooden slats on the bench and because it was bolted to the side, supported herself as she stood for the first time. She placed her palms on the tile, pushing until she was balanced and was standing on her own without aid.

Each movement was slow motion for her. She allowed the water to wash off all the blood, rinsed her mouth, taking more drinks of the precious liquid, and emerged, trying to avoid the growing pool of blood forming from the gash in her captor's neck.

Using the doorway as a brace, she stepped out and into the hallway she knew led to the living quarters.

Her own clothes were left on the floor in the storage closet where they'd been discarded next to her purse. Though they were dirty, she welcomed something familiar, something that smelled like freedom, grateful for shoes she would need to run through the forest to find help. Pawing through her purse, she found her cell phone and anxiously checked for service.

Her stomach leapt as she realized the battery was dead. She placed the phone back in her purse, slung it over her shoulder, picking up a couple of bananas and a half-full bottle of water and exited the dwelling.

Outside, she heard Middle Eastern music pumped loud, echoing throughout the long building on her right. She was grateful for this. Whomever was inside, then, could not have heard the screams of her captor. She bent her knees, crouching, and slipped into the edge of the forest. Once protected by the cover of greenery, she began to run. She knew right where she was going to go.

CHAPTER 37

LUCAS HELPED COOP bring the drone cases. Kyle had Fredo continue to monitor with SOC, so he could lead the team. They all had their specialties. Armando was their best shooter. Coop was their medic with the most deployments with SEAL Team 3, but if he was working the drone, T.J. would take over in that department, with nearly the same experience.

Lucas was also trained at the Army course at Ft. Bragg, certified by the SEAL instructors there. He was also their second sniper. Fredo was their communications and explosives expert and had lovingly said to Lucas one time when they were relaxing, "If they don't want to talk, I send a little fire their way. And guess what? They talk!"

As a unit, everyone was trained for one specialty, but cross trained to be able to work in more than three others, if need be. Lucas breathed slowly and deep to calm his nerves. He was put up on the ridge out of sight, but nearly fifty yards from Armando. Fredo was next to Armando working the comm. Coop was over on Lucas' side, getting his drone out, clicking the wings into place. With a flick of the switch they heard the soft whir of the drone's belly. The small tablet screen lit up as the drone was readied for it's mission.

Coop searched his spot, searched the sky and then leaned over to Lucas. "Eyes for their birds, Lucas. I got interference, I need to know."

"Roger that, Coop," said Lucas.

Cooper stood, leaned back, clutching the drone in his right hand, then propelled it forward and let it go. At first the white bird swooped down, then was corrected to stay high until Coop got her tracked. With a thumbs up to Fredo, Kyle was told, "Eyes in the air, Kyle. Good to go."

Jake and Tyler had disabled the sentries when they first took up their positions. The sentries were bound, gagged and tied and wouldn't wake up for several hours. They now joined the plateau where Lucas and Coop were perched.

With his high-powered scope, Lucas followed the two teams below, who separated, coming from different directions. Two SEALs were left near the entrance to disable the guard shack after their breech was discovered. Everyone else was going to go through the holes they were cutting in the fencing material. One breech was behind the long warehouse, the other was in the area of the camp's vehicle storage, well masked behind a fleet of white vans.

Their Invisios clicked to life. "On three, two, one, go!" Kyle's voice commanded.

The front gate exploded, the doors bursting wide open. Small explosive devices and smoke bombs were tossed into the long warehouse, starting a fire as chemicals began igniting, ending in plumes of flame nearly fifty feet high. Several earth-shaking explosions took out the side of the metal building, sending burning debris and pieces of twisted metal all over the area. The thick black smoke nearly made it impossible to see.

The team near where the hostages were was taking on fire. Armando picked off three combatants within seconds, sending others, who had ventured out into retreat. Lucas followed as several of them hid behind a storage tank of some kind. Lucas' one well-placed round caused the tank to explode in a hail of fire. Tires on several of the vehicles began to burn.

He studied the area where they knew the girls had gone yesterday and saw the front door to the structure open slowly. One gunman had the girl with a forearm across her throat, a pistol aimed at her temple. The sheik, whose robes were bloodied, walked behind one of the local girls. Lucas recognized her as the daughter of the contractor.

Armando was shifting position, adjusting his range, checking the wind and then, as the young girl stumbled in front of the gunman, took his shot. The blonde girl and the Sheik behind her were covered in the spray from the man's exploded head. The Sheik was armed with a small automatic and as he pointed it in the direction of the screaming young girl, Lucas took the shot Armando wouldn't be able to make and the tall man dropped to his knees first before one of the SEALs did the double tap to his head.

Having lost the two leaders, the rest of the group dropped their weapons.

Fredo was giving out information. The SEALs pushed the captives to the ground on their faces.

Lucas had only seen two hostages, but both appeared to be out of danger, for now. He spoke to Kyle in his headset. "Where are the other two?"

"We got 'em. Donna's okay."

Lucas breathed a sigh of relief. Something about Donna told him it was important she didn't have to stay overnight in the camp.

THEY UNLOADED THE girls over at the dorms where the soccer team was staying. Coop worked on the girl from Michigan while Donna sat by her side, holding her hand, speaking to her in broken Pashtu. Donna herself had a pretty good-sized bump on her forehead, but was completely focused on the girl.

She nodded up to Lucas and smiled her thanks.

The blonde girls were brought food and drinks by the soccer girls, allowed to shower and were given changes of clean clothes. Jenna called her dad, who was on his way over. Sheriff and fire crews were on their way to relieve the SEALs who had stayed behind with the prisoners.

"I think she's gonna be good to go here," Coop said. "See if you can get me an ambulance, Lucas."

"Sure thing. What about Donna?"

"I'm staying with her. I'm fine. But let's get her to the hospital," Donna answered.

Lucas ran the hundred yards to their buildings and sent an EMT crew over to the ladies dorm.

DECOMPRESSION WAS A bitch, Lucas thought. Easier to stay pumped up, but when you went through a firefight, and usually they were short and sweet, like this one, it took awhile for the adrenalin to subside. Everyone retreated to their own brand of recovery while their bodies adjusted. The mission was a success, but wasn't really cause to celebrate. This was, after all, an operation on U.S. soil. They had gotten all the way over here, had set up a camp—hell, had set up multiple camps—and nearly pulled off a tragic loss of American life. It was all handled small, which was their way of saying it caused as little disruption as possible.

When his cell chirped, Lucas jumped, having forgotten he even owned one. It was Nick. That's when he realized there were two other calls from Nick as well.

"Hey, what's up, Nick?"

"Man, you're not going to want to hear this, but we just got a call from Marcy. Devon and I were sick with worry when she didn't come home last night."

"What do you mean? Marcy's in San Diego."

"No, she's not. She's up in Sonoma County. She left yesterday to go look for a place to stay—"

Fuck me. I've messed up again.

"—escaped, she thinks she killed one of them. We've called the cops."

"Where, Nick?"

"Cloverdale, man. She's at your cabin."

"What the fuck?"

"There's one of those groups up there. She escaped, but she's all alone in the cabin waiting for the cops. Just wanted you to know."

Lucas searched his memory

Immediately Lucas' heart began to race. He had to find Kyle. Somehow he was going to have to get to her, even though he was clear across the country. He knew he was probably too late, but nothing in the world would be able to keep him away. He just hoped the Navy would understand.

CHAPTER 38

M ARCY WATCHED AS the bars went back down to zero on her phone. She knew Nick would send the police. She knew she'd feel more relaxed when her cell had enough power to be in permanent communication.

She looked through the windows, searching for evidence the camp members were coming after her, and wondered if they even knew about this place. She'd broken the bedroom window, the same one that had been used for the thieves—and then it hit her. They *did* know about the house, because they were here!

The remaining captors were all young, and she doubted they would have done the damage to the place without their leader, so perhaps she was safe. Maybe they had outside help. Maybe they'd be blinded by revenge. Every bird, every sound coming from the forest put her at edge.

Lucas told her earlier that there were no guns stored in the cabin. So that meant she was going to have to improvise. Other than knives in the kitchen, she couldn't find anything else that would work as a weapon. She did have a broom handle that looked solid. She picked up pieces of glass stuffing two of them into her pockets where she could safely hide them until needed.

Nick told her he'd be right there, but Cloverdale was nearly an hour from their home in Bennett Valley. She just had to get through the next hour, or however long it took for the police to arrive. She hoped they'd not get lost.

Her eyes wandered over the cabin where she'd spent a beautiful two days. She could smell him. When she closed her eyes, she saw what he looked like when he talked to her, the angle of his head, the way he smiled, what the touch of his kiss on her lips felt like. So many little things came racing through the fog of fear.

She prayed she'd have the chance to tell him all this.

It startled her when her cell phone rang.

Lucas!

"Is that really you?" Her heart was pounding, and surely he would be able to hear her ragged breathing.

"Absolutely, baby. Are you hurt?"

"I'm okay."

"But did they hurt you?"

"No. Big goose egg on my forehead."

"God, Marcy, I've been a total and complete fool."

"Where are you, Lucas? I'm all alone here and—"

"Nick called me. We just finished up an operation and I'm coming to California right now as we speak. Waiting for the transport. Won't get there for a few hours. Nick says the police are on their way."

"Good."

"You have battery on the cell phone?"

"It was dead, charging it now."

"Okay, nothing to do but hang tight. Let's hope they decide to bale instead of coming to the house."

"What do I do if—" Marcy saw three of the young boys come out into the clearing at the kitchen side of the house. "They're here!"

She heard Lucas swear on the other end. "Get a knife. Hide in the bedroom closet. There's a hatch there in the floor of the closet. See if you can get yourself in there before they come. Leave the phone on, but try to hide it."

"Right. Bye." She placed the device on top of the refrigerator where only part of the cord showed at the attachment to the plug in the splashboard.

Marcy wanted to say more, much more, but she knew they'd find the broken window and she didn't have much time to get herself hidden.

The closet floor was covered with empty bags and a suitcase. She brushed them aside and found the ring of the hatch, pulled it toward her and saw the dirt beneath the cabin floorboards. Carefully, she pulled the closet door closed, and tried to distribute the bags so they would fall over the hatch opening, perhaps giving her more time. She was small enough to slip down through the square hole and then touched the ground, stopping to listen.

Chatter from the young men trickled down to her from on top as she heard them climb through the window and begin searching the house.

She wondered why Lucas had asked her to leave her phone on, but she guessed he wanted to listen to whatever was going on, since he couldn't be there.

Fingering the glass chard in her left hand and the serrated knife in her right, she sat on the cool dirt and waited without making a sound. Her stomach growled so much for a second she wondered if they'd be able to hear it. She wished she had the water she'd left on the counter, or the bananas she'd brought from her escape. No doubt the boys would find them and realize she was near.

Orders were being given between the men. They removed themselves from the place the way they'd entered, and soon all was quiet.

Except for the crackling she could hear. Then she could smell it.

They'd set fire to the house.

CHAPTER 39

LUCAS HEARD THE unmistakable sounds of fire raging through the cabin. Already at thirty thousand feet, there wasn't a thing he could do, except text to Nick and Devon and let them know. He'd lost connection to Marcy' cell. He hoped she'd be able to get out before the smoke got to her, as this was more of a threat than the fire itself.

Lost contact with Marcy. House on fire.

Holy shit. I'll call the PD. They should be there by now. You in the air?

Yes. Taking direct to SF. Renting a car.

Hold it, let us pick you up.

If you can, sure would appreciate it.

Okay BRB.

Lucas was crammed into the oversold airplane, but because he was active military went to the head of the standby list. He texted Kyle to let him know he was on board. Kyle let him know the soccer team was leaving and Donna still wouldn't leave Alfari's side.

Good. I think she needs it, Lucas texted him back.

Thinking the same.

He decided not to add any further worry onto his LPO's shoulders, so didn't tell him about the fire.

He relaxed the seat back and pulled his baseball cap down over his eyes, and attempted some sleep. No telling what he would be doing later. He'd be no good to anyone if he was exhausted.

An hour into his rest the phone pinged with a message from Nick.

Fire out. No sign of Marcy or the others. Will update if any news.

Lucas managed to sleep the whole rest of the flight. The stewardess tapped him on the shoulder and asked him to reset the seat to its upright position. He barely had enough time before the wheels hit the pavement, in a landing far from smooth, the big plane swerving and rocking as if driven by a fighter pilot landing on a carrier. He checked his phone as they taxied to the gate and there were no further texts. His stomach turned over. When he mentally counted the hours since he'd last eaten, he discovered it had been nearly twelve.

He followed the line off the plane, his legs and neck stiff from sitting in one position for so long, but all the same, he was grateful for the shut-eye. Now he needed to find Marcy. He was hoping Nick had something he could go on.

Nick was waiting by baggage claim, but since all Lucas had was his carry-on, they made it out to the curb just in time for Devon to slip by and pick them up. The two men sat in the back seat of Nick and Devon's Land Cruiser.

"Not going to lie to you, Lucas. The cops in Cloverdale and the Sheriff's Department have an ongoing battle over the hearts and minds of the town, with the public pretty much split. So anything that is slightly controversial, you can bet there's a fair amount of finger pointing."

"Okay. I'm sort of used to that, on a much grander scale," Lucas answered back. "Shit, we never know who to trust, so we don't trust anyone."

"That would probably work well in this case, too."

Devon made a quick swerve to avoid a small car with blackened windows from hitting them. They had merged onto the freeway and took the overpass headed to 280 North.

"You okay, honey?" Nick asked as he leaned forward and put his hand on her shoulder.

"I'm fine. That asshole just doesn't know how to drive is all."

Lucas knew she was hauling ass to get them up to Sonoma County as soon as possible, while they had some chance to do some searching in the woods. But he wanted to get there without an incident, and he could tell Devon wasn't used to driving fast.

"So you were saying there's a pissing match going on. Is anybody focused on finding Marcy?"

"Oh yes, nothing like a murder to get the community all worked up. You know Cloverdale is a small town. That's part of the problem. Everyone knows everyone else's business."

"Right now, I'm thinking that's a good thing," said Lucas.

"See, I made the mistake of calling the Cloverdale P.D. But your cabin is in the County, Sheriff's jurisdiction."

"So who did you tell about the trap door?"

"I told the Cloverdale P.D."

"Okay. So who's taking lead here on the search?"

"That's what gets kind of interesting. We got some worried about stumbling onto a pot farm and getting shot."

"Shit. We got terrorists with a training camp and they're worried about pot?"

"Nope. They're not worried about the pot. They're worried about the gangs who guard the pot."

Lucas checked the passing lights as they swung their way onto the five-lane 280 Freeway. There was practically no traffic. He tried to think about where she would go. Could she have gotten herself safely out of the house and was hiding in the forest? Or, did they capture her as she was forced out, take her some place else? Marcy had told him about the neighbor and the young boys. Lucas didn't think they even knew how to drive.

"Someone's helping them. We just have to find out who that is," said Lucas. "The one in Tennessee? They had a whole house filled with paper money. Floor to ceiling. They've been making so much money selling drugs, they have plenty to buy political favors. They did it in Nashville. Those guys run the prison there. They could do far worse in a little town of less than ten thousand people, no problem."

During the two-hour drive, Lucas and Nick discussed all the scenarios they could think of. If Marcy was on her own, it would only be a matter of time before she'd find a way to contact one of them. Eventually, she would. If she could stay hidden.

But if she was being held by yet another group, or worse, being transported to one of the larger training camps up in Oregon, they were screwed. That would involve a plan taking up hundreds of man hours and probably the FBI, just like when they had a large scale drug bust. The jurisdictions fell all over themselves for the percentage rights to the drug spoilage, but they had to play nice with the Bureau.

Lucas wasn't prepared for the site of his little piece of Heaven, looking more like a burned out building in Bagdad or Mosul. Smoke still filtered up to the darkening sky. Perimeter lights had been set up, juiced to one large engine unit from downtown Cloverdale. Blue and red lights flashed, the vehicles fanning out like at a drive-in movie. Lucas walked like a zombie through all the noise of the radios, the generator and sound of the water pumps occasionally kicking in as a four man crew continued looking for hot spots.

The fire investigator introduced himself. He was one of the only men who wore a yellow jacket, but did not wear a hat.

"How did it start?" Lucas asked.

"They found something as an accelerant. I think you had lighter fluid or cleaning supplies under the sink, like most people? We think they poured it, ignited it and left."

"Can I?" Lucas asked, pointing the charred spines of the once-beautiful cabin.

"Sure, just walk the perimeter. There are still hot spots inside, so don't step there."

"No problem." Lucas and Nick began walking around the edge of the debris field.

"We cut the power of course. Your propane tank exploded," the inspector said as he followed behind them pointing out the highlights of the destruction, like he was giving them a tour of an art gallery. "Any idea why someone would want to torch this place?"

"No clue," Lucas answered him. "But it was broken into and vandalized not more than a week ago. Kind of a teenage thrill thing, we thought at the time. This goes along those same lines."

"What did they take?"

"As far as we can tell, nothing."

"I'm told you never met these people?" the inspector asked Lucas.

"That's right."

"The woman who is missing, Marcy Gelland, saw them," offered Nick. I did see the break in, helped with the cleanup, and Lucas is right, it did look more like some kids having fun at his family's expense."

"And what makes you think it was kids, like the kids from next door?"

"Because they shredded some girlie magazines, right, Nick?" Lucas turned to Nick, who confirmed it.

"They peed on them, too."

"So all they did was destroy? They didn't take anything?"

"Not a damned thing." Lucas made his way over to here the bedroom closet would have been, swiped the charred detritus to the side with his shoe. The hatch cover was burned all the way through. Partially burned pieces of furniture and flooring had dropped down into the five foot space. Lucas remembered his grandfather telling him it was the safest place to hide if anything dangerous happened to them. He remembered playing in it when he was a child. It earned him a fair share of scoldings.

Lucas jumped into the space and searched the walls with his penlight flashlight. Someone had written "Boathouse." He looked up to the inspector. "There a lake with a boathouse around here?"

"Over toward the camp there's a man-made lake and I think a small shed protecting a pile of stacked canoes," answered the inspector.

"Wonder how the hell she knew about that," said Lucas. "Where is this lake?"

The inspector gave him a hand up. "If she came over from the compound next door, she would have run right past it."

"Wonder how the hell she got out while the house was burning," muttered Nick.

"I have no idea. But I hope to God she did. Let's go."

AT THE FIRE scene, Marcy had managed to scramble out through the flames, the smoke giving her cover. She hid in the scrub behind the cabin, undetected. A green van picked up the boys, who had obviously been waiting for it. The van barreled off down the road before any of the emergency vehicles arrived. The driver's door was marked with some sort of official insignia she couldn't read.

She wondered if other men were still at the complex and would soon be looking for her. She needed to make it to the boathouse so, if need be, she could wait it out until she was safe. Until someone she trusted showed up.

Seeing the coast clear, she ran as fast as she could until she got to the old red structure, pried open the locked wooden door and let herself in. She stayed in there while emergency crews were working in the distance. She wasn't going to go out there in her sooty clothes and be arrested for being an arsonist. The only people she would reveal herself to were Lucas, Nick or Devon.

None of the fire crew or investigators even came close to looking at the boathouse, so she began to feel safe. She worked to stop from falling asleep in the warm space but was having difficulty. She was tired, dirty, and her lungs were filled with soot. She desperately needed a drink of water.

Marcy scrambled out the back of the structure, stooped down, lay against the dock landing on her belly, and splashed water on her face, taking long sips of water to quench her thirst. She quietly returned to the relative safety of the wooden structure.

Finally, the number of flashing lights diminished, and several vehicles left the scene. In spite of her efforts not to, she leaned against the doors of the little structure, and fell into a deep sleep.

Hours later, she was jarred awake when she heard a noise. Through the slim crack between the doors, she saw four figures jogging straight toward her. She braced herself, waiting until they stepped into the moonlight and out of the shadow of the forest, her hand firmly gripping the knife handle. If it came to it, she'd go out fighting. She was ready for the final showdown.

CHAPTER 40

LUCAS CONSIDERED THE message might be a trap, but his heart couldn't afford to wait any longer. If something had happened to Marcy, if she was injured or being held, or worse, the sooner he could find her the better. Devon held back to the shadows, just in case, while the three men approached the door.

As he got to within twenty feet of the outside of the building the red doors burst open and Marcy came running out, jumping into his arms.

"God, you're safe, Marcy. Thank God," he whispered as he held her shaking body. He felt her break down, as sobbing overtook her.

"Shhhh, shhh. You're safe. We got you. Nothing's going to happen to you anymore." He was rocking her from side to side. Nick put his arms around both of them. Within seconds Devon was there as well.

"Are you okay? Are you hurt in any way?" Lucas asked as he set her down. He brushed the hair from her face, blackened from the fire. He noticed a patch of her hair had been singed, but other than that, she looked pretty damned good.

"I'm fine," she beamed back up to him, tears making white lines down her cheeks. "I was hoping you'd see my message." She glanced over at the inspector.

"This is—"Lucas turned to the investigator with an apology.

"Russ Butler, ma'am. I work for the Cloverdale fire district."

Marcy nodded and allowed Devon to grab her, but her eyes came back to Lucas.

"So glad you're okay. What an ordeal. You held up like a champ,

Marcy," said Devon.

The long looks Marcy was giving him as she spoke with Devon and Nick speared his heart.

"Come here," he finally said as he opened his arms. She nearly collapsed into him. She was mumbling words he couldn't make out. "It's all over, Marcy. Nothing is going to happen to you. I'm here now."

IT TOOK NEARLY an hour to finish with the Sheriff's Department. Lucas was still combing through the rubble for anything left untouched by the fire and was coming up completely empty. The house was gone, completely gone, but it had done its job and protected her from harm, just like his grandfather had instructed those many years ago. Little did he know that some day those safety instructions would save the life of the woman he loved.

He had a new appreciation for how fragile life was. He also knew that he wouldn't be able to put anything in front of his feelings for Marcy, and for her safety again. They needed to have a talk. He hoped she felt the same.

On the trip back to Bennett Valley, she leaned into him as they sat in the darkness behind Devon and Nick up front. His arm was draped around her shoulder as she snuggled into him. It had never felt so good to have someone need his protection.

His fingers traced up and down her upper arm. Marcy brought her right palm to his face as she lifted herself to look him in the eyes. "Thank you, Lucas. Thank you for everything."

"No, sweetheart. You are the hero of the day." He bent down to brush his lips against hers. "Not sure what I would have done if anything had happened to you, baby."

"You were there. You told me what to do. You gave me the courage I needed, Lucas. I would not have been able to survive without your help. I—"

He covered her mouth with his and allowed her wild scent to completely overtake him. Her lips needed him. He was trying to be gentle at first, but her need slammed up against his chest and he was soon consumed in the flames of her desire again. Her breathing became deep, their tongues mingling. He heard her faint moan which caused him to hitch his own breath.

"Sweetheart, love you, sweetheart," he whispered between kisses.

She grabbed his hand and kissed the center of his palm, then looked up at him with her twinkling brown eyes and placed his hand against her breast, and squeezed.

He chuckled. "Honey, if you don't think I'm getting the message, you're not as smart as I thought."

He knew Nick and Devon were aware of their fooling around in the back seat when he saw Devon take Nick's hand and they shared a smile.

Marcy slipped his hand under her bra and he felt the pillows of her flesh, warm and fragrant, waiting for him to enjoy. His pants were getting tight. He squirmed in the seat as she ran her fingers over the bulge in his jeans and she squeezed his package.

"We need that shower in a hurry, sweetheart," he whispered.

"I need you, Lucas. Your ass is mine until I tell you it's okay to go back to work."

"Yes, ma'am. The Navy doesn't own my body. You do."

"Glad to hear it, sailor. I have plans for you."

"I can't wait."

THEY ARRIVED AT the winery. Nick handed Lucas his backpack and winked. "Guest house is all ready for you guys. I think Devon and I are going to sleep in tomorrow," he said as Devon wrapped her arms around her husband. "Depending on when we all surface, we'll have food should you be in need of some nourishment."

"Thanks, man," Lucas said. "Thanks for everything." He gave Nick a quick hug, hugged Devon, giving her a peck on the cheek, and took Marcy's hand, squeezed it, and led her around the back to the guest house.

He could see shadows inside the main house as lights were turned off, including the bright patio light that threatened their privacy. With the crickets chirping in the background, a light cool breeze running off the rustling grapevines all around them, he placed his hand to Marcy's neck, letting his fingers lace through her hair, tilted her head back and looked down on her glowing face. Her eyes smiled back at him. "Seeing your dirty face is one of the most beautiful things I've ever seen, Marcy."

She drew her arms up around his neck. "Lucas, I need you to undress me."

"Of course," he said, thrilled. "Wouldn't want to—whoa," he said as she quickly unbuckled his belt and shoved her hands into his pants.

"I bet I get you naked before you even get started," she whispered through half-lidded eyes.

"Not a chance." But he got snagged getting her pants off. The feel of the lace of her panties against her smooth rear end put him in a trance he wanted to savor.

He kicked off his shoes and his pants fell to his ankles. He stepped out of them, kneeling in front of her as she pulled his shirt off his back from his waist up over his head.

"See, you're slow," she teased, removing her own shirt and bra, her breasts in full view.

He reached up and squeezed, watching her arch her back with the pleasure of his touch. He dropped his hands to his thighs, his erection pointing to the stars above.

"I'm going to go real slow Marcy. I'm taking my time. I'm gonna make you beg me to stop."

"Another promise you won't be able to keep. There's no way I'll ever stop. You'll have to peel me off your body a week from now."

He stood, taking her hand and leading her into the little cottage.

The room was lightly scented with a fresh vanilla aroma. She followed him to the tiled shower. After turning on the warm water, he soaped her arms and neck as she pressed her backside against the wall, watching his face as he smoothed gel all over her body. His fingers kneaded down her spine, starting just under her hairline, and one by one, working his way down to the crack in her butt. With both hands, he pressed her forward against his groin, squeezing her cheeks, lifting her as she pushed against his hardness. She raised one thigh over his hip and rubbed the lips of her sex over his cock.

She gave him a long lingering smile. "My turn."

She placed her palms on his shoulders, moving him to sit on the tiled bench seat. His fingers found her opening, but he massaged all around it as she arched back, took some gel and rubbed her palms over his chest, his neck, his shoulders, and then lower stroking his cock and squeezing his balls. She stepped aside and let the water sluice off him, and then she placed her knees on each side of the bench and lifted her lithe body up over him. In one long fluid movement, her breasts leaving a hot trail down his chest, she angled her pelvis and came down on his shaft.

She began a slow rhythm up and down, raising and lowering her body on him, writhing like his private dancer. He buried his head in her chest, bit her nipples, helped her move up and down on him by palming her butt cheeks, and supporting her body's weight. She ground down against him, kissed his temple, hugged his face to her chest, massaging his temples with her probing fingers. Into his ear she whispered, "I want you to come in my mouth."

"Yes, baby," was all he could say.

She began to lift off him, and he grabbed her hips and ground her down on him again. "Please, Lucas. I want you in my mouth," she whispered again.

This time he allowed her to slide off him as she kneeled before him on the slower floor. The water was starting to get cold, so she arched her upper torso and turned the valve off. As the steamy water dripped around them, the drain gurgling, she placed her lips at the tip of his head, running her tongue over him, sucking him gently.

He moved his pelvis forward as she fully took him in her mouth. One hand found his balls and squeezed as she swallowed all of him deep. Back and forth, her movements were long, careful, and needy. He never wanted it to end. He felt himself get harder the more she worked on him. She registered her pleasure with little whimpers, coaxing him up and down. Several strokes later, he was bursting inside her mouth as she sucked against his pulsations.

He was near completion. Her fingers formed a ring at the base of his cock and one last time she squeezed the full length of him, then sucked his tip. Rolling back on her haunches her sultry smile teased him further.

"Let's rinse off and try something else," he said to her. His fingers had already found her opening before she could stand.

He turned her around and pressed himself, still hard, into the soft valley between her butt cheeks. She turned on the water as he continued to rub against her soft flesh, stimulating him further.

He pulled her to him, spreading her cheeks, finding her opening and helping himself inside her. Marcy moaned, pressing the wall with her palms as he entered her, thrusting up deep. His thumb pressed against her clit from the front, and she jumped, spreading her knees and pushing him deeper still. He stroked in and out of her tight opening, making her little organ stiff, feeling her give way, start to let herself go.

The cold water was delicious. He bit her shoulder, the side of her neck as she melted into him, giving him full access to all of her. He felt her juices begin to flow as he pressed her clit again, holding firm while he impaled her deeper still. She stopped breathing, held her breath and then exhaled as her body began the rolling orgasm he knew had been waiting for him right at the edge.

She covered his hands with one of her own, the other against the wall, giving her traction as she helped his fingers press against her while she came.

THE FLUFFY WHITE bath sheet wrapped around both of them, hot and sticking to her thighs as they lay together in bed. Marcy was going to try to keep her promise, but more importantly, she wanted to keep up with this brave warrior. She needed to show him she had all the stamina he had, and perhaps a little more, if possible.

When she found his cock, he angled his pelvis, pressing against her, a smile affixed to his lips. The morning sunlight made the sheets whiter, and the scruffy beard on his chin and cheeks gleam golden in the new morning light.

He opened his eyes as she massaged him to a full erection. "Will it be like this every morning, Marcy?"

She nodded her head. "I promise."

He touched her cheek with his fingertips. "You happy?"

"Never happier."

Lucas inhaled, rolled on top of her, spreading her thighs with his knees. "Every morning, then," he whispered and bit her ear lobe. He kissed her ear, sending an erotic zing down her spine.

"Every morning. Night too. I'm in for it, the whole way," she heard herself say.

She was looking for some hesitation on his part, some indication she'd gone round the bend faster than he had. Was he uncomfortable with the intensity between them that had started nearly from the moment they met?

He was bending down, watching her.

"What? Something wrong, Lucas?"

"Not at all." He pressed his cock against her opening, waiting for her to make the next move.

Marcy watched his eyes change as she grabbed his cheeks and pulled him deep inside her. It began to build an intense session that left them both wrung out and gasping for air.

"I HAVE SOMETHING for you," he said when she woke up. He was sitting across the bedroom in an overstuffed chair, still deliciously naked.

"Well I thought you already brought something. And then something else, and then another one, and so on. So get over here and give it to me," she laughed back at him.

He jumped back into bed, his long warm body lying against hers. He held her hand up, kissed each finger, inserting them one by one into his mouth. When her fourth finger came out, it was wearing a ring. It was a beautiful dark ruby in an antique setting.

"Belonged to my mom. I want you to have it."

"It's beautiful, Lucas. Thank you." She kissed him, then examined the ring again.

"I asked you once, and you said yes. Marry me, Marcy. Say yes again."

"On one condition."

"Shoot."

"Ask me every day. Ask me to marry you over and over again. I promise, the answer will always be yes."

"Done deal."

"But Lucas, we still have the same problem."

"Problem? What problem?"

"You gotta get divorced first, my love."

ALEX

Band of Bachelors
Book 2

SHARON HAMILTON

CHAPTER 1

ALEX KOWICKI LIKED blind dates, *in a fucked up kind of way,* he thought to himself. It was an opinion shared by his housemates— other bachelor members of his SEAL Team. It was considered a sport, seeing who they could rig him up with and how he would escape.

"Sort of self-preservation. If we don't get you good and laid, we can't play with you," Jake told him yesterday. He was one of Alex's roommates in the now-infamous bachelor pad overlooking the bay.

"We live vicariously through you and all your sexcapades," Thomas added. The SEAL explosives expert was halfway in and out of his own house. The divorce was not quite final so there was survivor guilt and make-up sex all over the place. The men were taking bets which way it would turn out.

Alex was amped with more than his usual dose of excitement today. He was almost manic. The timing for this was good—too good. He would be leaving early Sunday morning to drive up to Sonoma County with Lucas and several others to help Nick and Devon with the winery. But there was discussion amongst the group about perhaps purchasing some land and doing an all-SEAL winery too.

This was going to be his usual Friday night blind date, which meant he could woo the little lady all night—and all day Saturday if she was spectacular. And if not, well, he could get out of Dodge and wouldn't be back for over a week. It also saved the hassle he knew girls went through waiting for a callback from him. If he was leaving, there was no expectation of a return call. The pressure was off!

He was full of expectation, as if his life was about to change forever.

They didn't tell him anything about her, except for the fact that she was tall. Really, really tall. They always said that with a smile when describing her to him, so he was prepared for a lady maybe six feet in height. He loved tall, long-legged girls who liked to wear those Jesus sandals that laced nearly up to their Holy of Holies. He was praying for the chance, just once, to be able to untie one of those types of sandals and have the tiny leather shoelace be so close to her crotch the backs of his hands would be singed from the proximate distance to her heat. An easy couple of millimeters to go, and he'd hit pay dirt. The angels would sing.

Alex was getting hard just thinking about it. When he woke up this morning with a boner, it interfered with his early skydive. Jumping out of an airplane would take the edge off his nerves, he thought, but he wasn't that lucky and nearly did a three-point landing like a tripod on the moon.

Her name was Sydney, they'd told him yesterday. He immediately asked them if she was a virgin, because that was always a game-stopper.

"Hell no," Jake had said. "You think I'd put a virgin babe in your hands, you asshole?"

"Gee, thought we were buds. What about *my* feelings?" he'd feigned a whine to one of the bachelor SEALs he cohabited with. The other SEAL wives and girlfriends used the term "domicile" in quotes. It was more a crash pad. Raunchy posters of darkly-greased women in torn T-shirts and thong panties adorned their apartment walls, conjuring up visions of writhing around on an auto body shop floor. Several days' worth of cereal bowls and coffee mugs waited until the number of their cousins in the cabinet diminished to zero before being allowed a proper bath in detergent, meanwhile hosting a variety of life forms with white or dark green fuzzy outlines. The smell of sweat was always present, like the elixir of life it was. It was the way they measured the worth of everything: the more sweat, the better it was for all concerned.

"Your hurt feelings? You'll heal, Alex. And if you don't, who the fuck cares?"

Well, true enough.

The fact that this blind date made Alex super excited didn't bode well for the encounter. Usually when they seemed too good to be true, they were. Disaster could be looming right around the corner. He didn't doubt he would let himself go all double-SEAL on her, make it difficult for her to walk afterwards, which was the kind of fun he was, quite frankly, hoping for. He chalked up his reservations to age. Still, at nearly thirty, he was one of the old guys on the Team. Old in terms of tours as well as marriages. Only one of those marriages counted legally, but that one was bad enough.

He wasn't about to do what his friend Lucas had done—gotten himself tied up with a hottie before the divorce papers were signed. It would have been way smarter, not to mention way less of a negative adventure on Lucas's kids and everyone else on the Team, if he could have parted with Connie before he started round two. Alex had been smart enough not to make that mistake at least. But it had been said before, some SEALs feared being alone. Alex knew Lucas was one of those. He wondered if he might be the same.

Alex had gotten seriously in lust with Brandy, the buxom waitress at the Pink Bunny bar in Coronado, who gave head he was ashamed to admit he loved better than sex. So he and Ryan had married their ladies in a double wedding ceremony presided over by Elvis one evening in Vegas. He barely remembered that night, each SEAL drawing energy off the other in what could only be seen as a mercy mission to the Love Boat of Eternal Bliss. Oddly enough, that was the name of the chapel: Eternal Bliss. He'd told Ryan it sounded more like a funeral parlor. In a way, it was.

His marriage lasted three months, but his boners hadn't stopped every time he thought about Brandy. Her attractive smile was not her best feature and was often overlooked by the SEALs Alex hung around with. She also lacked domestic ability, except in the bedroom.

Brandy didn't get pregnant like Ryan's wife did, yet Alex knew he was the lucky one. Not that he would have minded being permanently connected to Brandy no matter what she wound up doing with her life.

He loved kids and knew one day he'd make one hell of a father. He wasn't littering the globe with children like Jake had done. But having a couple little Alex urchins, well, it was something he'd like to do. Not now, of course.

Women think this way.

He was one of those guys who would love the kids and put up with the wife.

The last date had been with a personal trainer and martial arts expert. But she'd neglected to tell him she frequented the bondage bars in San Diego and was into women as much as she was men, especially women who liked to get tied up. He should have known better when she actually dug the posters and promised him she'd give him some of her personal collection to enhance his room. She didn't have room for them at her own place.

Alex's sister was a nun, which he took as a sign God was watching out for his mother after all the crap he'd put her through growing up. But that still left one unresolved score to settle: there were no grandkids. Talk about not caring who he married! She just wanted grandkids around, and heck, she'd even raise them if he'd let her.

"Don't have to fall in love. Just find someone who will raise your spawn, and I'll do all the rest."

Good old Mom. She'd even picked up on Alex's language, much to the horror of Joanne, his sister. Alex nicknamed his sister *Joan* after the famous one. And, of all things, *Joan* was a pacifist. Only good thing about that was there was little chance any of his Team buds would ever get their hands on her. One less woman to defend, and that was indeed a very good thing.

Alex showered and began to shave, then considered going with the stubble for the bad boy look he liked. His dark features against his naturally pale skin made him resemble a vampire or evil dark angel of the underworld, he thought. He could look like a choirboy one minute, and the next, he swore his eyes glowed red, judging from the reaction he occasionally got.

When he arrived at the Rusty Scupper for fortification before meeting Sydney, he expected some of his SEAL buddies to have brought their wives or girlfriends too. But no, as Alex sauntered in and took his seat amongst the clean-shaven group, he picked up he was to be the evening's entertainment.

Whistles filled the room. Jake started with the evening's insults and smack talk. "Look at you all duded out. You look like a college kid."

"Alex, you going for a job interview or something?" joked Thomas.

"A funeral. It's gotta be a funeral," Carter added.

"Shut the fuck up." Alex studied the small group in front of him. "Hey, I thought this was to be a coed, group thing," he scowled at Jake, Thomas, Jones, and Carter.

"Still could be, if you want," Carter quipped. Alex narrowed his eyes suspiciously at the African-American SEAL's offhand behavior and the way he sought out grins from the other bachelor Team members.

After the chuckles died down, Alex barked like he was giving his LPO's orders. "So I want to see a show of hands who's met her."

Only Jake raised his hand. "But only from afar."

Alex grabbed his chin at the perfect angle, cracking his neck so loud that one of the patrons at the bar whipped around on his stool. Though Alex's neck felt better, his spine was stiff, his butt cheeks were tight, and the backs of his thighs locked up. He had to take a pee.

"Jake, you keep her company if she arrives early while I go pee, will ya?" He wanted to sound casual, but knew he failed when the little conference guffawed behind him.

The bathroom was plastered with Polaroid pictures of vehicles and brothers-in-arms, some with faces cut out. One had been varnished into the wall because the picture had been stolen so many times. There was the meek-looking Saddam Hussein in handcuffs and orange jump suit, his hair going in all directions like a homeless man's. It had been taken soon after being captured and before his execution. It existed so no one got it wrong what this place was, who frequented it, or who the real heroes were. Alex wondered how many other men gave this picture the three-finger salute every time they pulled their dick out to pee like he was doing now.

Returning to the table of SEALs from Team 3, he took up a seat next to Jake.

"So tell me about her."

"We were coming in from a swim and found her on the beach," said Jake.

"You and who?"

"None of these guys. They'd give you way more than I'm going to if they'd met her, trust me," Jake said, pointing at the other faces at the table. "I was with Coop, Kyle, Danny and Zak. Not an official swim. Working with Zak, you know?"

They didn't laugh this time. Everyone was pulling for Zak, who had lost an eye from an assassin's ricocheted round and was working hard to make a place back on Team 3. Alex had been injured in the same attack, but his were only scars. Zak had lost much more. Again, Alex was feeling lucky.

"So what's wrong with her?" Alex inquired.

Jake leaned back and gave him the Cheshire Cat grin of the century, showing off his pearly whites, his blue eyes sparkling in the low light. When Jake slapped Alex on the back, he nearly dropped his beer.

"Not a damned thing, my man. Not a fuckin' damned thing."

Alex was hard all of a sudden. Last weekend had become a long time ago for his usually nightly booty worship exercise. He looked from Carter to Jones, then around to Thomas and back at Jake. "You're full of shit."

The whoops and hollers began in earnest. Alex let their voices fade as he tended to the burgeoning in his pants. He talked to himself like an older brother. *Don't get your hopes up. Remember, one man's babe is another man's nightmare. You're leaving the day after tomorrow to go up to Sonoma County, and you'll never see this girl again for the rest of your life.*

It was the ideal set up for a casual and nearly anonymous date.

But something was wrong. Something was grossly different, like he was being led with golden chains to some kind of hot female house of pain. It scared him, but it also excited him more than he wanted to admit. Jake's words—*Not a fuckin' thing*—crawled around his brain like a black cat in heat. The rest of his beer was gone. He ordered another. His ears buzzed as the happy banter flew back and forth. The legendary smack talk they all did made muffled, unintelligible background noise.

He tapped his lace-up, lightweight Oxfords. His normal cargo pants and canvas slip-ons were back at the apartment. Today, he wore his faded Levis and a long-sleeved shirt.

Holy fuck.

His button down shirt was yellow! Now, what kind of a message was he sending the guys and the lady he was about to meet?

Better than a fuckin' pink shirt.

He sat back, closed his eyes, and raised his forehead to the ceiling, composing himself like when he used to pray. As he settled his jaw and made a small adjustment to his shoulders, he opened his eyes.

For a second, he could have sworn Coop's six-foot-four frame had blocked the sunlight at the entrance to the Scupper, like he'd seen a hundred times. But as he looked closer at the shape, he noticed a slim waist, curvy thighs, and a gait that was nothing like their tall medic, Calvin "Coop" Cooper. She nearly had to duck to get through the doorway, which meant she was no six-foot lady.

She was probably *taller* than Coop.

She headed right for him as if she'd known him her whole life, like she was following a tractor beam to the Death Star. He'd seen girls with radar for SEALs. This one was honed and toned and on a mission. Her shirt must have been made for an eight-year-old, but her forty-something at least D bra size was bulging for release. He clearly saw ten inches of tanned midriff, and it was all muscle.

As he remembered himself and brought his body to stand, he noticed she wore sandals with leather straps crisscrossing up her shapely calves, over her knees, and disappearing under her incredibly short jeans skirt.

He was weaving. The snickering at the table brought him to attention, and he stood erect, in every way he was capable. She looked right at his crotch and smiled.

"You must be Alex."

"You must be Sydney."

"I am." Her voice was husky and sultry. Alex's usual casual demeanor and smooth-as-glass countenance under pressure evaporated. "Been waiting to meet you all day, Alex."

He knew if he shook her hand it would be the end of something. Maybe his dignity.

He did it anyway.

CHAPTER 2

S YDNEY LIKED THE feel of the SEAL's hands. She also felt the adrenaline pulsing through his veins. He was good at control, which she liked as well. His hands were callused, verifying he was indeed a SEAL and not a poser. She even liked the fact that his voice broke when he spoke to her for the first time.

Alex looked good, really good.

The country music at the bar and the low-level sports channels on the three big screen TVs overhead, the occasional laughter and male banter faded into background noise. She could have been standing in the middle of a men's locker room. The view was that nice.

She slipped her hand from his as he held on just a tad longer than he probably meant to. Scanning the table, they had not made room for her, so she looked up, and before she could ask the question, Alex offered her the head of the table, standing behind her chair.

"A gentleman," she purred so softly she wasn't sure he could hear her, and took a seat. His hands gripped her shoulders briefly before he took his place perpendicular. "Hi, fellas," she waved to the table and got muffled acknowledgements back. "So Alex, this is a group thing, then?" She knew it wasn't, but couldn't resist the poke at his expense.

One of his friends was laughing. At Alex. She didn't take it as a sign of any disrespect to her. Alex sported a bashful grin and was nodding.

Did that mean she'd passed the test? She'd spent the whole afternoon getting waxed every place she could and getting her nails done in a white French manicure which matched her toes. They nearly glowed in the low light of the famous hangout.

She saw the pictures of young handsome men plastered over the walls above the liquor bottles, beneath the TVs. "Our Heroes" was hand written on a white sign that she'd seen over the years growing up in San Diego, when she and her high school girlfriends used to try to stop by and pick up a SEAL. They'd always gotten kicked out.

This time, they surrounded her.

Alex asked her what she wanted to drink, got the waitress' eye, and ordered her Merlot. "I'd share one with you, but I prefer beer."

"No problem. To each his own," she assured him. The chocolate brown of Alex's eyes and his dark hair made him look boyish and younger than he surely was. She'd been concerned she'd be older than him, but as she studied him she began to relax.

After she received her wine glass, they toasted the beer and the Merlot. "Here's to blind dates and…" Alex stumbled for what to say.

"How about just blind dates so we don't get ahead of ourselves?" she whispered.

When he smiled, she found the dimple at the right side of his full lips intoxicating. Her fingers itched to smooth over his jawline and feel the beginning stubble growing there already.

Sydney wasn't sure how long they'd been staring into each other's eyes, but the table began to clear out, and one by one the four other SEALs waved good-bye, winking and patting Alex on the back or socking his arm. She noted they horsed around like brothers in a very large family of boys.

"So, what do you do, Sydney?"

That's when she realized he'd not been told anything about her.

"I'm three years out of college, playing the beach volleyball circuit for now, looking to rack up enough wins to claim a good sponsor and an even better partner."

"Partner?"

"You've seen them play on the beach, I'll bet. Two ladies. Lots of suntan lotion. Skimpy bathing suits and shades?"

"Oh yes. All over the place here."

"Southern California is big beach volleyball country. The best players in the world live here. All I need is one. My last partner tore her rotator cuff and will be out for months. We'd come to the end of our game anyway. Looking for a new partner, probably someone better than me." She watched his reaction. "If I can."

"Why better than you?"

"I won't get better playing with someone who isn't better than I am. I might have strengths my partner might not have. But I'm looking for someone who can set my spikes."

"As in hitting it back over the net?"

"Yes, so it will come at you at ninety miles per hour and land five feet or less from the net."

He was checking out his beer glass, in deep thought. "Not a whole lot of people could return that ball. I know I sure couldn't."

"Oh, I guarantee you couldn't." She followed it up with a smile when his eyes darted to meet hers. The challenge was on. The best part about dating someone new was learning where their hot spots were and then pressing them. She liked pushing her limits, but she liked pushing the limits of her dates even more. Funny thing was, she was reeling herself in. This was her being nice, and already she was alarming him with her intensity. But if he was sensitive, she needed to know that, and know it quick. No sense wasting time.

He recovered nicely. "So, how many times have you jumped out of an airplane?"

That was an excellent scene-changer. Ask me about something I've never done. Expose my weak spot. Well, good for you, sailor. Her follow-up to that move would be to pretend he nailed her. And then she'd finish him off.

"Never." She didn't let up on him, staring him full in the face. She gave him the innocent shrug and puppy dog eyes. It worked.

"We'll have to fix that sometime." He winced, almost imperceptibly, perhaps second-guessing his words.

"I like fixing things."

"I'll bet you do." His low, rumbling cadence sent her blood pumping. He wouldn't look at her anymore, but he smiled, knowing she was watching him, telling her he didn't mind the scrutiny. Yes, he could handle the heat, she thought. He'd do just fine.

He was one of the handsomest men she'd ever seen. His shoulders and arms were huge, barely fitting into the long-sleeved shirt he was wearing. Just by the way he sat, she could tell he wasn't used to dressing up. The jeans looked new and the shirt had been taken right out of a laundry box, the fold marks not pressed out.

"So you wanna go to a movie or something?" he asked.

"Sure. As long as it isn't a sad one."

"I hate mushy ones too." His chin wrinkled as he frowned, adding a slight inclination of his head. "What *do* you like?"

"My favorite? My very favorite movies?"

"Yes. Of the movies playing now. At the theater, as opposed to renting—"

"Zombies."

His eyes closed for a moment as he took in what she'd said. He licked his lips, leaned on his right arm, and studied her. "Really?"

"I love horror films."

"I'll be goddamned." Alex shook his head, casually perusing the room. Then he finished his beer, running his tongue over his lower lip again, and whispered with a sexy smile, "Let's go get you the bloodiest, creepiest zombie movie playing in the whole county then, Sydney. Would you like that?"

Her insides were cheering. He had no idea what he'd just said to her, a huge green light the size of the moon staring her in the face. The burning muscles in her thighs from today's workout were painful, but still felt good. She knew she'd be stiff when she stood, and stiffer still after a long movie. It was an admission price she was willingly going to pay.

"Yes," she returned, "I'd like that very much, Alex."

He hesitated a few seconds and then leaned across the table and whispered, "Well then, why don't you check your phone for movies and times, while I take a leak. Sound fair?"

"No problem." Sydney didn't look up as he walked to the rear of the Scupper. Within seconds she checked the movie times of the film she knew was opening this weekend. The theater was about a half hour away, and the movie started in forty minutes.

Tapping on the screen of her phone, the trailer began, showing white-faced flesh-eating monsters growling and drooling into the foreground. The dripping red movie title oozed down the length of the picture frame.

"The Zombie Rebel Alliance Returns," said the announcer. The last shot before the screen froze was a greenish-gray hand with flesh peeling from it, showing bones and cartilage, trying to reach out from the phone to grab her.

Perfect!

CHAPTER 3

A LEX KNEW IT was a bad sign to be in the men's room twice before he and Sydney exited the Scupper, but his bladder was acting up. With the cups of coffee at the dive airport and the protein drink he'd had for breakfast, he guessed his liquid intake had been huge. He'd not been paying attention, and that was very unlike him.

He decided to confide in good old Saddam.

"You ever get nervous when you were dating way back when?" he asked as he began his stream, which relieved him immediately. The muscles in his lower belly relaxed and his back stopped hurting. "She likes horror films. Should I read anything into that?"

He didn't get a response from the sad photograph.

Sydney stood when he returned to their table, announcing, "Got the perfect one, but it starts soon. We gotta book." She'd put her jacket on, and slung her purse over her shoulder, looking like a little girl ready for an ice cream.

Alex studied the theater's address on her cell phone screen and nodded. "I was there last weekend." When he noticed she'd frowned, he assured her, "No worries, I haven't seen this one yet." Her eyes softened, but maintained their eager expression. "I guess we should leave your car here. Pick it up later?"

Her lips formed an "O" and then she licked them, her tongue brushing-over her bright red lipstick. Her sexy smile spread slowly, getting him dangerously close to being inappropriate. Teasing his self-control further, she smelled wonderful, the very definition of a woman heavily laden with pheromones. She was so damn kissable, he wanted to just take her in his arms and try to change her mind about the movie. But he also knew he wanted her primed and excited. Her energy was addicting, and for now, all he wanted to do was to get her good and stoked.

She lowered her eyes, giving him the ripe opportunity to gaze at her chest, which lusciously rose and fell with her heavy breathing. "My girlfriend dropped me off," she said as she raised her chin. "So I'm afraid I'm going to rely on you getting me home." Her eyelids fluttered just a tad as an exclamation mark he couldn't miss.

His pants were so damned tight, he worried the zipper would break. He'd thought it impossible he could get more aroused when she suddenly touched her forefinger to his lips and he found himself sucking her digit to beyond the first joint. Her eyes were transfixed with how he fed off her, devoured her essence. He reached for the back of her head, intending to run his fingers through her beautiful, honey-brown hair and pull her into him, but she stepped back.

He nearly gasped. Her eyes became dark, as she must have sensed his need, his total desire for this women he'd only spoken a few words to. It was indeed a chemical reaction he'd never felt before. His knees began to weaken. He realized she was waiting for him to speak, but he couldn't find his tongue, having nearly swallowed it.

In that way women do, she entangled her arm around his, drew him close to her body, and whispered, further binding him with the golden threads of enchantment and desire, "Let's not miss the movie, okay?"

THE THEATER'S THICK red carpeting had a gold scrolling pattern embedded in the fibers. The smell of popcorn made a trip to the snack bar a must, even though they were short on time.

"I'll have a quad latte," Sydney said to the tatted help behind the counter. The young lady attendant chewed on her bottom lip, rolling her tongue over her lip ring.

"Make that two," he interjected. "You like chocolate?"

Sydney lit up like a Christmas tree. "Absolutely! A food group."

She was perfectly formed, which indicated to Alex she only drank quad shots of espresso and munched down chocolate and popcorn on special occasions. He desperately hoped he was one of those.

She pointed to the boxes of chocolate covered mints, and as Alex was paying for them, she ripped open the box and dumped them into her popcorn. Then, she tossed the mixture like a gourmet salad. When she caught him staring at her, she stuck out her lower lip with the beginnings of a frown. "Don't tell me you're one of those guys who likes to separate his food and eats in a clockwise direction."

"Not a chance, Sydney."

She extended her arm as they ambled over to theater eleven. Alex carried the coffees while Sydney held the popcorn mixture. "I like the sweet and the salty together. Try it." She stopped like they had all the time in the world. He hadn't expected it, so gently ran into her body, which wasn't an unpleasant feeling. His brain practically groaned at the sensation of being pressed against her curves.

He allowed her to feed him a fingerful of popcorn with one Junior Mint in the middle. Her eyes were transfixed on his lips again as she intently watched him eat and react to her concoction.

Alex had to admit, he liked the taste. He held her coffee while he took a chaser from his cup, watching her again. The familiar zing down his spine gladdened his spirits. He put his palm at the small of her back and gently led her into the darkened auditorium. She was putty at his touch and took his direction without resistance.

God, have I died and gone to Heaven?

The credits had just come on and the background music was eerie. Because of her height, Sydney adjusted herself lower in the cushioned seat. Alex hunkered down next to her, peering over the large box of popcorn. Her eyes looked scared at first as she focused on the film, filling her mouth with popcorn and the chocolate mints. He was fascinated just watching her eat.

He didn't want to stare at her the whole time so he tore his attention from her occasionally, but he doubted she noticed. The movie was big on loud, bloody screams, and Alex noted her eyes began to grow wider with every one.

At one point, a girl was franticly looking for a hiding spot from a male zombie and had decided to use the closet. But the whole audience knew the zombie was in that closet, waiting to attack.

"No!" Sydney shouted, which brought several heads in the theater turning abruptly. "Don't be stupid!" she followed.

Alex was nearly jerked from his seat at her outburst. Didn't she know it was only a movie?

"Shhh," he whispered, putting his arm around her shoulder. He could feel her blood pumping as her upper torso began to shake. He took that as a sign she needed the shelter of his arms, and he was only too happy to oblige. She ducked under his chin, pressing her breasts into his ribs so hard he could feel the lace of her bra.

Of course the male zombie tore the girl in the movie to shreds. This made Sydney hold onto him tighter, something Alex as grateful for. But when she grasped his dick and squeezed hard, he dropped his coffee with a loud "plunk."

Her expression was confusing, as the movie played in the background. He started to dip his head, hoping for a kiss that would lead to her releasing his balls, which now started to burn. But on the large screen, the hero arrived, using a large sword to slice off the top of the zombie's head, right above the ears. The view of the unfortunate zombie's putrid, dark green brain matter and deep maroon blood spurting caught Alex up short and he forgot the pain in his pants.

And then Sydney interrupted his confusion.

"Woot! Woot!" she screamed and air-fisted several times, releasing his balls.

By now, half the audience was mumbling. A few chuckles were sprinkled in as well. Sydney was unfazed. She was about to give another shout when the hero sliced the zombie in half at the torso, but Alex held his palm over her mouth.

"Shhhh, Syd. Quiet or they'll kick us out."

She threw his hand away, dropping her popcorn box. Using both hands, she climbed up on his lap, her leather laces cutting into her soft flesh, and drilled him a deep throat kiss. "Gawd, Alex, I'm so hot right now, I don't know what to do." She fumbled under her skirt, and then pushed his hand underneath.

Alex knew exactly what to do. And the audience wouldn't mind one bit.

"I'm taking you home."

"Fuck me, Alex."

The teens behind their seats were having a good time listening to their interaction. He heard one of them whisper, "I'm right here, baby. Come on over."

Alex glowered at the youths. He had been trying to come to his feet, grabbing her hand and yanking her up to a standing position. She had hold of his balls again.

"Fuck me, Alex," she repeated her plea, this time a little louder.

The audience was erupting with complaints, while he attempted to scoot in front of half a dozen people seated next to them. It was all he could do to keep his balance to avoid stepping on someone's toes, and at last he had to stop and remove her hand from his groin. His blood pressure was skyrocketing.

"Fuck sake, Sydney, keep your hands to yourself or—"

"Shhh!" came someone's loud reprimand.

He wanted to go punch the asshole who tried to shush him. Exhaling, he blurted out, "Okay, we're leaving. Leaving right now." It was loud enough so the whole room heard him.

Alex made huge strides down the side aisle, turning toward the exit. He could feel Sydney having difficulty keeping her balance as he tugged on her arm, her sandals doing chicken scratches on the concrete floor. Just as they descended the ramp to the exit door, someone shouted, "Have a good time you two!"

Fuckin' Christ. He didn't know whether to be upset, or just give her what she seemed to want, a very public screw on the well-padded, deep red floor of the theater lobby. But he knew this wasn't conduct becoming a Navy SEAL, and nothing was worth jeopardizing that. At least that part of his brain was functioning.

"Geez, Sydney. What's the matter with you?" He threw her hand down like a dirty rag.

At first she seemed taken aback. Then a deep furrow formed between her eyebrows. She tilted her head to the right as if she hadn't heard him properly.

"Horror films make me horny as hell. What can I say?" She shrugged. "I guess I should have warned you."

Alex took a step away from her and nearly ran into another couple rushing to enter the theatre. "Anything else I need to know?" he finally asked her.

He was dead serious, but she took it as a joke. It was no joke to him. His string of recent blind dates had him wary all of a sudden.

"Like whatever do you mean?" she answered, batting her big brown eyes.

"Like do you like to tie men up, that sort of shit? Because, sweetheart, I'm not into that. I once dated a girl—" His words were truncated by her palm, which quickly covered his mouth so hard it was nearly a slap.

"I don't want to know anything about that. Don't ever bring up other women again." Her voice was low and deep, bubbling with anger.

Holy shit. I just met her. Why didn't I see her as the nutjob she is?

He was going to seriously have words with the boys in his apartment who had set up this date. This was going to be the last time. He was done with these blind dates that were more a horror film than the one they'd just come from.

He valued his life and his career too much to risk it just for a piece of ass.

CHAPTER 4

SYDNEY KNEW SHE'D blown it with the SEAL.

You were going to take it slow. Get that little demon tied up and sent to the closet so she didn't act out inappropriately. She cursed herself for not working out harder today. That was the solution—that and staying away from caffeine and chocolate. But she couldn't help herself today.

She'd dated much older guys, even a couple of former SEALs, but it usually took four or five intense dates before they'd go flying on their way. That part she didn't mind. She was usually tired of them by then anyhow.

But this one was different. He had a mild, quiet manner about him, yet she could tell he could handle the crazy life, just didn't like it in his ladies. It was okay if he did stuff halfway around the world that any adventure-seeker would pine for. At home, he wanted to be surprised, but not blindsided.

And she'd blindsided him tonight. She came onto him without much of a warning. It was too strong, and now, perhaps, she'd lost him. She'd never get a chance to have a second date. Her over-the-knee leather laces were hurting her now. She couldn't wait to get them off.

They'd taken turns clearing their throats during his drive to her house, but no one spoke after she gave directions. He wasn't going to bring her to his apartment. He didn't have to explain it. That part was obvious.

What wasn't so obvious was why he was denying the chemistry they had between them. One taste of his tongue and all the toggles got flipped to full on. She was a starved animal, or a wounded animal protecting something. Maybe both.

What?

She tossed the thought out the window and tried to act like she wasn't disappointed, but the closer they got to her place, the sadder she felt.

"I'm sorry, Alex. Really sorry."

He nodded and chuckled in spite of himself. "You should come with a warning label."

"I don't know what came over me," she lied.

"Sweetheart, I think you had it all planned. You don't fool me one bit." His words were sharp and it hurt.

She was quiet, waiting for him to apologize. If she said something right now, the opportunity would be lost, maybe forever. At last, her silence paid off.

"Look, Sydney, I'm sorry, but I can't tell if you did this on purpose or just—"

She turned toward him, placing her knee on the bench seat of his Hummer. "Yes. I'm really that way. Horror films turn me on. The coffee, the popcorn and all that chocolate—all those things are triggers. I get horny just walking past a See's Candy Store. I can't watch movie trailers for zombie movies in mixed company. But I am sorry. And you're right, I should have told you."

He wasn't buying her explanation. He shook his head and mumbled something.

"Do my buddies know about all this?"

"Your buddies? What do your buddies have to do with this?"

"The guys who arranged the blind date."

"I don't remember meeting any of your friends. My girlfriend and I were playing at the beach. She told me she had someone she wanted me to meet. Since I am unattached, I was game. So I agreed."

"So the guys didn't talk to you?"

She found this to be really funny, throwing her head back in a full-throated laugh. "I talk to guys on the beach nearly every day. I play beach volleyball, or did you forget that about me?"

Alex didn't say anything else for a few minutes. The silence was killing her.

Then it hit her. He thought she was some kind of freak. Well, he was partly right. As long as she exercised she could keep the crazy thoughts from overtaking her. She worked out and played hard, harder than most men. She knew she could take down most of them or handle herself in a dark alley. Physical contact didn't scare her at all.

But Alex thought she was a freak. This made her mad.

He pulled up to her bungalow. Her roommate's car wasn't in the driveway, which would have been a good thing if their relationship was going any further, but she noted it without celebration.

When he stopped the truck, she opened the door and hopped out, headed straight for her front door without waving good-bye or saying a word. The sooner she could get to that hot shower and then her well-lubed vibrator, the better. She didn't need a man to get off. But she had to get off.

"Hey," she heard him shout. She pivoted on her heels and saw him standing outside the driver door. "You just going to walk off like that, not say a word? What kind of manners is that?"

"I thought you made it perfectly clear, or have you changed your mind?"

"Changed my mind?"

"About fucking me."

He swore and shook his head. He was laughing when his gaze met hers a few seconds later. "Christ, Sydney. Are you okay? I mean, I've never met anyone like you before."

"And I'm supposed to do what with that?"

"No, it's just a manner of—"

"In case you hadn't noticed, I'm tanked up, ready for a hot shower and some hotter sex with my devices than I'll ever get out of you. No reason to put a bow tie on the fact that we're incompatible."

His square jaw and stern glare showed her some intensity she really liked. She'd picked a scab. He was angry.

Serves you right.

She turned and didn't check out the slam of the truck door behind her. But she did note that the engine had been turned off, and then there were the footsteps that got closer until she felt the tug on her arm. Before she could protest, he had her in a lip-lock, sucking her tongue into his mouth as one hand found its way to her panties under her skirt.

"Sydney, we might be totally incompatible, but can't we still fuck?"

Hallelujah.

She checked to see if any of her nosey neighbors were peering out their windows. They were used to watching her parade her trophies up and down the front walkway.

"Well, sailor," she said before he could plunge his tongue down her throat again, "that's more like it."

His hands were all over her ass while she unlocked her front door. He didn't spend any time looking at all the sports posters on the walls, the pictures of her on the cover of Sports Illustrated, or the trophies overflowing from her bedroom, burdening the living room bookshelf devoid of books. She checked for a note from Carole and found it taped to the mirror.

Be back in the morning.

They had this rule, if one of them was going to be gone all night, to let the other one know.

Alex bent her over the hallway chest, urgently pulling her panties down over her trussed thighs to her knees. His hand accepted the gift of her breast as she was pressed forward onto it. Her nipples were taught and ached, especially after he began pinching them. She groaned, spread her knees further, and raised her tailbone, rubbing her sex against the front of his jeans. She heard the zipper and then the drop of his pants.

"Honey, you got something?"

"I'm on the pill."

"Is that enough?" He kissed her neck.

"God, I hope so. You—you want to wait?"

"It would be smarter." But she could tell he was unconvinced.

"I don't sleep around, Alex." He was trying not to, but she could feel the tip of his cock brushing against her butt cheek.

He backed away for a second. "I do. But I'm always careful. I just wasn't prepared, and I'm so sorry about that."

She sighed. "Thank you, Alex. But I can't wait. Please…"

His low growl at the back of her neck sent chills down her spine. The warmth of his body pressed into her, as one arm wrapped around her waist. He spread her cheeks, letting a finger slip inside her core just before he rammed his cock inside her.

"You like that, baby?"

"Yes," she answered breathlessly. He took up a slow, deep rhythm, his hips undulating in a circular motion. He was getting harder. "You gonna let me come?" she finally found the words to say.

He didn't stop his thrusting as he raised her with his thighs underneath hers so that she was pinned on him and perfectly balanced.

"Nuh-uh. Not this time, sweetheart."

"I like it when I come first."

"I do too, but, baby, don't make me stop. I'm like you were at the theater, I want to fuck you senseless. Maybe next time?" His breath hitched as he groaned. She could feel his release was eminent.

She quickly whipped her body around and fell to her knees in front of him, putting her lips on his glistening member. She curled her tongue over him, sucked, and then ran her teeth over his head.

He appeared to be in shock at what she'd done, but powerless to do anything about it. His climax was overcoming him quickly. His cock began to spasm as she felt the warm come spurt down her throat. She inhaled deep, and pulled him down her throat, sucking up his balls too.

Alex was gasping as he gripped the chest top and struggled to stay on his feet. Sydney's hands scratched his buttocks and then squeezed his flesh until he started to scream.

"Wait!" he shouted.

She couldn't talk because he was totally filling her mouth, but she relinquished her hold on his ass. Her fingers feathered his butt cheeks as she drew her elbows together and squeezed her tits on either side of his left thigh until they hurt. He attempted to go deeper down her throat until his spill was complete.

She teased his cock as he began to withdraw, curling her tongue up and down his shaft, kissing and licking his underside in long strokes. He held her head with palms over her ears, and then let his fingers lace through her hair, pulling her onto him further, before releasing her.

"God, Sydney, I've never—"

"Shush," she said to his member. "We've only just begun. It's going to be a long night."

THE SHOWER WAS their next encounter. He went through the ritual he'd seen in his mind so many times—the fantasy of untying her leather sandal straps. She'd stepped out of her panties and thrown her top and bra to the side, but she still had those leather laces crisscrossing her shapely thighs and calves. Her nude little honeypot swayed from side to side as she walked towards him.

"May I untie you now?" he asked.

"I'd like that. She leaned slightly forward, hands on her lower thighs, her breasts firm and nipples knotted. He knelt before her, worshiping her body at first, looking at the smooth texture of her browned skin and the thin band of white where her incredibly small bathing suit sheltered her pussy from the sun and other prying eyes.

He touched her clit and then licked his lips.

"Just one lick. Then you untie me."

Alex's tongue slid down into her channel, the tip rimming her core and then playing round robin with her little nub. He noted her little jerking motions as he worked the little organ. He violated her rules and leaned in to put his lips on her, but she strong-armed him and held him back.

"No. You had your lick. Now untie me."

It felt like an order. He wasn't sure he was up for this, but a look down at his cock and he knew there wasn't going to be much she could say that would weaken his ardor.

After moistening his lips slowly, he said, "I like how you taste, Sydney."

"You've got a nice tongue, Alex, and you use it well. I hope you'll use it again."

"Without a doubt." He began to lean forward, but she stopped him again.

"Now you untie me," she said firmly.

Just like in his dreams, his fingers moved over the puckered flesh underneath the strapping, until he found the top ends of the sandal laces. He was careful to untie the first one, and then, just like in his dream, the upper part of his hand was dangerously close to her nude pussy again. He teased her by allowing her moist, warm lips to kiss his hand there, making him shiver and causing his cock to bounce. He began to extend his forefinger, working to impale her, but she stopped him gain.

"Untie me first, Alex."

Slowly, he untied the second knot peeling the leather strap away from her leg, kissing her inner thigh and tracing his tongue along the indentations the trusses left there.

"What do you like?" he whispered to her as he fingered her clit.

"I like that," she said in his ear.

"And this?" he asked as he slipped two fingers inside her.

"Um-hmm."

He was tasting her again.

She drew him up to a standing position, and led him to the shower. It was hard to focus, seeing the lines still embedded in her flesh as she walked. She examined him over her shoulder.

They stepped inside and she turned on the water. Taking his place behind her, he began kneading and spreading her cheeks, enjoying the luxurious feel of her flesh as he squeezed and released her butt cheeks. He inserted fingers inside her again. She hissed at his touch, the way he explored her, pinching her clit and asking her if she liked it.

She removed the oscillating spray wand from its holder, turned on the sharp, pulsing vibration and handed it to him. On his knees, he licked over her anus and then positioned the wand against her, spraying the water directly inside.

He sat on the bench. "Come here." He dropped the wand.

As she turned to face him, he hungrily searched her body before gently pulling her knees apart, inserting his thumb against her clit. Sydney squealed. His mouth was right there. He pulled on the lips of her labia with his teeth. His tongue massaged her clit. He leaned back and rubbed the water wand against her, allowing the jets to fill her while his fingers massaged her opening. He could feel Sydney sparking, readying herself to accept his cock again.

He gently turned her around and, without using his hands to guide him, slid his cock down the cleft to her vacant and wanting opening. And then he was inside her. Deep inside her.

She threw her thighs over his, straddling him, giving him deeper penetration and allowing her to move up and down on his shaft. He drew the wand around her front and pulsed against her clit again, while he pulled and pinched the little organ.

"Tell me what you like, Sydney," he whispered to her ear while he twisted her nipple.

"I like the way you are so deep, Alex."

"Yes, baby." He continued to lift his hips up, raising her feet off the shower floor, digging deeper inside her. "Like that?"

"Yes!"

The water had begun to go cold so Sydney turned it off. The remaining steam muffled her squeals as he plundered her. They adjusted. At one point, he was pressing her into the tile wall of the shower, her leg bent, and foot resting on the bench. Then she rode him from the front, her knees beside his hips on the bench seat. She pulled his hair as he felt her begin her orgasm. Her desperate moans rumbled throughout the enclosure, sending vibrations up his spine. She was losing control, urgently wrapping her legs around his waist as his pace quickened, building her climax to the brink. Her muscles clamped down on his member. His long strokes became faster and faster until he exploded, filling her.

They stared at each other without saying a word for several minutes, each exploring the other's face. Her fingers squeezed his earlobes as she bent to kiss him.

"I'm glad you stayed," she said between kisses.

"Me too. I almost didn't."

"I know." She played with the hairs that had fallen down across his brow. "Should we try the bed next?" she asked, kissing him on each eye.

"I think I'm up for that."

SHE FELT JOY emanating from the knowledge that he liked to screw with intensity. And he wouldn't be surprised, nor would he object to them going a third and perhaps a fourth round. And then they'd wait to see what the morning would bring.

She was already wishing it would never end.

CHAPTER 5

ALEX WOKE WITH a start, not sure where he had landed. He could tell bright light poured into the room, because the edges of his closed eyelids were rimmed in fire. He dared not to open them, for risk of an enormous headache, until he could adjust the shades. Experienced with Saturday morning wakeups, he waited for his head to tell him how bad the hangover was going to be before he attempted to make things worse by getting up.

But I feel fantastic!

Warmth and excited anticipation was pulsing throughout his whole body. Even his dick got hard, and then he felt her hand squeezing over it. All of a sudden, her lips were on him again, and oh boy! Was this number five? Six? Did it matter?

Alex squinted through the brightness as he adjusted his gaze. At first, the vision of Sydney straddling him, her long hair dropping to cover his thighs and her knees tightly hugging his knees, was blurry. But as she coaxed him and made loud sucking noises without trying to be delicate or ladylike, he was getting so hard and big, he felt he could screw all day.

Her head bobbed up and down on him. Her sultry eyes showed him how she liked to give orals, another very welcome surprise. He had a vague recollection of another person who liked this—oh yes, Brandy! Try as he might, he just couldn't see Brandy's face.

You're a dickhead. You can't even remember what your ex looks like?

Guilt began to rise inside his chest, like someone had stuck a rusty hook in it to fester. But then he felt those lips of Sydney's nearly sucking his cock right off the stem.

Holy Mother of God—Sorry, Joanne. He closed his eyes but still saw a faint vision of his sister, her arms crossed, a scowl on her face, white wings flaring from her upper back.

He was yanked back to the bedroom as Sydney looped her tongue around him again, sliding him deep and gently past her canines, her strong fingers squeezing his balls.

Alex lifted his head and watched her. God, she was a sight. Beautiful and strong, her tanned shoulders and upper chest bathed in morning sunlight as she worked, really worked to get him off. He so appreciated a lady with a sense of purpose, who was self-motivating. He got the sense she'd never quit.

Should I worry about this? Hell, no.

Her eyelids remained closed as she concentrated, pulling him deep inside and down her throat as her thighs powerfully pushed his legs together. Her cheeks got concave as she sucked hard. He felt her sex hungrily drill down on his left leg, rocking back and forth there, up from his knees to mid-thigh in a slow arc. When she held herself steady against him, he felt the warm wetness extracted and could feel her muscles working. He watched her ecstasy bloom over him.

For a moment all time stopped while he watched her come. Her eyebrows drew together. Her elbows pressed her tits together, showing the hardened nipples he was hungry for. But he didn't want to interrupt the perfection of her orgasm, performed like a dance, a private dance, for him and him alone.

She sat up, arching backward and moaned, clutching his legs, fucking his thigh. He reached for her clit and pressed a thumb against the little organ, and Sydney moaned again, then began to shudder. He continued to press and rub her nub back and forth. He wanted to tell her she was beautiful, that he loved watching her fly. That if he didn't come all day, he could be satisfied just watching her take her pleasure with him—any way she wanted.

His cock remained pointed to the ceiling after she removed her hands, her chest heaving for air. She had leaned back like a bow, hands bracing at his ankles. Her chest was sweaty already, her breasts like firm melons, and tiny beads of sweat formed on her upper lip. The vision of her letting the orgasm wash over her was the perfect way to start a new day.

Then she rounded her shoulders, drawing her elbows forward to squeeze her tits together, making them double in size. She lay her hands over those beautiful orbs, eyes barely open. She tweaked her nipples as she groaned again, watching him observe her pleasure.

He couldn't stay a bystander for much longer. His cock was anticipating an out-of-this-world encounter, and damn, he was going to feed it that. He needed to be inside her and feel the power of her pleasure.

He quickly drew to his knees. She allowed her body to fall back, knees bent, legs spread, ready for him. Her eyes flew open and a warm, light pink smile appeared on her full lips as the head of his cock entered her.

"Baby, I want to watch, but I need to feel it too," he said as he plunged in.

"Yes," she whispered. She threw her head back and drew him inside with her muscles.

She was slick and her lips were swollen. The wince at her right eye told him she was experiencing a little pain from their numerous lovemakings, but she bore it with pride. He didn't want to hurt her, so he asked, "You okay, sweetheart? I mean—"

She threaded her fingers through the back of his hair and pulled him to her, nibbling on his lips, "Don't say that. There isn't any part of this I don't love. I'm not a china doll."

He lost himself inside her mouth, inside her channel. He swam through all the sensations of her touch, her taste and the heady smell of their combined bodies. Each thrust made him need her more. She was no china doll. And he was so glad, he could hardly keep his heart from exploding.

She was just like him.

ALEX

ALEX WAS LETTING the day fill up with sex, and he didn't feel a bit guilty. Sydney's sleeping form was draped across his chest. He was proud he'd worn her out and didn't have to be careful around her or worry about her being fragile. But his chest swelled with the full realization and pride that he'd fucked her hard, and she loved it and wanted more, but in the end, she'd collapsed. All his worries about her fled. As long as she stayed in his bed, in his arms, she would be safe. She didn't need protection. She needed a man to rock her world 24/7. She needed it like the air they breathed.

He was the same way.

With other women, Alex always felt he had to hold back. Now he'd found someone who loved intensity in life as much as he did. She was more than rare. She was the one in a billion woman he could be with for more than a few weeks of fun. He gladly accepted the addiction of her being.

Her skin was tanned, with sexy tan lines showing a thin patch of white skin on her incredible ass. Her legs went on to forever. Her thighs were more developed than most guys he knew. And man, did she know how to use them! In bed, he didn't notice their difference in height. He would get used to seeing them side-by-side, her at least four inches taller. His private Amazon. Unleashing all that intensity on him and, hopefully, him alone. He'd gladly take whatever it was she wanted to dish out.

The walls of her bedroom were light pink, which seemed odd to Alex as he didn't think of Sydney as a girl with pink things but a woman in full dress camo, or scuba gear and rebreathers. He wanted to show her how to jump out of airplanes and fire weapons. He'd never felt that way before. There was always part of himself, as a SEAL, he wanted to keep stored safely inside. But now, after this brief encounter, he suddenly wanted to share with her everything about his lifestyle.

A glass bookshelf was overflowing with trophies. Posters signed by male and female volleyball players were hung in frames on every available wall space. Some of the faces he recognized. He noticed a fitness magazine with Sydney on the cover, her arm arched back, ready to take a swing. Her ribcage showed, her back in a perfect bow shape, and her feet some four feet off the sand. The red and white volleyball floating in the air slightly above her eye level was the defenseless target of her aim. He marveled at the power of her physique.

He saw several medals hung on red, white and blue ribbons, and a team photo with the ladies holding flowers on a beach somewhere in Hawaii. She had framed the cover of an Italian magazine featuring her in her signature skimpy bathing suit, riding a scooter, her long hair flowing out under her bright red helmet.

He noticed she'd traveled all over the world, as pictures at the Great Wall of China and the Kremlin in Moscow attested. It was obvious to him that she wasn't just a beach volleyball player, but a world-class volleyball player.

It was a shame, really, that he would be leaving tomorrow for Sonoma County. He'd have to tell her soon. Over food. When they got around to eating, that is.

All the past mistakes the Team had made fixing him up with girls were forgiven. They'd found Sydney for him. Yes, they'd had a rocky start, and she definitely had some odd quirks, but then, so did he. Jumping out of helicopters at midnight with a hundred pounds on your back, into enemy territory where they burned people alive just for the fun of it, wasn't exactly normal either.

No, he would forever be grateful he'd finally found a woman just like him.

CHAPTER 6

S YDNEY WAS ANNOYED when Alex told her he was hungry. Like food was as important as sex.

Guys think like that? Thought it was the other way around.

For her, it sure was. But she humored him when he allowed her to pick the menu.

"Oysters. You need some oysters, Alex."

He looked surprised, and then he blushed. Water sluiced over his massive shoulders as he ducked under the spray and rinsed shampoo from his scalp. Man, what she could do with shoulders like that. She could spike a volleyball all the way to China if she had arms and shoulders like that.

She rubbed her thigh along the outside of his, pressing her mound into his right butt cheek. His shoulders shook slightly, and she could see he was laughing to himself.

"No," she said.

He turned around to face her, his brows coming together, a question on his lips as the glistening water dripped down his face. "Excuse me?"

"The answer is no. You were going to ask me if I ever stop needing sex."

She stood perfectly still and didn't smile, but looked deep into his eyes as if she could soak up all the deep blue she saw there. She knew she was a lethal form of something and that he had no idea what he was getting into. She hoped the excitement she saw in his return gaze held just a little fear.

A little fear is good. I'll take some of your fear, Alex. I might even be able to take a lot of it.

His eyelashes briefly dropped as he perused her body, his back to the shower head. She knew he was studying her, making a plan. Making his mind up about something. Soon he sported a wicked smile.

"What am I going to do with you, Sydney?" he whispered, stepping to her and pressing his erection between her legs. She was going to wrap her fingers around him but he pushed them away.

His right hand slid along her slit as his shaft rooted to find her throbbing honeypot. All of a sudden, he turned her around, bent her over and spread her cheeks. His cock was inside her to the hilt with one forceful thrust. Sydney saw stars. She felt like she wanted to bite the tiles off the shower walls.

SHE HAD NEVER been to the seafood grill down at the inlet. It was filled with junked boats of various sizes and in various states of repair. The small fishermen's village was more populated with dogs than fish this time of day. The grill served breakfast all day and was a favorite Team hangout after Friday night dates, he told her.

"Especially those that didn't go so well. It has some of the freshest fish in town, as well as a steady supply of oysters from all over the US."

"Perfect choice. I like it," she said.

She loved the feel of her swollen sex as Alex led her across the tiled floor. Small, rustic wooden tables were set out on the balcony. Inside, the oilcloth tables were nearly half filled. The smell was salty and aromatic in a wild sense. Sea birds hovered over piles of overturned crab pots and netting, looking for a morsel.

There were chalkboards over the bar, listing all the varieties of oysters, eggs, and beer and their prices.

Alex let out a faint groan as she leaned her back against him when they studied the menu. He drew his arms around her waist and held her tight.

"You can have all the oysters you need, my dear." His whisper was raspy. He followed it up with a tiny bite to her earlobe. Sydney's chest began to pound and her ears buzzed.

"What do you recommend?" she asked.

"I like Hog Island. Drake's Bay are good. The barbequed ones are stellar, and so are the garlic pesto."

She hadn't known there were so many varieties. She turned to the side in his arms, careful to let her left breast press against his. "Aren't the raw ones best for you?"

He was smiling, getting ready to say something when a heavyset cook in a white apron slapped him on the back.

"How the hell are you, Alex? Haven't seen you since the—"

The cook had clearly started saying something that shouldn't be repeated in mixed company and abruptly stopped.

"Since my freedom party? That's okay, Griff." He stepped back and gave Sydney a tiny push at the sides of her hips, placing her between him and the cook. "Griff, this is Sydney. Sydney, meet Griff."

She extended her hand and felt the swollen callused paw of a man who worked hard. "Nice to meet you, Griff." Her squeeze was returned in kind.

Griff gave Alex a wink. "You guys know what you want?"

Sydney was suddenly starved. "Yes. I want blueberry pancakes, double the butter and syrup, a dozen of the barbeque oysters, and a dozen Hog Island raw with salsa." She turned to see Alex's surprised smile. She decided to push the envelope a bit more. "What are you having?" she asked him.

He stepped back. "Whoa. You really going to eat all that?"

"Yes. Why, you don't think I can?"

"I know better than to challenge you on that." He nodded toward Griff. "While she's protecting her pancakes from my fork, I'll have a seafood scramble." He checked her face and added, "I'll take a dozen of your garlic pesto."

He led them outside to the balcony overlooking the inlet. The crisp breeze tickled her cheeks. It was the right kind of invigorating. A light gray fog hovered over the cove.

Griff served them each fresh squeezed orange juice. "On the house," he said as he turned to the kitchen. Stopping, he asked, "Coffee?"

"Sure," Alex answered. "That okay?" he asked her. "I mean, it's a little caffeine. No chocolate in our menu this morning."

"Not for me, thanks," she said to Griff, who went in search of Alex's coffee.

She loved that he'd remembered and was trying to calibrate something. "Meaning, is it safe?"

He grabbed her hand and kissed her palm. "Just checking your temperature, sweetheart."

"Since you asked, I do have to watch caffeine and chocolate, especially together. I work out hard too. Occasionally, I can ease up on one of the three. As far as zombie movies? I have no clue. And I don't even want to find out, either."

He laughed. "So we just happened to hit the perfect trifecta last night."

"Yes, in more ways than one, sailor."

Alex began to blush, which was a huge surprise. He continued to hold her hand as he lay it back down on the table. She wondered if there was something on his mind he was struggling with. His face dropped the smile as he looked up. "I'm going on a little trip up to Sonoma County tomorrow and I'll be gone a couple of weeks, I think."

She sighed. Of all the bad luck. Maybe this would be good. She could focus on traveling to some venues to check out other players in her partner search. She didn't have a tournament for a month. Perhaps this time she'd really train the way she knew she was supposed to. Unless he was asking her to go with him.

"I'm going with several of the other guys, and we're staying with friends, or I'd ask you to go along."

She liked that he'd asked, at least. "Thank you. I have to get prepared for a tournament next month, and I'm still scouting the talent down here."

He nodded.

"Do they even have beaches in Sonoma County?"

"Not like these." He put his elbows on the table and leaned in, taking her hand in his again and kissing it. "But they do have oysters." He followed up his kiss with a wink.

"That's useful information. I'll have to file that away for future reference."

The food arrived. Sydney lathered her pancakes with butter and syrup, but before she could take a bite Alex scored a large slice and had it in his mouth.

"You were right about that. I do have to protect my pancakes, don't I?"

"Yup." His smile was deliciously covered in butter and syrup.

They ate in silence. Since there was a time limit to their encounter now, Sydney wanted some answers.

"So tell me about yourself, Alex. You ever been married?"

"How do you know I'm not married now?"

"Because I think you wouldn't do that. I'm rarely wrong. A married man has a different way about him. They make you walk through the back door. They have secrets, big ones. I don't get that with you. Am I wrong?"

"Nope, sweetheart. I'm divorced. And yes, this was the scene of my freedom party a few months ago." He sipped his coffee. "I live in an apartment with three other bachelors. But I was married, for about three months." He wiggled his eyebrows up and down, checking her reaction.

Sydney's radar was piqued. "Impossible to know everything about someone in a month."

Alex shrugged and examined his empty plate, and then noticed hers was nearly empty too. "We did good work here. Mission accomplished. Now I won't be able to move all day."

"That's too bad." She allowed her lip to droop. "So you were telling me why you were married for a month. Why bother?"

"It was sort of dumb. You'll probably not think very highly of me. Ryan and I—Ryan's my roommate—we went to Vegas with our girlfriends. It was just a lark. Her name is Brandy—my ex."

"I'll bet you didn't know much about her either."

"No. We don't talk that much. She's kind of a dancer."

"Ah." Sydney was having too much fun dragging the details out of Alex. But she did notice he didn't describe her in the past tense.

"We took them up to Vegas, and we had a fun weekend. A little over the top. We got a little smashed. It seemed like a good idea at the time." He stopped, inhaled and then continued. "Well, we did a double wedding at the Elvis Chapel."

"I hear that happens a lot up there. I had a friend who married a guy from Spain when we were over there playing. Had a terrible time getting it annulled. Alcohol was involved in that one, too."

"No, she knew. I mean, it wasn't that serious. I should have never done it. We laugh about it now."

There was that present tense again. "That how you look at marriage?" She needed to watch his reaction. He was being tested again, and yes, the return glance he gave her indicated he fully understood.

"Of course not, Sydney." He released her hand and sat back. "When I find the right girl, it won't be like that at all."

"So you still see her or are you fully single?"

"That's a lot of questions so early on a Saturday morning."

"If you can't handle it, I'll stop." She saw him flinch. She needed to turn on the syrup a little more. Her direct approach was beginning to scare him. On the other hand, it was important to know whether seeing him was a waste of time. She didn't like to waste time.

"Why don't we reverse this for a few minutes while I finish my coffee. And then I'll have to be moving on, okay? Gotta get ready for my trip."

She hesitated. He was good at brushing people off. Regardless of their world-class evening and morning, he could separate that. He could walk away. Her heart fluttered slightly as she realized perhaps she could not. Or just didn't want to.

"So what do you want to know?"

"Who are you, Sydney?"

And boy was that the right question! Not who are you dating, who do you hang around, what do you do all day? This was usually the question that came up after the second or third date, just before she was about to exit stage right.

Her answer was measured and well-practiced.

"I want more out of life than life's given me so far, but I'm not complaining. I just want more of it. I want the *juice* of life, not to *live* life. I'm looking to get a good partner and travel the world playing volleyball until my knees ache and my back or shoulder gives out. And after volleyball? Who knows what I'll be able to do at eighty?" She gave him the smile she'd given so many other dumbstruck men over the few years since she'd been dating. It was always the same. It also usually got the same reaction.

But this time, she saw something ignite inside Alex. The backdrop of lonely sea gull cries, the salty gentle breeze and sounds of metal clanging as work began late at the docks, only enhanced the excitement brewing in her belly. She was struck with the beauty and power of something maybe dangerous about this man. And also something so beautiful her eyes watered.

CHAPTER 7

T HE GOOD-BYE WITH Sydney had been slow and sensual. She nearly got him naked again. He was trying to act casual, but the parting irritated him. They exchanged phone numbers so they could stay in touch at least by text. He normally didn't do this, but today it had been his idea.

On the drive up to his apartment he couldn't help but chuckle. Yes, he was satisfied in several departments, but just when he'd finally met a woman he could spend the whole weekend with, he had made other plans.

He thought about their parting. His mood suddenly soured. He had turned, gotten in his Hummer and never looked back. That wasn't how he wanted to leave it, but what the hell was he supposed to do?

He pushed those thoughts aside and took a deep breath, donning the psychological clothes he needed for his brotherhood encounter. It was time to get the guys, get his gear and get out of town. End of story. That's all there was to it.

Nick, the former member of SEAL Team 3, had just medically re-tired and was now full time at the winery in Sonoma County. Several other guys who had put their ten years in and were suffering from some tough injuries were looking into getting into the wine business as well. Although Alex was completely short on funds, as were a couple of the other men, he seemed to be the glue that held everyone together. Besides, he'd promised Zak's new bride he'd keep an eye on the one-eyed SEAL. Both Zak and Amy were from Sonoma County so a move and change of career might be a good fit.

Coop was waiting for him at the apartment.

"You're late."

"But I'm fed and showered. Just got to get my duty bag."

Coop followed him up the stairs, passing the elevator they never took. "Kyle's not coming, kid." The tall medic always addressed him that way, and it had nothing to do with age. Coop would be going on his eighth deployment with SEAL Team 3, having served on an East Coast Team for his first tour. Alex only had three tours and five years to his name, so he was senior to all the froglets, but junior in rank to Coop. Kyle was their platoon leader.

"What's up with that?" Alex opened the front door. The apartment smelled awful. A young woman in a skimpy silk teddy ran around the corner from the kitchen, waving at Zak as she dove into Cory's bedroom and slammed the door without saying a word.

"Remember those days, Coop?"

"I do, I do indeed. Although they never got too far in my Babemobile. And slamming doors was not in the program, mostly because those doors don't slam."

"I've heard stories about that thing. You still have it?"

"Oh, I let one of the froglets borrow it for a couple of months—he's got it back at the beach, waiting for his housing allowance to kick in. Libby says it's an eyesore, and she makes me park it down the street at a gas station when it's home."

"Can you blame her, Coop?" Alex noticed that Cory's friend had made coffee. Although early afternoon, Alex was happy for the steaming cup. He poured another one with lots of cream.

"You want one?"

Coop scrunched up his nose. "Nah."

"Okay, well, I'm taking this in to Cory. Maybe this will help him get up."

Coop shrugged and walked to the glass sliders leading to their balcony as Alex approached the closed bedroom door. He banged on it with his fist, being careful not to damage the hollow core surface. "Hey

Cory, you in a gentlemanly pose so I can bring you some coffee?" Alex cocked his head and leaned his ear against the pressboard door. He could hear whispering and the tussle of sheets.

Cory's normally neat appearance was completely obliterated by the dirty-looking stubble and tufted light brown hair resembling the corn stalk scalp on a rag doll.

"Thanks, man," Cory said as he reached for the mug.

"Coop's here. Everyone's gonna be arriving in like ten minutes. Where's Ryan and Jake?"

"They're with Lucas and Zak, picking up supplies. Don't worry, they'll not want to hold up Kyle."

"Not Kyle you have to worry about. Coop's in charge."

"Kyle's not coming?"

"Coop says no." Alex heard the shower going off in the background. "You think you can wrap things up and get your butt out here?"

"What's got you all hot and bothered? Didn't it work out last night with the volleyball chick?" Cory sipped his coffee.

Alex wanted to punch him, but he quickly reeled it in. The irritation surprised him. He tried not to say anything, but he could see Cory was going to poke him with that big fat needle until he spilled. "She's fine."

Cory grinned from ear to ear. "Sweet."

"Yes, asshole. You guys are off the hook for awhile."

"Even better. Well, Alex, you see, miracles happen every day. So if it can happen to you, it can happen to me. Not that I'm looking, of course."

"Of course not. You're just sampling the merchandise."

Cory cleared his throat as the lady behind him walked past the crack in the door without a stitch of clothing on. Cory managed to roll his eyes, balancing his hot coffee mug, stepped outside the doorway and closed the door behind him. "Kinda glad no one came home last night, if you know what I mean."

Coop approached the bedroom. "What the fuck you doin' Cory? Get your butt out here. The guys pulled up downstairs so you're the last one to get ready."

"Yeah, not cool, man. You live here," added Alex.

Cory held up two fingers and quickly retreated behind the closed door.

"Honestly," Coop said as he stepped back, "you bachelor guys got no responsibilities. You'd think you could be on time for once. Heck, I had to clean up dishes, fold my own clothes, change a very nasty diaper and mow the lawn before Libby would let me out of the house, and I'm the first to be ready here."

"Coop, don't see how you do it."

"Well there's a little secret to that," Coop said, following Alex into his bedroom. While Alex pulled out a large duty bag, stuffing it with clothing and his medic's kit as well as his personal items, Coop continued. "I make sure it's worth it to her. That's the secret. It's so fuckin' simple. I don't know why guys can't figure that out."

Alex partially zipped up the bag, and after almost forgetting, pulled a toothbrush and a couple other small items from the medicine cabinet and threw them inside. "Happy wife, happy life, right?"

"That's it."

Pounding on the apartment door followed. It had enough force to rattle the windows. Cory beat them to the door and let Zak, Lucas, Jake, Ryan, Mark and Luke burst in, carrying grocery bags and ice chests. Mark had four bags of chipped ice balanced on his shoulders.

"Where's Kyle?" asked Lucas. Zak stood behind his friend, rubbing underneath his eyepatch with his forefinger.

"He's got some event Collins wants him to attend. He'll follow us in a couple of days," Coop informed them.

"We going early on our next vacation?" Ryan asked.

They used the term vacation whenever they were not sure about their security. No one took this lightly. Last week, someone on one of the other Teams had discovered one of the SEALs' apartments had been bugged.

"Nope. He didn't say that," Coop informed them.

For the next five minutes, the team worked silently, packing the chests, organizing it so nearly every square inch was filled. They added the ice last. Cory's date made a quick exit and the team followed her down the hallway, but avoided the elevator she took. They loaded the gear in three separate vehicles as she peeled off and drove away.

This was to be a road trip, of course, but it still was a mission of sorts. That meant that talk was minimal. If there was pressure, there'd be the classic smack talk and some mild jokes being pulled. But today, the muted caravan of two Hummers and one four-door, long-bed pickup headed off the island and toward the freeway north.

ROUGHLY SEVEN HOURS later, they arrived at Nick and Devon's winery, *Sophie's Choice*, in Santa Rosa. Alex was driving the bachelor contingent, Coop had Zak and Lucas, and Mark came with Luke. Alex had only been up one time before. He whistled. "Wow. This is spectacular!"

Though it was night, the buildings and driveway were lit up and it appeared there was some kind of reception going on. A catering truck was parked along the left side of the tasting room.

Their headlights flashed on green vines and well-tended rows bursting with tiny green fruit. Alex rolled down his window and inhaled the crisp night air. Colorful gardens were illuminated around the brand new tasting room entrance. The building's copper roof spires extended into the sky, above the guests on the balconies overlooking the vineyards and valley below. There was music coming from the downstairs level, carrying across the valley floor.

"Lookin' good. So I guess the winery business is booming," said Jake.

Nick met Mark's truck, which had been first in the driveway. He directed them all to drive around the back. The parking lot to the tasting room was filled with several black and white limos as well as a dozen or more expensive cars.

"Damn! I didn't come dressed for this party. You know about this, Alex?" asked Cory.

"Nope. Mark made all the arrangements."

Alex parked next to Coop's Hummer, and they began exiting the vehicles. He recognized Devon, wearing a shepherd's white top over a gathered skirt. She wore red, flowered gardening boots and had flowers pinned to her hair. The white top accentuated the huge bulge in her belly.

"Mamacita! Look at you!" Mark said as he ran to her and gently picked her up in his arms. Devon was giggling. "No briefcase, no suit, no high heels. Wow. You look fantastic," he said as he put her down.

Devon appeared to glow in the evening light. Alex could see she was embarrassed.

"Guys!" Mark said enthusiastically. "This is Devon, Nick's Devon, the lady of the house." He turned back to her. "You shouldn't have thrown a party for us. That was really nice of you!"

She grinned. "No, this was very last minute. We book up fast, but we had a cancellation. It's a private wedding, a fellow vet. But from some of the ladies I've met tonight, I don't think they'd mind if you crashed the party. I'll have to ask the bride and groom. Wasn't sure you guys would be up for anything like that with the long drive."

"Seriously, Devon," began Ryan, "I think with a shower we'd be ready for anything. But I didn't exactly bring dress clothes."

"I think they might like you just in blue jeans. I was going to gift you the lavender winery T-shirts so you wouldn't be expected to dress up. You could go as part of the staff—and yes, sorry, but they're lavender! If you want them, they're yours."

"Yes, ma'am," came the uniform response.

Jake scrunched up his nose and whispered to Alex, "Lavender? We gotta wear lavender?"

Alex stepped on his foot to shut him up.

Nick took his place beside his wife, placing an arm around her waist. "Come, and I'll show you guys where you're staying. Leave your gear. We can unload all that in a bit."

The group followed behind Nick, who was punching and chatting with Mark. Alex knew the two of them had been close, and Mark had at one time been a special friend to Nick's dying sister, Sophie.

Nick addressed his audience just as a scream and then clapping went up inside the venue hall. "I'm guessing someone might have been showing off in there. Either that or the cake fell over."

Alex liked it here. The evening was warm and filled with excitement.

"We have a nice guest house, behind our place. It's got beds, if some of you don't mind bunks. We get a lot of families staying here, especially during crush. Ecotourism is a new thing here in Sonoma County."

He led the way around the side of their modern two story home made from recycled material, to the bunkhouse behind. He stepped up on the wooden porch, lined with five rocking chairs. In front of the porch was built a stone fire pit encircled with log stools. Nick propped the door open. "Welcome to Sophie's Choice."

Everyone piled inside. The space was rustic, but had an efficiency kitchen and a large community table. The fireplace was already roaring.

"Bedroom is through that doorway, and it's set up to sleep eight," Nick shouted. Jake headed for it. "Only one shower, I'm sorry to say. We got an instant hot water heater, but if you guys aren't careful, some of you will still have to take a cold one." As an afterthought he added, "Unless some of you want to shower together."

He got a pillow tossed at him for his efforts.

MARK BROUGHT HIS stuff into Nick and Devon's house, since they had a room set up for him in there. Coop walked up behind Alex saying, "You knew about Mark and Sophie?"

"His wife?"

"No, his wife is Sophia. Met her after Sophie, that's Nick's sister, passed on. I know Mark's a little emotional about coming back here, but he's fine. Good that they're taking him in the house. Probably have a lot to catch up on." Coop slapped Alex on the shoulder. "Can you give me a hand with one of these ice chests?"

In a half hour everything was stowed, beds selected, showers completed. Their favorite workout music was booming in the great room, choruses of angels and titles like "One Against The Thousand." It was battle music they also listened to when they were heading out to a halo drop. It drowned out the music in the hall. The group, all in lavender T-shirts except for Jake, took stock of themselves before heading over to the party.

"I'm going to post naked pictures on FB of anyone who takes a shot of us in lavender," Zak said.

"As a matter of fact, gents, leave your cell phones behind so you won't be tempted to do something really stupid," Coop demanded. "That's not optional. It's an order."

That was never a guarantee, but Alex was glad he requested it. Ladies and alcohol and being away from home made for one dangerous combination.

Just before he lay his phone down, he noticed he'd gotten a text from Sydney.

Did you arrive safe and sound?

He answered back, *yes, ma'am.* Then he turned his phone off and left with the group.

CHAPTER 8

SYDNEY WAS GOING to run over to one of the local beaches to check out a tournament that was nearing a close when she got a call from her girlfriend, Carly.

"Hey, Syd. I've been thinking about your offer. Maybe we can have a shot."

"Seriously?" Sydney was elated. Carly had been a competitor in college, but they'd become close friends. They'd played together in a couple of side tournaments before Leah was free, and they worked well together. "Let's try it."

"You haven't found anyone yet?"

"No, and Leah's looking doubtful. I hired Jack to help me train. We're scheduled to do a mixed tournament next month. I haven't done one in nearly a month."

"Ouch. Sounds like me. We'll have some work to do, then. So, when I get back to San Diego later in the week, let's talk."

"Where are you?"

"I'm living with my old my roommate, you remember Jenn?"

"I do. The soccer player?"

"That's Jenn. Got herself coaching junior high girls here. I came up for a little R & R, and, well, I got hooked on the area and started coaching high school girls and now some Club ball. I thought about your offer, and I think I'd like to try it. I think it might work, but we need to talk first."

Sydney couldn't believe her luck. "Of course. That's way cool.

When will you be back?"

"A couple of days, maybe longer, but I think I'll head down Thursday at the latest. Can you wait that long for our sit-down?"

"Shoot, I've been looking for three months now. You were my first choice, Carly." On a whim, she asked, "Where do you live now?"

"Little town up here called Healdsburg. Sonoma County."

Sydney's pulse quickened. "Is that near Santa Rosa?"

"Yup. Just a couple of towns up the freeway from there. I train in Santa Rosa."

"Want some company? Or, would I be intruding?"

"You? Come up here? You're kidding, of course."

"No." She tried to tone down her eagerness.

Breathe! Are you completely nuts, Sydney? Think about this!

"I think Jenn would be cool with it."

"I'll stay at a motel. No worries."

"God, Sydney, you seriously want to come all the way up here?"

"Why not?" Of course she had some nagging doubts about what Alex would think. And how the heck would she even find him? It would be a needle in a haystack unless she called him.

After another shower, her second after her first steamy one with Alex that morning, she examined the tousled sheets on her bed. She dropped her towel and stood naked in the afternoon sunlight, staring down at the evidence of their exciting romp together.

There hadn't been enough talk, she noted. Probably too much sex, although he didn't seem to mind that her need had been off the charts last night and this morning.

I'll blame it on the Junior Mints and the caffeine.

She sat, spreading her hand over the comforter, smoothing the lines and wrinkles, then pulling it up tight. She picked up the pillows, put them both to her face one at a time and inhaled his scent, getting lost in the sensory memory of how his body felt next to hers. After the fluffing was completed, she replaced them in their respective slots.

Did men know they left a scent? It was as distinctive as perfume on a different woman or cologne on a man. She knew it was biology.

Somewhere inside her sensitive body was a delicate scale that measured and weighed everything. Along with the taste of his mouth, the feel of his touch and the sound of his breathing, his manly scent was part of what she would miss. And now craved.

Stop it, Sydney. This isn't you. But unlike other times, she just couldn't get Alex out of her mind. Though the encounter had been intense, it was still way too short.

This wasn't fair. She doubted men had the same bodily mechanism as women did. She'd heard someone give a lecture in college about how natural selection gave off the pheromones that in ancient times told a woman the man she was attracted to would pleasure her greatly and give her healthy children. This would happen long before the first kiss, but was *sealed* with the taste of him on her tongue. Was it something every woman thought about like she did? That first kiss was the clincher. "The taste of *the other*," her professor had said, "becomes the total object of the female's desire. When he is no longer *the other* but recognized as home and hearth and part of the woman's protection, they are truly joined as one. It's not sex. It's biology. The will to build the species."

It was a concept she believed in, though had never experienced herself until now. Most of her life, in relation to men, she was busy making sure she was in control, making sure she was protected in case they let her down. Making sure she would not only survive, but come out on top. She was into taking chances, but not if the price was too high. And after all that, she made it sport. The sport of it became the frosting on top, made it fun.

She threw on her clothes, slipping on her well-worn workout shoes last. At the bottom of the closet was her weekend bag. She stared down at it in the shadows, half covered by a long dress hanging overhead. Stooping, she picked it up, examined its empty belly, and then threw it on the bed, as if it had burned her hands.

No Sydney. This isn't wise.

Her inner mother was scolding her as she grabbed several pairs of underwear from her top dresser drawer, several T-shirts, sports bras and bras. One lacy one in black. A black nightgown she only wore in mixed company.

No. No. No.

Her toilet kit, favorite brush, two baseball caps, two pairs of sunglasses, extra suntan lotion, a pair of flats, a sweater and one dress—left on the hanger, still encased in the plastic wrap from the cleaners.

She checked her Apple Watch. It was barely two o'clock. She'd driven to San Francisco once in a hurry in less than six hours. One to two hours more and she'd be in Sonoma County. She could find a place to stay, have a good meal and plan for her meet with Carly tomorrow.

With the tournament coming up, it isn't wise. Stay home and train, her inner mother shouted.

But it isn't one of my qualifying tournaments, just something to keep in shape, something to help my mindset, which is pretty focused right now, she argued. She knew she was justifying something that made no logical sense. Because it wasn't logic. It was something else.

Your future on the pro circuit is a figment of your imagination unless you get your body in shape, Sydney.

She knew it was true, but she continued to pack anyway.

This mixed doubles tournament was with an old coach of hers who she later became involved with in college. Although competitive, the only thing Sydney had to concern herself about was him keeping his hands to himself. Even his new wedding ring seemed to make little difference to him. He was a player and was still playing, even though married. He would never change, even though he had helped her train in the past. Now, without a partner, she needed his expertise because he knew her ability better than anyone else on the circuit. He knew what a competitive machine she was, what her strengths and weaknesses were. It was worth it to put up with a little of his BS. She was focused on the game and hoped he would be as well. Maybe he'd agree to coach the both of them. Her partnering with Carly solved more than one problem.

Again, Sydney, you're justifying. You're going to have to make a stand with him.

She nodded. "Yes. I can handle him. I can handle anyone. I'll deal with it later."

She zipped her bag up, determined to go on that road trip. If she ran into Alex, would he understand or would it scare him away? She knew it was a risk.

What are you doing, Sydney? Stop. Just stop right now and think.

"I can do this. I'm focused on the goal. I just have to make sure I keep it between the lines. She was taking a risk, stepping outside her normal routine for a chance at something she'd just had a taste of. Was it wrong to go after that chance or forever regret not doing so? That was something she wasn't willing to do.

She slung her bag over her shoulder.

At the doorway, she turned and took a look at her pink trophy room, as she'd always called her bedroom. Now she saw it for what it was. It wasn't her future. It was her past.

THE TOP WAS down on her Murano, and as the sun began to sink low in the horizon, it began to get cold. Several times she'd had the same nagging doubts she was doing the right thing. She considered calling Alex several times, but restrained herself.

She turned on the heated seats as she descended into the Bay Area. Approaching and then driving through Palo Alto, she recalled competing in tournaments at San Jose State and Stanford. She'd spent time as an Olympic hopeful at a training camp there two years ago, and had earned a bid to try out for the US Women's Volleyball Team. Of course she was disappointed when she wasn't chosen even as an alternate. But now she was free to go after the lucrative sponsorships the pro Beach Volleyball circuit had to offer.

Crossing the Golden Gate bridge at sunset was a treat she hadn't expected. The red steel contrasted with the darkening blue of the sky and the gray fog beginning to roll in. Looking west, she saw the Farallon Islands.

That means luck will be on my side.

To the right, a long container ship was making its slow way out of the mouth of the bay. The little boats were returning to shore, a couple of tour boats still hovered around Alcatraz for a few more stolen minutes.

Through the Rainbow Tunnel she held her breath, just as she had done as a little girl when her dad would drive her in his convertible to a volleyball camp somewhere up north. She'd grown up tall and very quickly. He called her his little giraffe.

She allowed herself a few tender memories of the happy days that existed before her father had taken ill.

Her phone chirped. It was Jack. She looked for evidence of a Highway Patrol, then carefully installed her earpiece and answered.

"Hi, Jack."

"You up for dinner? Thought we could make a workout plan for the next couple of weeks. I'm free. Barb's at her sister's."

"Sorry. I'm on my way to do a little scouting. I'm already in San Francisco."

"San Francisco? Who are you checking out?"

She wasn't going to tell Jack until she'd had the talk with Carly. "Actually I'm meeting an old friend from college. She knows some ladies who are looking. Haven't met them yet."

"Uh-huh. Okay, then. How long will you be gone?"

"Oh, just two maybe three days. Not long."

"Sounds like you're driving."

"Of course! Gives me time to think."

"Just wish you'd think a little more about us."

Her belly clenched. "Jack, there is no *us*."

"Well, there sure used to be. You ever dream about those days?"

She was about to hang up on him. "That was a long time ago and never should have happened. You were my coach."

"*Former* coach. Sydney, I'm still a good coach. You never give me a chance."

"You promised, Jack. Remember? You bring this shit up and I walk. Remember that promise you made?"

The other end of the line was silent. She didn't work to fill the air space, making it easy on him. She had to be tough with him or he'd never stop going after her.

He finally sighed. "Okay then. Let me know when you're on your way home. And be safe. I've got some big plans for the summer. You'll love them."

"Will do, Jack. Give my best to Holly." She hung up before Jack could react to the fact that she knew Holly McGiver, the six-foot-seven middle from UCLA was his current flame.

She's probably on a recruiting road trip with her team.

Even if Sydney had been interested in Jack, she wasn't going to be his or anybody's number two or three. She was only interested in being a number one.

SYDNEY ARRIVED IN Santa Rosa after it had gone dark outside. Taking a motel downtown, she put the top back up and carried her things to the room. She had her third shower of the day and sat naked on the bed. Her hand hovered over her cell phone, as if some secret power would lift it up to her palm.

She texted Alex. *Did you arrive safe and sound?*

The answer came right back. *Yes ma'am.*

She asked him another question. *Having fun? How are your friends?*

She waited for several minutes. When the answer didn't come, she turned off her phone and tucked herself into bed. The cool, unfamiliar sheets felt soothing to her skin as she made a mental list of all the things she'd need to do tomorrow.

Would it be fortunate or unfortunate to run into Alex? Would he be happy to see her? Then the import of her decision hit her.

What if Alex was up here to meet someone *else*? Could there be another lady in his life?

CHAPTER 9

T HE PARTY WAS in full swing when the SEALs entered the reception. They were spotted immediately. Alex and several others had dance partners who'd had a lot to drink. Coop declined all invitations, as did Zak and Lucas, but the bachelors were in clover. Mark found Nick. He and Luke stood in the corner laughing at the spectacle of members of SEAL Team 3 in lavender shirts, while Coop, Zak, and Lucas hit the chow line.

Alex became extremely self-conscious when someone began taking pictures. He hoped it hadn't leaked out who they were and what they did for work. He looked for Devon but couldn't find her in the undulating crowd.

The next set was a slow dance, and he found himself holding up a pretty blonde in a bridesmaid's dress. She peered up at him dreamily.

"You a friend of Brandy or Josh?"

He could tell she was having difficulty talking. Her balance was off as well, and soon her chest pushed into his. She hung onto his shoulders and then slipped one arm down around his waist. Alex could hardly move. He was literally dragging her across the dance floor.

"I think you need to have a seat, Missy."

"Oh, such a gentleman!" She giggled in his arms and lost her balance again.

"Let me help you. I think you've had a little too much champagne."

"Yup. Guilty." She winked at him, but her other eye didn't focus at all. "You've heard the story, ever a bridesmaid, never a bride. That's me."

He thought perhaps she'd start to cry on him. He searched for a chair nearby before she started to resist him.

"No. I wanna dance." She tried, and this time was successful at righting herself before she pressed her body tightly against his. "I got myself a handsome young stud. I intend to take full advantage of it. Make all my pretty girlfriends jealous." She gave him a sheepish grin. Alex chuckled.

"You're pretty."

"You think so?" She still had a tinge of Texas in her accent, but it had been stomped out by years of living in California. She batted her eyelashes at him, raised one eyebrow, and licked her lips. Without warning, she leaned backward and Alex had to bend quickly to catch her before she hit the floor. He righted her, with effort, and was grateful he hadn't strained his back. Several of the other ladies on the dance floor squealed and came over. Alex felt like a tree covered in butterflies.

"Again," said one ginger-haired little thing.

"Yes! We want to see it again," said another.

Alex's dance partner gave him a wicked stare, albeit still not focusing or making eye contact. "He's all mine," she said and then collapsed against his chest again. "Hands off. You're too late." She regained her balance and twirled in his arms, winding up with her back and considerably sized rear pressing against his groin. But it was the position of his hands that drew the attention from the crowd. Both palms were on her breasts. "He's mine, girls!" She threw her arms in the air so they could see her total surrender. Alex quickly adjusted his grip on the drunk blonde, while still propping her up. Their audience melted into the crowd, but the whole room was looking at him in his lavender T-shirt.

Alex scoured the room for one of his team buds and at last found Jake, who immediately understood the situation and sprang into action.

"So, do you think I'm sexy, Mr. Body Builder? God, would you look at those arms? You lift weights for a living?" She'd gripped his biceps, stubbornly not moving her feet.

Alex used what little balance he had left to lift her off the ground and deposit her in a chair. When Jake arrived to assist him, the girl looked between the two of them.

"I think I've died and gone to Heaven." She blinked several times, waiting for a response.

Just in time, Nick arrived. "I've got it, boys. Sorry about that," he whispered under his breath.

"You want me to get Devon, or someone?" Alex asked.

"Go get the bride, if you can find her. You're one of the bridesmaids, aren't you, sweetheart?" he said to the girl.

The blonde was enjoying the sight of now three handsome men in front of her.

"Lordy, I just cannot believe my luck." She fluffed her hair up and began to focus on Nick.

Alex tore through the dance floor, scoured the sides for something white, looking for the bride. He felt the tap on his shoulder and heard a familiar voice.

"Hey Alex."

Pivoting slowly, he came face to face with his ex-wife, Brandy. She was dressed in all white: the bride. When the bridesmaid asked him who he was friends with, it never occurred to him it would be *his* Brandy.

"Oh wow." He cursed himself, but he couldn't think of anything else to say. "Brandy. I didn't know—"

"Of course not. How could you?" She delivered him a nasty, hurt look he felt he deserved fully. "You never returned any of my calls."

"I'm sorry, Brandy. Weren't we on deployment?" She quickly shook her head and put her hands on her hips. He drew his hand up to the backside of his neck. He honestly didn't remember getting any calls from her. Not that he would have returned them. He sucked it in and decided to just apologize. "I'm sorry, sweetheart. I really am."

"Ahh. Such a heartbreaker. I wish I could believe you. And now you've come to gloat. Ruin my wedding, is that right?"

"No. Absolutely not. That's unfair."

"When Devon told me some friends of Nick's were here, and asked my permission, I thought to myself, *What are the odds?* Well, no matter. That's all history now." She turned in front of him. "How do I look?"

"You look gorgeous, Brandy. I really mean that."

"Sure."

"No, I'm serious. I've never seen you—"

The music had stopped between songs. Alex heard his name shouted above the crowd.

"Alex!"

He'd forgotten about Nick.

"Brandy, one of your bridesmaids is really, really drunk, and—"

"The one you were feeling up? Her name's Daphne."

"No, Brandy, she's drunk. She's out of her mind. Please, can you help us out?"

"Honestly," she said as she gripped her gown and kept pace with him across the dance floor. "You would think a bunch of SEALs would know how to handle this."

Daphne was passed out in Nick's arms, who had shielded her from falling over backward in the chair. Alex couldn't find Jake anywhere.

"Let's get her over to the couch. You take her feet," commanded Nick. While they were moving her, Nick raised his head. "I see you guys know each other?"

"She's my ex," Alex whispered.

"Oops. Sucks to be you, then."

They placed a pillow under her head as Daphne regained consciousness. Several of the other ladies moved in around them and took over, bringing water and a cool damp towel.

Coop presented himself. "I should take a look, Nick," the tall medic said.

"No. Don't want you involved Coop. We have to call the paramedics. Those are the rules. Don't want you involved."

Coop still watched to make sure no one was doing anything that would further aggravate Daphne's condition. She was soon able to sit up and drink a little water, and then devoured a finger sandwich. The music began again and the crowd turned back to their partying.

Brandy grabbed Alex's arm. "Come on, Alex. One time for old time's sake?"

"Well, I'm not quite sure this is proper. I mean—"

"Oh come on. I finally get to wear a gorgeous white gown, have my wedding in a beautiful place, officiated by a minister who doesn't wear sequins. Humor me, Alex. Give me the sendoff I deserve."

She had a point. "What about your husband?"

She perused the room. "Well, he's not here to object. Besides, he knows you."

"Say what?"

"Dance with me, and I'll tell you."

The song was a little too fast for a slow dance, which was a relief to Alex, who didn't want to be touching Brandy right now. He'd already managed to get his share of scowls.

But she was the bride after all. So the deejay changed it up to a slow song. She gave Alex a sweet smile, with those pink, pouty lips he tried not to stare at.

Damn.

It was hard to pretend not to have any connection with Brandy. And he did feel bad about what had happened. He never should have married her in the first place. They'd used each other all they could, and then it was over quick. She was uncomplicated and just lovely. But not really the type of woman he needed.

"Josh is a SWCC Team guy," Brandy said, throwing her head back and raising her eyebrows.

He was impressed. "You said he knows me?"

"Not really." She was wicked beautiful, but very dangerous. "He used to come in almost as often as you did, toward the end." She swung her chin up, her little sparkling crystal earrings dangling, catching light from all around the room.

"I see. Did you—?" What the hell was he doing? What difference did it make?

"There was a time when he was leaving and you were coming back.

But just a little." Her smile was shy.

"When we were married?"

"Only once."

Shit. This was turning out to be such a bad idea, getting worse by the minute. As he tried to move over the dance floor, his legs felt like glass. He wanted to throw Brandy over his knee and give her a good spank, and he had absolutely no right to do so. But he was coming off the rails. His control was slipping and the awareness of this only made it worse.

He needed to do a jump, or go swim in the ocean, or run ten miles. It was all feeling too civil for him. And here he was in a lavender fucking T-shirt. He was a trained killer, a Navy SEAL, for Chrissakes. This wasn't the life he was supposed to lead. This was the pretend cardboard life of someone else who should be standing here holding Brandy and giving her everything she wanted. He felt like an alien species.

He smiled down at her. She wasn't even trying to be present for him, but was more interested in how the crowd saw the two of them dancing. She enjoyed pressing herself into his thigh, but not so obvious that the crowd or her husband would see. He wished she wouldn't do that. He wanted to be anywhere else but here.

Alex remembered what he'd been doing just this morning. He wished Sydney was up here. He'd take her skydiving when they got finished at the winery. Maybe he'd take her to the shooting range.

But of course that was a stupid thought. Right now, he was locked in a tense drama for the pleasure of his ex, the new bride, like an actor playing a part on stage. The song couldn't end fast enough for him.

THE MEN STAYED behind to help Devon and Nick with some of the work not being done by the party planners or the caterers. Chairs were stacked and garbage bagged up. Every time Devon tried to do something, one of the SEALs prevented her.

It was good to see her laugh. It was good to just be with their own kind after the caterers and their helpers left. It was getting to be that

Alex didn't feel he could have fun unless he was with his buds. He always felt on duty around the general public. Just something that came with the territory.

"Love it up here. So easy. Beautiful. Made for fun," Alex said. "Great place to relax."

"Looks can be deceiving," Mark added.

"He's right." Nick brought up something that recently appeared in the local news. "They found a Golden Gate Transit bus abandoned in Santa Rosa. People in our community and some of the retired cops I've talked to think it is terror-related. You gotta keep your eyes and ears open at all times, guys."

"Whatever happened with that property near Lucas' ranch up north? They ever find all those assholes who ran that terrorist training camp?" asked Alex.

"Devon said it went to auction, and another church group bought it," Nick answered.

"What the heck would someone want with a bus?" Jake leaned on his broom.

"Fill it full of explosives and park it on the Golden Gate Bridge, Jake." Coop's answer was smooth as silk. He didn't stop his quiet chair stacking to bother to look at any of them.

"A concerned neighbor made the call, and perhaps that thwarted the event," followed Nick. "Like I said, keep your eyes and ears open. They are looking for unexpected opportunities to create a huge loss of innocent life, and do it spectacularly. We're not DC or Coronado, but we're not immune."

But Alex had already had all those thoughts back in San Diego. It had been going on for weeks, ever since his divorce. Something was in the air. Strange people, sounds, bulges in pockets, whispers, dishonest glances—all these things were noticed. So were people with shifty eyes, or people who didn't look at you directly, or had a limp handshake.

It was late when they returned to the bunkhouse. Alex wanted to crash, but a couple of the guys stayed up to watch a movie. Mark said his good-byes and returned to Nick and Devon's house. Someone was in the shower. Alex threw himself on a bottom bunk and checked the time on his cell. He saw Sydney's text.

Are you having fun? How are your friends?

He placed the phone on his chest and looked up at the wooden slats of the upper bunk Cooper would be sleeping on later. She'd sent the text message nearly two hours ago. Should he return it? Wake her up? What were the odds she was also alone tonight? He hoped they were good.

Having fun, yes. But I think I miss you. Headed for bed. Nite Nite.

He hoped she didn't read anything else into his message. But then he wondered, what was he really trying to say?

CHAPTER 10

S YDNEY HEARD THE beep of her cell because she'd put it beside her on the nightstand. She wasn't sleeping well anyway. She sat up and cradled it, wondering if she should text him back, and decided not to do it. She wasn't sure yet whether she would try to contact him. It would be a miracle, but so much better if she could just run into him somewhere.

Where's your nerve, Sydney? Her internal mother was scolding her, which of course was going to keep her up further. She reached for a book, thinking it might make her sleep, and got snagged on it. Two hours later, she wasn't tired, but she knew she needed to get some sleep. The night before she'd had little, but no doubt about it, she was wide awake now.

"Fuck!"

Just admit it, Sydney. You want to see him again. You don't like it, but you do. That's why you came. Be honest with yourself.

The phone said 2:10 AM. More than likely he'd turned the sound off, so if she messaged him, he wouldn't get it until morning. Except he'd know she sent it in the middle of the night. And it would make her—*eager, Goddammit!*

Which was exactly why she balanced her phone on her thighs and sent her message.

Miss you too, Alex. Hope you're sleeping because I can't.

She didn't bother to wait for a response. Instead, she walked into the bathroom, washed her face, and brushed her teeth. While she was brushing her hair, she heard the ping and her heart leapt from her chest.

She nearly tripped on the way over to the bed.

Alex had texted, *Me neither. Wanna talk?*

If it's okay, she sent back. She wrinkled her nose at how dumb that sounded.

Just one second, let me wake up the guys and ask them.

No don't!

Are you kidding? I'd never do that. Headed outside to the porch. I'll call in 5.

She threw on a pair of sweats and a tank top. After pouring herself a diet coke from the minibar, she sat in the large, overstuffed chair in the corner by the window and waited. The minutes ticked by slowly. He called thirty-three seconds late. She let it ring twice first before picking it up.

"Hi, Alex. I'm sorry if I woke you." She toyed with the can of Coke. It was not caffeine free. *Crap.*

"Are you kidding? I thought I'd crash after the long drive, but now I'm wired."

"Tell me about it." She clapped her hand in front of her mouth. "Sometimes driving long distances does that to me too." She hoped she'd recovered well.

"We got up here in good shape. Our friends own this winery, and it's beautiful up here. There was a wedding."

"You were in a wedding? One of you guys got married?"

"No, but as it turns out, I knew some people here."

"Ah. And so all the flirting with the lovelies didn't make you tired?"

"That's a dumb question. Men don't get tired around lovelies, Sydney. You should know that."

She inhaled quickly. Yeah, that one served her right. "Of course. I forget." The pause was a little dangerous. "So, tell me about your friends, the part you can tell me, that is."

His chuckle sent a tiny zinger up her neck. "Not anything to hide here. Except the bride was my ex-wife. How's that for timing?"

"No way."

"Trust me on that, sweetheart. Had I known, well, I wouldn't have come."

"You're serious? Your friends didn't know about this?"

"Well, not like we were married long enough for them to meet her. I've only been here one time myself."

"So you're at a winery. Are you staying there, then?"

"Yep. They have a bunkhouse where people can come and learn about winery production, the cultivation of the vines and the soil, harvesting, crushing, that sort of thing. Sleeps eight. Except for the snoring, we're doing fine here."

"And you happened to stumble on a wedding for your ex? You have dark clouds above your head all the time, Alex? Or you just like to live dangerously?"

"Funny. I thought of you while I was dancing."

He paused. Sydney held her breath.

He continued, "I was thinking if you were here, I'd take you skydiving tomorrow. Seriously, that's what I was thinking when I was dancing. That's kinda nuts, huh? You down in San Diego and me up here."

It was her time to pause. It wasn't in her plan to tell him, but opportunity made it feel right, somehow.

"Did I say something wrong?"

Sydney recovered quickly. "Thing is, I got invited up here to visit my old roommate in college. So I'm actually staying in Santa Rosa."

"No fuckin' way."

"I didn't tell you because I didn't want to intrude on your plans. I drove up yesterday afternoon and got in late. That's when I texted you, Alex." She hoped her lie would hold.

"So where are you?"

"The Vintage, right downtown Santa Rosa."

She heard the long sigh and maybe the wheels turning inside his handsome head. It was probably a bad idea to tell him.

"Maybe we can meet for breakfast?" she added. She wanted to get him off the hook. "I've arranged to meet Carly at ten at Beach Inc. It's a huge volleyball complex over off Airport."

The heavy sigh was enough. It didn't matter what he said, because she could tell he wanted to see her, and that was all that was important.

"Let me see what I can do here. We're supposed to go over some plans. We've got some land to go see tomorrow—actually this morning, now. I gotta stay here. But tomorrow night?"

Sydney gulped down the rest of her Coke. She felt the tingle already coursing through her veins. "I'd like that. Now I really won't be able to sleep."

"Yeah, same here. You be careful around the caffeine, Sydney."

Too late. She'd heard all she needed to hear and didn't want to push her luck. "Promise. I'll be a good girl in the morning."

The deep chuckle in his voice was setting her on fire. "Why don't I believe you?"

"No horror films on TV. I know because I checked. Not enough chocolate in the minibar, either."

"Oh, Sydney, Sydney, Sydney. Whatever am I going to do with you? Now you're making me hard as hell."

"Just hold that thought until tonight."

"Not sure I can wait."

"Music to my ears, sailor."

"Man, this is nuts."

"Welcome to my world."

"What's your room number?"

"Five Twelve."

"See you in fifteen."

He hung up. Sydney's pounding heart was making her breathless. She dashed to the shower, then afterward donned the little black nightgown she'd brought. She drank one of the bottles of water and then fingered the chocolate bar in the refrigerator but decided against it. She really wanted a run, but the stiffness from sitting so long in the car was beginning to evaporate. Some leg stretches and back bends helped, thirty pushups against the wall, and then…

OMG there was a knock on the door!

CHAPTER 11

H E BURST INTO the room without greeting, his hands under her nightie, her body pressed against him, her legs around his waist. She tugged at his shirt and pulled it off. His bare chest against her warm, shaking body was more than he'd hoped for tonight. Stolen moments. They wouldn't have the long luxurious time they'd had before. But this was just fine. It was urgent. It had to be done. It was what they both needed.

Her lips melted into him. Her little groan set him ablaze as he ran his teeth at her neck and bit her earlobe. Pushing her hands inside the front of his pants she found him. He helped her unbutton his jeans and slide them down off his hips. She grabbed his ass and pulled him into her, wrapping one thigh up and around his waist again.

The clothes had fallen away and at last they fell naked on the bed a tangle of arms and legs. Her hair was splayed over the pillows, the long lovely body of hers hungry, her sex wet with anticipation. She smelled of fresh soap and her arousal. His fingers slid over her thighs, reaching to that magical juncture between her legs as his thumb pressed her nub and he felt her lithe body arch under him. He owned her with that touch. He dipped his head down to taste her and she pulled his shoulders up, begging him. He was more than happy to do whatever she wanted.

He was hard as granite, sliding into her wet channel. She pulled him deep. He was lost in the feel of her lips against his, her little squeals and moans as he explored her with kisses. He started slow, rooting deep, encouraged and rewarded with her hands on his ass squeezing him tight. He picked up the pace as her eyes flashed open—the grin on her lips all he needed to see. She'd take all he could give, which spurred him on further.

FOR THE SECOND bright sunny morning in a row, she was draped across his body. If she was an addiction, he didn't want to be rid of the need. They didn't know each other at all. Had barely talked. He was used to having sex with lots of girls, one-night stands that were exciting, good for his ego, and probably good for theirs as well—or at least that's what he told himself. But this time, being with Sydney, all of a sudden he wanted to know all about her. He wanted to know where she got that drive, that extreme call to action to live full-out.

He watched her sleep, as she hugged his upper arm, burying it into her chest, looking like a little lost girl, like she'd never let go. Her face, with a soft crease between her brows, indicated perhaps she'd had a sudden bad dream. Maybe that's what wakened him. Carefully, he used his other hand, drawing the strands of brown hair from her forehead to watch her more closely. She clutched his upper arm tighter, rolling her hips against his thigh in her sleep.

He'd not been attracted to women who liked to dominate and possess. It had always been a total turnoff, no matter how stunning they were. Part of his DNA was not to be owned by anyone. When he found the SEAL brotherhood—working with the Teams—he discovered he'd been created for this job. These were the only guys he would ever trust.

It had been a sad fact of life that with all the intensity of his job and the life-threatening things he'd learned to handle, even the ones that haunted him and reappeared in dreams or whenever he closed his eyes—he'd never really wanted intensity when it came to women. The fair species were complicated and not to be trusted.

He'd give them protection and affection. No problem doing that. But he wouldn't go down that rabbit hole of emotions, and didn't want to be needed, and certainly didn't want to need.

He'd chosen his job because protectors were in short supply in this crazy world, and that was something he *could* do—to protect—even give his life for innocents. But he never wanted to go beyond the point of actual full-on engagement with his female relationships. Even his marriage with Brandy was half-hearted, and although he'd wished it could have been something more, it wasn't. Just wasn't.

But with Sydney, he wanted something larger, something more. He couldn't get enough of her. That had never happened before.

He cautioned himself as he laced his fingers down her backside. This was so damn quick and there was so much about her he didn't know. His first impression of her was that she was a total freak of nature. Could he now say that he really did trust her, or was it just the incredible sex? Was he just now awakening from a dreamy fog land of lust and the need to immerse himself in the warm waters of satisfaction and recreational enjoyment? It couldn't be anything more. Or was it?

Did it matter? *Yes, somehow it matters.*

As the light in the room brightened, he began to worry. His equilibrium was off. Perhaps storm clouds were about to appear on the horizon. It reminded him of the way early dawn looked overseas in the sandbox. On deployments, the question came with each pinkish-orange sunrise: "Is this the day?" He knew everyone thought about that.

What would his last day feel like? Would he recognize it? Would there be something in the air or a sound that would tell him his time was up? Would it be in a sandy divot without anything familiar but his brothers, or would it be in a soft bed like this, an old man, surrounded by his family? He'd never allowed himself the luxury of looking into his future.

Why was this coming up this morning? Was this bed so dangerous he should have these worrying thoughts? Dr. Death drinking at the side of the road, a hitchhiker waiting for him to pick him up? An unwelcomed partner, but an inevitable one?

Something had shifted these past two days, revealing a deep cavern inside. It lured him, like leaning too far over a high railing. Something here was dangerous. He just couldn't put his finger on it.

Next he knew she was rubbing her breasts against him, nibbling his neck, making his mouth water for her kisses. There was no question his body had surrendered to her in every way it could. Was there danger in the fact that she literally owned him? That he couldn't help himself around her? He would have to be careful not to let her know.

She'd been whispering, "...the way you kiss me, make love to me, Alex. I can't get enough. Do you hate me for this?" Why did she say that? Was she still asleep?

"Hate you? Absolutely not."

Sydney startled, and for a brief second he saw fear in her eyes, like she didn't know where she was. She quickly recovered and then it was gone.

What the hell was that about?

"Sydney. Are you all right?"

Her frown told him she wasn't happy with his question. "Of course. I'm fine." And then the cool veneer of her "I'm fine" mask disappeared. She became pliable again, soft, as she wrapped her legs around his thigh and pressed into him. "Never better."

EYE CONTACT WAS difficult over breakfast downstairs, which surprised him. He thought perhaps it was the distraction of the other people in the coffee shop. Alex was also getting texts from the team about his presence being required. Coop reminded him he'd promised to be back in time for their early meeting, and he intended to keep that commitment.

She played with her eggs but drank three cups of coffee. He raised his eyebrows as she took another long sip.

"You sure you'll be okay with all that coffee?"

"I'm not a child, Alex." The look she gave him was abrupt and cold.

"Just trying to be helpful. It's my nature to be protective."

The softness he'd enjoyed just a few minutes ago had vanished. He noticed she was about to blurt out something and then held it back, smiled, and patted his hand. "Thank you. But you know I'm a big girl." She watched his reaction and added, "Besides, there's no chocolate anywhere in sight. No zombies, either."

Her words coaxed a smile from him. "Good to know." The awkward silence between them still worried him. Something was brewing, or was it just his imagination?

Unknown territory. You are home. Drop it. Don't overthink this. He was well aware he could create a problem out of anything if he dwelled on it too much. Best to shed it like yesterday's clothes.

His phone buzzed again. He checked it and looked up at her. "Sydney, I'm afraid I have to go."

"Yes, and I have a workout to do with Carly."

"You want to get together later on? I have no idea when I'll be free. We're looking at this winery property today, and this morning doing some planning." He pointed to the phone. "They're basically waiting on me."

"I understand. Let's just see how things go today, okay?" Again she didn't meet his gaze.

"That sounds good." He was compelled to say something rather than leave on such an awkward note. "Have I upset you?"

That got her attention. "Of course not, Alex. Don't be silly."

"All this happened so fast. Did I miss something here?"

"You mean the chitchat? The small talk about who we are and why we're here? That sort of thing? All we did was screw."

"And that's a bad thing? Is that what's bothering you?

"Not in the slightest."

Her answer surprised him, as he waited for more, but could see it wasn't going to come. The girl had demons. Powerful demons. He felt how tight she'd wound herself, masking something she wanted to hide from him. *What you think of me is none of my damn business.* That was sound advice, so he put that to work for him. But the hot and cold of her demeanor was worrisome.

"Well, if I offended you in some way—"

"Alex, would you fuckin' stop it? You haven't done anything to hurt me, so just quit this. Leave it alone. This isn't you. It's all me. Don't pry where you don't belong."

And there it was. Her shell of protection coming out like battle armor, telling him no matter what, she didn't need anything from him. "Well, I'd like you to know I had a wonderful time."

Her pert smile was efficient. "Me too."

He stood, but she remained seated, focused on her plate. He slipped his bag over his shoulder and heard her explanation.

"I'm going to have one more coffee, and then I'll be on my way too."

"You still staying over tonight?" he asked.

"Haven't decided." She didn't ask him if he wanted her to or mention seeing him tonight. Where was this distance coming from? Why was this so awkward?

"We'll touch base later on, then. Bye, Sydney." He leaned over, looking for a good-bye kiss, but when she didn't offer her lips to him, he gave her a chaste peck on the cheek.

The woman had demons. Perhaps she'd done him a huge favor.

ALEX GOT THE ration of crap he knew he'd get from the guys, who were just finishing up breakfast in the bunkhouse. Devon and Nick were clearing the table, with the help of several of the guys. Alex felt himself relax the instant he was back in this culture.

"Whoo-hoo, lover boy. Oh, lover boy!" Jake crooned like the song.

"Shut the fuck up," Alex blurted. "You were the ones who set me up with her."

"Whew, I was hoping it wasn't Brandy, for some reason. The way your ex looked at you, all dressed up in her finest..." Cory continued his description of the way Brandy danced with him, exaggerated touching of breastbone to breastbone she'd done, which had embarrassed the hell out of him.

"Who do you think I am? You seriously think I could do something like that, you dumbass? I was just playing along. You fucking don't think I enjoyed myself, do you?"

"You say so," Cory continued to needle.

Alex wanted to grab him by the lavender T-shirt he was still wearing, and throw him on the compost pile. "I'm fuckin' *here*. That's all you guys need to know. Besides, I wasn't sleeping anyway. She *called me!* I didn't know she came up to see a friend." Alex shrugged trying to tone it down. A couple of deep breaths and he was right as rain. He poured himself a coffee from the machine on the counter and hoped they'd drop their line of questioning quick.

Coop leaned across the table on his elbows. "You wanna run that one by me again? She came all the way up here, what, just a coincidence it happened to be the same place you are? You're not reading anything into that? Ever hear the word *stalked?*"

"Not like that. Consenting adults and all that. I'm not sure we're gonna see each other for awhile, if you must meddle in my affairs."

Someone whistled. "Testy," Jake whispered.

"Hey, can we talk about something else? Besides, who could sleep with all of you snoring your butts off last night? I say you issue noseplugs, Coop."

"No kidding," Coop agreed. "Everyone wear earpieces tonight, and that's an order. The room is much smaller than we're used to. Surprised the windows didn't shatter."

With the table cleared, everyone was seated. Devon made more coffee.

Nick began, "So, I think you guys should look at this place Devon found. Not formally on the market, since the owner has just passed away. A nice forty-six-acre piece with a couple of okay houses on it. Vineyard has been allowed to overgrow two, maybe three seasons, from what we can tell."

"What does that mean?" Ryan asked.

"They have missed the last two years' prunings, so there's more than normal work to be done. It will affect the first harvest. And we also don't know the condition of the vines as far as disease. But we *do* know it produced pretty good Merlot when it was tended. They have a pond and a great well, which is always a plus in the valley." Nick handed out parcel maps and copies of the land description from the tax rolls.

"I'm getting reports in the next day or two," added Devon. "We've had to wait until after the funeral. The immediate family doesn't want the out-of-town relatives to know they want to sell."

"Don't they have to sign off on it?" asked Lucas. "If they're part of the estate—"

"They aren't in the will," answered Devon. "There are a couple of relatives hanging around for the reading, but we don't expect any surprises. We just want it clean and simple. The family is very private, and there are parts of the extended family that can get undesirable. At least that's what I've been told," answered Devon.

Alex noticed the tax rolls had the property valued at two million five. "Says here it's worth only two-five. Why are we supposed to pay four point two?"

"The tax rolls don't adequately reflect the true value, Alex. Happens all the time. We've seen a spike in sales prices, mostly because of some large buyers coming into the area."

"Why don't they go with them?" Mark asked.

"You can't be a vineyard owner up here without property disputes with the adjacent neighbors. Lots of issues. Water, drainage and grading, spraying. Vineyards are planted in different ways, some for deep watering, like the old ones were, others shallow, requiring more water. One of those big land owners is right next door. Marco Zapparelli. Ever heard that name before?"

"The movie director?"

"The one and only." Nick nodded. "And he's got a huge reputation for being really tough when it comes to negotiations. He rules by intimidation really. Doesn't care if he's liked or thought of as a good neighbor."

Devon added, "Of course up here, everyone smiles to your face while they stab you in the back. Maybe he's just putting everyone on notice, perhaps being more honest about it. Things are very competitive here and getting worse every year."

"So, when he gets wind of this property, he's going to have a cow that it wasn't brought to him," Nick finished.

"Entitlement," Mark whispered.

"Worse than that. He thinks he's the king of the whole fuckin' valley," Nick complained.

"See guys, size does matter," quipped Zak. "Although in this case, based on his track record and ours, he might be a bigger bully with his millions—"

"Ah, the pirate speaks!" barked Jake.

"Devon thinks it's billions, Zak."

"Like I was saying, even with those numbers, and that kind of size, I'd still take our odds over his anytime. I mean, look what he does every day and look what we do?" Zak's eye patch was slightly crooked.

"Whoo-Ya, Special Operator Chambers," followed Coop.

Zak had been unusually silent all morning. Mark fist-bumped him. "Welcome home, brother."

CHAPTER 12

SYDNEY LINGERED AT the breakfast table as if she was hanging on to a memory of something fading away forever. The empty plates, water glasses, silverware and coffee cups were evidence two people had shared a meal, a conversation, and then a good-bye. She was hoping the longer she stared at it her body would react, but all she felt was the ice water in her veins, steeling herself from something she didn't want to feel. She was waiting for something. Waiting for warmth or some emotion to evolve. It never came.

Alex had left money on the table for breakfast without asking. She glanced to the view of the parking lot and thought perhaps she saw his Hummer exit toward the freeway entrance. Something melted inside, and she discovered a lone tear coursing down her face. Her cheeks were flushed and her hands were shaking. Glancing around, she looked for signs someone noticed, but found no one paying attention.

The thaw had begun. Before it got any worse, she exited the restaurant and walked down the wide, carpeted hallway to her room. The last time she'd walked down this runway she was holding the hand of a man. She wouldn't say his name. She refused to see his face or recall the feel of his touch. But her body knew it anyway.

The latch on her door clicked and flashed a green light. She walked back inside to the room still filled with the remnants of something deep. A place that bore witness to something she wouldn't allow herself to feel.

Their room, she corrected herself, coming dangerously close to that emotion again. The bed was coming apart. One pillow was on the floor. The evidence of a passionate play that had occurred between two people who—

Inside, she was caving. She sat down quickly, burying her face in her hands. She'd been cold to him, holding him off at arm's length. Refusing to let him inside her heart. It was her pattern. She'd done it over and over again without consequence, or at least not noticing one, if there was. But today, she was shattered.

The tears would not stop.

What is this? Get hold of yourself, Sydney. She didn't want to be pulled back to something dark, hiding in the emotions driving her tears.

Sydney straightened her back, wiped her face with her hands and then stood. With a wetted a washcloth, she dabbed her eyes, examining for signs of redness, and found none. Satisfied that the jumbled feeling inside wasn't visible on the outside, she pulled her hair back into a long ponytail. She brushed the ends, adjusted her sports bra, and put on her workout sweatshirt. With everything packed into her canvas workout bag, she filled the metal water bottle and tucked it into the netted pocket on the end.

Looking over the room again, she examined the evidence of their joining—the short story of their morning's passion and the path she'd taken to find him here out of the briar patch that was her soul. She'd found him, and he'd touched her. Again. It was dangerous. Risky.

And probably exactly what she needed.

Holding her key card, she hoisted her bag, and left the warm room behind.

Sydney considered checking out of the motel when the clerk asked her. She hadn't made her decision. She had to wait to see how the morning went, so she arranged a late checkout just in case, and promised to call later to let the hotel know for sure. The clerk was more than accommodating.

"You have until noon, perhaps later, so feel free to take your time. And, if I don't see you, thank you for staying with us at the Vintage."

Sydney noticed she was at the precipice again, stuck between leaving and staying. Time to set it all aside and put her game face on. Get her mind mentally prepared for a fierce conversation, hard workout, and driving herself to exhaustion and beyond. It was what always worked. It would certainly work this morning.

She arrived at the Beach Inc. complex twenty minutes early. Already the parking lot was filling with Suburbans as scores of high school girls' teams poured into the main gym, knee pads floating above their socks at their ankles.

Sydney walked through the heavy glass doors and heard the roar of voices, whistles, and team shouts. The air was cool, electric with excitement and purpose. She could feel the competitiveness hitting her flush in the face, and she loved it. Drank from it. Inhaling, she discovered she'd been holding up the entrance, so stepped aside to let several young players and their chaperones enter.

Carly had reserved a sand court, she'd told her. Sydney walked further into the space and noticed the two-story structure had perhaps a dozen traditional indoor courts arranged on both floors. Large expanses of glass divided the playing areas, with skylights bathing the whole interior in natural light. The state-of-the-art facility was impressive.

Several games were in progress. Sounds of whistles, the never-ending "sideout" and team cheers echoed throughout the huge structure. Parents and other team players sat on padded seats on risers instead of the standard metal or wooden benches Sydney was used to.

An Hawaiian-themed snack bar was down at one end of the building, near the four sand courts. Beach Boys and Margaritaville music boomed while two attendants in flowered Aloha shirts helped the customers. A short line of thin giraffe-like girls waited for smoothies and bagels for breakfast. Sydney had been one of them not too long ago. The squeal of an espresso machine pierced the air and surprised her.

Sydney smiled and shook her head. This was not what her growing up had been like. She'd played in hot, smelly gyms all over California, from brand new courts in the Central Valley to dingy inner city courts lined with graffiti and exploded toilets in the Bay Area and LA. She'd attended summer camps at colleges that didn't have gyms as nice as this one.

"Hey, bitch!" Carly's voice streamed across the room. "You ready to play, or are you going to go have a smoothie?"

Carly was a more compact version of Sydney's body type, with long legs and arms, but her height was well below six feet. Her blonde hair was tied up in pigtails, although it was hardly long enough to stay put. The little golden strands looked more like horns. Her skin was paler, which told Sydney she hadn't been playing outdoor, even grass courts, recently. She was dressed in black, barefoot, and ready to play, holding a burgundy and white striped volleyball.

"Damn, Carly. This place rocks. Who owns it?"

"Believe it or not, a bunch of local businesses got a Title Nine grant. Some of the schools were pissed."

"I'll bet."

"But it's a nonprofit center. Major benefactor here in Sonoma County left them a ton of dough, and all they can spend it on is youth sports. So the schools can train here, have fundraisers. They even do birthday parties." She pointed to the second level where a bunch of balloons were tied to one of the open glass doors.

"Wow. I'm seriously impressed."

"They've done a couple more of these elsewhere. It's great for the girls, and the Beach has a couple of boys' and men's league teams as well."

"This is a serious draw for the community," Sydney remarked. "I don't think San Diego has anything close to this."

"Probably not. I think one's planned for L.A. Lord knows the schools don't have the money for anything these days. And the little private schools love it. They don't have to build a gym at all. I coach a public high school girls' team, and we have to ask each family to purchase a volleyball so we have enough for practice. It's *that* bad."

Sydney could only shake her head. "So that's what you've been doing, then? Coaching?"

"A little. It doesn't pay well enough to be full-time. I don't have a credential, so I'm always on the chopping block. They hire a P.E. or English instructor who can coach and I'm out of a job. Each year it's the same."

"You've done this more than one season?"

"Second year for Club volleyball. Starting second school year. They alternate, just like when we were growing up."

Sydney's mind was flooded with questions. "How are you going to work on the AVP thing if you live up here?"

Carly motioned for them to be seated at the edge of the court. She released the volleyball to the sand. "See, that depends. I can give up the school season if this works out. That comes up this fall. I have camps and some stuff here all summer long, but I'm replaceable. I have a few personal coaching one-on-ones, but"—she shrugged—"I'll have to give them up." She looked at her hands, then brushed them together, removing sand. "My assistant might be willing to take the varsity. I have to finish the Club season which ends here in a month."

"Okay. So what does it look like for us, then? Everything I see scheduled is down south."

"So we travel."

"*We?*"

She turned, extending her arm out, palm up. "This could be our training court."

"There are no beach games up here, right? I mean real beach."

"This is real." Carly scrunched up her nose.

"You know what I mean."

"There are a few facilities in the Bay Area. San Jose has a complex. They're building one in Santa Clara. For the beach scene, well, we'd have to drive a couple of hours south. Santa Cruz. There's also San Francisco, but the training could be here. Only difference, really, is we'd be watching the tournaments from onscreen, not live. We train for the qualifiers next year, Sydney. We give it a go and see where it takes us."

Maybe that would solve some of the other issues plaguing Sydney. She felt like she was in a fishbowl down south, everyone watching every move she made. The circuit knew she was looking for a partner. Knew it was a long shot she could get qualified to try out for the spots on AVP. She'd only get the points by winning qualifying tournaments. She wasn't aware of any of them indoors or many qualifiers up in Northern California. But she could get her conditioning done here. She could work on sponsors. She'd have a world-class place to train. She'd be out of the prying eyes of the field in Southern California.

"Okay, Carly," Sydney said as she lifted her sweatshirt. She drew down her pants and slipped off her shoes. "Let's see what you got."

They bumped back and forth over the net, chatting as they warmed up. In between short volleys, Sydney stretched, worked her shoulders, and practiced sprinting and jumping. She had no aches or pains today. Her game body had showed up this morning.

The two of them gave up the soft passes and started placing balls to make each other dive. After several good digs in the sand, Sydney felt the familiar sting in her knees.

Carly asked a couple of Sonoma State girls to join them. They worked across each other for a bit, then Sydney invited her back to her side, and they went two against two. Carly's hands were good. The players on the other side were young Sonoma State teammates who also worked at the Beach. Although competitive, Sydney had no problem hitting Carly's sets and getting a kill every time.

"Hey, old lady," Sydney shouted to her, "Your hands are still nice and soft."

"Told you, bitch," Carly hissed back and set another perfect ball for a kill.

They took several five-minute breaks, but Sydney wore them all out, demanding Carly get vocal. They had to work out their play dominance.

Close to noon, Carly held her stomach. "Man, Sydney, you don't play like you've been out for a bit, girl. If anything, I think you're stronger than when we used to play in LA."

"Been working out with Jack. He kicks my butt."

"Well, as long as that's it, he's good."

So the rumors had lingered. "We're not an item, Carly. Just want to be up front with you. That's all in the past."

"I got you," she said while continuing to catch her breath, leaning forward, her palms resting on her knees. "So, you wanna go get some lunch. The girls have teams they have to coach, and I think some reffing assignments."

Sydney checked her Apple Watch. "Good. I could use some food. I definitely need another water."

The place had premade sandwiches and chili, so it saved them from having to drive. And they could eat as they dressed without being hassled by the general public. Only thing that annoyed Sydney was the noise. Between the beach music and the whistle-blowing, it was hard to understand each other.

"Logistically, how do we pay for this space to train, Carly? I'm not made of money."

"How do you do it now, Sydney?"

"I have a little I've saved from my Dad's estate. I get my last chunk when I turn twenty-six. Enough to live on for a couple of years, if I'm careful. I'd rather invest it somewhere."

"Buy a house up here."

"Not sure I could qualify. I'm not on the tour yet."

"We could get you something here, if you wanted it. But I guess you'd have to rent some place. I have a studio. Maybe we shouldn't live together too, if we're training together. You know the pros and cons of that."

"I do."

"Way cheaper than San Diego rents. And if you work here, we can get our court times. Plus"—she held up a key on a ribbon key necklace—"we can train day or night. He who has the keys wins, in this case." Carly wiggled her eyebrows and with her pigtail horns looked ridiculous.

She made it sound very attractive. She knew Carly was capable of playing pro-level ball, which was dependent on training and working hard. She'd been one of the most competitive players she'd known in college.

"Why didn't you go on to play more afterward? What brought you up here?"

"My family's from here. I grew up with my mom in LA, but the rest of my family is up here." Carly continued on with her story. Sydney thought about her comment about parents living in two places.

Sydney knew about that. Growing up, she'd heard the fights at night between her parents. She used to will it to stop, covering her head with a pillow to drown out the sounds when she was in grammar school and beyond. By the time she began to play volleyball in middle school, the coldness had dug in and her parents never spoke to one another. She became the bridge between two icebergs.

And then came the divorce. Sydney had wished for, and now had, an end to the arguing. But she lost the company of her dad in the process. When her mother went on a serial boyfriend circuit, Sydney requested to go live with her dad. It became the best two years of her life.

Something familiar crept up on her shoulders and added dark weight. The hairs at the back of her neck stood out, then the tingling spread up to her scalp. In just a few seconds, her eyes filled with water.

"Hey, Sydney. You okay? Have you heard a thing of what I've been saying over the past couple of minutes?" Carly's hand was placed against Sydney's forearm. "Did I say something that upset you?"

There it is again.

"People keep apologizing around me today. Sorry, Carly. It started happening this morning."

Carly looked off to the side. "Yeah, the past hurts sometimes. Everything okay at home?"

"Home?"

"As in, your family, your love life."

How could she answer that? "There hasn't been any family for me since high school. I got a mom somewhere out there. Haven't seen her in over three years. Even graduation." Sydney paused because this was more difficult. "As for men? Fuck 'em."

Carly gave her a high five. "Damn straight, fuck them all to hell! I'm with you there."

She liked the way Carly picked up on the need for a change in vibe. Something unspoken between them had started already. It was a very encouraging sign.

"So I guess the next thing is, we gotta get you hired here. Would that make it easier for you to get a place to rent?"

"I'm guessing it would."

"Let's try it on our own in separate places first. If we have to compromise, we can always do the roommate thing. But we're going to train hard. We'll need our space. There are days when I'm not going to like you very much." Carly's playful lilt to her voice was a great way of covering some serious boundaries and guidelines.

"Well said. I can see you could be one major bitch."

"Damn straight."

Sydney liked her more than she thought she would. "Carly, I'm going to tell you exactly what I think of your play. I won't sugarcoat it."

Carly put her hands on her hips. "Another one of those, are you?"

"What does that mean?"

Her new playing partner put a cool towel to her face, then her neck. "What it means is, when you dance, I'll bet you lead."

No truer words were ever spoken.

CHAPTER 13

A LEX LIKED THE bright blue sky in Healdsburg, but the air was dry. Blue and white ocean and breaker views were replaced with bright green rows of vineyards looking like cornrows on a young girl. The gently sloping land could easily resemble a woman's body, all the curves and smoothed ridges and mounds, just like he'd seen in large expanses of African desert he'd flown over during deployments. Something about the land and its shape and shadows reminded him of a woman's curves and hollows. One *particular* woman.

A cool breeze caressed his cheek, whispering things as it swirled through the large plate-like leaves of the vines on the hillside they were hiking. Sections were bare or contained brown dying vines, while others remained dark green.

They'd spent the morning creating a very rough business plan, identifying all the decisions they had to make, who would be general partners, how the partnership shares would be divided and how decisions would be made. They left blanks for people's names to be inserted. They would need a chief executive officer, a chief financial officer, and a board of directors.

Next, Nick told them about the winery and how much work was required, especially taking over someone else's project mid-cycle. That led to the creation of a chief facilities officer position. Over lunch they discussed what qualifications would be needed for all these job descriptions without mentioning any names. They agreed to fill the positions in-house with the SEALs first, wherever possible. And they knew the

CEO and CFOs would more than likely need to be someone who was getting off the Teams. These were not part-time jobs, so a salary would have to be paid, unless the people filling the slots were able financially to contribute their time, recouping it later on when they were making a profit. Nick and Devon would stay on as advisors, and perhaps partners too, depending on their cash situation.

As they drove up to the property, Devon looked in her element, still decorating her hair with bright red clips to hold what didn't hold up in a crystal comb. With her large belly and rosy cheeks, she didn't resemble the focused mindset of a star soft-pitch player or all-business attitude of the top-selling saleswoman in Sonoma County.

"I'd want to get Robert Minor from Davis to give us an evaluation," she said. "He'll be able to tell us if this is lack of water, or something systemic in the soil."

"Could it be that virus they talk about? What's it called?" Alex asked.

"Phylloxera, you mean?" Mark shook his head. "No, we got worse things here. Mildew, fungus. Those are our problems now." He stopped to examine a turning leaf, showing Alex a white powdery substance that could be scratched off with his fingernail. "When the old dead wood from the prior season isn't hauled away, it's a haven for pathogens. Here we got dead fruit, leaves, branches and other things blown in, all mixed together."

Jake asked the next question. "So the fact that the vineyard hasn't been properly tended means we have to understand what's here, what we have to fight."

"Identifying the enemy!" Coop confirmed.

"Yes." Mark walked down between the rows, kicking the dirt with his boot, stopping to pick a leaf here and there. He scraped the base of the vines with his toe. "Of course, one thing is for sure, this is prime Dry Creek Valley soil. Some of the most expensive vineyard land in the country. Perhaps the world."

"Let's go see the houses, shall we?" Devon asked.

Alex turned to Lucas and Zak. "You guys think you could live up here, do this?" They ambled over to the front door of the big house.

Lucas was first to speak. "I'm not ready to leave the Teams. You're not, are you, Alex?"

"Hell no. But someone will have to. That is, if we manage the money for the down payment."

"I'm game. Not sure how much longer they'll have me," Zak said. He had taken to wearing his black eye patch all the time, even though Alex knew he could sense some diffused light on occasion. The patch did more to hide the scarring around his eye than anything else.

"I know you're not the only one, Zak. Shoot, it coulda been me over there on the Canaries." Alex had always felt lucky his injury was to his leg, and not his face, like Zak. The mission was aborted without loss of life, except for the three would-be assassins against the Secretary of State. The public still wasn't aware how close they were to losing not only the Secretary, but several of the SEALs and State Department security team as well. Running a vineyard in beautiful Healdsburg seemed like a whole lot safer thing to do, and a pretty darned nice way to make a living.

But he wasn't ready to detach. Alex knew he'd fight a medical discharge tooth and nail.

They stepped on the large wraparound porch at the main house first. Built near the turn of the century, but Devon said it wasn't on the Historic Register. "Just some old guy who lived here forever. Think he bought it after World War II."

Inside, the home was still furnished with 1950's-style pieces right from a vintage House Beautiful magazine. The overstuffed upholstery still smelled of the man who was only dead a few days. A chill wiggled its way up Alex's spine.

"You get used to this sort of thing, Devon?" he asked her.

"What do you mean?"

"Looks like he's coming home anytime now. Just went out to do some shopping and will be back for some lunch and a nap."

"He's taking a nap all right," Cooper said.

The owner's pictures made one perfect row, lined up on the fireplace mantle. Old and yellowed, they revealed snapshots of a wife and children. Several other photos of graves and land without grapevines completed the display. As Alex looked around the living room, he didn't see any evidence of a feminine article indicating a woman had ever lived here.

They continued searching the rooms and timidly looking into closets. Most were empty. The master bedroom was different. The bare mattress looked out of place. The closet revealed gray and brown sweater vests, jackets hanging next to light tan pants and several wool plaid work shirts. Alex noted the man's boots were well worn, but clean, with two pair lined up next to one pair of polished black dress shoes.

"I see the shoes, but no suit to go with them," said Zak.

The two SEALs looked at each other and said at the same time, "He was buried in it."

Devon opened a dresser drawer. "Oh man, look at this."

Alex stood behind her, peering over her shoulder. There were several rolls of socks, organized by color, all rolled in the same direction.

"Okay, let's not open anything up until after the family has had a chance to inventory it," Devon added.

Despite the warning, Alex pulled on a broom closet knob at the end of the kitchen counter. The small storage area was nearly filled with stacks of brown paper bags, all folded in the same half fold, all facing the same direction.

How do some people live this way? Although Alex could appreciate the order, he couldn't understand the lack of anything entertaining or frivolous. An old black and white Mixmaster sat in one corner. The rolled Formica countertop was slightly spongy, containing swirls in turquoise, burgundy, yellow and black, and was edged in a one-inch metal strip tacked into place. He remarked how this could have been a June Cleaver kitchen just waiting for some cook from the 1950s to come home and prepare dinner for her family.

The TV in the living room looked like it was one of the first color models. No VCR or CD player of any kind. An unfamiliar electronics box on one of the open glass shelves was probably a record player.

"I'll bet there are some stories here. It would be kinda neat, if I had the time, to go through all his things and try to figure out who he had been and what he did."

All Alex got were blank stares and frowns from his Team buds. Devon's brow wrinkled. She pulled her briefcase onto the kitchen table and sat. Opening up her screen, she tapped a few keys and read before she looked up. "We have a couple of reports, but not the ones I was hoping for." She leaned back and cracked her back. "So, who's in and for how much?"

They went around the room, each SEAL giving their answer. Ryan and Cory were not sure they would go forward. Luke had gotten approval from Julie to pledge support. They didn't add Kyle, who had expressed interest. Several others might be added later.

"I got a signing bonus I'm due, but was going to use it for a house down payment," Alex added.

"Save it for the down payment, but we'll count you as in, without numbers," Devon responded.

She added up numbers she'd copied down. Lucas had no money to contribute, since he was in the middle of a nasty divorce, but mentioned he was willing to participate with labor. Coop noted his father-in-law was interested. Dr. Brownlee was also invested in Nick and Devon's winery as a minority partner. When it was all done, they had a commitment for nearly two hundred thousand dollars.

Alex whistled.

"That's not going to be enough," said Devon with a frown. "Not even 10 percent. On these deals, you will need 50 percent."

"So ask them, Devon," Nick insisted. "Tell them who we are. See if they'll take paper. You think there's any chance of that?"

"Not a snowball's chance in hell, Nick. I think they want the money. Maybe as a lease option, but honestly why would they do that? It ties the property up and all they get to keep is the option money if it doesn't work out. You're just buying a chance to bid on it in the future."

"At a set price, though," added Coop. "At least we know what we have to raise. Maybe that will give us a couple of years to do it."

"Couple of years?" Devon's grimace and near shout out echoed throughout the house. "I won't let you get into this with less than five to seven years as the option. Maybe some of you forget, you're still Uncle Sam's property. And you can't exactly order fertilizer and pay the help from the sand pit with PayPal."

"Yeah, the terrorists pretty much screwed up PayPal for overseas stuff," muttered Mark.

Nick wouldn't give up. "Just ask them, sweetheart. See what you can do." He gave her a peck on the cheek. Everyone was smiling but their realtor.

"You guys are completely nuts," she blurted out.

Most everyone nodded and made some effort to verbally agree.

"You have no idea what you're getting yourselves into," she added with emphasis.

"Been there, done that," answered Jake.

"You forget, Devon, we all believed the bull our Naval recruiter told us when we signed up. So far, nothing has been anything like what he said." Lucas looked to his teammates for agreement and got it 100 percent.

"We could start working on the property as soon as they sign the agreement," said Alex.

"What agreement?"

"The one you're gonna create," he added.

She searched for a set of sympathetic eyes, turning from one man to another. At last she stood in front of her husband, Nick Dunn. "You can't let them do this, Nick."

"I'm not going to do it. *You* are. You just meet with the people. See where they're at, and then we'll see if we can put some cash together and help with the details." He took Devon in his arms. "Devon, you're good at what you do. This is a walk in the park. We're the ones doing all the work."

Devon collapsed into his chest, mumbling, "I never thought you meant it, Nick."

"Come on, Devon," Zak interjected. "The least they'd have is a place that would be better than when they started."

Devon turned in Nick's arms, facing them. "You're not going to prune and cultivate some forty-six acres by yourselves, guys. You gotta hire that. And it costs money."

"Yup." Coop was nodding his head. "Gents, I think we've got some reading to catch up on. And Devon? Please get that consultant over here ASAP. I know he'll not do it for free, but we can cover that."

"Coop, it's likely to be several thousand dollars for the preliminary study." Her eyebrows were raised but Coop wasn't paying attention. Alex could tell he'd made his mind up and so had the group.

"I think this would be a fun caper. Bunch of SEALs going into the wine business. I can see it all now." His palm moved across the air slightly higher than his forehead, "Frog Piss Cellars."

That got a "Hooyah!"

Coop's cell rang. He stepped outside to take it in private. Everyone inside could hear him greeting their LPO, Kyle Lansdowne. That meant that he was either on his way up, or they were on their way out.

CHAPTER 14

SYDNEY WAS ABOUT to sign the employment form. Her pen was poised above the document.

"You sure you don't want to think about it first? Go back to San Diego, try on all these ideas and make sure you're doing the right thing?" Carly was revealing her concern. Sydney noted how hard she was trying to hide it.

"I gotta do *something*, Carly. Timing's right. Someone asked me what I do. Asked me what makes me tick. I told them,"—she pointed down at the form—"this. I said I wanted a good partner, and then I wanted to focus on making it to the AVP circuit. I wanted to be the best of the best. I intend to be."

"Boy, you make your mind up fast."

"Feed me some caffeine and chocolate, and you'll see some rather swift mood changes too, my friend."

"I'm all in, Sydney. I think you can do it. Right now, I have nothing else either. So, who knows? Maybe we do this. Maybe we start something really big. Maybe we have an epic fail. You figure?"

"Does it matter?" Sydney said after she'd signed the form.

"I say we go until we can't any more. That's all." Carly's eyes were sparkling. Her bright smile was infectious.

"Let's find out where our limits are, Carly. Let's just test ourselves, find out how far we can go. It's not a win or fail thing. We just don't give up, until we have to." As soon as she said it, Sydney knew who she sounded like.

"I like that attitude." Carly picked up the signed contract and put it in the general manager's in basket. "Done!" she said as she swept her hands together.

The day was coming to a close. "You staying at the Vintage again tonight?"

Sydney's internal smile warmed her belly with excitement. Memories. She would sleep soundly with the double session workout today. "Yes, ma'am. Are you starved, because I sure am?"

"I could eat a tire right now."

"Why don't you change and meet me at the Vintage? We can walk a couple of blocks to some restaurants. You know the area." Sydney might have offered to eat something simple at the diner at the hotel, but didn't want to be reminded of this morning's breakfast with Alex.

Carly agreed. They fist-bumped and went their separate ways.

When she returned to the motel, Sydney greeted the front desk clerk and headed to her room. In the back of her mind was concern about whether or not to contact Alex. She had hoped her decision would be clearer by the end of the day.

The workout had been grueling. She'd eaten healthy, not skipped her lunch. That was usually all it took to get her head level. But when it came to Alex, something inside her was ringing off the wall. An unanswered phone at an abandoned phone booth.

Her room was clean, but she could still smell the pheromones and visualize the look of them on the bed, as if she were gazing at a mirror while their bodies blended, went on that fantasy ride, trying to get as close as possible, indulging in the intensity without holding back. These sexual workouts were like fuel to her soul. Instead of settling her thoughts, the encounters brought energy and life to her world.

So, it was a conscious choice. *Do I look for that recharge of my batteries or go for logical forward planning?* She wondered if Alex thought that way, and realized perhaps it worked in him the opposite. In a firefight, there certainly would be the emotions of just staying alive in a dangerous place, saving each other. But through the fog of war, he was trained to think. Trained to use what they'd taught him. She could see why SEALs would have trouble assimilating into the "real" world, whatever that was. He was addicted to being the best Alex he could be, the killer machine.

Sydney had heard it said many times a good coach could tell which team was going to win by the intensity of their warm-up or their training for the week. She knew it was impossible to hide a lack of training, especially playing against a good opponent who would exploit the weaknesses they discovered. If her opponent saw she had difficulty with one particular type of serve, guess what she would see over and over again? That's if the opponent was talented and had the control to exploit it.

So too with Alex and the SEALs. It wasn't the superior equipment or firepower. It was their training, and something else—their mindset. She'd seen those poor guys down at the beach getting wet and sandy. Some of them were focused, others were checking out the pretty girls and showing off when they thought they could get away with it. But the ones who were going to make it could have been surfing on an iceberg like a polar bear, soaking up what little solar heat came from the crystals of ice reflected. They took advantage of every chance they had.

She sat on the bed and searched the empty walls of the motel room. She had a lot to do. She had to go back and pack, say good-bye to some friends, deal with Jack, gather her things in a rental trailer, and get herself back up here in two or three days' time, find a place to live, and start her new job. There wasn't a lot of room for second guesses. Overwhelming.

So maybe the good-bye she needed to do with Alex needed to be done in person, up here.

And, unless she was crazy, Sydney picked up that he expected her to contact him before she left. Maybe he was already on his way home too.

Am I ready for this?

The answer was a resounding, *yes!*

CHAPTER 15

C OOP BROUGHT EVERYONE together in a huddle. Devon walked outside with two of the heirs, both granddaughters of the late Mr. Santos.

"That was Kyle just now. Danny has gotten word Ali's paperwork has been stalled. As most of you know, he's been trying to bring the little guy here to the States."

Alex remembered seeing pictures of the little brown-haired boy and his poor father, the former Iraqi captain, who had lost the rest of his family, but deserted to spend his last days trying to protect his four-year-old son.

"I thought he was already at the orphanage north of Bagdad," Luke said. Alex and the others nodded in agreement.

"Perhaps you didn't hear the news. Parts of the city have been taken over by ISIS and other renegade fighters. The UN workers have been ordered to leave," Coop added.

"So what happens to the kids?" asked Alex.

"We don't know. I'm afraid once the aid workers leave, they'll be on their own."

"Those *assholes*," shouted Jake.

"Kyle says we're to get our butts back down to San Diego tomorrow. Alex, you, Lucas, Jake, Mark, and I have been given the opportunity to volunteer for 'Operation Ali Baba.' Luke, Ryan, and Cory, you may be needed so we're asking you to return home with the others too." Coop walked over to Zak, placing his hands on the one-eyed SEAL's shoulders. "Zak, you've been ordered to stand down for this pending further orders."

"I'll help in any capacity that's given me," croaked Zak. Alex could see he was emotional about not being selected to serve even in a support role.

"You'll be staying in San Diego, Zak. But we'll see if we can get something for you to do. Or you can stay here."

"No, I want to go with the rest of my team."

Nick stood next to him and placed an arm around his shoulder. "We need you to stay here, Zak. They can reach you by phone just as well from here as San Diego."

Coop nodded. "You're still cleared for time off up here. I say you stay and help Devon." He examined the faces of the rest of the team. "If any of these guys want to start talking vineyards, soil analysis, escrow instructions, or financial statements, you're our go-to guy. Got it?"

Zak accepted his fate and agreed to stay behind.

"Danny must be beside himself," whispered Mark. "He's going too, right?"

"Yes. On his way. He and Luci are building a house on the Res. He, T.J., Fredo, and Rory will meet us in San Diego tomorrow. We can catch a flight out of Schulz Airport early tomorrow morning, then fly out oh-one hundred Monday morning for the pit. Kyle and the staff are making all the arrangements."

"Or we drive. Fuck, I'm leaving tonight," said Mark. "I could use some company to take turns navigating so I can get some sleep. I don't want to wait until tomorrow. I won't have any time to say good-bye to Sophia."

"If we fly out, how do we get the trucks back home? We gotta drive, Coop," said Ryan.

"I need to run it by Kyle first, but if you want to, don't have a problem with that. You'll get home before we will. Who wants to go with him if it's approved?"

Everyone raised their hands, except Zak and Alex.

Coop walked up to Nick. "Sorry, man. That work party's going to have to be delayed some."

"Hey, you guys, this is important, way more important than the winery deal. Devon will try to work her magic while you're gone, and Zak and I will see what we got when you get back," Nick said.

Coop and the rest of the team focused on Alex. Coop asked, "So what's up with you?"

"Coop, if it's okay, may I fly back tomorrow morning? I can say my good-byes up here. I'll leave my truck with Zak here, although you sonofabitch put a scratch on it with your one-eyed driving and I'll personally come back and poke out your other eye."

The light-hearted laughter was welcomed and eased some of the tension of the upcoming mission.

"Okay, lemme get Kyle back on the phone. And one of you guys has to ride with me. I'm not driving that whole distance without some shut-eye. Lord knows we won't get much rest bouncing around in that box of rocks getting over there."

Devon was shaking hands as the two daughters looked through the doorway at the group of SEALs in the kitchen. One of them smiled and waved, which was returned by several of the guys.

Devon burst through the ten-light door with a confident smile on her face. "I have great news!" When she saw a lack of excitement on the long faces of her husband and the rest of the team, she asked, "So who died?"

"We've had a change of plans, sweetheart." Nick took her hand. "Everyone's got to go back to San Diego."

"What, now? How will we get a contract signed?"

Nick pulled Zak to him. "We've got the bossman here. He's staying behind to help put together the deets, just in case we can."

Devon was searching for some clue as to what had occurred while she was outside doing her sales pitch to the two girls. Nick gave a pleading glance at Coop, who decided it was okay to let her know a little bit about the mission.

"Little Ali, the boy Danny has been trying to get cleared to come here, is in trouble. We're being called on to help rescue some aid workers and the kids who stayed behind. That's all I can tell you and you can't say anything, Devon."

"No problem."

"I would like your good news, though," Alex asked.

"The heirs are several months away from making a decision on what to do with the money, working with accountants and attorneys and such. Since they know it will take time to do your proper research, and they're not ready yet to part with the place, not to mention clean everything out, they will entertain an option to purchase, first right, for a nominal fee."

"How nominal?" Coop asked, ever the frugal one.

"Only fifty thousand dollars. They'll give a two year, with an automatic two year extension for an additional fee."

Alex heard several whistles. Coop swore, "That's nominal?"

Zak began to lighten up. "Shoot, I think my wife's father and his buddies on the force would be interested in helping out with that one. They could raise that kind of dough, no problem."

"Zak, why don't you have her come up, and you can stay with us?"

Coop interrupted. "Going to make that call," he said as he exited to the outside.

Alex mulled over his possibilities in case Kyle nixed his request. He could just leave the truck for Zak to use and fly back to San Diego or ride back with Cooper. There were a lot of things about the mission he had questions about since he hadn't been involved in the original rescue of Ali a year ago.

Or he could attempt to see Sydney one more time. Only question was, would it be smart to call her or let her call him? She'd been obvious she wanted her space. And maybe she was already planning to return or had started the trip back. He knew he had to find out.

Coop walked back through the kitchen doorway. "Okay, Alex, you're set to fly home tomorrow at oh-six-hundred. Don't be late. The rest of you, we get back to the winery, load up, and leave."

Devon locked the door behind them. "We never got to see the guest cottage. There are outbuildings too. I'll show Zak tomorrow, and we'll send pictures to all of you. Maybe do a podcast?" She smiled and patted Zak on the back.

"Yeah, we'll make a YouTube video," answered Zak, who appeared to be warming up to the idea of staying behind.

ALEX GAVE COOP some gear he wouldn't be able to bring on the plane. He never went on the road without packing. He doubted the small airline and airport would be forgiving of him bringing any firearm on the plane.

He walked into the bunk room, sat on a creaky chair, and called Sydney.

She picked up, with music and the sound of a crowd in the background. "Hold on a minute, Alex. I can't hear well."

He waited. His heart was pounding in his chest.

"Okay. Sorry. I'm having dinner with my friend."

"Oh, good. That work out for you, then?"

"Yes. We're excited about working together."

"That's great, Syd. Say, I just wanted to say good-bye. We're leaving for an overseas gig tomorrow, and I'll be gone for a while. I know I wasn't supposed to call you—"

"No, it's all right, Alex. I'm glad you did."

"Well, I wasn't going to. I was going to give you lots of space, which it sounds like you need, especially now that you're focused on your training."

"Thank you."

The silence hung between them. It was almost as heavy as the lump in his chest.

"I appreciate your restraint, Alex. I really do. I've made some plans. Maybe after dinner we could talk? If you're not busy."

"You want me to give you a call then?"

She paused. "I—I know if you're leaving tomorrow you'll want to get some rest, and I wouldn't want to keep you up—"

"Come on, Sydney. Nothing I'd rather do than talk to you again, and I think you know that about me by now."

"Are you free in person?" He heard her heavy breathing, belying her nervousness. It sparked his need all too quickly.

"I can be free in person. Is that what you'd like?" She didn't answer him, so he persisted. "Sydney, you gotta tell me what you like."

"Well, if you're going to be gone, maybe a proper good-bye? So yes, I'd like to see you."

"Me too." He worried that he sounded too urgent.

She paused. Her words were calculated, careful, well crafted.

"Well then, I'll try to keep the talking down to a minimum."

"Promise?"

"Maybe."

"That's good enough for me, sweetheart. I have to be at the airport at 5:00 a.m."

"That should give us just about enough time. Barely."

"I can hardly wait. How much longer will you be with your friend?"

"Stop by and I'll introduce you two. You should meet Carly. We're at the Mexican place on the square."

"Near the motel?"

"That very one."

"I'll see you soon, then."

Hanging up, he wondered what doorway he was entering tonight. And was it a good idea before stepping through the gates of Hell?

But that's what life gave him, and he'd always been one to make the most out of what he was given.

The future was always uncertain, but tonight was a pure gift.

CHAPTER 16

SYDNEY KNEW ALEX had entered the restaurant and was approaching her back from the reaction on Carly's face. Her eyes got huge, her chest got blotchy, and her normally composed friend fiddled with an errant strand of hair at her temple.

"Um, there's some really big guy coming toward us, Sydney. Tall, dark, and dangerous."

Sydney smiled. "I think you're about to have an Alex encounter."

"Holy shit," Carly said as she retreated to her margarita and kept her gaze down.

He sat down next to Sydney, putting his arm around her shoulder, drawing her sideways into him, and giving her a kiss on the cheek. He left his large hand at the base of her skull to massage the upper vertebrae there, which warmed her all over.

She worked up the nerve to turn and face him. His soft eyes said all the right things. "Hey you," she whispered, with a smile chaser that was returned.

Alex abruptly drew his attention to Carly, extending his hand over the table. "Name's Alex Kowicki. So you must be Carly, is it?"

"Nice to meet you, Alex," she said as she took his hand and then withdrew. Her scrutiny going back and forth between Sydney and Alex telegraphed she was piecing together clues of a very strong sexual pull.

"Well, I imagine I'll be seeing more of you, then," Carly started. "Alex, you live up here in Sonoma County?"

"No, ma'am. San Diego. I'm in the Navy."

"Of course you are!" Carly's little laugh was suddenly sharp and a little too loud for the room, turning a couple of heads. "Well, I'll let the two of you get on with your evening, then. Sydney and I are just about done, right?" She ended her statement with raised eyebrows and bowed head in Sydney's direction.

"Yes, I'll touch base with you tomorrow, before I leave."

"Leave? You're leaving?" he asked her.

"Yes, I've decided to move up here and train with Carly. She's got me a job and everything. I'm going home to get my things, and then I'll be looking for a place to rent."

"Oh, and she can stay with me until she does. Not to worry," Carly piped up.

"I see." He was looking deep into Sydney's eyes without a trace of a smile.

"That's why I thought it would be a good idea to have a talk before you go back, Alex," Sydney whispered.

"Oh! That's why then." He smiled, taking her hand in his. Unashamed to show affection for her, he kissed her knuckles. Peripherally, she could see Carly had closed her eyes briefly. His lips were warm, lingering slightly longer than a normal kiss. She felt the tip of his tongue press slightly between her index and middle finger. She focused on his wet lips and the tiny flare of his nostrils as his thumb rubbed persistently on the underside of her palm. She had totally surrendered to his touch. Again.

"Okay, that's my cue." Carly's voice was laced with a nervous edge. She stood, and Sydney did the same, giving her a hug.

"I'll call you tomorrow, Carly. Thanks for everything."

Alex was picking off Sydney's plate.

"We can order you something," she said, watching him inhale the food.

"Nope, I like yours here." He smiled between bites. "You okay with this?" he asked pointing to her near-empty plate with his fork.

"I'm totally okay with this. I like watching you eat."

He winked at her, grabbed for a tortilla chip and, after piling on more salsa than she thought possible, lobbed it in his mouth. He wiped his lips with a napkin and stared at hers. "You ready to talk?"

"Whenever you are."

"Let's see how far we get. You want another margarita?"

"Sure." Her insides were melting like butter.

Alex stood and drew their waitress over, ordering a large strawberry margarita. "We're sharing," he said as he scooted closer to her. "So, Sydney, you've been a busy girl in the last few hours. Tell me about your plans."

"Carly has some really good hands. Her setting skills are great, she digs as good as I can, and she picks things up quick. She'll be a good partner for me."

"That's cool. What else?"

"There's this first-class facility here. She coaches a couple of teams, and then works at the gym. We'd have practically unlimited court time, so staying up here, especially after she got me a job there, seemed like the logical choice. I've decided I'm moving. The choice was simple."

"Sounds well thought out. You can tell that much from one workout with her?"

"No, we've known each other, played against each other in college. Otherwise, yes, you'd call it an impulsive decision. But being up here, out of the big scene down in Southern California, is healthier for me."

He was watching her. She could feel his eyes on the top of her head as she examined her fingers.

"And what's the downside?"

"Well, not being around the circuit live, maybe my intensity will wane?"

"You?"

She laughed with him. "Well, I guess I could stock up on Junior Mints, caffeine and popcorn."

"But stay away from the movies, sweetheart. At least until I can come up for a visit."

"Another downside too. I wouldn't get to see you as often."

"Well, as it turns out, we might be coming up a bunch more when we get back from the sandbox. Looks like we've located a property to purchase. A rundown winery property. I'll be coming up now and then to lend a hand if they go through with it."

"That would be fantastic." Sydney traced over some of the banded tats on Alex's forearm. She walked with two fingers the three-toed track marks inside his right arm. "What are these?"

"Just something we do on Kyle's team. We all get frog prints. You know, we're frogmen and all."

"Right." Her fingers touched his chest. He placed his hand over hers and drew it over his heart.

She could tell he wanted to say something but wasn't quite comfortable with it.

"So you leave tomorrow. Can you tell me what you'll be doing or how long you'll be gone?"

"This isn't our normal workup. Usually we train, then go, and afterwards have a few weeks of light duty stateside. This is something that came up, sort of an emergency mission, involving a friend."

"Okay." She could still feel his heart beating as he hadn't removed her hand from his chest. "But it's dangerous?"

"Dangerous everywhere, sweetheart. Getting worse by the day. One of the guys you met had his lady kidnapped by a terrorist group up north over a year ago."

She shivered at the thought of the loss of life happening on the other side of the world.

"Nothing for you to worry about. We got this."

"I've heard that line a few times in movies recently."

"Yeah, those are the cocky bastards who go running in until the zombies get them." Alex's grin was infectious. She found herself laughing at the dark humor.

"I'm glad you'll be here with your friend. Just keep your eyes and ears open at all times I wish I had time to drive back to San Diego with you and bring you back, but no can do."

Sydney lowered her voice to a sultry whisper. "Well, I have other ideas how we can spend the time together. None of them included riding in my van or your Hummer for ten hours."

"Well, we agree on that, for sure."

ALEX DROVE HER to the Vintage only two blocks away. Sydney noticed her mood was calm, the result of a good day's physical exertion. Her emotions were between the lines. Even her heightened arousal and sense of anticipation didn't take her off kilter. It was the first time she'd felt this way around Alex.

She noticed little things, like the way he sat, removed his shoes, and took his shirt off and laid it over the easy chair carefully. His jeans were folded on the seat. His American flag boxers were also folded. His T-shirt was draped carefully over the arm of the chair, and then smoothed over by his palms.

He hadn't looked at her while he did these things, or watched her while she undressed. When at last they were both naked, he on one side of the bed and Sydney on the other, they both paused without saying a word. His muscular body had a number of scars and tats she'd not noticed before in their urgent lovemaking of the last two days. His arms were longer than she'd remembered. The little finger on his left hand angled to the side, a little out of joint. He had a crescent-shaped purple scar over his upper thigh, dotted with evidence of old stitches now healed. A fresh bruise and scrape was on one knee. His body had worked hard in his nearly thirty years. His years as a Navy SEAL had taken their toll.

She had more delicate scars, like the surgery she'd had to her left elbow, a tiny scar from being smacked in the face with a glass wall when she tried to play handball and dove like she did on the beach. She had a crooked toe to match his little finger, but Alex wouldn't be able to see it.

She pulled her ponytail band from her hair, which was the signal for him to slip under the sheets. His tanned torso lying back against the stark white cotton pillowcases nearly took her breath away.

Whatever she'd done to come to this place, this right now, she was grateful for. Life was uncertain. Love could be cruel. Expectations were the darkest and sometimes the ugliest emotions in her soul. But tonight, she had none of them. She was on equal footing with this man who was a trained killer, a man who knew how to win and adapt to his environment. And he was waiting on her, watching her now as she pulled back the sheets, sat, and slipped her feet under the covers.

In seconds her body came to his like a heat-seeking missile, merging with the length of his thighs, and she felt his coarse hands slipping over her body. The taste of his careful, slow kisses sent a shiver down her spine and nearly brought her to tears. He covered her body, resting on his arms at her sides, sliding her long bangs from her forehead, dipping now and then to nibble under her ear or extract a wet kiss with the promise of something deeper. Her fingers touched his cheekbones, and she curled her other fingers behind his ears and then laced through his hair at the back of his head. She brought him forward to speak to his lips.

"You asked me, Alex, who I am."

He dipped his head lower to kiss her, but she placed her fingers between their lips.

"I'm that shooting star in the night sky. Going on a long, long journey, on my own trajectory. And then I ran into you. And it feels like I've planned it this way."

He chuckled. "Game of chance. Dangerous and beautiful, an exciting combination."

"Yes," she said. "Even our first date was a gamble. Arranged by others."

"Amazingly so." He was moving against her, angling his hips as he kissed her from her collarbone to just under her ear. And then he whispered, "Sydney, you promised."

She searched for the answer he was seeking. "Promised what?"

He continued nibbling down her neck, across and under her chin, holding her arms over her head with one of his hands, tucking his hip beneath her left thigh, raising it slightly over his waist so he could find her and slip home. But just before he did, he answered her question.

"You promised not to talk too much."

CHAPTER 17

IN THE EARLY morning hours, there is truth and honesty, Alex thought to himself. The distractions of daytime and the clashing of needs versus the time available, the sorting and choosing of tasks for specific purposes—all that was washed away in the early morning, honest hours of the new day.

Here, rising from the stupor of a love-lust indulgence, his heart still racing with the intensity of their lovemaking, becoming as close as he possibly could be to her, this magical angel who had stumbled into his life, he had no defense. Nor did he seek cover. He was as engaged as he could be without wearing her skin. But even that he would do if it would bring him more of the pleasure of her being.

It was strange that he'd never realized the hole that was there in his heart, even with the touching demonstrations of human kindness and cruelty he'd experienced being an elite warrior. He'd played his role, more as a means to test his own limits. And now he had something too that could be sacrificed, something larger and more important than his own life.

This time he was going off to battle with the taste of her still sweet on his tongue, something that could be taken away from him forever. Something he never wanted to lose. It was more than the loss of his favorite mutt growing up, or the girl he didn't get, or the loss of his cousin in the Twin Towers, the early passing of his grandmother, the number of times he'd sworn at his sister Joanne even though she told him he was going to Hell, and the father he never knew. Those were also regrets, scars that certified he was a human being and could feel, could love, could lose.

But never before had he willingly lifted his soul out on a silver platter and handed it to someone else to take, to discard, to not nurture or pay attention to. It was that trust in the space between where she was and where he was. All he wanted to do was show her, tell her that it had never happened to him before.

For the first time in his life, he didn't have a plan. This had never been a goal of his. Wasn't a direction he consciously moved towards. But he was here now. And in his arms was the most precious thing he'd ever experienced. It wasn't just the sex, although that was part of it certainly; it was the unrelenting life force of this lady who knocked him on his butt and made him look at his life as something incomplete without her.

And everything that had occurred up until now was just the path leading him here.

He wished she was awake, but he enjoyed the warm sweaty feel of her body halfway laying across his. She liked to be on top, he mused. His eyes watered as he felt her stir.

Then he'd be her foundation. He'd be her rock until he could no longer hold the bounds of his being together before letting it all fly off to Heaven.

Her forefinger encircled his nipple. Her breathing became deeper as her lithe body awakened to his day, charming every place her skin touched his. What a glorious way to wake up. Warriors throughout history were sent off to battle by the women who loved them, but none so grand as he was being sent by today.

"You're deep in thought, Alex. Share a little sample with me," she whispered and then kissed his chest, exploring with her tongue.

"I hesitate to say anything. I admonished you for talking too much last night." Her head popped up, and they shared a friendly smile. "And I so enjoyed the punishment, Alex."

"I need you to speak into my phone, so I can hear you say my name. I want to play it like a hundred times a day."

She arched on her elbows, bracing on his torso. His fingers luxuriously laced up and down her back, smoothing over her ass. The contour and feel of her body was even better than the view.

Sydney had been studying him. "So I pose the question again, talk to me, Alex."

At first he couldn't speak. She lightly traced the ridge of his left ear, slipping her three fingers down his cheek, following his jawline and then over his lips. Her thumbs moved upward, gently rubbing his eyebrows. She squeezed his earlobes between her thumb and first two fingers. He could feel her nipples harden against him as she inhaled what he was thinking and could not find words for.

She angled her head and smiled again. "You can't can you?"

It was true. He had no words. He drew his hand up to cover his eyes, and she captured it. "Then let me say it."

His breath hitched like he'd been exposed to a cold wind. He waited for what she was going to say next, hoping it would be something that wouldn't shatter their last morning together.

"I don't want you to go. I don't want this day to end with a goodbye."

He clutched her buttocks, bringing her into his groin. He quickly slipped from under her and pressed her into the bed, his hands on her face as he kissed her smile of pleasure. "Say it again, Sydney. Tell me again."

"I don't want you to go."

Could it really be? Could this be the dreaded "L" word creeping into his world? Is that what this feeling was? She was already a part of him, the *best* part of him, the part of him that would ache like the dickens on that airplane all those hours while he missed this, the part of him that would make him crash through anything and any obstacle to come back to her. His woman.

He angled himself to enter her as if it was the first, as every time was for him now. The words were there, but his tongue wouldn't cooperate. There was a frog in his throat. He arched upward as she pulled him inside her, her fists grabbing the flesh of his butt cheeks. He looked down on her smiling face as the wash of wonderful flesh on flesh consumed him. "Sydney," he whispered.

She waited with that knowing smile, matching his movements but her eyes remained tightly fixed on him. She knew. She knew what he so desperately wanted to say.

Her warm channel hugged him. Her thigh slung over his hip, reminding him how much he needed her body to show him how to be a real man.

She was shattering beneath him, almost as if she were suffering bravely. It was tears she was holding back. They thickly rolled from the corners of her eyes, onto the pillow with dark gray stains. Her body began to shake, but she wouldn't stop looking at him.

Was he somehow hurting her, while his body demanded satisfaction? He could not stop.

His arms slid between her warm, beautiful back and the mattress, as he pulled her up into his arms. She let her head roll back as if she was in a freefall. He held her shaking body wishing he could find the words he knew she wanted to hear.

His seed came with satisfying grace, so much more intense now that he knew whatever he felt between them, she felt the same.

He watched over her, tenderly kissing her while her orgasm pulsed, wearing her body out like a rag. He gently guided her home, back to the here and now, back from the peak of their passion to the real world where they stood side by side, as the perfect team.

He'd defend her to the ends of the earth. Nothing in the world would keep him from coming home to this woman. No price was too great to pay, no sacrifice too dear. She had opened up the future to him, and he knew he would never be the same.

CHAPTER 18

T HE TEAM ASSEMBLED in their SEAL Team 3 hangar, even the men who were staying behind. Kyle had asked that they bring every extra piece of firepower they owned, since they'd be riding military all the way and wouldn't be under the restrictions of commercial travel. There was government issue, and then there was every man's personal tastes when it came to weaponry. It also indicated to the men that for this fight it was important to use what they were comfortable with and accustomed to using—a sure sign they were in for some rough times.

Alex sat beside Cory and Ryan, his other roommates. Luke sat in front of them with two other team guys who were also not going on the mission. Coop and Fredo sat in the front row near Kyle.

Danny Begay was not his normal stoic self, nor was he sociable. The Navajo weapons and explosives specialist sat all alone in the last row of their little theater while Kyle went over the drill.

"Begay, you with us?" Kyle barked.

There was no quick response on Danny's part. Alex could only imagine how the man felt. He'd been trying for nearly a year to get the little boy out of Iraq after the sacrifice of his military father. Alex knew Danny considered it a debt to be paid in full and would not rest until it had been.

As SEALs, they could cut through anything and be the ones to "get 'er done," as their training required. But cutting through bureaucratic red tape was something they had trouble with. No one could understand how anyone could object to Ali and the other orphans in the temporary shelter coming to the States to families who would give them a new life. While everyone held their breath and waited, the children were looked after by some UN aid workers. And now something was seriously wrong with that arrangement. Alex was about to find out how wrong.

Danny looked up slowly, but kept his crooked slouch position, one boot on the crossbar of the chair in front of him, his hands in his lap fiddling with a bright red slingshot. The man was legendary how accurate he was with that thing, especially with the stainless steel balls he carried. But he could be just as accurate with a pebble or piece of glass. With his hunting skills, he was the most lethal killer the Team had when it came to perfectly silent hand-to-hand combat. When he threw knives, Danny never missed.

Ali was Danny's project and although he sat alone, the whole Team was there to make sure this time Danny got to bring Ali back.

"So here's the problem with our mission. The kids and aid workers—and we think there are four workers and ten children now, down from twelve kids—" Kyle flashed a stern look back at Danny who appeared as if he wanted to punch someone "—so we go in not knowing who's still alive. Our intel has told us only that they took the group up near Mosul, to the ISIS-held territory. The aid workers who were going to be released are now being classified as hostages. We have two from Uganda, one from Sweden, and one from Bulgaria."

T.J. Talbot raised his hand and barked before being given permission. "When was this? And are we sure they aren't still on the road?"

"They were picked up by an Army personnel carrier, one of ours, by the way, a present to the Iraqi forces upon our departure, except it got captured or sold to ISIS. They traveled along with supplies for their training camp, which we think is here." Kyle pointed to a red X slightly south of Mosul. "Although not spotted, we believe they made it up there in five hours due to road conditions. We have satellite images to thank for that. Unfortunately, most APCs look alike and from the sky don't tell us who is in them or in what condition."

This was an area the SEALs had known well, since earlier operations involving snatch and grabs were conducted in nearby villages before the SEALs were tasked to train Iraqi forces who would turn so they would later become their opposition in the killing fields. It was never lost on any of them that they had trained their adversaries to fight just like they did. And the US forces had generously left them great equipment to use as well. Some of the fighters were formidable, and they had an endless supply of willing recruits ready to die for their cause if they failed.

"We're going to drop in here. The Kurds will get us to the border, but we're not using any Iraqis except for your terp," Kyle pointed to a thin man who was dressed in camo, but without the tats and bulging arms he looked more like a shopkeeper.

Coop was on his feet so fast he literally bumped into T.J. who was rushing to the terp's side. "Jackie!"

Alex had never worked with this man before, but he knew the Iraqi interpreter had saved many of their lives over the tours his other teammates had gone on. His nickname was Jackie Daniels, his alias given him because it was easy to remember and didn't give the man's true identity. It was a huge asset to have him along, especially if they had to embed in a village or town and not be noticed.

Alex took his cue from Kyle, who watched the hasty reunion with little joy. He wondered if Kyle wasn't getting tired of seeing people he loved and respected placed in harm's way, especially for something that should not have happened. It was becoming a broken record these days. Missing machinery, parts, ammunition, people killed due to lack of preparation. Lives sacrificed while reaching for another weapon to help defend their brothers.

He saw in Kyle's face the wear and tear of the burden of planning, executing and bearing the brunt of the decisions, and then the burden of the explanations when things didn't go as planned.

Alex knew that although tired and nearly thirty-five years of age, having spent over fifteen years as a SEAL, Kyle would tell him, if he dared to ask, that it was the job he was made for. That gave Alex courage. Someday he'd transmit that courage to younger SEALs coming up the ranks. Take their testy asses and make men out of them. Men their mothers would love in life and honor in death if need be. It was a man's work to defend the innocent. At some point in the development of a hardened SEAL, the laughter and smack talk happened only to let off steam and not to be a hotshot. It was the way they kept the cobwebs that preceded Dr. Death and his absurd zombie ambulance crew from claiming any of them.

The rest of the instructions went quick. He fist-bumped Ryan and Cory, who already looked up to him because he was chosen to put his life on the line, and they were chosen to be backup.

"You keep their focus here, okay? Something happens, you guys yell and scream and make sure we aren't cut off with our dicks hanging, hear?" He followed it up with a smile just so they didn't think he was really serious.

Except of course, he was.

OF ALL THE rides to the sandbox, this one was the worst. Maybe it was because he'd spent so much time smoothing and kissing Miss Sydney's silky skin, and listening to subtle changes in the way she breathed, in the way she talked to herself when she didn't think he was listening. He could see her standing on a beach in her skimpy bathing suit.

Damn, I've not seen that action. When he got back, he intended to have her show him all her best moves. He'd reward her with kisses anywhere she wanted and he'd make love to her in the sand if she wanted it bad enough. Made no difference to him. Even going shopping for fresh fruit, red meat, and wine would be an orgasmic experience for him. These were all things he now realized he had never had.

He'd fix that shit soon as he returned.

Mark was throwing up from the ride, heaving into a plastic bag. Coop let T.J. tend to him, finally giving him a shot for his nausea. Fredo was discussing child rearing with Coop. Alex knew damn well Coop could only hear every other word, and with Fredo's heavily accented Spanglish and "isms," his phobias for health food and anything green except chilies and cilantro, Coop was probably hearing a story or an opinion he'd heard already twice today. Fredo never seemed to catch on that he could be boring as hell. No one had the heart to tell him because of the size of his dedication to the Team.

Kyle was asleep, and Alex was glad for that.

He looked at all the faces of the men he served with, all of whom left someone special at home. All except Jake. Because Coop probably told Kyle about Sydney. The ones left behind were single. He wondered if that was intentional.

Damn right it is. There wasn't anything Kyle did that wasn't in a plan. But he also wondered why he sent the married or committed ones in and not the unattached. Maybe it had to do with the children, and what these men might be able to emotionally handle. Maybe he didn't want the ones who could detach from the sight of kids being abused.

They landed after dark in the northern border region with Turkey. A small band of Kurdish fighters checked them out carefully, making eye contact with each of them. The shared expression of resolve gave the mission a higher likelihood of success. It was always the same with them. Tough as nails, defending their land filled with refugees from all over, camping out in fields their grandfathers had farmed, sharing their cattle, their water, maybe their women, but fighting just the same to preserve what they were forced to share.

He liked these guys. They were smart. Worst thing about their situation was that they didn't have the pull with either the US or with Turkey, and certainly not with the Bagdad government. He'd spent an afternoon pawing through dead bodies after one especially bloody engagement with the enemy on his first deployment. No ammunition could be left behind for two reasons: it either could come back to get you or it would leave a good Kurdish fighter without the means to defend himself, or you.

After his first tour, that dream of checking pockets and vests, finding pictures of wives and babies amongst the dead enemy, looking for intel and ammunition, had kept him awake at night. It wasn't the sort of thing he could get rid of with a few beers or a woman who wanted to impress a SEAL with her own moves. He just had to wait it out until the bright memory faded into a gray fog.

When those visions stopped fading, that's when he knew he'd be done. Or when going to bed became something he dreaded because he couldn't do it any longer. If he needed pills, he was done.

They moved quietly in a convoy without lights. The mission had been planned for a full moon, and the stars were always bright in this region of the world because of the lack of big electric grids. Moonlight made the roadside look wet like they were jeeping it down for a midnight swim in San Diego. Only thing they couldn't see without their NV headsets were the whites of the animals who dared to live here despite the carnage. Mostly skinny dogs. The fighters told him at one time the land was plentiful with small animals.

The building they were to sleep in for a few hours was an abandoned school that contained a fallout shelter, of all things. Two Kurdish men had guarded the place so they didn't have to take up valuable time clearing the structure—except Kyle insisted they do so anyhow.

The yellow radioactive sticker was nearly removed from the latch cover to the shelter. Some enemy forces had been routed out six months ago, but not before they had created a tunnel system that went who knows where. Figuring that out was going to be their job, but not until the light of day came upon them. Right now, they had to settle, eat a little, and get some sleep, taking turns.

Jake handed him a piece of goat jerky he'd picked up at the village in Turkey. It was actually quite good.

"They make this for us, you know. They don't eat goat in that village, but they have a rather good cottage industry selling it to Special Forces coming through. Look how they spell Teriyaki."

Alex laughed at the "Terri Yaqi" label. "As long as it isn't poisoned."

"Nah. They said it was okay," he answered pointing to their transportation and guard team.

"Gives you terrible farts," Jackie added. "Careful or it will announce your approach."

Alex and Jake chuckled.

"So you have two little ones now, Jackie, right?"

"Yes, Mr. T.J. Trying to keep up with you. But see, I'm a smaller man. You are the virile American."

"Horseshit. Being tall has nothing to do with it. It's how healthy you eat," said Coop. Fredo scowled and turned to the wall, pretending to take a nap.

Danny was listening to the wind above them. Little pebbles were pinging on top of the metal roof of the school. "Sandstorm," he whispered. "And I smell rain."

"No shit?" Jake said. "You can smell rain?"

"Personally, I think it's donkey piss," said Jackie with a grin.

Danny leaned into the three of them, "Do you know the worst place you can be during a lightning storm and flash flood?" he asked.

Alex knew what he was going to say before he actually did.

Jake was going to be the wiseguy. "On an all metal, fully-lit-up Ferris wheel?"

"Shush," Kyle whispered. "Get some rest because tomorrow's a big day."

Alex sat back. If it was ten hours' difference, then it would be close to noon at home. He'd be lounging by the pool, trying to coax that suit off Sydney, and making her dance for him on the diving board. And then he'd let her dance on his lap and send him to Heaven.

CHAPTER 19

BEFORE LEAVING FOR San Diego, Sydney previewed an apartment in a new complex on the north side of Santa Rosa, not too far from the gym and close to the freeway. With the move-in bonuses, she only had to leave a $100 deposit. Subject to her credit, which she knew was excellent, the attractive two-bedroom place on the top floor was hers. The large balcony off the living room faced east, but wrapped around three sides of the apartment. It would be perfect for having morning coffee or breakfast after an early morning run or workout.

She dictated notes for all the details she had to handle when she got back to town. By the time she got to her place and connected her computer to the Internet, the list would be transcribed and waiting for her. Next, she dialed her roommate.

"Okay, Sydney. As usual, your timing's perfect. I'm moving to Florida."

"Seriously?"

"Got a coaching job there."

"Awesome."

"Was just going to stay here for the summer to not leave you in the lurch, but since you already did that—"

"Oh, come on. I would have helped you pay for it, if I left you stuck with the full rent."

"I know. I'm just jealous. Things are really looking up for you. And there's a new man in your life. About time."

Before Sydney could respond, her roommate interrupted. "Oh gosh,

Jack said to give him a call. He's been a pest."

"I'll bet."

"Says he's been trying to get in contact with you for several days."

"He knew exactly where I was, and I've only been gone four days total." Sydney checked her phone, which was on vibrate and sure enough, there were several messages from Jack. And one voice message. "Okay. I see them. I'll call him next."

She stopped by her landlord's real estate office and told her about the move. There was always a waiting list for little houses down by the beach. Moving out quickly wasn't a problem because the rent always went up for the next person in line.

So that left Jack. At first she got the sound of his message recording. "Okay, Jack, sorry I didn't call you back—"

"Sydney! You're back. You were going to let me know."

"I told you where I was going. Sorry, I forgot to call." Her stomach lurched with what she had to tell him next. "Um, Jack, things have made a dramatic shift for me. I'm excited to tell you I've chosen a partner to train with, but it will mean I move up to Sonoma County."

"Really? Wow. I thought—"

"I know. This is sudden for me too, but I really like the direction everything is headed. So I'm going to withdraw from the co-ed league. I hope you can find a replacement for the tournament coming up. Maybe Holly?"

"Stop it, Sydney. Now you're making fun of me."

Only Jack would take a photograph of himself and think it was a cartoon. "I think my plan is going to work. And I like the idea of training in some degree of privacy."

"How are you going to get to games?"

"Well, it's not like we'll be in the middle of Africa. They do have cable and satellite here. And we won't be ready for qualifiers for several months, maybe a year."

"Of course. Dumb question."

"So, I'm afraid this is it. Hopefully, in about a year you'll see me at the beach events with Carly."

"Okay, kid. You'll be the one that got away."

"Aw, Jack. The way I see it, maybe you'll stay married longer this time."

"Ouch." After a brief silence. "Okay, best of luck, Sydney."

BACK AT HER bungalow, she removed her trophies, plaques, and her pictures, some of them taken in high school. She saw one with the Golden Gate Bridge in the background as she stood with her dad when he was healthy. She touched his image with her forefinger as if she could make the connection again.

Her resentment towards her mother for having forced her father to leave their home hadn't waned. With her mother's radical mood swings and wild ideas and boyfriends, Sydney had become the parent and her mother the child. The woman wasn't capable of taking care of anyone, including herself, and went from loser to loser, each "friend" a little scarier than the last. Finally, Sydney'd had enough and reached out to her father, who welcomed her with open arms. He put braces on her teeth, spent hours helping her with homework and bumping the ball around the yard. She had never felt so safe or so loved.

She packed the photographs and picture albums with the trophies. Under the blotter on her desk was the funeral notice for her father's service. She'd forgotten she'd saved it there.

After her father died, they had to wait three days until they could find her mom, who had been partying in Las Vegas with future ex-husband number five or six. Sydney was grateful she and her dad had talked about her future and his finances. He left a sizeable trust fund administered by an attorney friend of his. It had been the first thing her mother inquired about, and it didn't surprise Sydney one bit.

She read over the Order of Service, and the thank you from the family, and then discovered the message she'd written just for him:

"You were the best dad a girl could ever want. These past two years with you have been the best I'll probably ever have. I'm not sure how I'll get over missing you, but I know for sure I'll never stop loving you. I will make you proud, Dad. Your Favorite Gi-

raffe."

She'd forgotten he used to buy her stuffed giraffes. All arms and legs with practically no meat on her, she fit the description of his favorite nickname for her.

The notice was tucked carefully between two glass-framed awards, the awards added to a box, and one by one, all the boxes were stacked in the living room.

The next morning, moving men came, loading boxes, various pieces of furniture including her bed, desk, the dining table, and her big screen TV. Into her Murano she placed a few of her valuables, her favorite pillow and comforter, and some other personal items for the return trip to Sonoma County. She said good-bye to the movers, who would keep her things in storage for a week until she made it back up to Santa Rosa and called for them.

When she moved to San Diego two years ago, the first thing she did was sit on the deck at the Hotel Del Coronado and have chowder and a margarita overlooking the ocean, then walk down the beach and watch the young men in their boat crews trying to pass this little segment of the grueling BUD/S course required before they could move on to SEAL Qualification Training. Her friends had told her about this special breed of men, one in a thousand regular Navy ever getting to apply. And the pass rate for any of them to become full-fledged Navy SEALs could vary from 5 percent to maybe 20 percent by the time all was said and done.

So this being her last day in San Diego for a time, she decided to do the same again. The restaurant was packed since it was near the weekend. Outside, she had to share a section surrounding an unlit fire pit with several couples of various ages, celebrating birthdays or anniversaries. Though she felt out of place, she hoped someday to be one of those couples.

She finished her chowder and her drink, but picked up her French bread and took the wooden steps down to the white sand. She could barely see orange netting separating the beach from the training area. As she got closer, there was a crowd of people taking pictures, sitting and watching the men pick up the little rubber boats, put them on their heads in teams of ten or twelve, and navigate them over a rocky barrier that was sharp, craggy, and slippery. The boat was never allowed to touch the rocks or it had to be brought back to starting position. Once the rocks were scaled, the boat was put into the water.

Some of the boats capsized, dumping everyone out into the surf. Other teams drifted right out through the whitewater and into the inlet area, waiting for permission to come ashore. The same drill was done over and over again. Teams were yelled at by instructors with bullhorns. Two recruits were doing sit-ups in the surf for some sort of infraction. One boat crew was allowed a rare moment of rest, sitting at the edges of their rubber boat, oars pointed to the sky, watching all the activity before them. They cheered encouragement and shouted warnings to their fellow Team members. Other teams that groaned or occasionally complained were rewarded with a wet and sandy. Another team with several men who laughed as they ran by their fellow recruits' bad luck were ordered to join them in the surf.

The first day here and now the last day, she paid homage to these brave young men. With any luck perhaps one would permanently become a part of her life.

She blew the young men a kiss, turned on her heel, and headed back to the parking lot and then to the highway leading north.

THE APARTMENT WAS just as lovely as she'd remembered it. With no bed or furniture, she wrapped herself in her comforter, took a water bottle out on the balcony, and sat gazing at the red glow of the sunset. Tomorrow she and Carly would have their first real training day. She'd found her old workout schedule from college to use as a guide.

She closed her eyes and wondered what Alex was doing.

Be safe, my love. Come back to me.

CHAPTER 20

KYLE ASKED ALEX and Danny to accompany him on a scouting mission to see if they could locate the missing children. He'd had limited contact with the drone handler and not much had been learned, except the armored personnel carrier hadn't moved from the large hall adjacent to a bombed-out factory of some kind. Thinking it might be left there for a quick escape, they decided that's where they'd check first. They were mic'ed up. Cooper and Fredo were to listen in and comment if necessary from their bunker.

The Kurdish fighters struck up a conversation with Jackie in a pigeon Pashtu common to all of them. Jackie addressed Kyle.

"They say they've heard noises, perhaps an injured dog or something. They are not sure." Jackie shrugged.

"Maybe one of the kids?" asked Danny.

"My bet would be one of the aid workers," answered Kyle. "Those animals won't let them alone, and maybe that's a good thing in disguise. Gives the kids a fighting chance if the guards are preoccupied."

Jackie began the guttural singsong conversation again and then nodded. "They have not seen any women here for some time. And they do not know the exact number of guards."

Alex thought that whatever was going on in there, if this was the right place, it was fully self-contained, and he commented so. Kyle nodded.

"Ask them when their supplies come in, and if they ever leave to do a perimeter search or take a leak," demanded Kyle.

Jackie gave them the answer. "No leaks, no one comes and goes. But they are fastidious about taking out the trash. They leave white garbage bags outside the door first thing in the morning. A truck comes by once a day to pick up all the trash."

"So we steal one of those bags. That will tell us what is going on inside," said Kyle.

"I should go with you, Kyle," whispered Jackie.

"We're not here to talk, my friend. I need you to listen on the com in case we're overrun." He ordered Fredo to give him a mic. "You're more helpful telling me what I'm hearing, okay?"

"Okay, boss."

"Armando, you be ready. T.J., you help Fredo get out some flashy stuff we might need. See if there is anything here you guys can use."

"Roger that, Kyle. Do I have permission to move around outside?" answered T.J.

"Not yet. I can't take the chance someone saw us come in and is waiting in the wings to pick us off one at a time or radio for help. Stay invisible."

The town was without power either day or night, but at night the SEALs had the aid of specialized equipment. It gave them two very good reasons to explore then: it was cooler and it was easier for them to maneuver undetected.

There was one gas station operating with a generator attached to one pumping station. Dogs barked in the distance as they drew nearer to the building.

The roar of an oncoming jeep or large truck had them ducking into a doorway of a bombed home. The truck continued on its route without stopping at the warehouse building. Alex heard relief in the sighs of the men.

They kept to the shadows. There were lots of partial walls and piles of debris. Of biggest concern were explosive devices either left on purpose or left behind by retreating troops of either side. A no-man's land that technically was controlled by ISIS, there was no way to tell what fortification or level of manpower they'd encounter up ahead. The drones wouldn't be out until dawn, and they didn't have the intel on the ground that SEALs had used in the past. Their heat monitors showed nothing but small animal signatures, but the bright moon was interfering with the map.

A pinkish glow had just formed on the horizon, and at first Alex thought there was a fire up ahead. It turned out to be the toxic sunrise generated from burning oil fields. A measured sniff confirmed that detail. They'd have to be quick about getting back or lose the element of surprise.

The thick walls of the warehouse were not yielding anything from their new Graphene Sensors. Alex wondered if the bad guys had gotten smart about not positioning anyone inside against the perimeter walls.

One by one they hugged the perimeter and still no heat signature. Of concern was the fact that there were no windows or doors except the one in front facing the street. Alex guessed the enemy had selected this building carefully, knowing a rescue operation might ensue. This would be easier to defend or to control the outcome on the insides if compromised. Though this forward planning was disturbing, he'd been trained to read the enemy's intent and use whatever assumptions they had against them. Heavily laid plans were easiest to thwart with the element of surprise.

He guessed Kyle would create a breach of the walls of the building rather than attempt to use the entrance where they'd be expected.

Kyle was relaying intel back to the camp when they heard voices and someone coughing, coming from inside. And then they heard the distinct whimper of someone in pain, unable to control it. It did sound like an animal, like a dog. But it could also be a child.

Danny's jaw was set, and he closed his eyes, focusing on the noise. Someone was whispering a word they couldn't understand.

"You hear that?" asked Kyle.

"No, sir," came Coop's response.

"Sounds like *motley*, something like that," Kyle answered. Danny and Alex nodded in agreement. "See if you can get a translation. Jackie?"

"No, boss. I've never heard that language."

"So get some help. Coop? Swedish? Bulgarian? Ugandan?"

"Swahili, sir."

"What does it mean?"

"I'm just saying it would be Swahili, not Ugandan."

The coughing continued, followed by another moan, "*Mauti.*" Muffled voices and more coughing ensued from multiple sources. Danny opened his eyes at the sounds, which brightened his countenance. It appeared the coughing was intentionally done to hide the sounds of the injured party's moans.

"I'm confirming multiple persons, and I'm going to say they do sound like women or children. More than a handful," Kyle said to his earpiece.

"Roger that. Will relay," said Coop. "Working on *motley* too."

Kyle motioned toward another old storefront with the roof caved in, missing all its windows. It was located at the rear of the subject building, but still gave them a vantage of the street. The APC gave them partial cover, but blocked their view of oncoming traffic under the carriage or around the body of the APC.

The sky began to turn lighter gray with a pink tinge to it.

"We're coming back in five." Kyle pointed to his eyes, asking Danny and Alex to search for something they could use. Danny came up with some strips of cloth and a leather belt. Alex found two metal tins opened by a key, covered in what appeared to be Russian writing. The rolled edge was sharp enough to cut through a thick hide. A couple of cardboard boxes looked familiar, and they were surprised to find a board game of some kind using colored marbles. Danny was ecstatic with his find and filled two pockets with the little glass orbs.

They slipped down the back alleyway, again hugging the shadows of buildings, stopping to check out if anyone had eyes on them.

They heard the distinctive metal sound of a latch being pulled back and a door on creaky hinges being opened.

A small figure with a mop of dark hair held a plastic garbage bag, depositing it in the street, just before a hand yanked him backward and

shut the metal door. The boy's anguished yell drilled fear down Alex'
spine, but Danny was grinning from ear to ear.

"I swear that's Ali. He's alive, guys. We're gonna get him," said an
animated Danny.

"Hold that thought. We got a bunch of incoming. You guys make
yourselves invisible and hope to God they're just moving through," said
Coop.

The trio quickly ducked into another hovel of some kind. They
could still smell food, as if someone had lived there recently. A makeshift mattress in the corner, made up of rags and old hides appeared to
have been someone's bed for a time.

Soon, four large Russian military trucks drove through the dusty
downtown area, turned right and then proceeded without stopping.

"I'm gonna get that bag," said Danny.

"No wait." Kyle directed his next comment to Coop. "Anything
more?"

"I think we're clear for now."

Kyle nodded. Without making a sound, the Navajo SEAL ran with
lightning speed, picked up the white garbage bag, tucked it under his
jacket and returned without breaking a sweat.

"Good work. We're coming back, with a package," whispered Kyle.

CHAPTER 21

S YDNEY WENT FOR a five-mile run before she got to the gym and still
was nearly twenty minutes early. The bookkeeper, Mrs. Beeson, let
her in and signed a key to her name. The heavyset black woman
waddled in shoes that squeaked as she showed Sydney where her
personal locker was and where the equipment and supplies were stored.

"Don't you worry none about your first day. They might have you
work the café just so you get to meet the girls. In time, you'll get to
know the coaches and the mothers who practically live here. But I'm
gonna let Ruthie figure it out for you, so you just sit tight and wait for
Carly, okay?

Sydney liked her kind eyes and gentle demeanor.

"Can I help you with something, Mrs. Beeson?"

"Oh lord, child. I gotta concentrate on that new payroll system they
purchased. I don't get those checks out, and you know what'll happen.
You just don't worry that pretty little head of yours."

On the way back to the sand courts the woman turned to her.
"How'd you get to be so tall?"

"Genetics. Can't be the food or the water. I grew up in Southern
California."

"My son Mason was a tall boy. If he was still around, I'd be trying to
fix the two of you together," the woman said.

"Well, in my case, I have a boyfriend, so it wouldn't work. Maybe
Carly though."

"No, I'm sorry, the Lord saw fit to take my Mason overseas. That's not anything a mother should ever have to get over. He was a good boy." She walked to her desk, picked up a small school photograph and handed it to Sydney. She stared down at the picture of a handsome young man in a maroon graduation cap and gown.

It took all the effort she had to hand the picture back to Mrs. Beeson and thank her. Mrs. Beeson was talking on and on about how he'd enlisted right out of high school, would have played football in college, but he wanted to serve his country.

"Shouldn't have happened to a war hero. Did I tell you he was a hero?"

Sydney's hand was shaking. She needed water, and she couldn't get air all of a sudden.

"Excuse me, I have to go to the ladies room," she said and dashed down the hallway. She sat on the closed lid of the toilet and put her head in her hands. Recognizing she was having a panic attack, she wet down a paper towel and placed it at the back of her neck, sat back down and waited until the coolness settled her nerves.

When she heard Carly's voice, she stood, splashed water on her face, blotted it dry with her tank top, washed her hands again, and dashed out into the hallway to meet her new partner.

They shook hands. "They say all partnerships are never as good as your first working day together," Sydney said. "So, welcome to our first and perhaps our best." She was forcing her smile but found it worked.

Carly chuckled. "Yup, the new car or boat effect. You're absolutely in love with it that day. Only later do you find all the flaws you'd forgotten to think about or discounted as not being important enough."

They started taking turns setting and bumping while they talked casually. "You get a run in earlier?" Carly asked.

"Sure did."

"You tell me when I can pick it up," Carly said.

"Any time, bitch."

They played opposites and lobbed the ball back and forth over the net, angling it just enough so that the other person had to really stretch to keep from letting the ball hit the ground. After they got to the count of one hundred, Sydney picked up the pace. First she served, hitting the ball as hard as she could, nearly getting an ace every time. Carly didn't show her any mercy and did the same for another twenty five serves against Sydney. It didn't take long before Sydney wished she'd worn her suit, not the spandex and sports bra. She was covered in sweat and had downed half a gallon of water already. She only drank lots of water during trainings, never during a tournament until the play was over.

Two freshman players from Sonoma State approached after Carly waived them over. The four of them played hard, alternating partners, until at last Carly and Sydney worked together, which was a combination that was practically impossible for the new girls to defend against.

Sydney began to feel the rhythm of what their play would be like.

Over lunch, she talked about her workout from her college days.

"I knew you were a beach player. Now I wish I'd come to watch you before," said Carly.

"One of my teammates showed me the beach scene one summer. And man, I was hooked. But the scholarship was for indoor team play. And, as you know, when they're paying for you to go to college, they own you."

"It's a job."

"It is." Sydney dried her face off with a white fluffy towel. She pulled out her workout folder and the notebook she used to track her daily events, sharing how she alternated between doing heavy cardio and weight training, going lean and then binging. How she set up focus work such as serving, digging, and working on her foot speed with the ladder and the vertical leap trainer.

"We don't have those. Sort of a liability for the gym," Carly said pointing to the devices.

"I get it. I'll order them, okay? Not sure about the jumper, but I'm sure the ladder I can carry around in my trunk. If we go out to the coast, I'll have it. Make a training day out of a nice drive."

"Perfect! I'm going to modify this for me, too. This is excellent, Sydney."

After their lunch break, they worked side by side serving, then practiced roofing each other by working at the net. In regular team play, most opponents were ready for Sydney's killer spikes, and she'd been known in high school for breaking a good number of nose cartilages. She'd developed a quick swish move at the net so that instead of drilling the ball, she lobbed it carefully to a strategic place that was nearly impossible for Carly to reach.

They took a water break later on, and she watched the high school players parade in again like yesterday.

"It's an after-school league. Works because they get to play on a team with players whom they normally are competing against."

It made sense. *You always improve faster playing against an opponent who is better than you are.*

She watched them giggle, fix their ribbons and adjust their knee pads. They talked about sparkly nail polish and where they were going to go on vacation. Sydney watched the young players as if they were some alien species. She never had parents on the bleachers cheering her on during her last high school days.

She moved back in with her mother after her father passed. Her mother began leaving for several days at a time, which was a blessing. Sydney drove herself around to practices in her father's old BMW and agreed to pay rent as long as her mother never brought her boyfriends home. Her father's money paid for coaching and memberships on traveling teams, as well as recruiting trips. By the time she was a junior in high school, she was maintaining a heavy traveling schedule and was being sought after by several colleges Though she still lived at home, she was pretty much on her own. Graduation came and went. Her mother was a no show, and Sydney celebrated with the family of one of her teammates. She couldn't wait to get out of town and get to college, to have that life of her own. Her college scholarship was her way out of Dodge.

She studied the kids and their doting parents. It was even worse than down south. The spoiled little girls gave nasty looks to their mothers when they didn't care for the way their hair had turned out. They left half-finished sandwiches and tossed bottles of water after a couple of sips.

They have no idea what they're throwing away.

BEFORE SHE LEFT that day, Sydney made a copy of her workout plan for Carly, and they agreed to meet again in the morning for a run first. "Tomorrow you start being useful here. I'm going to give you a boy's team that comes in on Sunday mornings. They're a lot of fun. In the afternoon, you'll do your first birthday party, but I'll be there to help."

"Cool."

THE TALK ABOUT going to the beach made her think of this part of California's coast. She put the top down and drove the half hour to watch the rough surf crash down on the beach, which was more rock than sand. A couple of surfers in wet suits braved the cold waters of the Pacific, ever mindful of sharks and sinkholes in the dangerous Northern Californian coastline.

It was a different scene than the one she'd been at in San Diego. Less crowded and way colder with a brisk wind pulling fog behind it. She knew she would sleep well tonight having inhaled her fill of this fresh ocean breeze. Since nearly everything she did today was a new routine, her systems were overloaded. It had been years since she'd felt so relaxed.

Though it had gotten chilly she kept her top down and turned on the heated seats, playing some satellite country music she could sing along to. The hills were beginning to turn golden brown the further away from the ocean she got. Unlike other parts of the country, the biggest changes in colors occurred between the green of spring and the golden yellow-brown of summer. Dairy cows grazed and occasionally got onto the roadway, causing her to veer. She could see herself living here year-round. She planned on finding out what Sonoma County had to offer.

And then of course there was Alex. What would he want for her? She wondered what he was doing right now, if he was allowing the sights of a strange sunrise in a foreign land make him miss her. She

hoped so. She hoped he was finding answers to what they were searching for. Hoped there was some important mission being executed
flawlessly.

Come back to me soon, Alex.

CHAPTER 22

D ANNY DROPPED THE plastic bag in the middle of their little circle.
The two Kurds looked at each other and then turned down their
lips in disgust as Cooper carefully undid the twist tie, just like in any
kitchen at home. Coop held up the red fastener band with tiny metal
wire threaded through it.

"Glad bag."

Alex nearly lost it. If the citizens of the US could see them now,
huddling over a garbage bag in the night, in a dirty cave with no heat, in
the middle of the killing lands between two opposing armies, they
would question the millions of dollars spent training them all. They
might even ask for a refund.

"I'm going to examine the patient very carefully," Coop said as he
placed a facemask over his mouth like he was about to operate. Holding
his gloved hands in the air, twirling his fingers he added, "The patient
has but one orifice and I'm going in to explore now." He frowned,
opened wide the plastic bag and stuck his head inside.

Team members were darting worried glances all around until Coop
abruptly pulled his sandy brown pelt of a scalp up. In his best Dr.
Frankenstein imitation he held between his thumb and forefinger a
small, odd-looking, one-inch-long bug, it's bulbous body and crablike
legs wiggling, trying to get loose. "It's alive! It's alive!" Coop said in a
sinister whisper.

The Kurds whispered urgently in their own tongue, and Jackie
laughed, pointing out Coop's find, "They lay their eggs in the bellies of

dead camels. So, they are called camel spiders," he said, barely able to maintain.

"I understand they are quite good roasted," Coop said, his eyes still wild. Jackie nearly fell over backward laughing. The Kurds distanced themselves even further.

"You sure that bug didn't bite you?" asked Kyle.

"Gimme that thing," said Fredo, who yanked the insect from Coop's claws and burned it alive with a cigarette lighter. He tossed the still flaming carcass to the side. "Problem solved."

"They are harmless, my friend," Jackie said with a grin.

Fredo picked up what was left of the bug, squeezed the body and a green puss-like fluid came out. "This shit?" he said as he pointed to it. "You get this shit on your skin, and it will itch for five, count them, five days, comrades."

"Did not know that," said Kyle, very matter of fact. Armando and Danny were punching each other, hiding their chuckles behind their gloved hands.

T.J. was always the adventurous one. "Where'd you learn that, Frodo?"

"In an outhouse." Fredo's defiant stare gave way to his need to share. "I sat on one, that's how I know."

There were snickers all around the tunnel. Alex was streaming tears.

One of the Kurd fighters tapped an earpiece and said a word to Jackie.

"Listen up!" Jackie whispered. "They say a single truck is about three klicks out, heading this way."

Coop dove back into the bag and the horseplay stopped. He peeled back the plastic so everyone could aid in the search. They found several plastic fruit juice containers and straws. He nodded as he held up a bloody woman's sanitary napkin. "This is why the trash has to be taken out every day."

"So one of the aid workers is alive," whispered Alex.

"Or one of the children is of age," said Jackie. "They consider puberty to be at nine years, my friends."

But what Coop found next disturbed them all. There were bloody bandages made from strips of torn cloth. The discharge on the cloth was a light brownish yellow, mixed with blood.

"Someone's got a helluva infection. I'm not seeing any evidence of antibiotic creams, and I sure as hell don't think that person's on oral meds," Coop said after he sniffed the rags.

They quickly went through every piece of trash, saving cups, straws or anything that could aid in DNA identification if it came to that. Coop snipped off one section of bloody bandage and placed it in a plastic sandwich container. They found unfiltered cigarette butts, which could also be useful in identification since it was unlikely the children or the aid workers smoked.

At the very bottom, placed in another plastic bag, were pieces of magazine pages used as toilet paper.

He quickly returned the contents to the plastic Glad bag, refastened the twist tie, and handed the bag to Kyle. Danny grabbed it and departed their sanctuary.

"Alex and Armando, you watch him. Armani watch them tight."

Headlights flooded the abandoned buildings three houses down, and then flooded the roadway in front of their bunker with light. Armando trained his 300 Win on the driver, following the path the enemy's head traveled until they heard the squeal of brakes and a grinding of gears. The truck lurched, sputtered, and died halfway between their lookout and the entrance to the building housing the children.

In the moonlight, the white garbage bag shone like a giant free-formed pumpkin. Alex couldn't see Danny anywhere. The driver got out, walked to the doorway, picked up the bag, walked the short distance back to the truck and hoisted the bag into the back. With a backfire, he started the truck back up, nearly flooding it and was on his way into the town center via the winding descent.

Armando dropped the scope, surveying the horizon, which was now getting light bluish gray. All at once, Danny was right there in front of them. Alex felt like he'd jumped ten feet.

"Whoa. I didn't hear a thing. One minute I was looking out there and the next, boom, you were there," said Alex.

"That's kind of the point," returned Danny.

Aware they were not entirely invisible, the three team guys retreated to the safety of the underground bunker.

Kyle was on the phone with the Headshed discussing their options. Though they had heard someone complaining, the lives of the children didn't look in imminent danger, but that could change at any time.

"They're going to get a heat-seeking drone. We've ordered three birds since I'm hoping we can get everybody. We confirmed an injury, someone in pain who might be the same person, and a relatively healthy and brave little boy," Kyle's voice wobbled. "We go at oh-one-hundred, which means we rest up now and into the heat of the day. If we're not disturbed, we find another spot for tomorrow if we're still here, since the shed thinks it's likely our drop was spotted."

Alex listened while peeling off his vest and unbuttoning his shirt to get rid of the restriction he felt about his middle and get fresh air. He needed to drift off into a deep sleep quickly. Maybe it would all be over in twenty-four hours, and he'd be on his way home. He saw green fields waving in the breeze and vineyards stretched across hills in tight, perfect rows.

Kyle's words were droning on and on until at last they were coming from Sydney's lips and Alex was back in her bedroom as she rubbed against him and whispered battle plans.

HE AWOKE TO the smell of baby wipes. Danny had already been out and stolen a bag of oranges he'd found in a home recently bombed. The delicious fruit was literally inhaled by the group after they washed their faces and hands with the wipes.

Alex alternated with some bits of the dried goat jerky. Jackie passed around some glorious jasmine rice he'd brought from home. With bottled water that almost tasted sweet it was so pure, he was well satisfied in minutes and ready to start his new day at nearly midnight.

Kyle had good news about the extraction. Based on movements that had been tracked by satellite, it was determined the ISIS leaders had been planning an offensive on the north side of town beyond the town center. So the concentration of manpower was some five or six klicks away, which gave them a decent window to do a full-on raid.

Weapons checked and rechecked, each man had the laundry list of personal things they brought into battle. Their Invisios were adjusted and synched so their command could hear the chatter. Alex watched Danny stow a small red slingshot matching the larger one he'd been practicing with earlier and knew it was for little Ali.

They marked time and left the safety of their compound.

Fredo and Danny set charges along the back wall of the building. T.J. and Rory would cover the street, with Coop, Lucas and Mark going in behind the front door when it was breached. Armando and Jake took their perches on top of two abandoned buildings. That left Alex to attend to the breach of the back wall with Kyle. Danny would handle any problems with entry in case more explosives were required and then would accompany them. Jackie would follow behind. Fredo would man the alleyway behind and take care of escapees or signal any reinforcements coming to the aid of the guards inside.

The timed devices went off exactly as planned. The building construction was so weak, half the roof collapsed in the rear, so instead of crawling through a neat square hole, they had to navigate over rubble and falling debris from on top. The front door had been loaded with charges from the inside as well, so most the front of the building had collapsed, T.J. reported. Immediately Alex heard automatic weapons from the front of the building, which meant someone was on sentry detail.

The interior was thick with smoke but his night vision goggles clicked in after the initial blasts, and interior walls and doorways began to form. He heard children screaming and the staccato commands of guards who were scrambling for their weapons.

He and Danny found the children huddled in one corner of the room with two women standing defiantly in front of them to protect them.

"We're from the United States of America, and we're here to get you out." Danny's voice hung in the room like thick smoke. Through the wall of children out came Ali, who ran straight for the big SEAL. Danny kneeled to accept the hug of the little boy. "We're bringing you home," he said over Ali's head.

Alex guarded the doorway, hearing spotty gunfire and the ever-present "clear" as each room was searched and neutralized. He turned, counted ten children and three adults, and gave the count to Kyle and the others.

"And looks like Danny has Ali."

"Anyone injured?" Kyle's question was answered all around in the negative.

"Kids appear okay," said Danny.

Jackie raced inside the room and spoke with the aid workers, who did not speak Pashtu. "Swedish. I need to go to language school in Monterey, learn some Swedish. My Russian is so poor, the Bulgarian girl cannot understand me," he said as he shrugged.

"You're all right, Jackie. We like you just the way you are," Alex reassured him.

Alex asked the workers in English and crude sign language where the fourth was located and they pointed to a litter in the corner covered with a bloody rag.

"Hold it, we got injured or worse, one of the workers. I'm checking now," Alex said. He pulled back the sheet and found the chalky face of one of the Ugandan workers and checked for vital signs finding none. "One worker dead." He recognized the bandages from the garbage bag. She'd suffered a large gash to her lower leg, hugely infected and still swollen at the time of her death. Her body wasn't yet stiff so the death had occurred within the past few hours.

"Hey, Danny and Jackie, we gotta be ready to move out," Alex reminded his teammate who was hugging the children and giving them water and small granola bar rations. Jackie was explaining to the children they would be going on a helicopter ride soon. That news was met with much enthusiasm.

Kyle appeared from down the hall. "We're all clear, Alex. Let's get these kids out the back."

"None of them have shoes. We're gonna have to carry them," he told his LPO.

"Okay, hear that? Everyone who isn't gathering intel, we need help with the hostages."

One by one the children and three remaining workers were carried over the rubble of the back wall, herded together and led on foot back toward their bunker. The familiar *whosh, whosh, whosh* of the birds was music to Alex' ears.

A box of cell phones and some maps were recovered. An old computer was also taken, but looked like it hadn't been used in months. As Alex left with one of the girls, he glanced back, stopping to watch Coop and T.J. gathering blood samples from the four KIAs. One of them appeared to be a boy of around ten years of age. T.J. was swearing profusely.

"Looks just like this kid," Coop whispered, pointing to a teen who lay dead beside him. Everyone scrambled with their precious cargo, some holding two kids, and exited what was left of the crumbling building within seconds.

Mark ran back to gather their duty bags left in the bunker and to sign off with the Kurdish fighters.

Everyone was safely loaded. Ali was in Danny's lap and clung to him with all the energy he could muster. Alex heard Danny reassure him he was taking him home. "California, Ali. You're going to California."

Alex watched the faces of the other children, some girls but mostly boys and all below the age of nine or ten, when they heard the word California. He could see there was hope that those plans might include them as well. Alex wished he could take them all, wished he could forever protect them from the horrors they must have witnessed in a war that was already underway the day they were born.

As they lifted off Armando clung to his perch in the doorway of one of the other Black Hawks while Alex guarded his. They could see a line of lights as a small convoy was heading toward the building they'd just liberated. He was surprised to see the air clear of counterattack measures from the ground.

As they ascended further and headed north to Turkish air space, Alex pulled back to take his seat amongst several of the children, one worker and two SEALs. Mark was chattering. Everyone was elated the mission had gone off without a casualty. Before long, two little girls were wrapped around his upper torso, crying into his uniform. He murmured unfamiliar words to the tops of their heads he knew they fully understood though they spoke no English.

"You shoulda seen those Kurds, man," Mark began. "I got the bags, I thanked them, called them brother, we high-fived it, and they just walked into the countryside and disappeared into thin air. No one was coming for them, they just walked out. I'm telling you, those guys are tough."

Alex wondered what was going through their minds when they saw the Americans and the hostages being flown to safety, if there was such a place in the region. But he understood the fight was on their turf and they had innocents of their own they needed to go home to and protect. The mission was over, but the war continued and probably would for many years to come.

Alex began to relax as he leaned against the seat and allowed himself to breathe in fresh mechanical-scented air.

I'm going home.

CHAPTER 23

S YDNEY GOT THE call she'd been hoping for.
"I'm back on US soil."

"Oh, so wonderful to hear your voice, Alex. Did everything work out?"

"Yup, about as good as it could have."

"Where were you exactly?"

"Sorry, sweetheart, no details over the phone. And I have to run, but wanted you to know I'm safely back."

"Thanks. I'm so relieved. So when will I see you again?"

"Not for a while. We have debriefing to do and interviews, like exit interviews. I'm going to be tied up for at least two weeks before I can get back there. It would be the same if you came down here, too."

Sydney was disappointed, but she knew it came with the territory. "I got it. Well, call when we can chat a bit. I'll let you go, then."

After another brief good-bye, they hung up.

He had not asked her how things had been going on her end. The call, after such a dangerous separation, was all too brief. She knew she should reel in her emotions and deal with the reality that it would always be a tug of war of priorities, but because of the nature of what he did, his life and career would most likely come first. She had never had this type of relationship with a man before, since Sydney was usually the one in control. She wondered as the weeks went by how this would settle with her.

Missing her dad was the most painful part of growing up. Maybe that's why she had such a tough exterior to most guys. Maybe that's why she tried so hard in everything she did. Was she making up for something she'd lost and would never find again? A man who unconditionally loved her, like her father? Or an adult relationship with someone who wouldn't abandon her like her mother?

She attributed her thoughts on these matters to a lack of focus and vowed to pound it out of herself. Over the next few days, she threw herself into the new job and her training with Carly. Some evenings they'd sit at her apartment and watch matches of the AVP qualifying tour. They caught up on gossip about the players they both knew.

Her conversations with Alex were the highlights of her week. Although awkward not being able to talk about his work, she told him what she was doing and he encouraged her.

"You find little things to focus on, make up stories in your head when it seems you're at an impasse. You remind yourself you can do way more than you thought," he said one day.

"Don't you have doubts?"

"Every day. But I trust the training. I trust the men I work with."

"Okay, I get that. You assume you have the skills, you just work to apply them."

"Exactly," Alex answered. "I'll bet you're way too hard on yourself. The only times I doubt are when I think of all the things that could go wrong. That's not a place I go. If I feel that way, then I haven't trained enough. Train for every eventuality."

Though she would have preferred to speak about other things, the fact that he was talking about something he was passionate about, gave her some hope. He wasn't keeping everything to himself.

"I agree, Alex. Everyone is always looking for the most talented athletes. What they sometimes overlook is their dedication to their training. You've heard the stories too, about future Hall of Fame athletes who got beat out on school teams because others were better players. But when those players didn't practice or hone their skills, they were passed over in favor of the athlete who would train so hard he'd become great."

"Yup. You got it."

"Someone wrote a book about talent being overrated."

"Everyone wants the short cut. Only the few greats are willing to dedicate themselves to their work." The awkward silence lingered until he broke it. "Buy the way, speaking of being prepared, I meant to tell you that several months ago we had an altercation with a home-grown terrorist cell up there in Cloverdale. We think they got rooted out, but stay safe. Keep your eyes and ears open always."

Sydney had never heard about this and decided she'd ask Carly tonight.

Hanging up was one of the hardest things she had to do, and she couldn't wait to see him again. He was still postponing coming up to visit, blaming it on his change in work situation, which annoyed her. And though logically she couldn't put her finger on it, she was feeling him distancing himself from her with each phone call. They needed time alone together again. The loss of the intensity between them was beginning to sting, but she tried not to let it show in her conversations.

She was put in charge of working with some of the younger, inexperienced coaches. Sydney discovered she was good negotiating with parents. Playing time was always a sensitive subject. Many of the young coaches who worked with teams at Beach had difficulty expressing themselves or speaking with authority. Sydney had no problem with this and often helped bridge the gap. And there were also times when her direct approach was too much. There were occasionally tears on the part of the coaches or the players. She had her share of fierce conversations with parents out of earshot of their daughters. She asked several to leave their program.

But what was difficult for some also made her worthy of respect with others, who knew her no-nonsense style was like a brick wall. The Beach's general manager made her the director of coaching, and with it came a raise. After barely three weeks on the job, she was making a serious impact on the operations of the gym.

The competition for college-level play was even worse than when she was in high school. College scholarship monies had to be shared across several women's sports teams now, not just volleyball. And while volleyball was popular, it didn't bring in the revenue for the schools like football, baseball or sometimes soccer. This increased pressure made it so a girl who might be talented would have no chance competing for the best schools unless she had more than just school team experience. Sydney's summer camp program filled up within days after it was announced on their website.

Sydney began a scholarship for players who could not afford the league fees, subsidized by several local businesses. It was just a small first start to something she hoped would expand. She began to talk about their programs at civic group meetings, and a very favorable article was printed in the local newspaper.

When it came time to promote their league season launch party, she created a volunteer group to do community outreach. Their group targeted some neighborhoods with high refugee populations where she knew funds would be lacking, and she'd met several promising young players who would never have been exposed to volleyball or have had a chance at a college scholarship.

It was delivering on the promise to the community as well as her personal convictions that sports for young women was very important to their development. She wanted to see that every girl who wanted to play could find a team regardless of the family's financial situation. It made her proud to be part of such an organization and to share her American lifestyle, especially with those who sought sanctuary in this country.

And although making the AVP circuit was still her goal, she could see a life for herself outside her own volleyball play.

The new work must be satisfying, she thought, because each night she crashed into bed, often forgetting to change into her night clothes. Mornings came too soon.

But then she began to feel her energy waning during the play. Carly noticed and, true to their commitment to each other, one day after practice spoke the truth that Sydney was just becoming aware of.

"You getting enough sleep, Sydney?" She poured water over her head and waited for her answer.

"God yes. That's all I do when I get home. I'm beginning to think working with so many people, you know, the coaches, parents, and the players, it's taken more out of me than I'd thought."

"You just seem to run out of steam. Not like before."

"I'm adjusting. We both have a lot on our plate."

But over the next week, she began wondering when the tiredness would go away, and if there wasn't something more serious wrong with her.

Alex was leaving for a two-week training exercise in Alaska, and hinted perhaps he'd come up for a quick visit the following weekend, which thrilled her. She lay in bed, dreaming what it would be like to see him again, and mourning the fact she wouldn't be able to talk to him for what seemed like an eternity. Watching the reflection of the early morning sun play across her ceiling, she shook her head at what a sap she'd become. How she'd worried he was perhaps losing interest. She almost felt lazy, wallowing in—what was it? Whatever she and Alex had to work out, she was confident their next meeting would send all the doubts away.

Showtime!

She rolled out of bed, stood to stretch, and immediately was hit with nausea. She ran to the bathroom and threw up, but as she looked at her face in the mirror afterward, she realized she could count on one hand the number of times she'd been that sick to her stomach.

And then she knew. Of course, she'd have to verify it, but the way she'd been feeling over the past days came flooding back to her.

On her way to the gym she stopped by the drug store. After her morning setup routine, she went into the stall bathroom and conducted the urine test and watched the results appear with her own eyes.

I'm pregnant.

CHAPTER 24

ALEX HAD BEEN ruminating over the discussion he'd had with Kyle and Lieutenant Garrison two weeks before.

"We think you might have what it takes, son, to be part of our DevGru Team. You'd have to try out, of course, and I won't lie, most men find it even more challenging than the BUD/S training. Question is, is this something you can see yourself doing?"

He watched Kyle's stoic face and was given neither encouragement nor doubt. Kyle was going to leave it entirely up to him.

"I'd be lying if I said I wasn't flattered." Alex had met a couple of the Team 6 guys at joint operations before their last deployment. They were the stuff of legends. They were often referred to as the professional players. Kyle's group was one of the best squads of any of the Teams, but DevGru was the place where the big boys played and played hard. He knew them also to be made up of a bunch of crazies who occasionally strayed off the farm.

"You think it over. It will be four months before the physical try-outs. We have about the same percentage of passes as BUD/S, so you'll want to get into the best shape of your life, or it will literally kick you on your butt. You understand?"

"Yes, sir."

"I have things I have to go over on my end if you decide to give it a try, so make sure you come with a firm decision."

"How long do I have?"

Kyle stood up from his perch sitting on the edge of the Lieutenant's desk. "Most men say yes to the LT, Kowicki. But the formal answer to that question is, *yesterday.*"

That little conversation had changed his entire focus. All of a sudden, he had to ask himself if he was ready for that level of commitment. He couldn't deny that he'd found a family in SEAL Team 3, and leaving them would be like cutting off his arm. If he didn't make the workup, there was also no guarantee there'd be a spot on Kyle's squad if he detached.

He was hesitant to discuss it with any of his bachelor friends. Coop was off at a medical training in North Carolina. Lucas was still having child custody issues with his ex, Connie. The ensuing battle was postponing his marriage to Marcy. That's all Lucas talked about, and it used to entertain him but now was annoying. Danny was settling in with Ali, getting his medical checkup and shots and dealing with a host of issues he'd inherited by bringing the boy stateside without permission. No one had the heart to tell him he couldn't come with Danny, but the fallout was considerable. It was even threatening Danny's career.

So Alex decided to risk a conversation with Kyle.

"I can't help you there, Kowicki. Just some guys know it's for them. For me, when they asked me, I'd just made this Team's LPO, which is what they do. They not only want leaders, but good operators too."

"How did you decide?"

"I didn't look at them and say to myself, *hey, that's me.*"

"You think it has to be a calling?"

"It's for guys who think of nothing else. I'm not that guy, Alex. I got Christy, the kids. But even before Christy was in the picture, I knew there would be someone, and I wasn't sure I could put them behind my career."

That gave even more for Alex to think about.

"Don't let him force you, muscle you. Make sure it's your decision. But you know, if you do it, give it everything you've got. You decide once. Everything else is execution."

"Thanks, Kyle. Appreciate it."

"One more thing. The new little lady. How tight are we there?"

Alex smirked. "She's pretty damned good for me, Kyle. But she's focused, like we are. She has some goals to achieve before anything else can happen in her life. I wouldn't want to be the one to get in the way of that."

"So, she'd be okay with it?"

"Does it matter? I mean, I've heard some of the wives don't take to it."

"No, they don't. So will that be okay if that happens, Alex? Gotta know the answer to that question."

"I guess I better find out."

"Roger that. But don't forget, it's your decision. It's not a democracy. You're the one who knows whether or not you want it. And that better not be situational, Alex. You gotta love it no matter what."

"Thanks."

"Oh, and by the way, congratufuckinlations! That's awesome they asked you."

OVER THE COURSE of the next couple of weeks, he'd wondered what Sydney would say if she knew he was considering this new assignment. Of course, he might wash out. Would she be okay with that?

But then he kicked himself around the block a bit. *Since when do you have to get permission from anyone when it comes to your career?* Perhaps it was not a very good sign he was considering her opinion at all. He was an elite warrior, doing what most other men could never do. The last line of defense. Wasn't that a higher calling?

And then the doubts would begin flooding in. His old self was scolding him, just like Joanne or his mother would, asking how he could be so callused.

Alex decided he needed to settle some things between himself and the other women in his life. He called and asked for a meeting at his mom's house.

JOANNE LOOKED PALE and had lost weight. "You okay, sis?"

"Of course I am."

She worked in a Catholic school that provided convent housing. He honored the fact that she had the will to be of service, putting her own needs behind the needs of others, but he knew she still harbored ill feelings for all the needling he'd done growing up. And he didn't think she was happy, really happy.

"Don't get into it with your sister, Alex," said his mom. "We all live in glass houses."

If there were two polar opposites, his mother and his sister would be at different ends of the scale. His mother was bright, attractive, highly opinionated, cynical and undisciplined. Her somewhat unconventional lifestyle had always bothered him. She didn't surround herself with big thinkers, but she had a saint for a daughter. Alex felt that was a burden to her, a thorn in her side.

"So what's so big you have to call a meeting?" his mom said as she lit up her cigarette.

"Mom!" squawked Joanne.

"Oh, come on, you know I've been a smoker for over twenty years."

"I think what Joanne is saying is although it's *your* habit, she has to inhale it too." Alex knew his mother would find fault with this. He wasn't wrong.

"Oh, Christ!" She put her cigarette out without apologizing for the swearing either. Joanne rolled her eyes.

"Well," started Alex, "now we can see why we don't get together much anymore." He stood and paced in front of the women. Joanne was examining her hands in her lap.

Alex knew the meeting was a waste of time. He was suddenly filled with regret for having called it. He didn't want to talk about his invitation to try out for SEAL Team 6.

"Just thought we should be more in touch," he lied.

"Which is code for you've met someone," his mother said.

"No, Mom. Well, yes, I have, but that wasn't the reason I'm here."

"You don't fool me one bit, Alex. So you're going to dangle this little relationship in front of my nose? I've been asking you when you were going to get married for now—what—four years?"

"Probably longer," Joanne mumbled.

"Ever since I was out of diapers."

His mom chuckled at that comment.

Alex looked at the two of them seated on the purple velvet couch in his mother's small living room. Like everything surrounding her, the room was filled with splashes of color so bright it nearly hurt his eyes. No wonder she'd never remarried. No one would be able to stand living here, he thought.

He scratched the back of his neck. He hated being in these kinds of conversations. Sticky, undefined, everyone coming at him from different directions with motives he didn't trust. If this was family life, he never wanted anything to do with that. He'd rather get his teeth drilled without Novocain than have to spend a significant amount of time around these two women.

What the hell was I thinking?

Sydney was just as strong-willed, but she was—spectacular. That was the word he'd used to describe her to other Team guys. And even in her spectacularness, his mother would get a royal charge out of her zombie and chocolate fetish. That would be something he'd actually like to see.

His mother stood and came over to him. Putting her palm to his cheek, she began, "Alex, it's not that hard. Her name is…?" She waited, her eyebrows tented up.

He carefully peeled his mother's hand away. "Her name is Sydney. She's a beach volleyball player."

His mother smiled. "She wears those skimpy suits, all tanned and buttered up all the time." Her eyes sparkled with glee.

"Mother!" Alex shouted.

Joanne scowled at him, then faced his mother. "What is the matter with you? Let him say it in his own way. You're making him feel like an insect in a jar."

Alex was grateful his sister thought to stick up for him. "Like a camel spider," he added.

Both women looked up to him and said in unison, "What?"

"I saw one over in Iraq. Ugly things. Look like potato bugs, you know with the funny legs and big blue-green bodies." The women weren't reacting, so he added, "My co-worker sat on one."

"You see, Joanne, if you let him talk, this is what he does." His mother spoke to his sister like he wasn't in the room. He hated that.

Joanne looked up to him like she'd used to when they were kids. He saw a warmth there he hadn't seen for many years. "I'm ready to listen, Alex, when you're ready to talk about it. I'm not judging you. Just want you to know that."

"Thank you." He meant it. "Her name is Sydney, as I've said. I like her a lot." He opened his palms. "And there you have it. That's what I came to say."

All the way home he felt like a shit. Confusion wasn't natural for him. Only thing he knew to settle his nerves was to go for a skydive. Maybe his mother was right after all. All of them were freaks.

It just seemed like he should tell someone he was seriously considering doing something so dangerous that most men turned it down. He wasn't most men. His family wasn't like most families, either.

No, he knew who he needed to discuss this decision with. He'd been putting off the meeting, and now it was time. When he came back from Alaska he'd see her, and let her know how much he appreciated their time together.

And then he'd end the relationship. He had no business asking anyone to wait for him or grieve when he was gone. Besides, he was just learning how to get over his childhood. And this would give Sydney time to pursue her dreams without the distraction of worrying about where he was and what he was doing.

Now you're justifying again, you asshole. Maybe it was easier to commit to the SEALs than to a woman, even a spectacular woman like Sydney.

He hoped the cold of Alaska would freeze that burden out of him permanently.

Yup. Jumping out of an airplane at thirteen thousand feet today was sounding pretty good right now.

CHAPTER 25

SYDNEY DIDN'T TELL Carly about her pregnancy or the clinic appointment. She wanted unequivocal proof before she'd start talking about it with anyone. Faced with the choices she had to make, the decision whether or not to have the baby weighed heavily on her. She knew Alex would have a reaction and had a right to know. She knew it was the right thing to tell him, but she wasn't sure what effect it would have on their relationship. How much should that weigh on her decision?

And then, of course, was the issue of her AVP goals. That would also impact Carly. The Beach had stuck their neck out for her, giving her a safe space to train, to afford to live, to have whatever it was she wanted of her future goals. She told herself that included Alex, but this was totally not what she'd expected, having been on the pill.

Now she understood the difficulties other single women had in making this decision. It was ultimately a decision she had to live with the rest of her life. While she was thrilled at the possibility of raising a child of Alex's, it wasn't right to do that without his input. And she'd always disliked the decision others made to terminate a pregnancy. She thought the decision would be an easy one for her, but now she knew the truth of it.

The clinic was filled to bursting with pregnant women, usually alone, but occasionally with a mother or a boyfriend or husband. Some of the women were very young, not much older than the girls she worked with on her teams at the Beach.

She tried not to study the faces of the girls waiting, as if the burden or the joy of their situation would somehow affect her.

Her name was called by a hoarse woman in a lab coat covering blue jeans and a T-shirt. Suddenly, she felt guilty for not having waited to get a proper doctor's appointment in a discreet, private office somewhere.

But she wasn't one to shirk her responsibilities. Pregnancy had been the least of her worries when they were having unprotected sex. She'd been stupid. Really stupid, she thought as she followed the woman to the exam room.

"How far along are you?"

"Not long. Less than a month."

She was directed toward a chair. "So you've missed one period?"

"Oh my God. I didn't even think of that. I play sports, and sometimes when I'm heavily training, like now, I don't have one for several months.

"You must be aware of the fact that nearly a third of all pregnancies terminate themselves in the first trimester, right?"

"Yes, I think I knew that. I did the home test, and it came out positive. I repeated it again yesterday and the results were the same."

She answered a number of questions as the clerk went down the list of items on the form Sydney had filled out while waiting. She held her emotions inside and told herself she was here for the facts, that the decision didn't have to be made today or even this week. She'd be out of contact with Alex for another week. She was hoping that time would point her in the right direction.

"Any discharge, cramping?"

"No."

"We'll have to do a physical exam, but probably not today. You're sure on the dates?"

"Positive."

"Okay, let's get the blood test done. I'll need a urine sample too."

She was given a plastic cup and shown the way to the bathroom. The clerk had her wait while she dipped the test strip into her urine. It came out bright blue.

"That would be a yes," the woman said.

They made plans for a follow-up visit. Sydney was given a packet of information on the services they provided at the clinic. "So you can make an informed decision. I'm required to give you all of this, even if you're going to go through with having the baby. And we have counselors' phone numbers on the backside here and other resources too, all listed."

She thanked the clerk, took her packet and her appointment card and walked out through the waiting room without looking at a soul. The outcome was what she'd expected. She was waiting for her emotions to show up. But she'd done such a good job stuffing them down, they were MIA.

It wasn't until she saw a young mother with a baby in a Snugli pack that she felt her eyes ache and then tear up. Inhaling deeply and looking away helped. She'd way underestimated the flood of images of her father, family photographs she'd seen growing up and then cherished when he was gone. She knew what he'd say, what he'd be thinking if he were here. And she felt ashamed she was even considering the cruel alternative—something she was sure she'd regret the rest of her life.

At home that night, she put the brochure into the top drawer next to her bed and tucked it away, deciding for now she was going to put it all out of her mind. The first person she would tell was going to be here in a week. Then she'd go from there.

ALEX WAS COMING in on the eight-thirty direct flight from San Diego. She needed to pee again as she shifted her balance between feet, her hands tucked into her fleece jacket pockets. She didn't want to appear nervous, but she couldn't stop from sweating, and her breathing hitched unevenly as if she couldn't get enough air. Her mouth was parched. Her stomach lurched when she watched his plane land. She dug her hands out, placing them on the glass divider, leaving foggy handprints from her heat as she examined the string of passengers exiting the plane.

There was no mistaking Alex from everyone else around him. Not the tallest of men, he was certainly the best built, and with his sharp dark features and strong jawline, he was the one people noticed. Men moved away from him, giving him a wide berth, as if knowing what he did for a living. Women did double takes, sometimes whispering to the person beside them. It would forever be hard for Alex to walk into a room and not make the whole place sigh. She imagined him dressed to the nines, wearing a tux.

His long gait made fast work of the distance between them. His smile warmed her whole body. She held back the tears and regretted she couldn't just run and tell him about the pregnancy. Sydney was going to have to pretend everything was status quo until the right time. Playing this little game of hide and seek, which might have been thrilling in their past encounters as the sparks engulfed them, now felt dishonest. She had always been so sure of herself. Now she had to do the right thing, whatever that was, and worry she'd send him away, never to return.

In the warm embrace and the chaste kiss at the side of her face when he entered the lobby of the airport, she lost herself in the scent of the man she ached to love. She hated the barriers that now loomed large between them.

"Welcome back," she whispered, her arm wrapped around his waist, her head leaning into his shoulder.

His answer shocked her. "Thanks."

Not, *It's good to be back,* or *Missed you.*

"Where are you parked?" His voice was warm, but efficient. Something was wrong. A wave of nausea began at the pit of her stomach as her spine became stiff, her skin clammy, and her emotions prickly. Underneath it all was not only dread, but anger.

She handed him the keys, and he opened the door for her, placing his large bag in the second seat. Walking around to the driver's door, she saw through the windshield he was staring off into the distance and his left eye was narrowed, his lips pursed.

Instinctively she lay her hands against her stomach, willing it to stop flip-flopping between excitement and nausea. As soon as he'd strapped in and turned on the engine, she removed her hands and breathed in a wish upon that star that had always done so well for her. She didn't know what she was praying or wishing for. It was just a thought.

Please.

Alex cleared his throat. "Sydney, I have some things to bring to Nick. We didn't talk about arrangements, so they have the bunkhouse set up for me."

She whipped her head around, storm clouds brewing just above her eyebrows. "You're staying *there?* But I thought—"

He pulled over to the curb. They had neared the toll gate exit from the parking lot. He got out his wallet.

"It's free." She handed him the ticket. "Just give him this."

Their eyes made contact as he pulled the ticket from her fingers. Too late she'd discovered she was holding onto the paper, and he had to do a last minute tug.

His eyes softened before he answered her. "I know how busy you are. I just thought it would be easier."

She broke away and peered out the windshield at a pretty blue sky and green vineyard day, at a world that was moving along so normally. And she wasn't a part of it. The disappointment and anger building made it easy to control the tears that had been threatening. She didn't look at him when she answered, "We've not seen each other for over a month. You've been overseas on a dangerous mission you can't talk about. I've been working hard to focus on the training and all that supports it. These were the goals we stated when you left. These were the things we said we wanted to accomplish when we spoke on the phone."

He was heading to the toll booth, rolling down the window, when she turned to him and asked, "What's changed?"

He continued through the frontage road, towards the direction of the freeway. "I didn't want you to feel like you had to entertain me."

"And why not? You didn't seem to mind last time you were here." She held back the venom she was feeling.

His chuckle began to melt her frostiness. "No, that's true, Sydney. Those were some mighty wonderful times, and I think of them often." She saw his smile in profile.

"So where's the but?"

"I didn't want you to feel obligated, you know, just in case—"

"Just in case I'd changed my mind about seeing you? You honestly think that would be anywhere within the realm of possibility? Alex, just level with me. Have you changed your mind? What am I missing here?"

Sydney watched as he peeled off the freeway to the country road his friend's winery must be on.

"We need to talk. I'm crazy about you, Sydney." He grabbed her hand. "Your hands are cold." He kissed her knuckles, which further melted her defensive exterior. "But some things have happened, and we need to talk first. This time, we *have* to talk."

No kidding!

"So, I'm going to drop off the things I brought for Nick, and then maybe you and I can go have a private chat somewhere."

His cell phone chirped. Sydney could hear a man's voice on the other end. It sounded like Nick was telling him they were on their way to the hospital.

"That's great news, man. We're probably ten minutes away. I'll drop off your order if someone can let me in."

There was chatter.

"That'll work. Give me the name of the hospital." He turned to Sydney. "Santa Rosa Memorial? Okay, I think we can find it. Maybe see you in an hour? Give you a chance to settle in?"

She heard more chatter. "Well, call me if something changes. Hey, man, congratulations! You're almost a father. That's cool. Very cool."

Sydney looked out the passenger window as they wound under the freeway and down the two-lane country road.

"Well, that kind of changes things a bit. They're off to have their baby. Mind if we stop by?"

"Of course not," she said to the window.

She felt his hand on her shoulder, shaking her slightly. "You okay?

Everything okay?"

"Everything's fine."

When she didn't look him in the face, he dropped his hand. Soon, they were at the gravel driveway of Sophie's Choice Winery. She remarked how beautiful the golden hills were that bordered the bucolic valley of green vineyards and olive trees. They came upon a field of lavender before arriving at the tasting room entrance. A large water fountain embellished the entrance. The parking lot was empty. Alex drove around the side to the back where several modern structures and a warehouse were located.

From his large bag, Alex took out a long black nylon zipper case Sydney recognized was for a long gun. "I'll give you a tour," he said.

The back door to the main house was open. He took her hand. "You'll love this place. Come on."

He seemed to warm the longer they were inside. Alex led her up the wooden staircase to a set of double doors leading to the master bedroom. He placed the case on the floor of a walk-in closet. A large four-poster bed dwarfed the room. Antiques and hand-hewn furniture decorated the space. The ambiance of the home was lovely.

"There's Devon's office down there. Nick has one of the spare bedrooms up here for his. Downstairs they have a guest room and bath." He grabbed her hand tighter this time. Her unease was beginning to dissipate. They stopped at the top of the staircase, overlooking the living/dining/kitchen great room downstairs. Straight across clearstory windows showing the lush green of the rows of vines. "You like?"

The whole house and surrounding property made her breathless. "What's not to like? It's incredible. So this, this is what you guys were talking about doing up here?"

He gave a half laugh. "You understand Nick and Devon have been working on it for several years. All her income and what he inherited from his sister went into making this place what it is today. Took a lot of work and a lot of money. We don't have the luxury of either. But we're working on it."

"But this is the inspiration, the vision, right?" She felt the heat from his body as she stood close to him. She leaned against the railing bending one knee so that when their eyes met, they were level to each other. He watched her mouth as if it was the first time he'd noticed her.

The tug of the chemistry between them was still there. His hand came up to the back of her head as he pressed his lips to hers. She let her inner demon out and pulled him into her, which made him chuckle through the deepening kiss. "Don't tell me you're staying anywhere else but my bed, sailor. Don't you dare tell me that."

"Well, all right," was his answer. His sigh was music to her ears. He was falling into the urgency of their proximity to each other. The attraction was undeniable and just as strong as it had ever been.

And then he pulled away. "Come on. We have to talk." He led her down the stairs to the kitchen, pulled out two glasses and poured them each ice water from the dispenser, handing one to her. "Just a minute while I check on something first." He disappeared around the corner and returned a minute later. "Zak and Amy are up here. Thought maybe they were staying in the guest room. But we're alone."

Sydney sat and waited for whatever he was going to tell her. The knowledge that he'd not lost his feelings for her buoyed her spirits. But something had come between them, and there were some things she feared more than others.

Alex pulled up a chair made out of rustic branches from a pine tree, and sat across from her, his knees touching hers. She leaned forward. Whatever he was going to tell her, she was going to face head-on. She was anxious to get it over with.

"I've been invited to try out for the DevGru Team. That's more commonly known as SEAL Team 6, although the group has special forces from other branches as well. Kind of a boys' club with all the badasses in all branches. They do all the high-level stuff, not that we don't on Kyle's team, but these guys, these guys are the best of the best."

"Okay. So what does that mean?"

"Well, I have to try out. They have to vet me as well, with interviews. Someone high up must have recommended me, because you don't ask to be on one of these, and it's an honor to even be approached."

"I'm proud of you, Alex. That's quite an honor."

"It is." He leaned in further, taking her hands in his. "But it means I will be gone much more. It also means I could be gone for longer periods, part of that in training missions or training other forces. I wouldn't really have a home life, so to speak."

She was beginning to understand what he'd been struggling with. It pained her, but she realized he was telling her she would not, could not, be as prominent in his life as perhaps she wanted, or they'd planned on. This was the change pushing him away.

"And you think I'll be whining at home, baggage under your feet. You do know I have my own set of plans."

"Yes, that's why I thought perhaps this would work. But as much as I'd love to just move forward with us, if I take this job, our relationship, everything about us has to go on hold."

"So this is for uncommitted guys."

"No. Some are married, but they came into the program married. Or they sorted it out and got married. But what I'm saying is that I can't do both right now. And I don't want you to sit with any false promises or expectations. I might not make it, which means maybe I'd be reassigned to another team, maybe back East. If I do, I wouldn't be home much for the first couple of years. This is more than a full-time job. And it requires my complete attention. Complete."

Their eyes met again. She found it in herself to not show him the disappointment she felt. What she showed him instead was how proud she was, because that was there too.

"So you've told them yes, then?"

"In a manner of speaking. I've not filled out the paperwork. I've talked it over with Kyle, and, Sydney, I'd like to try doing this. I'll never know if I don't give it a shot."

Now she knew she wouldn't be able to tell him about her secret. He'd made up his mind without her counsel, which was totally appropriate. So that meant she had to make the same decision for herself without counseling him. But it still didn't sit right with her. She knew then and there she was going to have this baby, with or without Alex at her side. And she'd have to wait to tell him.

That was the hardest thing of all. Telling Carly would be a piece of cake compared to that. But some day, when the time was right, she'd tell him. But that day wasn't today.

"Go for it, Alex. I hear what you're saying and not saying. You're asking me not to wait for you, that you might not want me when you're done. I understand the stakes, believe me. And maybe this is as close as we're ever going to be."

He released her hands and sat up straighter.

"I—I guess you're right. I didn't think about that."

It was so incredibly hard, but she'd find the strength within herself to make him fall in love with her all over again. Make it hurt when he went away. Make him find he needed her more than ever, and he'd for sure come back. If there ever was going to be a chance for them, her job would be to blow his mind so that he'd never forget her. "So what you're saying is your ass is mine this weekend and then I got to get over you."

He started to object, but she cut him off.

"Ah?" She put her finger in the air. "Hear me out. If you come back, and I've met someone else, you'll have to accept it, right?"

"Well—"

"It *has* to be that way, Alex. You have to give me the same freedom you are asking me for."

"Well, I guess that sounds fair. Sydney, I'm not sending you away."

"Oh, but you are. You're telling me that your job is going to come first. I get it now." She sucked in a big gulp of air, masking her nervousness. "I can do this on one condition."

"And that is?"

"If we're agreeing to walk away after this weekend, you better show up, at least for the next two days. I mean fully. Do we have a deal?"

CHAPTER 26

ALEX HELD HER hand as they drove to the hospital. "This will be a first for me," he said, kissing her knuckles.

"Me too."

Sydney had been quiet. He couldn't believe how incredibly understanding she'd been. He was expecting the weekend to be painful, and then he'd go home to San Diego, sign all the paperwork to start the application for SEAL Team 6, and just move on with his life, trying to forget her. That was for her sake, not his. Otherwise, he'd have a weak moment between tours or trainings, look her up, have a weekend of sex and then not be able to offer her anything else—going back to work and knowing he used her. He respected her too much to do that to her.

So he'd also decided not to try to force himself on her, arranging to stay at Nick and Devon's. That felt like taking too much advantage of her.

So why am I here then?

Because he wasn't a heel. He wasn't going to just give her the phone call, or write a letter and end it. She deserved to hear it from him in person. When he'd left for Iraq so much had been unspoken, but he knew she felt it too.

When the DevGru guys contacted him, suddenly he found he was willing to put himself through that one more test. He wanted her to understand that. And he thought now she did.

He hadn't considered *this* alternative she gave him. The good-bye weekend. Something special to remember each other by. It was beyond his wildest dreams that he'd finally met someone who was okay letting him be who he wanted to be and not some stuffed-shirt replica of her idea of the perfect boyfriend. He could walk away with no regrets, and the best part of it was she could too.

She was the strongest woman he'd ever met.

He didn't want to think too far out into the future, but he could see that after the next couple of years, they could seriously have one together. As long as he wasn't pressured before that time.

He also liked that she had something she was as passionate about as he did. She wasn't living her life through him, depending on him to bring it to her. She had her own. How had he gotten so lucky?

As the minutes passed, he found it safer to touch her, to hold her hand. He felt her unthaw as well. Her stiffness had gone away, her smiles had returned, and she became more lighthearted. Suddenly the weekend looked to be a real adventure. He might even suggest another zombie movie. She'd love that! And he'd let her bring it on however she liked, as long as it was started on her side of the fence.

The Labor and Delivery unit was on the third floor. A check-in volunteer led them to a cozy waiting room which was empty. The attendant left after promising she'd let Nick and Devon know they were waiting.

"Hey there, Alex!" Nick was dressed in blue jeans. Alex expected he'd be in scrubs or something sterile, so he hesitated to give him a hug. The two were not close friends yet, but the occasion was a celebratory one, so they embraced quickly. "So how's it going? Is it baby time yet?" asked Alex.

"No. We have a ways to go. But right now, Alex, I'm higher than a kite, right there with her, man."

"Where's Zak? Thought he was staying with you guys."

"Haven't been able to get hold of him yet. But they're staying with Amy's dad. A couple other guys from Team 3 came up yesterday. They're probably partying." Nick stuck out his hand, reaching for Sydney. "We've not been introduced, but man, I feel like I know you from somewhere."

"Oh God, I'm sorry," Alex blurted out. "Nick, this is Sydney Robinson. Sydney, Nick Dunn."

Sydney shook Nick's hand and smiled. "You've probably seen me play on the beach down south."

"I've been up here almost three years now. I'm thinking it was that sports magazine cover? The one where you were—" He demonstrated by raising his arm from the shoulder, elbow high in the air, with his back arched. "That was you, wasn't it? Little yellow thong, showed waay too much?" He quickly checked with Alex and then finished in a whisper. "I had that picture on my locker at Gunny's before I moved up here and got married."

Alex knew just what picture that was since Sydney had it framed on her bedroom wall in San Diego. He'd stared at it that morning after.

Sydney blushed and put her hands on her hips, slouched to one side since she towered over both of them. Alex could see she liked Nick. "I'd love to be in that kind of shape again someday." She glanced at Alex. "I'm going to go use the restroom, if you don't mind, okay?"

"Sure."

Nick tilted on his heels to get a good shot of Sydney walking down the hallway. He shook his head and punched Alex in the arm. "Don't know how you guys do it."

Alex ignored him and asked about Devon.

"She's a trooper. She's already dilated four centimeters."

Alex had no clue what that meant.

"When Sydney comes back, I'll let you guys go in and see her."

"Whoa, no way, man. This is your time. I'm not going to infringe on that. Besides, I've just come from a plane stuffed with people. We're only here to give you moral support."

"Oh relax, Alex. Not like she's naked and you're going to see her parts and all. She's in a nightgown, except she has monitors stuck to her all over under her gown."

Sydney returned.

"Nick says we can go in and visit for a little bit. You want to?"

"I don't want to impose. Sort of a strange time to meet someone when she's in labor and all. I'm not sure I'd want to meet strangers under those conditions."

"Oh, she's totally fine. She said you guys could come in. The nurses are cool with it too. Whatever keeps her calm." Nick motioned for them to follow. A nurse stopped him in the hallway, and he told her his wife was expecting them.

Devon's hair was done up in pigtails, like the day he'd attended the wedding at the winery. "Hi there, Alex. I guess today's the day!"

Her face was flushed, and her forehead had wetted her bangs. She had a bright red floral shawl over her shoulders. The light in the room was turned down low and some sea music was playing on her cell phone.

Alex leaned over the bed and gave her a peck on the cheek. "Hey, Mama. You look beautiful."

"Oh please, you're such a liar."

Once again, he'd forgotten to introduce Sydney. Devon was angling to be able to greet her. "You must be Sydney."

Alex put his arm around Sydney's shoulders and then brought her toward the bed.

"Nice meeting you. I—I hadn't planned on barging in here. So sorry."

"Oh, nonsense," said Devon as she made a face and exhaled. "Hold that thought for a minute. Here comes another one." She leaned back into the pillow. Nick was at her shoulders, giving her an upper spine massage, running his fingers up the back of her neck and into her hair. She took deep breaths, letting it out slowly until the contraction appeared to be over.

"How long's it going to be?" Sydney asked.

"We have no idea. But she's coming along. We're making progress, aren't we, sweetie?" Nick squeezed his wife's hand.

"It's up to the baby. We're on her time," Devon said.

Sydney spoke up again. "You know it's a girl?"

"Nope. I want a girl. He wants a boy. We don't care. It's a friendly argument."

Nick was perched on the edge of Devon's bed. "Have a seat for a little bit. You want something? They have custard and Jell-o down at the nurses' station. Other stuff too I don't want to tempt her with."

"No, we're fine," answered Alex. "But can I get you something, Devon?"

"I'd love a cool towel for my forehead."

Before the men could get up, Sydney was at the sink wetting down one of the folded washcloths stacked neatly there. She squeezed it tightly, then brought it over to Devon's face. "Here you go." She pressed the white cloth to her forehead, lifting her bangs before doing so. She dabbed her cheeks, then under her chin, across her lips and down her neck to the top of her chest. "That feel better?" she asked.

"Heavenly."

Alex watched Sydney's tenderness. Something about the scene touched him. Some kind of invisible bond had already formed between the two women. It added to his respect for the mystique of woman-hood. He wondered why some women had it and others, like his mother, didn't seem to have a clue. Or maybe she'd stopped trying when life got too hard at home.

"Devon, Sydney is a beach volleyball player," Nick whispered. He turned up the noise of the ocean. "This probably makes you feel at home too, Sydney," he added.

"It actually does," said Sydney.

A nurse came in. "I'm gonna ask all of you to go outside now while I give her a check. You can come back when I finish updating her chart."

Alex, Nick, and Sydney exited to the waiting room. A very young father was on a cell phone even though signs posted around the room advised all phones be turned off.

The trio walked through the double swinging doors back into the lobby just outside the surgery waiting room which was three times bigger.

"So how long are you up here for?" Nick finally asked.

"Just today, tomorrow and part of Sunday, when I go back."

"Oh, that's too bad. I'm sure Devon would have wanted you to see all the things she's discovered about the property. Zak and Amy have already started with cleanup. Supposed to get the appraisal done next week."

"I guess Coop's in-laws are investing in it too?"

"Think so. We'll need a final head count and tally of moneys we have to work with, but Devon says they want us to have the property. Zak's got several of the single guys agreeing to come up here occasionally for a work party."

Alex wanted to know about Zak. He was hoping the transition to civilian life wouldn't be hard on him, especially with the loss of his eye.

Nick reassured him. "Seems to feel quite at home. We've been talking about labels, which is getting way ahead of ourselves. Something with the pirate theme, maybe a drawing of Zak with his eye patch."

"Pirate piss wine."

"Actually, we were thinking about brewing some beer too. We kind of liked the name Frog Piss, maybe make it green or put it in green bottles."

"I'm glad he's adjusting." Nick went into detail about the land while Alex watched Sydney. She observed several pregnant couples arriving at the birthing center. Another woman dressed in a hospital gown like Devon's was walking between a man and an older woman who appeared to be her mother.

Sydney caught him watching her, and abruptly she looked away.

Nick discovered he was being ignored and started asking Alex questions about their visit to Iraq.

"You got Ali, right?"

"We sure did. None too soon, either. We took out four bad guys, one kid really young, the rest teenagers. Nobody high level, or at least the DNA didn't give us anyone we knew about. We think they were there just to make sure the kids or the aid workers didn't escape. Our terp said they expected someone big to arrive and choose which children to take."

"Sick bastards. Glad you got out without injury."

"Me too. And it helps when we get accurate intel. That doesn't always happen anymore."

Nick agreed, but refocused his attention on Sydney. "So how do you like it up here? It's different than San Diego."

"It suits me fine. Got a great training partner, and the facility is awesome. Ever heard of it? Beach Inc."

Nick shook his head.

"They have four sand courts in addition to the regular gym floor. That's where I train. But I'm also the director of coaching, so I get to work with girls of all ages, from just starting out to gals from Sonoma State and the J.C."

"I'll bet you were a find for them, then."

Sydney rolled her shoulder and shrugged. "It's the perfect arrangement."

"Well, after the baby's born, we'll have to come down and watch you play."

"Thanks. Even Alex hasn't seen that yet." She winked at him.

The nurse poked her head outside the double doors and told them she was finished with Devon. Sydney held Alex back.

"I don't want to stay too long. I don't care if she wants us there, I'd like to give them private time."

"No complaints from me." He slipped his arm around her waist. "You doing okay?"

She darted a quick look at him, low-level defensiveness showing just under the surface of her flawless tanned skin. "Sure. Why wouldn't I be?"

He squeezed her tighter to his side. "Just checking."

Devon was having another contraction as they walked back inside, and this one had her nearly swearing. Alex waited until she regained concentration to indicate he and Sydney would be leaving soon.

Sydney bent over and gave Devon a hug. "Best of luck. I understand being a mother is the hardest job you'll ever love. I know you two will make great parents, from all I've heard about you both. I'll be thinking of you today."

"Aww. Thank you, Sydney. What a lovely thing to say." Devon's face was flushed with a bright smile. "So glad I got to meet you on this special day." And then her face scrunched up as another contraction began.

Alex loved Sydney's soft features as she wafted past him, leaving the hospital room to wait for him outside in the hall. He felt awkward for a second, with Nick attending to his wife and Devon focused on her delivery. He gave a thumbs up, which Nick returned.

All the way down the corridor, down the elevator and across the parking lot, he held Sydney's hand loosely. Neither one said a word.

CHAPTER 27

SYDNEY WAS MOVED by the hospital scene with Alex's friends. She'd been there to witness a miracle, the start of a new life, and she pondered the impact it would have on everyone around them. Even her.

She was even more sure of her decision than she had been earlier in the day. Something inside her soul had settled. And yet, there was so much unknown about the future. She was proud of herself. Instead of fear, she was changing, rising to the opportunity to face this new challenge with grace and dignity, bearing the emotions and the fear and doubt she knew would come along as hitchhikers for a time here and there. She wasn't being a Pollyanna about it. She stared reality in the face and reality blinked. She did not. Would not.

Out of the corner of her eye she could see Alex give her furtive glances. That was good, she told herself. He had noticed a change in her. It would be the first of many. She chuckled at the remembrance of their first date, only a few weeks ago. The zombie movie and the popcorn and—

"What in the devil are you thinking, Sydney?" he asked.

She examined his face in profile as he drove. "You'll take this off-ramp and go under the freeway here." She pointed and then went back to feasting on his handsome face. "I was thinking about our first date. And don't ask me why I thought about it just now."

"Why did you think about it just now?" he said with a grin.

"Funny."

"No, seriously. Why?"

"I can't believe I was so out of control."

Alex raised his eyebrows. "That's an understatement. I wasn't sure you were safe to be around."

She speculated on what he would look like in twenty years. He'd stay handsome, stay rugged-looking, and lose what little boyishness he had, which wasn't much. He'd probably stop getting tats, but maybe not. His hair would be streaked with white perhaps. She smoothed her fingers through his temple, letting them delve into his scalp, and then squeezed the back of his neck. "I think you'll be even more handsome when you're in your forties or beyond."

"And I think you'll always be that volleyball goddess everyone had pinned to their lockers."

"You think so?" She liked that at least he tried to lie for her benefit. It was a lie she could live with.

She finished the directions, and at last they came to the complex. He was at her side of the car in a flash and opened the door for her. As he leaned past her and grabbed his bag, the scent from the proximity to his muscled neck nearly made her weak at the knees. She resisted the urge to kiss him there, figuring there would be time for the fog of lust, if that was what was to occur. She was orchestrating something, now. There were things she urgently wanted, but she had to put some of them on hold. It actually felt good to be more in control of her emotions. She wanted to walk through the doorway of this day and remember it all. Remember tomorrow and Sunday. Remember how she felt on Monday and thereafter.

He walked beside her as they climbed the three flights. He was barely out of breath when they got to the outside of her apartment. She turned, her back flat against the door, her hips at an angle. "Kiss me, Alex."

He bent forward, dropping his bag and placing both hands at the side of her face and then nourished her with a loving kiss that sent chills all the way to her toes. She knew she'd always remember that special kiss. It was life-giving. She hoped the tiny child she was carrying could feel it too.

She placed her fingers over his mouth. "I love your kisses, Alex. I just want to say that."

"I have lots more."

"I was hoping so." Looking down, she examined her keys. "I want to take it a bit slow at first, if you don't mind. Not because I don't like the fun and the intensity of the other way, but I just want to honor our last weekend together."

Emotions were beginning to steep inside her, her heart fluttered a bit, as some of the old fear reared its head. Her eyes were beginning to water, but she faced him anyway and let him see all of her.

"Syd, I'll take it fast, slow, any way you want it. You have nothing to fear from me, sweetheart."

It would be so easy to just drown out all logic, let herself go, and set up the make-believe world of the Happily Ever After and deny herself the opportunity to show him what a real lady she was. Yes, she was a character. But she was also a lady, and she was going to be a mother, a task she willingly took on with pride. It didn't matter if her baby's birth day wasn't shared with him. He could be halfway around the world in some hellhole, doing things she didn't even want to know about. It would make it no less sacred a time. No less important. She'd make it the best day of her life, like today was for Devon and Nick.

Once inside, Alex watched her set her keys aside and kick off her shoes, which was always her routine. He was still holding onto the canvas bag, the strap hanging from his shoulder.

"Where do I put this?" His sparkling eyes and little boy smile cheering her.

"Unless you'd rather sleep on the couch, I suggest the bedroom."

"Yes, ma'am." He'd left his jacket behind when he returned. He approached, wrapping his arms around her waist. His fingers removed a couple of long errant hairs from her forehead. "I'm getting used to kissing you on my tiptoes. The first time it happened, I wasn't so sure it would work for me."

She met him half way and they melded together as though there were no distance between them. Sydney took his hand and directed him to sit on the couch. She sat crossing him, her legs nearly touching the end. "I have a couple of ideas of some things we talked about. Some things I'd like to do this weekend, if you're game."

His large hand massaged the top of her spine, something she loved almost more than morning sex. "Okay, shoot."

"Wine tasting. There's the rugged coastline. Oysters at Marshall's Cove. You game for any of that?" she asked.

She noticed he was keeping his hands to himself. "And I'd like to talk more. I want to know about you and your family."

"You mean you want my pedigree?"

She was embarrassed she'd come that close to coming right out and telling him she wanted to know what she would tell their child some day if he wasn't going to be in the picture. Sitting as she was on his lap, that seemed less likely. "You're being cute. There must be something you want to ask of me."

"Yes." He inhaled big and leaned forward, holding her face in his hands again and kissing her deep. "Among other things, I'd like to see you play volleyball."

"Really?"

"Yes ma'am. I'm as serious as a heart attack."

She scrambled to her feet, pulling him up. "Carly will be there now. If we go right now, we can show you what we're working on."

"I just want to watch you jump and spike and do all those things I've been fantasizing about in my mind. I couldn't stop thinking about it when I was over there."

"Let's do it. Let me get changed and we'll go, okay?"

"You need any help? It's been driving me crazy." He pulled her to him again. "I wasn't going to go anywhere near that, but honey, I'm afraid I'm a flawed man. I can't help myself."

She liked that he wanted to dally. Pressing her lips to his, taking nibbles as she did so, she whispered, "We have all night, Alex. I promise to make it up to you, okay?"

He held her at arm's length and examined her face. "Going to make me wait?"

"The anticipation will make it sweeter. Trust me on this. If you want to see me play, we have to leave right now or we'll miss Carly."

"Call her."

"Good idea." She waved to him, standing there with his long arms down at his sides, his shirt halfway pulled out of his jeans, and his hair messed up. His lips had a bit of her red lipstick that lingered and made him look sexy as hell. Those eyes and his playful smile promised kisses she loved all over her body.

Carly didn't answer her cell, so she left a message. "Hey there, Alex and I are coming over, so don't go anywhere. He wants to get a personal tour and watch us play a bit. See if you can get some of the older girls to stay behind too. See you in like ten. Bye."

The sight of his black bag and jacket placed on her bedspread sparked her with excitement. She used the restroom quickly, then rummaged through the top dresser drawer where her underwear was located. She hadn't worn the little yellow outfit in over a year. She slid off her clothes, tossing them into her hamper in the closet, and then stepped into the tiny thong bottoms, sliding them up her flat abdomen, the arch of the panty coming just below her hip bone. Then she slipped the bra top over her head, pulling it down until it lifted and supported her breasts. She examined herself in the mirror, turning around to make sure everything looked right.

"Vera vera nice," Alex said wolfishly. "You're sure we couldn't fool around with this little outfit for a few minutes before you get it all hot and sweaty?"

"Oh, but I like things hot and sweaty," she said as she slipped past him, making sure to brush against his growing package. "All good things come to those who wait. And in this case, you won't have to wait very long. We'll do a late lunch, or just skip lunch and come back here. Unless you have a better idea."

Her fingers brushed over his lips again. He grabbed her arm and pressed her palm to the outside of his jeans.

"Nice," she whispered. "but if you want to see this gal jump and show off for you, your private volleyball player, you're gonna have to hold that thought until just a little later." She kissed him quickly. "Come on."

She stepped into her black workout pants and fleece jacket with the Beach Inc. logo on it, while he slipped on his jacket, taking something from his pocket, and then adjusting his waistband.

She slipped on her shoes, and they headed down the stairway to her car.

The early afternoon traffic was heavy for a Friday. They got to the Beach in a little over twenty minutes. The parking lot was full of SUVs and only a couple of sedans. She recognized Mrs. Beeson's car. Two large white vans were backed into the rollup doors at the rear side of the building. Sydney didn't recall any tournaments scheduled or team scrimmages. Without markings and windows, she assumed perhaps a private delivery service was setting up some new equipment the general manager had ordered.

As they exited the Murano, Alex got a call from Zak. He placed his finger up in the air while he answered the phone.

"I'll go get warmed up. Take as long as you like," she whispered to him, then gave him a kiss on the cheek. She plugged her earbuds into her cell phone, unzipped her jacket and snapped the device into the Velcro holder on her arm. She liked warming up to the *Rocky* theme song and played it as she jogged toward the entrance.

Closer to the lobby, a mother with her child was walking back toward her. Sydney removed one ear bud.

"Oh, Sydney, thank goodness you're here. They've got it locked. I knocked and no one came," the mother said.

Sydney cocked her head, concerned. "Well, I have the keys, let me open it for you. Someone's little sister must be fiddling with the door lock mechanism."

"Well, I know someone's inside, with all these cars out here," the mom said.

Sydney got out her keys and no sooner had she inserted the metal fob into the dead bolt when the door swung open and she was yanked into the dark cave of the dark gym. Someone else had the young girl in a choke hold, brandishing a knife. The girl's mother screamed and got slapped across the face for it. Not more than a second passed before the door slammed shut behind them, cutting off the only light. Sydney's eyes started to adjust as she wondered if Alex had witnessed any of this from his vantage point in the car.

The girl was dragged to the back stairs leading to the smaller gyms on top. She struggled keeping her balance to such an extent another masked man with a semiautomatic rifle grabbed her feet around the ankles, and the two of them brought the wriggling teen down into the back.

Through the glass partitions, Sydney could see two gym spaces up-stairs holding people crowded together, their hands and faces plastered against the glass. On one side were the young players. In the adjacent gym were parents. Some were standing near the partition to their daughters' side, others sat stoically, and some looked down below to watch what the screaming and commotion was all about. In the middle of that crowd she noticed the unhappy face of Mrs. Beeson.

Sydney scanned the people, looking for evidence of a male figure somewhere, and sadly, found none. She located Carly sitting down nearby, her head in her hands resting over her knees.

Two metal ladders were set up under the overhang of the gyms up-stairs. Near the top of the ladders, two men were wrapping something over a metal beam. Sydney's heart started racing when she realized they were duct taping something to the underside of the gym flooring. The objects were the size of a shoebox.

"Your purse," a masked man demanded. One of the men on the ladder looked across the gym and Sydney knew him as the older brother of one of her Somali players. In fact, Sydney thought most of the men were young, and now recalled seeing several of them coming by to pick up their sisters or relatives.

She handed the gym bag to him, letting go of the handles before he'd grabbed it, which sent the bag to the floor at his feet. The masked man stepped closer to Sydney, nearly touching her, his red eyes wide with fear he was desperately trying to mask. His right temple was pulsing, and she could see perspiration on his forehead and upper lip. He appeared high on some kind of stimulant.

The nearly one-foot difference in height proved a distraction to him. He said something in an Arabic-sounding language and unzipped the bag, dumping the contents on the gym floor. He tossed the empty carcass into the corner piled high with other purses and bags.

Sydney was ordered to sit while the masked man pawed over her bag contents and spread them out over the concrete floor. She knew he was looking for her cell phone.

He was called away, but not before another guard was sent to stand over her. She was surprised they did not tie her up.

Underestimate me at your own peril.

After several minutes, the masked man returned.

He pointed to her earbud, still lodged deep, playing the Rocky theme that was perfect for her current situation. Her mind was racing what to do next, and expected to hear banging on the door from Alex's attempted entry any time. He'd know something was wrong if it was locked. But what would be her fate? The girls? Mrs. Beeson?

"My iPod," she insisted, pulling out her plug and handing it to the man so he could listen to the music. "For my workout, you understand?"

The man shouted and the boy she knew from the ladder immediately came running over. His eyes were downcast, as he realized Sydney had recognized him. There was a back and forth exchange between the two of them, and the boy gave her the command, "He wants your cell. He knows it's not an iPod. You don't want to play tricks with him. Very bad man, understand?"

Sydney figured that was all he could say. She took her phone off the armband and handed it to the younger man, with the ear bud still dangling. The bud was removed and the Rocky music blared from the microphone, reverberating throughout the gym. This seemed to irritate the masked man and she worried he'd destroy it. It was tossed into a box outside the office doorway with several others.

She glanced up at the group of girls and the relative of the boy was not among them, nor did there appear to be any from their immigrant family. She wanted to ask him why they were doing this, but knew she wouldn't get anything satisfactory. At least the girls were relatively calm, although several were quietly crying or hugging one another. She was grateful they could not see what must surely be two explosive devices hanging in the metal frame of the structure, right below them.

The younger man translated several bursts of language.

"He says our leader wants to use you as a hostage negotiator. If everyone cooperates, there will be no loss of life."

Sydney could tell he was lying.

An even shorter man came from Mrs. Beeson's office. He had a cash box, a couple of computers and some Beach Inc. sweatshirts in his arms. The masked man pushed Sydney in the direction of the office and she complied, but her anger was coming to a full boil.

"What would Alex do? How can I get a message to him?"

She heard lecturing coming from upstairs as one of the attackers said in perfect English, "You will cooperate or you all will die. I promise you that. You do as I say, make no problem for us, and you may live."

Response to the man's words was immediate. There was collective moaning and sniffles as the young players began to understand the danger they were in, and they began to panic. Their mothers huddled in small groups, whispering.

Just as Sydney entered the doorway and was pushed into Mrs. Beeson's rolling office chair, she remembered her Apple Watch, and understood she had the power to text. The other thing that made her happy was the fact that Mrs. Beeson always had a loaded gun under papers in the locked file cabinet. If she could find her key, there might be a way to defend herself, Sydney thought. But how could she defend herself against so many men? And how many of the girls or mothers would be injured or worse if she tried something bold?

But she knew she couldn't just sit idly by and allow the standoff to continue.

On the desk and side table were several white vests with multiple pockets sewn into them, like a fisherman's sport vest, except these pockets were jammed with small white plastic bags. It didn't take much imagination to understand that vests like this, with wires connecting the bags, were made for a suicide bomber.

A clean-shaven unmasked man walked into the office and greeted her with an almost flirtatious smile. He appeared very Westernized, and he was sporting an expensive haircut. His cultured English told her he'd been well-educated. She recognized him as the one shouting instructions to the girls above. He picked up a vest from the pile, extended his arms to Sydney, and placed it over her neck and shoulders. It was heavy.

"I am sorry, but you must wear this. But you won't be the only one," he said as he tenderly pulled her ponytail from her collar.

He smoothed the canvas material over her fleece jacket, lingering a bit too long over her breasts. He placed his palms at her upper shoulders and smoothed down over her arms.

He wore expensive cologne. His well-polished shoes looked as out of place here as he did.

"Why? Why are you doing this?"

He shrugged, then pointed to her vest. "That's a good look for you."

"Why?" Sydney insisted. She hated the man and her odds. Playing with the lives of innocent children enjoying their freedoms. Who was he to take all that away? She wasn't afraid to let him see her disgust for him.

"What is it you do here?"

"I'm a coach."

"Oh, so I think maybe you are the coach everyone talks about."

"Yes, I've coached girls from your family, perhaps. I'm doing it because it's the right thing to do."

"This I respect. But surely you understand there is a war going on."

"Not here."

"You are wrong, coach. You take away our way of life. We do the same to you. You kill women and children—"

"Because you hide amongst them."

He laughed. "Why, you don't believe we have wives and girlfriends? Children of our own?"

"You drag them into your filthy war."

"Coach, you are an ignorant woman. You should be duct taped. You should learn to have respect for those who have been trained properly. This is what's wrong with your country. You listen to too many women."

Sydney bolted out of the chair. She knew she only had one chance to get this asshole, because if she failed she would be duct taped there, perhaps for the rest of her life.

Caught off guard, he wasn't prepared for the kick Sydney delivered to his groin, but since she was wearing only flip flops, it didn't do the damage she'd hoped. He groaned and bent over, then turned and gave her a backhand to the left side of her face. She heard a crack, and knew he'd probably shattered her cheekbone. She screamed as loud as she could as a warning. She heard answering cries from upstairs.

The noise brought the other men. They were ordered to hold her down with force as her vest was removed with near delicacy.

"You stupid fool," the unmasked attacker spat out. "You nearly sent us all up to Allah."

"Isn't that what you want?" Her lips felt numb and the sputtering of blood sent droplets flying like tiny magnets, depositing themselves on the man's expensive shirt, slacks and pullover sweater.

She was brought a wet towel and a bottled water for her face. The leader received a cell phone call and went into the main gym area to seek privacy.

Temporarily, Sydney was left alone. She was satisfied they didn't notice that she also had an Apple Watch on her, and with that she could text Alex.

She extended her fingers under the sleeve of her left hand, which had the watch on it, and felt the tiny divots for the keypad on her sport model. She wasn't sure how close she came, hoping it wasn't all gibberish, but she attempted to text,

SOS Alex. Suicide bombers have everyone held hostage. Help.

She could tell the text went through because she heard a tiny swooshing sound and then a short vibration on her wrist. She hoped to God it was the right number.

Her thumbnail clicked off the sound so the attackers didn't catch on.

She shouted out to one of the attackers outside, asking to use the restroom. The younger boy walked into the office and denied her request, "You pee here if you need to." He pointed to the corner of the office, where a metal wastebasket stood.

They finally tied her to a chair with duct tape secured around her ankles and wrists. Mr. Cleancut poked his head in the doorway. "You will become famous now, Coach. Get yourself ready, say your prayers. If you do a good job, perhaps you'll survive this." He stepped inside the office, leaning closer to her and whispered, "In my country, I would have celebrated slitting your throat and watching you bleed all over yourself."

They both left the room, closing the door behind them.

SYDNEY COULD STAND with the chair strapped to her. She walked herself near the bookkeeper's desk and found scissors in the top drawer. She tried to finger them, but they slipped from her hand and dropped to the floor.

Damn it.

She eyed the telescoping back scratcher next, but ruled it out as not helpful at all.

She heard voices come near the doorway, so she kicked the scissors further under the desk, and headed back to her corner, still very much attached to the chair.

The man with the expensive cologne came into the room first.

"What is your name?"

"Sydney. S-Sydney Robinson,"

"Well, Miss Sydney Robinson, lets see how skilled you are in negotiations. I am going to dial a local TV station, you will tell them who you are, and where you are. You will not leave anything out, but only when I give you the sign that it is okay to do so. Can you do this?"

Sydney nodded her head, but kept her evil eye on him for emphasis.

"Good." The man put his hand on his heart. "My name is Youssef. I am a messenger from God."

Sydney tried not to react. She was getting adjusted to her situation. It had been over twenty minutes since she'd walked into the gym and still there had been no knock on the door. No attempts to contact her. She hoped Alex would locate the authorities.

Youssef was not wearing a vest, like some of the others had begun to put on. Then she recalled the white vans outside the gym.

They're going to take some of us somewhere! But there wasn't enough room for everyone.

Sydney inhaled and drew courage from the satisfaction of knowing they had other plans than to just blow up the gym and everyone in it. They had enough room for maybe thirty of the girls or mothers. Perhaps they'd leave the others alone. She needed to know what his timetable and plans were.

But before she could ask Youssef, everyone left her alone again and gathered outside the doorway, joining arms over their shoulders. They spoke softly. It wasn't a meeting.

It was a farewell.

She couldn't text Alex, and panic set in as she realized the phone call to the TV station was probably just to draw news crews for publicity. She could tell, as Youssef handed out the remaining vests, none of them were going to survive.

She struggled with the duct tape, trying to dislodge it from her wrists, and ankles. Her strong leg muscles worked hard, and finally, she was able to free one ankle. She extended her toes and slid the scissors closer toward her. She balanced the tool on the inset of her shoe, bringing it up to her lap. She tried to maneuver the blade but was unable to have it reach any tape to cut.

She was getting frustrated and needed to calm herself. As a brief reminder, her stomach lurched and she resigned herself to wait until they asked her to phone the TV station. That's when she'd make her last stand.

Then she noticed a piece of the metal trim had been dislodged from Mrs. Beeson's desk top, probably from the scuffle with Youssef. It was sufficiently sharp to use as a knife. She turned around in her chair and rubbed up and down until one wrist and then the other was freed.

She quickly undid her other ankle.

The men were still occupied outside. She fired off a text to Alex.

"They are preparing to end us all. Must hurry."

"On it. I got help. Location?"

"They're in the center. There are 8. Vests."

"Bomb vests? Hostages?"

"Yes. All upstairs, except me. In ofc down. Hurry."

"Dive under a desk and wait. Lock yourself in?"

"Yes."

She moved toward the door, but her actions drew the attention of one of the men, who spotted her through the door's window, and raised his weapon. She got behind Mrs. Beeson's large wooden desk just as the room was filled with splinters from the rounds the semiautomatic made. She didn't have a chance to lock the door and knew they'd be on top of her any second. She was defenseless. Mrs. Beeson's gun was in the lower locked file drawer, and she had no key.

Damn.

She heard the girls screaming upstairs as there were more weapons fired. Smoke started to fill the room. Sydney held her breath for as long as she could, but then she was forced to inhale the smoke fumes and it made her cough. She was getting dizzy and sick to her stomach again.

When would the man spray the room with gunfire again? Would he figure out she was behind the desk and come for her? She heard the gun go off, but not in her direction. She knew it would be very soon now, and she was on borrowed time.

Would this be the last of anything she would hear? Were they going to get her—never give her the chance to feel the life of her baby inside her? Someone would tell him. And then he'd know. But he'd hear it from a policeman, or a counselor, and not from her lips.

Everything she'd always wanted was being taken away from her.

And then she heard the most wonderful sound in the whole world. The man she loved was shouting her name over and over again.

The happy shock of his voice made it so she couldn't move. And then his face was in front of hers.

"Did they hurt you?"

"No."

"Are you sure?"

She tried to think. "I'm not sure. H-he hit me. Can you check?"

He was on his knees in front of her. "Your face is bruised, but looks okay. You can come out now, sweetheart. Zak and the guys got here just in time, or I was going in alone. But we got the bad guys, Sydney. You helped us save everyone."

His large dark eyes scanned her body as she huddled under the desk. She began to shake. Her vision was suddenly blurry as hot tears streamed down her cheeks. The salty tears stung on one side.

"It's okay," he said as he pulled her towards him, still on his knees. "You're okay, Sydney." He rocked her from side to side gently. "Everything's okay now. I'm here, and you're safe. I'm not leaving."

She pulled back and examined his face. "Never?"

"Well, you know, go to work, but I don't want to leave you alone. I would not be able to live with myself if something happened to you, Sydney. My place is here. I'm going to stay here."

"So no Team 6?"

"Not yet, sweetheart. Maybe someday. Not now."

"You sure?"

"Positive." He gently took her hands in his. "Come on out of your cave. Let's see how you are."

She let him lead her to a standing position. A new wave of nausea hit her. He brought the metal wastebasket over for her, but she stubbornly willed the nausea away.

"Those flashbombs are nasty stuff, but not lethal. Nothing to make you sick. But they're nasty."

"Good."

She collapsed into him. The one-eyed man she'd met in San Diego who helped set up her date with Alex was in the doorway. He had two other men with him.

"Alex, we've called the fire department and cops. Everyone's okay. They didn't hurt anyone, and no one's missing."

"Hear that?"

She nodded, then buried her head in his chest. Alex whispered to his friends, "We'll be out in a second. She's in a bit of shock."

His warm body against hers was what she'd wanted to feel. She knew she needed to stay calm, for the baby.

OMG! The baby!

He was saying things to the top of her head while letting his strong fingers give her a firm neck massage. She heard him say, "I thought I'd lost you today. I never want to feel that way again. Can you see yourself married to a sailor? Would you do me the honor?"

She inhaled his words, letting them wash through her as he held her trembling body. It wasn't what she'd expected on a day with all sorts of other plans. Savoring the moment, she was willingly stringing it out for as long as she could make it. Because now she was going to have to say something that might change everything. And she'd have to make that okay, whatever the outcome.

"Sydney? Did you hear me? I want you to be my wife."

After just a few more seconds of being nourished in his arms, she was ready. "You need to know something first."

"No, baby. No bad news. We'll talk about all this tomorrow." He hugged her tighter. "Only good things today. Tell me you'll think about it. Promise me?"

She separated from him enough to look directly into his eyes.

"It isn't bad news, Alex. Not bad at all. What I mean is yes, Alex, I'll marry you. But there's something else you need to know first."

"Whatever it is, we'll get through it. We'll overcome anything you and I."

That made her smile. *How in the world does one overcome a lifetime of raising a child?*

"What is it, Sydney? Tell me."

She splayed her fingers over his warm chest, feeling the solid wall that was his body—willing and capable of shielding her, protecting her, risking his life for her. This wasn't going to be anything he'd trained for.

"Sweet Alex, what I wanted to say and was afraid to tell you was, I'm pregnant."

CHAPTER 28

A LEX COULDN'T BELIEVE what she'd just said. Sirens were going off as the rescue squads arrived. Zak and the other two Team guys had backed away, giving them the privacy they obviously needed. With a tornado of activity going on all around them, her tear-streaked face still smiled back at him. And yes, she looked a tiny bit worried about his reaction. So he'd have to tell her something.

He didn't have to dig very far. He knew it just as soon as she said it. He was overjoyed with her news.

"Baby, that's the best thing I've heard all day, honest to God."

He felt her knees buckle. Her eyes closed as she collapsed into him.

"Sweetheart, are you okay?"

A heavyset, graying female paramedic rushed into the destroyed office, surveyed the scene, saw Sydney's weakened state, and ordered Alex to put her down on the gurney brought in by her skinny male partner behind her.

"She's—she's pregnant," he told the paramedic.

"Gotcha. Hon, you get hurt anywhere? They do anything to you or you fall, sweetheart?"

Sydney tried to sit up and was gently restrained.

"Hold on there. We just want to check you out." She glanced up at Alex. "You got some water so I don't have to get it?"

As he maneuvered around the gurney, Zak threw him a fresh bottle. He heard Sydney say, "There's some—oh wait, my bag is over there on the pile."

"No, he's already got you some fresh water, sugar. You just relax and let this nice-looking young man take care of you. It looks like he's the right kinda medicine for you!"

Sydney smiled, and then began to laugh. "He sure is," she said after she gave him a bashful expression. Alex lifted her head up and placed the cold water to her mouth. A bit spilled down her neck, and he dabbed it with the blanket. He set the water down on the desk nearby, and then grasped her right hand between both of his, kissing her knuckles. He had never been more proud.

"God, I can't wait until you get fat. I don't even care about the volleyball anymore. I just want to see that belly get huge, Sydney."

The paramedic's eyes sprung to mock alarm right in the middle of extracting Sydney's arm from under the soft blanket. "You hear that?" she barked.

Sydney was streaming tears, her lower lip quivering. She could barely say his name. "Alex—"

"Right here, baby." He leaned over to kiss her and she grabbed his neck, hooking it with her right arm. "Whoa! I'm not going anywhere, Sydney."

"All I can say—" the paramedic began as she pushed up Sydney's workout top, wrapped the blood pressure cuff around her left arm and began pumping. Alex glanced upward for the result. After a few seconds, she added in a whisper, "She's fine, blood pressure amazingly normal." Placing her very large hand gently against his chest, she added, "Give me a little room, sugar. There will no doubt be time for that later." She followed it up with a wink.

Alex stood straight and let the woman check Sydney's cheek, her eyes, and then she moved her head back and forth gently on the white cover. She removed her hands and adjusted the blanket. "You getting more comfortable now?"

Sydney nodded.

"Like I was sayin', this one here—he's a keeper! Any man who says something like that, you keep that man around. Don't you dare let him stray, you hear?"

Carly, Zak and the two other SEALs were chatting in the doorway but stopped when they heard this.

"Carly!" Sydney shouted out, extending her arms wide. Her friend bolted past everyone and wrapped her arms around Sydney's upper torso.

"Oh, Sydney, you put yourself at too much risk for all of us. I don't know how you managed to get these guys here to show up, but I'm damn glad you did." She glanced between the SEALs. "Thank you all."

"So good to see you well, and the girls?" Sydney asked.

"Oh. My. God. They're going to have stories. I think the tweets have already started, once they got their cell phones back." She gave Sydney one last hug. "I need to go check on the girls." And then she left the office.

"Show's over folks," the paramedic said. None of them moved. "Oh, you must be with him." She crooked her thumb over her shoulder. "All these guys looking all kind of wonderful. Give her some space, let her catch up. Now I gotta go check on some skinny butt, anorexic teenagers. I'll be back. Don't leave with my cart, okay, darlin'?" She winked at Alex in an unabashed flirt.

She parted the wall at the doorway and then stopped, turning around, "Young lady, you remember what I told you about him. Keep him around, and I hope you have a beautiful baby. Oh, and I don't think anything busted up here," she pointed to her own cheek, "but best get an xray soon anyhow. You rest for a couple of days. Take it easy. Let this guy get all nekked and wait on you hand and foot. You make him shake that fine ass—oh yes, I saw it. You didn't think old Muriel here would notice such things, but I still do!"

When she left, the room seemed empty.

"She's right about the rest, you know," said Alex. He brought his arms around her, scooping her waist so she could feel how badly he wanted to hold her.

"The rest of what?" Sydney whispered, arching backward, her arms above her head.

"The rest. Bed rest."

"Well then that means you're gonna get lots too, Alex. I'm going to need an awful lot of tender loving care. Your very best."

"You'll have it. You'll always have it, Sydney. Forever."

He loved that her softness was coming back. The panic in her eyes was gone, the distraction, masking the hurt and pain. Girls started walking by, and he had to share her with several of them.

"Oh my God, Miss Robinson, we saw you down there, and were like, *'Oh no!! Leave her alone.'* We were ready to just bust out and take over those guys, but then they started shooting!" With her braces, the enthusiastic teen was slurring her words and spitting all over everyone. She glanced over at Alex. "Is he your boyfriend?"

"No, he's my fiancé, Janine."

The girls screamed. Several jumped up and down. "Oh, that is so cool. You were saved by your fiancé. Oh my God. That is just so romantic!"

Several others had similar things to say. Zak and Kurt and Eric stood near the wall, sucking in their waists and expanding their pecs, their arms crossed, exposing a lot of ink.

After the bevy of well-wishers and mothers were gone, Alex lifted the blanket. "Come on, sweetheart. Time to get home, get showered up, and get your butt in the bed where it belongs."

She placed her arm around his shoulder and neck, and he lifted her in his arms. Out in the main gym area, several white sheets covered the bodies of the kidnappers. Two were still alive, being escorted by police. Sydney waved to one of them as they passed by. A news crew was trying to gain entry and was barred at the doorway.

"Does the investigator need to speak to me?" he asked Zak.

"Not today. I filled him in. He knows you have to take her home. You sure she doesn't need to go to the hospital?"

He turned and spat out his answer at the same time Sydney did. "No!" Then he softened. "We'll do that after she's rested up."

BACK AT HER apartment, he insisted on carrying her up the stairs. They'd retrieved her wallet at the gym along with the bag, which he'd slung over his shoulder. He unlocked the door and carried her over the threshold.

"I guess I better enjoy this while I can. I won't be able to carry you much longer, will I?"

"Oh stop it, Alex. I'm not going to get that big."

"Oh, but sweetheart, you get as big as you want. I honestly don't care."

"I'm pregnant, not fat. I won't get fat."

He set her down but couldn't keep his hands off her. "And I believe you, I honestly do! Just want you to know, Sydney, it's okay with me. We want a healthy baby. That's all that matters."

"So I guess that means skydiving tomorrow is out?"

"Absolutely it's out. After what you just went through today?"

"Well then, whatever can we do?"

"Well,"—he scratched the back of his neck—"I'm thinking of a few things we could do, once you're settled." He added, "You should take that warmup stuff off, to begin with."

"Okay. Why don't you sit right there?"

"Yes, ma'am," he said as he fell back into the easy chair.

She unzipped her top, slowly. Too slowly. She carefully revealed the yellow top he'd seen on those darned magazines. He licked his lips, suddenly parched for the taste of her. That brought a smile to her lips.

She let the top drop to the ground, then stepped out of her shoes. Next she pushed her pants down those gorgeous thighs, and then stepped out of them all together.

Her little yellow uniform was on parade as she slowly turned. The woman didn't have an extra ounce of fat anywhere. Her calves were well defined, even her toes looked sexy. She angled her hips as she presented her backside to him, the thong not covering one damn thing. Her butt cheeks were tight and compact like ripe fruit.

He was glad he never saw her play on the beach in the flesh. He'd have been so jealous, he'd have gotten into trouble. But she wore her outfit with complete confidence. Not an ounce of self-consciousness in her. She was a lean, mean spike and jumping machine. Her long muscled arms hung down gracefully at her sides, her wrists small, her cherry-red fingernails splayed out.

When she was facing him again, she slipped one strap of her top over her shoulder, then the other. The little halter top was pulled up and over her head. Her arms crossed, revealing her washboard abs. She stood with her right knee bent, her hips at an angle, her awesome form now naked from below her navel up. She threw the top at him. Hard.

That got to him. He was on his feet, pursuing her as she screamed and scampered into the bathroom, trying to close the door. He forced it open, enjoying the chase, enjoying her strength and her defiance of him. She had him wrapped around her little finger.

She turned on the shower, stepping inside with her little thong still intact. Her eyes taunted him, as if she thought the shower would make her safe. He kicked off his shoes and stepped into the stall fully clothed. Warm water drizzled down his back, soaking his shirt. He fell to his knees, almost in a beg, as he reached over with both hands and gripped the thong pulling it down her backside. As it fell to her knees, he buried his head in her crotch.

She was sweaty and salty tasting. But once he got his tongue inside, her moistness was sweet. He sucked her bud and heard her moan.

"Are you for real, Sydney? Is this all for real?"

She was backed into the corner, one foot balancing on the tiled ledge, exposing herself to him intimately. His forefinger rubbed the wet length of her slit, before he gently inserted two fingers and watched for signs this was not allowed. He bit the delicate folds of her labia and swirled his tongue over her little nub.

Quickly, she was on him, her long legs wrapped around his waist. She ripped apart his shirt, the buttons popping on the floor of the shower. She bit his nipple and then kissed up his neck. At last their mouths connected while she pulled his shirt off one shoulder and then the other.

He sat her on the ledge and removed the rest of his shirt, throwing it over the glass enclosure. He began to unbutton his wet pants, but she was suddenly on her knees, hungrily doing it for him, shedding the wet jeans to his ankles. He felt her hands inside his shorts and then they slid the elastic waistband down his thighs.

She pulled herself up on him, her powerful thigh muscles hugging his waist, as she angled and then found him at her opening.

They were face to face, the water splashing from his shoulder into her eyes. While the large droplets sluiced down between them both, she forced herself down on him as he held her buttocks, squeezing hard and pressing her deeper.

He knew he couldn't hold out long at all especially as she began riding him up and down. She increased the frequency until he could hold on no longer. She didn't stop while he pumped her full until he felt her internal twitching. She pressed herself hard against him, holding on to him with her incredibly strong arms, nearly squeezing the air right out of him.

They began the slow descent together, touching and kissing, rubbing gel on each other. She kneeled at his feet and helped him step out of his wet boxers and jeans, depositing them outside the shower door. Still on her knees, she poured the lemon-scented shower gel over his legs, smoothing his calves, knees and thighs with her delicate fingers. She washed his cock, squeezing his balls before moving up to rub gel all over his chest, down his arms, and up his neck. Then she turned him around and did the same to his back.

He turned back to face her, "I'm supposed to wait on *you*," he whispered to her wet hair.

"I know," she said, outlining his lips with her forefinger, "but I couldn't stop myself. Somehow, I'm always out of control around you."

"Me too, sweetheart."

"Promise me something."

"I promise."

"Promise me you won't be gone when our baby is born."

"Sweetheart, I can't promise that, but I'll try." He didn't want to ask, but he had to. "Are you saying you want me to get out?"

"No, Alex. That's who you are. I just want you to be there. Not on a monitor somewhere else. Don't let them take that away from us."

"It really does depend on what we get. But I won't volunteer for anything if there's a chance it will interfere. That's the best I can do. I'll work miracles to see to it that I'm there. I do promise that."

"That's good enough for me. I want you here for all the big events in my life, in our lives. In our baby's life."

"We'll find a way, Sydney. Maybe I won't re-up. Maybe I'll stay here and we'll do the winery. You can continue to coach, if you want. Or go for the AVP tour after the baby's here. Anything you want, sweetheart. What do you say?"

"If you're by my side, anything is possible, Alex. Anything."

It was his time to kneel. He kissed her firm belly, rubbing his palm over the flat, toned flesh, and whispered, "I'm your daddy. And I'll love you both forever."

JAKE

Band of Bachelors
Book 3

SHARON HAMILTON

CHAPTER 1

H IS HEAD FELT like someone had sucked out his guts and injected them into his skull right above his eyebrows. His tongue was stuck to the roof of his mouth. He heard the stretching of huge rubber bands, high-speed drills, and a car horn, which forced him to try to open his eyes.

Except he couldn't. They were stuck shut. He tried to pry them open with his fingers and had no sensation past his wrists.

Of all the fucked ups I've fucked up, this is the most fucked up I've ever been fucked up.

He tried to roll over and discovered why he couldn't feel his hands. Forcing his eyelids open by sheer concentration, he determined his arms were drawn above his head, his wrists secured with red ribbons, double-tied in knots wrapped around the metal bedframe. Whoever had done it was serious about immobilizing him and leaving him that way long term. Judging from the numbness in his hands, it had been hours.

The room was big and crusted in red and gold colors worthy of a high-end whorehouse, which wouldn't be a first time for Jake. It wouldn't be the tenth, either. And he'd been to them all over the world.

Where the fuck am I?

It felt like desert, but not the Sandbox of the Middle East. Desert as in the Southwest. New Mexico? Arizona?

He heard traffic outside. Some bump and grind music echoed down the street. Hucksters. Millions of little flickering electric lights sounded like gnats.

Las Vegas!

The slit of bright orange light crept across the room and fell over his bare feet. Thankfully, those he could feel. The window was framed in red. Like the rest of the room, the brocade curtains were peppered with red hearts. Red sheers poked out from the sides like ruffles on a petticoat.

He was stark naked. Good thing it was a hot day. His rod was ready, always a bad sign. Not a condom in sight. No protection, totally risky behavior, again.

Dammit! You said you'd stop this shit.

He tried to roll up to his shoulders and push against the metal frame, but the ribbons were secure. As he yanked on his bonds, a warm glow began to develop in his hands, and they felt painful and swollen. He couldn't move his fingers.

"Help!" he screamed, sounding like a teenager. He cleared his throat and concentrated. "Somebody, help me!" This time his shout was more manly.

Listening for the welcome sound of a key being used. running feet, or voices outside the door, he was soon disappointed. He scanned the room again for his clothes and came up empty. He did find his cell on the floor by the bed, face down, so he couldn't tell if anyone had tried to call him. And then he thought about something else.

My wallet!

It had happened before. Surely they had taken his wallet. *She* had taken his wallet.

She? Was there a she?

One thing was for sure, it wasn't going to be a fuckin' *he*. No matter how drunk he got, there'd never be a *he*. Or at least he better look like a she.

Oh, fuck.

"Somebody? Somebody get a manager!" he screamed. He held his breath and listened.

Nothing.

He sunk his head back into the double pillow, closed his eyes, wiggled his hips to try to get some of the weight off his stiffy, which only made it worse, and then just gave up and tried to think.

Images of Las Vegas and what his past had been like here replayed. Lots of weddings for his SEAL buddies on Team 3. Fredo and Mia got married here. Ryan and Alex married their wives in a double Elvis. Hard to forget that one. Boy, he nearly wound up in jail, running through the casino stark naked. There were the showgirls. Someone had dared him to streak the dressing room, but they pointed him to the wrong one so he ran past well-oiled dudes who were more than a little interested in him. His buddies could always be counted on to put him in the most embarrassing situations.

Okay, Connor was sent to Alaska and missed his own wedding here. T.J. had threatened to send Frankie—poor Frankie, who was so in love with Shannon he drooled on himself whenever he talked about her drunk. They brought him home and buried him next to the plot they'd all chipped in and gotten for Gunny.

He concentrated on the celebrations, too. Like the divorces, including both of his. The first one he definitely needed. Ginger had been just too hot to handle, but God, how he loved her. He tried to think of her as Wife #1, but it was no use. Even though he married Karlene, then lived with Monica, and had more kids with both of them, he still loved Ginger. His carrot-top daughters looked just like her, and they'd be driving all the young SEAL sons crazy in a few years.

Are you crying, you dumb fuck?

Sure thing. *Those tears are running down my neck and sinking into the pillow. I have nothing to feel sorry about—that is, unless I can't get untied and I die here. Well, I've almost died several other places before. At least here there's a soft mattress, and—and—some ladies' things hanging over the chair.*

His headache had roared back to life, but stalled a bit as he examined the light peach underwear and fuzzy slippers under the tall-backed chair done in red heart-patterned fabric. He tried to re-create his steps by imagining who might walk around for him right now in those unmentionables. Just do a little wiggle, maybe lean over, and let him have a taste of whatever fell out. Underwear was a big thing for Jake. Half the time, he liked his ladies to leave it on. It was a major turn-on for him.

Captain Commando was enjoying the stimulation, chuckling at him.

"You shut up!" he told his dick. Old Captain winked back at him and just laughed. It had gotten him in so much trouble, even ruined a perfectly good marriage—well, didn't ruin it, but the misunderstanding festered, and they were done. A real shame, too. But after that? Oh yeah, it had ruined one relationship after another. Seemed like they were always on the outs when they'd get pregnant. Jake had child support that technically exceeded his pay. Now, the Congress should investigate that sorry state of affairs. But no, they worried about the Russians and Tweets and fake news.

His eyes went back to the lingerie. Nice stuff. Not just bought at a sex shop. The panties had a satin crotch, a little red heart embroidered on the backside to the left. Quality. The bra had ample lace and a big cup size. What did it look like on the lady? This one was definitely a lady. Not a hooker. Someone special. But why couldn't he remember?

He closed his eyes again and told himself he was going to stop drinking. Oh yes, now he remembered. He was going to the spa to get a massage. And—and—he waited while the image came—his brother was there! Gerud would know what happened. He was making fun of him in the shower, getting ready for their massages. He drank the ice water and got to the treatment room, and those lovely hands began to work on him and he was—*out!* That's the last thing he remembered. The padded table was warm. The flannel sheets smelled wonderful. A candle was burning before he put on the eye mask and lay down on his belly. She'd oiled her hands, and he was feeling a little woozy, and then nothing!

Jake's LPO, Kyle Lansdowne had requested he start going to AA, and he began at a Men's Meeting on Saturday mornings. The condition of those sorry guys worried him, and he didn't go back. He didn't want to sit and remind himself of his problems with drinking, but he knew that if he didn't do something about it soon he'd be just like them. Sober was the right word for it—in all its meanings.

So he'd tried, really tried, to taper off the beer at first. Then he compromised and gave it up during the week. It had never been a problem during deployments. Somehow, he could stay sober. He was with his buds the whole time, so he couldn't slink off somewhere and get plastered.

He peered at the peach lingerie again. Maybe it was the ladies. There weren't any ladies like he liked overseas. And never the opportunity, unless he was off for a couple of days, staying over after a deployment. Then he could have some fun. And that always meant finding someone to spend a few days with, because he told himself he wasn't just a "love them and leave them" type.

Of course, that's exactly what he was.

Okay, so all those thoughts were getting to Captain Commando. "Got you, you little bastard," he mumbled to his unit. "You're not so feisty now, are you?"

Enough.

He had to find a way out of this bondage situation, because now it was beginning to worry him. The red marks on his wrists would remain after he was untied. Maybe someone was trying to do him in!

Could it be someone's husband, ex-husband? Holy fuck! Another Team Guy? Is this payback for something?

He didn't think it would be something from one of his exes. They'd want the child support. Even Monica, who'd come after him with an ax on their last day together and actually thrown the damned thing at him, wouldn't do this. And this lingerie? That wouldn't happen if someone wanted to off him. It was a tease. Someone knew his tastes and that he appreciated expensive lingerie, satin crotches and all. And if a guy was going to do it, well this MO wasn't like anything his SEAL buds would do. Divorces and breakups were common. Everyone in the whole community understood that there was no way a guy would take another man's girlfriend or wife, unless they were free to do so. It just wasn't done. No matter how fucked up he'd gotten, he would never knowingly do that. No sisters, either, for sure no daughters or, well, there were a few mothers that looked pretty good at forty, but just a couple. Shannon's mom, for one. And that lady definitely had the eyes for younger men. But no way.

Okay, time to get serious. This was unhealthy, and something had to be done.

"Help!" he shouted. "Somebody get the manager! Help me!"

He jammed his shoulders into the bedframe, making it rock against the wall. He kept it up. "Help!"

Sure enough, he heard a knock at the door.

"Mr. Green, is everything all right?" the muffled voice of someone on the other side of the door spoke.

"No. I need help!"

"Sir, I'm going to call security. Can you give me five minutes?"

"Go ahead, but I need to get out of here!"

"Calling right now, sir."

Jake heard the walkie-talkie burping someone's response and the voice of another stranger or two, probably people who had called to complain about the noise.

"They're on their way, sir."

"Great."

"Are you in pain? Have you fallen?"

"No, goddammit. Some one has tied me up, and I can't get loose."

"We'll be right there, sir."

About thirty seconds later, he heard a keycard slip into the door lock, and he was faced with a manager in a red sport coat and a huge black security guard, armed to the teeth. They looked first at his outstretched arms and the red ribbon. Then both gentlemen focused on Captain Commando, who was waving hello.

CHAPTER 2

G ERUD GREEN SIPPED on his Bloody Mary and then checked his watch, chewing the celery stick. He picked up his cell, but checked again for a text or call from Jake. It had been nearly two hours. Time to check his brother's room.

He left a generous tip for the buxom cocktail waitress, avoided the slots, and wandered the winding trail to the Desert Oasis elevators. Jake was on the top floor, the Wedding floor.

The dedicated penthouse elevator was all done in red hearts. A young couple Gerud guessed were barely legal were going to town, dry humping in the corner. He pretended not to look, though he was convinced people didn't do that in public unless they got off on it.

The doors opened, and he stepped back, motioning with his hand for the couple to exit in front of him. He followed behind as the young man put his arm all the way to his elbow down the girl's pants and made her squeal.

These types of things didn't affect him anymore. He was on a mission and had the luxury of having no choices left. He was driven to earn back the respect his father had lost in him. If he could help Jake turn his life around, that might get him in his dad's good graces again. If he could marry right this time, fix the rift in the family, and repair the hole Jake had created, Dad would be grateful.

Gerud was counting on it.

A hotel manager was standing in the hallway, speaking into a radio. He eyed Gerud suspiciously. Had something happened to Jake? Panic washed over him. Was he injured, or worse yet—dead? It took a second for him to figure out what emotion pooled around in his stomach. Jake's death or injury would be a bad thing, not a good one.

So he sucked up his gut, which did not resemble his brother's in any way, held his breath, and decided to be ready with tears if he had to create them. He tented his eyebrows, puckered his lips in an "O," and addressed the manager, who sneered at him.

"Excuse me. This is my brother's room. Is there some problem?" He tried to glance past the man, but the manager held out his hand and stopped him. "I'm sorry, sir. You'll have to keep out."

But then he heard Jake's voice.

"Gerud! Get your ass in here."

He stared at the manager's eyes and discovered one was blue, one was brown. "Is that invitation enough for you?" His grin was delayed just so the man knew it was insincere.

The manager stepped back and answered a call on his radio.

Inside the room, Jake sat on one of two cherry red chairs on either side of the window overlooking the strip. He was wrapped in a sheet. A huge security guard was standing next to him.

"What's going on, bro?" Gerud asked.

"How should I know? I have no idea how I got here." Jake rubbed his wrists.

"We found Mr. Green tied to the bed. You know anything about that, sir?"

Gerud shrugged.

"Mr. Green claims not to know who did this."

"I'm his brother, not his social secretary," Gerud answered. "He's a fuckin' Navy SEAL. He can usually take care of himself with the ladies."

Behind the security guard's back, Jake gave him a three-finger salute.

"Where are your clothes?"

Jake gave him a sour look. "Beats me."

"You've been streaking again, then?"

That got the guard's attention. "Mr. Green, the Desert Oasis doesn't allow nudity in the public places."

The obvious elephant in the room was the fact that what their cocktail waitresses and showgirls wore wouldn't be classified as clothes, either. Nudity was what the entire hotel was fashioned around. That and the healthy sexual innuendos one could practically get pregnant hearing, Gerud thought.

"Well, if I could find out who did this to me, I'd probably find my clothes."

"You can't walk around in a sheet, bro. You honestly don't remember a thing? How the hell does that happen?"

The security guard gave a smirk. He didn't say it, but Gerud could tell he was thinking, *it happens all the time.*

"Okay then. I'll file an incident report, and you let us know if anything further happens. And your wrists, you want to get them checked out by the medical staff here?"

Jake held his hands out in front of him. "Wow."

"Sir?" the guard asked.

Jake held up his left hand, showing Gerud the wedding ring there. "Something else I don't remember, brother."

"Geez, Jake. Now you've done it."

The guard closed his metal clipboard box with a snap and rolled his eyes. "You guys try to stay out of trouble, ya hear?"

Jake shook his head.

The guard waddled to the doorway and, just before closing it, barked back, "Y'all have a nice day."

Gerud put his hands on Jake's bare shoulders. "So who did you marry?"

"I'm serious. I have no idea. I don't remember a thing. I went in for that massage, and then, boom. I wake up here."

"Well, we had that massage around six or seven. When I left you, you were chasing cocktail waitresses and feeling no pain."

Jake swore under his breath.

"You told me you were done with all that. You were going to just gamble a little and go to bed early."

"Well, apparently I ran into someone I thought would be a good fit for Wife number three."

"Four."

"Nope, three. I never married Monica."

"Huge point in Monica's favor. Didn't stop you from creating a baby with her, though."

"Having babies and getting married are two distinct things, or don't you remember?"

Gerud winced. He'd married, but discovered he couldn't father children, which landed him a big fat zero on both scores, since the marriage failed because of it. But Jake just had to sleep with someone one time and she'd get knocked up. Life wasn't fair, he thought. Notch something else Jake could do that Gerud couldn't. Their mother loved all four grandchildren and lavished attention on them generously. The brothers agreed, their mother loved the grandkids more than she loved raising her own boys. Gerud's gene pool wasn't part of that affection, either.

"So get your butt into the shower. I'll bring up some clothes and let's do a bit of shopping."

"Gerud, I have no idea where my wallet is."

He pointed to the counter in the bathroom. "Right there, kid. You think she cleaned you out?"

Jake beat him to the bathroom, grabbed his wallet and found money and credit cards in it. "A little light on the money," he said.

"Maybe she took out her fee."

"Shut up, Gerud. I got a wedding ring on. That *means* something!"

"Yeah, asshole. If only you could remember her name."

CHAPTER 3

JAKE COULDN'T GET the wedding ring off, even after trying it with soap in the shower. He was hoping that in time, when the swelling went down in his hands that he could get it.

"So you gonna sleep in the suite tonight or are you coming back to our room?"

Jake stopped the fork of eggs halfway to his mouth and thought. "Didn't think about that."

"Better find out who's paying first," said Gerud.

"Good point," Jake said, pointing his fork at his brother.

"I mean, aren't you curious to see who you married? It could be important."

"Curious? Yes. But if it was important, I'd remember. So, it couldn't be that."

"You do know Mom thinks marriage is a sacred vow. Something spiritual, stuff of angels and shit."

"Well, she'd have to think that to put up with Dad and all his drinking and womanizing ways. He hurt her real bad, Gerud. You remember."

Gerud was watching him very carefully. "I do. Sort of like how you treated Ginger."

Jake nearly spit out his orange juice. "Watch it with Ginger, bro. I never cheated on Ginger. Not once. Hell, I even cheated with Ginger on wife #2, and nearly once with Monica until one of the kids walked into the room."

"Surprised you can keep them all straight, my man. Well, at least you got a couple of carrot-heads out of it."

"Carrot tops."

"That's what I said."

Jake threw his napkin at his brother.

"So we have tickets to Circus Bare tonight. You game?"

Jake was thinking about the peach underwear and especially the satin crotch panties, curious to see the woman who filled them out.

"Don't you think I should ask my wife first?"

"No problem." Gerud mimicked searching the room for someone. "Oh that's right, you don't remember her name or what she looks like."

"Fuck you."

That got the attention of their waitress, who wore slightly more clothes than the ladies who served in the bar. "Coffee? Espresso?"

"Espresso, please," said Jake, "Thank God you have a machine."

"And you?" The waitress made a point to show Gerud she didn't find him as attractive.

"I'll have one, too, because this guy's paying." Gerud was good with the sarcasm this morning.

While she was off getting their drinks, Gerud pointed to the over-sized golf shirt—his golf shirt—that didn't fit Jake. "We gotta get you some decent duds."

"Where the heck do you think my clothes went?"

"Maybe you got them wet? Threw up on them? Your lovely blushing bride is off washing them for you?"

"You know, Gerud, wouldn't she at least have my cell phone number and call me? I mean, if she came back, knowing I didn't have any replacement clothes?"

"Dunno, Jake. But I think we better get you some clothes just in case. Then if she doesn't return, at least you can tag along with me to the show."

"So you think the bag I came up with was in the room, too?"

"I have no idea what you did with that. You probably don't even remember taking it. When we left for the massage, it was right there beside your bed. Can't say."

They took a taxi to a Native American outlet mall where he bought a nice pair of jeans and a long-sleeved shirt. He turned down all the Aloha shirts, especially the ones with naked women on them. It was time to clean up his life. Although he was supposed to celebrate his release from Monica, none of his buddies had been there for him this weekend, or were tired of celebrating his exes, but Gerud was only too happy to tag along. Jake figured he wouldn't be a SEAL forever, so it was time to start figuring out what he was going to do with the rest of his life, starting with eventually looking for something that would pay better so he could support all those kids.

He was okay with the fact that none of his former relationships were big time career women. He liked that they wanted to devote themselves to being a mother first. It was time for him to step up to the plate, and like the guy had said in the AA meeting, become a man. A real man.

Gerud was still trying to get him to buy the thong underwear and low hip hugger French stuff, but he bought a two-pack of boxers with red white and blue stripes and stars on them. A couple of tee shirts, plain white and plain light blue, and some canvas slip-ons rounded out the purchase. He knew the hotel had shave kits and toothpaste, so the only other thing he bought was some bargain cologne at the checkout counter at the jeans store.

"The high school kids shop here," Gerud said.

"Yeah? Well I've got about as much money as a high school kid, probably less. And I've got four kids to support, so about time I started taking austerity measures."

Gerud chuckled. "Never gonna happen. You'll change when you're good and ready to."

Heading out to the car, Gerud asked him, "What ever happened with Monica anyhow? I thought she was crazy about you. That girl was fine."

"You know, I think some women figure hooking up with a SEAL will solve all their problems." Jake shook his head. "Man, that's just the start of their problems. We're gone all the time, and when we come home, we can't relax unless we get shit-faced, or all we want is to stay in bed, and not necessarily to screw."

"You didn't like to screw Monica? I find that hard to believe."

"I'm not gonna talk about my marriage with you. That's between her and me, but I'm just saying I knew it wasn't going to work out, so I wouldn't marry her. And then when she got pregnant, well, she thought for sure I'd marry her. I told her I loved her, that I'd love the baby. But my track record sucks."

"And then that's when she got out the ax."

"No, that was the next day." Jake wondered where Gerud had gotten his information. "Who told you that, anyway?"

"Can't remember."

Jake was certain he was lying.

JAKE CHECKED WITH the registration desk and verified that his room had been comped by the manager based on prior Gold Club usages, and that two keys had been issued, one for him and one for Mrs. Green, whoever that was. He asked for a new key for security, telling the clerk he'd lost his key at the pool.

A lot of the Team guys liked staying here because the manager was a former Team guy as well and knew their base salary was less than being a dealer on the floor. They were putting their life on the line every deployment, and it was getting worse and worse out there. But a constant was the fact that they got paid very little for doing so.

And that was okay with Jake, or was before he had so many children. It wasn't why he became a SEAL. He just felt like it was something he could do, was compelled to do. In his heart, he was a protector. And not a killer. He was there to preserve life. And yes, he guessed God put him on this earth to procreate, too, since it was so easy for him.

"Okay, man. You get some shuteye and I'll come up and get you about six or so? We can get some drinks and something to eat. Show's at eight."

"Sounds good. Just the two of us, right?"

Gerud frowned. "Of course. I wouldn't set you up. That happens next time you come up here, okay?"

Jake was fiddling with the wedding ring, which still hadn't come off. His hands weren't back to normal yet, and the purple marks where the ribbon had been too tight were starting to scab over a bit. Whoever had tied him up had an attitude Jake wasn't so sure about. He was happy he got out of the restraints before too much time had passed or he might have incurred some serious damage to his hands.

When he opened the door, he looked for the lingerie first, figuring she'd definitely want that first. But it still lay draped over the chair. He hung up his new shirt and put the shorts in a drawer. He found the headache medicine and tossed back four with complimentary bottled water. He lay the shave kit and toothpaste down and stripped, stepping down into the shower.

He let the water drizzle over his pounding forehead. He knew he could dull the pain a bit with a beer, but decided against it. It was a small victory, but an important one.

He dried off and headed for the bed naked, after latching the door for total privacy. He stopped by the wingback chair and fingered the lingerie.

The bra and panty set was brand new. He knew about such things.

CHAPTER 4

G INGER AND KAREN took their seats in the theater. A troop of clowns was walking around the audience, stepping on the backs of vacant chairs while the audience arrived. A slow drip of water drizzled from the ceiling, landing right on the part in the middle of the red-haired clown's head. He immediately put up his umbrella and looked all around. The droplets of water splashed off and into the laps of the audience members sitting nearby.

Another clown on a bicycle rode down one of the aisles backwards and collided with the clown with the umbrella, and they both sprawled on the stage. Yellow-bodied fairies with blue wings drifted from the ceiling and landed on stage as their helmets lit up, glowing shades of blue and green.

Vampy clowns followed audience members who were looking for their seats, imitating the walk and mannerisms of the unsuspecting tourists.

The activity settled Ginger's nerves. Karen squeezed her hand down low between them so no one could see.

"You're doing fine," whispered Karen.

"Is he here yet?"

"No. Stop talking about it. Just forget about it. We have an hour until intermission."

She sucked in air. She'd had her hair done with a fresh style, giving it some curl, but no color was needed since her bright naturally-red hair was a showstopper anywhere she went. That fact wasn't lost on one of the clowns who bowed to her and extended his hand.

"Go," whispered Karen, pushing her toward the aisle.

She wanted to peek behind her, but then she heard Karen whisper, "He's not here yet."

Ginger stood and curtseyed to the clown in the aisle. She was wearing a very low-cut, formfitting knit dress, showing just the right amount of ample breast and leg, and of course highlighting her hair color since the dress was a shade of pinkish orange.

Her heart racing, she accompanied the clown, giggling in spite of herself. It was so unlike her to get up on stage anywhere, and here in front of a thousand people in the Grand Oasis Theater, it was so large she felt like she was walking through an airport terminal.

Two other clowns walked over and surveyed her. The first clown turned her around while the others scratched their chins and nodded. They took turns dancing with her. One of the actors whispered in her ear, "Relax. You're the most beautiful woman in the theater. Allow us to let you glow. Just enjoy it."

She gazed into his green eyes, the same color as hers, and found a friend there, behind war paint. "Thank you."

"Tell me you are not here alone."

Ginger smiled. Another clown took her in his arms and twirled her effortlessly like a professionally trained ballroom dancer. She had a bit of training and knew the best thing was to just relax and go with his rhythm and not try to keep any sort of time. The beautiful thing about dancing, she thought, was that the man was always in control, so she gave herself up to him and just allowed him to make it appear she was gliding.

The third clown cut in and grabbed a rose from a flower cart nearby. Placing it in his teeth, he swung her in romantic sways back and forth, and then bent her back nearly to the floor. "Magnifico!" he whispered.

The first clown tried to cut in. The audience was clapping to the Latin beat. One of the blue and yellow fairies danced with her, and then she danced with a large sea creature of some sort wearing a tall head-dress with bright shades of purple and red.

Her original suitor presented himself and she took his arm as he led her in the direction of her seat to enormous audience applause. He stopped her, bowed to her, encouraged the audience to clap louder, and let her share the moment. She couldn't see any of the faces of the two balconies above, but she was awash in the flash of lights from everywhere.

She wondered if Gerud had also arranged this reception. She bowed to the audience again and then resumed the processional to her seat, the other clowns and fairies in tow behind her.

Of course, just as they were coming upon her section, she saw Jake and Gerud seated just behind where she and Karen sat. Jake looked like he'd seen the Virgin Mary or some such thing.

The clown air-kissed her on both cheeks, as did the rest of the entourage before she sat down to thunderous applause.

She felt Jake's presence directly behind her and glanced up to her left, catching a wink from Gerud. She immediately faced the stage as the lights went dim and the performance music began.

"I've never seen you so radiant, Ginger. You took my breath away," came the voice she knew so well.

She turned her head in profile and said across the aisle, not facing him, "Thank you, Jake. What a nice surprise."

"Yes, it is."

Karen grabbed her hand, and the show was off to a magnificent start.

If someone had asked her what the performance was like, she wouldn't have been able to tell them about any costumes or acts, except the look of the three clowns and half dozen fairies she'd danced with. She could tell anyone the color of the velvet seats: burgundy. She could tell someone that fleur d'lise patterns were stitched into the carpeting that went up the aisle. The stage was a light tan canvas, tiny markings drawn in it only the dancers could see. She could tell you about the purple glove of the first clown, or that his eyes were green as emeralds and he had lots of chest hair that extended up over his red and white striped shirt.

And he smelled nice. And streaked his face paint with sweat.

But she could also tell anyone what it felt like to sit in front of the man she loved, had always loved and hoped to win back again. She was a wicked woman on a mission to lure him back to her. She'd been planning the takedown ever since she'd heard Jake's newborn had arrived and he and Monica were fighting constantly. Her ex-mother-in-law made sure she understood that Monica was all wrong for her son. Ginger got good at laughing it off, even while her girls longingly looked up to her just to check and see if there was a chance Daddy would be coming home to stay.

All had been artfully planned. She'd waited too long the first time and missed Jake in his flurry to get married and thought she'd lost him forever. Monica was the result of a weekend in Mexico that lingered for two years.

But this was her time. She would make him see the error of his ways. She would have him back if it was the last honest, or perhaps dishonest, thing she did. She could play stealth and execute a plan just as well as any of the SEALs on Team 3, maybe better. They had no idea what five years of regret had wrought. And if this didn't work, so be it. She'd go on and have a good life with her daughters and would do her best to bury Jake in the cemetery of her lost dreams.

This little clown parade had helped. Oh God! It had helped. She owed a lot to Gerud, who had been the one with all the ideas. She'd find some way to repay him for giving her the one thing she wanted: a chance with Jake again.

Intermission came quickly. As she turned, expecting Jake to avert his gaze like he always did when she'd drop the girls off or he brought them home, this time, he just examined her directly, like he was seeing her for the first time.

Gerud was asking if they wanted some champagne. Karen was all for it. Ginger shrugged. Just being in Jake's proximity was refreshment enough, but she said, "Sure."

The four of them walked up the aisle, Karen and Gerud in rapid conversation with sprinkled laughter thrown in. He turned several times to wink at her, and she showed her appreciation with her best smile.

The plan had been to make Jake jealous by being a little flirtatious. They were to go dancing afterwards, and Gerud would show him how much he admired his ex. All she had to do was not look at Jake very much, avoid his eye contact if she could, make him want to stare her down, take her away from Gerud. Jake's brother was a genius at reading people. He knew exactly how she felt about it and how desperate she was to get Jake back into her life.

And it was a miracle Gerud had agreed to help!

They had to ease their way through a throng of people on their way to the bar. Several couples stopped her and commented on how talented she was on the stage, asking about her hair color, if she was part of the cast or just a bystander or audience member.

The questions came so fast, she didn't have time to answer them in order. Finally, Jake took her hand and dragged her toward Gerud and Karen by the bar.

"Ginger's got all the attention tonight, Jake." Gerud said. He put his arm around her waist, pulled her to his side away from Jake and planted a kiss on her cheek.

This made her blush. Karen giggled. Jake turned his head stiffly like a robot and stared at his brother.

Gerud handed her a glass of pink champagne, matching Karen's and his own, and asked Jake if he wanted something.

"Water," he said, his voice gravely. He extended his left hand and that's when Ginger noticed his wedding ring.

She knew Gerud had placed it on his finger, but she was supposed to act surprised, and more than a little disappointed.

She leaned into Gerud closer, "Congratulations, Jake. You didn't wait very long this time."

Jake pulled back his hand without taking the water, as if he'd burned it. He adjusted his sleeve over the still-swollen wound from the red ribbon sashes.

She knew he would be at a loss for words. That was the plan. Ginger knew there was no real marriage or wife, but she thought she would enjoy watching Jake squirm, trying to figure out what to say to her. But his wrist injury had her distance herself from Gerud's embrace.

"What's the matter with your hand? Did you injure it?" she asked.

Jake scanned from Gerud to Karen and back to Ginger again before he'd answer. His happy mood had soured. Ginger was concerned.

"Just another case of bad judgment, I guess. Isn't that all what you're used to from me?" His right eye twitched. He walked away from them, into the crowd.

Ginger was crestfallen.

"What is that—that—red mark on his wrist?" She alternated between Karen and Gerud. Karen shrugged. But Gerud hung his head.

"I improvised."

"What did you do?"

"I added a little bondage scene to his pass out."

"You did what?"

"I tied up his wrist, well, both his wrists, to the bedframe. I thought they were loose enough he'd get them undone and then fall asleep. But apparently I was more thorough than I thought. He must have slept that way."

"Gerud, that's terrible!"

"Ginger, I'm sorry. I guess part of me was concerned he'd fall off the bed."

She could see even he didn't buy the excuse. And now she had a problem. She had to tell Jake. She had to take responsibility for what their plan had hatched. What had started as a fun caper—though she'd never been totally comfortable with the sleeping pills—what she thought would be a joke they could laugh about turned out to be something much more. He could have been seriously injured.

What was she thinking?

"Ginger," Gerud grabbed her arm but she wrestled free.

"I have to tell him, Gerud. This isn't right."

"And if you do, everyone in the family will know. Your parents, your girls. Everyone."

"But I didn't do this!"

"No, but you were an accomplice."

"Not really. I didn't expect he'd get hurt! What were you thinking?"

"That you'd do anything to get back with Jake. You even told me so several times. Desperate was the word you used, I believe."

Karen was looking down at her feet. Other patrons were pushing past, trying for a spot at the bar, annoyed they were taking up space. The three moved out into a corner. Ginger watched Jake standing near the entrance and thought perhaps he was going to bolt. She felt horrible, and tears began to collect in her eyes.

Karen put her arm around her shoulder. "Go to him. Just go talk to him, Ginger. He seemed interested, earlier."

With a last minute death stare at Gerud, Ginger did just that. Just as she got close, Jake started for the exit.

"Jake, wait a minute! Can I talk to you?"

His scowl was familiar to her. It was the expression she saw most often in their last days together, just before their breakup.

"So you and Gerud, huh?"

"What are you talking about?"

"You let him get his hands all over you? How long have you been fucking my brother, Ginger, Miss High and Mighty?"

"I'm not sleeping with your brother, Jake."

"I didn't say *sleeping* with him. I said *fucking* him."

"That's unfair. I'm not."

He put his fingers to his eyes and squeezed them. "God. Can't do anything right."

"Look, can we just go somewhere and talk? I'd really like to just talk to you."

"Is that what this, this setup is, then? You and Karen getting tickets right in front of me and Gerud?"

She tossed her head and agreed. "Yes."

"Your little dance on stage?"

"No! That was just coincidence. I don't know how they found me.

They just pick people from the audience, Jake. Honest, I had nothing to do with that. I have no clue how come they picked me."

His eyes roamed over her body, scanning her neckline, up to her eyes, then focusing on her lips. "Probably because of how beautiful you look tonight."

Tears pushed up and spilled over her lower lids as her cheeks flushed. He'd not said that for years. They were words she'd wanted to hear ever since the day he'd left.

"I'm sorry. I shouldn't have said that. I didn't mean to—"

"Didn't mean to what? Cause me discomfort? How in the world would you think you telling me I'm beautiful would cause me any degree of pain, Jake?"

The air cleared for thirty seconds as they gazed straight into each other's eyes, unlike anything they'd done since the breakup.

"Okay, are we set to go back?" Gerud's voice cut through the moment like Monica's ax.

"You know? I'm going to go have a cup of coffee," said Jake, avoiding eye contact. "Would you excuse me?" He followed up with a half grin that looked more like a grimace.

"I understand the grand burlesque scene at the end is a showstopper, Jake. Don't want to miss it!" Gerud seemed unaffected by his huge blunder. Ginger feared he didn't even feel remorse.

"No thanks." Jake held up his hand. He glanced back and smiled. "Nice to see you again, Ginger."

Her heart melted. As he turned, she caught his arm. She'd come all this way, had made a terrible mistake in doing so, but she was still on her mission. It was still the right thing, done the wrong way, but still the only thing that mattered to her anymore. She risked appearing needy, but she knew deep down inside her it was the honest truth. She was so crazy in love with her ex, she'd swallow her pride and take her chances, because not doing anything left only one outcome.

His face showed surprise.

"You want some company, Jake?"

He glanced up at Gerud and Karen and then returned to her. "I'm not very good company this evening, Ginger. Kind of been a rough few hours."

"Let me be the judge of that." She had to add, "But you decide."

"Well, sure, I guess we could get a Starbucks. They're right across the street."

She noted Gerud looked like the life had been sucked out of him. Without expression, he turned. Karen waved and nervously followed him back into the theater as the call came.

She was alone with Jake at last. The timing was all wrong. So much of this evening was all wrong. She regretted everything she'd done, been a part of, and even regretted that she had felt so desperate. All her old fears about not being worthy enough for Jake and his bravery and not being strong enough for his demons, came haunting her once again.

She brushed those thoughts aside, grabbed his hand, and led him out into the Las Vegas night air. For coffee. For a chance. Just a chance. And if it failed, well there was the life she'd been living before, raising his girls, teaching them to honor their father, and looking for a partner who would never measure up to Jake, flaws and all. She'd have to make do with that, but only after she went for the brass ring and hoped she didn't fall off the horse.

CHAPTER 5

J AKE ORDERED THEM both lattes, without checking with Ginger first, because he knew her that well. He still remembered what she liked. He understood more about her than she even realized. He'd thought more about her over the years than he wanted to admit to anyone.

Boy, did he need a drink. But the latte was reassuringly warm in his hands as he shuffled to the corner table with his ex looking fine in that beautiful peachy-orange glow she always seemed to have. She'd been a ray of sunshine in his life at one time. He'd very nearly put that light out, and he figured she'd been much better off, the girls, too, with him gone.

"Here you go. Hope you don't mind I didn't ask you."

She studied him with those green eyes of hers, those honest eyes that didn't miss a thing. That was always the thing with her. She saw everything about him. Noticed everything. Everything meant something to her. The intense flame that was her honesty was still there, in that commanding beauty he finally couldn't take.

"Thank you."

Again, she stared.

"So, here we are, Ginger. What did you want to talk about?"

She broke off and followed her finger rimming the top of the latte cup, dipping in the foam and making a mockery of his heart. She had no right to hold such a claim on him, but she did. Her smooth flesh was moist from the humid coffee shop lobby, the cleavage between her breasts heaving and settling, her hair of spun fibers of orange framing her face in a new cut that featured her jaw and cheekbones. Her lips were pale pink with a hint of rose from the lip-gloss she liked to use, not the heavy lipstick the showgirls sported. It made her lips the color of other parts of her he'd enjoyed during those early days of their marriage, when all they could do was lay in bed together and feel how incredibly wonderful it was to fuck, to be so much in love, and to want to just die doing nothing but that.

He didn't wait for her to return his gaze, deciding he'd indulged his fantasy too long. He inhaled, sitting erect in the chair and stared out the window.

He fingered the wedding ring still fuckin' stuck on his digit. He'd go get it removed tonight. Probably was a jewelry store open somewhere. He'd go there alone. They probably knew what to do and saw it all the time in this place of broken dreams and fantasies of impossible proportions.

"So can you tell me how you managed to get that ring on your finger if you aren't really married?" Her face was pure angel. The right side of her lips turned up in a sexy crease he watched deepen and then disappear. His heart was in his throat. He hated experiencing being so helpless.

"Well, you, of all people understand me, Ginger. Always unpredictable. Surprises. I was expecting to see the little lady come tonight and claim her prize!" he extended his arms to the sides and gave a sarcastic chuckle. It would have been funnier if he'd been drunk. "But like all the rest of the women I've loved and love still—" He watched her blink twice. "She's abandoned me. Left me here in Sin City."

He could tell she was at a loss how to react to him. He leaned in and suddenly decided to take a chance, tucking her hands in his. "Funny thing is, Ginger, you were the one I always wanted, even after I went out and got crazy. It was just a rebound thing. Twice. That's the God's truth, and I'm sorry."

He watched her eyes fill up with tears. Now he'd done it, made her miserable with a come-on she probably thought was generated by some desire to get even with Monica. Or anger at being left at the altar with no wedding night to consummate.

He was about to pull his hands away and leave her alone when she moved one thumb over the top of one of his hands and didn't say a word. He knew that look. It was pure flame.

She examined their entwined fingers. "I always thought we never finished what we started. Things got in the way. If they weren't there, we would have been different."

"I didn't like disappointing you all the time."

"You scared me, Jake."

"I scared myself." He had to break away. He put his hands on his thighs under the table, checking out the bizarre assortment of people sitting in the coffee shop. The crowd was nearly as colorful as the cast of the Circus Bare.

She was doing that thing again she always did when things got tough. She inhaled and was holding her breath, steeling herself from exploding out of control. He hated he had that effect on her.

He loved her, but it was so bad for her that he did. The best thing in the world to do was to let her go. He wished she'd find someone else, because he hated the idea of hurting someone he loved so much.

"Ginger, I loved you so much it hurt. I want to be a better man. A man who wouldn't disappoint you all the time. You are way too good for me, honey. Way too good. I'm not worth it."

"Stop it, Jake. That's not true. You just don't want to try."

"Try?" He sipped his latte and noticed she'd barely touched hers. "Come on, finish your coffee, and I'll walk you back across the street."

"Sure," she said as she smiled to her coffee cup.

He finished and watched her push hers to the center of the table. "Take mine."

After studying her, he posed the question he'd been dreading. "What was it you wanted to talk to me about, anyway? We're here. Relatively alone except for the freak show behind me."

She liked that and smiled.

"What was so important?"

Her answer was quick. "I miss you."

"You miss me?" His blood pressure began to rise. "Miss all the misery I caused you?"

"I caused some of it, too. I pushed too hard."

"No. You had to lay down the ground rules. We had two kids. I was a terrible husband. I drank, I stayed out all the time with the guys," He stopped and pointed to the ceiling, "But I never cheated on you. Not once."

"I think I can believe that now. Doesn't mean you didn't go away, though."

"Yes. I did leave. I just couldn't stop."

"I wasn't enough for you to want to stop."

"No, Ginger. That's not fair to you. You were all I ever needed. I just was afraid I was going to let you down. All the things I was seeing over there, the killing, the crazy-assed stuff that part of the world does to their women and children. Good people getting killed, and bad people laughing about it. I went a little insane. I didn't want to bring it home, but I did anyway."

She had left her hands on the table and now reached for her coffee. Shaking, she took a sip and set it back down.

"It was never you. It was all me."

"I still love you, Jake. It's not that I just miss you. I still *love* you. I think perhaps I always will."

He so didn't deserve her and yet part of him, the selfish part, wanted to take her in his arms and rock her world like he knew he could. But it was unfair. It was taking something and not giving her anything in return. She was too good for that.

Perhaps the old Jake wouldn't care, but the person he was today, who had walked into that meeting and faced the old drunks that didn't stop when they were young, that Jake didn't want to pile on the garbage of broken promises he'd made to her over and over again, and then repeated to the other women in his life. And then would say some day to his children. Some day they'd be old enough to hate who he'd been. The mess he'd made of his life.

"I don't know how to bridge this cavern between us, Jake. I can't predict if we ever will. But I'd like to try. I'd like to show you who I really am and what I'm really about."

"The right thing for me to say is no."

He saw that sparkle in her beautiful green eyes. "So am I seeing this properly then?" She leaned into the table so he could see her cleavage, so her face was nearly close enough he could lean forward and kiss her. "I'm giving you the come-on, telling you I'm hot for you, Jake, that I want you more than I've ever wanted you before, and you're going to say no? Is that right?"

She knew she could wait and he'd come around to the idea. It was her way to get him right where she wanted him. She always could do that, when she had the energy. And boy, she had some energy tonight. Her unmistakable desire for him, his absolute soft spot, where he had no defense.

Dammit. She was right.

But this time, he didn't hate her for it. This time, he wanted to believe that she still belonged to him.

She'd always been the stronger one. He desired to give her some of that back, show her he was a different man. He didn't mind drinking from the well of her soul, but he needed to replenish what he was taking. Maybe it was the elixir that would heal him.

CHAPTER 6

WALKING NEXT TO Jake again had her feeling twenty, the way she felt the first time she'd kissed him. He was the experienced Navy SEAL, crusty, irreverent, the one all the girls watched and wanted. Her little circle of friends, including Karen, had told her he liked fast women, faster cars, and all the things that were dangerous.

But she saw something else. He was a grown man, but he was a lost boy trying to behave like a man. He'd taken on the impossible task of doing things no one else would do, to show the world he didn't mind. That he could handle it.

It was Jake's belief in the world, in the little things of the world that needed protection, that made him the man he was. Not the bravado or joking jackass he could be in front of his friends. He danced with abandon, he drank with abandon. She never thought he noticed her. But she'd been watching him, and something inside her was snagged and caught.

That night when he finally fixated on her, she'd blushed and turned away a dozen times. He loved the chase. She was the one he couldn't charm the pants off of. She said no when he tried to grab her in the hallway.

"You're such a pretty little thing. How come you never say anything? What goes on in that head of yours?"

"Not much."

"Liar. I'll bet your libido is as strong as the color of your hair."

He was right, but she didn't know it.

"That's not what I'm looking for."

He tented his eyebrows. That's when she knew she had him. He couldn't take his eyes off her.

They'd meet at parties when she'd arrive with her friends. Then the boys would suddenly be gone on a mission. She always held her breath to hear he came back whole and without injury. They'd lost a couple one deployment. They had some who had to retire from injuries. Some of them went through divorces from hell. But Jake was always the same. Never changed. The tough demeanor that she suspected she could get up under to experience the man underneath.

It had happened at the beach around a bonfire for their good-bye ritual. It was special that she'd been invited. He'd sat behind her, and over the next twenty minutes he'd crept closer and closer to her until his thighs had lined hers. She felt his breath at her back, his heartbeat. She felt him swallow. Heard his laugh. She was nervous that this strong warrior of a man was coming to claim her.

She felt his fingers walk up her spine, and then slip her hair to the side. He had whispered, "You're so beautiful. And I like the way you smell."

Her girlfriends grinned from the other side of the bonfire. One by one people left, but Jake remained with her until they were the last ones on the beach. He didn't even say good-bye to the friends he'd be flying out with the next day. It was understood. Jake had found someone. There was no hiding it, denying it. No running away from it. She belonged to him, and she'd never loved a man before, never taken her clothes off in front of anyone before.

She wished tonight she could give something so precious to him again. She wished they could do a re-set and take back all the tears that had been shed. Bring the girls into the world with him at her side, one by one. To see that fresh quirky face of his above the hospital gown, holding their little red daughter with the bright red curls, despite the fact that Jake had black hair. The girls had her coloring.

"Carrot tops," he'd said. He was so proud as he held their second girl. "I should have known. Thank God, they take after you, honey."

Those were wonderful memories they had. And they'd chosen to push them aside, turn their back on them. Maybe it could be repaired. Just maybe.

His hands were the same. He cleared his throat in the elevator as they stood side by side amongst drunk partygoers. Women with greasy faces and streaked mascara. Bachelors hoping to misbehave. Everyone was headed to the Wedding floor, where every single room would be filled with couples doing God knew what.

His arm was protective. She fit well with him as they walked down the hallway, in the opposite direction of the rowdy groups. He took a key card out from his pocket and opened the door a crack. But he blocked it, held her head in his hands and kissed her like it was the very first time.

The familiar scent of his chest, the way he groaned when her tongue followed his, the way his fingers grabbed her hair as if telling her the thrill ride was almost too much for him as well.

He brought her to his chest, his hands protecting her head and pressing her against his beating heart. "God, Ginger. I've been a fool. How could I have ever—"

The waver in his voice made her heart sing. When she checked his face she did see tears there. "You have no idea how many nights I've wanted to feel this, Jake. You have no idea."

She was crying, too.

"Look at us. Divorced. Parents of two kids. We walked away from all this, Ginger."

She placed her fingers against his lips. "Shh, Jake."

He was mumbling.

"Jake, can we go inside the room?"

"I just want you to understand something first—"

"I know. I know it all, Jake. Let's go inside. I get what you're trying to say and I agree."

"What a complete ass I've been—"

"Jake." She found the whole thing funny. "Don't tell me. Show me. Please, show me."

He shook his head, laughing. "Come to my room, little girl."

She followed him as he walked backwards into the dark space with the glow from the Strip splashing color all over the walls, sound bouncing everywhere. When Gerud had described it as gypsy chic, he'd been right. There were more red hearts than a stationery store at Valentine's Day.

The door clicked closed behind her. The finality of her being alone with him again sent a shiver up her spine. Then when he touched her, she nearly fainted. He pulled her hair from her neck and kissed her there. He whispered into her ear, "I'm so sorry, Ginger. Truly I am, honey. Let me make it up to you. For everything I've done."

She turned. "No, Jake. Not from that place. From this place," she said as she put her palm over his heart. "Bring me what's here, what's always been here, like you told me at the coffee shop. Bring me what you have, all that you have. That's what I bring you. Everything I can give. If you'll have me."

"God, Ginger." He fell to his knees and she held his face to her belly. His fingers lifted up the hem of her dress as he kissed her belly button through the fabric. He clutched the material all the way to her waist, one hand smoothing over her rear, fingers slipping into the back of her panties. His other hand lifted her dress over his head and between her legs he kissed her on the flat of her lower abdomen.

She jumped when he slipped his tongue under the elastic of her lace, layering a wet trail all the way before his fingers gently pressed her thighs apart. His tongue slipped down the slit at her sex, and he was delicate as he sucked her bud and tasted her, following up with a finger. She began to vibrate. The heat of his breath between her legs and the feel of him tasting her set every nerve ending on fire.

She pulled her dress off, watching the top of his head feasting between her legs, moaning as his hot tongue foraged deeper.

He abruptly rose, unbuttoning his shirt while she unsnapped his button fly and felt the velvety goodness of his cock. She squeezed him and heard his guttural moan.

He quickly removed his jeans and shirt while she slid his boxers down to his ankles. She stood in front of him in her panties and bra. He just watched her in the glow of the lights. As laughter and cheering erupted down at the Strip, as the squeal of tires and the sounds of music filled the air she let him take in every part of her, understanding that she belonged to him. His cock bounced in the air. She reached for it and held him firm.

"Are we ready for this?" he whispered.

"You mean after your tongue has been inside me, after you've gotten me all worked up and nearly coming from just being close to your naked body, Jake, after all that, you ask me this?" Her heart soared. "I'm just as ready as that night you made me a woman, honey. There has never been anyone else. There never will."

They fell to the bed together. Ginger remembered what it felt like to be with a man. Like before, when she and Jake made love the first time, the experience for her now was fresh. His power, his strength and his need scared her but brought an explosion of exhilaration. Years of anticipation were enveloped in his kisses as he found all her spots, as he pleasured her to the peak of her consciousness. Jake read her body well, made love to her with his kisses and his tongue, all the while heightening her senses for the final dramatic act of becoming one with him once more.

His massive shoulders loomed above her as his thighs pressed her open to him. His arm dove under her waist, lifting her pelvis up as he pressed against her. Just before he entered her, he held her head in his hands, like they did that very first night, as they did for their married years, and even during the years they fought. His eyes hungrily watched as she experienced the exhilaration of his cock seating deep inside her, claiming her for his own. He was relentless, slow and deliberate so she could fully experience every long delicious stroke.

He suddenly held her arms above her head, and she wrapped her legs around his hips, arching up to meet him deeper still, pounding against her with thrusts pushing her deep into the mattress. And then he held steady, waited, until she felt the delicious ripple of an orgasm coming. She touched their joining while he resumed his strokes, reveling in the hardness of his muscles working to pleasure her. She tasted the sweat dripping from his neck, pressing her breasts against him and hearing his satisfying groan.

The foreplay and kissing would have to come later. Right now they were made one again. All the rough, sharp edges of the years of pain and the difficulties before the separation were being loved out of her. Her bones became rubber, and her body shattered beneath him. And out of the ashes of her old body, she had come alive again.

CHAPTER 7

LOVING GINGER WAS all about the little things. Her soft skin glowed under the lights of Sin City. Inside and in his bed, in his arms, was the angel of his life. He could get turned on by just the hint of a dimple, whether it was the pair of them atop her perfect ass or the one she had on the left side of her cheek when she smiled with her lips and eyes closed. The way her lip looked like as she bit it, those eyebrows furrowed in ecstasy as she came.

Ginger had always been more than a wife, more than a lover. She was a phenomenon of nature, of softness and power, patience and resistance, light and shadow. The contours of her body were revealed to him, familiar and new at the same time. An enhanced version of the woman he'd first awakened.

Tonight he was accepted by her body in all the ways he could be. He didn't leave an inch of her unkissed, even the backs of her knees, her ankles, the nape of her neck, and the warm sweaty flesh beneath her breasts that tasted of her arousal.

They'd just finished another long lovemaking session as the early morning sun began to glow pink in the sky and the cars and crowds had dwindled away. The music was gone. But the desert air washed through the gauze fabric of the curtains all night long as they opted for the dry heat instead of air conditioning. It would be hot within an hour. Her back was glistening. Her hands grabbing the headboard rails still, the pillow under her belly raising her rear as he watched himself softly stroke her from behind. Her hair was on fire, her cheeks flushed from his stubble. Her forlorn moan told him she had come again.

"Yes, baby." He waited for her to finish, kissing her softly up her spine.

"Jake," she sighed. "I don't see how I'm going to be able to walk," she whispered as she moved against him, then giggled into the pillow.

He pulled the covers up from the floor, throwing them over her beautiful peach skin and lay beside her, watching her breathe. Watching the perspiration on her upper lip evaporate in the heat of the early morning.

She flipped to her side to face him, and they kissed.

"Didn't know I had it in me, Jake. Sort of like the old days, right?" She smiled sweetly, little ridges furrowing her forehead.

"Oh, I knew it was there, sweetheart. Pent up and waiting for me. God, how you make me feel."

She traced his nipple with her forefinger. "It won't be always this beautiful, Jake. Sometimes it'll be hard."

He looked down at his groin. "Not yet. Give me an hour or two. At least that long."

"Liar," she said and kissed him on the nose. "But I could use the rest."

He didn't remember how long before he fell asleep, but he knew she did immediately. Statuesque and perfect, naked or clothed, in her sleeping state she was even more beautiful. Her smell was what he decided he'd missed the most, that musky scent of her arousal, mixed with her favorite orange and flower blossom perfume. Even her hair smelled wonderful.

He drew the backs of his fingers across her cheek as she lay against the pillow next to him. "Welcome home, Ginger. I've missed you, too."

But her sleeping form didn't respond.

THEY SLEPT UNTIL housekeeping walked in close to noon, and abruptly shut the door again. He ran to the door and turned the privacy lock. Then he closed the window and turned on the air.

She was laying on her back with one arm over her head, the bedcovers down about her waist, watching him.

"Should we order room service?" he asked as he headed for the bathroom.

"Only thing I could eat this morning is pancakes."

He washed his hands and brushed his teeth. Leaning against the bathroom doorway, he shot her a wink, "Pancakes it is. Butter and maple syrup."

"Lots of maple syrup."

He sat on the edge of the bed and ordered room service, then slid under the covers.

She grabbed his hand and fingered the wedding ring.

"Still don't know what happened," he murmured.

He thought perhaps she hesitated, as if she were about to speak.

"You want to stay another day, Ginger? I don't have to be back in San Diego until Tuesday. We could fool around in the shops, go swimming. Did you bring a suit?"

"My things are in the room with Karen. I should call her."

Ginger rolled away from him and got out of bed. She picked up her dress and lay it over the chair with her other things. She fingered the lingerie, holding the panties up to her.

"You like?"

"Very much. Just your size."

"And this?" She held up the bra against her own breasts."

"Very nice. Put them on. They look like you, Ginger."

She stepped into the panties and strapped the bra together. Staring down at the floor, she whispered, "I have a confession to make."

He watched her, liking the excitement of a secret unfolding.

"Go on. Tell me all your secrets. I love true confessions."

Her face was sad, her brow furrowed. "I haven't been completely honest with you about all this."

"What?"

"This. The room, the Honeymoon Suite. These," she said as her fingers brushed against the lace of her bra.

He couldn't possibly imagine what she'd tell him next. "Jake, I conspired to bring you here, to have you wind up here, in this room. I'm not proud of it. Gerud helped me. I thought he was someone I could count on. And it was wrong of me."

He sat up. "You mean you guys did this?"

She nodded.

"And this?" He held up the wedding ring."

Again, she nodded. "But the red ribbon thing, your wrists, that was never the plan. Gerud went overboard, but I have to take responsibility for that. I'm sorry."

Jake chuckled. It was such a relief.

"So you planned all this, then. You did all this to get me back?"

"Well, I helped do it, but it was my idea, yes."

"You are so in trouble, Ginger. You've been a very, very bad girl."

"You're not mad at me?"

"How could I be mad at you? I'm mad at Gerud for fucking with my wrists, but it all makes sense now. You little vixen. I never thought this was in you."

"I've changed. Again, I'm sorry."

"On the contrary, it worked. I'm glad. Now get your phone call in to Karen so I can properly punish you. You're gonna pay for this, Miss Ginger."

Ginger bent over and gave him a nice view while she searched for the phone in her purse. Then she dialed Karen.

"Hi, there, it's Ginger." She came over to the matching red chair and sat, crossing her legs, twirling her hair, pouting her lips and pretending to ignore him.

"Yes, I am. We're just getting up." She grinned at Jake. "How was the rest of the show?"

He propped his head and watched her tease him in the lingerie. He called to her, curling his forefinger slowly.

"That's too bad. Why was he out of sorts?"

She listened, and Jake's curiosity was aroused.

"Oh, I think you're being silly. Karen, could you ask for a ride home with Gerud? I think Jake and I are going to spend another day, then I'll drive us home. That okay with you?"

Ginger frowned. "Okay then. Let me know what he says. Bye."

She replaced the phone and came over to the bed.

"You like?"

"I do. Come here, Ginger. It's time for your punishment. I'm going to get so even with you, it's not even funny."

She climbed on top of him and slowly pivoted her pelvis back and forth, rubbing his cock, pressing harder and harder with each move. His thumb pressed her nub encased under the satin crotch, and she pressed herself against him. He pulled the elastic of her panty leg to the side, massaged her sex with long lazy motions, encircling her bud and then pressing it. His other hand slipped under the bra and squeezed her right breast hard, pinching her nipple.

Ginger's expression went from sweet to siren in a matter of seconds. She rose up on her knees as he pulled the elastic to the side, and then allowed his cock to enter her as she pressed down and rocked her pelvis back and forth again.

He knew this wasn't really punishment, but he couldn't help himself. He needed to feel fully seated inside her.

After starting slow, he held her hips, urging her up and down on him, repeating the rhythm faster and faster until she stopped him, held her breath and he felt her internal muscles milking him. She held her hair up with one hand on top of her head and gave him that vacant look as he filled her.

He thought about the pancakes, but no way was he done with Ginger, or all the ways he could make her come. The waiter would just have to leave the pancakes in the hallway.

CHAPTER 8

THEY NEVER MADE it out after they retrieved the pancakes. She'd had gotten creative with the maple syrup and whipped cream. One thing led to another and it required another shower.

Karen had gone back to Coronado with Gerud. Although Ginger felt there was some unfinished business with him, she was glad she didn't have to speak with him until they got home.

They decided to take an early dinner, turn in and actually sleep, before heading home in the morning. Jake received a call there was another quick deployment coming up he'd be involved in.

"What do you think we should tell the girls?" she asked.

He was adjusting himself to driving her car, which was new since their divorce, and definitely did not have the power he was used to. She suspected he was a little frustrated with its handling.

Before he could respond, she addressed what she thought could be bothering him. "It's a *safe* car, Jake. I don't drive fast, but it's safe, and has all those features that will protect us, the girls and I."

He grinned and reached for her hand, which she gave him. "What do you say we just leave things the way they are right now? Let's just wear this for a bit. Get used to it a little."

She was a little tender about this, but let it pass. "No second thoughts, then?"

"Oh God, no."

But she could tell there was a bit of hesitation because he'd answered so forcefully.

"I have to digest it. Figure out what I'm going to say. Figure out what all this means. But Ginger, honey," he kissed the back of her fingers, "I'm in. We got together like an atomic bomb, and it was great. Not sure that's what I want to tell the girls, do you understand?"

"I do." It was the right answer. She would bide her time. Checking her insides with her outsides, she said something she'd had trouble with before. "I trust you, Jake."

He squeezed her hand. "That means a lot. I'm working to become a better man, Ginger. But I'm not there yet."

She let that one settle a bit before she answered, giving it careful thought.

"Just so we're clear. If this involves other ladies, and I didn't ask you last night if there were, the answer is no. I'm not sharing."

He grinned. "Neither am I." He kissed her knuckles again.

But there was still something there.

THEY DROPPED JAKE off at his apartment. Ginger took over the driver's seat, and they kissed good-bye, agreeing to get together after he found out what was happening with the Team.

Checking herself in the rear view mirror, she loved how she glowed. Flushed, full of that wonderful tired feeling from making love nearly non-stop for a day and a half. It harkened back to memories when he'd first come crashing into her life. God, how she hoped this time it was for keeps. This time perhaps she had the maturity to stand by when things got tough. Because she knew they would.

She dropped by her mother-in-law's house to pick up the girls and saw Gerud's car there. That worried her. She didn't want to have her first conversation with him since her return to Coronado under the watchful eyes of her mother-in law and the girls.

Mrs. Green was at the front door before she rang the bell. "There you are and looking so pretty today!" Adele Green wasn't exactly unattractive, either. A former model turned realtor to the stars in Coronado, she retired when she married Burt, Jake's dad. But the Green & Green house signs were everywhere. Everyone in the community understood it referred to the Mr. and Mrs. Green, and not the father and son Green. Gerud was still part of the realty office, but no one expected him to take over some day. His heart clearly wasn't in it.

"How was your little adventure?" she asked Ginger. Adele's eyes twinkled in that conspiratorial way, anxious to live her life through the younger generation, but living the luxurious San Diego lifestyle that only the older generation could afford.

Did she know about the little ruse to get back in Jake's good graces?

"Fine, Adele. It was just what I needed." Ginger tried to appear wholesome and proper, but her thoughts were in the gutter with all the things she and Jake had done the last twenty-four hours. She suspected that most mothers-in-law knew about such things and could smell sex and abandon a mile away on their daughters-in-law.

Adele leaned forward attempting to go in for the deets, but Ginger was spared by her two carrot-topped girls.

"Mom! We got a puppy! Gran got us a puppy!" squeaked Jasmine, Ginger's oldest, who was nearly five.

Ginger turned to her mother-in-law. "What did you do?"

Adele shook her hands above her head and closed the front door. "I know. I took the girls to the mall, and there were these adorable puppies being adopted out, and, well, the girls loved them. It was everything I could do to not come home with two, let alone one."

Little Jennifer came out holding a squirming fat puppy with her arm around its belly, the little legs trying to find purchase.

"Careful, honey," Ginger said as she stooped down and let the puppy come to her. "Oh he's adorable."

"She's a girl, mommy," corrected Jennifer.

"I don't blame you, but Adele, you should have asked."

Gerud appeared in the hallway, looking in a foul mood.

Ginger picked the puppy up and nodded to her ex brother-in-law. She doubted anyone else noticed how he scanned her entire body up and then slowly down to her shoes.

"Yes, you're a cutie pie, and what a little flirt you are, wiggling your way into this family's good graces," she said in puppy talk. The pup licked her face, her chin and tried to bite one of the buttons on her shirt.

"We've named her Fiona," said Jennie.

"No, we've named her Chelsea," argued Jasmine. "After my best friend."

Ginger put the puppy down, and it ran to the girls.

"She seems to really like you two already," said Ginger.

"Tell me about it. Slept with the two of them last night. They got up with her a dozen times—every time she cried. That little thing is going to be spoiled out of her mind."

"Thanks, Mom," Ginger said in mock praise. "So we've got a puppy now, who sleeps with the girls."

"Can't put her out in the garage, that would be cruel. Too cold." Gerud's voice broke the levity of the moment.

"Oh, I think she has to pee!" said Jasmine. Both the girls ran to the kitchen, the puppy in tow.

"Now you've done it. What do I do with her when I work?"

"Drop her off here. When I get the girls after school, they'll all play here that way."

"And just when will you have time for your other grandchildren? What if you and Burt want to get away?"

"Oh my God. Just seeing those two with the puppy, it's worth every vacation we've been on all last year. Nothing compares to seeing their smiling faces. You know how I like to spoil them."

Adele was off to the kitchen to close the glass door the girls had left open.

Ginger sighed. "Just what I needed. Another project at home."

Gerud stepped closer to her. "As if Jake wasn't a project enough, right?" He wiggled his eyebrows.

"Well, let's not get too ahead of ourselves, Gerud. We had a good time. We're just waiting to see where it goes. That's all. Would like to keep it low-key, if you don't mind."

"Your picnic, Ginger." They walked side by side to the kitchen, watching the girls play with Fiona Chelsea who was chasing their grandmother in the backyard.

"I'm going to have my hands full," she said to the glass door.

"Why? Won't Jake move back in?"

"Gerud, we're not having this conversation. Please, don't press me."

He shrugged and wouldn't look back at her.

"Oh, come on, Gerud. I'm not telling anyone. Jake knows, and that's all that matters, and he forgives me. As for what Jake and I discussed, about our relationship, that's between the two of us. Only the two of us. We're not ready to tell everyone. Not yet."

"You know old big ears will find out. Your funeral"

"Your mother is more interested in the puppy and the girls than anything else."

"Wanna make a bet? She's already guessed something's up with you two." He paused before asking one more question, carefully. "Do the girls know?"

"Not yet. Gerud, we want it left that way, for now. Do you understand?"

It was a thin line she was walking, but she wasn't going to let Gerud's mood affect her. Her ex-husband loved her, had never stopped loving her. And she could finally tell him back. Show him back with everything she had. She was almost as happy as the morning after they'd first slept together, before all the storm clouds appeared.

And then she found some levity there, and giggled.

"What's so funny?"

"Well, earlier you called it a picnic. My picnic. Now you're calling it my funeral. You honestly think it's the same thing, Gerud?"

"I guess it depends on which version of the truth you're comfortable with. You owe me a thank you, and I'll collect one day." He winked at her, and for some reason, Ginger shivered.

"But for now, it will be our secret." He wrapped his arm around her shoulder. She resisted the temptation to distance herself from him.

"I'm not proud of my involvement, but yes, the outcome was perfect."

"There you go. Just remember I got you two back together again. Just in time, too, because in another two weeks he'd have married again and probably fathered another baby."

CHAPTER 9

JAKE ENTERED HIS apartment that he shared with two other bachelors SEALs. Lucas and Alex had moved out, but Ryan Groves and Cory Brown, also men on SEAL Team 3, had stayed behind. They liked to rub it in they left Jake's room vacant so he could come back every time he became a bachelor again.

The place was deathly quiet, but it had the familiar bachelor pad smell. A few days of dishes filled with dirty dishwater were in the sink. A pan with a spatula and lid was still on the stove. The TV was turned on to a sports network, but muted. The same pallet they'd put it on when they first moved in years ago was its stand. The couch was still there, lumpy as hell, but vacant. Always grinning, waiting for someone to grace it and sleep off a drunk. A row of beer bottles was displayed on the gas fireplace mantle.

His stomach growled, but looking inside the refrigerator, he didn't see anything he wanted to risk eating, so he chose a yogurt, checked the expiration date, grabbed a spoon and went to his room, closing the door.

He'd had the master bedroom at one time, but this one did have its own bath, a tiny one with fiberglass shower stall. He tossed his bag on the bed, turned on the hot water and sat, finishing his yogurt. Before stepping into the shower, he heard a knock on the door.

RYAN WAS STANDING in a pair of boxers, bare-chested. "Have a good time?" he asked.

"Yeah. It was nice."

"Sounds boring."

"Well, first of all, I went up there with Gerud, which is never boring, but I kinda connected with Ginger again, and trust me, that was not boring."

"No shit? Wow, I would not have expected that. You have that planned?"

Jake could see hope springing from Ryan's eyes. He still loved his first wife, too. "Nope. She and a girlfriend were up there. But yeah, she planned it." He nearly blushed.

"Well, good for you, then."

The silence was awkward between them. Jake felt for Ryan, even though his Team brother had tried his best to drown out the memory of his failed marriage, just as Jake had. The collateral damage that being a SEAL created on families was hell. And he knew it was rare they ever got to live out their fantasies and get a do-over. Jake knew he was lucky.

He cleared his throat. "So, I'm gonna take a shower, Ryan, and then I guess we gotta get over to the Team Building. You guys both up?"

"I think Cory is still comatose. We watched soccer until two o'clock. I woke up on the floor, and everyone else was asleep, too. Sorry bunch of bachelors we are. I guess everyone got home okay cause I don't see the couch has been used."

"I'll be out in five. Better go wake up Cory, then."

"Roger that."

After his shower, Jake unpacked his things and found the clothes he'd been wearing the night of his massage in the bag, along with his other pair of canvas slip-ons. He wondered how this could happen, and then recalled that Gerud had kept up the ruse by taking him shopping, later replacing the clothes. The wedding ring had come off in the shower this morning, and he placed it on the highboy dresser, with fondness. If everything went as he hoped, he'd be wearing one again. He finished getting dressed and came out into the kitchen-living room area.

Ryan had made eggs and coffee. Cory was dressed, with his duty bag, but it was obvious from the way his hair stood out in all directions he hadn't showered. He was staring at a plate of eggs like they were the keys to his future.

"You good to go, Cory?"

"Nothing a little PT or a swim wouldn't cure. How was your lost weekend?"

"Good." That was all he was going to communicate. He could talk to Ryan straight, but Cory was a dangerous combination of fallen preacher's son and victim of child support hell. Jake had avoided those things by staying charming to his exes. He didn't want to be cut out of his children's lives like Cory was from his son's.

After breakfast, Jake cleaned up the kitchen.

"So you're all domestic today, Jake. Looks like you had a good weekend up there." Cory still had shaving cream under his ear, and Jake decided it wasn't manly to tell him.

"Well, funny thing about being in a clean room for two days. I walk in here this morning, and first thing I notice? We live like slobs, Cory."

"Not like our mothers come visit," Cory said stubbornly.

"No, but what Jake's saying is that the girls we bring home might notice, Cory, my man. He's trying to help us out."

"Shit, don't do us any favors, Jake." Cory had an extremely tough chip on his shoulder. "At least we've not been married three times."

"Two."

"I can count, shit-head," Cory said as he followed Jake and Ryan out the hallway toward the parking lot. "One: Ginger. Two: *Karleeeene*! Sweet Mother of God, she was fine. And then there was Monica."

"I never married Monica."

"Well, doesn't that make you goody two shoes, asshole?"

Jake stopped and grabbed Cory by the collar. He towered over his brother SEAL by at least five inches. Cory was built like a soccer player, all muscle and could run like the wind with more stamina than Jake and Ryan combined, but he had a nasty temper and was the first to complain about everything.

"I didn't screw girls in the back pew of my father's church. I didn't get married in a double ceremony with this asshole," he said pointing to Ryan, "by an Elvis impersonator singing *Nearer My God To Thee*."

"That *was* a mistake. He was supposed to sing *How Great Thou Art*."

One thing in Cory's favor was that although he had a nasty temper, when he was challenged, he backed down every time. He grinned and wiggled himself out of Jake's enormous paws.

"Just got the music mixed up is all," he said as he adjusted his clothing. "Singing from the Book of the Dead instead of wedding hymns sort of put a jinx on the whole marriage." Cory adjusted his shoulder and started to chuckle.

"We did have a laugh about that, Jake," mumbled Ryan. "Cory wanted his bride to hear *How Great Thou Art* and take the true implication of those words to heart."

"My daddy always said being well hung was a curse in our family. I didn't see it that way at all." Cory continued talking to himself while he headed toward Ryan's Hummer. Jake hit him on the back of his head.

"You are such a dumbass."

In the second seat of the Hummer, Jake looked at his two buddies and realized what a mistake it had been to room with them again. It was one thing when Lucas and Alex were bringing nice girls by. They helped with the cleanup and actually were fun to be around. But Cory and Ryan *needed* to get married so someone would take care of them. They didn't need a wife. They needed a mother.

KYLE LANSDOWNE WAS front and center, as was usual. A couple of the Viking crowd, Tay and his Team brother Kerk, stood off to the side, their blonde hair and striking tall bodies looking nearly like twins despite their difference in years. They didn't say much. Ever. Ollie had taken to standing with Tay during most off times, but Kerk was a true loner.

There were a couple local detectives and a gentleman from Naval Intelligence. It wasn't common to see the Commander show up for these meetings.

"Listen up," Kyle began. "We're doing a cleanup operation and the Commander thought perhaps you boys could help out. This is a mission of indeterminate length, and you'll be briefed on a need-to-know basis."

"As some of you have heard, we encountered another guns-for-drugs ring operating out of San Diego, smuggling guns into Mexico, and returning with drugs, mainly for US consumption. The cruise ship operation a handful of you went on several weeks ago was highly successful. But, as you know, it was only a drop in the bucket."

Jake knew Fredo, T.J. and Cooper were part of that raid and operation, which had occurred in international waters off the Mexicali coast.

"Last time, as it turned out, the guns were dumped in the waters off Baja and picked up by a troller. Our Navy halted a lot of the Mexican operation with the seizure of that ship. The crew are being tried and dealt with. Our government has isolated a few of these with long criminal records at some of our Supermax prisons. A few have been sent to Gitmo."

An intelligence officer, probably CIA, stood up. "You didn't hear that, gents. No one went to Gitmo."

Kyle looked annoyed.

"Okay, strike that. They've gone to places unknown." Kyle smiled down at the man in the gray suit. "They've been questioned. Some are cooperating. In the process, we've learned about some rather disturbing details of drug gangs in this area again working with disgruntled military, buying equipment and guns from active duty or retiring service men and women."

"Several have told intelligence a large group lives in a gated community in one of the luxury resorts in Baja California where they can mingle with the tourist population and attempt to find new recruits. They pose as resort employees. They are both American and Mexican Nationals, as well as others."

He went on to explain that half the squad would be heading down on a "training mission" and wander into the resort town of Baja Nuevo on the Baja coast, but infiltrate under the guise as tourists. They were told Santiago Garcia, a Columbian citizen and drug lord forced to flee his native home, owned a large share of the resort and was using it as his base of operation.

"This isn't a holiday. And we are doing this under what we hope is top-secret cover with cooperation from the Mexican government. Local authorities will not be privy to our mission, so you are to keep your mouth shut and act like you would, oh, say, going to Las Vegas."

Mumbling and chuckles erupted throughout the room, as various members whispered and recalled stories of some of their escapades.

"You will reel it in a bit, though. Understood?" Lansdowne added.

General agreement was given.

"You guys know who you need to check on the most. I don't want any fuck-ups. At the same time, I want just healthy ex-military types who are a little crazy to pose as possible new recruits. I think you guys are perfect for this caper."

After the meeting, his LPO came over to Jake, taking him aside. When Ryan and Cory tried to join them, Kyle pushed them away. Then he motioned to Cooper to join him.

"Jake, I'm giving you a fairy godmother here. Except she's way taller and hairier than a fairy godmother." He pointed over his shoulder to Coop. "I've spoken to him about my concerns with your drinking. You know he doesn't drink. I'm hoping you'll spend a lot of time with him so we can get you straightened out."

"Sir?"

"That comment about Las Vegas was intended for your ears, mainly. We want you in the mission, but I almost scratched you, giving you a medical for this one."

"I'm working to give up drinking. I've just made that decision, and so far, I'm doing okay with it," Jake said.

"Well, that's good to hear. You been to meetings?"

"Yessir."

"More than one?"

Jake hesitated.

"So that would be a negative then. It's not a hard question, Jake. I figured you'd been at maybe five or less. But one sounds about right to me."

"I didn't much care for what I saw."

"And that's the point. I didn't tell you to go so you could enjoy yourself. I could have sent you to a Padres game for that, except it would be a bit expensive. I wanted you to get a dose of reality. Not everyone can handle alcohol, and you're one of them, like Coop here"

Jake didn't know Coop had ever had a problem with it.

"Now, Coop isn't going to tell you his life's story, because, frankly, you don't deserve it yet. But he'll lay on you what he thinks you can handle. And if he tells you to come home, you're coming home. And if he says find a meeting, you find one. If he tells you to go see his father-in-law the shrink, you do that. Is this understood?"

"Yessir."

"Everything okay with the kids and the three ex-wives and all?"

"Two."

"Pardon?"

"Two ex-wives. I didn't marry the last one."

"Fuck you, Jake. You think that makes a fuckin' ton of difference?"

"No, it's just everyone gets it wrong."

Kyle stood within an inch of his face and poked his chest so hard it nearly sent Jake falling backward. "No Mr. Fuckin' Special Operator Green, you're the one who gets it wrong. About time for you to start getting it right."

As Kyle and Calvin Cooper walked away, Jake realized he'd just dodged a bullet and had very nearly ruined his career with his behavior. He wasn't proud of the fact that he was on Kyle's shit list. He was relieved he was being given a second chance to become the SEAL he wanted to be. The only thing that made him nervous was whether or not he really had the stones to shape up and fly right.

With four successful tours under his belt and nearly eight years of service, at nearly thirty years of age, he finally had to become a man.

A real man.

CHAPTER 10

G INGER GREETED BURT Green, who came home early from the office. She was exhausted from chasing the girls and the puppy all afternoon and listening to her mother-in-law's incessant gossip, which bored her to tears.

"So you see what Adele went and did, then?" Mr. Green asked as he passed her in the hallway, setting down his briefcase.

"Yes. Thanks in advance for all the late nights I'm going to have with that puppy."

"I told her she shouldn't have, but you know Adele." Green removed his sport coat and poured himself a stiff drink. "You have a good time? Jake was up there, too, or did you already know that?" He took a long drag on his drink, nearly downing it.

He was as stunningly handsome as his wife and played tennis with some of the elite of Coronado Country Club as well as others from neighboring beach communities. Ginger knew of his reputation of being a womanizer, but he'd been careful not to show her this side of him. His good looks and his enormous wealth had no effect on her, though.

Right now she was a little irritated that he knew Jake had been in Las Vegas.

"No." She decided lying was the best practice, under the circumstances.

He glanced up to her quickly, raising his eyebrows. "And why not?" His directness caught her off guard. She was not expecting the grilling.

Sucking in her pride, she answered the best she could. "That's classified."

He threw back his head, laughing. Then he quickly gave her a peck on the cheek, "Well done, Ginger. Your secret is safe with me."

He walked to the kitchen where his wife and son were discussing something. Gerud had hung around all afternoon as well, and Ginger thought perhaps he wanted to talk to her again in private. That opportunity never came.

Burt Green kissed her mother-in-law and didn't say anything to Gerud or address him in any way. There were times when Ginger couldn't imagine what it was like for Jake growing up in this family, with their stingy behavior when it came to affection and understanding. Something about it was very painful and cold. On the surface they appeared to the outside world like one big happy family. She wondered why she hadn't seen it before and wondered if the girls spending so much time here was actually healthy.

She wandered back into the kitchen. The girls were making the puppy bark, and she quickly came over and quieted him, putting her arms around the girls. "We're going to leave soon, so get your things. I'll hold Chelsea Fiona."

"Fiona Chelsea," said Jennie.

Jasmine stuck out her tongue at her little sister.

"Oh please, Ginger. I was just making a salad, and I ordered a pizza already. Cheese, with extra cheese!" said Adele Green.

The girls cheered.

"No really, I think we should be going," Ginger announced.

"Nonsense. You're staying and that's that," said Burt Green.

Gerud looked on like the fifth wheel he was. Ginger felt sorry for him all of a sudden. Her frostiness toward him began to melt.

Adele Green came over to her youngest son, patted him on the cheek and handed him some dishes. "Go set the table, dear." Her eyes followed her husband as he went into his study and closed the door. "Oh, he's in one of his moods again," she said nervously.

Gerud looked like a grown man acting like a teenager, in the wrong place at the wrong time. He said nothing and went about completing the task he'd been given.

The pizza delivery boy arrived. The puppy was put into a kennel and barked for nearly a half hour while they tried to eat, everyone talking over each other. Adele was lavishing chocolate milk on the girls and telling stories, while Mr. Green was grilling Gerud on a real estate deal. Ginger watched it all unfold before her, suddenly missing Jake.

While they were finishing up, Ginger got a text from Jake.

Can I come over tonight?

Yes, was her response. *I'm at your mom & dad's.*

Should I come?

Sure. Gerud is here.

Mr. Green frowned at her texting at the table. "New boyfriend?"

Ginger blushed. "No." She glanced up at Gerud whose expression was not something she could read. His lips formed a straight line as he clenched his teeth.

The ping of the phone interrupted again. "Let me just finish this, and then I'll shut it off. Sorry. Didn't realize it was on." She avoided both Gerud and Mr. Green's eyes, and looked at Adele. "That was poor manners of me. Sorry."

At the phone screen she saw Jake's message.

Don't tell anyone, even the girls. I'll come around 9 after everyone's in bed. Be naked.

Ginger's fingers had difficulty turning off the phone, and she dropped it.

Mr. Green pointed to her with his salad fork. "See? New boyfriend. She's a bundle of nerves."

Mrs. Green's frozen stare at her husband was frightening. Gerud looked at his lap. Even the girls were quiet, and then Jennie started to cry. Ginger rose and picked her daughter up and took her to a chair nearby, giving her a big hug. "What's the matter, Jennifer?"

Jennie stopped crying and squeezed her tight, burying her head.

"Honestly, Burt. You give her a hard time for using the phone at dinner, and then you make up some story about a boyfriend in front of her daughters." She shook her head and dug into her salad. She practically screamed at Jasmine. "Your mommy doesn't have a new boyfriend, Jasmine. Your grandfather is a—a—" Realizing she had nothing proper to call him, "—a silly goose."

Mr. Green hung his head for a while. Ginger knew if she and Gerud and the girls weren't present, he'd have said something cruel. It was the first time she'd realized the relationship between the two so seriously damaged. She'd been so caught up in her own events, she hadn't noticed.

"Pop, come on. That's the booze talking. Leave the girls out of this," Gerud added.

"You shut the fuck up!"

Everyone was stunned. Jennie burst into tears again and nuzzled her mother. Jasmine ran over to join them. The puppy barked, and Adele threw her napkin across the long table with the huge flower arrangement in the middle, and hit her husband square in his flushed face. Then she stormed out of the room, heading upstairs to the bedroom and slammed the door.

Mr. Green got up and made himself another drink at the mini bar.

Gerud began to clear plates.

Dinner was over.

CHAPTER 11

T HE HOUSE WAS dark except for the porch light, which Ginger left on for him. It had been their routine all during the years they were married, since he often came home at all hours of the day or night. When he turned the front door handle, he was smiled to find she had thought to leave it unlocked. She probably knew he still had his house key but wanted to make sure he felt welcome.

And he did.

He locked the door behind him.

Quietly, he tiptoed upstairs to the bedrooms, checking in on both girls first. What he didn't expect was a growling and yapping puppy that woke everyone up. The girls started screaming, and it was only seconds before Ginger was running to their room, still trying to put on her bathrobe. She had been naked.

"Oh, Jake, I'm sorry. Forgot to tell you about the puppy," she said.

"Daddy!" yelled Jennifer. She stayed in bed with the still-yapping puppy, while Jasmine ran to him. He gave her a hug, and then picked up Jennie, puppy and all.

"Who's this little fellow?" He asked. The puppy was trying to bite his chin.

"She's a girl," corrected Jennie.

"Chelsea Fiona," said Jasmine.

"Naaw. Fiona Chelsea," said Jennie.

"Girls, girls. It's time for bed. Daddy just came by to drop something by for Mamma, and he didn't want to wake you."

Jake let his hand fall at Ginger's rear outside of eyesight of the girls, and felt the delicious cleft between her butt cheeks. She struggled with her balance and tried to keep her composure.

"Please stay for breakfast, daddy," Jasmine asked.

"Will you take Fiona Chelsea out to pee, daddy?" asked Jennie.

He turned to Ginger who gave him a helpless grin and chewed her lower lip. "I'll come with you."

"You better." He whispered to the girls, "Daddy's afraid of the dark!"

They both giggled and settled back in their beds.

Ginger held the pup, and he followed her downstairs.

"I'm so sorry about that. I don't know what I was thinking. Actually—"

Jake stopped her with a kiss. "Give me that," he whispered as he took the puppy in one arm and let his other hand find the opening of her bathrobe. The dog was squirming so their kiss and his feel-up of his wife was cut short.

"She probably does have to pee, Jake."

"Oh, all right." He grabbed her hand, and the three of them made it out to the backyard. The puppy ran around the lawn in circles a couple of times before she abruptly stopped and nearly fell over trying to squat. Then she thought it would be a good idea to go for Ginger's bathrobe hem.

Jake pulled her up. "She's cute. Where did you get her?"

"Your mom."

"Ah!" He held the puppy up under her armpits. "So who do you belong to, the Greens or the Greens?"

"She's ours. I'm to bring her by when I go to work after I've dropped the girls off at preschool. Your mom's orders."

He set the puppy down, and this time she got serious examining a shrub on the edge of the lawn before she squatted again.

"So what does dear old Burt think of this?"

"Hard to say, actually. He was in one of his moods tonight. Came home early from the office, and boy he was on tenterhooks. I'm worried about them, Jake."

"Well, I'm sorry you had to see that. But I didn't come over here to talk about my parents and watch the puppy pee. He walked up behind Ginger, wrapping his arms around her waist and biting her ear lobe. "I actually was hoping I could get you to talk a little dirty with me tonight. Remember how you used to do that?"

She began to giggle.

"Ah, come on, honey, just a little come fuck me. Just a couple of times. I'll try to hold out as long as I can, but I'd like it if you begged."

She turned around. "You haven't changed a bit. So you came over here to fuck me?"

"Oh yes, most definitely."

"Not talk about our future?"

He hesitated, but then she pressed her palm against his dick and his worries evaporated. "If we're gonna talk, I prefer that we talk dirty. But we can talk about that other stuff, too."

"Other *stuff* as in what?"

Jake had thought about it all afternoon after the briefing. He knew exactly what he wanted, and he hoped she did, too.

"I was wondering what it would take to get my ass permanently ensconced in your bed so you could fuck me all night long every night, not just when I needed it."

She giggled again.

"As in, would I do your laundry for you if you serviced me?"

"Something like that," he said, slipping a hand between her legs. "If you did it naked I'd watch you bend over, and then I'd put my tongue wherever you liked it."

He could feel how wet she'd become. His finger moved lazily up and down her slit, and he felt her delicious shudder, her breath getting deeper.

"I think I could put up with that. It would be a sacrifice, though."

"Oh, I'd make you pay all right. I'd expect to extract a huge price."

He inserted his forefinger inside her opening. She grabbed his shoulders for balance. The puppy started to pull at her robe again.

"You have a kennel for this thing?" he whispered in her ear.

"She sleeps with the girls, but yes, there is one. But she'll whine all night long."

"That's a no go," he said as he inserted his second finger deep inside her, lifting her up with his other arm and letting her ride his thigh. "Only one I want to hear whimpering is you."

Jake let go of her, dropped to his knees and buried his head in her crotch. The puppy started barking again. From upstairs, they heard one of the girls shout out, "Daddy, what are you doing to Mommy?"

Jake froze before he could get his second taste in. He stood up, holding the puppy. "Daddy was just getting Fiona, honey."

He heard Ginger chuckle and follow him inside the house.

"That was most creative," she whispered in the dark as they padded through the kitchen, through the living room and up the stairs.

"Better than scarring them for life," he answered.

Inside the bedroom, Jake gave the dog to Jasmine. "Jennie, it's Jasmine's turn now. Daddy's very tired, and if you want me here for breakfast in the morning, you've got to get right back to bed, okay?"

"Okay, Daddy," came the answer in unison.

He closed the door behind them and grabbed Ginger's hand. "Enough with the interruptions and surprises." He dragged her down the hallway to the master.

The room smelled like Ginger, but she'd redone several things. Nothing was familiar except for her scent. By the light of the moon he peeled her robe off her shoulders and stared at her naked body while he disrobed.

She crossed her arms and he instructed her to stop it. "I want to see everything. Don't cover up, Ginger."

She remained standing with her hands flicking at her sides.

He dropped to his knees again. "I didn't get to finish kissing you there, honey." He pried open her knees and inserted his tongue in the warm folds of her sex, and then sucked her bud. Ginger pushed herself up on his shoulders, rising to tiptoes and gave him as much access as she could. He moved them over to the bed, and pushed her forward, bending her over the end of the mattress. His fingers found her wet and so ready for him he could not help but massage her with the tip of his cock. With long strokes he teased her up and down, until he snagged on her opening and thrust inside deep and hard, nearly taking her off her feet.

"Oh God, Jake!" she moaned.

"Yes baby? You like this?"

"I do."

"Do what?"

"I like it when you fuck me like this."

"If I fuck you harder will you talk dirtier to me?"

"Yes."

"I want to hear it."

He knew Ginger didn't have much of a vocabulary for dirty words, but he found it such a turn-on that she'd even try.

"You make me hot."

"You like being hot?"

"Yes. Jake make me come."

"Oh, I intend to, sweetheart. Just be a little patient."

"I don't want to be patient."

He picked her up and tossed her on the bed, spreading her legs and climbing on top of her. She was writhing beneath him, her lips seeking his, drawing his tongue deep inside her as she raised her knees, then wrapped them around his hips and moved against him as he stroked her deep. He picked up the pace, her little moans and love squeals driving him crazy. She clutched his ass, pulling him down on her, answering his thrusts with hip movements of her own as they joined frantically and finally crashed against each other in orgasm. Her muscles milked him, drained him of everything he had. All he could think of was to hope to God he could do it again right away. He never wanted to be left disconnected from her again.

CHAPTER 12

BURT GREEN STARTED off the day in the same foul mood he went to bed with the night before. His wife had slept in their master, which was locked. He had to pound on the door in order to retrieve his clothes for work this morning.

She was still angry with him, and her face showed it. Though she had been a beautiful woman at one time, he could honestly say she'd become very ugly, both inside and out.

"Not going to do any good locking me out of my own bedroom, Adele. Next time *you* take the guest room. I slept with dog hair and stuffed animals," he said tersely as he made his way past her.

"You're a sonofabitch, Burt Green."

"Well, you might as well not lock the fuckin' door. Not like I'm going to come in and ask for a quickie." He was sorting through underwear and socks, his shirt and slacks hung over his arm. "I'll shower in the girls' bath if I can stand all the rubber toys."

Before he closed the door behind him, he saw a pillow come flying at him, but fall short. He had a brief thought about what would happen if Adele started throwing axes, like Jake's last ex-wife. And what might happen if her arm or her aim improved. Then maybe he'd be the one to have to lock the door.

Fuckin' women.

He scooped up the toys so he didn't slip and fall, placing them in the sink and started his shower.

He knew he was an asshole. And he knew he, too, was getting ugly.

But the business was wearing him down. Several of his friends had retired to a luxurious lifestyle. Burt could only go on vacations as the "buddy" and be in the same country club, getting his $100,000 fee waived, because of the referrals he gave. He was good at cold calling and giving names of wealthy clients. The best in club history, they said.

His personal life had been a lot more fun when he was younger and could slip off for a golf weekend with his buddies and then find some pussy on the side. He didn't like professionals nor local girls. One was too impersonal, and he wasn't a dumbass to think they really liked him. But he'd tried anyhow. Local girls were too complicated.

His wife wasn't aware of one long affair he'd had, fathering a daughter who was sweet and dumb just like her mother. Burt had always cared for the woman, but couldn't be married to her. She wouldn't be able to tolerate the lifestyle, the other wives would chew her to bits, and he didn't want her to know what he was really like. Only Adele had the mettle to put up with him and the fast crowd they ran with.

So now Belinda was twenty-two, and he'd hired her to be his receptionist at Green & Green. Her mother told him she didn't realize she was his daughter, but some days, the way Belinda looked at him, he wondered. But Jill swore her lips had been sealed, which was the condition to be kept in order for her living expenses to be paid. He paid for Belinda's two-year Executive Assistant AA degree as well, and the poor thing barely graduated. But she seemed happy, and her mother was thrilled.

He shaved and dressed in the children's guest bathroom. They'd stocked it with packets of vanity items from the hotel stays they'd been at, so there was a full shave kit, shoe shine and mouthwash. He didn't have to go back to the master suite for anything except a good yelling, and only if he thought that would improve his day.

Which of course it wouldn't.

Fuckin' women.

Why couldn't Adele just accept what he was? She didn't do anything all day long anyway but spend his money. She had no trust fund like some of his buddies married into. Was a whole lot easier when a few seven-figure savings accounts could be merged into the marriage. But in the beginning he wasn't about that. He was going to be a self-made billionaire, and were it not for the fact that Gerud had picked a terrible shopping center to purchase in Hawaii on a beautiful golf course, he'd be living in clover, probably retired.

He should have checked before he bought the course from some aging Japanese icon of industry that needed money all of a sudden. He wondered why they sold it too cheap. Only after he wound up with the same liquidity issues, which at the time were only temporary, did he discover that if you defaulted on a commercial loan in the State of Hawaii they could make you pay every penny back, and if you didn't, they could take everything you had. And you could go to jail for it, too. You'd be shit out of luck in the rain forest, stuck with a Japanese lawyer and a Chinese judge who never smiled. You had no chance as a Haole.

Fuckin' sport of kings. He knew they made these laws to get even with the Haoles who came over, stole their women and transformed their island paradise into hotel chains, fast food chains, and tiki bars with umbrella drinks, where the girls wore fake grass skirts. Nothing like their proud heritage.

He tied his tie, applied some aftershave from the sample pack and went downstairs. He made a one cup coffee, grabbed his packet of vitamins he'd take at lunch, picked up his briefcase and left for the office in his leased Jag.

Something was going to have to change. He was getting too old for the pressure. Surrounded by a half-wit son with no backbone, an illegitimate daughter and old mistress who adored him, a wife who hated him—even his most proud accomplishment, Jake, was headed down Burt's path, running through the girls and the booze and throwing his life away jumping out of airplanes trying very hard to get himself killed. Burt shook his head. Everyone was either leaving him, or being a financial burden to him. He was all alone and hating his life more and more every day.

There were going to be only so many cocktail parties at the club where he could smile. Very soon, his alcoholism was going to mess with his brain. He'd be throwing chairs and tossing women into the pools any day now. And he'd start with Adele, who used her body and model good looks to impress all the wives into thinking the two of them had a hot sex life. The woman was about as warm as road kill. But he didn't mind being thought of as the stud of Coronado, and it helped him get dates on the weekends.

The infidelity and self-loathing was one thing. His one true regret was Jake. Jake had married the best woman on the planet, a solid gold lady who was brought up right, and even then had to throw it all away. Burt was going to offer him a position when he got off the SEALs, but now he didn't want Jake anywhere near the company, his half-sister, or knowing about what a mess he was in financially. That would be like showing his dick to the crowd at the Club, how small it was due to all his alcohol abuse. It always took a girl twenty minutes to get him hard enough to even have barely any penetration.

Gotta get that Viagra refilled.

It was his birthright to screw. The only pastime that gave him a moment's pleasure. Not even his beautiful grandkids brought him joy any longer. The carrot-headed girls were connected to Adele and were afraid of him. Monica's baby was old enough to hold, but all she did was spit up all over him. And Monica expected he'd have some influence over his son, which he didn't. Karlene's boy looked just like Jake. Burt stayed away. Watching Jake bounce him around and play with him made him want another drink. He saw a fatherhood he could have had with his son—with either of his sons. But he was too busy making money to have a relationship with them at all.

He figured they were better off if he just stayed out of their lives.

Belinda's fresh face was the first thing of the day that made him smile. She resembled her mother when she was young. Shapely figure, large chest, super small waist and perhaps a little larger than required ass. If he had had a daughter with Adele, the poor thing would be skinny with sunken cheekbones and a death stare.

"Good morning, Mr. Green," she said with a wide wholesome

smile.

"Good morning. You look lovely today, Belinda."

"Thanks, Mr. Green. Um. You have someone waiting in your office."

"Oh? They couldn't wait out here?"

Belinda leaned forward, "One of your daughters-in-law, sir. Sorry. She had the baby."

"Ah! I see." Burt was slightly annoyed Monica had started to stalk him again.

"Any other messages I should know about? Gerud around?"

"Haven't seen him. Only a handful in today. Caravan day, remember?"

"Yes, and I'll be going out later. We have anything on tour?"

"No, sir," she said frowning. The office had been losing listings, and there was a marked difference in the timbre of the agents who did come in. Word was beginning to get out, he thought, that his business was shrinking about as fast as his pecker.

Green knew that if he were a younger man, Monica would have been just his type. Feisty as the dickens, she could be inappropriate in all the right ways, and occasionally in some of the wrong ones, which always added variety and excitement. He could live with those.

He closed the door behind him as she got up and gave him a kiss on the cheek, which he returned at the same time. He was careful not to touch her in any fashion other than that. Just in case.

"So Jake went up to Las Vegas," she said, bouncing the baby on her knee. Burt could see the baby had taken a sudden interest in him and bestowed him with a smile. Little Samantha was cute, but there was no way Burt wanted to get spit-up on all over him.

"I heard about that. Baby's getting big."

"So does Jake have any news? Because I understand Ginger went up there, too."

"Monica, you know I'm not the one my son confides in. Least of all me. And just where did you get this information, anyway?"

"Gerud."

"Oh, well, yes, Gerud took him up there. He doesn't allow Jake to drive when they're together."

"He said it was to forget me. He was having a hard time forgetting me."

Burt looked at her pretty dark auburn hair in curls framing her rounded face. It was sad someone so pretty was so needy when it came to his son. And he knew exactly what a turn-off it was. But then there was this Gerud thing that bothered him even more.

"I don't think it's Gerud's place to tell you that. I don't think they speak on a regular basis."

Green stared at the baby and he knew that although Jake would do anything for the child, the mother was another thing. That's why he'd never married her.

"So, I don't think I'd put much stock in what Gerud says. He should butt out, and I'm going to tell him so when I see him today, Monica."

"Like he'd listen to you." Monica had a way of giving him little stinging mosquito bites when he wasn't looking.

Green narrowed his eyes. His irritation was beginning to fester. This was way bigger than an infected mosquito bite. It was a tiny stab wound.

"Monica, I have a lot of things to get done today, which is why I'm in early. And I'm not quite sure I have any answers for you."

"This is your granddaughter."

Burt was taken aback with the comment. "Yes. She's cute. I'm sorry, did you change the subject?"

"Don't you want to be a part of her life?"

Right now Burt was wondering if he even wanted to be a part of his own life, let alone this baby's or Monica's or either of his sons'.

He stood. "I'm going to ask you to leave now, Monica, and I think you'd better reconsider before you come in here threatening me. I am a part of her life. I'm her grandfather, for chrissakes!" He straightened his tie and adjusted his belt. "But who my son sleeps with is his own damned business. He doesn't ask me, and I wouldn't counsel him anyway. I don't consider myself much of a role model, either. So, like I said, I can't help you. Now, if you will excuse me?"

His palm pointed to the door.

Fucking Gerud.

His son had not only tied up his business in knots and a pile of debt, now he was inserting himself in Jake's personal life. He knew who he should contact about this. Monica'd be sorry she brought it up to tip his hand.

His phone rang. It was his business attorney.

"Burt, I need a word. Can we have lunch today?"

"Sure. I can be over at the club at eleven-thirty, how's that?"

BOB FELLOWS DIDN'T want to meet at the club, which meant it wasn't going to be a pleasant conversation. They met instead at a little Greek Taverna off the strand with blue and white-checkered tablecloths covered in clear plastic. The plastic was sticky.

Burt's cholesterol had been giving him some problems, and he didn't want an issue when he went back for his checkup and another refill of Viagra. So he picked up his Greek salad with Feta cheese with a few extra olives that the toothless woman behind the counter knew he liked. The two friends made their way back to their table. The restaurant was empty, but it was early for the lunch crowd.

"Thanks for seeing me so quickly." Bob took a deep breath and watched Burt dive into his romaine lettuce. "I got a call from a colleague of mine."

"Yes. First, so you don't string it out, does this have anything to do with Aloha Shores or Green & Green?"

"No."

Burt was relieved.

"But indirectly, yes."

"Bob, just get done with it. Just put it out there for me, please, will you? I'm not feeling well, and I think this conversation is going to make me feel worse."

"As your attorney, it's is only fair that I give you some information you might not possess. And help you make a decision."

"Okay." The lettuce was cool, and it was satisfying to be chomping down on the fiber, which blocked the strange Indian music coming from the kitchen. An Indian family who had immigrated to the US five years ago in fact owned the Greek Taverna.

"Do you remember Rob Peterson—used to work in your office?"

Burt thought about it for a second. "I think so. Boy, that was like what? Twenty six-no seven years ago? Something like that. Haven't seen much of him."

"He moved up to LA some years ago, and actually did quite well after he left your company."

"Okay." Burt was hoping perhaps the guy wanted to buy him out.

"Adele liked him."

Burt's gut grumbled, and a sharp pain hit the left side of his chest.

"She visited him several times in LA. During a couple of your golfing trips to Scotland, from what I understand."

"Okay."

"He thinks he's Gerud's father."

That fuckin' bitch.

"Is that possible, Burt?"

"Anything's possible. If he bought her things and was sweet about it, yeah, I can see her spreading her legs for him." His blood pressure was beginning to rise, and he didn't like it one bit.

"So, if he's not your son, you can cut him out of your inheritance."

"What inheritance?"

"I wanted you to know that you have a choice now. I understand how concerned you've been about the business venture. Rob Peterson is a very wealthy man, and he's dying, Burt. We aren't sure if he's reached out to Adele yet, but he wants to contact Gerud. Bob's attorney suggested I ask you first."

"So, what you're saying is that Gerud is about to come into some money. Not Jake, but Gerud."

"That's right. Bob is under no obligation to leave any money for either of them, but he wants to leave money to his son, or who he thinks is his son."

"No, he wants to send me a message he fucked my wife. He did what I cannot do, he fucked her and provided a nice nest egg for that fuck!"

Two faces appeared in the window each wearing black caps, with Bollywood music booming in the background. Burt inhaled again and resumed quietly. "He wants the whole world to watch as he gets even with me. Took my wife, gave her his kid, and now is doing what I cannot do."

"Well, there are two ways to look at it?"

"I only see one."

Peterson grinned, a proper lawyerly grin. "That's what you have me for."

"I'm waiting." Burt shoved the salad away to the side, suddenly not hungry.

"If he's not related to you, you can cut him out of your inheritance. But you can also sue him."

"He's been raised as my son."

"Under a ruse that your wife participated in. I'm telling you that if you wanted to, you could sue him for his mishandling of the Hawaii deal."

"You mean steal his inheritance from a dying man who wants to make it right by him after all these years? Not even I am that low."

"Well, you think it over. And after you do, come back and see me."

This was turning out to be an even shittier day than he expected.

"I'm not sure I want to do that, but you can start preparing something. Start with the will. Let's get him out of my will."

"Just the sole separate property part," Bob Fellows corrected.

"Which is the part that used to have a ton of real estate and now owns that big fuckin' piranha of a golf course shopping center, eating up all my assets like a starved zombie."

"Right, Burt."

"Not Adele's part with the house and the jewelry and cars and stuff. He's her son, and I'll let her take care of him. And then we can think about what to do next."

"Okay, Burt. I'll begin that today."

"Don't spend a lot of money on it, please."

"I won't."

"This isn't going to be a big complicated thing, now is it?"

"Doesn't have to be. Very simple, really."

"And Bob, get Belinda Matheson in. She's my daughter."

"You fathered another child?" His attorney nearly choked on his beer.

"I did. I've taken care of her, sort of. Something happens to me, if there's any money left, I want her to have some."

"You'll forward her date of birth and social security number? Do you have those things?"

"Yes, she works for me."

"Okay, Burt. Just get those to me, and I'll begin at once." He reached over and put a hand on his shoulder. "I'm here for you, Burt."

"Yeah, at a thousand dollars an hour, you're here for me."

Allen sat back, frowning. "I'll be on my way, then. Have a nice day. Let it sink in for a day or two, and then we'll talk."

It wouldn't be appropriate to cry, because Burt didn't have the same feelings for Gerud as he did for Jake, so it wasn't like he'd lost something he never had.

It was just that everything was so hopeless.

And everything was beginning to spin out of control.

CHAPTER 13

GINGER COULDN'T BELIEVE how nice it was to wake up in Jake's arms again. The lovemaking, after their first rushed encounter, was long and satisfying. Early morning sex was always her favorite, when the house was quiet and the day was a blush of possibility.

"Are you leaving soon, is that what they told you, Jake?" she asked him as he pulled her hair aside with his forefinger and lightly bit her earlobe from behind.

"Um hum." His fingers pulled her chin over to him, and he kissed her sideways, their tongues having to reach to touch.

"When do you leave?" She whispered.

His hands traveled over her thighs, up over her belly and were squeezing her breasts while she could feel him rooting to find her opening. She tilted her pelvis to give him a little help. He quickly dove under the covers and sucked her lips from behind. Then he slowly kissed up her spine and slid into her core with a satisfying sigh.

His muscled forearms covered hers, his fingers gripping hers as she moaned into her pillow as he plundered deep. Jake liked to work from every angle, pressing inside until she began to lose control. He slowed to give her time to tone down a bit, then as soon as her breathing returned to normal he began again, this time adding his fingers pinching her bud as he bit her neck and licked the knob of bone at the top of her spinal cord. He grabbed a pillow and slid it under her belly to raise her pelvis up. He held her by the hips as he rose to his knees, splaying her thighs further apart and sunk in deeper, picking up speed.

Her fingertips began to spark. The whole length of her hands, past her wrists and up her forearms tingled under the weight of his arms squeezing them down into the mattress. Again he sent his arm beneath her, reaching down to pinch her bud, which she could feel was swollen with need.

"Come for me baby." He pressed her there again and she exploded, drawing his cock up inside her, pushing back against him to keep him deep and tight against her cervix wall.

He pulled her up, putting her on all fours as he rammed inside from behind, then pulled her back against him. She arched, her head against his, allowing him to feel her long shapely torso, poking her belly button, squeezing her sensitive nipples and then landing again at her bud. Her head leaned against his shoulder. She was rocking against him, each time sitting back down on him deeper than before.

Jake had to know she was close because she was pulling on his ball sac. She looked down to try to see his penetration between her thighs, but all she saw was his fingers as they probed, pulled and slipped inside where they could find room. He touched all her swollen parts, her nipples, lacing fingers down the inside of her thighs, pinching and pulling her lips over his cock, and then encircling the stiff little bud until finally, she began to shatter with a long, rolling orgasm. Toward the end of hers, she could feel him spilling deep inside, holding himself against her.

His breathing slowed when he placed his forehead against her back, pressed himself one last time in a thrust deep inside and then released.

They rolled to the side. "Thank you, Jake."

"God, Ginger. I've said it now a dozen times. What a fool I've been. And this doesn't have one whit to do with sex, either, although," he kissed her in return, "I have to say, the sex is fantastic. You're unbelievable."

She slipped out of his grip and turned to face him, their legs entangled in the sheets and each other. "You know you're the only man I've ever loved, and the only man I've ever made love to. I always did belong to you, Jake. Even when we were apart, I was yours."

He thumbed her lips and gave her a kiss. She saw in his eyes the mark of devotion he'd had when they were first married. "I should have never left. I've made so many mistakes. How can you forgive me?"

"My biggest mistake was not trusting you. I believed what I was told. That you'd fallen for one of the girls down at the beach."

"That wasn't me, Ginger. I was probably with the guys, like every night. Running away from all that I saw over there. Some of it was pretty bad, sweetheart. Part of me didn't want to bring that back home. But of course, that's exactly what I did. What a fool."

"I should have trusted you, believed you."

"It really threw me when Frankie was killed. I came back a different man. Thinking about you and the girls. The one thing in the world I didn't want to lose, and what did I do? I screwed it up."

She traced his lips with her forefinger. It hurt her to think that he'd felt he couldn't return to their marriage, and had sought solace in someone else's arms. She didn't want to think about that right now, because this morning it felt like a lazy day, and a good day to stay in bed. But she knew they were on borrowed time. The puppy would be getting up, and so would the girls.

But for right now, everything was perfect. Her perfect life had come back to her. Finally.

THEY ATE TOGETHER as a family in the kitchen. The puppy was underfoot constantly, and Jake nearly stepped on her several times. The girls were asking questions, and Jake was honest with them.

"Your mom and I have some things to work out. You know how it is when you have a fight with someone? It takes awhile to stop being angry."

"Were you angry with Mom?" asked their oldest. Ginger decided it was time for her to jump in.

"Girls, it was a misunderstanding. And feelings were hurt, and we stopped talking. Now we're talking, so, we'll see."

Jake looped his little finger over hers as her hands pressed against the countertop.

"I don't want you to go away again, Daddy," said Jasmine. Her green eyes excoriated Jake, and she sported a frown.

Ginger knew Jennifer was too young to remember her father leaving. She'd been raised in this house, seeing her father over at his parents' house, or when he picked them up to take them places. But Jasmine did remember and at first had asked constantly when he was coming home. It had been the most difficult time in Ginger's life. But thinking he had been unfaithful, she steeled herself into bearing the pain alone and being a rock for her girls.

"Jaz, I'm always going to be your daddy. Nothing can stop that. Ever. And your mom and I are working real hard at communicating. Real hard," he said as he pressed against her behind.

"Don't worry Jasmine," she finally added. "It's all going to be okay. You'll see."

Jake offered to take the girls to school for her, which she accepted. He told her he had to report to the Team Building to send over some equipment they were going to need. He wasn't sure he'd be able to come back home tonight and would probably stay over with the guys on base, since they were leaving so early.

Ginger agreed to take Chelsea Fiona to Jake's parents' house, and then she'd head to the cooking store where she worked as a clerk.

She hugged and kissed the girls, who were delighted getting to ride in their father's big truck, and said her good-byes to Jake.

"About a week, you say?"

"Maybe two. It depends."

"Mexico? Really?"

"Yup. Wish it was with you."

"Maybe when you get home we can go sometime. Take the girls, too."

"Not this place, but somewhere, yes. I think a family vacation is in order."

"Will I be able to call you?"

"Sure. Call me anytime. We'll be in the same time zone. No worries there."

THE GREEN'S LARGE pink stucco home behind the gated community of similarly-sized homes was always a showstopper. A studio mogul had originally built the home in the thirties as a place to get away from the crowded LA suburbs for a life at the beach. So the art deco detail, especially the fine wrought iron fixtures and railing and use of colorful Spanish tile, always made her feel like a movie star in the age of silent films.

It also reminded her of some of the darker mystery films she'd loved growing up. The house had actually been used in a movie one time.

But none of that made any difference to Adele, who answered the door, her eyes puffy and red.

Ginger held the pup up to her, and before her mother in law could take her, she stopped, saying, "You sure this is okay with you to do this today?"

"You going to bring her to the kitchen shop today?"

"No, but if it's too much, I can arrange for someone—"

"Look, Ginger," she practically wrested the pup from Ginger's arms. "Your father-in-law is a royal asshole, and he's going through some tough times. He usually snaps out of it, eventually, and then all is forgiven."

"Adele, what I saw last night was serious. You should talk to someone about it. You guys were nearly violent."

Adele laughed. "Come on in for a sec." She let the puppy run to the kitchen where a fresh plate of dog food and water were prepared for him. They watched her devour the food and then make a sloppy mess of her water dish, until Adele called the puppy outside. Ginger followed her.

"I don't want you to talk to Jake about this, if you happen to see him."

"Okay. But don't you think he needs to know?"

"No. He doesn't. And I'm trusting you with that, Ginger. Besides, Gerud will probably tell him anyway. He can't seem to keep his mouth shut."

"You're being unfair."

"Am I?" Adele had gotten her hackles up. She poked her toe at several blades of grass before looking back up at Ginger. "Burt and I have lived through a string of bimbos and bad decisions. But I've never seen him so uncertain. I think whatever it is, some big deal or something, once it's over, he'll be his old self again. A son of a gun, but I'm going to see if he can get some rehab, maybe book him a stay in a clinic for a couple of weeks after all the dust settles."

"You mean a detox place?"

"Yes."

"He says he wants that?"

"No, as a matter of fact, he doesn't. But I'm going to ask him for a divorce if he doesn't."

Ginger thought the circumstance was similar to Jake's discussion with his LPO, Kyle Lansdowne. Jake had given her a brief rundown about how it was motivating him to go to meetings and become a better man. There was no possibility that she would divulge that information to her mother-in-law.

Adele agreed to pick the girls up again, like she always did. Ginger decided to let the girls tell Jake's mom about the fact that he'd spent the night at home.

CHAPTER 14

BURT GREEN WASN'T able to concentrate much during the afternoon after he got back from lunch. The conversation with his attorney had him worried. He wondered if somehow Gerud knew the truth about his paternity. And although he didn't trust him to make good decisions for clients and for the company, now Burt was beginning to distrust him for an entirely different reason. He wondered if Gerud had somehow set him up to take him down. A way of getting even for some wrong his son had thought he'd perpetrated against him.

Gerud was a boy who had always harbored resentments. He'd resented his older brother, going off and becoming a war hero. Jake was so easygoing, he allowed Gerud to spin his tales and weave his web, and Gerud was always getting Jake into trouble. He was also the first to tell them about Jake's problems with alcohol and women. When he broke up with Ginger, Gerud delivered the news almost with a smile on his face. Like he was happy Jake had screwed up so badly.

So this revelation about Adele's infidelity actually helped a few pieces of his life's puzzle fit into place. The more he thought about it, the more he was sure old Bob Fellows was right. It was time to excise Gerud from his life. If he was lucky, Adele would have no part of it and leave him. Might even let him off the hook so he didn't have to air the dirty laundry of their lack of funds in front of anyone. She could go live off the trust fund of her ex-lover. Better yet, she could go take care of the man, change his diapers and wipe his ass so she could get her hands on some freedom afterwards. She and her boy. And leave Burt and his bad fortune alone. He could liquidate, sock away a few things without paying taxes on it, and head for Mexico or the Caribbean and disappear.

But then he thought about Jake. And the whole plan went up in smoke.

He watched Gerud pick up a file folder and read over some things, then hand it to Belinda with a smile.

If he only knew.

He'd have to watch those two. If Belinda didn't understand Burt was her father, he could see the two of them getting involved, and that would be a huge mess. He didn't want to divulge anything, though, until he had to. And he didn't trust Gerud with the truth. Not yet. He knew Gerud was working on some kind of a plan because he'd shown an interest in real estate again and had actually been working later than normal. Something was up.

Burt knew whatever it was, he couldn't trust that plan, either. It wasn't something that would be good for Green & Green or for himself personally.

He decided to put Gerud to the test.

Coming out of his office, he approach Gerud. "I wonder if we could speak in private, son." That last word stuck like a thorn in his tongue.

"Sure, Dad," Gerud returned. Was Gerud mocking him?

After taking his seat behind the desk he examined Gerud's face for some sign he knew the secret Bob Fellows had revealed. Burt decided he did not.

"Has your mom taken any recent trips to LA that you know of?"

"Wouldn't you know about it? I mean, I don't live there. You do."

"In a manner of speaking. You understand we've not been getting along lately."

"I can see that, yes. I get you're under a lot of stress. Is there anything I can do to help you out? All you have to do is ask."

Burt allowed his evil chuckle to sneak out. "You can fuckin' get me out of that shopping center deal."

"Why don't you try to sell it? There has to be someone who might want it."

"That piece of shit is only good for one thing: money laundering. I haven't gotten to that point yet, but I wish it would just burn down. Be the best thing that could happen."

Gerud didn't take the joke.

"I was joking, Gerud."

His son shook his head. "I think people do it all the time. If I can find someone—"

"Oh, cut the crap, Gerud. I wasn't insinuating we'd have a *fire!*"

One of the salesmen in the office turned and looked through the glass window at the two of them. Burt lowered his voice.

"So I want to talk about your mom taking any recent trips by herself."

"Beats me. I'm not aware of anything about that. She's got her hands full with the girls. And with Aaron and Samantha. She's babysitting all the time. I don't think she has time to go anywhere."

"What about before these kids were born—what, about ten or more years ago? You ever hear her talk about, oh, I don't know, having a boyfriend in her past?"

Gerud's eyebrows quickly drew together in a nasty frown.

"Mom? You suspect something about Mom?"

"Yes, Mom."

"That would surprise me. You mean she would do to you what you've been doing to her all these years?"

Burt figured he deserved that. If Gerud knew about his real father, he certainly was being a hell of a good actor.

"It's different for men than women," he lied. "Take Jake, for example."

Gerud looked down at his hands in his lap. "Chip off the old block." Then he added, "You know I think Jake and Ginger are screwing again."

"Oh yeah?"

"I think so. Nobody's talking, but I think that's happened."

"So why did you go get Monica involved?"

Gerud glanced up quickly, appearing surprised. "Excuse me?"

"Monica came to see me today. Don't go getting yourself caught up in Jake's affairs. And don't go sending Jake's ladies to come see me, understand? One might think you were trying to cut a nice slice of meat for yourself, Gerud. Leave the ladies alone. Go find some of your own to play with."

Gerud stood up. "You prick!"

This time, several heads turned in the office.

"Always protecting Jake, watching out for him. Always defending him, covering up for him. Jake the perfect son. You always have and you always will."

"Fuck you, Gerud. You're fired!"

Gerud's face transformed into a huge mean sneer. "You can't fire me. This business is part of my inheritance. You owe me—"

"I should make you pay for your lack of doing due diligence on the Hawaii deal that's strangling me and—" he lowered his voice again, this time to a whisper, "practically putting me out of business. Now get out and don't come back. And if you talk any more about your inheritance, I'll sue your ass and take your leased Volkswagen, too."

Gerud ran to his desk, stuffed papers into a cardboard box left over from the last agent who quit, stopped by the reception desk, and picked up a file that he'd turned in, and left, slamming the door behind him.

"One down. One to go," Burt mumbled to himself.

CHAPTER 15

JAKE DROVE TO the apartment he shared with Corey and Ryan and
decided he'd give them the news he was moving back in with
Ginger and the girls. They deserved to know. Both the bachelors were
gearing up, bringing enough firepower to arm a small country. Each
man had his own black duty bag. Jake's had wheels on it and a handle
that slid out of one end for ease in carrying heavy loads.

He brought his H&K, his Glock and a sparse amount of ammo,
since Uncle Sam would provide him that. His helmet and night vision
gear also fit into the bag. He stashed a couple pairs of socks and boxers,
two fresh t-shirts, and one uniform which he'd wear on the trip the next
morning. His vest had extra pockets he'd had customized so he could
have access to his explosive charges, flash bombs, grenades and his KA-
BAR. His small shave kit also had a tube of antiseptic, a vial of alcohol
and his toothbrush, as well as tape, bandages, baby wipes and super
glue.

He stuck a few zip ties into the larger bag, as well as some long Velcro straps and an extra scope. His boots were at the Team building,
along with a second helmet and a shotgun.

The three of them rode together in Jake's truck.

"Where'd you go last night, bro?"

"I was over at Ginger's," he said over the back seat.

Ryan whistled. "Good for you, my man."

"Does Monica know? Because she came over earlier and asked
where you were," said Cory.

"I'll call her, but, no, you two are the first to be told anything about it. Figured you'd want to get someone to share the place with, since I'll be moving out when we return from deployment."

"You work fast, Jake," said Cory.

"I'd say it was more like I finally woke up and realized I should have never left. Ginger's the one. She's always been the one."

The two Team guys didn't say a word, and Jake knew they were each in their private fantasy about getting back with their exes.

"I'm going to be responsible and shit. I mean, these are my kids, and I'm going to protect them, take care of them."

"Well, we wish you well with all that, Jake. We really do," Ryan replied.

THEY WERE BRIEFED on the mission ahead of them. The group was going to pose as a sport fishing club down in Baja. That would enable them to have ice chests and lockers full of fishing equipment, but meant they could carry weapons without detection as well.

At dawn, the Team was loaded up onto the big military transport planes for the two-hour flight to Puerto Cortes on the Isla Santa Margarita, Baja California coast. The Mexican naval base there was only a landing pad for the SEALs. There they boarded a trio of commercial fishing vessels that catered to the tourist trade. The boats unloaded them at Nuevo Vista where three twelve-passenger vans were waiting for them so they could drive to the Baja Nuevo resort, their destination.

Jake texted Ginger.

Arrived. Been exactly twenty-four hours and already I miss you.

She returned the text.

Be safe. Love you. Miss you, too.

They were set up in several cabins and one long house near the water's edge, surrounded by white sandy beach and blue water of the bay. They left one van locked at their lodging, containing the bulk of their equipment, and piled into the remaining two, headed into town.

The place was full of tourists, mostly young couples, but several groups were American fishermen lured down to do some world-class sport fishing. The SEALs were able to blend in easily. They found a small local restaurant without a floorshow or fancy trimmings and settled in for some beers and incredibly good food, so they could watch the local population and the tourists mingling in the early evening air. The chance to just be together as a group, socially, was a good way to begin their mission.

"Anybody forget anything?" asked Kyle.

"My woman," said Tay.

They all laughed. Nothing discussed was out of character.

"Tomorrow we begin. Low key for now. T.J. and Fredo, you ready?"

"Fuckin' A," said Fredo. T.J. gave the thumbs up.

"Okay to wander off, but I prefer quads, okay?" Kyle whispered.

Jake hung with Alex and Lucas. They checked out several bars and looked into store windows. A couple of places with corrugated metal doors were open, selling beers, water and sundries from tiny holes in the wall. Several children holding iguanas came up begging for money and requesting they take a picture with the creatures. The men were always careful about being photographed and just gave coin and candies they'd brought with them for that very purpose. It worked well in the Middle East. Mexico was just the same. Poor children of the world all acted the same, thought Jake.

"Hey, congrats on the news. Marcy's pregnant?" he asked Lucas.

"Yup. Just found out. We're pretty stoked."

"Lucas here was hoping you could give him pointers about raising three kids, Jake." Alex and Sydney were expecting their first any day.

Jake chuckled. "Thank God they have wonderful mothers that don't fight over me, or at least, not yet." He hesitated to bring up his news, but decided if he didn't, they'd hear it from Cory and Ryan, and he wasn't sure what story that would be.

"I'm getting back together with Ginger."

"That's awesome!"

They heard a snap of firecrackers, and all of them jumped. It was unsafe to carry a weapon on these streets, but all of them instinctively reached for their sidearm, which was not there. Jake's was usually tied to his thigh or hidden behind his waist in his belt holster.

They noticed another group from the Team walking out of a bar to check out the noise as well.

"Just firecrackers and kids, a lethal mixture," mumbled Alex. He checked his cell phone and then darkened the screen and stowed it in a front pocket.

Jake grabbed his shoulder. "Hang in there, bro. I'm hoping we'll be home in time. But hell, you're only two hours away plus. Maybe Kyle will let you go home."

Alex thanked him. "It is what it is. This stuff doesn't wait on no babies. I was given a slot, I go."

Lucas shushed them, hearing an argument from one of the bars they'd just passed. Two men fell out into the street rolling in the dusty unpaved road. They gave a wide berth as a couple of military-looking security guards descended upon the two of them and threw them in the back of a van and took off.

"Now, you don't see that every day do you?" Jake said as he watched the van disappear down the roadway in the moonlight.

"Private police force. Paramilitary dudes," whispered Lucas.

"No badges. Unmarked trucks. We gotta let Kyle know," said Alex.

"Already got it," whispered Kyle behind them. "And watch your language. You don't sound like a bunch of fishing buddies."

CHAPTER 16

BURT WAITED AS long as he could to go home. The confrontation with Adele was going to escalate, especially if she'd spoken to Gerud.

He'd stopped by the Club and had a drink with a couple of his buddies, and had a light bite to eat to soak up the alcohol. Bob Fellows came over to his table after two of his friends left him alone.

"Got the paperwork you asked me for. Can I drop it by the office first thing tomorrow?."

Burt winced, took a sip of water, and crunched some ice. "Sure, I'll look it over in the morning when I go back in. Thanks for not bringing it here."

"I did."

"Well, tomorrow is good enough for me."

"You been home yet?"

"Nope. That's my next stop, I think." He looked around to see if anyone noticed him speaking with his attorney. "But I did talk to Gerud, and I fired him."

"I think that was a wise decision. He give you any trouble?"

"Just left like a bat out of hell, dumped his considerable work," Burt leaned over and whispered in Bob's ear, "He only took *one file*. Put it in a cardboard box and that was it. I'm going to find out soon enough if he went crying to Mama, but I suspect he didn't."

"Well, you call me if you need anything. You have my cell."

"I do, and those after hours calls are expensive, so don't hold your breath, Bob."

"So you told him, or does he already know?"

"No, I fired him because he's incompetent and he was starting to insert himself where he doesn't belong. Messing with Jake's wives, getting them all thinking God knows what."

"Kind of weak excuse for a firing. Gotta be careful there, Burt."

"Well it was that and the fact that he gave me a lecture about keeping my pants zipped, and comparing himself, which he always did, with Jake. He's gonna blow a cork when he finds out. I just figured it would be easier for me if he wasn't around."

"Jeez. You do have icewater in your veins. Remind me never to get on your wrong side."

Burt looked at his attorney's round baby-face, his soft hands and black horn-rimmed glasses and his expensive unwrinkled suit, and decided he wasn't going to utter what was on the tip of his tongue. The man didn't have the chops for the real down and dirty fight that was sometimes needed in business. Burt wasn't afraid of those fights. He didn't like to lose.

That old familiar line washed back over him, *I never lost until I bought that fuckin' shopping center.* That thought led to the anger in his gut toward his son, and that led to the sharp pain again in his chest. He was going to make that doctor's appointment first thing in the morning and get that checked out.

"Bob, you won't ever have to worry about getting on my bad side because we're on the same team, remember? And as long as I keep paying the bills, we always will be, right?"

Bob gave him a meek smile. Burt could see his attorney was beginning to figure out how much of a hole Burt had gotten himself into, and that there was some smoke. No fire yet, though.

"You got that right, Burt. But take it easy with Adele. Go easy on her. It might be the smart way to handle things. Don't go do anything rash."

"Good advice."

He watched his advisor walk away, veering around an older couple dressed to the nines, just arriving for an elegant dinner by the pool. Burt didn't want to watch someone else celebrate an anniversary or special occasion. He needed to get home. By now, the yapping puppy and the girls would be gone. That meant he only had to deal with Adele.

HE WAS RELIEVED to find Gerud's car was not parked in the driveway. Lights were on in the house, so she hadn't taken off on him. The front door was locked, so he used his key and shouted out to the house, but no one answered. He set his briefcase in the study, deposited his keys on the desk and started removing his tie as he walked into the kitchen. The pool lights were on and the sliding glass door was open. He could hear water from the pool being disturbed. He walked to the open doorway and peered out into the lush backyard.

Adele was swimming at eight o'clock at night, which was very unusual, since she never used the pool except to bring the grandkids in the shallow end. And that was during the day only. Her towel was draped over the metal pool fence. She was doing laps.

He quickly made himself a drink and then walked outside, leaning over the railing.

She stopped when she got to the edge closest to her husband. Being married a long time, he knew she had wondered if he was coming home at all. He wasn't going to ask her if she was okay, since it was obvious something had changed.

Now what.

She leaned onto the stone edging, her chin resting on the backsides of her hands. "I understand you had a visitor today."

Her frostiness was gone. But Burt didn't have a clue which visitor she meant.

"I met with a lot of people. Who do you mean?" He finished his drink and held the glass down by the side of his leg.

"Monica."

Burt was relieved. That's exactly what he was hoping would happen. This was the type of stuff Adele loved meddling in. "So she called you?"

"Of course. Said you practically threw her out."

"So now you've got opinions on how I run my office? When people stop by I didn't invite?"

"She's your daughter-in-law."

"Jake would quibble with you, but what does that have to do with it? I have to entertain the women he sleeps with now, is that what you're saying?"

"Oh, for God's sake, Burt, lighten up. What is the matter with you?"

She got out of the pool and headed toward him. She'd kept her model figure, and her face was still less lined than most of her friends even without surgeries. It was what was going on with her soul that bothered and turned him off the most. But she still was an attractive woman.

"I thought you said you weren't interested in quickies anymore, Burt," she said, nailing him on the look he'd given her. She concentrated on dabbing herself off without paying further attention to him.

He was big time busted. He didn't like being confronted with the fact that he still found his wife attractive. Even without the Viagra he was actually beginning to get hard.

She opened the squeaky gate and walked past him to the kitchen, the towel thrown over her shoulder. Burt was left out on the patio watching her flat ass move in the moonlight and decided he'd rather have another drink.

Adele's footsteps were lightly tapping the steps to their bedroom. Burt made his way over to the bar, made himself another Scotch and downed it. He rinsed the glass in the sink, checked the sliding door, turned off the backyard lights, then checked the front porch lights and front door locks and headed upstairs himself.

At the doorway to their bedroom suite he leaned on one hip. Adele had turned off the shower and was drying herself off again. He sat on the bed and watched her. He had two needs. First, he needed to confront her about Gerud, and he guessed she hadn't heard anything from him yet or it would have been the first thing she'd thrown at him. But second, he was curious and a little excited to wonder what it would feel like to have sex with his wife for the first time in nearly two years.

Maybe longer.

Bob Fellows had opened up Pandora's box with the knowledge that Adele had slept with another man, and apparently had some feeling for him, too. And the guy wasn't some bastard pool boy or casual screw, she actually had a relationship, bore a child by him, and apparently did all this without Burt's knowledge. He'd thought she was pretty much an open book. But now he saw her in a slightly different light.

The two needs couldn't be met at the same time, because if he discussed her boyfriend and his bastard son, he would more than likely be sleeping in the granddaughters' bedroom or in a motel tonight. And that didn't satisfy the other need.

So he just watched her until she looked up at him. He wondered if she found him attractive at all. He'd stayed in shape, not like Jake of course, but he wasn't flabby. He didn't exercise as much as he used to. He played less golf because he was working harder trying to keep the business going. But she was definitely checking him out.

Holding the towel up to her chest so she hid all her girly parts, she spoke softly. "Burt, I propose we set a truce, for the sake of the kids and grandkids."

Now he definitely knew she hadn't talked to Gerud. So he swallowed his pride. He decided he could try to believe in forgiveness. She was as damaged as he was, when it came right down to it. They'd been a pretty hot pair at one time. Maybe there was something left.

"I think that's a good idea, Adele. I have a lot on my mind, and I'm not myself sometimes. I'm sorry if I was harsh to you and to—to—" He wanted to say *your son* but knew that was cross purposes to what he really wanted. "To Gerud and Ginger and the girls."

She came over and knelt in front of him, the towel still stuck beneath both her armpits. She placed her hands on his knees. "Is there something I can do, Burt? Anything I can do to help?"

He blinked a couple of times, not quite sure he'd heard her correctly.

"Well," he said as he pulled the towel from her chest and watched her eyes get wide. "We could always try this. But I'm afraid I'm going to be honest with you, I need a little help in that department."

He was surprised at his own words. The Mini Me inside him was jabbing his calf with a pitchfork.

She suddenly got up, and Burt thought she was going to storm out, but she returned with a blue Viagra pill. "Is this what you mean?"

"Where did you get that?"

"Never mind. I just had a few."

"But where the fuck did you get this? I'm out, so it couldn't have come from my bottle."

She narrowed her eyes. "Do you want to fuck me or not? Or would you rather argue about where the pills came from?"

It was a difficult threshold to be on for Burt. Both sides of the doorway were bad choices. But in the end, his male ego won out. He grabbed the pill and swallowed it.

But he just couldn't let it go.

"Where did you get it, Adele? I want the truth."

She showed him her backside and brushed her hair, and then took her time applying some red lipstick, the shade he liked. Then she put on some perfume and dabbed a bit on her belly button and rubbed her palms together and worked them down her thighs. In a sultry voice, she answered him, "Go take your shower, Burt. And when you get out, if you still feel like asking me that question, I'll answer it. But take your shower first."

He tore his clothes off, got into the shower with anger on his mind. If he had another drink it could interfere with the drug, which he'd been told he should never do, so he was just going to seethe as he quickly got heated from the water, and then felt his rod start to get hard. It would be cruel to fuck her and then tell her he was cutting her son out of his sole separate property. But she'd been in possession of Viagra, and that didn't come from his stash. He kept it quietly tucked away in his Jag on purpose in case of emergencies. Those sorts of emergencies would never happen at home, so she would never have access to it.

Which meant that she was still screwing the guy, or had been.

How recently?

The hot water made him slightly light-headed so he turned down the heat, finished his soaping and rinsing and stepped onto the bath mat still a little woozy. He drank a tall glass of water and brushed his teeth, then combed his hair. He grabbed his aftershave and hesitated.

Oh fuck, what difference does it make?

He decided he was all in. He applied the aftershave gently and then walked to the bedroom where it was not lost on Adele that he'd gotten hard as a rock. He was rather proud of himself.

She was sitting on the edge of the bed, focused on his groin, so he approached. Her soft hands reached out and touched him, then her fingers found his balls and gently squeezed them.

He wasn't used to this exciting stimulation, especially after the hot shower, so he began to weave. He braced on one of her shoulders as she slipped his cock between her lips and sucked him so hard he thought for a moment she was going to do a Bobbit maneuver. But she'd been practicing. And that thought, while it was exciting to feel, also made him angry.

He visualized her with this Peterson guy—hoped he was a balding son of a gun—going down on her. Her and those skinny legs of hers. Him calling her baby, and her telling him to fuck her or suck her or whatever. He saw it all, and his blood pressure began to rise. But his dick was also rising, getting huge and she was beginning to choke on his size.

No one could make Adele come like he could. He didn't care what this guy had, he was masterful with Adele, always had been, until she'd gotten so cold and angry. But now she was all purring, moaning and gagging while he was ramming himself down her throat and letting her squeeze his balls.

But then he saw this Peterson guy with his hairy ass in the air, he'd be flabby and maybe forget to take his socks off. They'd be argyle socks. His legs would be white because he didn't play golf and worked all the time, so he was white and a little flabby. And he was fucking Adele and she was clutching his hairy ass and he was moaning, too. He curled his toes.

Who fuckin' curls his toes when they screw? Maybe he was afraid of wetting the bed or coming too soon? Anything was possible. His mind was racing, getting more and more agitated.

With his cock buried all the way to the back of her throat he had to spoil it all and ask her.

"Where did you get them? Were they for your boyfriend?"

She didn't glance up at him but kept sucking and man, it felt good. When she came up for air her lipstick was smeared but she looked sexy as hell with her hair all messed up. She gave him an angelic smile, and started crawling backward on the bed like an upside down crab. He could see her pussy, she made sure of that.

"I still want to know. Who does it belong to?"

She grinned and used her forefinger to motion for him to follow up after her. Then she stuck her finger inside her pussy and wiggled it around like she was stirring a martini.

Holy fuck!

He scrambled on the bed after her, urgent to show her who was the commander of the situation. He grabbed her shoulders and thrust his cock deep inside her and then began to pump, to show her how he could still do it, how he could make her insides burn so hot she'd forget her own name. She was moaning, and he was delighted with what was surely going to be the sexual performance of his lifetime.

Then black circles appeared in his eyes. A sharp pain in his chest took his breath away. He cried out and held his throat, thinking he had swallowed his tongue or swallowed something and was choking. His arm hurt and he glanced down, expecting it to look bright purple and swollen. Adele's face was contorted with horror. She was screaming, but he couldn't hear a thing. It was all white noise and fading darker and darker. He gasped and collapsed over her body.

Everything suddenly turned black and was completely quiet.

CHAPTER 17

G INGER WAS FAST asleep when the phone rang.

"Burt's had a heart attack. I've got him at Scripps." Adele broke down and started to cry. "He may not last the night, Ginger."

"Oh no! Let me see if I can get a sitter, and I'll try to get over there. Are you all alone? Where's Gerud?"

"I can't reach him. I've left messages. I have no idea where he is."

Ginger thought about who she could call this late and gave Jake's LPO's wife, Christy Lansdowne, a call.

"I'm so sorry, Ginger. Of course you'll want to be there. I can't leave, but can you drop the girls off here?"

"Christy, my mother-in-law, bought them a puppy. I'm afraid I can't leave her in the kennel, and outside is too cold, and inside, well, you know what I'd come home to."

"Well, bring her along, too, then," said Christy. "I mean, my kids would have a ball with a new puppy to play with."

GINGER ARRIVED AT the hospital near midnight and took the fifth floor elevator up to the CCU. Adele came running toward her and nearly collapsed in her arms just outside the family waiting area. The older woman was sobbing uncontrollably. Ginger could only whisper encouragement and hold her tight, rubbing her shoulders and kissing the top of her head.

Ginger noticed a sign for the chapel down the hallway. She imagined many hours had been spent there by families such as hers, waiting for the outcome of a very long night.

"So what have they said?" she asked.

"Not much, except they don't want anything to upset him. He's sedated, and they're running tests. At least he's still alive, Ginger. And that's the main thing."

She brought Adele back to the tiny lounge, and the two sat down together on a loveseat. One of the nurses asked if they wanted anything to drink.

"How about some tea, Adele? Does that sound good?"

She nodded, unable to speak.

"I'll bring some choices for you two. Be right back."

"So, this happened at home or at the office, Adele?"

"At home."

"Thank God. And thank God you were there too. He could have been somewhere all alone and he'd be—"

"The doctor said he still might not make it, Ginger." Adele's face was red from crying. Normally, even in the morning, Adele would have makeup on, but tonight she wore nothing but a pair of yoga pants and a large sweatshirt. No lipstick, not even her hair was brushed. Her eyes pleaded for answers Ginger could not give her.

"Did this happen in his sleep?"

Adele chuckled and then began to gag and cough and then sneezed uncontrollably. Ginger leaned over the coffee table and grabbed a box of tissues and presented her with a handful.

"Not ever in my wildest dreams could I have anticipated this." She started to collect herself and was going to say something further when her emotions spilled over and she blurted out, "It's all my fault! Oh. My. God. I've killed him!"

"Come on, sweetheart. That's not fair. No way you could have," answered Ginger.

"I did. I'm going to rot in hell for what I've done."

Ginger held her, but was worried for what lay ahead. This family had been so fractured. She decided to be patient and wait for definite news one way or the other, and then she'd call Jake.

MR. GREEN'S DOCTOR came out nearly an hour later.

"He's holding his own right now, but these are the most critical hours. The longer he stays alive without further incident, the better the prognosis, so it's a waiting game. Every one is different. I wish I could be more encouraging, but I'd say you should prepare for the worst."

Adele became comatose, staring off into the corner.

"You'd best take her home. I don't think he'll be awake anytime soon, and she should get some rest. Nothing you can do here. And I'd make sure the family is notified, just in case."

"Adele?" Ginger put her arm around her. "I've got to give a call to Jake. Do you want to talk to him?"

"Where is he?" Adele looked disoriented.

"He's on a mission. They're in Mexico. But I'd like to get a message to him."

The doctor appeared concerned with Adele's state of mind. "Mrs. Green, you should just try to rest. I think you should let this nice lady take you home. Or we can make a bed up for you here, but the main thing is, you need to sleep, rest. Nothing you can do but gather your strength."

"Thank you, doctor. It might be easier if she stays here. There's no one at home who can help out, and I think she'd want to be here until I can get the rest of the family located."

"I understand. I'll have them make up a bed. I'll also have them give her something for sleep. Do you know if she takes any medications?"

"Adele, honey, do you take anything, any meds?"

She shook her head silently from side to side.

"Okay, just a moment." He left to get one of the nurses to set something up.

THE PHONE RANG only once before Jake's gravelly voice came on the line.

"What's up, sweetheart? Is everything okay?"

Ginger took a deep breath and held back tears. Though Jake and his dad hadn't been very close, she knew he would be devastated.

"He's had a heart attack, Jake. We have him in the hospital here. Scripps. Special cardiac unit. And—" her voice began to waver. "He may not make it, Jake. I just want you to know. We can't find Gerud, but I'm with your mom now in the hospital."

"Dad? You're talking about Dad?"

"Yes."

"Oh God. Does she want to talk to me?"

"They have her resting, and I think they gave her something so she'd sleep. That's all she can do. I think that's best right now. But she blames herself for some reason. Not quite sure about how that is wired up, maybe a little regret, who knows?"

"So were they arguing? I'll bet he was drinking."

"I think so, but she just breaks down when she tries to talk about it, so I haven't pressed. Doesn't matter now, anyway."

"That's right. He drives himself."

"Yes. I suppose there's no chance you could get released to come home?"

"Well, this comes with the territory. If there was something I could do by coming home, you know, if it was one of the kids, or something. Then maybe, in an emergency. But parents die. Grandparents die, family dies all the time when we're away, and most the time we can't be there. You know how it goes."

"You're right. I'm so proud of you for what you're doing. It's exactly what you were made for."

"I'm glad you're there with Mom, too. Wish I could be there to help, but hey, they got the A-team on board. She couldn't ask for a better person to be with her. Love you sweetheart."

"Thank you. Miss you so much."

"Me, too."

She was hesitant to bring up one more item, but overruled her doubts. "Jake, should I call Karlene and Monica?"

"Let me think about that." She could hear him sigh into the phone. "Oh man, that's a tough one. I'd say yes. But that's a lot to put on you."

"I don't mind. You know that. Just want to do what's good for the family."

"Let's wait a few hours, see how he does. I don't think Mom wants all the attention. I think you're the right person to be there. Keep it quiet. Keep her quiet. Keep him quiet. Say some prayers."

"You got it."

"That's my warrior princess. I love you so much, Ginger."

"I can't wait for you to come home. Be safe."

CHAPTER 18

I N THE MORNING, and on cue, T.J. and Fredo got into a fight. Thankful they had witnessed the altercation the night before, it was decided if the private force showed up, the Team wouldn't let their men be taken away, no matter what.

In seconds, a dark green four-door pickup arrived with another pair of private guards. Fredo argued in Spanish that T.J. was responsible for him getting booted from the Navy. T.J. didn't understand any of it, of course, swore in English and denied everything, instead, blaming Fredo. The Team separated the two of them, and Fredo walked off with Danny. The guards were hesitant to intervene. Jake figured it was due to the size of their group.

The rest of the day, the men saw to it that two others hung around Fredo to make it appear there was an anti-military faction that had split off the main group. Danny, who was Navajo, and could pass for being Latino, and Armando, from Puerto Rico both consoled him. For a time it started looking like the Aryan Brotherhood vs. MS-13, since Tay stood slightly taller than Coop and had nearly blond-white hair and eyebrows that looked like they were perpetually were tipped in frost. Ollie and Jake, Ryan, Cory and the others, including Kyle, stayed on the side of the "fake" Brotherhood with Tay and several others and allowed the open warfare to permeate anywhere in public they met up with Fredo's faction.

It didn't take long for a group of well-dressed locals to join Fredo and his cadre while they were drinking alone under a thatched roof palapa near the shore. They stayed away from the rest of the Team on purpose. Fredo was wired, though, using a tiny microphone he'd installed at the back of a button on his shirt. Coop monitored everything back at their cabin with T.J. while Kyle, Jake, Tay and Ollie strolled a block away, in case they had to jump in. Kyle and Jake were also wearing embedded Invisios and could hear every bit of Fredo's conversation.

"Order these fine gentlemen a beer, if you please," the newcomer said in Spanish to a young waiter making his rounds. Fredo turned and thanked him.

"I'd offer you a chair, but there aren't any."

The newcomer whistled, and another cabana boy brought over three rickety chairs, and Jake could hear their three new friends sit. Six more beers were delivered to the table and no money was exchanged, although Fredo had started to pull out his wallet and had been rebuffed.

"Not necessary," the newcomer said, again in Spanish.

"Gracias," answered Fredo. Danny and Armando mumbled thanks as well.

"Forgive me for intruding, but I couldn't help but overhear you have recently been discharged from the Navy, then, is that right?"

"Depends on why you're askin'." Fredo's voice sparked attitude and distrust, also something planned.

"I get you, my man. Well, if it is true, here's to your honorable discharge, amigo." He clicked his beer bottle to Fredo's. The man's two other friends similarly toasted Armando and Danny Begay.

"Discharged?" Fredo spat in the sand. "More like shit upon."

"Sorry, man. So I hear they're making everyone turn in their uniforms these days. What's up with that? They recycling everything now? Who is gonna go around in your Goodwill uniform?"

"Exactly. Nah, I didn't turn nothin' in."

"Which makes you a dangerous man, amigo."

A block away, Jake and Kyle high-fived and kept wandering through stores, pretending to look for sunglasses.

"Not *here*. I'm not that crazy. But yeah. I'll be ready for the zombie apocalypse, my good man." Fredo clinked beer bottles again.

"How about you guys?"

As was prearranged, Armando said he was still in, and Danny confirmed he'd failed a drug test. That last comment earned them all another round of beer in celebration.

"My manners are somewhat lacking, but I'm Rodrigo, and these are my two associates, Benji and Que Pasa."

"¿Que Pasa? Armando asked.

"It's a nickname. Cristobal Passa," the local on Fredo's right said.

Rodrigo pointed to Benji. "His mama was watching cartoons when he was conceived. She was a little young."

This also got Kyle and Jake's attention.

"So how long are you fellas going to be here?"

"We all came down to go sport fishing. We thought we'd drive down to Cabo and do a little exploring. But now, I think I'm ready to go home," said Fredo.

"I'm so sorry. It's lovely here. You are of Mexican descent?"

"That's right."

"What province?"

"Sinaloa. But my mother brought me to LA when we were kids," Fredo truthfully answered.

"Ah, I love Sinaloa. Have lots of friends there. Beautiful place. Althhough this is more peaceful, wouldn't you agree?" Rodrigo asked.

"I have no clue. I've not been down there since I was a kid. We have no family living there any longer."

"Yes, you have to be careful if you are American. But we travel safely without problem. You just have to know somebody."

"So I've heard."

They continued the small talk. A couple of local girls came over to offer back rubs and oil rub downs. Jake could hear Fredo turn his down, but Danny and Armando removed their shirts and accepted the massages.

"You like pretty girls?" Rodrigo asked.

"Who doesn't?"

"If perhaps you are homesick and need some company, these lovely girls can come cook and clean your place, and they give nice massages, too."

"They look young," Fredo answered.

"Young and untouched. The finest you can buy here." Rodrigo paused and Kyle and Jake heard him refer to Fredo's wedding ring, which he refused to take off, even if they were on an undercover mission. "But you are married, and so I respect that."

Rodrigo ordered finger foods, and Jake had to endure hearing Fredo munching down on fresh shrimp and Mexican lobster. Fredo was waxing eloquent about all the food, and Jake suspected it was for especially Coop's ears, when he added,

"I got a friend who doesn't eat anything that isn't organic. Tofu. Shit like that."

"Bean plastico," Rodrigo said.

"¿*Plastico*? asked Danny.

"They make it into a paste, and then bake it and make jewelry out of it, buttons, too. Hair clips. It hardens just like plastic. It's not intended for human consumption."

"I completely agree," said Fredo.

Jake smirked, and Kyle was shaking his head, hands on his hips. They both knew Coop was having kittens back at the complex.

"Well, I'm afraid we have to cut our little meeting short. That leaves all this food for you. They will wrap it up if you ask them."

"What about the bill?" Fredo asked.

Just before the three strangers walked away, Rodrigo softly told them, "My brother owns the whole town. The bar, the resort, even the airport. Your money is no good, my friend. While you are here, you and your friends may consider yourselves guests. You want anything? You just ask and it's yours."

"Wow. Thank you. I guess this is my lucky day."

"This evening, we are having a little party at my brother's home, which is up on the hillside over there. You see it? The big pink castle?"

"Yes, I see it."

"Here is the address. I've written it on the back of this business card. You shouldn't get lost, or should I send a car around?"

"No, I can drive fine. We have a van for all our equipment. Um, what time is the party?"

"Around here, parties don't start until about ten o'clock. There will be tons of food, so don't eat dinner beforehand or you'll get sick. Guaranteed."

All three of them thanked their host.

"My pleasure."

After some minutes had passed, Jake heard Fredo's voice again. "You get all that? I certainly hope so. Listen, I'm going to stay here a bit and finish off some of this awesome crab and shrimp and dip it into all this melted butter. I'd like to finish some of the fresh papaya and pineapple, too. But when we're done, we'll bring home a care package. After all, sharing is caring."

Jake knew Coop was swearing up a storm back at their lodging. And T.J. was probably laughing his guts out.

"HOW'S YOUR DAD?" Kyle asked.

"Haven't heard yet today. Ginger is supposed to call me if there's any change. So far, no calls."

"You know I could probably spare you, if something big comes up. But it's a pain in the ass to get it and will take me a half day. But if you need to go, we're good here. And it looks like we've met our target.'

"I appreciate that, sir. Your wife is helping out with the girls so Ginger can console my mom. So, I owe you thanks as well. You've done a whole lot already. But if I'm a third wheel, I don't mind paying for my own flight home."

"Let's play it by ear."

Jake got a text message from Ginger.

No change. Do I call the exes? If so, what numbers?

Jake returned the text message.

Let's wait a few more hours. You holding up okay?

Missing you.

Baby, me, too.

CHAPTER 19

A DELE HAD CALLED Burt's office and let them know their boss was in the hospital. So, just after lunch, his secretary showed up, as well as a couple of the long-term brokers who worked for Green & Green. Ginger was introduced to everyone as Jake's wife, which alarmed her somewhat.

"Is he expected to pull through?" Belinda asked her.

"We're hoping so. The longer he goes without further incident, the better it is for him, but they said he's still not out of the woods yet."

"I'm so sad. He's a young guy, really, and pretty healthy, too."

Ginger looked at Belinda's sweet face and suspected perhaps she was Burt's new interest du jour, but when she didn't pick up any animosity from Adele, lay that thought to the side. She was younger than Jake, about Gerud's age.

After realizing Mr. Green's care was still in the air, Belinda excused herself, gave her condolences to Adele, and promised to go back to the office to keep the doors open and inform anyone who was inquiring after him. Of course, she was not only telegraphing about the health of the owner, but the company as well.

"You make sure to tell *everyone* not to worry, that Mr. Green will be back at work in no time. Tell them he's getting better," Adele said as she delivered her command.

"I will certainly do so," Belinda said without an ounce of opposition.

Adele did look rested and was beginning to get more organized. She called Burt's attorney. Concerned that her husband would be in the hospital for some time, she let Bob Fellows know she'd have to be put in charge of the financial affairs, something that had been put in place years ago. She was a fifty percent owner in the company, she reminded him, so she needed banking authorization so that checks could be written and deposits made. Fellows told her he'd bring paperwork and go over what had to be done when he got there.

Ginger offered to retrieve Adele's makeup and a fresh set of clothes from the house, but she declined, instead insisting Ginger stay, and left to take a shower and bring back some things for a more prolonged stay.

Shortly after Adele left her alone in the family waiting room, until, the attorney arrived. She'd met him before at gatherings at the Green house, and she recalled he had attended her marriage to Jake.

"Good to see you, Ginger, although I'm so sorry it's under these circumstances."

"Yes, same here."

"Any change?"

"No. He's still sedated, but as far as I know, there have been no more incidents. He had a couple very minor ones last night, apparently. But we are glad he's still looking stable, for now."

"Where's everyone else?"

"Adele went home to get some things, and take a shower. My girls are over at Jake's boss's house. We haven't been able to find Gerud. Adele's more concerned about him right now. But, I'm sure he'll show up. Burt's secretary dropped by and promised to keep the office informed. And Jake's on deployment, but I've called him and. Unfortunately, it's not likely he can come home."

"I see. Tell me who the secretary is? I've forgotten her name."

"Um, Belinda, I think. Pretty little thing. Very loyal."

"Okay, that's good. Anyone else stop by?"

"Like who?"

"Is there any other family that you need to call or are waiting to see him?"

"No. Not unless you consider Jake's other wife and former girlfriend."

Fellows frowned and put his hand on her shoulder. "Burt liked you very much and hoped that you'd get re-connected with Jake."

That forced her to look away, a blush forming on her cheeks. When it occurred to her Mr. Fellows had used the past tense in referring to Burt, it worried her.

Just then, Gerud strolled down the hallway with determination. Behind him, Monica was in tow, wheeling Jake's newest offspring in a stroller. Monica made it obvious she wasn't the least bit anxious to bury the hatchet, literally, and ignored Ginger.

Fellows stiffly gave Gerud a handshake and made nice over Monica's baby and her introduction.

"Has Jake been here?" Gerud asked.

"No, he's on deployment. I don't think he can come home."

"Oh darn." Gerud was rocking back and forth in his boots. "Mom's coming soon?"

"Yes, she spent the night here, just went home to freshen up and bring back some things. They were very nice, made up a bed so she could sleep."

"How you holding up?"

"Fine for now, but I've been up all night. Your mom should be back any minute now."

"Gotcha." He looked at Monica, who had kept her back to Ginger and he whispered something to her ear and then waited for her answer.

Fellows sat down, his briefcase on his lap, watching Gerud and Monica carefully.

"Listen, Bob," Ginger said, "I'm going to give Jake a call, now that you and Gerud are here. I need to give him an update."

"Okay. Ask him if he wants me to say anything to dad on his behalf, Ginger," her ex-brother-in-law said from clear across the hall.

"Sure. Will do," she returned. The attorney just nodded.

Ginger could hear mariachi music in the background when Jake picked up her call.

"Hey, baby. How's Dad?"

"The same. Gerud's here. So is Monica and the baby. And your dad's attorney stopped by, too. I guess your mom has to sign something?"

"Beats me. I never talked to dadDad about any of that. Must have to do with the business."

"Yes, I think it does. How are things there?"

"Good. We're progressing. Kyle says I might be able to come back early. Are you okay? You get a chance to catch some sleep?"

"No. But I'm okay. Just missing work, and Christy has taken the kids. I'm sure they're having a ball. The puppy is over there, too."

"Oh, boy. Not telling Kyle that. Bet the kids are thrilled. You picking them up tonight?"

"Probably."

"Well then, get some rest sometime this afternoon if you can. You up to calling Karlene?"

"If you think it's time."

"With both you and Monica there, I think she'd expect a call. I don't want to do it from here."

"Just text me the contact and I'll do it."

"Look, I gotta go. I'll try to call in the morning. We've got some stuff to do tonight."

"Sounds good. Love you."

"Miss you and love you more."

"Not possible."

"Can't wait to duke it out with you when I get home."

"It's a date."

Ginger called Karlene who decided she'd bring her son over after school. She sounded brittle when she heard Monica had already been there and Ginger had spent the night without calling.

"It's been a little exhausting, Karlene. Adele has been a mess. I wanted to focus on being there for her. Don't read anything into it, please."

Karlene apologized. "I'm sorry. Everything is so complicated."

That was the understatement of the century, thought Ginger.

"Well, I'm sure if he wakes up, he'll want to see his grandson. That's the main thing to focus on. And we can always use some extra prayers," Ginger said as she noted the chapel sign again, and hung up the phone.

She needed a neck rub. She needed to get off her feet. She was about to ask if she could lie down on Adele's made up bed, when the doctor came into the hallway, surveyed the group and announced, "He's awake. I don't know how long for, but I can't let all of you in. Just two at a time, please."

Gerud bolted for the door. Monica was right behind him, shoving the stroller ahead of the attorney's feet and making it through the doorway of Jake's room before Ginger could even react.

Bob Fellows was pacing back and forth, glancing up to the darkened room, his expression somber. Several times he sighed, and waited, listening to hear any conversation coming from Burt's bedside. His briefcase looked heavy, and Ginger felt sorry for the man.

"You want something, Bob? Can I get you some tea or some water or something??" she asked him.

"No, thank you. I don't need a lot of his time, and I don't want to miss my chance." He glanced into the room again.

The doctor came forward.

"Doctor, listen, I have some papers for the business. It's critical they be signed. Adele isn't here, and she'd want these things handled. I'm afraid, with Gerud and—"

"I understand," said the doctor, who disappeared inside.

Ginger heard voices being raised and the unmistakable sound of Burt swearing a blue streak. Gerud was returning fire, and the baby began to cry.

"Jeez!" Fellows mumbled.

The altercation was getting more and more heated, and finally it was the doctor's voice that rose and demanded Gerud and Monica and the baby leave the room.

Burt was coughing.

Gerud and Monica stormed past her, past the waiting area, arguing amongst themselves, the baby wailing at the top of his lungs. They disappeared into the elevators without saying a word or stopping or even glancing her way.

"You literally have not much time at all, sir. I shouldn't allow you access," she heard the doctor tell Fellows.

"It's critical. And I need you to witness the papers. I have to have you stay."

The doctor sighed and allowed entry. Ginger came to the doorway and was shocked at Burt's pale coloring, a light shade of greenish-purple. His lips even darker. He had a tube running across his face, hooked on his ears, giving him air. His coughing stopped, and he slowly opened his eyes fully and slowly recognized her. He raised his hand meekly and waved with fingers wiggling, and then dropped it heavily to the bed.

Ginger was shocked how weak and unhealthy he looked.

The doctor was on the window side of Burt's bed as Bob Fellows brought out several stacks of paperwork and placed them on a wheeled tray in front of Burt, handing him a pen and showing him where to sign. Burt tried to lean forward but couldn't, so the doctor stepped aside to allow more light into the room.

Burt began to sign where he was instructed. He coughed as another sheaf of papers was presented to him and the original set was given to the doctor to also sign.

A loud intercom page for the doctor barked in the hallway and startled everyone. Another pile of papers was hurriedly shoved at the doctor and he began to protest, but Fellows insisted. Burt began to cough again as the doctor left the room in response to the page.

In between coughing fits Burt attempted to complete another signature, while Fellows helped stabilize his wrist and hold the paper, but midway through, Burt's hand fell back to the bed, the pen still gripped in his fingers. His head drooped to the side. His eyes were still open, staring at the ground.

Ginger flagged the nurse and directed her toward Burt's room.

As suspected, Burt was gone, the nurse confirmed. The attorney was picking up his paperwork and stuffing them back in his briefcase.

He headed for the door.

As he passed by, he stopped. "Tell Adele I'll phone her. I'm afraid he left us before I could finish so nothing is signed. I'll explain it all to her when I talk to her."

"I will." Ginger watched Fellows head toward the elevators as the finality and sadness of Burt's passing hit her. Now she was all alone with her former father-in-law. Jake was in Mexico. The whole family had been ripped apart, admittedly by their own actions. And even run out on each other.

Even the dignity of Burt's last breath was stolen from him. He died over a pile of papers, which was how he lived.

She slid down the wall, bending her knees, buried her head there and sobbed.

CHAPTER 20

BACK AT THE lodges, the Team was in an upbeat mood. Kyle called a meeting and lined out what they were to do. T.J. brought out the beer, and Fredo laid out the fruit from his brunch on the beach, courtesy of Rodrigo. He zapped the leftover tamales and finger foods in the complex kitchen and placed them on the table in the middle as well.

Jake squeezed a lime into the long-necked beer and had it half downed before he felt something wrong with the taste, and then remembered his promise to stay sober. He set the bottle down, sliding it toward T.J, and went in search of a bathroom.

Sounds of laughter and music coming from the living room didn't match his mood. He was upset with himself for the slip with the beer and hoped Kyle and Coop didn't notice. He'd given his word. This was Day 4 of his new clean and sober lifestyle. He cursed himself for having forgotten so soon, and then realized it must have been the pressure from not knowing what was going on with his dad. He had never considered the possibility Mr. Green was more fragile than he normally looked. But Jake also knew what pressure could do to a man. Drive him literally insane.

He washed his hands and stared into the mirror. It was funny how that half bottle affected his nerves. Took the edge off the pain. He hoped his father recovered and made a vow to repair his relationship with him first thing when he returned.

That and re-marry Ginger. Something small and intimate.

He re-hung the hand towel and decided he looked acceptable. As he reached for the door handle he noticed his hands were shaking.

Jake sat on a bench with Fredo, rather than the couch sandwiched between T.J. and Armando.

"So, Fredo, Danny and Armando will be going to the Pink Palace," said Kyle. "I'll have Ollie and Tay hang back and give cover in case we have to do an emergency extraction. Alex, I'm putting you up on this rooftop here. Looks like it's a storage room for the complex. All three of you bring your long guns and your night gear, okay?"

"You think I should get miced up?" Asked Fredo.

"No, because then someone's got to monitor it. I'm trusting you guys on this one. We're in, we don't want to get caught with an Invisio in our ears and blow the cover."

"Could use one of my button minis," suggested Fredo.

"Nope. I'm going to nix it. We'll have a com between us, but you guys inside are gonna have to be quiet. Can't risk it. This will be a fast-moving party, I'm guessing. We're here to get the introduction cemented so we can catch them at home. The Feds are going to make the arrest. We're here to help them build a case, and protect American citizens.

It made perfect sense to Jake. But since he didn't hear his name called, figured he'd be part of the second round of backup shooters, or relievers.

"No drones?" Ollie asked.

"Not at nighttime. Line of sight is compromised and with all the revelers, I just don't want to tip our hand."

This was the part of a new operation that was exciting. Jake knew every one of the SEALs felt like he did, and if they didn't feel that adrenaline and determination driving them to an effective outcome, that was the time to quit. Scanning the room, he saw faces of men who would lay down their lives for him. Everyone came with their own baggage. He'd been dosing and medicating himself with alcohol, and just now began to realize how much of it was unconscious. He needed to admit he was afraid sometimes. He worried sometimes, but rather than get a crutch, he'd use the crutch of their training, the abilities of men on both sides of him who would not give up.

No matter what.

Across the table his long necked beer with the lime stuck in it remained half consumed. It was his trophy. A symbol of him becoming a better man. A better husband, lover, father. A better son, even if his father wouldn't live long enough to see it in him.

And if he had the opportunity, he'd be kinder to the man who had helped create him. He'd give him a break. He'd do what he could to lift the man's spirits and perhaps help him repair his soul. Because he knew his dad had always been a warrior and was driven. But somehow he'd lost his way. Jake might be able to help lead him back. Ginger had given him that opportunity to be the father and husband he'd always wanted to be. She believed in him. Jake decided he needed to start bringing some of that to his dad.

Coop saw him staring down at the bottle, but his face showed no emotion.

"Everyone good? Speak up now if you have questions," said Kyle, finishing off his briefing.

Quietly, the group prepared. Backpacks were adjusted, loaded up with supplies for danger and for safety. Each man was responsible for carrying with him the tools of the trade. His favorite sidearm. His favorite clips and straps. Ammo, scopes, goggles. First aid kits were checked and replenished. Something for heat, something for pain. Something for staying awake. Maybe even something from home, if they dared.

He thought of his dad, lying in a hospital bed, and wondered what he'd think if he could see him right now, preparing for the unexpected, doing his job. Doing what he'd been birthed to do for people he'd never meet. Only because he was that guy who could do it.

Even with all the fears that made other people quit or run away.

I'm still here.

PT and training was always filled with music and bravado. Getting ready for a mission and doing that was like spiking the football before the goal was achieved. Some men listened to music or something inspirational. Others listened to a favorite song because that was their lucky routine. Jake just sat with his pack on his thighs, waiting for the group to move out. Some were prepared with funny-looking backpacks and Aloha shirts, canvas slip-ons and backwards-turned baseball caps, with a sidearm strapped some place hidden and quickly accessible. Others were wearing all black to blend into the night, carrying long gun duty bags, black backpacks or vests with custom pockets stuffed with their own tools. They'd be driving in two separate vans. One was for the tourists. One was for the security detail. Both were equally important.

Kyle approached. "How're you feeling, Jake?"

"I'm good."

"You need to check in before we go?"

"If there was news, they'd call me. No news is good news right now."

"So you know you have to go dark until we're done here. You okay with that?"

Jake looked his LPO in the eyes. Kyle was not always the fastest or strongest, but he would always go emotionally where none of the other guys would go every time. And that's what made him a leader. He never ran away.

"You mean, would I be okay if I learn that my father has died while I'm here and dark? That what you're asking?"

"Yup. That's it."

"My focus is on my job, Kyle. I'm not going to lie and say I'll not think about it, but I'm going to think about how good it will be to shake his hand again and give him a hug. That's what I'm going to be thinking about."

"You're a good man, Jake."

When Kyle walked away, Coop was on him. Kyle was giving the instructions to move out. Jake stood up, adjusted his pack over his shoulder and walked with Coop.

"I liked what you did over there," Coop said, pointing to the half empty bottle at the table. "So that's the battle you forge every day, man. You made the right choice today. Some days you won't. Today you did,

Jake."

Jake gripped his hand, and then the two walked away because nothing more had to be said.

The squad piled into the two vans and both took separate routes out of the driveway, one to the right, one to the left.

JAKE, COOP, ALEX and Jameson hiked up the forested ridge behind the pink complex. At night, the jungle-like foliage was teeming with bugs and reptiles, and small mammals frightened by their footsteps. The moon was full, so they didn't have to resort to any Night Vision gear. If the clouds kept coming and the moon was obscured, they'd need their enhancements.

But he was glad he'd brought extra repellant, because the biting bugs were all over the place and several fell down his back and pinched his flesh, but didn't hang on. He stopped trying to smash them after awhile and just dealt with it.

Coop motioned to the warehouse building on the right on a slight rise above the main house, where Alex was supposed to get set up. It would give them an unobstructed view of the approach to the front door, but not the door itself. They split up into two groups, each scaling the wall and then lying flat on the corrugated metal, being careful to stay quiet. Normally, Armando or Luke would be their lookout-shooter, but tonight Armando was bait and Luke had a little one expected any day so wasn't tapped for the trip. Alex was good, but everyone knew he was number three shooter, tied with Jameson. But he had more experience on the Teams, so it was his job tonight to be the sniper.

When Kyle wasn't present, Coop would take over leadership, unless he was tending to someone, since he was their number one medic. T.J. had become a very close second, and he was with their other group.

Alex was set up and in place in less than two minutes.

They observed Fredo's van pull up to the house and park where directed, down a small driveway offshoot to a secluded parking lot. The trio of Amigos looked like normal twenty-year-olds looking for a party with hot girls and plenty of recreational substances. Fredo had put extra pomade in his hair to slick it down, and unbuttoned his tropical shirt one button too many, exposing the gold chains he wore, along with a prominent cross that actually was something he wore that had belonged to his dad.

Armando was looking cool with his shades on even though it was dark. With his Hollywood good looks and shiny light grey silk shirt over jeans, he too had applied extra hair wax but was more discrete on the chest hair exposure. He walked with a smooth gait. Jake knew in the back of his pants, underneath the untucked shirt was a Glock, unlike Fredo, who liked to be strapped on the calf.

Jake didn't know where Danny was stashing his piece. With his proud Navajo features and his unusually tall height from his mother's Northern California tribe connections, he wore only a turquoise pendant and white tucked-in long sleeve button-down shirt like it was the only one he owned.

All three of them were dressed well, were greeted and checked over by a two-man security team outside the entrance, and were inside like they did this sort of thing every day.

Music echoed down the canyon and over the water. The view of twinkle lights from a handful of small craft anchored off shore was peaceful. The air was warm and there was a slight breeze, which helped with the insects. Now it was just hunker down and wait.

He heard Coop give Kyle the ready-in-place sign, and it was show-time.

"Jameson and Jake, you guys can take a rest if you want. I'll get you to spell Alex in an hour, okay?" Coop nodded to Jameson who nodded back.

Jake turned to his back and watched the stars. Smoky clouds with long tendrils of opaque covered the sky in patches, but in general the weather was mild and non-threatening. He thought about his dad, lying in the hospital bed and hoped, if he survived, perhaps he could start working with him to get a healthier lifestyle. Maybe take him to Coop's father-in-law, who was a shrink Kyle wanted him to see. As the unofficial Team headbanger, the guy was supposed to be pretty good with the SEALs. Might be good for his dad, he thought.

He warmly thought of Ginger, holding the whole fuckin' family together, relaying messages and having to deal with his exes. And the kids he'd brought into the world. The lady was a saint. Why the hell hadn't he seen that before?

But it was like what he'd learned from one of the old Team guys: *Circumstances don't make a person, they reveal a person.*

She was holding up better than he had any right to hope for. He was going to work hard not to let that coldness and fear grip him, that worry that she'd leave him because he had to keep so much inside. He was afraid of hurting her by telling her some of the things he'd seen. And done. Better to keep her soft and innocent. Better to have her believe in the goodness of mankind, to stay tender and not hardened. Only needed to have one warrior in the family.

But she was being one. He hoped the call with Karlene went okay. He'd left and dumped all that on her, not on purpose, of course, but just because he never really handled anything. He knew how to kill, to protect in times of conflict, to react, to train harder than anyone else he knew, and to fuck like there was no tomorrow. In her quiet way, she met all his intensity with a metal all her own. Her own weapons and tactics. Her own inner strength. She had the ethos.

She'd be the one, like that quote says, who would be the warrior who would bring them all home. He'd left his family in good hands. Of that he was sure. And he'd make sure he came home to help take that load off her as soon as he could.

He thought about the way her hand felt when she grabbed his as they crossed the street just four days ago. Like she was saying, "Jake, are you ready to be the man I married?" And just because she had extended that hand, she helped him to believe he could be that man. Now he'd have to make sure he could do it even if she doubted him again. Things were good now. They were in love again, but he knew, just as sure as he was breathing on top of some building in Mexico, a long way away from home and his family, that there would come a day when he would be tested.

And that's when he'd know for sure if he could do this, have it all again, or if he had to walk away.

CHAPTER 21

G INGER FELT A strong arm on her shoulder and looked up to see the kind face of the young Indian doctor gently peering down on her.

"I'm so sorry. Would you like to lie down?"

"No." She allowed him to help her up. Brushing the tears from her cheeks she wanted to tell him what she'd seen, but knew there was no way she would breathe a word of it until she could talk to Jake. "I have to find out where his wife is. Call everyone. I'm the only family here."

"I understand. But, if you need to rest up, things are simple now for us. Let us handle the relatives. Give yourself a few minutes."

She needed to call Adele, Gerud, everyone. And Jake. But she nodded as she allowed the nice young doctor to lead her to the chapel, which was mercifully empty. Yes, everything could wait just a few minutes. Give herself time to process it.

"I'll make sure you're not disturbed," the doctor said. "Take as much time as you like. Mr. Green's door will be closed and posted with a sign. You just come out when you're ready."

She gave him a big hug, nearly bringing back the tears she'd been shedding, holding on to him, the one person she could physically touch who cared anything about what was going on with her. But then the realization began to sink in. He was not Jake. He was just a kind stranger. She had to hold on a bit longer.

When the doctor left, she took a seat midway on the right. The simple room décor, with lighted stained glass window above an altar with a fresh lace runner on it, bearing a small brass cross, was calming. The signal was there. Life came. Life went away. One day onto the next. The finality of parting and death was staring her right in the face, in a serene and peaceful setting. Almost orderly.

Poor Burt wasn't surrounded by those who loved him. He was surrounded by those who used him. And perhaps that's what he'd done to them. But it still was a horrible way to die, and something she wished she'd never seen.

She took several deep breaths until the urge to cry left her. Her focus returned. Her mind started to tick off the things she had to do, one by one. She didn't want to forget anything, anyone.

And it began to make her feel better. She had a job to do. Time to focus on her role.

The hallway was still sparse. The family waiting room was now occupied with an older woman and her friend or sister, one consoling the other. Ginger walked past them to the elevator lobby, pointing to her phone as she caught the attention of the nurse's station.

First, she dialed Adele and got voicemail.

"Adele, I need to speak with you right away about Burt. It's urgent."

Then she called Gerud who picked up on the first ring.

"Anything new?" he asked. He sounded nasally, and tired.

"I'm sorry, Gerud, but your father has passed away."

The scream on the other end of the phone was full of pain as he shouted *No* several times.

"Is Mom there?" Gerud said through tears.

"Not yet. I've left her a message to call, but she does not know."

"I'll call her. I'll go by and get her. She shouldn't be driving. I will go pick her up."

"Just get here as soon as you can."

She called her friend, Karen, and they spoke briefly until she got the call she'd been expecting from Adele. "Karen, I'm going to have to go. I'll let you know."

Karen had offered to watch the girls if she needed it, which she appreciated.

"I'm in the parking lot, heading for the lobby. Is he—?"

"Yes, he passed away a few minutes ago, Adele."

"I'll be right there," she said and hung up.

Ginger called Karlene and left a message. And then she tried to reach Jake, but the phone went right into voicemail, as she'd expected.

"Jake, sweetheart. You dad is gone. I wanted to tell you in person, but just wanted you to know as soon as possible. Call me as soon as you can. I love you. So sorry, sweetheart."

She waited, heard the ping of the elevator doors, and met Adele in the lobby.

Adele gave her a stiff hug and then asked, "Was he alone?"

"No. The attorney was there with him."

"Bob Fellows?"

"Yes."

"Was he signing papers?"

"Yes. I think so. He told me Burt died before they could be completed and he'd give you a call."

She glanced down at her cell phone. "Did he say anything else?" Her forehead was lined with worry.

"No, he didn't."

"Do you want to see him now?" Ginger asked. She was surprised she had to ask, but understood grief did strange things to people.

"Yes. I should go do that."

She came dressed comfortably in a light blue pants set, her hair done, makeup on, wearing a colorful scarf that matched her shoes. Flawless and attractive. In contrast, Ginger felt dumpy and wrinkled, and suddenly very tired.

She stopped at the doorway with the no admittance sign. The doctor appeared, placing a hand on her shoulder and spoke to her gently. "He's at peace now, Mrs. Green. Nothing horrible to look at, so don't be afraid. He's just resting, while we await you and your family's instructions, okay?"

"Okay," she said meekly.

Since the doctor was with Adele, Ginger opted to wait outside. She'd already seen the time of his death once, and didn't need to be reminded of it. She wandered back down the hallway and dialed Christy Lansdowne.

"Oh, I'm so sorry, Ginger. Does Jake know?"

"No. He said they'd be out of communication, but I did leave him a message. I guess that's okay, right?"

"Oh, of course. These guys are tough. He'd want to know right away. Dealing with news is much easier than waiting and worrying about it. But I know he'll be missing his father though. Maybe Kyle can get him home sooner."

"I hope."

"So how are you, then?" she asked.

Ginger heard screaming on the other end of the phone.

"Hold it a minute."

Christy's scolding voice and the sounds of a little fanny getting spanked and someone else crying were normal sounds Ginger was actually grateful for. Oddly enough, it brightened her mood.

"I'm sorry. Brandon is just being a brat. Nothing to worry about, but he plays a little too rough sometimes."

"I understand. The girls adore him."

"He's quite the charmer. Organizes all these games and things. Gets the kids all participating in these big projects, acting out things. He has to run the show, of course."

"Of course."

"Yeah, wonder where he gets it, right?"

Ginger laughed. She gave a deep sigh. "Thanks, Christy. I needed to hear something I'm used to hearing. This is all so strange over here."

"Oh you poor dear. Well, don't worry about the kids. And I have to tell you, there are going to be tears at our house when we have to give that puppy back. What an adorable little things she is."

"She is, isn't she? Hope that hasn't been too much work."

"Nonsense!" She hesitated. "So, you need some company? We do that, you know. Want someone to come over and sit with you? Keep all Jake's relatives at bay so you can think?"

"Oh, that's nice. Actually, Jake's mom is the only one here right now. But maybe later. Just knowing the girls are doing okay is wonderful, Christy."

"You want to tell them, or?"

"Oh, God no. I should do that in person. And the last night with Burt, well, it was strange. He scared them, Christy."

"That's too bad. Hang in there. I better go. But you call me, and I'll get you whatever you want. And I can tell Kyle if he calls, right?"

"Of course."

"We'll get Jake to call you as soon as he can. Just don't worry about a thing until—until—oh, whatever, you know what I mean."

Ginger was eternally grateful for Christy's matter-of-fact attitude and honest advice. She was, as Jake had told her many times, the mama bear of the whole team.

CHAPTER 22

S OUNDS OF VEHICLES arriving woke Jake up. Coop was already looking at the new arrivals.

"Girls," he said in a disgusted mumble.

Alex had them in his sights. "They're young. Fuckin' children."

Jake removed his binoculars and focused them on the gravel approach to the front door. He saw three men carrying women over their shoulders,—women with their wrists and ankles bound with zip ties. Two of them were very small girls who appeared to be preteen at best. Their long hair was braided in tandem. They wore tennis shoes like they'd been taken right from a shopping mall somewhere. White gags were tied securely across their mouths.

The third girl was slightly older, and barefoot. Her gag had slipped down around her neck and one shoulder, and she began to scream. The noise echoed down along the hillside and rolled its way off into the distance. Dogs barked and a house on a lower street lit up all of a sudden.

The girl was nearly dropped to the ground by her handler, who was getting ready to kick her in the belly, but a fourth man ran up and stopped him. Together, they held her roughly on the concrete porch, a palm pressed against her mouth while she tried to wiggle, until one of the men slapped her across the face so hard it sounded like her cheek bone had fractured. They hurriedly untied the rag, and re-cinched it so tight the girl moaned in pain. Her pants were covered in caked blood, and her long dark curly hair spewed out everywhere. She was hoisted up over the handler's shoulder so rough they heard her grunt.

"Fuckin' looks like Mia," Coop whispered.

He was right, too. The girl did resemble Fredo's wife, Mia, who was also the younger sister of Armando. But this girl was a much younger version of her. Mia herself had been kidnapped by a San Diego gang several years ago, and when Armando tried to come to her rescue, he himself was captured. It forced several on the Team to go in and rescue them both. Those who had been in on the rescue mission were reliving it again right now as they watched these girls hauled into the house.

Introducing this girl to the party both Fredo and Armando were trying to infiltrate was going to put a wrinkle the size of the San Andreas fault right in the middle of the Team's mission. That meant Plan A was pretty much DOA, and Plan B was to be implemented immediately.

Jake checked the time. It was nearly twelve-thirty. He'd been asleep for over an hour.

"Fuckin' perverts," whispered Jameson.

Coop spoke to Kyle on the com. "Lannie, you getting this?"

Everyone heard the string of expletives in response. "No way they're gonna let that slide inside," Kyle finally announced.

They'd been prepared for the illegal substances and the weaponry. Excesses of party behavior was somewhat expected, but they'd not planned for the importation of forced child prostitutes. Jake knew that virgin girls stolen from the cities commanded a high price in some circles. It was the same all over the world and had been spreading, especially with displaced populations.

A loud roar from the house marked the entry of these new partygoers. Next thing Jake expected to hear was gunshots. But none came.

"So I'm thinking out loud here," Kyle began. "We don't storm it, we introduce a little bit of our own brand of surprise."

"You're thinking?"

"T.J. here is loaded up with some small loud and harmless stuff. I don't want him going in alone to pick a fight with Fredo. I can't spare a man here. So Jake, you're it. You and T.J. make your grand entrance and make all kinds of noise.

"Roger that." answered Jake. "On my way."

He slid down the backside of the storage building, which was on a rise above the main house, and quietly rendezvoused with T.J. At the corner of the house, Jake watched him remove a small flashbomb from his vest pocket, and strike the fuse, tossing it into the bushes on the other side of the driveway. With the music blaring inside, no one there could hear, but the two security guards readied their short-barreled automatics and began to investigate.

Jake and T.J. overcame them without either being able to scream or fire a shot. Their element of surprise was intact.

T.J. handled one of the weapons, balancing it on his palm and shaking his head. "We're better off without it."

He flicked on the safety and tossed it into the canyon. They quickly tied the guards' wrists and ankles, and secured their mouths with two wide patches of duct tape, and then rolled them into the brush out of eyesight.

Though they both had Kevlar plates in their vests, it was a risk going in without having scoped it out beforehand. They had to find their three Teammates quick, hopefully get the girls and then get out.

"Going in," T.J. said.

Instead of bursting through the door, T.J. just opened it slowly and walked in like he'd been invited and checked out. Jake had been right behind him. At first no one paid attention, since the girls were put up on the pool table where they attempted to huddle together, their eyes wide with fear. Parts of their clothing were being removed as the audience taunted them, laughed and enjoyed their reaction.

Jake saw Fredo and Armando in a dark corner and tapped T.J. "Right corner, ten degrees."

All four made eye contact. This time, T.J. hung back behind Jake, as if he was trying to sneak up on Fredo, buying them more time. Jake crossed over by making a large swing to the right, with Teammate in tow. He heard the whisper com report, "We're in."

Jake knew the others were drawing closer as he spoke to Fredo.

"Where's Danny?"

"Sent him to get the van," whispered Armando. He'd acknowledged their arrival, but his eyes burned with hatred for what he saw paraded and fondled on the pool table.

"Five minutes," Kyle whispered through the Invisio. Jake held up his fingers to indicate that to Fredo.

"I can feel a pain coming on," Fredo said. Jake turned and discovered Rodrigo Garcia and two of his goons headed straight for them.

That was T.J.'s cue. He gave Fredo a swift upper cut that Jake could tell he tried to couch, but landed a little too hard. Fredo was knocked backward and was out cold.

"Motherfucker," T.J. yelled at Fredo and spit on him.

Garcia aimed a pistol at the back of T.J.'s skull. "Wrong party, sport."

Jake didn't hesitate. He knocked the weapon out of Garcia's hand just as one of the goons landed a blow to his gut, sending him to his knees. Armando scrambled for the weapon that was scooting across the floor but he was soon tackled by two very quick partygoers.

Simultaneously, T.J. and Jake pulled out their sidearms and delivered lethal head taps to Garcia and both his lieutenants and then aimed toward at the crowd, which sent the innocents screaming to the corners but signaled the active shooters to get ready.

The music still played, but all movement stopped. Jake knew it was the quiet before the gun battle. He'd seen close combat shooting before in Iraq where nearly all innocents were killed. He saw the women and children lying in a heap of bloodied clothes, pictures plastered over the news that claimed the SEALs had conducted a massacre and had extracted revenge against the non-combatants. All B.S.

But this was one of those no-win situations. They only had a few seconds to make the right decision. He saw movement, a weapon, and he sent someone into the corner. A volley of return fire exploded, shots coming from behind him as he recognized Kyle and the rest of the Team had arrived. A dark figure rushed him on the left while he heard automatic fire next to the pool table on the right. One of the rounds hit the guy below, who then crashed into Jake as he was readying to aim. From his knees, he adjusted to the target. The girls screamed and one of them lost her balance, falling against the others. Jake had already taken aim and fired. He watched in horror as his shot hit the young woman instead.

He wouldn't look, but peripherally, he saw her fall to her knees, the other girls screaming, falling over into a huddle.

"Fuck!"

T.J. took out the asshole on his left. Armando had cleared the pack and aimed Garcia's pistol at the shooter near the pool table. Jake and T.J. backed up to the wall for protection when they heard the sound of a vehicle approaching the opened front door, and he hoped to God it was Danny.

Kyle and Lucas approached the girls as T.J. and Jake were joined by Coop, Alex and Jameson, holding the nasty looking crowd at bay. Weapons were dropped without a word being said. The girls were lifted off the table. Coop scooped up the injured girl, ran past them and carried her out first.

That's when Jake snuck a peek. She had a chest wound, on her left side, right where her heart was. She was not breathing.

CHAPTER 23

GINGER WAITED UNTIL the rest of the family arrived. She hadn't seen Jake's son with Karlene since he was a baby. He was the spitting image of his dad. The boy at only two, had a penetrating gaze, and she could see in his big brown eyes he'd be a heartbreaker just like his dad. He was smart, and observed everything, she noted.

She didn't agree that he should be brought, not only because it was very late for his age, but she didn't think it was necessary. Karlene wasn't paying attention to making sure there wasn't an accidental sighting of Burt's body on the hospital bed. She had her back turned, talking to Adele. So Ginger took advantage of keeping the boy occupied. She squat down to be at Aaron's eye level.

"So Aaron, you like preschool?"

"Yes." He had a plastic airplane clutched in his fingers.

"What do you like the best."

"Playing."

"Good for you. Playing is very important. You like to fly?"

"Yes!" He demonstrated with the plane.

"Where did you go flying?"

"To the moon!"

"To the moon? Wow. You're been somewhere I've never been. What else do you like to do?"

"I read."

Ginger was impressed. "That's great. You must be very smart."

"Yup, I am. I'm the smartest."

Ginger smiled and put her palm on his chubby cheek. "You hold on to that thought, Aaron. I'm sure you are a very, very, good little boy, too."

He crossed his arms over his chest. "What's your name?"

"I'm Ginger. You can remember that because I have orange hair."

He reached over to touch it.

"It looks like fire, doesn't it? But you won't get burned." She smiled and he poked a forefinger into her bangs and quickly withdrew his hand.

He leaned into her. "Is Bompa sleeping?" he whispered.

"Yes, sweetheart. He's going to be sleeping for a very long time."

"Do you know daddy has another baby now, who doesn't live with me?"

"Yes, that's little Samantha. She's very pretty. Have you seen her?"

"Nope."

"Do you remember Jennie and Jasmine?"

He crossed his arms to think.

"They have red hair, too, like mine. They are a little older than you are."

"I don't remember."

"Ah, well, they are your daddy's babies, too."

Aaron frowned and uncrossed his arms, and grabbed on of his mother's long legs, then poked his head around her and watched Ginger with one eye. She stood and waved at him.

She examined the little crowd of family, *her* family, by marriage, except she was divorced from the man she loved, and getting back together. But, she wasn't married. She had two children. She was looking at two ex-wives and two other children her husband had fathered. And Jake was gone.

She had witnessed some horrible family interactions, and suspected there was more going on she didn't know about.. Jake would have to spend time with everyone here, and that left less time for the two of them, which she immediately recognized as a selfish thought. He would be coming home from a deployment and he always needed his down time, but now he'd have to plunge himself into the family dynamics of his father's passing as well as deal with his own personal grief.

She wasn't really sure what the relationship was between Jake and his dad, but she knew it was practically non-existent when they were married. She watched Monica and Karlene, both beautiful, younger women, with long legs and of course gorgeous children. She heard Jake's name come up several times, but no one actively included her in any of their family talk. They had closed ranks. Ginger felt like an outsider.

It was a lot to take in. She wondered if she had the courage to face it all. She knew that it was worth it, but she was beginning to doubt her courage. Maybe sleep would help.

Ready to leave, she wove her way through the small group. Monica still didn't look at her. Karlene was vying for Adele's attention. But Ginger finally just interrupted the conversation and announced she was going to pick the girls up and go home.

"Adele, you let me know if you need anything now," she added.

"Thanks, Ginger. You've been a dear. We're all here, except Jake."

"I'm not sure when he'll be back, but I've left a message."

"Oh, so he knows?" Monica asked.

"Well, it's a message. I suspect he'll call you whenever he can," she addressed her comment to Adele, accepted a hug and kiss from her, and turned to go.

Gerud followed after. "Hey there, so you and Jake, huh?" They kept walking toward the elevators.

Ginger noted her stamina was waning. She'd been up for nearly twenty hours. She really needed to decompress. But she gave Gerud the time he was asking.

"We're just waiting to see where things take us. He's trying hard, Gerud. But now there is this with your dad, the family."

"Have him get in touch with me right away."

"I'm sure he will. You know they have to go dark. I might not talk to him for a couple of days. But I'll be sure to let him know."

"So, you happy with how Vegas turned out, then?"

Ginger stopped walking. She hadn't thought about that for days, always thinking she'd have time after Jake got back.

"To be honest with you, I wish I hadn't had any involvement in that. He was hurt, Gerud. I look at that whole thing as a mistake."

"Oh, so you're gonna blame me for that too?"

"No, of course not. But what exactly do you mean?"

"You gonna tell Jake?"

"You're not yourself, Gerud. He already knows about the suite. What's done is done. Leave it alone. I'm tired, exhausted. Go be with your family. They need you right now."

"You were always the smart one, Ginger."

"Listen, your brother is over there putting his life on the line. Your father's just died. Your mother needs some attention. You were the one who upset him so much and then he had his fatal heart attack. Where are your brains, Gerud? Get hold of yourself and stop making wild accusations and stories."

He righted himself and squinted. "So that's how you're gonna play the game. Blame me for dad's death?"

"I'm not playing any kind of game and I didn't say that. I wasn't there. It was you and Monica!" Ginger began to realize Gerud's world was collapsing.

"But you'll tell Jake that I killed our father."

"Stop this. This is insane!" She saw out of the corner of her eye that Monica was on her way down the hall, pushing that baby stroller like it was a *Clean Up On Aisle One*. Adele and Karlene were frowning. Karlene was holding Aaron in her arms as if for safety.

"You leave him alone and stop harassing him." Monica said as she inserted herself between she and Gerud. She inhaled, and Ginger knew she was going to get her best, something she'd probably wanted to do probably for days. "You know, this family is way better off when you're not around. Why don't you take your pissy little daughters and butt out of our lives?"

Adele came running down the hallway. "No! No! No! Monica, please stop. You don't understand. We need to come together." Ginger saw the anguish written all over Adele's face.

Monica appeared ready to punch her ex-mother-in-law. The baby woke up and began to cry. The two women began shouting back and forth, their voices echoing down the hallway.

Looking back toward the nurse's station Ginger saw one of them on the telephone. Karlene was on her cell, still holding Aaron. Gerud was trying to pry the two women apart. Adele reached for Monica's hair. For a few seconds, Ginger thought she might actually see her mother-in-law and her husband's whatever-she-was girlfriend/wife rolling down the hallway like they were at in a playground fight in grammar school.

Ginger stepped back against the wall, wishing to be anywhere but there, just as two security guards ran around the corner from the elevator and ordered everyone to be quiet. One took hold of Monica's arm and the other tried to grab Adele, but instead grabbed Gerud.

"All of you, outside! Lower your voices or we'll call the police and you'll be arrested!" The larger of the two guards was built tall and skinny, like a high school basketball player. His hat sat low over his eyebrows, too big for his head. The other one was stocky and nearly as wide as he was tall. Gerud towered over him.

Adele, Monica and Gerud were issued orders to exit down the elevator. Ginger stood back in shock, trying to collect herself. Just as they turned the corner, the taller guard hailed her. "That means you, too, Miss. We gotta clear the hall."

Karlene was the only one left behind, with little Aaron, who wanted to run after his grandma, wiggling in her arms, crying for her. He threw his plane down on the floor in anger.

Once in the elevator, Ginger stared at her feet. No one was talking. Monica was sniffling. Adele slid over and put her arm around Ginger's waist, but said nothing.

As soon as the elevator doors opened, everyone scattered to their cars. At first, Ginger couldn't remember where she'd parked. So much had happened in the last day, just being out of the confined space of the hospital made her feel like she was escaping from jail. She used her alarm on her car's key and as soon as it went off, was able to walk straight to her vehicle.

She watched several other two cars leave the parking lot, and realized she'd finally been left alone. In the privacy of her own space, she folded her hands over the top of the steering wheel, and cried.

CHAPTER 24

JAMESON DROVE THE van while Kyle got directions, linking in to an excellent trauma center. Jake, Lucas and Alex gathered the bags and equipment in one area, stacking them to make room for passengers and their patient. Armando cracked open the window in the back, looking for signs of anyone who might have followed them, his H&K at the ready. T.J. and Coop were working on the girl, but were somber, and Jake couldn't see her chest move and her color was turning ashen. The other two girls were wrapped together under a blanket Fredo placed around them, and out of eyesight of the third girl.

The second van was close by, so Kyle ordered Armando and Fredo to stay with the girls, to obtain as much information as possible about their kidnapping. Coop and T.J. were ordered to stay working on the injured girl, and everyone else to leave. He handed the keys to the second van to Jameson.

"You get these guys home and stay put." He gave Jake a hard stare. "You okay?"

Jake looked at his boots.

"It happens, kid. Glad it wasn't you that got it."

Jake shrugged. "I'm good. Just what we do." He was glad his voice didn't show signs of the shaking going on inside his ribcage. His lips felt cold, and his fingers were stiff and numb. He tucked them under his jacket to keep them warm.

"And those fuckin' girls shouldn't have been anywhere near that place," whispered T.J. over his shoulder.

"Boy, would I like to get those assholes. The whole operation," said Alex.

Everyone agreed.

Kyle continued with his instructions. "No calls in or out. Stay put until either I call or we get back, understood?" he said looking at the crew just before they stopped. "You hang together. No TV, either. Get some rest if you can. Get cleaned up, shower. We might be taking off soon, so make the most of your time."

Jake, Alex and Lucas concentrated on transferring bags and equipment to the other van, since it was important no weapons be found on the SEALs with the girls.

He heard Fredo whisper to Kyle, "They don't want to go to the police. They want to go to the local padre at the catholic school. Can we do that?"

"I'd say take them where they feel safe. They probably know better than us assholes." He assisted in the last transfer. "Okay, we'll be back as soon as we can."

Everyone nodded and climbed into the van. Jake was in the second seat, behind Jameson. Kyle walked up to the window and hit his open palm on the glass. Jake returned it with his own on the other side of the glass, and then they both gave the thumb's up.

Both vans sped off, Jameson trying to keep up with Kyle in the first one, but they finally got away, speeding to get to the center. Jake had a bad feeling about that outcome.

No one said a word on the way to their lodge. Tay and Ollie greeted them and learned about the evening for the first time.

"Fuck," whispered Ollie. "You okay, Jake?"

"Other than the fact I have poop in my pants, yes." He was kidding, of course, but trying to stay light. He didn't want to descend into that dark pit of a place he felt was sucking him in.

"Good thing it was remote, or you'd be in jail," Ollie added.

"Where did they take her?" Tay asked.

"Kyle got hooked up with some world-class trauma center," said Jameson.

Everything was unloaded, wiped down, re-stored back in their cases carefully before anyone got into the shower. Inventory was taken of remaining ammo, equipment counted to discover anything missing. Nothing was.

"I should have gone with them," said Tay. "Maybe I'll take the van."

"No, man," objected Danny. "Kyle said we stay put. Don't answer anything until Kyle calls us, no TV, we stay right here until they get back. And to be ready in case we leave right after that."

"So what was the scene like?" Lucas asked Danny as Jameson headed for the shower.

"These guys were players. Never seen so much jewelry and flashy bling. Drugs. More girls than guys. They had a small group meeting going on we were just about to be introduced to when the girls were brought in."

"So they were from town?" asked Ollie.

"That's right. It's a girls boarding school. They had no chance and no security. The two girls were students. Probably about thirteen years old. Fuckin' perverts." Danny pulled out several beers from their refrigerator and placed them on the table in front of the group. "The one who got shot was their teacher."

Jake sat by himself on the couch and stared at the floor, feeling worse than ever. Alex offered him a bottle. He grabbed it, taking a swig before he remembered he was going to have to do this solo. And fuck, he didn't want to. His father was dying, the girl was dying, and all he could think about was having a beer. He knew the most important thing for him to do in the next twenty-four hours was not to drink. Stay sober, and keep his shit together.

He handed the beer back to Alex. "I do that again, you can punch my lights out, Alex."

Nobody gave him any guff.

The unspoken rule is no one would bring up the shooting unless Jake brought it up. Up to the man to determine if it needed to be talked about. Oh, he'd talk about it with the shrink, and with Kyle and others. But the Team didn't go digging where they weren't invited. It was as bad as dating someone's wife, or daughter or sister without permission given.

He wanted to check for messages on his phone, but he had promised not to. He focused on his breathing. As the others were done with their showers, it was Jake's turn.

Under the warm water he cried for the first time as a SEAL. It wasn't fair that she'd been shot. He'd killed a lot of bad guys. He'd probably injured civilians that had been used as shields or gotten caught in the crossfire. In some cases, those were people who knew the risks and were willing to die for it. Some were just innocent people held hostage by evil men.

But the SEALs were sent in, to break the mission, to save these girls when it was determined saving innocent lives took precedent over the overall mission. Jake was supposed to be the one to be counted on to protect her.

Instead he'd killed her, or nearly killed her. He couldn't be trusted.

The water felt good. He couldn't hear a thing, and couldn't feel the tears, either. Under the gurgle of the steamy water, he let his angst and worry and self-loathing melt away.

It was no more than a few seconds before the water got stone cold and Jake jumped out, toweled off and put on fresh boxers and a tee shirt. Alex was listening to music on his iPod. Jake's bedroom he shared with Lucas, but Lucas was already sawing logs and making the windows rattle, so Jake figured he'd retire to the couch. He was also glad Alex was staying up a bit to keep him company. Danny and Jameson were in a quad room they shared with several of the others. Tay and Ollie retired to their room, while Coop and Kyle had their own place next door.

"You suppose they'll send us home tonight, or do you figure tomorrow?" asked Alex. Jake knew he was just shooting the breeze.

"I'd like to get out of Dodge. From some of my trips down here, you get involved in a shooting, you don't want to get the authorities involved."

"Roger that."

"Man, I wanted that beer tonight. But I can't do it anymore."

"I'm not six-foot-six, either."

Jake chuckled. It was as simple as that. He was allergic to his pastime. Probably his dad was as well.

Sure sign of battle fatigue was when he started wondering what his bank account balance was, and if he'd remembered to lock the apartment door behind him. He wondered if he'd remembered to pay the PG&E at the apartment and if he'd forgotten to mail his truck payment.

And then he thought of Ginger. Just like in the shower, thinking about her brought tears to his eyes.

Alex had dozed off, his music still on. Jake watched him through watery eyes. She was all alone dealing with his dad and mom, who could be a real handful, especially if they were arguing, and they had been doing that a lot. He was glad his girls were over at Kyle and Christy's and not with her at the hospital, waiting, nowhere to play and be loud.

He hoped she was holding up okay. Would she change her mind about re-marrying him if the family was too weird?

Lights in the driveway signaled Kyle and the rest of the Team were back. Alex came to attention and shut off his device. Coop crossed the room as soon as he saw Jake, the front of his shirt bloody, blood on his hands all the way up to his elbows, where he'd rolled his sleeves up. He knelt in front of Jake.

"We lost her, kid. I'm sorry," Coop patted him on the knee. "She was dead when we brought her in."

Jake held his breath.

Kyle stood behind Coop. "Nothing you could have done, Jake. Your reflexes were good. Lots of moving parts going on in that house tonight. We're lucky none of us got shot the way everything was going."

Jake looked up at both of them. "Did the girls get back to their school?"

"Yup, we escorted them, and told them about the other one, the teacher," answered Kyle. "We're being picked up at oh-eight-hundred, tomorrow, flown back to the island and immediately back to Coronado.

We can't break Mexican air space unless it's an emergency, and they have to get permission in the morning. But we're leaving. So, get your rest. Coop, you get in there and then burn those clothes."

Coop leaned over and tapped Jake on the shoulder. "Tough break, but you're tougher, Jake. Now let's get out of this hell hole, okay? We don't forget, we just put it past us. That sound right with you?"

Jake nodded. It wasn't about eliminating the memory. It was just tucking it to the side of his mind so it wasn't the first thing he thought about when he opened his eyes and the last thing he saw at night.

"Everything's packed and stowed. We're all set here," said Jake.

"Good," said Kyle.

"Can I call home to find out about my Dad?"

"Not yet. And that's not coming from me. They're already looking for you, Jake. We don't want to give them any way for them to track you. We get to the island, you call then. Nothing you could do anyway."

It was true. Finding out about his dad wouldn't change anything. But what he needed more than anything else was to talk to Ginger.

He watched everyone leave the room and knew they'd all have to take cold showers, thanks to him. Another fuck-up.

He lay down on the couch, using his jacket as a blanket and prayed he could get to sleep quickly. He wanted to count angels. All he could see were three red-headed angels, two little ones and one who looked just like Ginger.

CHAPTER 25

CHRISTY WAS WAITING for Ginger when she arrived. She found herself running up the steps to her warm arms and bursting into tears.

"Oh, sweetie. I'm so sorry all this is happening. Come on inside. Let's have a cup of tea, or do you just want to get home?

"It's so late. I really should get home. I do have to work tomorrow."

"Don't be silly," Christy said as she put her arm around Ginger's shoulder. "They have to understand you're trying to manage all this with your husband gone. So much falls to your shoulders now."

"But I feel like I've already taken so much time off. The trip to Vegas, was a couple of days—"

"An investment in your long term future health, Ginger," Christy argued. "Come, lets have a little tea, or would you like some hot chocolate?"

"Tea sounds great."

Ginger looked around the house for signs of destruction, but found none. The toys had been neatly put away in bins. The Lansdowne's dining room was a playroom for the kids, since the house was so small.

"Everyone's racked out. That puppy insisted on sleeping with your girls. I put Brandon in bed with his sister."

"Hope they were good."

"Brandon is the handful. Big instigator of things. Anything that goes wrong, he's right in the middle of it. Your girls were easy as pie to take care of. So sweet. Maggie adores them."

"Thanks. And the dog was a hit?"

"Oh. My. Gosh. Kyle doesn't know it yet, but I think we're going to have to get one."

She brought two mugs to the kitchen table and offered Ginger a chair.

"So tell me how it went."

Ginger wanted to unburden herself about the papers the attorney had Burt sign, but was going to hold to her own resolution and keep it quiet until she had a chance to speak with Jake.

"Where do I begin?" She took a sip of tea. "Mr. Green has never been especially close to his family, working all the time. Driven, I could say driven. He and Adele have a curious relationship."

"Curious?"

"He is or was a womanizer and drank heavily. It seems more so now than before when we were married. I get the impression things are not going very well at the Green & Green offices."

"You know, rumor on the street is that they're going out of business soon. Lost a lot of their good agents. My broker has picked up quite a few from them. They did better when Adele was selling, I hear." Christy was also a realtor in San Diego, but was now working more part time to be with the kids.

"Gerud works there, Jake's brother."

"Oh, I didn't know he had one. Don't think I've ever done a deal with him. Has he been a help?"

"Kind of the opposite. It's hard to explain, really. He kind of sought me out after Jake left Monica. He knew I regretted the divorce in the first place. I don't know, I considered him a friend, but—" Ginger could find no path to the discussion she wanted to have. "Let's just say it's complicated."

"No kidding. I'm sure Jake will appreciate all you've done when he gets home."

"I hope so."

"I think you're going to be very good for Jake. He needs someone like you, someone level-headed, to ground him. I'm not supposed to express opinions, but I'm going to anyway. I never liked those other two, and I could never figure it out. I could tell they'd never fit into the community, the lifestyle. It's hard on women. They think they can, but in the long run, drives some of them bananas. They run the household and make all the decisions, and then the King comes home and all of a sudden he's running things. You saw that, right?"

"Yes, I did. That wasn't the hard part. Jake just never talked about things."

"He can't, Ginger. Not allowed to, and probably wants to keep it from you. I know Kyle has done things he never wants me or anybody to know about. Has seen things he doesn't want anyone to know about. I honestly think if he did tell me about all that stuff, it would be worse for us, not better. I sort of have to trust him with all those secrets."

"Yes. That's what happened with us before. And when Jake felt I didn't trust him anymore, that's when it was over. He didn't wander back and forth at my doorway, he was just gone and never looked back."

"And now you have a second chance."

"Yes." Ginger felt her cheeks flush. "I feel like a newlywed."

Christy threw back her head and laughed, fanning herself. "Whoo! Now you're giving me dirty thoughts! What I wouldn't give to feel like that again. I can't complain, though. Kyle tries really hard. Can't do anything if only one person is pulling their weight. Has to come from both sides."

"I agree. I think we're there, but just beginning."

Christy gave her a big hug.

"Listen, I have a great idea. Why don't you stay here tonight?"

"No, I couldn't possibly."

"Yes, you can. You can sleep with me in the master. The girls would be thrilled to wake up and find you here. I can lend you some clothes, if you need it. Seriously, Ginger. You've spent your whole day being with people who probably weren't a whole lot of fun and not on their best behavior. Spend a morning with us, the kids, here. And tell your boss to shove it if he doesn't let you."

"Seriously?"

"Absolutely. I'll take Brandon to school, but the girls can play. I'll keep Maggie out of preschool if you want to. The three of them would have a ball with that puppy."

"They need their friends too, but I think it would be fun for them for just the day. I'm not sure I'm going to resume Adele taking care of them after school anymore. I don't know. There are so many things up in the air. I want to wait to see what happens with Jake."

"Of course. Now. No more decisions or too much thinking. Go have a nice hot shower, or do you want a bath?"

"Shower would be great."

"I'll get you some pajamas, and we'll head for bed. Tomorrow, hopefully, we'll still be all together and maybe we'll hear from the men. How does that sound?"

"Sounds lovely."

"Good. Now the master bath is down that way." She pointed to the left. "I'll leave your pajamas in the bathroom for you."

"Great."

Ginger hugged this nice woman, the Mama Bear of SEAL Team 3. She was every bit the rock Jake had told her she was, and that hadn't changed since the first time she met her. She was smart, compassionate, and not afraid to speak her mind. Her part time work supplemented Kyle's salary. She was every bit the leader and resource for the Team wives and girlfriends as Kyle was the leader for his squad.

The shower felt wonderful. Christy left the folded pajamas on the counter for her. Ginger looked in the mirror at her face and swore she had more lines than she'd ever had before. Her right eye was slightly bloodshot as well. It was clear. She needed rest.

Christy was getting ready to climb into bed.

"I'm just going to check on the girls, if you don't mind."

"Sure, mind if I peek?"

"No problem."

The two women tiptoed to the first bedroom, where Brandon and his sister were sleeping hard. Brandon had rolled himself up in the comforter and it left Maggie with just a sheet. Christy added another throw to Maggie's side, and they quietly left the room.

The second bedroom was Brandon's room. The two girls were snuggled together with the puppy sprawled between them. The dog scrambled to the end of the bed and greeted Ginger without barking. She picked her up and whispered to her.

"She's so cute," Christy whispered, scratching her fluffy head. "I'm going to be in serious withdrawal when you go home, sweetie."

Out of the darkness, they heard Jennie's voice. "Mama? Are you back?"

"Yes, sweetheart." Ginger handed the puppy to Christy. "I'm right here." She bent over and gave her a kiss. Then Jasmine woke up and wrapped her arms around her neck.

"Can you sleep with us?"

"Well, no. This is a single bed. Too small for three people. I'm going to be just down the hallway with Christy. Not far."

They said their good nights, and placed the puppy between the two girls. Christy and Ginger tip-toed down the hallway to the master. As soon as Ginger got situated, she heard the door open.

"Mama, can I sleep with you?" Jennie's little voice rang out.

"Go ahead," whispered Christy.

"Come on in."

Jennie climbed into bed, and Ginger wrapped her arms around her. A few seconds later, she heard another voice. "Mama, I'm scared all by myself. Can I come in?"

Christy giggled. "Oh heck. You guys take the big bed, and I'll sleep in Brandon's room with the puppy, unless—"

This time Fiona Chelsea sat, looking at the tall bed she couldn't jump up on, and barked. Christy put her with Ginger and the girls, and then left the room, closing the door.

Ginger lay on her back, one girl on each side of her. She couldn't see the ceiling, but she imagined stars and wondered if Jake was seeing the same stars in the sky. Her heart was healing, and having her girls close to her was a big part of what felt so normal and right. Christy had been right about that. But another big piece of her heart was down in Mexico, and she hoped he was out of harm's way and would come home to her soon.

Love you, Jake. I need you to come back to me, safe, and I'll do all the rest. Just come home to me.

The puppy circled, looking for the right place to land, until she dropped to the bed, centered between Ginger's outstretched legs.

CHAPTER 26

A T THE BASE on Puerto Cortes, their leased plane landed, greeted by Mexican authorities, waiting for them to deplane. Kyle's attention piqued when he noted a C-212 Aviocar parked near their Naval military transport, which thankfully had arrived ahead of them. The Mexican military used the 212s for transporting small bands of troops. Two crewmen from the transport were on their way, jogging to meet the greeting party, but the plane was still running and the pilots in place. Jake knew they intended to leave as soon as the clearance was given.

Jake and Kyle shared a look without either saying anything.

"You guys wait here while I find out what's going on. Didn't expect this welcome committee."

Kyle motioned to Armando to accompany him, and the two walked down the gangway. Jake and several others kept in the shadows on board, but had a perfect view of everyone congregating below.

He watched Armando translate the introductions as the two American airmen without uniform arrived, taking their place in line with the Mexican officials.

Armando began translating, "It has come to our attention that members of your SEAL Team 3 murdered an innocent girl at a party at Baja Nuevo resort. There are many witnesses, and also several who were killed defending her honor." Armando's eye twitched as he translated that last sentence.

The airman interrupted and removed a letter from his notebook, which had the insignia of the CIA or some government agency on the outside.

"Excuse me, gentlemen, but I have a signed letter from Admiral Adam Wellesley, Commander of the Pacific Fleet. I think you should read this first."

He presented the letter to the Mexican General Cortez, who handed it over to his aide.

Armando whispered, "He's not happy with the letter. Says he thinks it's a hoax designed to embarrass the Mexican military." Armando continued as Cortez addressed the group in English, shoving his aide aside.

"You will wait one minute here. No one leaves. Not you," he pointed to the American flight crew, and certainly not you." He pointed to Kyle. He turned on his heels, formally, and disappeared into the airport offices.

Kyle shook the hands of the two American crew. Jake couldn't hear what they exchanged.

"Well, you got an Admiral at your back, at least, Jake," whispered T.J. as he slapped his shoulder. Thank God they got here first or they'd not be given permission to land."

"Yeah, how does it feel to be so wanted?" Fredo sneered at him.

Coop whispered, "Too bad we couldn't make a run for it. But that would cost us everything, maybe even our lives."

"Roger that. No. We don't do that. We got an Admiral working for us. If need be, I think we stay right here until we get further word." T.J. looked up at the Mexican pilot who had come back to overhear the conversation.

"I have to return the plane. You must all go. Go now!"

"Hold on, buddy, we're not going anywhere," said T.J. "You wanna call someone, go right ahead, but we're staying aboard this bird until we get our orders."

"No, I cannot stay here. I do not want to get involved." Jake could see the pilot was terrified.

Kyle looked up the gangway. "We got a problem up there?"

"It's the pilot. He wants to leave."

"Well, he can leave as soon as we are allowed to board that plane." He nodded to the airmen. "Keep those engines running. And you better call the Admiral."

Kyle made a call as well.

Jake asked Coop. "Can I make one? Can I find out about my dad?"

"Shoot, Jake, I sure hope so. Wait a minute and let me find out." He leaned into the doorway, "Kyle?"

Their LPO interrupted his phone call. "Jake needs to call about his dad. Can you grant permission?"

"Tell him go ahead. In fact, everyone get on the phone and call home. I'm on the line with our liaison now. You get everyone to start calling the Spec Ops Center, and someone call Congressman Denkins. Somebody got his number?"

"Okay, Jake. You're cleared," Coop repeated. "And say what, Lannie?"

"I don't know. Tell them the Mexican government is holding a whole squad of Navy SEALs against their will."

While Jake was dialing, he could see several of the Mexican officials who spoke English nervously speaking amongst themselves. They all were peering at the little office shed, waiting for the General to bring them some news.

"Hey, I got KTLA on the line," said Alex. "Old girlfriend is the weather girl on the weekends there."

T.J. started to chuckle, "Holy motherfucker. I guess the shit's gonna hit the fan now." He shouted down to Kyle. "You're gonna be on the evening news, Lansdowne."

On the fourth ring, Ginger picked up.

"Hey baby, we're coming home. At least we think we are."

"Oh my God, Jake. So good to hear your voice!"

He heard cheering in the background. "You still at Christy's?"

"Sure am. I spent the night here."

Jake heard the voices of his daughters fighting over who got to talk to him. Ginger was trying to navigate getting away from them so she could talk.

"Hold on, honey. Listen, we got ourselves a situation here. You gotta tell Christy to get hold of someone over at SpecOps and to put the lady SEALs on it. We need some help getting released."

"What's going on?"

"Some General wants to hold us. We made a dirty exit. I can't give you the details, but nothing you hear is going to be right, so don't bother."

"Oh, Jake. Are they going to put you in jail? A Mexican jail?"

Jake looked around the plane at his friends. He was aware what kind of firepower they had on board, and he knew there was a skeleton crew on the defunct Mexican Naval Base, mostly deployed taking apart equipment and old planes and selling them for scrap. He knew if a fight broke out, unless reinforcements were sent in, it wouldn't end well for the locals.

"Not a snowball's chance in hell. Only question is, how's it going to go. So, you tell Christy to call Kyle, and let me talk to the girls, okay?"

"Okay. Miss you, sweetie."

"Same here. I'll feel a lot better when I get home. Get back on California soil."

"Girls, girls, who wants to talk to Daddy?" he could hear her say.

"Oh, Ginger, what about Dad? I almost forgot."

"Jake, I'm sorry. He had another heart attack."

He closed his eyes. Something in him knew it was so.

"Thanks."

"Hi, Daddy!" Jasmine's voice shrilled over the phone. The puppy was barking, and he could tell the girls were in a tussle over who was going to hold the phone.

"Hey, Jasmine. You share with Jennifer, okay? Daddy doesn't have a lot of time, so I want to talk to both of you."

They agreed. "Are you coming home now? Are you in America?"

"No, sweethearts. I'm still in Mexico, but I'll be home soon. Maybe tonight. Would you like that?"

"Yay!" came their voices. Someone dropped the phone. Jennifer was the first to come back on the line. "Daddy, Chelsea Fiona is getting big. And she's a girl."

"I should hope so, with a name like that," chuckled Jake.

He heard a whistle from outside, and T.J. gave the cut sign.

"Look, sweethearts, Daddy's got to go. You tell Mama I love her, okay. Gotta go."

He hated to disconnect, but there was a flurry of activity. He heard his name being called out.

T.J., the pilot and others moved out of the way to allow Jake to stand at the top of the gangway. He saw Kyle motion for him to join him on the tarmac.

"Jake, I'm afraid we need to see you, buddy."

Several of the guys patted him on the back with encouragement. He noticed the General was stoic. The decorum didn't look dangerous, but Jake reminded himself it only took one gun to kill someone. He still had his tucked into his waistband. T.J. put his palm there before he started down the steps, and whispered, "You sure?"

Jake hesitated, and T.J. took the Glock back.

"Wise choice." Jake heard as he made it down the ramp.

"General Cortez, this is Jake Green, Navy *SEAL* Jake Green. My entire squad attempted to rescue two children and their teacher last night. In the firefight, Jake is the one who accidentally shot Ms. Lopez, who was the girl's teacher. These girls were kidnapped from their boarding school, along with their teacher. Our Navy is prepared to issue a full report to your government within twenty-four hours, and if necessary, accompany Special Operator Green here back to Mexican soil to answer to any outstanding charges. But under no circumstances, and I have it on the highest Naval authority, are we to be detained any further on Mexican soil. These gentlemen," he pointed to the transport plane crew, "have been tasked by the Admiral of the Pacific Fleet to bring these boys home."

General Cortez gave Jake a dangerous look. "You shot that girl?"

"The man I was shooting at was behind her, sir. They had all the girls up on a pool table and were undressing them, sir. She ended up in the line of fire. It was an accident, sir." He was speaking louder than necessary, but part of it was to keep himself from shaking. He was also about to lose his stomach contents.

He did not flinch at Cortez' stare. He'd seen bad guys much worse than this guy—guys who lived their whole lives for one purpose only: to kill Americans. This man didn't have the taste for killing that Jake had confronted face to face.

The General flinched. He said something to his aide, who produced a cell phone and they took Jake's picture.

"Here, you wanna take another one, please?" said Kyle. He gripped Jake's shoulder and whispered, "Smile." The aide took a second picture of the both of them, smiling.

The aide asked for the correct spelling of Jake and Kyle's names, and then gave approval for them to go.

Jake nearly collapsed in Kyle's arms, which wouldn't have been a good thing.

"You okay, there, buddy?"

"I'm fine."

"Sure you are. How's your dad?"

"He's not so fine."

"Damn shame." Kyle looked up at him. "Then we go home and start to pick up the pieces, right?"

"Hell, yeah."

"Okay, everyone," Kyle shouted, "Get your shit and let's get back to California."

One by one they brought their equipment and ice chests full of ammo, plus a couple of fishing poles they'd brought just to enhance the cover, and loaded up the transport. Kyle waved to the pilot and handed him an envelope. He also gave the General an envelope, and saluted the man, who saluted back.

He ran after his team and was the last to climb aboard. Within seconds the big machine lurched forward. Kyle was still strapping in when he sighed and said, "I was thinking of taking Christy to Cabo for a nice long vacation this fall. I'm liking the Caribbean much better."

When they lifted off the ground every man cheered.

Even Jake was laughing and cheering his lungs out.

CHAPTER 27

CHRISTY AND GINGER watched as news reports showed Jake's picture as being the Navy SEAL detained by Mexican authorities for shooting an unarmed Mexican woman. Depending on the news media they watched, the story ranged from stories about how the SEALs were killers of women and children, to the fact that a secret mission to rescue innocent hostages used in a prostitution ring had been successful, even with one loss of life.

"Where do they get off telling these lies?" wondered Ginger.

"They make it all up. Whatever their audience wants, or so they think. But I imagine they're not exactly getting much cooperation out of the Navy, either. And no one will ever report what exactly happened."

"I don't think Jake will tell me." Ginger watched the girls taking turns chasing Brandon.

"Do yourself a favor, and don't ask. Just don't ask. Pretend they were on a fishing expedition and things happened. That's it."

Ginger had taken extra precaution to look good. Christy had lent her some clothes and makeup. They washed the girls' clothes so everyone looked their very best for the two daddies to come walking through the front door. That's the way Christy did it, she told Ginger. She always waited until Kyle was ready to walk through her front door, and then she knew he was back. Until then, he was still a SEAL, and he was still hunting the bad guys.

"When he crosses my threshold, his ass is mine, and he knows it,

Ginger. He belongs to me, and I get to do anything I want with him."

Ginger was more nervous than Christy was. Whatever Jake came home with, she'd deal with it. If he didn't want to talk, she'd remind him, just like Christy said. That seemed like the only plan that made sense.

At two o'clock the two Hummers pulled up. Christy and Ginger waited, with the kids dressed, pressed and clean, standing in front of them.

Kyle was the first one in, and Brandon did a flying leap into his arms. Little Maggie hugged his leg, but Kyle was headed over to Christy, and nothing was going to stop him.

Ginger stepped aside and watched as he and Christy got lost in themselves.

And then Jake was at the doorway. He had a four-day-old beard, but his eyes were clear. Jennie and Jasmine erupted into screams and ran to his side. He got to his knees and hugged each of them, one at a time. Both the girls were sobbing. Ginger's cheeks were glistening with tears as well.

Jake stood up, all six-foot something of him, with that almost bashful gait he had, the smirk on his lips, his eyebrows raised. He was nodding, and taking his sweet time to get over to her.

"Damn you, Jake, get over here!" she screamed. He did exactly that, picked her up and swung her around the room. Fiona Chelsea barked at the intruders, but Jake was undeterred. He put Ginger down, held her face between his hands and kissed her.

"I'm home, Ginger. I came home to you. Nobody but you."

His embrace nearly knocked the wind out of her. She tried her best to match his strength, knowing she'd fall short.

The tearful welcome lasted nearly an hour as the children told stories of what they'd been doing while their fathers were away. The time was given entirely over to them. Several times Ginger saw Christy smiling at her from across the room. She saw her negotiate with Kyle, holding the puppy up, trying to convince him to get one for their kids. Brandon didn't leave Kyle's side, but stayed connected however he could, looping his arm around his dad's, or hanging on to a pocket, or his leg.

At last it was time to go home. Ginger thanked Christy for her support, and for showing the way.

"You'll do it some day, Ginger. You'll see some little girl who hasn't got a clue what being married to a SEAL is all about, and you'll just take her under your wing, and you'll show her why she's in love with the best kind of guy in the world. Not perfect, but you're gonna tell her what a great choice she made. Especially when she doubts it."

"I will."

They said good-bye. Ginger followed behind Jake's truck. The girls wanted to ride with their dad.

She thought about everything that had gone on these past few days. How her life had changed since that evening in Las Vegas. How she'd had the courage to confront a mistake she'd made long ago in forcing Jake from their home by withholding her trust of him.

She put the girls to bed while Jake unloaded his Hummer and stowed his things in the closet of their master in a special compartment he'd built years ago and was still there.

He stripped off his shirt and left his tee shirt on, being called into the girls' room to say good night.

Ginger watched as he kissed each one and had a little thirty second prayer with both girls, very personal, out of earshot of anyone else. She'd forgotten that had been his routine at one time, and her heart swelled to see it had come back so easily.

It was agreed that the puppy would start out sleeping with Jennie. Ginger knew they'd be up most the night playing with the pup and making sure she was taken outside.

Jake pulled her backward and shut the girls' bedroom door. He led her to the master. "I need a shower, and I know just the right person to get me feeling clean and whole again."

"Your wish is my command." She slipped off her clothes and before stepping into the shower, Jake took her in his arms, and they stood together naked. "I meant what I said, Ginger. I came home for you."

"This is your home. It's always been your home. I was a fool."

"No, no. I was. And then I kept being a fool. I should have turned right back around and come back. I wanted to, honey. I thought about it every day. I was out there looking for you, and you were here the whole time."

"It's all about the future now, Jake."

In the warm spray of water, she found Jake to be tender, careful, and patient. Her fingers smoothed over his hard muscles, as the bubbles from the lemon wash floated tantalizingly over his hard body. Her most favorite part of Jake was the place right next to his heart, where she could hear him breathing, where he sometimes groaned his need for her. He was like a solid wall of man who would always be there for her.

But his big stubby fingers were tender. She loved how they smoothed over her skin, hands that had seen bloodshed and war, but hands that were caring and dedicated to saving innocents.

Their exploration and play became more intense. Jake turned off the water.

"Showtime!" he said as he threw a towel at her.

In bed, his fingers laced through her hair as he kissed his way from her neck down to between her legs and watched as his tongue on her nub made her jump.

His thighs lifted hers as he angled down on her, relentless in his pursuit to mount and consume her.

Tonight he would take the lead. Her body was ripe for him to take control of their lovemaking and show her his tender side. She'd learned in their early marriage this was a routine he favored when he got home from deployments. She'd give him the control tonight, and early in the morning she'd wake him up just so he knew how much she needed him. She wanted to surprise him, make it so he never wanted to leave her bed, or however long he wanted to make love, she belonged to him.

He grabbed her arms above her head and pushed deep inside her. Back and forth he softly stroked, needing and giving, wanting and taking. She arched as she got close to shattering, and he slowed, kissing her neck.

"You like that, baby?"

"I never want it to end."

"I'll do my best to make it last, sweetheart."

In the darkness, the shadow of his body looming over hers as he groaned, placing his hands beneath her rear and raising her up to accept him. His massive hands held her hips in place as he moved his hips back and forth, stretching and stroking everything inside that needed filling. She pressed her hands to his buttocks and squeezed and heard his muffled cry next to her ear.

The layer of sweat that covered his chest shone in the moonlight. Balancing on his hands he was looking down on her, waiting for her. "Take me, baby. Take me to the moon," he whispered and bent down to kiss her. "Come for me, sweetheart."

Her body erupted out of control. She arched first and then sank back into the bed as her internal muscles took hold, desperate to be devoured. He shuddered and held her still, so they both could feel the delicious coming together as he filled her.

Their lovemaking had always been beautiful, but tonight she was overcome, tears streaming down her face.

"Don't cry, baby," he whispered. "Everything's going to be okay. You'll see."

"God, I thought I'd lost you, Jake."

"Never, sweetheart. I'll always be here. Not going anywhere."

It wouldn't be easy, they had told her, but it would be worth it. It was a night she never wanted to end. And it was the start of a life together that would last forever.

JAKE 2

**Band of Bachelors
Book 4**

SHARON HAMILTON

CHAPTER 1

IT WAS AN exceptionally beautiful morning in San Diego. Bright fuschia bougainvillea vines covered the Spanish style First Presbyterian Church in the downtown Gas Light district. People filed into the weathered building wearing black. This was no wedding, but the funeral for Navy SEAL Jake Green's father. It was the church Jake and Ginger had been married in, the same place his parents had attended church, along with the rest of the country club crowd who were neither Jewish nor Catholic. Ginger had the girls dedicated there when they were old enough, but Jake was never a regular attendee.

The service had been paid for by Burt Green himself prior to his death. Jake's father had been on a roller coaster ride, with the recent "downs" outweighing the "ups" of both his personal and business lives. A prominent and respected broker in town, Green & Green was synonymous with old money and status, even though the company had fallen on hard times recently. Jake didn't think his father anticipated his heart attack and subsequent death, but he obviously wanted to ease a little of the firestorm that would be created in the aftermath. And so at least he planned his own funeral and didn't leave any room for anyone else's input, good or bad.

But the family had overruled Burt and urged Jake to speak, which was a noted departure from the order of service. Jake's mother, Adele, talked down her other son, Gerud, when he felt left out of the process. It was a foretelling of future events. Jake took his spot at the lectern, sucked in air and let the exhale calm his nerves. This was the last thing he wanted to do. Public speaking was not his strength. He'd much rather jump out of an airplane at midnight, land in a quiet cove and swim to shore silently with his Team buds from SEAL Team 3.

"My father and I had a very close relationship, made fonder the more we stayed apart."

Jake waited for the snickering to die down. There wasn't anyone there to object, and he doubted his father was anywhere at all, since his dad didn't believe in the afterlife.

The audience was peppered mostly with people he'd seen only a time or two. Others he knew by reputation or by his father's descriptions from the Country Club crowd. Burt Green had been a larger than life character on all fronts. He lived hard, he played hard, and he died hard, according to what Ginger had told him. But the hardest of all was the way his dad lost. That was never done with any kind of grace or decorum. It was as if old Satan himself pulled Burt down through the black ooze of a tar pit in the center of that one horrible investment in the Hawaiian Golf Course shopping mall that threatened a lifetime of good investments. He could nearly hear his father screaming under the bubbling goo and still blaming his other son, Gerud, for the mistake.

Jake glanced over at his father's casket just to make sure Burt wasn't really screaming obscenities. Then he made a mental note to get an appointment with Coop's father-in-law, the shrink, to discuss some of Jake's residual PTSD. He wanted a drink too so it was time for another meeting, and he really didn't want to go.

Several from his SEAL Team 3 were in the front seats to the side, which required some of the family to sit in the second row. Jake nodded to Coop, who gave him a lopsided smirk, as a thank you. He needed those guys right in front of him today, and he was glad Coop knew enough to make it so.

He gripped the lectern edges because people started coughing. He'd taken too long to give them sentence number two of the eulogy.

"I used to think he was the most fearless man on the planet. Nothing my dad couldn't handle, even if it didn't exactly turn out the way he'd intended."

There was another small rumble of titters. Were they making fun of his dear old dad?

"I think he cared about things very deeply. About people very deeply. But he worked very hard not to show it. His costume and his game face got stuck and after awhile, it was a permanent fixture to him. But one thing was for sure, he loved his grandkids probably most of all."

The front row burst into grins. It was filled with Jake's three exes and his children. Karlene kissed squirming, two-year-old Aaron on her lap as Monica gushed and then kissed her treasure, the sleeping baby Samantha in her arms. Those were his most recent exes. Karlene had been his wife for nearly a year but Monica he never married. He glanced at Ginger, his first wife and mother of his two oldest red-headed daughters, sitting together like three angels on a perch, next to his mother, Adele. Ginger was the one he never should have left. And now he was going to try to negotiate his way back to a more permanent station with her again.

So, although it would be easy to talk about his father's flaws, Jake knew he had even bigger ones. This was a reminder to him that life was short, and that he'd better work overtime to plug those holes while he had the strength to do so, before the whole boat sank.

He noted that his brother, Gerud, sat in the second row next to Belinda Matheson, the Green & Green receptionist and personal assistant to his father—rumored to be his dad's sometimes mistress. And next to her was an older woman who looked like she could be Belinda's older sister. While he watched, Gerud put his arm around sweet Belinda's shoulder, triggering a scowl on the attractive older woman's face.

"He'd be the first one to tell you he was a self-made man. I've seen first-hand the value of not quitting, and my father was certainly not one of those, even when it might be in his best interest. He wouldn't give up. He didn't give up on people, even those who irritated him endlessly. I don't think he ever forgave, and he certainly never forgot. It took a lot to impress him, and he liked people who didn't have to try very hard. Being genuine was a big thing to dad. And he didn't like pretending, except to keep someone from getting hurt. He lived with his mistakes and honored those who were loyal."

Jake's mother was in the half-state of shock and poised to defend her husband, thus protecting her own reputation, if Jake went too far. So she looked to be on the edge of an eruption of some kind. Jake smiled at her.

"Mother, you did an awesome job being his wife. It wasn't easy to do."

Adele Green was forced to smile, even though her right eye twitched and her jaw clinched. She shrugged as if to show anyone sitting behind her that it was all in a day's work, water off a duck's back, and a dozen other trite comparisons one might think up.

"You were a good team. The only one brave enough to be his partner."

The room was silent, a lot of people holding their breath. Jake knew there were secrets and pledges of keeping the secrets. Burt was adept at making alliances, stringing friendships and opportunities together to form a netting good enough to ensnare just about anyone. He'd been unfaithful to Jake's mother for years and just about everyone in the room knew it and would pretend they didn't have any idea about it.

Adele sucked in air, and for a moment, Jake thought perhaps she was going to shut down the whole affair.

"I guess if there's any takeaway here, it would be that none of us knows how long we have. Some of us seek danger as part of our job responsibilities."

He nodded to his front row comrades, and they almost imperceptibly returned the nod.

"Others take risks in the corporate or banking world. My father was not one to run away from those risks or the mistakes he made. He didn't make many. He didn't tolerate incompetence, but he didn't expect perfection because he was imperfect. He was sometimes too abrupt for a young boy, but one thing I can say is that he made me the man I am today. For that, I'm grateful."

Examining the sea of faces, he tried not to seek approval. And he saw none. He saw no judgment from his Teammates. But they stood with him. They were there for him.

His eyes finally fell upon Ginger, who looked stunning in black. Her red hair naturally made her whole face glow. He hoped the last thing he saw on this earth was her sweet smile transmitting all the love and passion he knew she bore for him. He'd been unfair, but unlike his father, he still had time to make total amends.

Forgive me, Ginger.

He said it to himself even though he'd said it to her many times in the last month, ever since their Las Vegas second honeymoon. And every time she'd forgiven him. He intended to spend the rest of his life being the man she thought he was.

His two girls grinned back at him, basking in the glow and certainty that their mother and their father loved each other. Again. And hopefully forever.

"I'm hoping that however you think of my father, you remember him as a fierce competitor who played at one hundred percent and enjoyed winning. It's really the thing he loved more than the people in his life. But I honestly think he did it *for* the people in his life."

Several heads nodded. Some dried their tears discretely with tissues. Adele did not cry one tear, her face still showing shock and dismay.

Jake turned to address his dad, lying too pink in the casket, with red lipstick he would have hated. His gray hair looked too stiff and filled with spray. He didn't appear to be sleeping. He looked like he wasn't there.

"Good-bye, Dad. You leave a big hole behind you and big shoes to fill. But none of us will ever forget you."

He couldn't say he loved him, because he really wasn't sure that's what he was feeling. Today, he didn't want to pretend, or lie about anything. Jake knew his father would understand, even if the crowd wouldn't.

THE RECEPTION THE Presbyterian Women threw reminded him of the wedding reception they'd done for his big day with Ginger. It had been without the lavish frills she so deserved. Ginger didn't have living parents, so Jake's family paid for everything. She'd insisted it be simple, so simple it was.

He was holding hands with his oldest daughter, Jasmine, who wouldn't leave his side. Ginger shook hands with several of Burt's friends, people she'd known from their early days of marriage. He noticed how well she was regarded. Their other daughter, Jennifer, was close beside her, soaking up all the praise and head pats from the fawning and adoring Club crowd.

His SEAL buddies gave him a wide berth, and maintained their little enclave near the alcohol. He knew exactly what was going on as they scanned the crowd for pretty girls. It was just a SEAL thing. Just something you did at weddings, funerals, or celebrations. It would always be the same.

Belinda and Gerud approached. Gerud was struggling, his eyes red and his chest heaving. Jake had noted a slight argument with Monica earlier as they'd left the church when she'd tried to give him a hug. Something in Gerud's demeanor told Jake all was not well with his brother. But Belinda Matheson brought him over and whatever it was, Gerud was dealing with it.

"Jake, I thought that was a beautiful message. I think your father would have loved it," Belinda said sweetly. "If there's anything I can do for you, please let me know."

Gerud opened his mouth, took a deep breath, and blurted out, "Jake, you did him proud. I couldn't have said it any better." His gaze darted to the side in nervousness and then finally landed on Jake's face. Jake held his attention for just a few seconds before Gerud looked away.

"You okay, man?" he asked as he placed a hand on Gerud's left shoulder.

"Sure. Just emotional. That's all. This was harder than I thought it would be. So final. I can't get out of my head I'll never see him again. I feel like he'll just walk back in here and laugh at all of us."

"Now that's a frightening picture, bro." Jake welcomed the chuckle he managed to elicit from his brother, which seemed to break the tension.

Belinda's ripple of laughter worked like glue, connecting all of them. She nudged Gerud. "Come on. Let's get something in your stomach." She took Gerud's arm and pulled him around and away.

He looked down at little Jasmine. "How are you holding up, Jaz?"

"I don't know all these people."

"That makes two of us." He tousled her hair and caught a glimpse of Ginger smiling at him across the room as she talked with an elderly couple. "I'd say we go out for pizza afterwards, just the four of us. And maybe some ice cream. You up for that kiddo?"

"Awesome, Daddy! I'm going to go tell Mom."

She ran to deliver the news to Ginger.

A very frail older man walked up to Jake, resting his weight on a cane, having difficulty with his gait. He held out his hand, which was shaking in an involuntary tremor.

"Jake, I'm not sure if you remember me. Last time I saw you was over twenty years ago."

Jake took the cool hand, more to steady the man. "I'm sorry, I don't remember, sir."

"I'm Rob Peterson. I used to work for your father way back then. I just wanted to pay my respects. Burt was a fair boss and I learned a lot working under him."

"Thank you for saying so. I appreciate you coming."

Peterson turned with difficulty and searched the room. "Your mother was such a help to him in those days. I used to tell her she was a better salesman than Burt was."

Jake chuckled at that. New information about his parents and a slice of life he'd never encountered before.

"I don't imagine he'd like hearing that."

"Oh, most definitely not. I never told him. I wanted to pay my respects, but I don't see her anywhere."

Peterson adjusted his stance carefully.

"I'm not well, so I'm afraid I can't stay, but you give her my regards, will you?"

"Sure. Rob Peterson?"

"That's right."

Jake watched him shuffle across the room and out the sunny glass doors where an attendant waited with a wheelchair. They departed from view.

Monica saddled up to him and didn't stop until her large breasts brushed against his upper arm. Samantha was grabbing for her mom's hair and then smiled as she noticed her daddy and raised her arms up to be held. Jake took her and bounced her up and down, which made the happy child giggle.

"Look at you, little princess. So pretty."

"She sure knows her daddy all right. No mistaking that smile. It's reserved only for you." Monica's big eyes and oversized lips attempted a major flirt in front of the whole group. All it did was make Jake uncomfortable.

The baby grabbed Jake's tie and tried to pull it into her drooling mouth.

"Whoa there, darlin'. That's not exactly on your menu." He pried her arm loose, turned the child around so she faced the room and just bounced her.

"So how've you been, Jake? You should stop by, now that you're home."

"I will, Monica. I'm doing fine."

"You staying with Mom?"

"No, I'm over at Ginger's. I'm sure you know we're getting back together."

"Yes, incredible as it is, Gerud told me. So you're gonna make the same mistake one more time?"

Jake knew the mistake had been leaving her in the first place. "I think this time I've learned my lesson. If she'll have me."

She responded to the baby's searching arms and pulled her to her ample chest. "Well, when that doesn't work out, my door is open. For now. But I wouldn't wait too long. We had some good times, Jake. Not exactly cheating if you're screwing your ex-wife now, is it?"

"Monica—"

"Whoa there! Jake! Where've you been hiding this lovely lady?"

Teammate Ollie Culbertson was holding a long-necked beer and knew it wasn't improper to give Monica the attention she wasn't getting from Jake. Two other Team guys stood by in case he needed assistance.

"And she makes pretty babies, too," said one of the waiting Team guys. "This one of yours?" he said as the baby stretched her arms to him. "Hey there, little angel."

The baby was coddled and bounced around amongst a handful of SEALs, which drew Monica to the group and left Jake alone.

Adele made her way over. Jake threw his arm around her shoulder and she leaned into his chest. "Ah, Jake, I can't believe he's gone. I spent so many years fighting with him, and now, I've just got this big empty house. Why don't you move on home, honey, and spend a few days with your dear old mom?"

Jake wanted to say yes, but he knew it wouldn't be good for either of them.

"I've already promised Ginger, Mom. But we'll come over and visit. The girls would love to swim. We'll make it a family thing."

"Very well." She detached from him. "I'm getting tired. I hope people start to leave."

"Mom, this is for them. A chance for them to pay their respects. Let's let them do this."

She tilted her head from side to side.

"Hey, there was a guy here who said to tell you hello. You used to work with him at Dad's office before you retired."

Adele's head flipped up quickly. "Who?"

"Said his name was Rob Peterson."

Her eyes widened. "Rob Peterson was here?"

"Yes, Mom. He said he was looking for you. But he asked me to tell you he stopped by."

She searched the crowd.

"He's gone, mom. Someone with a wheelchair took him just outside that door." He pointed to the glass doors that led to the parking lot.

Adele left him without saying a word and stood at the door, examining the parking lot. But she didn't go out. Standing with her face and hands pressed against the glass, Jake thought his mother looked like a little girl lost, poised somewhere between her past and her future.

CHAPTER 2

G INGER WAS LETTING Jake banter back and forth with the girls, who were taking turns with silly jokes from the second seat of the car. The funeral for Jake's dad went longer than she expected. Although Burt Green had selected the order of service and what would be read, Adele Green made insertions the reverend was loath to reject.

There were so many stories, personalities that clashed, friends, lovers and who knew what else. Burt had slept with many women, Jake had told her when they were first married. It left her with a warning sign that lodged itself in her gut and never went away. She blamed her distrust of Jake on his dad's history. It affected her so much that when she thought Jake been unfaithful to her, she had asked him to leave. It had been a difficult decision and a horrible mistake. But Jake hadn't fought it much, and before she could catch her breath, before logic and sense crept in, Karlene was there and already announcing her pregnancy and another wedding.

Jake had grown up a lot since those days. He didn't handle the relationship thing well at all. But he didn't mind fathering babies, and that wasn't something she knew before. He just didn't do the confrontation with his women very well, so he went along. The big tough SEAL could never say no to a woman.

And thank God, he couldn't say no to her again. This time, she intended to keep him forever at her side. She was grateful for her second chance and promised never to doubt him again.

So she took the attention the other two wives (well, one wife and one live-in that resulted in pregnancy) garnered with their offspring, and tried as best she could to accept them and the children and to make sure there wasn't a wall or barrier between her family and theirs. After all, Jake was a part of it. It didn't matter that his DNA was spread all over the world. She shuddered, wondering if that could really be true. Could Jake have fathered more children she didn't know about?

She took a deep breath and let it all out, watching the landscapes whoosh by as her former husband and their two daughters sang and joked and laughed. As the houses and trees, cars and dogs, people outside watering their brown lawns, kids playing at the school yard danced by the picture frame of her car window, she saw the streaming that was life all around her. And she felt blessed. It wasn't perfect, but it all was a blessing. Her problem was that there was so much life, it was nearly too much to handle.

Drop that thought. Be thankful for everything you've been given. Because in it came the gift of Jake returning to you. And that is worth every ounce of pain, worry and stress.

Jake gently touched her hand, and she discovered he was smiling at her. Those blue eyes, ingrained laugh lines at the top of his cheeks, bringing his promise of secrets and desires he couldn't hide.

"You okay, sweetheart?" he asked.

"I'm fine. Just tired."

"I think when you get home, we'll all go down for a nap. Then perhaps later we can go have pizza, and some ice cream. How about that?"

The girls, with ears that would hear those comments a mile away cheered. Jake was gaining big brownie points today.

She leaned back into the headrest and winked at him. "I'm game." And with that little signal, she let him know she was open for a nap with benefits.

He drew her knuckles to his lips and kissed her softly.

"Who was that woman sitting with Belinda?" she asked.

"I think it was her mother."

"I've never seen her before."

"Neither have I. Mom knew her, though. I think someone from the club, but I'm not sure." Ginger knew he wanted to say something more.

"Go ahead, out with it."

Jake chuckled. "Am I so transparent?"

"Totally." Ginger was happy that Jake's serious mood during the funeral was easing. She suspected he was relieved the whole ordeal was finished.

"Mom had a mystery man show up at the funeral."

"Mystery man?"

"Yup."

"Who was he?"

"Someone who used to work at the office when Mom was an agent there. He knew me when I was a boy. Seemed like a nice guy. He told me to tell her hello, and Mom freaked."

"Wow. Your family has more secrets than a spy novel."

"You can say that again. I suppose we'll learn more when we do the reading of the will next week. I want you there, Ginger."

"Of course I'll be there."

"The other—" he winced mid-sentence and Ginger saw he was still uncomfortable with her acceptance of his past relationships.

"Jake, I signed on for this. I knew full well what I was getting myself into this time. Just call them your wives. We don't have to keep bringing up the fact that Monica was never official. You made a baby. She was your wife. End of story."

She scanned the street, checking her insides, and discovered she really was okay with it.

"You're too good for me."

"Only if you cheat on me."

"I never did—"

"Would you stop it? The girls are in the back seat."

It had gotten very quiet back there, and their big ears had no doubt picked up everything.

"We're not going to hide anything, Jake. Best thing is to just be honest with them, with all of the kids and the wives. I am not a fan of labels." She delivered this without looking at him.

He took her fingers again and kissed them tenderly. "Except, sweet Ginger, you're mine. That's a label you'll wear for the rest of your life, honey."

Ginger couldn't wait to get home.

WITH THE PROMISE of ice cream and pizza for dinner, the girls went right to bed, shedding their dark dresses and patent leather shoes and sleeping in their long slips.

After settling them down and opening the windows, Ginger entered the master bedroom and found Jake naked on the bed, waiting for her.

"Now that's a picture I won't soon forget," she whispered as she closed the door.

"Come here, Ginger. Let me take that dress off you." His low sexy voice sent tingles down her spine. The whisper was meant for her ears only.

She sat on the edge of the bed, feeling the covers shift. Soon, his fingers were at the back of her neck, smoothing up and down the little twist she'd done with her hair. He removed her rhinestone wire clip, and her hair fell loose. His fingers slid over her scalp, sifting through her hair, pulling slightly, as he angled her head to one side and placed a kiss on her exposed neck.

"You have such a lovely neck. And the red hair drives me wild, Ginger. It always did." His lips touched her ear as he continued, "I feel so lucky you came back to me, sweetheart. I would have missed all this."

His fingers worked the zipper down slowly. He kissed each inch. The heat of his massive frame and the groans he tempted her with had her ears buzzing. A driving need inside her had her bonfires stoked.

With both hands, he slid the dress off her shoulders. He knelt at her back, unlatching her bra and looping the straps forward and down her arms. She let her dress and bra pool at her waist. Behind her, he pressed his chest against her back, his arms reaching around to tweak her nipples and fondle her flesh. She leaned back against him and turned to plant a sideways kiss on his cheek. He pulled her over, cradling her and then set her down on the bed as he pulled the rest of her clothes down her hips, taking her panties too.

She arched as his head was buried between her legs, heightening her passion. His expert tongue did all the right things, but she wanted him deep inside her now, so pulled under his arms and begged him to crawl on top of her. With the taste of her own arousal on his lips, he kissed her deeply and found his way inside.

Their bodies mated in tandem. Jake brought her to the brink of release and then slowed her down several times before their explosive finale. Sometime during that afternoon of lovemaking, she knew they were bonded and mated forever. As his blue eyes searched her face afterwards, his fingers wiping the sweat from her brow and his lips still feeding off hers, she felt the glow of new life and all the possibility that meant. Everything was starting all over again. The cycles of life had just expanded to include yet one more reason to never leave this man's protective arms.

She curled up under his chin and hugged him close, their legs still entangled, as he pulled the light peach sheet up over both their bodies and let her doze off into a deep, contented sleep.

CHAPTER 3

J AKE WAS INFORMED they'd be going on deployment in a week, back
to Baja Mexico, which was way sooner than any of the Team had
planned. They were to do a revisit of the Santiago gang—who, among
other things, were running guns from the US to Mexico for use in their
drug trade. But last deployment they discovered the gang was also
responsible for kidnapping young girls and selling them into the sex
slave business all over the world. By chance, Kyle's squad had stumbled
upon the three innocent girls, only able to rescue two of them. Jake had
accidentally shot their teacher in the gunfight that broke out during the
rescue.

But the main reason Jake was uncomfortable going back was the
fact that a certain General Cortez had nearly detained him due to the
shooting. He wasn't looking forward to meeting him again. They'd been
lucky the last time. The quick-thinking crew of their transport manu-
factured a letter on CIA stationery, forged the Director's signature, and
presented it as evidence the entire SEAL team was due home on an
emergency basis. By now, the Mexican authorities would know the
letter was a ruse. The General wasn't the type to take these sorts of
practical jokes very well. So he asked Kyle the obvious when he got the
call.

"You really think it's a good idea I should go back down there, LT? I
mean, my dad's just died. We have the will reading. Plus, I've got all
sorts of things to complete as executor. I'd be fine if you said I could
skip this one." Jake was hoping Kyle would agree with him.

"Already asked and answered," he said over the phone. "We're to show no fear in dealing with the authorities. Our liaison thinks they've been given the word to fully cooperate with us."

"In all fairness, Kyle, he's gonna be pissed he didn't grab me when he could. He might just do it out of spite, this time."

"Nope. You're part of the package. We're doing a show of force. Gonna work a joint operation to pick up these cretins, but let's assume they want the mission to go as planned so they can get some reward the US is offering. That's the carrot, Jake."

"I don't like it, sir."

"But you'll do it."

"Of course."

"When's the will reading?"

"Monday."

"Well, you're right. Timing sucks."

On Monday, the clan met at the office of Burt and Adele Green's attorney, Mr. Bob Fellows. The firm occupied the top two floors of the prestigious San Diego skyscraper shaped like a long grey-blue crystal.

Adele was about to take a seat next to Jake and Ginger, when Bob Fellows came over to her and whispered he'd like a private moment with her.

"No, Bob. Let's get this over with. Or is there some problem you're warning me about?"

She'd said it a little too loudly, so the private conversation was not going to be very discrete. Fellows sighed and rolled his eyes at Jake when his mother wasn't looking.

"What was that all about, Mom?"

"Oh, beats me. I suppose we'll find out shortly. I don't honestly know why we all have to sit here. Some firms just mail out the paper-work to people so they don't all have to cram in here." She turned and frowned. Jake followed her gaze.

Entering the office was Belinda Matheson with Gerud. Behind the couple was the older woman who had been at the funeral.

"Good Lord," she whispered under her breath and then stood up abruptly. "What the hell are you doing here?" She was speaking to Belinda, but for a second, Gerud thought she was talking to him and was shocked. She hadn't noticed the older woman behind them yet.

Everyone in the room examined the trio. Bob Fellows broke the silence.

"Come on in and take a seat. I invited them, Adele."

When he got a raw glare from Jake's mother, he ignored it and rubbed his hands together, ready to begin.

"First, I wanted to take a moment and let you know how all this works. As you will see, certain family members have been given responsibility to handle specific aspects of Mr. Green's estate."

Adele stiffened and blinked without expression.

"I would ask that you just hold your comments until after I've read everything. I also need to let you know Burt intended to write a letter to each of you individually, but he passed before he could complete this task. So if the words in this codicil seem rather cold and unfeeling, that's the way they're supposed to be. They were to be softened by his personal message to all of you, which with only one exception, was never written."

He cleared his throat and gave a nervous smile. He sat back behind his desk and took a drink of water and began reading over provisions of the will that Jake was sure were boilerplate legalese that bored him to tears. Until Fellows came to the part that read:

"I hereby appoint as my executor, my son, Jake Green. He shall have full power to dispose of all my sole separate property, the company known as Green & Green, and my half of the assets I now hold with my wife, Adele Green, as he sees fit."

Adele was on her feet. "What? When did he write this? This isn't anything we discussed."

"Please, Adele, have a seat and we'll go over everything when I'm finished."

Jake stood, wrapped his arm around his mother's waist, and brought her down to sitting position again.

Several items were listed separately, gifted to individual people as part of the will itself. Burt had an old car that he gifted to his grandson, Aaron, which brought the room down in laughter, since Aaron was only two years old. Karlene's face looked like an ugly smear. Several rental houses were listed, two that were left to Karlene and Monica. The rest would be sold off or held as the executor saw fit. All of the houses were heavily encumbered, as Jake recalled, so he wasn't sure there would be any benefit to keeping them. He was going to have to use Christy Lansdowne or someone in her office to give him an evaluation to help him figure out what to do with them.

Burt's half-interest in their main home fell to Adele as community property. But there was a cottage in Hawaii he'd bought and no one else knew about, which he gifted to Ginger. Jake found that curious. The proceeds of the sales of properties, minus the business debts, would be distributed amongst all the heirs.

Adele got out her Kleenex, bracing for round two.

"I hereby bequeath the home at 345 Belmont Court to Belinda Matheson, my daughter, and to Jill Matheson, her mother, in equal shares.

Jake could tell Adele was going to erupt in a murderous rage and was glad they'd not had that little nip before they left the house. It had taken some doing to talk her out of it, but Jake sensed this reading could leave some bombshells behind, and he'd been right.

Gerud discretely took his arm off Belinda's shoulder and clasped his hands between his legs on his lap. Jake also noticed he did a slight lean in the opposite direction, making a small space between himself and the woman he now knew was his half-sister. Belinda was whispering something to her mother. Apparently, this was a surprise to her as well.

Monica, Karlene and Ginger were all left modest savings accounts for benefit of the grandkids for college, or to be held in trust until they turned twenty-one.

But most remarkable was the statement why Gerud was not left anything at all. Jake's heart broke when he heard the news.

"Gerud has been treated like my son all his life. For reasons only his mother knows, I am leaving any remaining inheritance he would receive to his mother to distribute as she sees fit."

A gasp overtook the room. Bob Fellows stared directly at Adele as Gerud bolted out the door before Jake could stop him.

CHAPTER 4

A DELE INSISTED SHE have a private meeting with Bob Fellows, but Fellows requested Jake stay, since he was the executor of the estate. Everyone had cleared out of the room, except Ginger, and Jake told her he'd get his mother to give him a ride home, and not to wait up for him.

Adele said she felt light-headed. Fellows opened his liquor cabinet, but Jake discretely shook his head out of sight of his mother. She was brought a glass of mineral water and lime, another glass given to Jake.

Fellows sat on the edge of his desk, loosened his tie, and sighed.

"Adele, I am so sorry about all this. You can, of course, contest it. I could recommend you get other counsel, and perhaps the *not to sue* clause could be challenged."

"Bob, if I was going to sue someone, it would be you, you son-of-a-bitch! How could you call yourself a lawyer? You were supposed to represent both our interests."

"But, Adele, this doesn't affect anyone but Gerud."

"He made Jake executor? Where did that come from?"

"I don't know. He changed it a few days before his death. And it had something to do with some information I'm afraid I gave him. But first, let me ask you, didn't you anticipate something like this would happen?"

"No."

"Look. We all know Burt wasn't a good boy. Turns out, he fathered Belinda, and he wanted to provide for her and her mother. I didn't realize you didn't know this."

"Obviously not. That little slut. I should have known. He helped her sell her house when her husband left her. Oh, she cried her way right into Burt's bed. I should have seen it coming, but I was too busy working my tail off selling subdivisions while he was just chasing tail. Oh my God, have you looked at those chunky thighs and her plain features? The woman doesn't know how to curl her hair or apply decent makeup. She's a slob."

"Mom. This isn't helpful," said Jake.

She stood, arms straight down at her sides, made into fists. She stamped her foot and screamed, "It's just not fair!"

One of the secretaries opened Mr. Fellow's office door.

"Everything okay?"

"We're fine here, Claire. Nothing to worry about."

"Shall I stay to lock up?"

"No, that won't be necessary. I'll see you tomorrow, and thanks."

The secretary closed the door quietly behind her, and once again, the three were left alone.

"So, what did you tell my dad?" Jake asked.

Fellows stood, adjusted himself before sitting behind the desk again, leaned forward, and clasped his hands together with his forearms resting on the blotter. "About a week before Burt's heart attack, I got a visit from a colleague of mine who said he represented Rob Peterson."

Jake recognized the name from the older gentleman at the funeral.

"You remember him, don't you, Adele?"

She was fidgeting in her purse to find some Kleenex. Jake leaned across the desk and dropped the whole box in her lap. Adele was careful to dab under her eyes and at the sides of her face, pressing the tissue into her laugh lines that would have been prominent on a happier day.

"Of course I do." She blew her nose and wasn't very ladylike about it. "He worked for us."

"Well, Mr. Peterson believes he is Gerud's father, Adele." Fellows leaned back in his chair, which squeaked, making her jump. With his hands at the back of his head, he asked her, "Is he?"

"I was trying very hard to keep it our little secret. I wish he'd have kept his mouth shut. No one needed to know. I told him I'd deny it, but since this was done in such a public forum, I don't see how there's any way I can manage to keep my reputation."

"Mother, this is Gerud, your son, my brother, we're talking about. This isn't about you. Can you imagine how *he* feels? Are you that cold?"

She squinted at him, parts where she'd missed her running mascara making rivulets down the top of her cheeks. "Says the man who jumps into bed with anyone. You're a serial baby-making machine, Jake. Hardly one to talk."

"Well, at least I care about the people I hurt."

"And that excuses it? Really, Jake?"

"You should have told Gerud. You should have told Dad. Can't you imagine how he must have felt finding this out from old Bob here?" Jake was beginning to boil inside.

"Not like it was any secret your father and I weren't that close. Heck, we were not even very intimate until that last—" She placed her hand over her mouth, and tears overflowed. Broken and heaving forward, she barely got the words out, "I killed him with sex."

Jake nearly spit his water out all over Fellows' desk. He knew better than to look at Fellows, or they'd both embarrass themselves. Jake had always wondered why his father had been found on their bed, naked, when his mother insisted she was out at the pool and didn't hear him in time to call for quicker help. She'd been *with him* when he had the heart attack that eventually killed him. He shook his head in disbelief.

Jake finally had the courage to sneak a glance at the attorney. "So where do we go from here? Say we're not going to contest this. Gerud might. I can't imagine he'd put up with all this. I know for a fact he put up with a lot from my father for years and years. I had a lot more respect for Dad until today. I can't believe he'd be so cruel and heartless, even with this news."

Adele was mumbling in her chair, lost in her private thoughts. Her whole world had collapsed.

"Now I regret telling him," Fellows returned. "Didn't realize he had a heart condition. But, Jake, your dad had reason to think this would work out for your brother. You see, Mr. Peterson isn't well, as I'm sure you noticed at the funeral."

"You saw him?"

"I kept Adele away from him. That was a scene I didn't want you all to watch."

Jake was getting sicker by the minute. No wonder his father had been so angry. It was like the whole world had conspired against him. It was one thing to deal with the hand he created, but he was sure his father felt sucker-punched.

"Adele, Rob Peterson is dying, or so his attorney tells me. I have instructions to give you this letter. He'd like to see you one time before he passes over. I wouldn't wait too long."

Adele stared at the sealed envelope with both their names on the outside in a scrawl she appeared to recognize. "What about Gerud?"

"It's all in there, I'm told. Peterson would like to visit with his son as well. He'd like you to bring him. Mr. Peterson is a very wealthy man, and I could be wrong, but I believe he means to help you and your son, if you can see your way to visiting him again. You'd regret it, Adele, if you allowed your pride to get in the way. It might be the last chance Gerud would ever get to meet his biological father."

Jake thought the attorney had given very good advice. Now he understood why his dad was so angry. Someone else was going to be able to provide for Gerud in a manner he couldn't any longer.

It was just like his dad. He liked to win. This news probably made him feel like a loser, in more ways than one.

ON THE WAY home, Adele tried once more to twist Jake's arm about staying over at her place for a couple of days. She was laying the guilt trip heavy, being all alone in the big house, having just lost his father, and now all the work of the estate needing to be settled.

"I can't do it, Mom. I made a promise to Ginger and the girls. Not like I'm just home from college. I have a family. I wish you'd ask Karlene or Monica to come stay with you. Or Gerud."

"Would you do it?"

"I'm not taking sides here. But listen, it's really your place. And if you don't want to be left alone, come on over to our place. Our house is tiny, as you know, but you're welcome any time."

"Thanks, Jake. You've been a good son."

"I still am. You're not going anywhere, Mom."

"I know, but you just are able to manage everything. Going off to the Middle East, off to war, doing all your SEAL things. Your dad was sure proud of you."

"That's nice to hear."

"I know, he never told you, did he?"

Jake thought about that for a bit. "He was starting to change, Mom. Things were coming unraveled. You know what was going on?"

"Money problems. But he hid all that from me. When I left the office, that was it. I never heard anything else about it. He wanted to work with Gerud, but there wasn't the level of trust he had with you. A completely different relationship, almost as if he knew all along Gerud wasn't his son."

"*Did* he know?"

"I swear not. Even with all his playing around, I couldn't bring myself to tell him. And I thought Gerud would bear the brunt. As it was, he did anyway, so I guess I should have been honest with everyone."

"So tell me about Gerud's father?"

She gave him a nostalgic smile. "He was everything your father wasn't. He was attentive. I was starved for attention, and it caught me by surprise. We had a wonderful few weeks while your dad was off golfing in Scotland and traveling in Africa with some of his friends from the club. He was gone practically the whole summer. I was running the office then, working myself to the bone, and Rob was just, nice to be around. We were friends at first. Later, well, I think it was loneliness that got to us both."

Jake watched the traffic and thought about how his parents interacted in those days.

"When Burt came back, I found out right away I was pregnant with Gerud. I felt so guilty. I was so confused back then. He begged me to leave Burt, but I had you. What was I going to do, abandon you for this new life with Rob and a new baby? I had to end it. I knew there was no changing him. Burt was like Clinton, "one Bimbo eruption after another." But I still couldn't break away, so, Rob moved to LA and we occasionally saw each other, but by then, we were just friends."

"Didn't he want to meet Gerud?"

"Oh, he definitely did. That was my doing, though. I didn't want to put Gerud in the middle of my mistake. He wasn't the one to have to pay. It was my own fault."

"So you stopped being in touch."

"He always sent me a birthday card on Gerud's birthday every year. Burt never noticed. Always sent it a week early. Just a simple card, no note or anything. No news about him. No pictures. Just letting me know he hadn't forgotten. I never wrote him back or tried to contact him after Gerud started school."

Adele turned off the freeway, headed for Coronado. Jake couldn't wait to get home.

"It just doesn't seem natural for a man not to want to see his child." Jake could never imagine not being a part of his children's lives.

"Well, I'm going to fix that. I have to talk to Gerud first. And then, if he's agreeable, we'll go together on that road trip."

"Listen," Jake said as they pulled up to the bungalow where Ginger and the girls lived. "I'm deploying at the end of the week. Not quite sure how much of the estate stuff I can get done before I go. I'm going to need you to run some interference with the rest of the family. The girls will be impatient."

"You aren't going to sell my house out from under me, Jake. I won't let you do it."

"Of course not, Mom." He placed his hand on her shoulder. She remained clutching the steering wheel and looked at him warily. "I'd never do that. I have to find out what's going on with the business, and I'll only be able to start the process. The rest I'll have to do when I get back to California."

"When will you return?"

"We never know. Not more than a month, though. But you know that could change. I asked for permission to stand down for this deployment, but it wasn't granted. So I'm going."

"Where?"

"I can't tell you, but think about tamales and rice and beans."

"Mexico. Same place?"

"I can't tell you. And if you knew anything about it before, you have to forget."

"Well, you were on the news, KTLA for heaven's sake."

He didn't want to show his apprehension about the trip, so he told a little white lie. "That was all disinformation, Mom. It was all made up as a cover."

She seemed to accept it, and he was grateful the lie worked.

"I'm spending as much time as I can with Ginger and the girls before I go. Just don't go expecting miracles on my end. I had my priorities set before today's reading. Nothing changes that fact."

Adele nodded. "Well, we each have our adventures, don't we?"

"I think it will be good to get it all out in the open, Mom. Good for Gerud, too. He needs to know someone cares for him. I've lost my dad. But Gerud is about to find his. I'd say that makes him pretty lucky, wouldn't you? Maybe this is the second chance you both need."

He hugged his mother in the front seat of her car and then gave her a peck on the cheek. "Let me know when you guys leave for LA, if I'm not gone by then."

CHAPTER 5

G ERUD WAITED NERVOUSLY for his mother to return to the big house. He made himself a drink and sat at the dinette table in the kitchen, overlooking the backyard and pool. The view of his mother's gardens and the turquoise water normally had a calming effect on him, even as the alcohol dripped into his bloodstream. But this evening he was furious and wanted answers.

He heard her car pull up into the garage and remained seated as she walked through the kitchen door.

"Hope I didn't scare you," he said, sullenly. He noticed his words were already beginning to slur. He hadn't eaten any lunch before the reading so he was getting hammered on just one stiff drink.

"I saw your car outside, Gerud. I'm glad you're here."

He doubted that and felt he was on uncharted ground. It was like a giant earthquake had shaken his world, put back the pieces, but nothing was familiar or recognizable. He crossed his arms over his chest.

"So what was all this, Mom? What did I ever do to earn Dad's wrath?"

"Oh, sweetheart, I'm so…" She hovered closer to him, and he put his arm up.

"Don't touch me. I don't need any mothering, if that's what it can be called."

Adele tossed her purse and keys on the kitchen countertop and went in search of a drink for herself. When she returned, she pulled up a chair opposite Gerud and stared across the table at him.

"I need answers. What the hell happened? What does it mean, *'for reasons only your mother knows?'* What did I do to piss him off so much?"

"It's not anything you did, Gerud."

"Well, there's something you're not telling me, and I want answers, and I want them right now!"

Gerud watched as his mother jumped in her chair, blinking her red eyes.

"He was under a lot of stress. He wasn't thinking right, Gerud."

He tried to remember what had gotten his father so off-kilter, but finally gave up. "So how come I was cut out of the will? I worked with and for the man for what the last six, seven years? And he treats me like this?"

His mother downed the rest of her drink quickly and then rubbed her right temple. "I have some news you might not like to hear, son."

"Oh boy, more good news. I can hardly wait! Might as well get it all over with in one day. Please." He held his palm out to her, asking her to proceed.

"Burt Green was not your father. Your father is Rob Peterson, and we're going to go visit with him as soon as you're able."

"You've got to be fuckin' kidding me."

"No, I'm not. I should have told you—"

"Damn straight. So is that what sent him to the hospital, then? You guys have a fight, and you screamed at him and told him he wasn't my father? Or did he know all along?"

His mother hung her head sheepishly to the left and then closed her eyes as the tears started streaming down her face. With great effort at composure, she spoke softly in almost a whisper, "No. Bob Fellows told him just before—that afternoon he had the heart attack. I never got a chance to speak to him about it or anything else."

Gerud could see she'd been wounded. He also couldn't understand why she'd withhold that information from him. "So out with it. Give me all the sordid details." When she continued to stare at her fingers on the tabletop, it irritated him. "Damn it, Mom. I deserve to know everything!"

He knew she was ashamed, because she wouldn't look at him in the eyes. He began to manufacture a host of other things that could be, things that could be even worse, wondering if he had been conceived as the product of a rape or some other horrible event.

"Mom! I fuckin' went out on a date with my fuckin' sister. Do you have any idea how that makes me feel? Can you even imagine—"?

"Stop it, Gerud. She's not your sister. She's not even related to you. She's not related to me, either, so quit being so melodramatic."

He did the math and agreed. It had been what he was thinking all the way over here, the one thing that bothered him more than anything else and the reason he needed to dose himself on the Scotch. But if Burt wasn't his father, then Belinda wasn't his real sister, either.

Thank God for small favors.

"Your father lives in LA. He came to the funeral to pay his respects. I didn't see him, or I would have introduced you."

"And I'd have punched him in the nose, too."

"Which is why Bob Fellows discretely preoccupied us both until the gentleman left. Jake met him."

"Of course, Golden Boy met him. I suppose Jake knows all about this, too."

"Yes, he does now."

"Okay, that's all I can handle today." Gerud got up and put his glass in the kitchen sink. "Jake has a dad, the dad I thought was *my* dad. Yet Jake got to meet my dad. Me, though? No, I was sheltered from all this. But Jake is the one who can do no wrong. The pure son. Not the son from an illicit affair. That's what it was, right, Mom? An affair? A fling?"

"Just stop it right now, Gerud. You're being a child. Sit down and I'll tell you the whole story."

The fury and pain pulsed in his veins so fast he thought he was going to burst. "You can skip it. I don't need to hear it." He turned to go, passing the dinette table on his way to the front door, when his mother shouted out to him.

"He's dying, Gerud. Your father is dying."

"Oh I see. So the man I *thought* was my father, whom I buried last week and grieved over, turns out *not* to be my father after all. A man whom I don't know and who is actually my father, is now getting ready to check out. So I'm Oh for two."

"Stop being so selfish. He wants to meet you. And it was never his idea that you not know him as your father. It was *my* decision. So you can heap all that blame on me."

She was shaking, barely able to stand. In that moment, he saw her pain and the distress all this had caused her, and he felt sorry for her. He couldn't bring himself to give her a hug, but he could return to the table.

He sat back down in his chair and folded his hands together. "I'm ready to listen."

She sat as well, grabbing a napkin from the holder and dabbing her eyes again and then blew her nose. She reached for and was given Gerud's drink. Taking a sip, she sighed.

"Okay. Rob Peterson was a man I worked with at the office. Your dad was off most of the summer on a safari with some friends from the club. They also went golfing in Scotland. I was left running the whole business that summer, as well as taking care of Jake. I was busy, and I guess that kept me from thinking too much about what your dad—what Burt was doing. Rob was a good friend, and, well, we got very close."

It wasn't the story he was expecting.

"Believe it or not, Gerud, I was happy. That was probably the best summer of my life. And then Burt came home, and everything went back to the way it was before, except I was pregnant. I didn't have many choices back then. Of course, I couldn't even conceive not raising you, so I never told Burt he wasn't the father. Rob had to move away, which was only reasonable. It was hard having him here with me being pregnant. Burt seemed to be more settled, and I just thought everything would turn out. I made a mistake, Gerud."

"And so now he wants to meet me."

"Yes. He's a very decent man. He never imposed anything on you or me. He let me control all that."

"So do I have other brothers and sisters?"

"I really don't know. I never talked to him after a few months of him moving away. He knew your name and your birthdate. That's all he knows."

GERUD DECIDED TO stay overnight in the house with his mother. They watched the late news together, drinking tea after she made them a light supper. She'd called his father, who was unable to come to the phone, but she arranged with an attendant for her and Gerud to meet with him tomorrow.

They retired after giving each other a hug.

"No more secrets, please, Mom, okay?"

"No more secrets, son."

CHAPTER 6

GINGER NOTICED A text from Jake's mother and carried the phone into him. He was in the hot tub with their two girls.

"Your mom's going to Los Angeles today with Gerud. You know about this?"

"Uh huh. Part of what we discussed last night. She's taking him to introduce him to his father. His biological father."

"That older man you were speaking with at the funeral?"

"Yes, ma'am."

Jennifer poured a plastic cup of water over Jake's head.

"Whoa! Okay, Missey, you're gonna get it!" Jake yelled.

Both girls screamed. Jennie was the first one to slip her leg over the hot tub lip, slithering over the edge, and was already running away. Jake had Jasmine by the ankle, pretending to eat her from her ankle to her knee as she screamed and churned from side to side like a fish in the warm water.

"Daddy! It's not fair. It was Jennie who poured the water, not me," Jasmine objected.

"But you gave her the idea. I know you did," Jake said in his mock troll-like voice. "Now you will pay the price for your crime!"

Ginger turned and went back inside, understanding it would be impossible discussing anything with Jake while he was playing with the girls. She jumped into the shower and soon had company.

"Hold it right there, sweetheart," Jake whispered in her ear. His large hands covered hers, pressed against the tile walls of the enclosure.

"With an ass like that, honey, you're downright dangerous."

She giggled.

"Hold it. Did I say you could move?"

She sighed as his hands smoothed over the curve of her right butt cheek. His fingers drifted to the crack between them as he tickled her there.

"I say spread 'em. And make it quick. I got urgent business to attend to." His mock growl and whisper sent her nerve endings on high alert. Showers were unpredictable things with Jake. He was so inventive and experimental when it came to gels, scents, and warm water.

He pressed his chest against her back, smashing her breasts into the cool tile. "I said spread 'em, sister, and I mean what I say."

She widened her stance, angling her tailbone back towards Jake's groin. His fingers separated her ass, and one of his forefingers made its way into her sex, just ahead of his cock. He continued to knead her butt cheeks, separating them so he could fill her channel. Bending his knees beneath hers, his powerful thighs lifted her onto him, his rod demanding a depth that made her shudder. Jake urgently slipped a hand to the front, and he rolled her bud between his first two fingers and his thumb.

"That little confounded thing is all swollen, honey. Feel that?"

"Yes," she sighed, thoroughly consumed in his manipulations.

"Am I deep enough, honey?"

"Yes—no. Deeper please."

He thrust upward, his thighs slapping against the backs of hers. "Like this?"

"Yes. But harder."

"Oh man. You're a demanding little thing, aren't you?"

"I want all of you, Jake."

"You liked to be fucked this way, honey?"

"I could stay here all night long."

That seemed to send a signal to Jake, his reaction was swift, grunting to press and hold her over his thigh. She felt the delicious pulsing of his release. She could barely breathe he was pressing her so hard into the wall, still with his knees bent, thrusting upward and holding her steady against him with his palm on her lower belly. She covered his hand with her own, smoothing up and down his fingers and arm as he worked to complete his job.

At last, he slowed, giving her a satisfied groan before removing himself and spanking her on one side. "To be continued. Next time, I'm gonna make sure you come first."

"Thank you, Jake."

He abruptly turned her around, took her wet face in his massive paws and kissed her deeply. He ended the kiss with little nibbles at the sides of her lips. "I like it that you never say no."

"Why would I ever do that? It's the best thing in the world, Jake. I need it."

"Yes, you do, and so do I."

Her fingers traced the lines of his face and over his mouth. The wonder of this man's love for her was totally inspiring. "I think I'm addicted to you."

The bathroom door burst open, and Jasmine and Jennie jumped up and down. "Mommie and Daddy are naked!" Jennie giggled, pointing to the lower parts of their anatomy.

Jake once again whispered in her ear. "I could do with some duct tape right about now."

JAKE GOT A call to do some PT with a ten mile run with several of the other guys. They were to have an early briefing on the new mission. Ginger took the girls to the grocery store and then stopped off at the library for a children's reading by an author she knew. She was hoping Jake didn't return home too late. They'd not gotten very caught up on their sleep the last few nights.

Luci Begay, the Dine wife of Danny, walked in with Griffin and their adopted Iraqi boy, Ali, who was now nearly six years old. She noted Luci grabbed the red slingshot from the boy's back pocket, something he kept with him night and day. That slingshot had actually saved his life in Iraq after Danny had made it for him from pieces they salvaged from the soccer stadium Ali and his father were hiding in. The Navajo SEAL, grandson to a WWII Codetalker, showed Ali how to use it, and while they'd been waiting for extraction, practiced hours at a time hitting objects with different sized pebbles and pieces of concrete. Ali now could actually hunt birds with lethal accuracy. Several car windows were suspected of being Ali's targets.

GRIFFIN WAS A chubby, roly-poly child, but Ali was getting tall and stayed skinny. His favorite target with the slingshot was Griffin, who had an assortment of bruises on his forehead to testify to that fact.

Luci waved with the red device and came over, sitting next to Ginger.

"Let's hope my boys don't terrorize your girls."

Ginger watched as Ali insisted on sitting between the sisters and Griffin sat down in Jasmine's lap. The children had spent so much time together it was only natural they be physically connected, touching constantly. They were one huge family, and Ginger was grateful her kids had this.

"Ali looks like he's on good behavior today, Luci."

"He's a challenge. Got him registered for every sport I can find this summer. I have to keep this kid moving, or he'll erupt on the playground. He's absolutely not afraid to tackle anyone, even the fifth graders in the school. He wants to play Rugby with the older boys, but Danny put his foot down on that idea."

"Wise, of course."

"Like he's got a spirit inside him. He even thinks he can fly."

"Seriously? You mean he dreamt it?"

Luci shook her head. "I don't know where he got the idea, but he swears he flew home one day. We couldn't talk him down off that. One of these days, he's gonna get his butt kicked, and perhaps he'll learn his lesson," said Luci.

Ginger squinted. "Really? You honestly think that will happen?"

"Probably not." The two SEAL ladies laughed. "So I hear you and Jake are back together now. That's wonderful, Ginger. I love Jake."

"So far, so good. You know his father just passed away last week. The family is in a bit of turmoil now. Jake's the executor of his dad's estate. This deployment is coming at the worst time."

"Oh, that's right. I hear it will be short. But we never know, do we?"

"Nope."

The two women agreed to get together during the Team deployment. They also agreed to set up a playdate for an upcoming birthday party.

"You hear from any of Ali's relatives?" Ginger asked.

"Not a word. Danny thinks they're all dead. He'd be difficult to convince to let Ali go off with anyone from his family. Danny really loves him, and so do I and Griffin."

AS THEY EXITED the library, Ali was transfixed by a gathering of several men on the corner, all of them wearing white robes. He dove into Luci's bag and grabbed his slingshot, holding it ready as they approached the little group. Ali dipped to pick up a couple of stones on the sidewalk.

Ginger noted these robed boys looked to be young, possibly early high school in age. She avoided eye contact with them, but Ali stared them down, completely unafraid. The boys took turns checking him out and their discussion halted as soon as they got within earshot.

"You know those boys, Ali?"

"They were from my auntie's village, I think. They've grown up, though, so I'm not sure."

He was an avid scholar, and his English was nearly perfect.

"Luci, you've done wonders with him. I can remember he couldn't even speak a word two years ago. Now you couldn't tell he wasn't a native speaker."

"He has to learn to mix in. I don't want him not understanding the reality of how many Americans see his culture and language. I do it for his own protection."

"You're doing a fantastic job."

"He's the brightest child I've ever taught. He doesn't sit still much, but luckily, he learns quickly, so he doesn't have to sit long."

Ginger made a note to tell Jake about the robed boys, who looked like religious students of some kind. She hoped that Luci and Danny were able to hold on to this little Iraqi boy and not be forced to return him to relatives who might call someday. But that was US policy. She wondered if Danny wouldn't take his family underground if it ever came to that. Ali was one of them now. Nothing was ever going to break that bind.

CHAPTER 7

"LISTEN UP," KYLE announced to the men at the Team 3 building. Jake sat between Alex and Calvin "Coop" Cooper. The whole squad for this mission was only going to be twenty men, and Kyle had told them they were each hand-selected.

"We're going back to Baja, landing again by transport at the old Mexican Naval base at Puerto Cortes, on the Isla Santa Margarita." He glanced Jake's way. "We hope General Cortez doesn't send a welcoming committee for you, son."

Coop put his arm around Jake's shoulder and rocked him.

"We're only giving them an hour head's up so we don't think they can muster that fast, and our liaison will get our permission to land and try to bypass the brass if she can. Not to worry."

Kyle proceeded to tell the group their purpose was to again pose as disgruntled former and current vets, looking for some fun, but also wanting to score some sales of military equipment.

"What about the girls down there?" Armando asked. "Can we check on them, maybe see if they have more information about the Garcia gang?"

In the previous mission, Santiago Garcia's little brother had been killed. In the gunfight, Jake had accidentally shot the older girl brought to the party they were attending and a schoolteacher at the Catholic school in town.

"No pink palace this time," Kyle answered. "The Federales did a major cleanup so we're hoping a lot of the old group is diluted. But

Santiago Garcia is back in residence, and that's why we're going down. He hasn't met any of us and we're banking his crew hasn't, either. But we tread careful. Invisios all the way, so you guys come with your ears cleaned."

"We need anything extra fancy?" asked Fredo.

"No rescue this time. No party. Just looking for the ones offering to buy our surplus equipment and someone big enough to lean on to get to Santiago himself. We turn them in to the Feds there, and they do the confrontation and arrests. We had to promise no gunfight this time. Of course, if you gotta defend yourself or a brother or an innocent, well, you know the answer to that one," Kyle barked.

"Kyle, they're gonna recognize Jake and T.J. They're the ones who started the gun battle last time," said Coop. "You sure Jake should go?"

"Thank you," whispered Jake.

"What Jake doesn't know is that he's to become a skinhead," answered Kyle. A wave of chuckles erupted throughout the room.

"Nice, huh? Headshed wants him totally incognito. You all can go as yourselves, but we gotta keep Jake out of harm's way, and yet I can't risk not taking him because of what he's seen."

Jake was dreading the haircut that probably would happen right after the team meeting. He knew there was no way Ginger would like the way he looked.

"You grow a beard, too. Can you do that in four days?"

"Sure he can," Alex interrupted. "His dick hangs down to his ankles. He can grow a beard just by pushing real hard to take a dump. It pushes the beard right out."

The laughter helped Jake feel slightly better about the situation he was being put in. It was just the way the Team operated, and indicated they were comfortable enough with him to give him a good razing.

"Okay, let's can the potty mouth, guys. I want you all to get some rest. We'll do a longer briefing on Friday when we leave. I hope to have someone from the State Department giving us some background. Now, I need some volunteers with barbering experience."

Practically the whole squad attended to Jake while Alex got out a pair of electric hair clippers. First, they did a Mohawk cut. Then Alex removed the ridge and made him as smooth as a cue ball. Jake had wanted to watch the process, but he had a SEAL on each arm and leg, and Fredo was sitting on his chest as he lay on the workout bench. His fingers smoothed over the porcelain of his skin, and he knew Ginger would have a fit.

"You get yourself an earring," said Armando. "A nice big one."

"Should I wear an eye patch, too? Red bandana?" Jake was half serious.

"The eye patch might work. Forget the bandana or they'll think you're gay," answered Coop. "And, Alex, don't forget to bring the shears. We need him to stay bald."

"Roger that."

Coop whispered, "You get your butt over to Flesh Graphix and have Daisy do the piercing, so it doesn't get infected. While you're at it, get another tat if you want. Something naked and nasty looking."

Jake pulled away. "I'm a family man. No way."

Coop and several others laughed. "Just pulling your leg, man. But Armando's right. Get the earring, but get it done right. Daisy will have some surgical steel earrings that will work. You don't want to get an infection in Baja."

"Probably wouldn't be the first time, bro," mocked Lucas. Laughter rippled through the group.

Someone put some masculine-scented oil to finish off Jake's lack of hairline, and the deed was considered done.

JAKE WALKED THROUGH the front door when he got home, finding Ginger, the dog, and the girls sitting on the couch watching a movie. Chelsea Fiona immediately reared up and barked at him, while Ginger tried to calm her down. But Jake hadn't counted on Jennifer being scared to death seeing the strange man walk through the front door. She screamed and buried her head in her mother's arms, adding to the drama on the couch. Jasmine didn't recognize him either at first, but then carefully ran to Jake to give him a hug, which was her custom. Her enthusiasm was lacking, and he knew she also was on edge.

Ginger was dumbfounded. After successfully calming down the mutt, she managed to blurt out, "What happened?"

"The guys got to me. It'll all grow back. Part of what we have to do for Mexico. And I have to start growing a beard." Jake shrugged. "Better than being recognized."

The dog had wedged a spot between Ginger and Jennifer, growled, and gave a final bark.

Ginger scratched the top of the mutt's head. "I'm just thinking it will feel like cheating on my husband with you in my bed tonight."

Jake waved his eyebrows up and down. "You can always close your eyes…" He winked at her and saw the satisfying blush on her cheeks. Jennifer finally broke away from her mom and stepped toward him. The dog followed, but stayed back a pace.

"Sorry, Daddy. But you did look scary, until I recognized you."

"No worries, angel." He came to his knees and hugged both his girls. Jennifer's warm little body was shaking, but she hugged him hard, as if asking for strength and forgiveness. Her courage in the face of fear moved him. Brushing the hair from her forehead, he spoke to both of them, "Daddy is supposed to look a little scary so the bad guys don't know who he really is. It's for my protection."

They both nodded their heads, and he kissed each on the forehead. The girls ran off down the hall to their rooms, the dog following. Jake stood up, yanked his pants, repositioning them on his hips, and then kicked off his shoes, laying them by the front door. Then he adjusted his pants again.

"You losing weight, Jake?" Ginger asked.

She got just close enough so he could grab her. With her back to his chest, his arms making a straightjacket so she couldn't wiggle free, he whispered in her ear, "It's all the sex, sweetheart. You've been making me a lean, mean fucking machine, and I've only just begun showing you how I feel about you."

He felt her giggle as she whispered back, "I kinda like that and am not sorry one bit. Your hip action is making me one happy lady, Jake.

One lucky lady."

He whipped her around. "I think you're gonna get lucky again tonight. It's all for you. Only for you, sweetheart."

As they parted, he gave her a squeeze on her ass and followed her to the kitchen. "What's for dinner? I already know what's for dessert."

Ginger's blush was a thing of beauty, the way her bright pink cheeks framed her face, making her red hair give her the impression she was literally on fire. He liked seeing her distracted, blushing, forgetting things and just generally being affected by his proximity. Her body offered up to him pleasures even when she took greens out of the refrigerator. It was sensual just watching her pour him a tall glass of cold water. He could lie in bed and watch her shower every morning, if he could keep himself from joining her. The way he felt about her was even better than when they were first married. He loved her like a man loved something so precious he'd give his life for it in an instant. His chest swelled with pride that this little sweet thing was his forever. He'd never been so happy.

They had a light dinner, and then the girls went off for a bath, followed by reading time, which was always reserved just for him. He took his time with them every night he was home, always finishing up the session with a kneel at their beds so they could offer what they had been thankful for and pray for others less fortunate.

The dog alternated who she slept with at night, and tonight, Jasmine had her tucked under her arms. Jake blew them all a kiss, turned out the light, and closed the door quietly.

Ginger had just finished up in the kitchen and was drying her hands. He removed the towel and slipped his arms around her waist, allowing his fingers to slide under her shirt. He discovered she was wearing something silky underneath.

"What the heck is this?" he asked as he lifted her shirt, revealing a white lace push-up bra. "Holy cow. Frosting!"

He scooped her delicate breasts up from the lacy cups that held them, kissing her knotted nipples.

"I like this. You brought the cherries, I see," he observed as he lingered over each nipple, sucking and making them peak. Her areolas were the same color as her peach lips, wet with desire for him. He pressed his mouth to hers and felt himself fall under her spell. His hands roamed over her tight ass. Then his fingers slipped under the front of her pants, undoing the top button and zipper. He felt satin again.

"Matching. I know you like things to match," she said breathlessly as his fingers breached the elastic waistband of her panties.

He kissed up the side of her neck, tasting the sugar-sweetness of her feminine scent when he bit her ear lobe. "No, darlin' I like you best naked. But until I can get you there, honey, matching is very, very nice."

She climbed up his front, wrapping her legs around his hips and waist, and he took off to the bedroom.

He watched her remove her shirt and pants as he disrobed. She was going to remove her bra, and he stopped her.

"You just lie back on the bed like that. I want to look at you first."

Ginger smiled, obliging by sitting on the edge of the bed, then turning and crawling slowly up toward the headboard. She peered around the perfect roundness of her ass. "Like this."

"Just like that," he said as he approached, fully naked and with an erection he felt might last all week. "Hold it! Right there. Don't move a muscle."

"You mean I can't do this?" She palmed her mound, rubbing up the crease in her rear with her fingers gliding over the smooth white satin. She spread her knees and, with her fingers still in place, pulled back the elastic slightly, just enough he got a glimpse of the lips of her sex.

"Oh, that was very bad, Ginger. But I have a cure for that. Yessir, indeedie I do."

He came up behind her, his thighs pressing against the backs of hers as he fingered her sex, sliding up and down until he tinkered with her bud, making his sweet Ginger moan in desperation.

"Dessert, sweetheart."

"Yes. Please." He could barely hear her.

He drew himself up and again pulled back the elastic of the panty.

He didn't want to take the time to remove anything. He slid himself inside her sweet channel until he was at the hilt. "There."

"Better. But—"

"Shhh. Talk dirty to me, Ginger."

"Oh. My. God. Jake, I need this so much."

"Dirtier."

"Fuck me, Jake."

"More, please."

"Make my pussy swell. I want you to fuck me until I can't walk."

"Whoa there, I just might be able to do that, sweetheart."

"And then wake me up and fuck me again."

"Perfect."

CHAPTER 8

GERUD INSISTED HE take Adele to breakfast before they started their trip to Los Angeles to meet his father. She objected at first, but Gerud had always been good at convincing his mother about things she should never say yes to. This was one that should have been an immediate yes, so they sat at the trendy diner just outside San Diego proper.

He had memorized a list of questions he wanted her to answer.

"So what's he like?" Gerud asked.

"Well, he was an athlete in college, so I remember him as tall and fit. He wore a business suit better than just about anybody at the office."

She'd gotten that far away look again he'd seen just about any time he'd brought up Peterson's name.

"It took a lot to distract me. I was so darned busy in those days. Then one day, he waltzed into my office and asked me to lunch. I told him I had work to do, and he told me to take the afternoon off. Well, we went to lunch, and then we went to the movies of all things. I'd never been to a matinee before. Honest."

"Swept you off your feet."

"Not at all. He said he was rescuing me from an early grave." Her fragile smile began to show her age. "I think he probably saved my life. Your fath—Burt and I were so driven to make it with the new business, we hardly talked. Hardly did anything together. Rob showed me a little concern and attention during that summer when Burt was away, and, well, I was certainly ripe for it."

"So how did you get together then?"

"We used to talk. That's how it all started. I came in early, as soon as I'd drop Jake off at the sitter's, and then work until past dinner. He'd bring me these wonderful fish tacos from a little taco truck he knew about. Otherwise, I'd skip my meals all day and only eat dinner. He was right. I was being reckless with my health."

"You said Burt was traveling?" It felt funny to call the man he'd always known as his father "Burt".

"He was gone that whole summer. Off to Africa with the Boys from the club—Jerry, Bob, and his friends. They went on golfing vacations together and, I supposed, got into trouble together, but always covered for each other, too. We all knew it. The wives never spoke of it in public, but we all knew."

"Must not have been very much fun."

"Oh, it was just the way things were then. I didn't like it at all, but Burt was brilliant in business and so driven. I allowed his excesses, as long as they didn't interfere with the family." She checked her wedding ring, flipping it around her finger loosely. "We had some fights, some real bad ones. But I think it was sheer stubbornness that kept us together all those years." She frowned, looking down at her nearly untouched plate of food. "But recently, well, you know. His drinking increased. He just couldn't seem to get away from it. I had hoped Jake could get him to meetings, but he was the most stubborn man I knew."

She smiled at her son.

"Thanks, Mom." He felt warmer to her today, just sitting across the table from her than he had in years. The dark cloud that was Burt's stormy personality was gone.

"For what?"

"For being honest."

"Oh that. Well, death has a way of softening the resentment I felt toward him these past couple of years. Everything was just slipping away from him. I felt sorry for him. But God, not that I could tell him so."

"You ready?" Gerud asked her. "You've barely touched your eggs."

"No time like the present."

As they walked to Adele's car, Gerud asked her one more question. "Do you have any idea what we're in store for once we get there? I mean, is there an agenda?"

"Not that I know of. Just a chance for you to meet your father. That's all it is. Something I should have allowed to happen much earlier in your life. I know I'm going to regret that the rest of my days, Gerud. Let's hope he's the same man I remember."

"Either way, I'm kind of nervous."

They both buckled up, and Adele continued toward the freeway. The morning traffic had thinned, and the bright blue sky was still clear. By the time they arrived in Los Angeles, the blue would turn light brownish gray.

THE RESIDENTIAL STREET Peterson lived on was wide, lined with massive old trees, which only barely hid the huge mansions behind them. Gerud hadn't seen so many large, beautiful estates ever. Crews of landscapers were working several front yards. Even the vehicles traveling down the quiet streets were expensive.

Adele's GPS announced they had arrived. A light tan, Spanish style stucco mansion dripped tons of ornate plaster bric-a-brac all over the front of the two-story structure. It looked like the type of home that would have been featured in a 1930's gangster movie involving a Hollywood mogul with a backyard full of starlets.

"Holy cow. I guess he has done very well. Did you have any idea?"

"No. I mean I figured he'd done well, but this will be a first time for both of us."

Although they were going to park in the street, a young man appeared at the front door and then motioned for them to drive up onto the driveway to park.

As Gerud approached the entrance, he heard classical music inside. Outside was the distant sound of a freeway somewhere, but the birds nearly drowned out that sound. He traveled the intricate brick pattern of the walkway and stepped up onto the stoop.

"I'm Alex, Rob's attendant today. You're Gerud?"

The young man extended his hand, and Gerud shook it.

"Yessir. Thanks, Alex. This is my mother, Adele Green."

"Yes, we've been expecting you. Rob is very excited. He's having a good day today, and now since you're here, it will be even better."

He opened the door and motioned for them to follow him inside.

The foyer was as large as the living room at the Green's home in San Diego. A walnut paneled stairway switched back on three sides leading to the top floor. The entry had a stained glass dome, letting in a shower of colorful light patterns over the marble floor. Leaning next to the doorframe into the living room was a handsome, but frail-looking man. His legs were crossed at the ankles, his arms folded chest-high. He'd been staring at Adele, but his focus switched to Gerud.

Carefully, and with great focus, he walked toward them both. His attendant appeared in the doorway behind him, watching his feet. His forehead bore sweat from the exertion he was making, but Gerud could see how important it was that he walk on his own. Though the man's skin was sallow and had lost its dewy radiance, his eyes sparkled with some fire from within. He first smiled at Adele and then turned his face to Gerud, extending his hands.

Gerud gripped the gnarled cool hands of a man in pain, yet working hard not to show it. The connection between the two was unmistakable as Gerud held firm and gave the man the gift of his youth and strength. His eyes were the same as Gerud's and the shape of his nose long and slender like his own.

"Nice to meet you, son, if I may call you that?"

"Of course. I—I'm still getting used to all this, so—"

"You can call me Rob. It is enough that we meet, at last. What you call me is unimportant."

He adjusted his upper torso with difficulty and addressed Adele. "And you look as lovely as I remember."

Gerud watched his mother bite her lower lip as her eyes filled with tears. "Rob, it's been a long time."

Peterson was going to reach for her, but his grip became unsteady. Instantly, the attendant was there to help him stand and then led him to the wheelchair nearby.

"You did very well, sir," he told Peterson.

The older man gave a dismissive wave off. "I'm afraid these days of being able to walk are growing rarer."

Gerud instinctively took his mother's hand and squeezed it.

Alex turned Peterson around in the chair and headed toward the rear of the home. He looked back at the two of them. "We've prepared some refreshments for you. He likes to go outside on the patio where it's sunny this time of day. Will you join us?"

From the back, Peterson's slouching form made him look twenty years older. Gerud was grateful they hadn't waited any longer to meet.

"Are they coming?" Gerud heard Peterson ask Alex.

"Yup, right behind us, sir."

A painted white table with a striped multicolored umbrella secured in the center was set for four. Peterson was positioned up to the table in his wheelchair. "Gerud, Adele, please sit on either side of me so I can hear."

Alex took his seat across from Peterson.

"So, now that we're all together, I'm afraid I'm a little shy. I've thought about it for so many years, and I was worried—well, you know."

It was unsettling to meet his father for the first time while also experiencing that he was leaving them at the same time. Visions of the funeral flashed through his mind, the sight of Burt Green's body lying stiff and unnatural in front of him being most prominent. That scene felt like it was happening all over again, despite trying to wipe his memory of it. Something bubbled up inside, some emotion he couldn't put a name to. All of this was uncharted territory.

"You want to ask me any questions, Gerud? I have no experience in this, so forgive me if I just make pleasant conversation until, hopefully, we can feel more comfortable being around each other. At least, that is my goal for today."

Gerud's heart was about to burst wide open. His eyes stung and he held a tight rein on any feeling that dared to escape. What was this going on inside him? He couldn't quite put his finger on it.

Gerud cleared his throat, which had become dry and parched. "Do you have a family?" he finally found the courage to ask.

"I always thought I would. But I was just working. Very involved in my business and my real estate investments. I had good friends I traveled with and worked side by side with. But one day, I turned around, and everyone had gone. They'd gotten married, or I'd lost contact with them. I never paid attention to that until it was too late. I figured maybe someday Adele would come visit me."

"I'm sorry, Rob. I truly am."

"No, you were honoring the deal we made. I signed on to it, too. We kept to that agreement, for Gerud's benefit."

Adele examined her lap.

"But you got my cards, right?" He turned to Gerud. "Not sure if your mother told you, but I sent cards on your birthday every year, just so she'd know I was still alive."

"She told me."

"I saved them all, Rob. Burt never knew."

"I was sad to hear about Burt. I know you loved him very much. Did your other son tell you I was at the funeral?"

"Yes, he told me. I didn't realize you were even there until you had gone."

"Well, Burt had been good to me, and if it weren't for him, I'd have never met you. So it was only fitting that I pay my respects to you all."

"Thank you," she whispered.

Gerud and his mother stared at each other as if deciding what to ask or what to say. He thought of something.

"I was told you invest in real estate. I have a Broker's license as well. My fa—Burt was teaching me things."

Peterson covered Burt's hand with his. "It doesn't bother me. You should call him your father because he was. He raised you, Gerud. I'm fine with that. He is owed the respect you show him by calling him such. Who knows? Maybe I would have been a horrible father!" He grinned. "Now, please go on."

"Well, I also am learning about investments. Probably not nearly like you do, but I'm interested in it."

"That's good." He tapped Jake on the hand. "How do you like the house? You want a tour after lunch?" Peterson asked him.

"Feels like a big old school building. It's huge," Gerud blurted out. "I mean—I'm sorry if that sounded—"

Peterson laughed, clasping his hands together. "Yes, kind of ridiculous for one person, I agree." He leaned into Gerud's side. "I used to get lost in my own house at first. But I bought it because it was a good deal, and because I could. Now that I've had it, well, that just takes one more thing off my bucket list."

Gerud returned Peterson's smile.

"My list is a lot shorter than yours. Things are getting kind of rushed these days," Peterson added.

Adele took his hand. "Rob, please. No more talk about all this. I don't want to spend our time here talking about—"

Just then, two staff members brought out lunch on trays, along with some iced tea and a pitcher of iced water. Gerud grabbed his cup and nearly downed it without coming up for air. Peterson raised a tall glass filled with what looked like a green smoothie.

"I get the super power lunch. Sorry I didn't offer. Alex and his buddies have me drinking buckets of juiced kale and claim to be able to cure me."

Alex smiled and continued eating. "You never know, sir. It could happen."

"No harm in trying. I have pancreatic cancer, and it goes very fast once it takes hold."

"And responds well to good, clean food. Lots of greens."

Peterson whispered, "I'll be the healthiest looking corpse in the funeral home."

Adele burst into tears. Gerud got up and put his arms across her neck and shoulders, leaned forward, and pressed his cheek against hers. "Don't, Mother."

She accepted his hug at first and then waved him off. "Oh, this has been building," she said between bouts of blowing her nose and wiping her eyes. She let out a big sigh. Alex handed her a box of tissues. "Rob, this is so hard for me. I'm not sure I can do it any longer."

"Sure you can. You're the toughest I know."

"Would you like something else, Mrs. Green?" asked Alex.

"No. I'm good." She lightly pushed Gerud away. "Go sit down. I'm fine now." She took in another deep breath and stared at Peterson. "Damn you, Rob Peterson. Cool as a cucumber in the face of—" She melted again and more tears came. "I can't even say it!"

Peterson watched her. He didn't console, but just observed with eyes that sparkled as if he was viewing her take a bath or swim with her long graceful body. Gerud saw more love in those eyes than he'd ever seen.

When she settled down, he asked her, "You okay?"

"Yes. I think I'm about cried out now."

"Of course. I've had weeks to get adjusted to my outcome. You two didn't know until the day before yesterday. I'm so sorry. It was thoughtless of me."

Gerud looked over the well-manicured lawns and formal gardens behind, full of blooming plants. In the center was a swimming pool twice the size of the one they had in his mother's yard. It was a garden oasis.

"I can see you like it here, Gerud. This is my favorite place in the whole property. I try to eat breakfast and lunch right here, because it makes me happy. I like to watch living things grow. When it's too hot, I sit just inside, right there by the window."

Gerud watched his mother's lower lip quiver occasionally and heard her deep inhales and measured exhales. She avoided eye contact with him, because he'd recognize the sadness that emanated across the table and enveloped him. If Peterson noticed, he didn't show it.

"So now to some unfinished business. First, Gerud, let me tell you what an honor it is to finally get to meet you."

"Likewise, sir."

"I've wondered over the years what it would be like to have a son.

Wondered what you were doing. Wondered what your challenges in life were. I've second-guessed our decision many, many times. But, on the whole, I think we made the right choice. Don't you agree, Adele?"

She nodded, but looked up at Gerud to show him she'd calmed down. "I'm sure your dad would have made me leave the house. I couldn't abandon Jake. That I couldn't do. Forgive me, Gerud."

"Not my place to forgive, Mom."

"So I've given lot of thought to our promises, our arrangement, and the future, whatever we all have together. I wasn't there for your growing up, Gerud. But I'd like to help you with the rest of your life. I couldn't be your father. But I can make you financially independent. If you'll allow me, I'd like to make you a very wealthy man—to be able to enjoy the things I won't be able to enjoy going forward. And nothing gives me more pleasure than the thought of this."

"Mr. Peterson."

"Rob."

"Rob. You don't have to do that."

"But I want to. This house, this will be for you and your mother to have. Or to sell and move anywhere else you want. I have funds set up in your name already, Gerud. I'm providing for your mother as well."

"But that's not why we came to visit. We weren't looking for a handout."

"I know that. But you're not going to turn me down, are you?"

Gerud hesitated.

"I want to do it because I can. That's the best reason of all. Consider me an investor in your future, your advisor in the clouds, so to speak."

He reached for and grabbed Adele's hand, putting it to his lips.

"Just knowing that your mother will enjoy seeing you live well and not have to struggle is the greatest joy I could ever receive."

Now Gerud felt he was on the edge of an outburst. Instead of holding them back, he let the hot tears roll down his cheeks.

"And, Sir, I promise to make you proud."

"I know you will, son."

CHAPTER 9

G INGER WAS MAKING preparations for a small get-together at the Green house before Jake's deployment on Friday. He wanted to get his whole blended family together—all the kids and their mothers. Of course he had asked her permission, but that wasn't something she could deny him. Adele was back from LA with some breaking news about her visit there. She'd been delighted to host the party at her house and insisted she have it catered.

Jake looked stunning in his new cotton shirt and slacks, even with his cue ball head. His beard shadow made him look rough and dangerous, and she liked it. The two of them had spent a little time together the day before, wandering the shops, having lunch, and just enjoying being a couple.

Ginger had bought a light pink dress with a lowered neckline Jake couldn't take his eyes off of.

"You know this is going to help me in the competition for your attention, Jake," she said as she paraded in front of him. He was sitting on the bed, watching her.

"Come here, and let me show you how I show my appreciation, then, sweetheart."

Putting down her hairbrush, she presented herself to him. "This dress makes you look like a good girl with really bad girl thoughts. I like seeing those ideas in your eyes when I kiss you."

"You do?"

"Absolutely," he said as their lips touched. He ran his hands from the backs of her knees up to squeeze her ass. "Are these the new pant-ies?" He lifted her dress and saw the peach-colored thong underwear he'd picked out.

"Why, of course."

"Don't you think you should drop those drawers and show me a little thankfulness."

"Not until tonight, Jake. I want you to think about it all day. I want you so distracted you'll forget the names of your kids."

"Unfair."

"You are more than welcome to punish me all you want, but after we're alone."

"We're alone now."

"You know what I mean." She knew it was past time for them to get over to Adele's. Her pulse had quickened, and she looked forward to her libido growing as the afternoon and evening wore on, culminating in what she'd hoped would be a mind-blowing event. Doing this helped her also cope with the thought of missing Jake in just a couple of days. It used to help her to anticipate the reunion rather than miss him. She'd adopted several tricks like this in the past. "I like the idea that every time you look at me, you'll know what I'm awaiting."

She grinned at him, planted another kiss, and began to move away.

"Hold on. You can't walk away from me that fast."

Her blood pressure spiked, and her panties got wet. But she man-aged to slip from his grip and walk to the bathroom where she applied her pink lipstick. When she looked back at him, he was still grinning on the side of the bed.

"I have a huge boner."

"Well, good. That's exactly what I wanted."

"All right." He stood, examining his crotch. "Dayam, woman. You are lethal."

"Count on it, Jake."

ON THE WAY over, the girls sang together. The back of Ginger's car was loaded up with towels, pool noodles, and floaters, as well as sun screen and some sodas and snacks the girls loved.

"I'm going to make a speech."

Ginger quickly scanned his profile. She hadn't gotten used to Jake's lack of hair. She liked the stubble growing, however. "Speech?"

"You'll see. Got it all planned."

"Have you really?" She was intrigued.

"See, I'm good at anticipation. Just like you wanted."

"You're beginning to have secrets like your father."

"No secrets, baby. We said that. We hold nothing back. Remember?"

Now she'd wished they were alone. Jake was seriously turning her on. "I like this new you."

He wiggled his eyebrows. "Good."

They arrived, finding it difficult to park. Two catering trucks parked end to end, and she recognized Monica and Karlene's cars, plus several others, including two Hummers Ginger thought might belong to Team Guys. Jake had to park Ginger's car nearly a half a block away.

The girls ran to the front door ahead of them. Jake was overloaded with baskets of things they'd brought. Ginger had made a plate of cookies and brought some sodas and juices the girls wanted.

Once inside the front door, Ginger caught the festive mood right away. Caterers had totally taken over the kitchen, while others were outside serving guests at tables and patio furniture under various bright umbrellas. The girls had already found the water and were playing with a couple other children she knew to be Team kids.

Alex and Lucas greeted Jake by rubbing his head and tried to hand him a beer, but he declined. Cooper and Libby were getting their two kids ready for the pool. Danny was in the pool with his two boys, riding herd on Ali, who was using his slingshot to lob water balloons at some of the adults until Danny stopped him. Kyle and Christy were sitting under an umbrella holding hands, but watching Brandon and the others in the pool.

The churning blue water was filled with more kids than Ginger had ever seen at the house.

"Just look at all that energy, Ginger. Isn't it grand?" Adele was dressed in a colorful kaftan, her face beaming behind huge sunglasses.

"Thank you so much. I had no idea this was going to be such a big event."

"You know they always get together somewhere before they deploy. No one has a house big enough for this crowd, so I volunteered when Jake said he wanted to throw a party."

"He knew about all this?"

"He made the invites himself."

Ginger took a glass of champagne from a silver tray an aproned girl presented her. Then she was shown a tray of stuffed mushrooms. "Adele, you've gone all out. I'm glad you're feeling up to it."

"You know, Ginger, I've been a pretty hard-charging lady most my life. Here I have all this beauty and family right in front of me. Why not share? This house was never a place any of you felt good about visiting. I mean, the kids always did because the pool and their favorite foods, but they're easy. I wanted to do something for Jake's brothers. It just seemed about time."

Adele slipped her arm around Ginger's waist. The affection she showed was touching.

"I'm glad, Adele." She noticed Monica was sitting with her baby on a blanket on the lawn, surrounded by three tatted and very muscular men. "She's having a good time," she said as she nodded toward Monica's group.

"I think Monica has a good time everywhere." Adele took her by the shoulders. "She and the baby belong here because they are family. But understand, Jake belongs to you, Ginger."

"I don't think he belongs to anyone, Adele. But thank you for saying so." Ginger searched the gathering, looking for Jake, and found him staring back at her. He winked and gave her a smile that nearly had her melt.

Adele had followed his gesture and her blush. "See what I mean?"

She enjoyed the feeling of a flushed face and that her former mother-in-law was reveling in it.

"I'm not sure I like the new haircut, though."

"It's for their mission. The beard, too."

"I see. Well, if it's necessary."

Then Ginger remembered what she'd wanted to ask Adele earlier. "You didn't tell me your news about LA. You said you had news?"

"Yes. Gerud and I went to visit Rob Peterson, his father. The two of them hit it off very well. Rob's going to help Gerud. I never thought it would work out this way. Really kind of a miracle."

"That must be a huge burden off your shoulders with the way Burt's will reading went."

"Oh God, that was a terrible day. Poor Gerud. I guess we must be the family of second chances, though. Somehow, we just always come out okay."

"So happy for you. How was it seeing him? It's been many years, right?"

"Nearly thirty."

"Wow. So how did you feel?"

"I think Rob was always the level-headed one. We could have had a nice life together. I say that now with no regrets for being with Burt all those years. The poor man did the best he could, but his demons got in the way."

"That's a good lesson for Jake."

"I agree."

"So are you going to see him again?"

"I suppose so. We set it up to talk. And I know he and Gerud will talk. I think Gerud would like to see much more of him. But sadly, Rob has not very long to live."

"How long?"

"About a month. And the last part of that won't be pretty, Ginger. I'm thinking he won't want anyone to see him then. But who knows? We'll just see what comes. I am glad he invited us over and we got to talk, finally."

Ginger was impressed with Adele's strength. "You deserve your happily ever after."

Adele examined her carefully. "Yes, but for me, it's enough that my children have one. I've lived my life. I've made all my choices. I do live for this." Her hand swept in front of her as they watched the crowd of families enjoying themselves on this sunny day in San Diego. Both women knew that there would be storm clouds ahead, but for today, it was perfect. "I only wish Burt were healthy and alive to see it. I really do. That's my only regret, but nothing I can do."

Christy Lansdowne came running over, her blonde hair tied up in a big clip. Adele left to join a group under one of the umbrellas.

"Ginger! So great to see you. Brandon was so looking forward to the girls coming."

"I didn't know you guys would be here. But what a great party, especially for the kids!"

"How's Chelsea Fiona doing?"

"Oh, she thinks she belongs to Jake, the way he's spoiled her. She even started following him into the bedroom like she could sleep with us instead of the girls, which was a non-starter. We didn't bring her today."

Christy also watched Monica laughing as one of the SEALs bounced the baby, Samantha. Karlene was nearby, talking to one of the SEAL wives. Aaron crawled at her feet.

"You know, I'm glad you're comfortable with all this."

"It's part of being with Jake, isn't it?"

Christy's pretty face was serious. "You're doing a great job, Ginger. This will help Jake come to terms with everything."

"I get along with the other gals, and the kids will be better friends the older they get. Wouldn't be fair for me to demand he stay away from a family he created. I have to embrace it. Like I said, it's part of Jake."

"You're a better woman than most. I've seen a lot of jealousy and insecurity on the teams with the wives. It can be rough. But if you're solid with your man, that's the main thing. And they need the support. Poor Lucas' wife Connie went nearly crazy. Those kids are way better off with him."

"Well, thanks for the encouragement. I'm hoping we can make this permanent. I really want to make it work."

"You will." Christy hugged her.

"Jake says he has a speech. Can you believe that?"

Christy beamed. "He's a character, all right. I'm glad he's lightened up considerably since his father's passing. That had to have been hard on him."

"Especially since it happened when he was away. But yes, things are more settled."

The rest of the afternoon went smoothly. More people arrived, and a few left early. Ginger enjoyed the play she and Jake made with their eyes. She also saw Jake speaking with Karlene and Monica on one occasion, together. He held Aaron, walking him around to introduce him to other partygoers, then had Samantha as well, carrying the both of them and appearing to enjoy his brood.

Adele announced that there would be a special dessert served. Jake was in the shade with all four of his children, kneeling to speak with Jasmine and Jennifer. Jennifer listened to her daddy and then slapped her hands across her mouth, jumping with exuberance. Everyone else faced Adele and waited.

Jake and the kids made it in the circle formed around Adele. Ginger walked closer to the edge to see what the plan had been, sure this was his speech. Her girls were holding onto Jake's leg, and Ginger could see they were excited. Jake handed the baby to Adele and let Aaron crawl on the grass at his feet.

"Ginger, come on down here for a sec," he said.

The crowd parted, making room for her to stand with Jake in the semicircle. Her girls ran to her and each grabbed a hand, dragging her over to their daddy. Aaron sat up and attempted to eat some grass, but Adele stooped down and removed it from the toddler's mouth. Samantha was squirming in her arms.

The girls presented their mom to Jake. He cleared his throat, glanced around the circle of Team guys, friends, and relatives, and began.

"Ginger, I've made almost every mistake a man could make, and still you're here, and you still love me. I'm not nearly worthy, but if you'll have me—" He kneeled down, and both girls giggled and looked up at their mother's face.

Ginger could feel the flush of her hot cheeks, but also the warm tears running down her face, dripping onto her new pink dress.

"If you'll have me, I'd be honored if you'd marry me, and this time it will be forever."

The crowd started to whoop and clap. Kyle shouted out, "Hold on, folks. We haven't heard her answer!"

"Say yes, Mommy," whispered Jennifer as the crowd tittered.

Ginger ran to Jake, threw her arms around him, wrapped her legs up around his hips, and whispered to his ear, "Yes, sweetheart. You didn't even have to ask."

"Oh yes, I did. And I had to get permission from our daughters, too."

CHAPTER 10

J AKE WAS GLAD the caterers had been hired by his mother. The girls had had too much sun, and playing in the water added to their fatigue. They snored all the way home. He and Ginger let them forgo their baths, book time, and prayers. Over sleepy protests, they got the girls into their nighties and let Chelsea Fiona choose Jennifer for the first part of her night. Before their door even closed, both girls were asleep again.

He took Ginger's hand, and they walked to the back after locking up the house and flipping on the night lights. He could tell she was nervous.

He turned on the radio to some light jazz music.

"That's nice." She lit a vanilla candle in the bathroom and let the golden glow create flickering shadows throughout the bedroom. Her pink dress slipped down her shoulders, and she hung it up, wearing only her new peach satin underwear for Jake's benefit.

He was naked, propped with pillows up against the metal headboard, tucked beneath the covers, waiting for her. "Ah, my investment. I'm very pleased with how it fits."

"I love it," she said as she fingered the circular outline of the stitching on the bra. "I think the cleavage is nice, too. Don't you think, Jake?" She leaned slightly forward.

"It's perfect. Why don't you turn around so I can see it from all angles?"

"Like this?" Ginger angled her hips, swiveling them back and forth and then bent over, showing him the smooth texture of the peach satin covering her rear.

"Just like that. You are so beautiful. I can't believe you said yes."

"I told you I was yours a long time ago."

"Come here. Are you ready for your punishment?"

"Punishment?"

"Remember, for giving me a hard on I had to endure all afternoon and evening? I told you I'd get even. A promise is a promise."

"Oh yes. Now I do. Will I like it?"

"I think you will. Get your little self over here so I can show you."

She crawled the width of the bed. Before she reached him, Jake removed the sheets and showed her his erection.

"That's my punishment?"

"No. It's your first test."

She straddled him, sitting back on his thighs, and used both hands to massage his member, pull on his ball sac, and finger his velvet tip. She licked her lips, and her eyes smiled at him while her tongue curled around his cock as she sucked and then took him in deep. He loved to watch her consume him, caress him, and kiss his sensitive member, her little pink tongue flicking the divot at his tip. She placed him between her breasts and squeezed, letting him root between her two delicious orbs. His precum presented a drop, and she was careful to lick it off slowly like a popsicle.

He sat up and drew her to his lap, spreading her knees and moving her hips back and forth, pressing against the ridge of his cock with her pubic bone. His finger found the elastic on her right side, opening a space, and he raised her up so he could press himself inside. His finger guided the way as she bent down and watched. Then her hand covered his, her fingers forcing his inside her and assisting his cock so it could gently slide into her wet channel. Fully seated, she pressed his thumb against her bud. Her back arched at her mournful moan.

Jake raised his hips, and she responded with an undulation, pulling him farther inside her as she rocked from side to side, raised and lowered herself to feel every inch of him slowly.

He held her hips again and thrust upward. Each time their coming together deeper than the last. He could feel her insides begin to pulse.

He quickly flipped her over on her back and removed her panties but left the bra on, creating lovely pockets of flesh where it restricted her breasts. He bit her nipples with his teeth through the fabric. His fingers found the lips of her sex, and he opened her to him and then bent down and tasted her creamy arousal.

She jumped, her fingers pulling his head closer, pinching his ears and feeling the connection his lips made on her core. He sucked her fingers and then sucked her bud. Her shuddering continued, and it heightened his arousal that she was coming to a huge climax. He wanted to ride with her until the very end.

He kissed her belly button and then crawled farther to slip his fingers under the tight band of the bra, squeezing and pinching her. He finally slipped an arm under her and released her breasts into his hands, letting his lips and tongue taste her.

He moved first her right and then her left forearm up and formed her fingers around the iron bars of the headboard. Sliding to the side, he opened the side table and removed two red satin ribbons, holding them up to her so she could see. Her eyes got full and round.

"My punishment?"

"What do you think?"

"Getting even."

"Oh no, not getting even. I'm getting way more." He smiled down at her sweet face. "Tell me you want it."

"I want it, Jake."

"Tell me what you want."

"I want you to use those."

"Where?"

"I want you to tie me to the headboard."

"And then what?"

"I want you to make love to me, Jake."

"Really?" He began to wrap her right wrist and then tied it to the metal rod going across the headboard. "Like this?"

"Just like that."

He laid gentle kisses from her belly button, over her right breast, and up under her arm. Then he kissed from the inside of her elbow to her fingers. Her lips were full and wet and begging to be plundered. He pressed his groin against the juncture between her thighs and kissed her deep as she wrapped her leg around his waist.

Then he secured her other wrist to the headboard with the ribbon. Her head was held with two pillows, and with her arms secured above her head and to the sides, he mounted her.

"Tell me what you like."

"I like this, Jake. I like being tied to you. I like being helpless underneath you, as you fuck me."

"Like this?"

He smoothly undulated his hips, digging farther into her, placing his hands beneath her rear and lifting her slightly for deeper penetration.

"Yes, Jake. Don't stop."

"Not to worry, Ginger." He increased the rhythm, feeling her losing control. When he kissed her, she sucked his tongue inside her mouth as her internal muscles pulled his cock deep. She struggled against the ribbons, her head thrashing from side to side. She pushed her pelvis against his, holding his hips with her powerful thighs.

Finally, she turned to putty beneath him. With sweat dripping from her chest, she moaned and then held her breath as a series of undulations took over her insides, pulsing against him until at last, he exploded deep inside her.

He laid his head over one of her breasts, reveling in the scent of her body, cradled in the rise and fall of her chest.

With one hand, he untied both wrists, kissed the slightly pink skin where the friction had caused some discoloration there and her palms, and buried his head next to hers, whispering, "You. Are. Mine."

"Always, Jake."

Her arms hugged him. Her legs entangled with his and held his right leg between her thighs.

CHAPTER 11

THE TEAM WAS briefed and took positions on the transport to Puerto Cortes on Isla Santa Margarita in Baja. Jake was relieved there was no presence of anyone official from the Mexican military, especially General Cortez.

They were again transported by commercial fishermen from the island to the gathering point for tours and charters at the port at Nuevo Vista, where their rented vans were waiting.

The rental agent was a skinny kid not more than about eighteen. Kyle used the credit card that had been issued to the Team for this mission.

"You will sign here and here, and Mr. Lansdowne, I am supposed to inform you that if you return the van dirty, you will be charged an extra five hundred US. It is necessary you must clean it first. No fish blood please."

Jake stiffened at the kid's words. This van had been used to transport the girl to the Emergency clinic—the one who did not make it.

"Sorry, but we had good hunting. We'll be sure we clean up better this time," answered Kyle. Jake felt several pairs of eyes on him.

After the agent left, Coop asked him about the comment. "You think that's a problem, LT?"

"I doubt it. I think he just was following instructions. Even his boss doesn't know he's rented to the Navy. Don't worry about it. Get your things aboard and let's stop by a market and get our stores."

Everyone piled in to the three vans, along with their fishing poles and ice chests and gear. The chests had been taped shut so no prying eyes could see the ammo and other explosive material they'd brought just in case.

The Super Mercado was brightly lit, so much so that it hurt Jake's eyes. The store attendant watched soccer on a big screen mounted in the corner next to a huge swamp cooler.

They'd been told the kitchen in their house was first class, so the Team stocked up on frozen dinners, local fruits, cereal, milk, yogurt, and eggs. The meat the market sold was of unknown origin, so no one took a chance on it. They bought several cases of beer and large bottled waters originating from California, even though they'd been told the local tap water was clean.

They once again posed as a group of sport fisherman down for a week vacation, but the real mission was to find contacts to the gun buyers. Kyle had been told to watch for an ex-Navy man who helped put the buyers together with the men who had guns and ammo to sell after discharge. After deployments, a large amount of equipment had been consistently missing from the San Diego area, and it was suspected this man, who had fled to Mexico rather than be subject to US law enforcement, was responsible for its disappearance.

Since he was a US citizen, they were supposed to bring him home to face charges. The task was too delicate to assign to local Mexican authorities.

Fredo asked the attendant as they were checking out if there was a gun range nearby, and the boy frowned and told him that guns were not allowed in Baja Nuevo. Fredo acted disappointed, but knew the seed had been planted, somehow the right people would be told, and it would spread quickly.

A Columbian drug gang, who also did their share of gun running, owned the Baja Nuevo resort. The last time, the team discovered they had involved themselves in kidnapping underage girls from the local village school to send up North as sex slaves.

Jake knew the combination was a lethal one. Baja was a favorite place to party, to get over a nasty divorce, or to just generally get into trouble. Though the resort looked well-manicured and serene with its golf course and lush grounds, the dark underbelly of crime lurked throughout. He could just feel it.

This trip, they rented a two story eight bedroom house near the beach. It was considerably nicer than the lodge type dwellings they had rented before.

"Hey, Kyle, who did you have to blow to score this place?" asked Alex as they pulled up to the huge structure that dwarfed some of the big beautiful homes in the San Diego area.

"Collins got us fixed up this time. I've been told to take real good care of the old broad," Kyle returned. "He said no parties. Not here."

Cooper whistled as they entered the tiled foyer. Jake followed him to the kitchen, done in dark granite countertops and teak cabinetry. It was everything it had been billed to be. The view from the eating area was all ocean and beach.

"I get dibs staying home. You guys can go out on the boats tomorrow and puke your guts out. This place is fine!" added Lucas.

"Let's get everything into the freezer and pick out your bedrooms. Then I want to have a team meeting downstairs in about twenty," ordered Kyle. "Now, get your butts in gear. Leave all the firepower and ammo in one of the vans, and pull them up close to the house. Locked. Got it?"

Without hesitation, everything except the taped coolers was unloaded and stowed. Jake chose to share a room with Kyle and Cooper. Some rooms had four, others just three occupants. Jake felt safest around Cooper, who also didn't drink.

At last, they gathered in the spacious living room. Sounds of the ocean pounding on the beach made for a pleasant background.

"We're staying here at the resort owned by the Garcia gang, but only because our intel has told us that's where all the gun deals are made. The guy we're looking for—actually Naval Intelligence is looking for—is Wade Seacord. He's a fifteen-year veteran dishonorably discharged due to suspicions of his obtaining equipment and firepower from retiring or discharged vets selling them to make a buck or two on the side. They uncovered a warehouse in Chula Vista chock full of all kinds of things, even drones, specialized robotics, cameras, and scopes used by a variety of Spec Ops community."

The Team grumbled. "Asshole," and other choice words were bantered around the room.

"No parties this time, so we're going under the radar, using the fishing as our cover for now. We want to find this guy and bring him back home to stand military trial. We're not to hurt him or anyone else. The last mission got us in a bit of hot water. It was cleared since it turned into a rescue operation for the girls, but no more of that. We're to avoid all interaction, especially with Mexican authorities. That said, don't get in their crosshairs. We don't know who we can trust."

Kyle went over other details and then ended with the "Cast of Characters," as he liked to call it. "Pretend you guys are in a live-streaming play and you're playing certain parts. In case we run across people we met before, Jake here has adopted this disguise. Jake,"—he pointed straight down at him—"You are never to take those wraparounds off, you hear?"

"Roger that, sir."

"I'll make sure he's shaved each morning, Lannie," offered Cooper.

"I brought the clippers. No razors, if you don't mind." Jake didn't want anything that could create a wound while away from home.

"Perfect!" Kyle listed a few more characters. "Armani, you're still in the Navy, but lookin' to get out and not likin' the new rules imposed on the rank and file. Danny, you failed a drug test, got booted, and have been unsuccessful getting onto any police or fire team. Fredo, you and T.J. have patched up your disagreements, but still not on good terms. If we need a good fight, you guys are it."

T.J. and Fredo fist-bumped.

"We've got a charter for the morning that will take six. The rest of you can wander the town and just generally be ears."

"Hey, Lannie, you got a picture of this character, Wade Seacord?" Jake asked.

"Good thinking, Jake. Let's see." He flipped through a folder and pulled out a black and white photo, a San Diego P.D. mug shot, which everyone studied as they passed it around.

"This was taken four years ago for a DUI, before they found the stash. He could be bearded, wearing glasses now, might be tanned—just look for anyone who looks like him. He has no accents. But he does have a big fuckin' dragon tat on his back, which should not be hard to miss. But he knows people are looking for him, so I'm thinking he'll cover up more than he used to."

"I've seen him at the Scupper before," said Armando.

"Good, excellent. Now, we're okayed to use the cells you've been issued so we can communicate. Remember, we want to look as normal as possible, so no vests. Don't go packin', and I know we all came heavy. Also, no earpieces."

Fredo swore.

"You got something you're trying out, Fredo?"

"This little microphone, I put it onto a button I can attach with a clip."

"Not yet, because you won't look natural monitoring it. Let's hold off for now. Anyone else have gadgets?"

Jake knew most the team experimented with equipment, special pockets to store things, so it was a valid question.

"So we got Ollie, Lucas, Alex, Tay, Jameson, and Tyler on the boat. They meet right where they dropped us off today at oh-eight hundred. For the rest of the afternoon, we walk the streets and just look like a bunch of goofy guys being tourists. You text me or Coop if anything comes up we need to know about. I want you in triples or quads today. Dress is ugly shorts and shirts that don't match. Except you, Armani. You can go designer if you brought any."

Armando smiled with pride, and the rest of the Team laughed, slapping him on the back.

JAKE WISHED HE could call Ginger, but had to obey the rules of silence while across the border. He, T.J., Cooper, and Danny wandered down a garden path until they found the dusty streets of the tiny fishing village on the outskirts of the newer town with its shops and malls. There they passed by older men sitting on metal canisters or plastic stools, mending fishing nets or cleaning fish. A pack of children chased a chicken with a stick until a woman appeared in one of the doorways and reprimanded them.

A fresh fruit vendor sold pineapple and other local fruits in white paper cones, drizzled with red hot sauce. They looked tempting, but Jake waved them aside for fear of getting sick. The sun was hot on his now-fuzzy head, and his new beard had grown out nearly an inch and itched in the afternoon heat. He was going to go for a swim when they returned to the house.

A pair of little girls approached them to sell handmade braided bracelets and dashboard dolls for pennies. Each of the men bought several and doled out their US dollars generously.

They noticed Tay and Ollie with Kyle and several others haggling with another street vendor selling necklaces made of shells.

With their pockets bulging with inexpensive trinkets for their kids, the four SEALs entered a small cantina where the food smelled great. Outside, the crowds of tourists had died down in the heat of the day. Upon taking a table in the corner, Jake and Coop ordered a mineral water, while T.J. and Danny asked for a local beer.

Sounds of a Jeep echoed through the little dive. The squeal of brakes and then the slamming of doors came just before the doorway darkened as four uniformed men entered the room.

They were dressed in the light brownish green colors of the Mexican military, not the black uniforms of local police. Each took a stool at the bar. The ranking officer removed his cap and set it on the vacant stool beside him. As he turned, Jake came face to face with General Cortez.

CHAPTER 12

G INGER TOOK THE girls to the library again for the Storytime hour and had arranged to meet up with several other wives and their children. On the way, she picked up Brandon and Maggie at Christy's and agreed to keep the kids at her place until Christy was done with work. Libby brought Gillian and Will. Luci brought Ali and Griff.

The eight SEAL kids sat together, some naturally holding hands or placing arms around each other's shoulders. The three mothers looked on to make sure they behaved.

Luci had taken away Ali's slingshot again just before the librarian was going to be hit with a wad of chewing gum as she sat to begin the reading. His mother quickly stashed it in her bag, out of sight.

"Honestly, I checked him before we left the house. He sleeps with this thing, and we have rules about him taking it to school, or to public places. But he's getting better and better at sneaking it or hiding it somewhere on his clothes," said Luci.

"A SEAL in training?" Libby smiled.

"Heaven help us, because I overheard him talking to Danny about learning to throw knives. I'm not going to have a single piece of wood paneling intact, and I know he'll practice on my throw pillows. I'm holding off on a decision until we can get some control here."

"Maybe that's how you make him understand. Tell him what the cost it would be for you," added Ginger.

"He doesn't really understand no. He thinks it's *no for now* or *no unless I can get away with it.* I think it's a cultural thing he learned as a street urchin in Iraq. Those kids made up their own rules. At least he had a father, up until the end. So many of those kids perish because they have no one except themselves to keep them safe. Very sad."

"Maybe that's why he's so attached to the sling shot Danny made for him. It did save his life, didn't it?" asked Libby.

Ali's last desperate run to the waiting arms of Danny, who was in the helicopter ready to take him away from the war and carnage, nearly ended in disaster when the boy fell. The fighter who pursued him, after killing his father, was not expecting the boy to scramble on the ground, pick up a pebble, place it perfectly on the rubber tubing of the sling shot, and shoot it smack into the center of the pursuer's forehead, knocking him backward. This skill Danny had taught him in the hours they practiced while waiting for their pickup, had actually saved his life. Ginger didn't blame the boy for wanting it by his side constantly.

But Ali's behavior at school was beginning to become a problem, she told them, since he fought on the playground not like a child, but like a young man in survival mode. He was so strong he could over-power even the older kids in school. His little brother, Griff, bore the goose eggs and bruises he received from the rough play with his adopted brother.

"I think you have a born warrior there. His father was military, and now he grows up in the shadow of Danny," said Ginger. "I'm glad I have girls!"

Libby and Luci laughed.

The story engrossed the kids, who were naturally inquisitive and not afraid to speak up. But toward the end of the story, Ginger saw Ali had lost focus sitting with her two girls and watched another group of preteen boys in white robes, sitting around a table, in an animated discussion. She recognized them from the last time they were at the library. She made a note to discuss this with Christy, Kyle's wife. She also decided to remark about it to Luci and Libby.

"Ali is watching those boys." She pointed through the open door-way to a table beyond, near the checkout counter, where the young boys had their heated discussion.

"Yes, last time he said he knew who they were," whispered Luci.

"We need to let the men know when they get back," added Libby.

"I'll be sure I tell Danny when I next talk to him." She examined her hands and Ginger knew she was sorry for the same reasons Ginger was sorry. She missed her husband and was hoping he hadn't found himself in harm's way.

After the reading, the book was given to one lucky child to take home on loan. That child would be the first person to let the book leave in his possession. The librarian smiled sweetly and presented it to Jasmine, whose eyes got as big and round as saucers. She hugged the book to her chest and came running to her mother.

Their whole group perused the shelves that had been specially arranged for the reading today, and chose books they wanted to check out. At the checkout counter, there was no sign of the young boys, so Ginger stopped looking for them.

But after the four kids held hands with each other and formed a human chain on the way to Ginger's car, she spotted the men again, lurking beneath a tree across the street from the library. It was scary when one of the youngsters broke away and headed directly toward them in a casual jog. When the boy was nearly upon them, Ginger noticed the sides of his face were deformed in a large reddish burn mark extending from his wrinkled eyelid down nearly to his jaw line. Though it was healed, it still looked painful.

Ginger advanced to her girls, picked up Maggie and shoved the other three behind her and whirled around to face the oncoming teenager. He held a large stubby stick in his left hand.

Ginger quickly finished loading the kids into the car and took off in the opposite direction. In her rearview mirror, she saw the other boys catch up to him and stand together in a group, watching her leave. She didn't see either of her other two friends. Her heart pounded, certain that if she hadn't acted quickly, the youth had intended on doing her harm.

She pulled over a few blocks away and dialed Luci.

"Did you see those boys?"

"Yes. Ali says he was a troublemaker from their old village in Iraq, the same boy he saw last week."

"We need to report this. If they're hanging around the library, we've got to warn the staff. I don't want to go back there."

"I'll call the library," said Luci. "Should one of us call the police?"

"I'm going to drop by the station. Hopefully, I won't have to wait too long if they see me with four children."

"I'm going to call Libby and check on her as well," said Luci.

"I didn't see her leave, so let me know, okay?"

"Will do. Let me know if we need to do anything further with the police."

Ginger explained to the kids she was going to take them to the police station, and Brandon cheered his lungs out. Luci texted her and said Libby had gotten home safely and had not seen the crowd of boys.

She had the kids hold hands and walked them all into the police station lobby. Behind thick glass, a clerk was sitting as she approached. She smiled at the kids. Brandon tried to climb up on the counter, but Ginger pulled him back.

"Can I help you?"

"We were just at the library."

"Your name?"

"Ginger Green."

The clerk wrote Ginger's name down on a tablet. "Okay, what brings you in here?"

"We were at the library just now, doing a reading for the children. These are my two, and I have two others I'm babysitting. There was aA group of youths gathered at the library, sitting around a table. They wore white robes. We saw them last week for the reading as well."

"Okay."

"Well, when we got ready to leave, they started to—well, one of them started to advance toward me and the children. He held a tree branch or something in his hand. He was menacing."

"When was this?"

"Just a few minutes ago, literally less than ten minutes ago. My other friend who was there with her kids has already called the library to warn them, but I think someone should go check out these boys."

"You say how many boys?"

"I think five?"

"And what were they wearing?"

"They all wore white robes, no hats or anything on their heads. They were like teenagers. But they weren't dressed western. I'm sure others have seen them."

Ginger gave her cell phone number and declined to write a report or make a complaint.

"If your officer checks with the library staff, I'm sure they've seen them there and could help perhaps with further descriptions. I just wanted to get out of there with the kids."

The information was relayed, and as Ginger put everyone back in her car, she saw a patrol car leave the garage, giving her a wave as he left in the direction of the library downtown.

The kids talked amongst themselves in the back seats. As she drove home, she wished she had Jake to talk to. He'd know what to do. Her heart was still pounding wildly in her chest. What had started out to be a nice afternoon with her friends at the library had suddenly become scary.

She'd always thought Jake had the more dangerous job. Today, she felt the weight and responsibility of protecting little ones in an ominous situation and now understood what Ali's father must have felt like as their city was crumbling all around them.

She was going to have to be more vigilant and observant. Her idyllic world had revealed some of its dark side, and she was more vulnerable without her protector. She needed him now more than ever.

Come home, sweetheart. Please be safe and come home soon.

CHAPTER 13

A S THE GENERAL turned to face the cracked mirror over the bar, enjoying his beer, Jake averted his gaze to Cooper, who was already nodding. He'd seen the General, too, and it registered that they needed to exit the place, but not do so as to attract attention.

He was hoping the cue ball look threw the General off in his recollection, but something in the man's eyes bore a twinkle of recognition. Despite the mineral water he was sucking on, his tongue stuck to the roof of his mouth and he had difficulty swallowing. He felt his palms sweat.

The lady bartender was keeping the military men happy, which meant the food T.J. had ordered wasn't going to come soon, which also meant that they should just finish up and leave. He couldn't get out of there fast enough.

Someone shouted in the street, which was followed by a high-pitched whistle and some cat calls as a group of young boys rolled up the narrow street, smoking cigarettes and chattering with a couple of local girls. The youths checked out the inside of the bar and as soon as they saw the uniforms were quickly silenced and gone from sight.

That was what Jake wanted to do. He wished he had the "disappear" gene so all he had to do was click his fingers and, like a genie, he'd be gone too.

A young girl brought a tray of hot beans, rice, and corn tortillas, as well as pieces of chicken and pork, vegetables, and a mound of shredded Mexican cheese. T.J. motioned for everyone to help themselves.

Jake rolled the tortilla with a generous mixture of steamed vegetables, adding the beans and rice, but didn't trust the cheese. It tasted divine.

The Cortez removed himself from the bar stool, stretched, and then proceeded to walk toward the rest rooms at the rear of the diner.

"I'm thinkin' it wouldn't be a good idea to take a piss right now," said T.J.

"I'm thinkin' it might be a good idea to shop for some sunscreen for tomorrow's little boat ride," added Danny.

"Too obvious. We don't run away," whispered Coop. "Just be cool. All will be well."

Jake clinked bottles with him, and he grabbed a jalapeno pepper and bit into it boldly. It didn't take long before his cheeks were lined in tears, but he refused to say a word.

"Fearless, that's you, bro'," laughed T.J.

"I think you fixed your plumbing problem, Jake. No more babies for you," Danny scoffed.

"Forget the sunscreen. Go for the Pepto, maybe some Prep H." Coop was grinning straight at him. "You know you love this. The fate of your life hanging in the balance, like jumping out at thirteen thousand feet."

"Shut. The. Fuck. Up." It was all Jake could say. He wiped his eyes with the napkin and then started to blow his nose when the General sauntered into the room. He took a detour and approached their table.

"We have some Gringos here, I see." He gently bowed to Coop. Jake kept the napkin over his nose as if he was going to blow once the General was gone, out of respect for his officialdom.

"Calvin Cooper, sir," Coop said in exaggerated Southern accent. "This here's Jack." He pointed to Jake, and he raised one hand, keeping the other on his nose. "We got T.J. and Danny."

Danny eagerly shook the General's hand while T.J. waved casually.

"Any of you guys military?" Cortez asked.

"Former," Coop said, pointing to his chest, "Former," he repeated, pointing to Danny. "Nope and nope," he said as he pointed to Jake and T.J.

Jake sneezed and blew snot all over the table and the food, which earned him some moans as one by one his buds wadded up their napkins and added them to the table. The General took a brisk step backward and scowled.

"That's just wrong, Jack, you asshole!" Coop barked.

Jake continued to wipe his nose and then quickly took a drink of water. His eyes were still running, and his nose felt bright red. He hoped it added to the disguise. He blew one more time, and this time the General had tolerated all he could. Staring back at Jake like he was a leper, he sneered and returned to the bar.

"We done here?" asked T.J.

"I need a fuckin' shower," Danny pouted and pretended to brush remnants of Jake's sneeze off the front of his shirt.

Cooper left extra money for the cook and waitress, and they all stood and smooth as silk, exited the cantina. Jake didn't start to breathe normally until they got nearly a block away. Normally, they would have browsed in some of the little shops and haggled with the street vendors again, but today, their gait was rather brisk. At the first available alleyway, they turned and got off the main road.

"Holy shit, that was close," Jake whispered.

"Only time I've been happy to be sneezed on. Was that all real?" Cooper was shaking his head.

"One hundred percent real," Jake answered.

"Timing's good, at least. Jake, you okay?" T.J. put a hand on his shoulder and examined his face.

"Now for my next trick, I'm about to have a bowel movement." Jake followed it up with a goofy grin.

"I wondered to myself why on earth Kyle let you come," Coop said. "Then I remembered. You're the comic relief, right?"

They continued through the alleyway and cut across another wider street, but kept to the alleyways all the way back to the outskirts of town, headed toward the rental house. Instead of hiking along the dusty roadway with no sidewalk, they moved onto the beach and walked in the clean, white sand close to the surf.

Jake realized how clean and invigorating the ocean was. His nose stopped throbbing from the hit his sinuses had taken with the pepper, and he began to swallow again. He reached down and held a palmful of seawater to his lips and nose and rinsed his face off.

The heat had been somewhat oppressive in town, but here by the ocean, a gentle breeze swirled around all of them. The sound of the pounding surf was so strong it was impossible to talk, so each of them went to their private places as they leisurely strolled down the beach.

At the house, they turned up toward the rear sliders, which were locked. Coop went around to the front and unlocked the sliders after he let himself in.

"I'm hitting the bed for a few. Wake me if we're doing anything?" Jake said.

Cooper was texting and nodded. "Um. Hum."

"I'm headed for the shower," said Danny.

"Coop? You want to go for a swim in the ocean?" asked T.J.

"Sure."

"I'll join," added Danny.

"I'm still headed for the bed. Have fun, mermaids."

From the upstairs bedroom, Jake watched his three Team buds dive into the surf and take turns swimming lanes back and forth at the outer edges of the waves. This would have been a great vacation to take Ginger and the girls to. They would have loved the shopping and had their picture taken with the little boy who had his pet iguana on his shoulder. They'd pay too much for trinkets and stare at the little girls their own age.

He hoped they'd be able to find the Navy asshole they were looking for.

He splashed water on his face again in the bathroom, careful not to drink any of it. He opened another bottled water they'd brought and stared out at the window one more time.

A line of four military uniformed men marched down the beach. He was relieved to note that none of them had medals.

Miss you, Ginger. Hope to come home soon. Kiss the girls for me.

CHAPTER 14

G ERUD BROUGHT THE plans for the shopping center expansion when he visited his father. He unrolled them over the sunny table in the older man's yard. Gerud watched his father's gnarled hands shake as his fingers smoothed over the drawings, stopping to check a legend and angling his head down to read some of the fine print descriptions.

"So, Gerud, from the looks of this, you are only about forty percent built out. Any reason for this?"

"Well, that's the way we bought it."

"So you own this yourself?"

"Actually no, my fath—"

"Just stop with that and say it. Next time you do that I'm going to be angry with you."

"My father and I own it together. My brother is in charge of his estate, but I'm going to see if he will let me take it over, since it is technically upside-down."

Peterson frowned and looked up at his son. "Why on earth would you do that?"

"Well," Gerud shrugged and talked to the hedge next to them as if it was an audience of investors, "To finish out our vision for the place. To show that it can be done."

"So you have an alligator, and now you want to make babies with her?"

Gerud giggled at the suggestion, which was damn funny.

"It's not funny, Gerud. If you continue to do business this way, you'll be broke inside a year. I'm deadly serious."

"Rob—"

"There you go!"

"Thank you. I think this is an alligator because it is too small and doesn't draw the traffic if it was built out. There are a number of stores that can't go in here because there is not enough parking, and the retail space is way too small for them. We've been contacted by retailers who wanted to know if we had expansion plans."

Peterson scanned the drawings and then put his fingers to his lips. "So the parking is here. Is that right?"

"Yes, at the present time. But look at that space if it was opened up. Not only would you have a huge lot in front of a big box store, you'd add great accessible parking to the smaller boutique shops by doing so. It's a win for everyone."

"At a pretty penny."

"Well, parking lots are cheap. The storefronts? That's where the expense is."

"So you need to attract a good anchor tenant, is that what you're saying?"

"Exactly."

Peterson sat back in his wheelchair and took another sip of his milkshake. "What are the features and benefits to an anchor tenant?"

"The obvious one. The golf course."

"And why is that?"

"Because on any good non-rainy day, and even some rainy ones, they get nearly twelve hundred people on or around this area, not counting families or others who are not golfing."

"But this is a golfing resort. Why do you think the golf course is the net draw? Look at the surrounding home sites?" His hand swept over the paper. "And here's a big problem for an anchor tenant." He placed his forefinger on the end of a cul-de-sac abutting the proposed parking lot. "There is no direct access to the home sites. Only access is either off the highway, here, or from the golf course parking lot, here."

Gerud looked at the map again and couldn't believe what Peterson had pointed out to him.

"Tell me, Gerud, would you battle the single lane nearly bumper to bumper traffic that I know exists there during heavy commute hours, and especially on weekends, to go from your driveway to the highway and then turn back to the center? If I was going to do that, I might go all the way into the next town where there are three big shopping centers."

"How did you see that?" Gerud asked.

"Because I own one."

He was dumbfounded. "Which one?"

"Doesn't matter. Any of them are fine. And we're all connected so we draw traffic for each other. We try to make it easy for people to get in and hard for them to get out. They'll spend a day there, or at least do something while they're waiting for the traffic to thin out."

Gerud scanned the map again.

"That, right there," he said, again pointing to the cul-de-sac, "is your alligator."

"So how do I get them to open it up?"

Peterson shrugged. "You give them something they want. What does the golf course and the Homeowners Association want?"

Gerud didn't have an answer for him.

"Have you ever gone over there and stayed at one of those vacation homes?"

"No. I've visited, and I've played the course several times. My dad and I have together."

"Do they have a post office?"

"No, they don't."

"And if you were going to attend a meeting, a small concert there, or a lecture, where would you go?"

"Well, there are three beautiful hotels here. Tons of convention space too, meeting rooms."

"Free?"

"Um, I would guess not."

"Exactly. And they go into Kapulua for their mail, don't they?"

"I believe so."

"In that ugly portable building that looks like an old school class-room."

"Yes."

"And they have a one year waiting list to get a post office box there."

"I didn't know that."

"Because the Homeowners Association doesn't allow mailboxes. What a smart idea that was."

"Wow. You really know your stuff, Rob."

"Gerud. You don't make money by accident. You have to plan your attack. A big new post office and a meeting room free for members to use would draw them to your center in droves, if you had good retail support. You have two ice cream shops, some little local retailers, and a good deli. I've been in it. He was a good addition. But for a sit-down meal, you have to go pay a hundred bucks at one of the resorts or the links restaurant. What if you had a family with children who can't afford that? They can't all eat ice cream every day."

"You're quite right."

"Sir," Alex interrupted. "You can."

Peterson threw back his head and laughed. "That's right," he said after he composed himself. "I'm special."

BY THE TIME they'd finished talking and Gerud had rolled up the plans, his father helped him make a list of things he could do to get his access to the housing development, even creating a plan for three places residents could enter the shopping center so that the burden didn't fall on one particular street. He had a list of items he was given as home-work, things to research.

"So, Gerud, all this is a no-go if you can't negotiate with your brother."

"Excuse me?"

"Well, actually, your first job is to negotiate with the lender on this property. Bank of Hawaii, is it?"

"Yes."

"You're going to have to tell them you won't be making payments for a year while you develop this. And tell them it might be two years."

"Wait a minute. Why would they do that?"

Peterson grinned. "Do you think you could sell this thing and get your money out?"

"Hell no. I've told them that when they threaten to take it all away."

"My point exactly. They are prodding you with something, the threat of doing something they have no intention of doing. Your father might have had assets they could go after. But he's gone now. And you don't. But if they think you have a backer, they'll give you time before they own this alligator for themselves, which will not look very nice on their balance sheet."

"A backer?"

"Me."

"You would do that, sir?"

"I told you I'd help you, but I intend to make money on it. This isn't a gift. It's a loan."

"Okay."

"I can see you have questions. Let me answer one of them. Will I be around to get my return? The answer to that is yes. Because if I don't, then I will haunt you all the days in the rest of your life!"

CHAPTER 15

G INGER FED THE kids lunch and then called Christy to see if she was okay with her bringing them to Adele's house for a swim. She was feeling the need of some extra eyes to help her with the kids, but actually to calm her nerves. The incident outside the library today still bothered her. Her own home felt small, and the neighborhood wasn't as nice as Adele's. She felt vulnerable. With the workmen and landscapers all around, she thought the sheer numbers of people around would make her feel more protected.

Christy was fine with it, so next she called Adele, who was delighted. "Monica is bringing Sam over this evening. She has a date with one of the men she met at your father-in-law's service."

"Really? That's nice. I thought the whole team was down with Jake."

"That's all she told me, sweetie. Someone new perhaps who didn't get asked to go? Or someone on another Team. But he's definitely a SEAL."

"Jake will want to hear all about it. And he'll check the guy out thoroughly."

Adele laughed. "Ginger, you are taking this way better than I ever guessed you would. You know, some wives would get downright territorial."

"Believe me, Adele, I'm learning every day. Every day is a stretch for me. Not at the breaking point yet, and trying to be accepting and flexible. But sometimes I'd like to drop kick Jake for being so irresponsible, and other times I want to drop kick the exes."

"Well, you come on over here when you can."

The children were all excited, except Brandon had a problem. He pulled on Ginger's top and asked her to bend over so he could whisper something.

"I don't have swimming trunks."

"Maybe Adele has some. She's got kids over there all the time. But if not, you can just go in your underwear."

Brandon fidgeted, biting his lip and staring at his pointed toe trying to dig a hole to China. He crooked his forefinger again, a signal Ginger better lean down again.

"What is it, sweetie?"

"I went commando like Dad does sometimes."

She was trying to hold it all inside and finally had to slap her hand across her mouth.

"Then I give you permission to wear those." She pointed to his shorts.

"What will I wear home, then?"

"You can wear one of my girl's dresses, or you can wrap your naked body in a towel, my man."

Brandon looked at her horrified, shocked that she'd said such a thing.

"Why don't we go to Jasmine's dresser and see if she has something that's plain enough to be worn by a handsome man like yourself."

"Absolutely no flowers," he said, pointing to the ceiling with his forefinger.

Ginger asked the girls to watch Maggie for a couple of minutes while she and Brandon went into the girls' room.

"Yuck!" Brandon said, examining all the pink on the walls and the pictures of Chelsea Fiona taken by a cell phone and then printed out. The dog streaked past them and jumped on Jennifer's made bed, waiting to watch what they were up to.

"It stinks in here."

"That would be the perfume Jasmine got for her birthday and Jennifer dropped. Sorry."

Ginger went to the third drawer in a painted bureau and started sifting through several pairs of long as well as short pants. She found a gray pair of stretchy shorts. "How about this."

"No. Doesn't have the thing, you know, there."

He'd been referring to the zipper or button enclosure like most boys' pants had.

"Oh, that doesn't matter. You just pull them down if you have to go."

"No, it will show my thing."

"Oh." Ginger noted that her lack of experience with little boys was showing. Inside, she was about ready to bust a gut. But she took his demands very seriously.

At last she found a pair of plain jeans shorts. It also didn't have an enclosure, but it had stitching to make it look like it had one, and that was acceptable to Brandon.

The problem was solved.

GINGER HELD CHELSEA Fiona under her arm when they walked through Adele's front door. "I hope you don't mind. I was worried she'd just yap and yap and I'd get in trouble with the neighbors."

"Nonsense! I'm the reason you got her. All my fault," she bent down, took the dog, and talked baby talk to him.

The kids ran through the kitchen and out onto the patio and into the water. Ginger had to run to catch up to Maggie, who was going to jump in, but didn't know how to swim yet. She hoisted the squealing child up in the air. "We have to change your clothes and take off that diaper, Maggie. And one of us has to go in the water with you, okay?"

Maggie let her considerable lower lip droop and curl down as she watched the other children play. Ginger removed the wet diaper and put on pool diapers and a plastic pair of elastic diaper covers.

"I'm going outside to find the water wings and the other toys," Adele told her and headed for the tool shed at the side of the pool under a large tree.

Ginger had her suit on under her cotton dress, but she retrieved her hat and the sunscreen and took Maggie out to the patio. There she smoothed the sun protection all over the jumping girl's pink, chubby body then slathered it generously all over her own fair skin.

"Whoa, you're using it all up, Ginger. You have enough for the girls and Brandon?"

"Sure I do. I used to tell Jake I could get a sunburn from a flashlight, my skin is so fair."

Adele took Maggie and the donut ring, applied the water wings, and brought Maggie down the pool steps until they were both in the water. Maggie splashed and kicked, trying to propel herself closer to the older kids, but Adele had a hand on the back of the donut ring, and Maggie finally gave up.

Ginger called each of the kids over to her patio chair and gave them heavy applications of sunscreen and handed the girls their goggles so they could spy on people under water. She made Brandon do the same, much to his protest.

They were playing a game of picking up colorful plastic rings tossed into the pool. Ginger took one and gave it to Maggie, who tried to throw it several times, managing to toss it only about a foot. Adele floated her closer so she could retrieve it and then repeated the process.

"Where's Gerud? Jake told me he was moving in with you." Ginger came around to the steps and began to enter the pool on the shallow side.

"He has, but he went to LA to visit Rob Peterson."

"That's nice. So I guess they're getting along, then."

"Very well, from the sounds of it. I owe him a visit as well."

"I'm glad to see you so happy, Adele. So much has changed since Burt's death not even a month ago now."

Maggie held her arms out, and Adele floated her over to Ginger. The two of them began to bob in the pool together.

"I think this was more a business meeting. I told you he was going to help Gerud, didn't I?"

"Yes. I'd say that's good for both of them."

"You know, Gerud always tried so hard to win Burt's affection, but it was always Jake. Jake was his favorite, and he never tried to hide that fact. It used to irritate me. I tried to make it up to him, but a boy doesn't want to take his mom as a substitute for a father's love. Fathers and sons are special. Now he has something none of the rest of us has. And it's not just a financial arrangement. I think Rob actually wants to get it right, to finish his life giving back. I'm so thankful, but we'll see where it goes."

"Why do you think Jake was favored?"

"Jake could do anything. He was the star athlete. Handsome. All the girls wanted to meet Gerud so they could be introduced to Jake. It was like he was Jake's shadow."

"But Jake loves being with his brother."

"Oh, I know. He's not the jealous type. Burt liked that, too. Gerud couldn't wait to hear him come home with all his adventures when he was off to the Navy. And the more he got caught up in it, got on the Teams, then married to you, I think the more Gerud thought he'd lost him. His little brother missed him terribly. So Gerud went to work for Burt. Did everything he could. And then they made that one bad investment, and it was like the man was broken. That's when all the arguments started. You saw them."

"I did. They were very vicious. Cut very close to the bone."

"No one was safe from those."

"Hey there, you lovely ladies!" Gerud crossed the lawn area and took a chair near the pool's edge.

"Uncle Gerud, come into the pool with us, please!"

"Please, please please Uncle Gerud," begged Jennifer, mimicking her older sister.

"In a couple of minutes. Let me talk to Grandma and your mom for a bit. Hey, Brandon."

"Hey, Gerud," Brandon returned.

"How did it go?" Adele leaned against the side of the pool and squinted up to her son's face. Ginger was still bobbing with little Maggie.

"It went fantastic. He's a genius." The roll of drawings was secured with a large blue rubber band as he held them up. "He took these, and we identified several things we could do to add terrific value. Maybe even do that expansion Dad wanted to do."

"How?"

"Well, like I said, I've never seen anyone so smart when it comes to investing. We came up with several action items I need to complete this week and fax back to him. And then we'll go one step at a time. Mom, Rob said he might help me finance the expansion. He says he's watching me."

"Sounds like if you play your cards right, Gerud, you two will be partners."

Gerud fiddled with his palm. "I wish we had more time."

The sobering thought left the three adults quiet. The giggles and screams of the three older kids drew their attention away from the awkward silence.

"There never is enough time. Before they know it, they'll be our age. And we'll be the ones they'll tell stories about." Adele wiped a tear from under her eye.

"They'll be great stories, Mom," said Gerud.

"The best," said Ginger. "Huh, Maggie?"

The toddler splashed water in her face.

CHAPTER 16

JAKE ROLLED OUT of bed early at sunrise to get in a morning run on the beach, since he hadn't exercised the day before. Running was easier for him, anyway, than swimming in the ocean, as nice and invigorating as it was. The peaceful sounds of birds and the splashing of little washes over the smooth white sand set his mood just right. It was the refresh and stimulation he was looking for.

A few other lone runners also traveled the same path in the first rays of morning light, a communion of souls with similar goals and, perhaps, similar demons of the heart.

He could see Ginger sleeping all alone in their big bed. He could hear her breathing, and the sounds of her stretching. He knew what it was like when she snuggled, half asleep still, wrapping her legs around one of his, curling her hands backward into fists, placing them under her chin and then resting along his shoulder or on his chest. He liked to let his fingers wander down her smooth spine, and then tickle her behind, waking her to him, and aroused.

He liked to be the first thing she kissed in the morning. She was always funny about it, wanting to go get her teeth brushed, but he wouldn't have her any other way. Her natural flavors were just as nice as the way she smelled when she had used her lemon shower gel and the special oil she liked to wear in her cleavage that drove him nuts. He liked how his finger would slip up and down in that oily spot then travel to the dark place between her thighs so he could watch her eyes open and gasp first thing in the morning. It was the right way for a couple to start the day. He would do it this way until their bones were too brittle, and then they'd figure something else out. It had become their ritual and the best way to say hello.

A light mist had traveled from the ocean to land, and it shrouded part of a rocky natural barrier with a brightly lit house sitting on top of the promenade. The beach took a holiday there right in front of the house, so he turned around and went back the other way. The tide had come in, and he didn't feel like trudging in thigh-high surf to complete his run.

As he turned, a couple of black watchdogs came to the living room window and barked.

Dobermans.

Whomever lived there was serious about their own security, as any guard dog owner could attest to.

Running past their rental, he noticed a dark, unmarked car tucked under a huge bright purple-flowered bush that threatened to take over the whole hill. All he could see was two people sitting in the front seat, but couldn't tell their features, age, or sex. He kept on running without appearing to take interest but thought he'd text Kyle when he got around the bend and out of eyesight of the detail. They were either waiting for someone to show up at the beach, or they were watching the house. Someone needed to get closer to make a determination if they were friendlies. He doubted they were, no matter what entity they worked for.

A weathered concrete picnic table that had been painted several colors in its past was a welcome sight. The cool surface felt good as he sat in his own sweat on the bench.

He retrieved his cell and sent the text.

Kyle's answer was quick.

Noted. Sending Danny out to check them out. Don't come back yet until we've determined they aren't looking for you.

This little text reminded him he was still a person who some thought should stand trial, which would be a farce. They'd just beat out of him what they wanted him to say, and until he gave them that, his body was theirs. He was going to make sure that never happened.

He continued to watch the sunrise as the warm yellow glow baked the sweat from his face, legs, and chest.

He thought about the drill of military guys on the beach last night near sunset and wondered if there was a police or Special Forces training camp nearby. But since he saw no more, he put the idea out of his mind.

Kyle texted back.

Private security. Danny got them to leave. Come back.

That suited Jake just fine. He picked up a flat piece of broken shell that had been weathered, exposing layers of beautiful pink colors. He tossed the shell and watched it bounce four times in the calm backwash.

Cooper had made some whole grain pancakes and set out some yogurt. They used up their two dozen eggs making a scramble. They also drank a half-gallon of orange juice. The pancakes were tasty, but instead of maple syrup, they'd only been able to find Agave syrup.

"We gotta get some real stuff here. No more of this cactus shit," said T.J. pointing to his pancakes with his dripping fork.

"You guys should go on a little buying spree. We already need more eggs and beer. Maybe some more waters, and who the fuck thought to buy this instant coffee?" Lucas was complaining, but Jake knew he was nervous about being first on the boat.

"You should drink some, Lucas. It will settle your stomach. The ocean looks a little choppy this morning," said Kyle.

Lucas peered out the picture window and appeared to turn a light shade of green as he confirmed a wind had started to whip up already. That meant for a rough day in the open waters.

"Where'd you go earlier?" asked Alex.

Jake swallowed the last of his eggs. "I went for a run. I missed the swim last night."

"Next time, get me, okay?" Jameson was frequently one of Jake's running buddies and he didn't much care for the long swims, either.

"You got it."

Tyler asked about bringing a lunch for the trip.

"It's supposed to be provided for. If you brought snorkel gear, they might stop at a quiet cove and do a little diving. They do that sometimes," answered Fredo.

"Okay, we'll drop you guys off at the harbor, and then we'll head for town. I need a volunteer to stay back at the house, just in case the security detail wants to get curious." Kyle looked over the three hands that went up. One of them was Jake.

"No can do, Jake. I'm not leaving you anywhere alone." Kyle chose Alex to stay behind. "Make it obvious you're home so you don't scare someone, okay?"

"Sure."

The five SEALs were dropped at the pier a half-hour early. Their charter boat hadn't arrived yet, but Kyle and crew took off toward town anyway.

Most of the shops were closed. There were a few cantinas and some palapas out on the beach where coffee and sweet breads were served. The crowd who'd never gone to bed could even order a drink. Since the resort owned the whole stretch of beach, no commerce was allowed, and so none of the usual street vendors peddled their wares. A couple of older Mexican men were fishing off an abandoned pier. Kids and dogs roamed in search of treasures abandoned on the beach. Jake knew it was smart to watch where he was walking, since some of the debris could be sharp pieces of glass or other hazardous items. A dead sea gull lay with its stiff wing partially arching into the air. It was missing eyes and one of its feet.

Their group was fairly large for the little tables and rickety chairs, so the group split into two and kept their distance. For authenticity, Fredo was with one group, while T.J., his pretend enemy, was with the other one.

Kyle and Fredo ordered coffee and sat back with the morning sun on their face, their arms outstretched to the sides. Armando shared their table and took an orange juice in a plastic cup from a little girl not more than six or seven years of age. She also brought some child-sized bracelets from her pocket and, without speaking a word of English, displayed them on the little tabletop for all the men to see.

Armando spoke to her in Spanish, and her smile became wide. He handed her a ten-dollar bill, and she nearly dropped the remaining orange juice glasses on her tray looking at it. She pushed all the bracelets, about a dozen or so, closer to his lap and took a bow and then disappeared.

"Good thing I wasn't hungry," said Fredo. "I think our waitress has retired for life on your tip, Armani."

"How in the world could you be hungry? You ate nearly a quarter of the eggs," said the handsome Puerto Rican SEAL. "Besides, it was just ten dollars. It means so little to me, and so much to them," Armando justified.

"Kyle, any known hangouts for this Navy guy?" asked Jake.

"We didn't get any of that. It was suggested we just hang, and those people just come out of the woodwork and find us."

"You have any idea where he lives? Does he own a place here?" Jake persisted.

"We were told he has a nice house in the complex. But no, no address."

Coop, Danny and T.J. walked to the water's edge and stood in ankle high water. Jake joined them, hopping along the way, due to the hot sand.

"I know the last time we came we said it would be nice to bring the girls. I'm not feeling a good vibe here, are you guys?" T.J. asked.

Coop searched the beach and looked at the empty palapas. "The place is a little too dead for me. If I took Libby anywhere, they'd have to have a cool disco and a special gym set up for her workouts."

But Jake liked the quaintness of the village proper and told them so. "I actually would like to window shop a bit. And of course, I need to add to my considerable collection of ugly shirts."

T.J. slapped him on the back. "But you wear them so well. All the ladies love them on you, sport."

"Anyone want to split off this group and go back to the village?" asked Coop.

Both Jake and T.J. nodded, and then Danny decided he'd go, too. They walked past Kyle and the rest of the guys. "Catch you back at the house, Amigos," said T.J., who then punched Fredo in the arm a little too hard. Fredo was on his feet in an instant, threatening to punch back, but T.J. backed up a couple steps and remained more than arm's length away, his hands in the air, flickering, as if to say he was done.

The four SEALs took a shortcut through an alleyway that was flocked with crisscross laundry lines, the white linens for several hotels nearby hanging in the breeze. By the time they'd traveled the length of the alley, they discovered it was a dead end and so returned the way they'd come in.

They made a right turn, and standing there, in front of his Jeep, was General Cortez and three other military men.

"Jake Green?" the General said.

Jake hesitated, but knew it would be pointless to try to talk his way out of it. Besides, no one in their group spoke Spanish. He didn't want to disrespect the nasty looking General, who was not appearing to have a very good day, but he needed to make his identity known and the reason for his visit.

"Sir, I am Jake Green. But I am here on official business."

T.J., Danny, and Coop stood close beside him. Of course, none of them had any weapons, but they assumed their normal wide-legged stance just the same. Jake could tell just by their breathing they were ready for anything, and if he wanted them to protect him or fight to get him out of this situation, they would.

One of the younger uniformed men stepped forward and spoke in fairly understandable English.

"You are wanted for questioning and the possibility of standing trial for the death of Juanita Orosco Lopez. You will please come with us willingly."

Coop spoke as the senior man in their little group.

"Excuse me, we are willing to deliver him to you. But we cannot let him go without our accompanying him. We are not allowed to leave his side. Like Jake said, this is official business at the behest of our Department of the Navy."

"He will be taken to our detention facilities at Puerto Cortes, and there held over for examination and questioning."

"We're going with him. We'll even deliver him, if you want. But we're all going together," Coop further insisted.

The young officer discussed the conversation with General Cortez.

That's when Danny recognized a man who had been watching the house. "This one here, in black, was one of the men in the car this morning. I wish my Spanish was better."

Coop was texting Kyle about their situation. Jake hoped that the slight delay would mean Kyle and the others would show up to help with the negotiations. The two Spanish speakers were in his group back at the beach under the palapas.

"We should have brought someone who speaks the language," Jake mumbled.

"No worries," Coop said as he stowed his cell. "Kyle and them are on their way. He's placing calls and got us tracked."

"General," Coop started. "With all due respect, our team leader is on his way, and the US State Department has been notified."

The translation didn't move Cortez. With his dark glasses, it was hard to tell his mood. But Jake noted he seemed to be in an eternal state of pissed off.

The young officer shouted, "If you are carrying weapons, you will disable them and toss them to the ground."

"We have none," said Danny. Everyone else in the group held their hands out to their sides, indicating the same.

Jake heard the sound of their rented van, and after first driving past the roadway where they were standing, the van stopped, backed up, turned down the road, and parked right behind the group. Kyle was out the driver's door in a flash, stepping up to the General to shake hands, but he was barred from doing so by the uniformed attachment who stepped in front of the General.

Kyle turned to Fredo, who had been doing something in the van and now jogged to stand at Kyle's side. He spoke with the General in Spanish, and soon, they began to argue.

The General gave an order, and two of his men stepped past Kyle and Fredo and grabbed Jake's arms, bringing him forward. Fredo continued to argue as the men ordered Jake to step up and sit in the back seat of the Jeep.

Jake's heart was racing. He'd never been in a Mexican jail or detention facility, but somehow, he imagined it wasn't a very comfortable place to be. Without his weapons, and with the order they were given about not engaging the military or police, he realized that he would have to cooperate, or someone would get nervous and the whole situation could blow up.

A crowd had started to gather. Armando began speaking to the group, keeping his voice calm, but before long, he, too was being contradicted and ordered to stop.

Kyle spoke to the officer who spoke English. "I am going to confer with my men. You understand we do not want any problems, and no violence or bloodshed. But we must consult our government since we are all here on official business."

The young man motioned for him to carry on.

Jake couldn't hear the conversations, but knew they were working out a strategy. Fredo translated for Kyle.

"You may take Jake to the detention facility, but we will follow, and we will see where he has been taken and under what authority. We request written confirmation he is in custody and the reason for his being held, so that we can present it to our representatives in the Department of the Navy."

The General blurted something out, and the young officer shouted the translation. "And there will be no fake letters from your Mr. Secretary of the Navy."

After conferring with his other men, the General nodded and climbed into the front seat of the Jeep. Two of his men sat on either side of Jake, one of whom placed handcuffs on him.

"No! No! No! This is not necessary!" Kyle protested, as Fredo translated. "He is not to be handcuffed. He is to be treated with respect. We submit to the questioning, but nothing else."

The General listened to his officer and then nodded. The handcuffs were removed. He spoke again.

"You will follow us now. Mr. Jake Green will be left at the detention facility until further notice. You may inform his next of kin."

The Jeep sped off, leaving behind a cloud of dust the van had to navigate in. But Jake could see they were not far behind. The Jeep headed for downtown where a fairly modern concrete and granite building loomed before them. They drove around to the back where armed men guarded the large rear doors. Jake was unloaded and escorted up the ramp way, and inside. His last glimpse of freedom was watching Kyle and the other men from his Team forming a small circle, Kyle giving instructions. Several men stayed with the van, while Kyle, Armando, Fredo, and Cooper walked toward the door.

He sighed with relief as they were allowed to enter.

CHAPTER 17

W ORD SPREAD FAST in the community that Jake was being held in Puerto Cortes. Sr. Chief Collins was monitored calls from the Team, annoyed that they'd managed to step in dog poop without a sighting of the person they'd been sent to get.

He spoke quietly so that the rest of the office didn't get wind of how out of control the situation really was.

"Kyle, we've got an attorney on retainer there, and he'll stop by in the morning and meet with Jake. You need to just tell your guy to be cooperative. You know the drill. Everyone stay calm and cool. We don't get into a firefight, understood?"

"Yessir," Kyle answered. "Can this attorney protect him at all?"

"Hard to say, son. We don't think General Cortez is necessarily rogue. He does command loyalty amongst his rank and file, but like most of them down there, they look out for themselves first, so he'll not take any risks. Just don't give him a reason to get angry with any of you. Don't make him feel nervous, because no telling how he'll react. We have to find out what the motivation is down there. Working on that. So just keep it real cool. That includes Jake."

"Roger that. I'll make sure it gets relayed. So is the mission blown, then? Should I send some of the men home?"

"I'm thinking you can send home the non-essentials. Definitely keep Fredo and Armando, Coop and T.J. Up to you about Danny. But everyone else I think should come on back. That leaves you two medics, one sharpshooter who better not be shooting anything but ground squirrels, two native speakers, and a couple of weapons and explosive guys with backup."

"Tay is asking to stay as well."

"Nope, you send him and Ollie home. I got some underwater stuff they can do here. He's probably going to be doing a temporary duty assignment for the Navy elsewhere, but he'll be back later in the year, I think."

"So I'm assuming you'll arrange pickup for these guys at the old Naval base tomorrow? We're to get them over there on our own?"

"You got that right. Not enough time for me to arrange it. I think you could do a better job. I'm going to get my ass chewed on this one. Already been one of our most expensive ops, and we've been at it, what, like two days now? Let's get everyone home safe and without collateral injuries, you reading me loud and clear?"

"Absolutely, sir."

"Next I've got to notify the next of kin and then arrange for your military transport to California."

"Sounds good."

"Oh, Kyle?"

"Yessir?"

"I'm looking at Jake's record, and he's got his mother listed as the next of kin. Isn't that kid married? I heard he'd done it like six times or something."

"Three, well, two really. One, he never married."

"So who the hell am I supposed to call?"

"You call the first wife, Ginger Green. And you call his mother, Adele Green."

"And his dad? Do they live together?"

Kyle chuckled. "Hardly, sir. Jake's father passed away during our last trip down here. You probably didn't know that."

"Ah, that sucks. So I got both those addresses for Ginger and his mother. Anyone else?"

"His brother, Gerud, but Adele would know how to locate him."

"Okay, I'm updating the file now. You see why this causes so much problem for us when they get so casual with the paperwork?"

"I do. My squad never expects they'll need those notifications. They're Superman, every one of them."

GINGER HAD JUST picked up the girls from gymnastics and had served them lunch when she got a knock at the front door. Chelsea Fiona barked up a storm, which scared the girls. Ginger picked the dog up and opened the door. It was their team liaison, Sr. Chief Collins. Her heart jumped to her throat, and she couldn't speak at first. But not seeing a chaplain meant that something had gone wrong, but Jake was still alive.

"Ma'am. I'd like to come in, please."

"Sure." She stepped aside and let the dog down. "Let her bark. She won't bite," Ginger said.

She let the girls greet their father's Team liaison. Both of them were good as gold and, upon Ginger's instruction, retired to their room with the dog in tow to take a short nap.

"What is it, Sr. Chief?"

"Can I have a glass of water?"

Ginger dutifully got Collins the water and ushered him to the living room to take a seat at the couch. She sat in an easy chair perpendicular to the couch.

"Jake's been held by the Mexican authorities for questioning in the operation they did last month. You heard about it last time on the news, which was unfortunate, but I'm sure Jake filled you in. We were able to use some trickery to get him out the first time, but this time, they're not letting him go."

"How long?"

"Oh, they have civil rights, but nobody down there pays much attention to it. There's so much crime, bribery is a real problem, so nothing's consistent. Of course, we can make it a big international incident, but in this case, we didn't and don't want that."

"So what does that mean?"

"Well, I'm afraid it means we've got to raise some money, possibly."

"Me?"

"No, not you, but if you had resources somehow, that would help. This is not exactly like negotiating with terrorists. That we never do, officially. But Jake did shoot that woman, and we have lots of detail on it being an accident. As you know, Mexico has been ordered around a bit by the new administration in Washington, and perhaps that's a factor. We're not going to launch a hostage rescue mission, so as long as he's not being tortured or beaten—"

"Tortured or beaten?" Ginger's senses switched into high alert. For the first time since she'd been with Jake, her fear he would be taken away from her was real.

"We don't think they'll mistreat him. In an odd twist of fate, we don't think they're trying to get any information out of him. They'd like something flashy for their television news media. Something to show that Mexico wasn't going to be bullied any longer by the US. Thumb their noses at the US type of thing. If it were information they wanted, it would be far more dangerous for Jake. However, being in that detention facility in Baja is no cakewalk. He's well trained, but he doesn't have a weapon, and that's a handicap. We're hoping we can get him removed from the general population to some place safe."

"I understand. So what can I do? You are arranging some money, then?"

"We have certain protocol we have to follow."

"How much are you trying to raise?"

"No figure yet. We're not even sure who the players are. No demands have been made. No ransom notes or anything, so it's a waiting game."

"I see. Well, just so you know, we don't have a lot of money, I'm sorry to say. But I'll discuss it with the family."

"Thanks. Now, I've got to go visit his mother, Adele." He stood and Ginger shook his hand, even though she could see he wanted to give her a hug. She was going to have to start enduring some sleepless nights, and there was no reason she should start out soft.

"Can I ask you one last question, Sr. Chief?"

"Go right ahead," he said as he walked to the front door.

"What are Jake's chances of getting home safe?"

"Well, Kyle and a few of the guys are down there, too. If I were the Mexican authority, I'd not bet against the SEALs. They can be pretty resourceful. Just not sure in this case whether their skills are a match for what's needed. But being calm and looking for opportunity is what it's all about. Once that little hole appears, we're pretty good at ripping that thing to shreds."

"Thank you."

GINGER GOT A call from Adele about forty-five minutes later.

"Are they going to allow you to see him?" she asked.

"I didn't even think about that, Adele. You think it would help?"

"Well, he said something about looking to raise some cash. What if we made arrangements so we didn't have to wait so long for the Navy to do it?"

"What do you mean?"

"I could go to Rob Peterson and ask him."

"Gerud's father?"

"It wouldn't hurt to ask. And I have some equity in this house. I could get a short term loan perhaps."

"The fact of the matter is, Adele, Jake's innocent. It was an accident. Shouldn't we just trust the system?"

"Honey, there is no system. I think that's what Collins came to tell us."

"I don't want to interfere with whatever they're doing."

"You need to talk to Jake's LPO, Kyle. He's still there, from what I understand."

"Yes, I was told as much."

"The guys have to know we might be able to assist in the money arrangements. I don't think they do yet."

"Okay. I'll get hold of Collins and see if he can get Kyle to give me a call. And you let me know how things are going on your end."

BY NIGHTFALL, GINGER had received several calls from other SEAL wives, which was the custom. Babysitting was offered, and meals were set up to be delivered. The community surrounded Ginger so she didn't have to endure all the worry alone. Kyle's wife, Christy, agreed to let her know if she heard anything from Kyle, and promised to encourage him to call.

The girls were in bed. She'd just gotten out of the shower when she got the call she'd been waiting for from Kyle.

"How're you holding up?"

"Hanging in there. Listen, I need to tell you there is a chance we can raise some cash to help with getting him freed, if you think that will do anything."

"We still don't really know who we're dealing with. General Cortez might be actually in the employ of someone else. We don't want to go offering cash or letting people think there could be a cash payout, because we could be bled dry, or it could create a competition for control over Jake's fate."

"Well, we're working on it. I wanted you to know. We'll keep on it, and you just keep it at the back of your head in case it's needed. I'll know more in a couple of days."

"Your mother-in-law is all in for Jake. That's nice she can do that. I hope we don't have to drain her bank account."

"Jake's brother might have resources we didn't know about before. Just stay tuned and let me know how it's going, and give us some idea how much we might need, if you can."

"Will do."

"So how does he look?" Ginger wasn't sure she wanted to hear the truth.

"Oh, he's fine. I mean, he's nervous, but you know how level he is in a stressful situation. It's the unknown that gets to hostages and prisoners. We're trying to get that worked out. Until we do, that's his biggest challenge."

"Any chance I can talk to him? Or can I come visit?"

"Oh no, sweetheart. You stay the hell away from him. This is no place for you to be. It's not a safe or stable environment. And Jake would worry himself sick if he knew you were coming, but I'll let him know you wanted to."

"Yes, please do so. And tell him I'm being positive. I'm shopping for satin and lace."

"Ma'am, Jake's a lucky man."

His deep chuckle wasn't Jake's voice, but for now, it would have to do. She knew he'd enjoy hearing about a homecoming, if that were possible.

But then this was Jake. Everything was possible with Jake. This was the life they were supposed to live. It was their turn. She wasn't going to let anything stop her from fulfilling her dreams of spending the rest of her days with him.

She forgot to tell Kyle she had another secret. But Ginger decided that would wait until the homecoming. That was something she wanted to do in person, whispered in his ear on a night filled with candles and soft music.

That vision became her new trajectory.

CHAPTER 18

T HE CELL JAKE was placed in also housed two other prisoners. The lack of a window made it impossible for him to see who they were or what condition they were in. He hadn't heard beatings, but he did hear lots of clanging and guessed most the people stored in this facility were chained by hands or feet or both.

The place smelled like feces and stale urine. He imagined it would be difficult to use the honey bucket he knew to be in the corner of the cell without missing, since there was no benefit of light. He tried to sit back on the itchy mattress he'd been given and soon discovered he was covered with fleas.

He knew it had to be mind over matter. The fleabites stung and then itched afterward. If he indulged, the itching would get worse, and then there would be the possibility of infection. That was always going to be his biggest problem. That and obtaining enough water to keep his brain functioning in such a stressful situation with little food.

One of his cellmates had a hacking cough that didn't sound healthy at all. Someone at the end of the hall was mumbling with fever, and the rest of his cell was complaining. He heard Spanish spoken, as well as what sounded like an African dialect. Jake imagined Baja was a magnet for people from all over the world to try to gain entry into the US, in a state that was lax on enforcement of immigration laws. With the added juice of a very healthy drug business run by cartels all around Central and South America, the clash of money, cultures and greed made for dangerous bedfellows. Jake didn't have to compete with all this distraction. He just had to outlast it all. Somehow, he had to remain alive long enough for a rescue, a fair resolution to his legal troubles, or a miracle. He was praying for the latter. He didn't want anyone risking their life for him today.

He could hear water dripping down the stone blocks of the cell's perimeter. The long corridor echoed in mysterious ways, sometimes making him think a voice was whispering in his ear, and other times not. He remembered on the tour of Alcatraz in San Francisco Bay that inmates on the rock could sometimes hear partygoers on expensive yachts berthed at the Marina just as if they were standing on the pier. Water and wind would carry the voices so the inmates could listen to what they were missing, even if they couldn't see it.

He started doing what he always did when he was gripped with fear. He counted his blessings. First on his list was his family—all of them, but of course mostly Ginger who had come back into his life when he didn't deserve it. He was grateful for those lush days and nights he'd had with her and for the chance to give her back the joy she'd given him. It was a dream he had no right to expect, but was the thing he would be clawing toward every minute of every day he had to spend in this awful place.

He was grateful his brother had found his father at last, that he had a new purpose in life, and was sure the best was yet to come for him.

He regretted his father had never taken care of himself and would be missing the growing grandkids and all the new family history that would be created in the coming years. He regretted not being able to tell his dad he loved him more often. He couldn't even remember a time when he had said it, recently.

He was grateful his mom could now devote herself to her grandkids and the rest of her family. He wondered, should he not make it out of this prison, who would finish his father's wishes as executor, but dismissed it as probably something his mother could do by default. And she'd do a great job of it.

Jake was grateful for his Team, for the guys who had sacrificed, kept him safe, and for those he had saved, both innocents and Team Guys. It was a job he wished most men could have the chance to perform. He was the lucky one doing all the things he'd done. He got to be a force for good, not evil, in the world.

He would need his strength and so willed himself to sleep, rolling down on his side and letting the tiny fleas have their way with him. He just pretended it was some exotic form of skin treatment, willing his body not to react, like he did with the adjustment to his heart rate. He remembered the rebreathing exercises he'd done in BUD/S, how some of the guys had a hard time with the disorientation exercises they'd done under water. But for him, he just held his breath and calmly conducted his tasks with time to spare, pushing up to the surface with smooth grace, loving the knowledge that he'd passed on his first try.

That was going to be how he'd survive this ordeal, just the same way. He'd remain calm. He'd listen and watch for opportunity. He'd look for a tool, a weapon, something to either defend himself or protect himself with. He needed to read every situation in the building and—just like in BUD/S—try not to stand out, grand stand, or express frustration or emotions that could tax him or make him slip. He was going to survive. He was made to do the impossible, the things that other people couldn't do. He was special, but not better. He was a super strong killing machine who loved with great passion. He would lie here and experience himself getting stronger mentally and physically and wouldn't give up. No matter what they threw at him, he would not give up.

That was what he was all about.

JAKE WOKE UP with a start. Someone in the next cell was being dragged down the hall, and the man was either dead or unconscious. The heavy iron bars rang with finality as they were shut behind the lifeless body and the lock reapplied.

He also was careful to take even, deep breaths, which renewed him with the flush of new oxygen carried throughout his body. He flexed and unflexed his leg muscles, to the point of making his lower legs cramp, and then let them relax afterwards, waiting until the cramping stopped. Then he repeated it with his arms, fingers. He rolled his neck and shoulders before moving slowly to a sitting position with his legs crossed, doing the power breathing exercise they'd all been taught. He held a forefinger against his right nostril and inhaled and exhaled, then did the same with his left. He tried to bring as much calm, cleansing spirit into his body as he could.

He saw Ginger holding out her arms to him and experienced his longing for her, causing his eyes to water. He let them stream tears, and knew that, if he was experiencing emotions, he wasn't dead, or even close to dead.

Again, this was another survival technique. All emotion could be regulated through breathing. It was not something to dread, but a proof of life. Controlling it stopped the destructive negative cycle of despair and turned his body into a vessel of bliss.

JAKE DISCOVERED HE was able to sleep in the lotus position when he awoke and was still sitting erect with a slight bob of his head. A door had been opened at the end of the hallway and light flooded into all the cells. Some dirty forms cowered and covered their faces from the brightness. He made his eyelids into slits, viewed the light sparingly so as not to damage his eyes, and realized he might have to do this for several days, perhaps longer.

Through the slits, he examined his cellmates. The man who had been coughing all night long was now in a deep raspy sleep, curled up to a stone wall, shirtless and with wild hair that appeared not to have been combed in weeks. Part of the sides was matted with early formations of dreadlocks.

The other man didn't have the darker complexion of their first cellmate. His skin was fair. His belly flabby. He was leaning against the wall, one leg out in front of him and the other bent at the knee. He had been wearing a white long sleeved button-down shirt when he'd come into the cage, but he'd rolled the sleeves up to the elbow. One arm was draped over his knee. Jake saw the outline of something familiar.

The man had an anchor tat on his left forearm midway between his wrist and the inner arm joint.

Formerly or currently in the Navy?

With renewed interest, Jake adjusted his arms and legs and tried to see the man's face.

Well, he'd asked for a miracle, and one had just been shown him. He'd created it with his own mind. The man who was his cellmate was none other than the man they were supposed to bring back with them: Wade Fuckin' Seacord.

CHAPTER 19

KYLE WAS PACING back and forth on the living room carpet. The calm beauty of the ocean view belied the danger present all around them. He had two goals for today. First, he needed to sit in on the appointment Jake had with his Navy-appointed attorney. Second, he needed to find out what kind of a man General Cortez really was.

Only one way would work before they had to exhaust the "nuclear option" which might entail him giving up his career as a SEAL team leader. Could also mean he spent some time in a military prison, stripped of his pension and separated from his family.

Nothing was worth that amount of pain to himself or his family—especially his family. But the other part of what made Kyle the leader guys would die for was that he wasn't going to let a man be left behind. He'd played several scenarios over and over again, and although he didn't have all the facts, he was confident somehow they'd get it done and get it done right.

"Lannie, you're wearing a hole in the carpet. Would you quit it please?" Cooper asked as he dropped his shoulders in frustration. He waved at the little enclave of SEALs trying to look busy examining gardening magazines and wedding books that had been left in neat piles under the coffee table for guests. "You're making us all nervous. So just quit it."

Kyle gave him the finger and continued pacing. Then they heard the sound of a Jeep pulling up to the front door.

"He came alone, Lannie." Danny's voice echoed down the stairwell.

"I'll be fuckin' fucked," whispered Kyle. Armando and Fredo frowned at each other and then shrugged in unison.

He waited for the knock on the door so he didn't appear too anxious. He opened it to find the General in civilian clothes. Rather nice civilian clothes, and once again, Kyle was surprised. He was about to piss his pants he was so excited.

"Welcome, General. Thanks for coming this morning."

Fredo stepped up beside Kyle and translated for the General, who then nodded, and spoke back to Fredo.

"He says this is his day off and that this is an unofficial visit, not part of his regular duties."

This time Kyle nodded. "Bueno." His attempt at Spanish brought the General's hand to his face, and he removed his sunglasses. Kyle saw an angry squint there and figured he didn't like his language being made fun of.

"Excuse me, General. I meant no disrespect. I am endeavoring to learn Spanish. It's really something I should have done years ago. No excuses, and once again, pardon me."

He waited for Fredo to translate.

"Si, si, si." General Cortez said as he swatted the air like it was filled with flies.

Kyle pointed to the couch, and the General took a seat.

"It has come to my attention that perhaps we have another way of solving our mutual problem."

The man looked confused. "Problemo?"

"Opportunity, let's say. It just so happens that my government is willing to pay you a reward for the return of this rogue Navy SEAL who killed one of your women."

The General corrected Kyle's interpretation that the woman killed was his woman. "I have a wife and three daughters, thank you. This is not my woman. I only have one," Fredo said.

"Me, too." Kyle rubbed his hands together. His forearms were balanced on his knees. "The point of all this is that we are prepared to offer you a reward for the return of this SEAL. You will be doing us a favor, and in return, we wish to do you a favor. Perhaps it's something you would share with your colleagues, or, perhaps," Kyle angled his face and dropped his voice, "you could use the reward to do good things for your town and your family."

General Cortez crossed his legs but not his arms. Kyle read that as he was interested. Without smiling, he held his fingers up and rubbed them together. "How much?"

"We are prepared to offer you fifty thousand dollars, in cash."

General Cortez took his glasses from his shirt pocket, reapplied them to his face, stood, and extended his hand.

"No, *señor*."

Kyle also stood. "Wait a minute. What amount would you think would be just compensation for such a wonderful job you have done apprehending our citizen? Bear in mind the good people of Puerto Cortes wouldn't have to bear the costs of a lengthy trial and court case. And, God forbid, what would happen if the SEAL were found not guilty?"

The General looked from Fredo back to Kyle. He held his fingers up again.

"*Cuanto cuesta?*"

"You tell me. Surely only you know about all your expenses. Perhaps this could help compensate for all the cases you worked long hours on for no compensation? And because of your diligence to do the right thing, perhaps you have to hire private security to make sure your wife and daughters are adequately protected?"

The General held up his palm, spread his fingers, and spoke to Fredo, who translated, "Five million pesos."

Kyle was taken aback. They weren't even in the ballpark. Suddenly, his hopes had been dashed. He shook his head, no. He was very sad and showed it on his face, made sure the General could see how painful it was for him to reject his offer.

Cortez scanned the faces of the SEALs sitting around him. He spoke again to Fredo.

"I am not an unreasonable man. Living here can be very difficult, especially when one has daughters and no sons. Perhaps one of your SEALs could marry my daughter?"

Kyle sat up when Fredo said this. "No, no, no. We're going in the wrong direction. These men here? They are all married. They all have children."

"He says you can choose the SEAL who marries his daughter."

Kyle stood and resumed his pacing again. "Jesus Christ, where does this guy get off asking for me to hook up one of his daughters with one of our members? Can you imagine what kind of a father-in-law he'd make?"

Armando rolled his eyes. "Details, details. You don't think we could find one bachelor SEAL who might be willing to take that trip down the aisle for the Team?"

Coop began to laugh. He was holding his gut. "I'd say you got yourself one hell of a problem, Kyle. Ask him if that lowers the price some. It also means they'd be first in line for immigration."

"I know what the fuck it means. I'm just trying to figure out if it's worth my career to find some poor asshole who would like to marry into this family. Get my drift?"

"Oh, I do. Indeed, I do."

The General interrupted and held his hands out to the side, asking what the discussion was about. Fredo spoke to him, and the man grinned and sat back down, smiling.

Everyone looked at Fredo. He raised one shoulder up and then smirked. "I told him you were looking for the best candidate and that you said yes, if the price was right."

"Holy shit, you did NOT say that to him, Fredo!"

"Oh, I did. I very much did."

"How the hell am I going to deliver that?"

"Let me see if I can work this out." Fredo spoke to the General again and after a little back and forth, both men shook hands. "So it's all settled then. You will deliver a SEAL who will wed his oldest unmarried daughter sometime this year."

"This *year?*"

"Yes. And in exchange, you will bring him four million pesos in US currency, which is a little over two hundred twenty thousand dollars, and he will exchange this for the bad SEAL man." Fredo crossed his arms and sat defiantly, taking turns staring back into the eyes of his SEAL buddies. "I dare you to do better. It's done, he accepts, and it's less than what Adele offered, so she'll be pleased."

"We didn't offer citizenship, did we? Because that's against the law to sell that, Fredo," said Coop.

"No, no promises of citizenship. But I explained that, of course, she would have to live with her new husband in San Diego."

Kyle saw no option but to agree. He extended his hand, nodding. "Tell him day after tomorrow. And I want Jake moved to a private cell if he's in a communal one."

After Fredo's translation, he delivered the General's message. "He says he will put Jake up in his finest cell, the one that was built for the Governor of Baja when he went to jail on corruption charges. It has internet and cable TV and a bed, no extra charge."

IT WAS ARRANGED Kyle would meet with Jake and his attorney this morning, so he and Fredo drove the van behind the General's Jeep and was waved through the security gate without delay.

Cortez gave them a tour of the facility, which reeked of all things horrible. The special suite created for the Governor of Baja looked a little better than a cheap motel room, but he knew it would be much safer than wherever he was housed now.

He and Fredo were shown an interview room where Jake would be brought. The Mexican attorney they'd hired was already present.

"I'm so sorry about all this," the nice-looking attorney said as they shook hands.

"I think we have just managed to secure Jake's release."

"On bond? They don't do bond here. If you pay, you are out the money."

"No, I think we were able to negotiate something to compensate the General for all the trouble this event has caused."

"Oh. Well, very good. So perhaps I won't have to mount a legal defense. I wasn't looking forward to it, because you never know what to expect. But I'm glad for your boy."

Jake walked through the door. Part of his face was swollen, but the smile on his lips was genuine and heartfelt.

"God, did they beat you?"

"Nope. Fleas. They have some fleas in there that don't just bite, they take chunks out of your flesh," said Jake. "But I'm good now. I understand I'm to be transported to the Presidential Suite?"

"Don't hold your breath, Jake. But yes, I think we worked everything out."

"Awesome. So when do I leave?"

"Day after tomorrow."

Jake grinned and leaned on the interview table. "Well, I want you to know that I fuckin' lucked out."

Fredo scrunched up his face. "You don't look very lucky to me, my man."

"You had to pay for my release, right? I mean, you got some money from the government?"

"Sort of."

"Well, ask them for a little bit more. Guess who my cellmate was?"

Kyle knew Jake must either have really good news or was delusional. "Who?"

"Wade Seacord."

"No shit."

"I'm telling you. He wants out real bad. Thinks I can score a deal so he can come home with me. How about that?"

"Holy fuck. I can't believe it."

Fredo was laughing.

"What's so funny?" asked Kyle.

"This is gonna cost you another million pesos."

Jake's eyes popped out of his head. "You spent a million dollars on me? Where did you get that kind of cash?"

"Pesos, that's about fifty-five thousand dollars," corrected Fredo.

"Oh. Well, then."

Kyle didn't want to tell him about the rest of the deal. But he gave him some basics. "Day after tomorrow, we fly in a private plane, which brings the cash. We load everyone up, all our equipment and such, and we take off. The General has agreed to give us permission to land, so we ought to be out of here about fifteen minutes after we see that plane. That work for you, sport?"

"So what we doing about Seacord?"

"What's he in here for?" asked the attorney.

"He didn't pay a prostitute. He thought the gal just liked him."

"Unbelievable."

THE SECOND NEGOTIATION was conducted in another interview room. General Cortez was in a very good mood, and Kyle was hoping he'd just give them a two-fer, but he had no such luck.

"Another American? This man is a SEAL as well?"

"No, just a former Navy guy. We can't let him rot here," Kyle said to Fredo for the translation.

"I don't know. Perhaps you could come back in thirty days or so, and I will think about this. I haven't researched the crimes he has committed."

Kyle tried to reason on humanitarian grounds. "He doesn't belong here. It was a minor offense. The offense of being stupid. He didn't recognize her as a professional. We just don't want to let a Navy guy get left behind. Can't you think of something you want we could give you?"

The General's face lit up. The twinkle in his eyes told Kyle it was going to be something outrageous, and it was.

"I have this picture here of the car I would like to get. It is for sale in Los Angeles." He pulled out a magazine ad, unfolded it and pushed it across the table to Kyle. There in the center of the page was a brand new, shiny Tesla, the one with all the bells and whistles on it. "This is what I want. I want it registered in my name. I want it delivered to the San Diego airport parking structure where I will fly in and pick it up and take the lovely drive home."

IT TOOK SOME more massaging, but Adele got the money for the purchase. Rob Peterson knew the dealer, so the price tag wasn't the full hundred and fifty thousand dollars. The dealer registered the vehicle in the name of Juan Cortez esquire, which was exactly what the General requested. A picture was taken of the car parked at the short term parking garage on floor 3, section A6. In the photograph was a picture of the registration confirming the car's ownership.

The private jet was arranged, and when it landed, Kyle, T.J., Fredo, Armando, and Cooper walked from the hangar to greet it. Several airport employees handled the ice chests and their other gear, rolling it out on a luggage train. First, a large strong box was unloaded, and then all the Team's equipment was uploaded to the belly of the sleek jet.

General Cortez opened the strong box and examined the contents in private, returning with a grin. "Bueno," he said in exaggerated Spanish like Kyle had done two days before. He motioned for Jake to be released, and with Wade Secord walking next to him, he made his way to the others, where he was greeted with hugs.

"You got rid of your beard," remarked T.J.

"Damn straight. With all those fleas, ew. I don't ever want another beard again. And as for this," he said as he rubbed his palm over the top of his skull, "it's already starting to grow back. I can't wait to get home!"

Seacord had no clue what was to befall him and was introducing himself to the team, sharing in the joy of the moment.

"Jake!" came a shout from the jetway.

Gerud ran to embrace his brother. "Would you look at this! I got to help my big brother out this time. Probably will never happen again, but who would have thought, right?"

"Thanks, man," said Jake.

"You don't have to thank me. We're family, Jake. I was happy to do it. Mom and I think it's the best investment we've ever made. Welcome home, almost."

General Cortez held up the Tesla keys and winked. "Gracias, amigo." He started to leave and then forgot something. He reached into his shirt pocket and took out a photograph, handing it to Kyle.

All the SEALs looked over Kyle's shoulders at the gorgeous picture of one of the hottest women they'd ever seen, posing in a bathing suit. Kyle smiled, tucked the photo in his pocket, and gave it a little pat.

"And the saga continues, gents. You're gonna have to help me with this one."

CHAPTER 20

T HE PARTY HAD been held at Adele's home where all the grandkids were invited to spend the night, as well as Monica and Karlene. This was done so Jake and Ginger could at last have some alone time.

His bites were nearly gone, thanks to medication Coop gave him. He walked with her up their front steps and lifted her over the threshold, bringing her inside.

"We'll be making this official soon, but I thought I'd get some practice in."

"I'm not that heavy, I hope."

"Nope. Just like to practice. You know, until I get it perfect. Like we do in bed."

"I do know. You are perfect. Perfect in every way." She opened the doors to the bedroom and turned around, stopping his entry. "I need to go put on the music and light the candles. I want this to be just like I'd imagined it would be."

Jake leaned against the wall and waited. The familiarity of their relationship, the smells of home, and the certainty of their evening together made him feel the happiest he'd ever been. It was so damned good to be home. To be part of the SEAL family and his own family. He knew it wouldn't always be like this, but for today, everything was perfect. His mother found the love she thought she'd lost years ago and sacrificed for her son. Mr. Peterson now had a family he never dreamed he'd have, and the contact and association with all the SEALs, the grandchildren, and the community actually energized him. Both Adele and Gerud thought he was improving, instead of going the other way.

The mission had been declared a success, even with all the twists and turns. Gerud was looking forward to his future, however long that would be, with his father. The dysfunctional family elements were gone. It was the start of a new life for him. He'd done it. He'd actually turned things around.

Ginger opened the bedroom door in her new bra and panties. These were bright red. Her hair once again looked like it was on fire because of the warm glow coming from the room. She had lit over a dozen white pillar candles all over the room, had turned on some soft jazz, and was waiting for him.

She tucked her fingers into her bra cup and slowly pulled out a red ribbon and then one other. "I've been saving these for you, my love."

Her soft flesh trembled under his touch. That little moan she always gave at the first kiss of their encounter finished him off. "Ginger, you're so full of surprises."

"I'm just getting started."

She unbuttoned his shirt, unzipped his slacks, and carefully laid his clothes on the overstuffed chair by the window. She took his hand and brought his naked body over to the bed. A red satin scarf waited in the center.

"What's this?"

"Just some things to occupy our time." She peeled back one corner, revealing a variety of sex toys including gels and lotions, a riding crop, black velvet ribbons, hand-held vibrators of various sizes and shapes, and a collection of some naughty DVDs.

"I had no idea you had this in you, sweetheart."

"I want you to teach me, Jake. Make me into the woman you'd never ever even think about leaving. Show me how to love you."

"But you do beautifully. I have absolutely no complaints. Honest, honey."

"But would you like to experiment a little? Would that turn you on?"

"Indeed, it would. I'd love to explore with you. I'll go anywhere you want me to go."

"And I have one more surprise."

"*Another one?*"

She touched his tip, let her fingers dance up his torso, and then pressed herself against him, as he bent to claim her mouth.

She kissed him on the ear and whispered, "I'm pregnant."

Did you enjoy this bundle? If you like binge reading, won't you consider leaving a review and telling other readers about it? Thank you!

And, speaking of Bundles, I have them for the original **SEAL Brotherhood** books, as well as the other SEAL series, as follows:

Ultimate SEAL Collection #1

Ultimate SEAL Collection #2

Big Bad Boys Bundle

Don't forget to sign up for my **Newsletter** here, so you won't miss a new release, read exclusive excerpts and special events and future writing releases and news.

authorsharonhamilton.com/newsletter

And if you like the community of other avid fans of Sharon Hamilton's books, won't you consider joining my **Rockin' Romance Readers** group? We have a great time, interview other authors, talk about books and things related to reading and loving romance. Join the family today!

facebook.com/groups/sealteamromance

Thank you, and God Bless!

ABOUT THE AUTHOR

 NYT and USA Today best-selling author Sharon Hamilton's award-winning Navy SEAL Brotherhood series have been a fan favorite from the day the first one was released. They've earned her the coveted Amazon author ranking of #1 in Romantic Suspense, Military Romance and Contemporary Romance categories, as well as in Gothic Romance for her Vampires of Tuscany and Guardian Angels. Her characters follow a sometimes rocky road to redemption through passion and true love.

Her Golden Vampires of Tuscany are not like any vamps you've read about before, since they don't go to ground and can walk around in the full light of the sun.

Her Guardian Angels struggle with the human charges they are sent to save, often escaping their vanilla world of Heaven for the brief human one. You won't find any of these beings in any Sunday school class.

She lives in Sonoma County, California with her husband and two Dobermans. A lifelong organic gardener, when she's not writing, she's getting *verra verra* dirty in the mud or wandering Farmers Markets looking for new Heirloom varieties of vegetables and flowers.

She loves hearing from her fans:
Sharonhamilton2001@gmail.com

Her website is:
sharonhamiltonauthor.com

Find out more about Sharon, her upcoming releases, appearances and news when you sign up for Sharon's newsletter.

Facebook:
facebook.com/SharonHamiltonAuthor

Twitter:
twitter.com/sharonlhamilton

Pinterest:
pinterest.com/AuthorSharonH

Google Plus:
plus.google.com/u/1/+SharonHamiltonAuthor/posts

BookBub:
bookbub.com/authors/sharon-hamilton

Youtube:
youtube.com/channel/UCDInkxXFpXp_4Vnq08ZxMBQ

Soundcloud:
soundcloud.com/sharon-hamilton-1

Sharon Hamilton's Rockin' Romance Readers:
facebook.com/groups/sealteamromance

Sharon Hamilton's Goodreads Group:
goodreads.com/group/show/199125-sharon-hamilton-readers-group

Visit Sharon's Online Store:
sharon-hamilton-author.myshopify.com

Join Sharon's Review Teams:

eBook Reviews:
reviewcrewsh@gmail.com

Audio Reviews:
reviewcrewaudio@gmail.com

Life is one fool thing after another.
Love is two fool things after each other.